11-06

Teen

D0949590

VIZ GRAPHIC NOVEL

MAISON IKKOKU™
WELCOME HOME

This volume contains
MAISON IKKOKU PART NINE #5 through PART NINE #10 in their entirety.

STORY & ART BY RUMIKO TAKAHASHI

ENGLISH ADAPTATION BY GERARD JONES

Translation/Mari Morimoto
Touch-Up Art & Lettering/Bill Spicer
Cover Design/Hidemi Sahara
Layout/Sean Lee
Editor/Trish Ledoux
Assistant Editor/Bill Flanagan
Director of Sales & Marketing/Dallas Middaugh
Assistant Sales Manager/Denya S. Jur
Assistant Marketing Manager/Jaimie Starling

Editor-in-Chief/Hyoe Narita
Publisher/Seiji Horibuchi

First published by Shogakukan, Inc. in Japan

Printed in Canada

Published by Viz Communications, Inc.
P.O. Box 77010
San Francisco, CA 94107

10 9 8 7 6 5 4 3 2
First printing, May 2000
Second printing, March 2001

Visit us at our World Wide Web site at www.viz.com,
our Internet magazine, j-pop.com, at www.j-pop.com,
and ANIMERICA at www.animerica-mag.com!

MAISON IKKOKU GRAPHIC NOVELS TO DATE

MAISON IKKOKU
FAMILY AFFAIRS
HOME SWEET HOME
GOOD HOUSEKEEPING
EMPTY NEST
BEDSIDE MANNERS
INTENSIVE CARE
DOMESTIC DISPUTE
LEARNING CURVES
DOGGED PURSUIT
STUDENT AFFAIRS
HOUNDS OF WAR
GAME, SET, MATCH
WELCOME HOME

VIZ GRAPHIC NOVEL

MAISON IKKOKU™ VOLUME FOURTEEN

WELCOME HOME

STORY AND ART BY
RUMIKO TAKAHASHI

CONTENTS

PART ONE
I LOVE YOU, BUT...

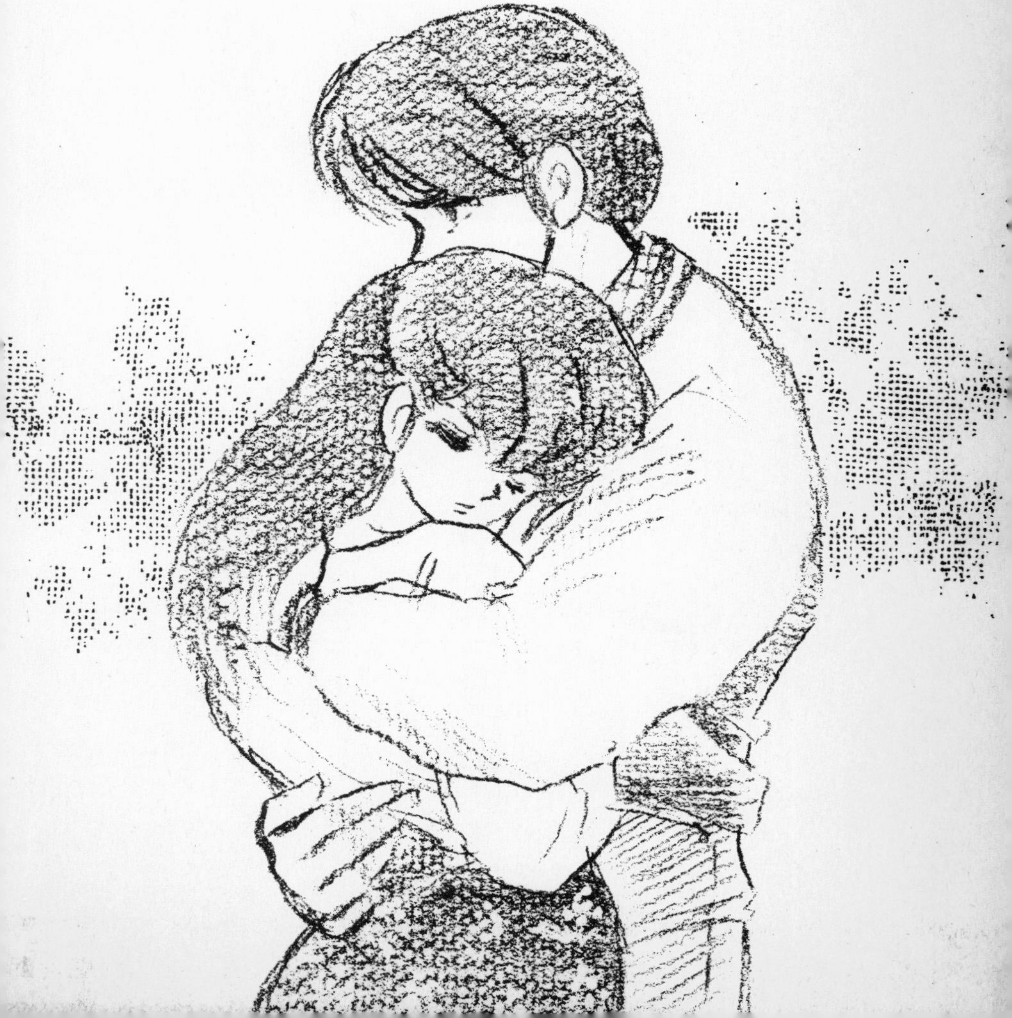

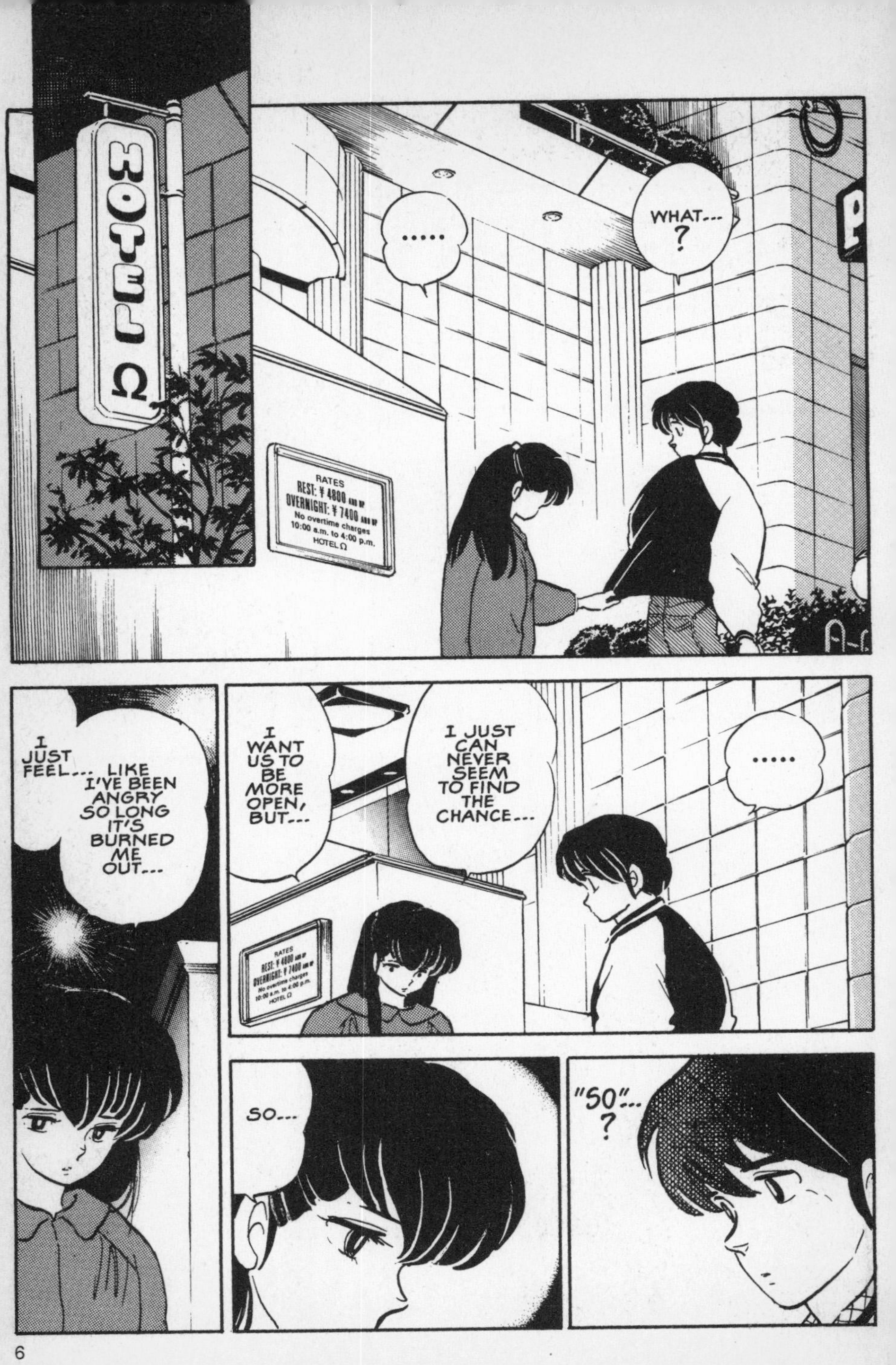
HOTEL Ω
RATES
REST: ¥4800
OVERNIGHT: ¥7400
No overtime charges
10:00 a.m. to 4:00 p.m.
HOTEL Ω
.....
WHAT... ?
I JUST FEEL... LIKE I'VE BEEN ANGRY SO LONG IT'S BURNED ME OUT...
I WANT US TO BE MORE OPEN, BUT...
I JUST CAN NEVER SEEM TO FIND THE CHANCE...
.....
SO...
"SO"... ?

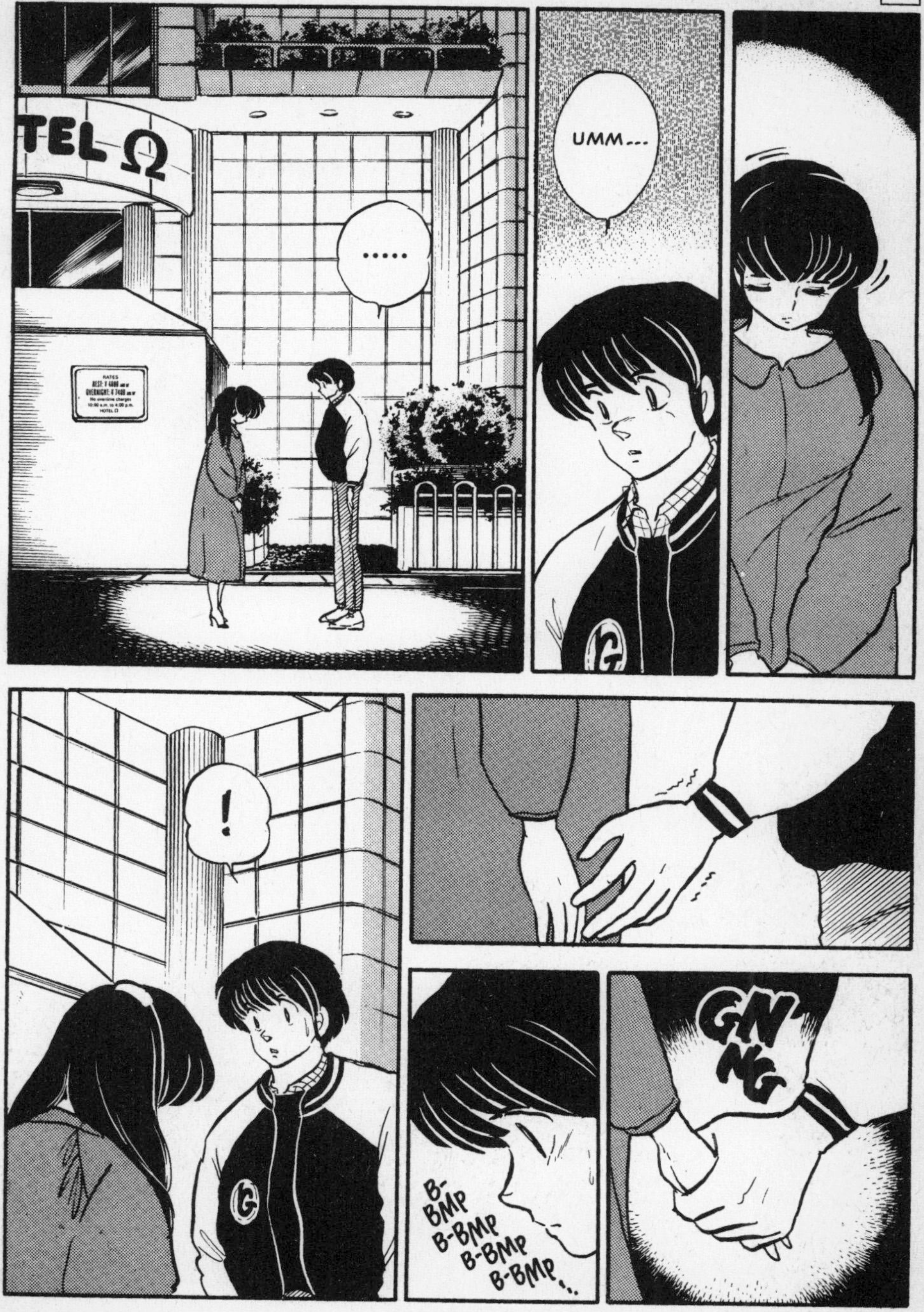
TEL Ω
......
UMM...
!
B-BMP B-BMP B-BMP B-BMP...
GN NG

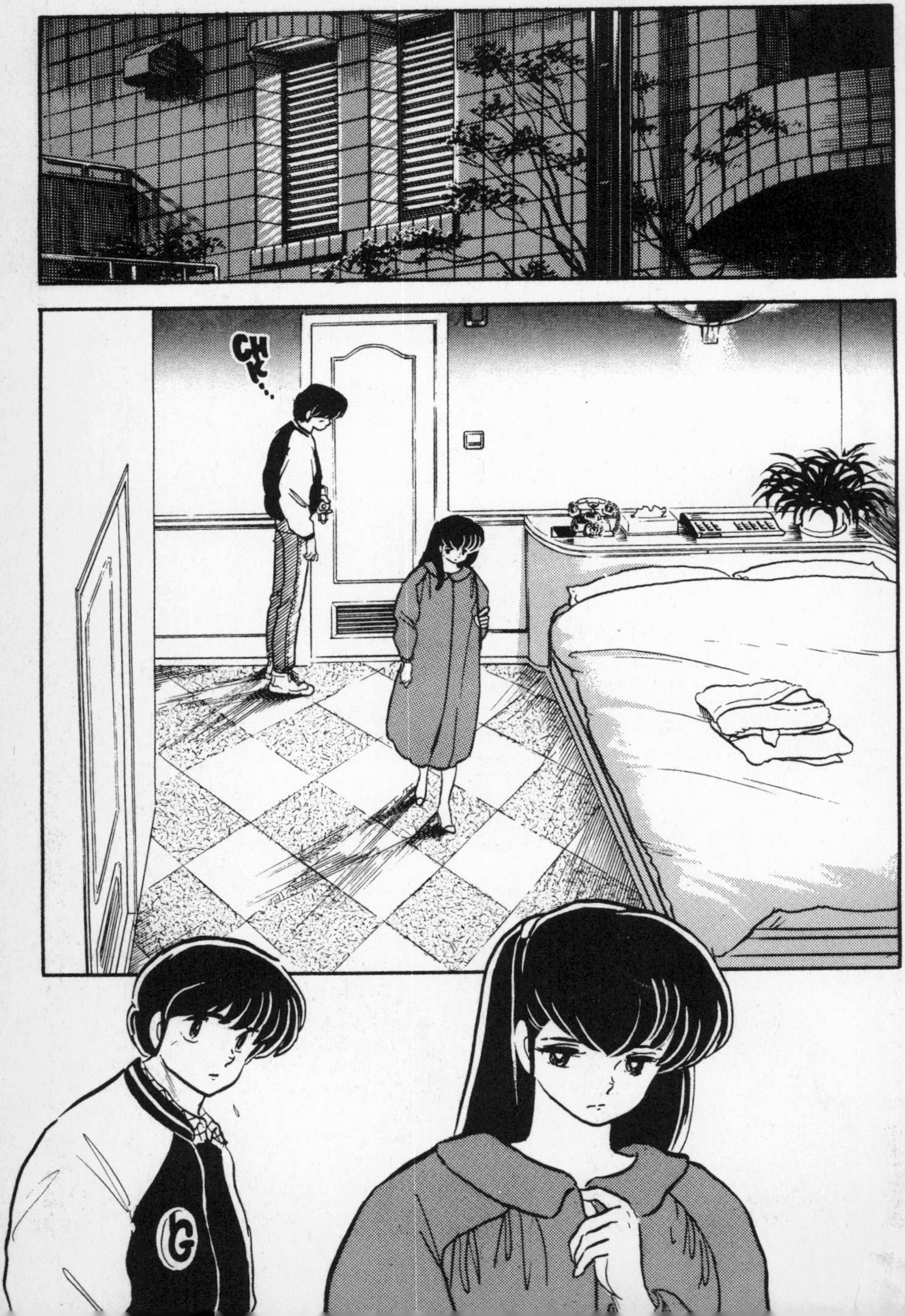
CHK...

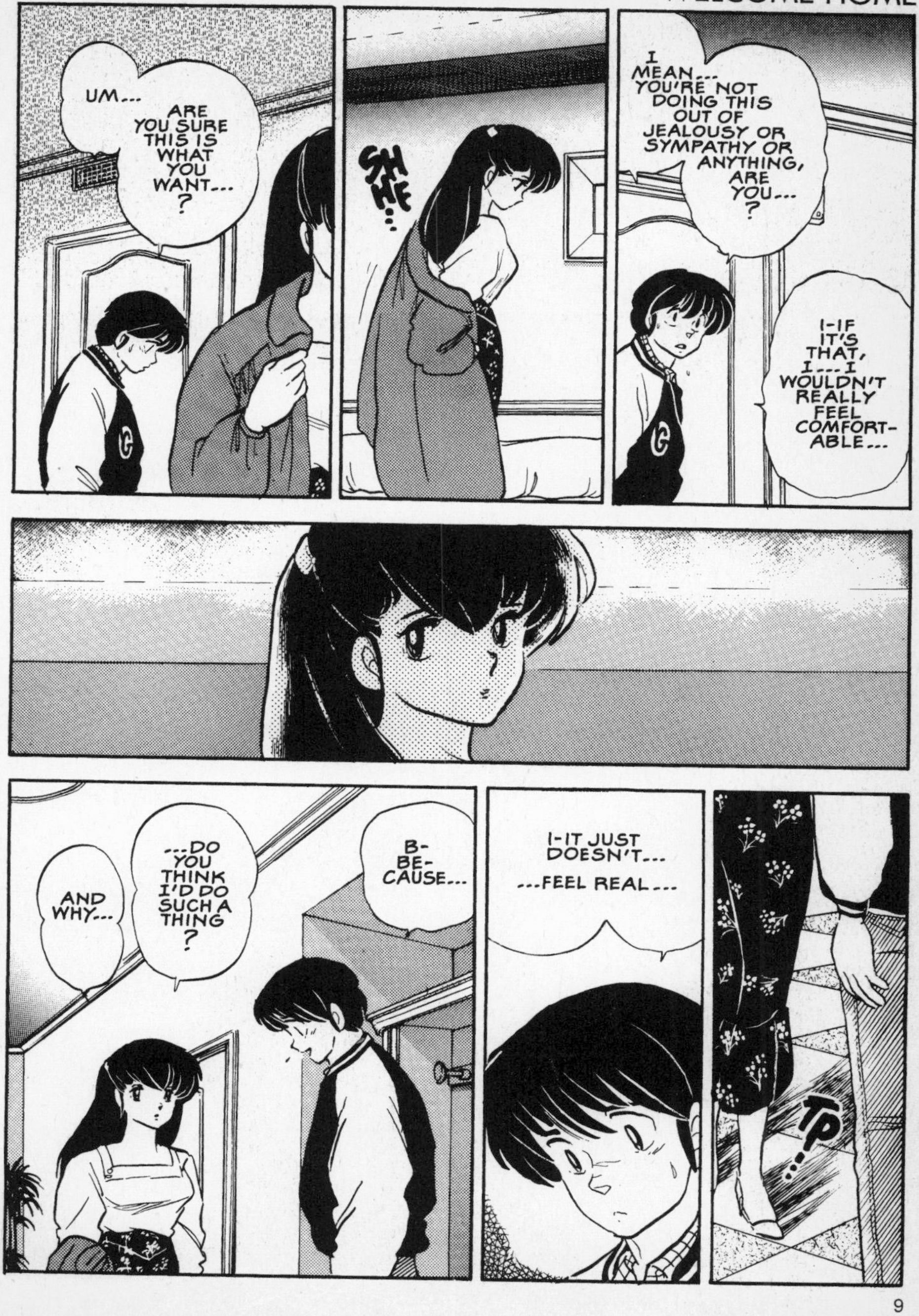
UM... ARE YOU SURE THIS IS WHAT YOU WANT...?
SHHF...
I MEAN... YOU'RE NOT DOING THIS OUT OF JEALOUSY OR SYMPATHY OR ANYTHING, ARE YOU...?
I-IF IT'S THAT, I... I WOULDN'T REALLY FEEL COMFORT-ABLE...
AND WHY...
...DO YOU THINK I'D DO SUCH A THING?
B-BE-CAUSE...
I-IT JUST DOESN'T...
...FEEL REAL...
TP...

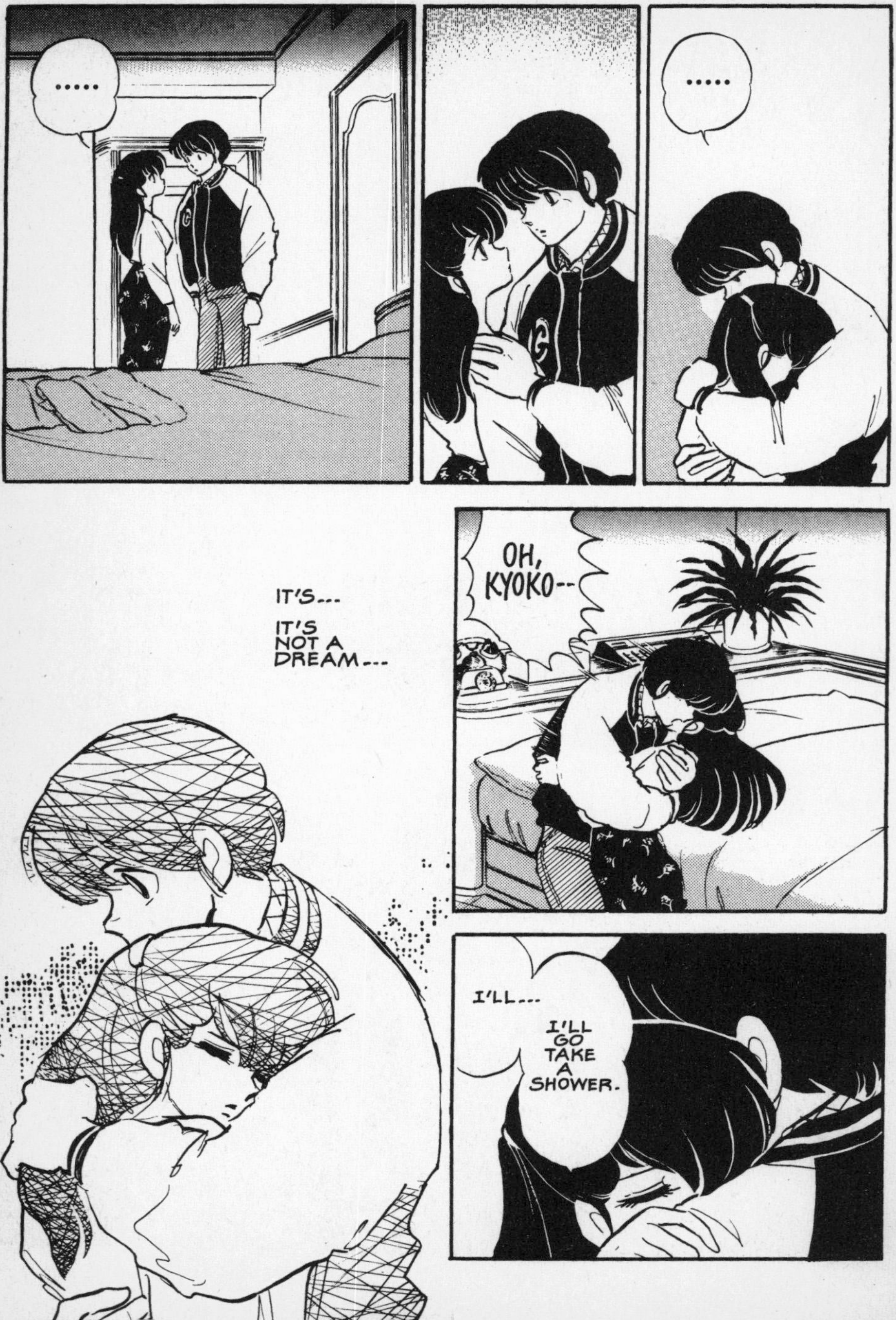
......
......
IT'S...
IT'S NOT A DREAM...
OH, KYOKO--
I'LL...
I'LL GO TAKE A SHOWER.

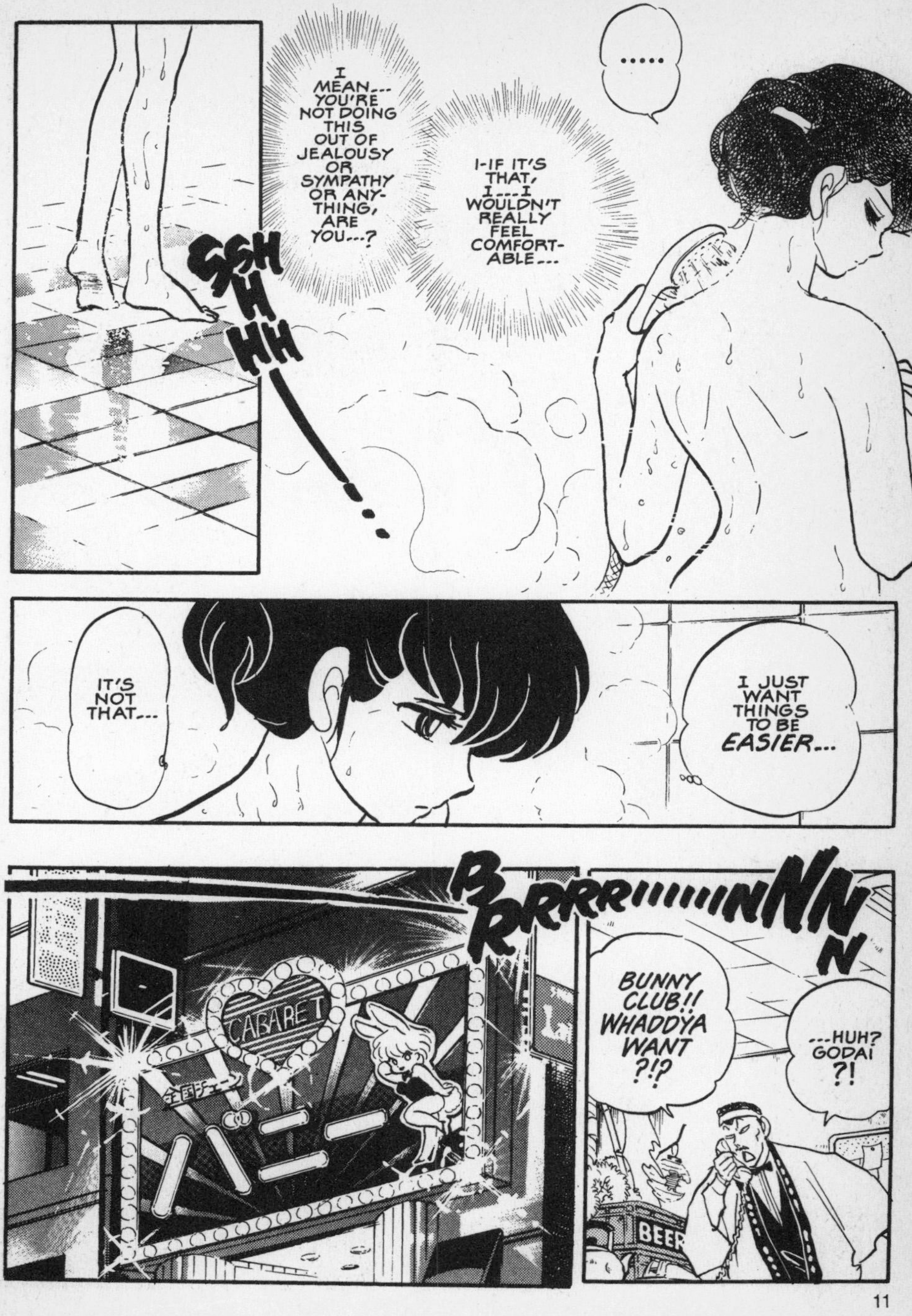
I MEAN... YOU'RE NOT DOING THIS OUT OF JEALOUSY OR SYMPATHY OR ANY-THING, ARE YOU...?
SSHHHHH
I-IF IT'S THAT, I...I WOULDN'T REALLY FEEL COMFORT-ABLE...
......
IT'S NOT THAT...
I JUST WANT THINGS TO BE *EASIER*...
CABARET
全国チェーン
バニー
BRRRRIIIIIINNNNN
BUNNY CLUB!! WHADDYA WANT ?!?
...HUH? GODAI ?!
BEER

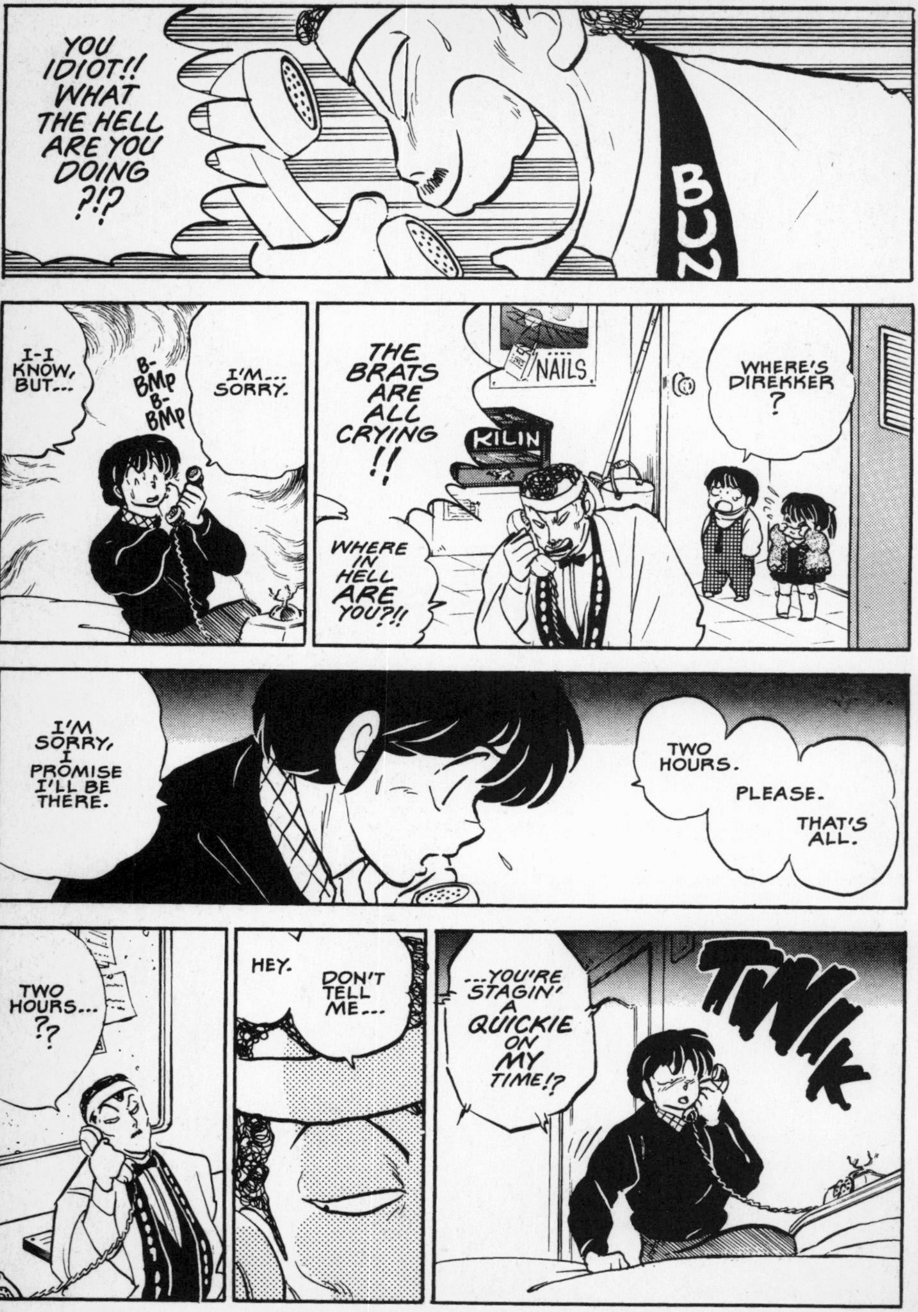
YOU IDIOT!! WHAT THE HELL ARE YOU DOING ?!?
BUN
I-I KNOW, BUT...
B-BMP B-BMP
I'M... SORRY.
THE BRATS ARE ALL CRYING !!
NAILS
KILIN
WHERE IN HELL ARE YOU?!!
WHERE'S DIREKKER ?
I'M SORRY, I PROMISE I'LL BE THERE.
TWO HOURS.
PLEASE.
THAT'S ALL.
TWO HOURS... ??
HEY.
DON'T TELL ME...
...YOU'RE STAGIN' A QUICKIE ON MY TIME!?
TWIK

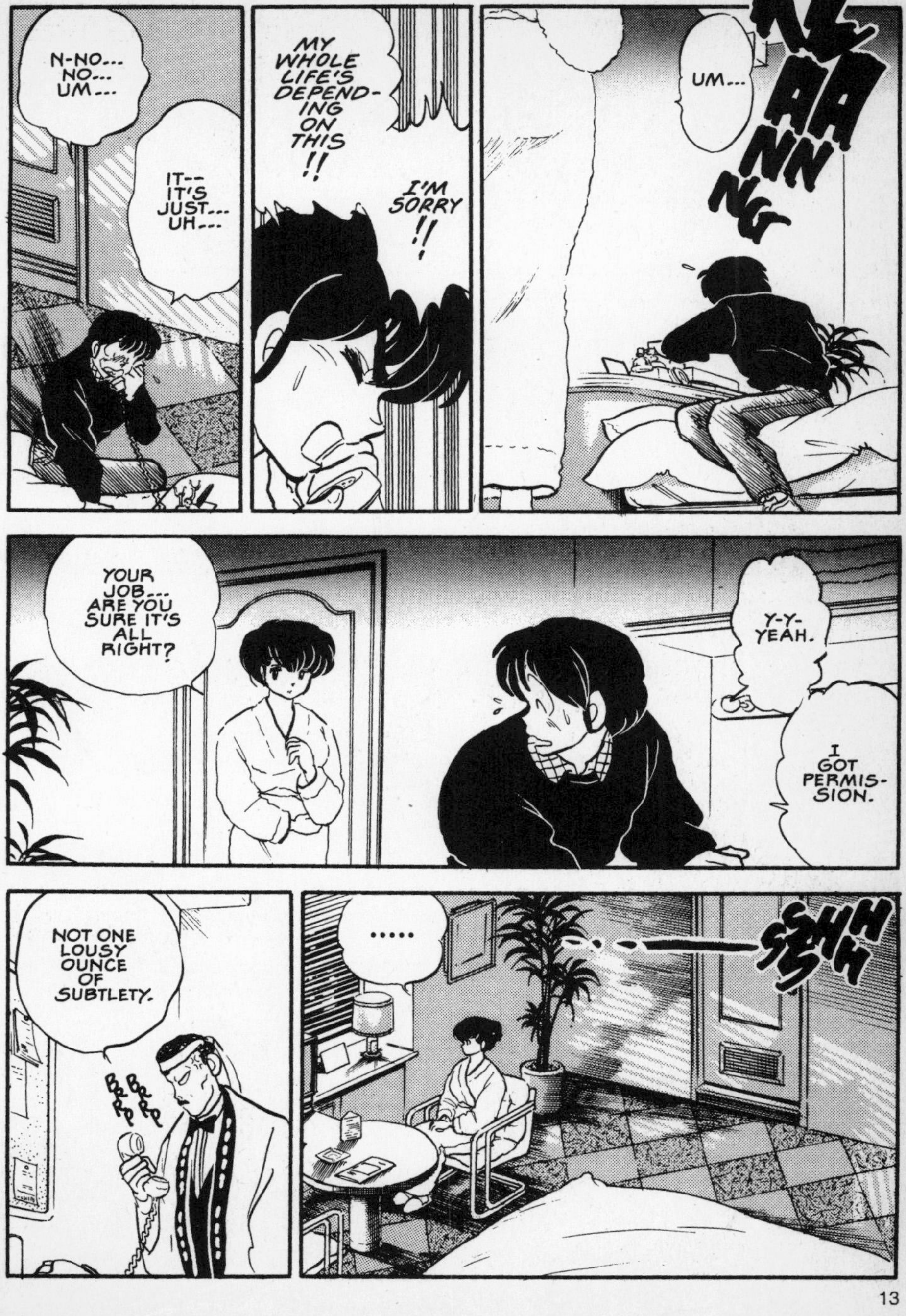
N-NO... NO... UM...
IT-- IT'S JUST... UH...
MY WHOLE LIFE'S DEPEND-ING ON THIS!!
I'M SORRY!!
UM...
KLAANNNG
YOUR JOB... ARE YOU SURE IT'S ALL RIGHT?
Y-Y-YEAH.
I GOT PERMIS-SION.
NOT ONE LOUSY OUNCE OF SUBTLETY.
.....

THIS *IS* WHAT I WANT... ISN'T IT...?

ABSOLUTE HONESTY ABOUT MY FEELINGS...

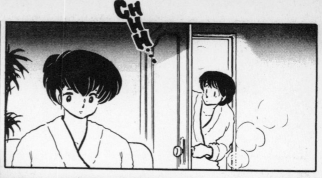

CHH...!

DMM

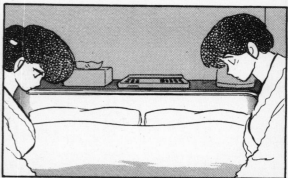

UH HH HH...

W-WOULD YOU LIKE A DRINK...?

NO, THANK YOU...

14

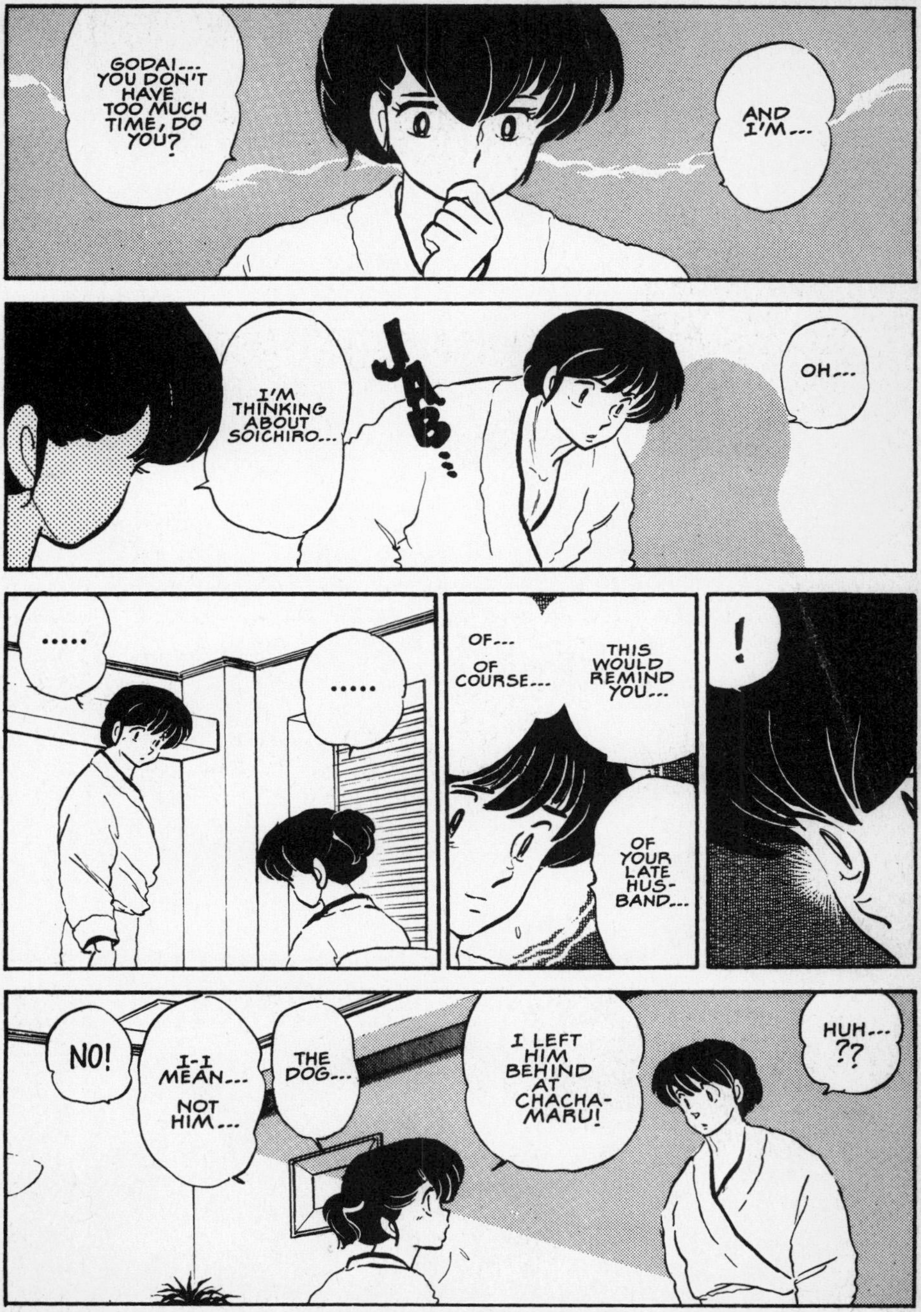
GODAI... YOU DON'T HAVE TOO MUCH TIME, DO YOU?
AND I'M...
I'M THINKING ABOUT SOICHIRO...
JAB...
OH...
.....
.....
OF... OF COURSE...
THIS WOULD REMIND YOU...
OF YOUR LATE HUS-BAND...
!
NO!
I-I MEAN... NOT HIM...
THE DOG...
I LEFT HIM BEHIND AT CHACHA-MARU!
HUH...??

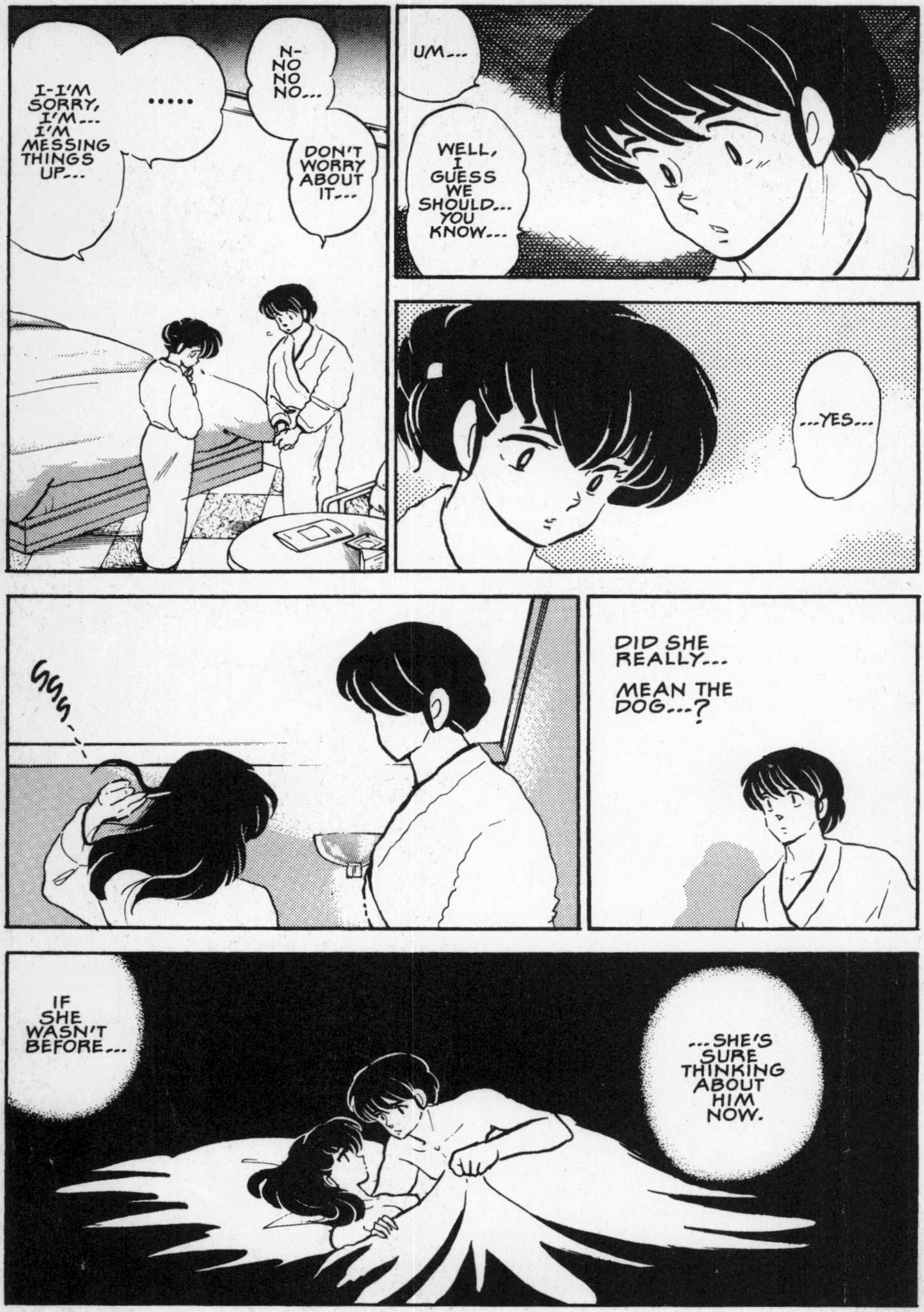
I-I'M SORRY, I'M... I'M MESSING THINGS UP...
.....
N-NO NO NO...
DON'T WORRY ABOUT IT...
UM...
WELL, I GUESS WE SHOULD... YOU KNOW...
...YES...
DID SHE REALLY...
MEAN THE DOG...?
IF SHE WASN'T BEFORE...
...SHE'S SURE THINKING ABOUT HIM NOW.

...I WONDER IF...

.....

NO. NO!

CONCENTRATE...!

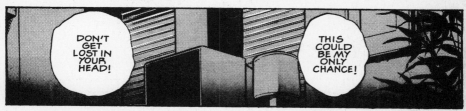

DON'T GET LOST IN YOUR HEAD!

THIS COULD BE MY ONLY CHANCE!

KYOKO...

OH, KYOKO!!

I BEG YOU... THINK ONLY OF ME.

FORGET ABOUT YOUR HUSBAND...

17

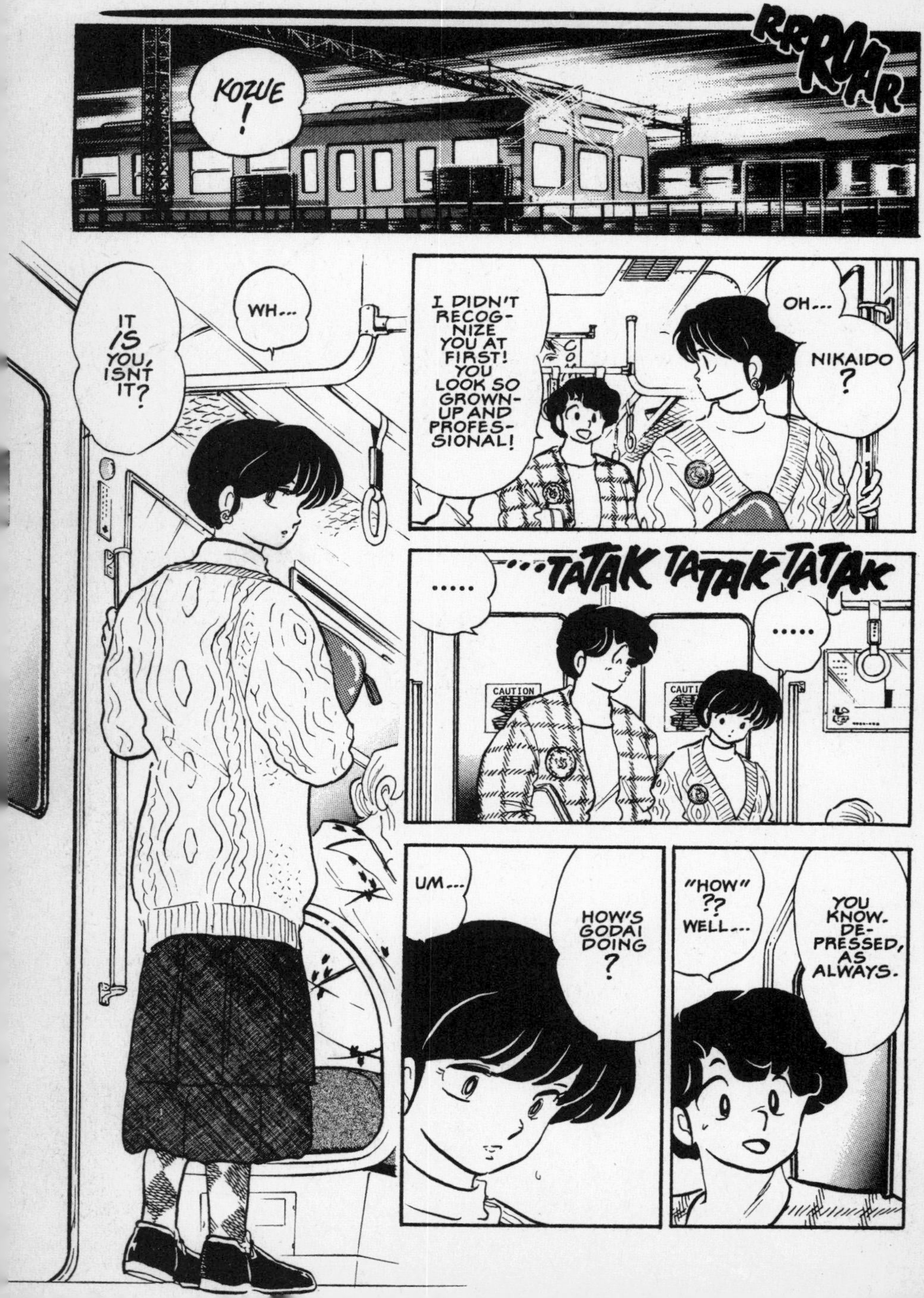
KOZUE!
RRROAR
IT IS YOU, ISNT IT?
WH...
I DIDN'T RECOGNIZE YOU AT FIRST! YOU LOOK SO GROWN-UP AND PROFESSIONAL!
OH...
NIKAIDO?
.....
...TATAK TATAK TATAK
.....
UM...
HOW'S GODAI DOING?
"HOW"?? WELL...
YOU KNOW. DEPRESSED, AS ALWAYS.

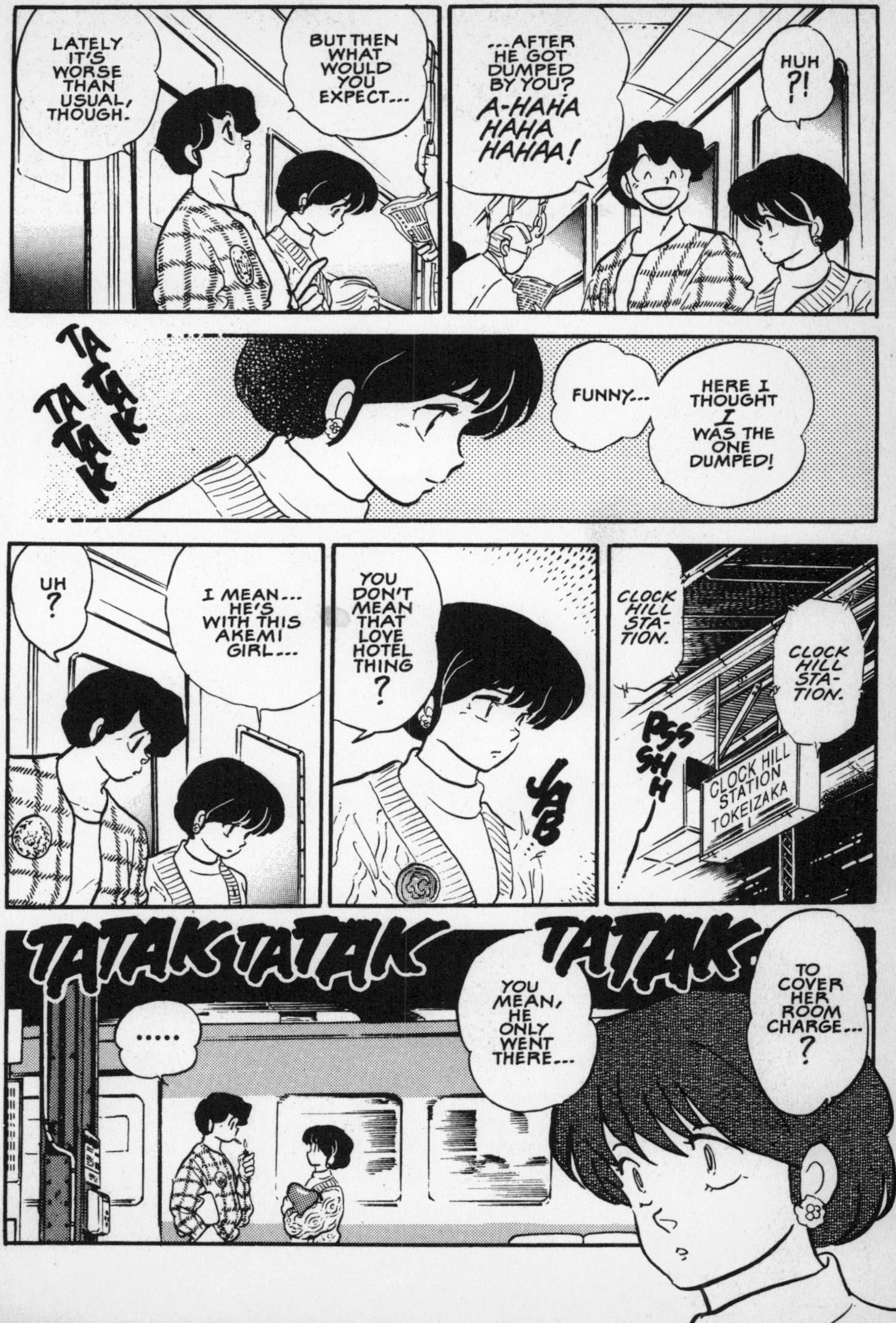
LATELY IT'S WORSE THAN USUAL, THOUGH.
BUT THEN WHAT WOULD YOU EXPECT...
...AFTER HE GOT DUMPED BY YOU? A-HAHA HAHA HAHAA!
HUH ?!
TA TAK TA TAK
FUNNY...
HERE I THOUGHT I WAS THE ONE DUMPED!
UH ?
I MEAN... HE'S WITH THIS AKEMI GIRL...
YOU DON'T MEAN THAT LOVE HOTEL THING ?
JAB
CLOCK HILL STATION.
CLOCK HILL STATION.
PSSSHH
CLOCK HILL STATION TOKEIZAKA
TATAK TATAK
TATAK
.....
YOU MEAN, HE ONLY WENT THERE...
TO COVER HER ROOM CHARGE... ?

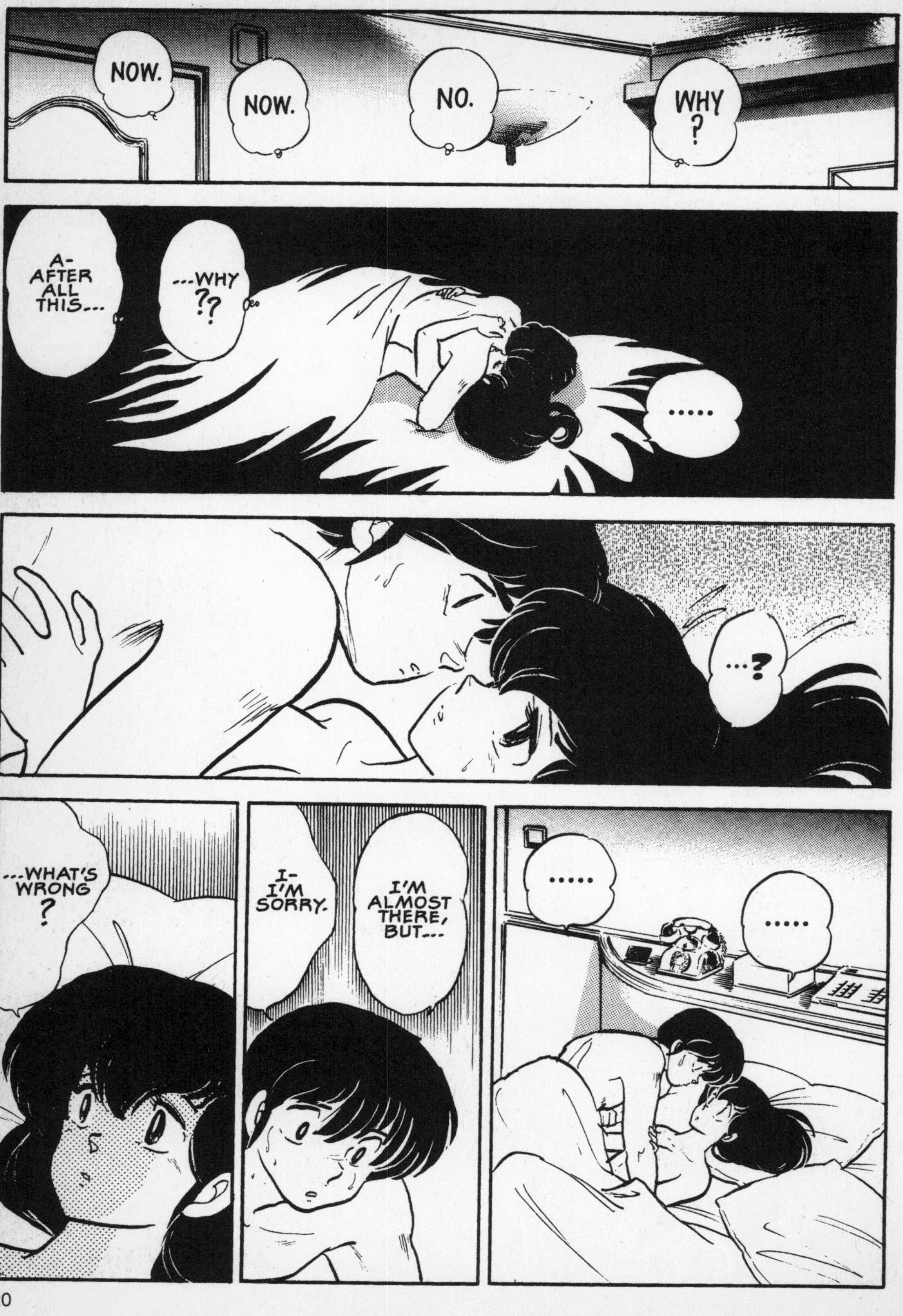
NOW.
NOW.
NO.
WHY ?
A- AFTER ALL THIS...
...WHY ??
.....
...?
...WHAT'S WRONG ?
I- I'M SORRY.
I'M ALMOST THERE, BUT...
.....
.....

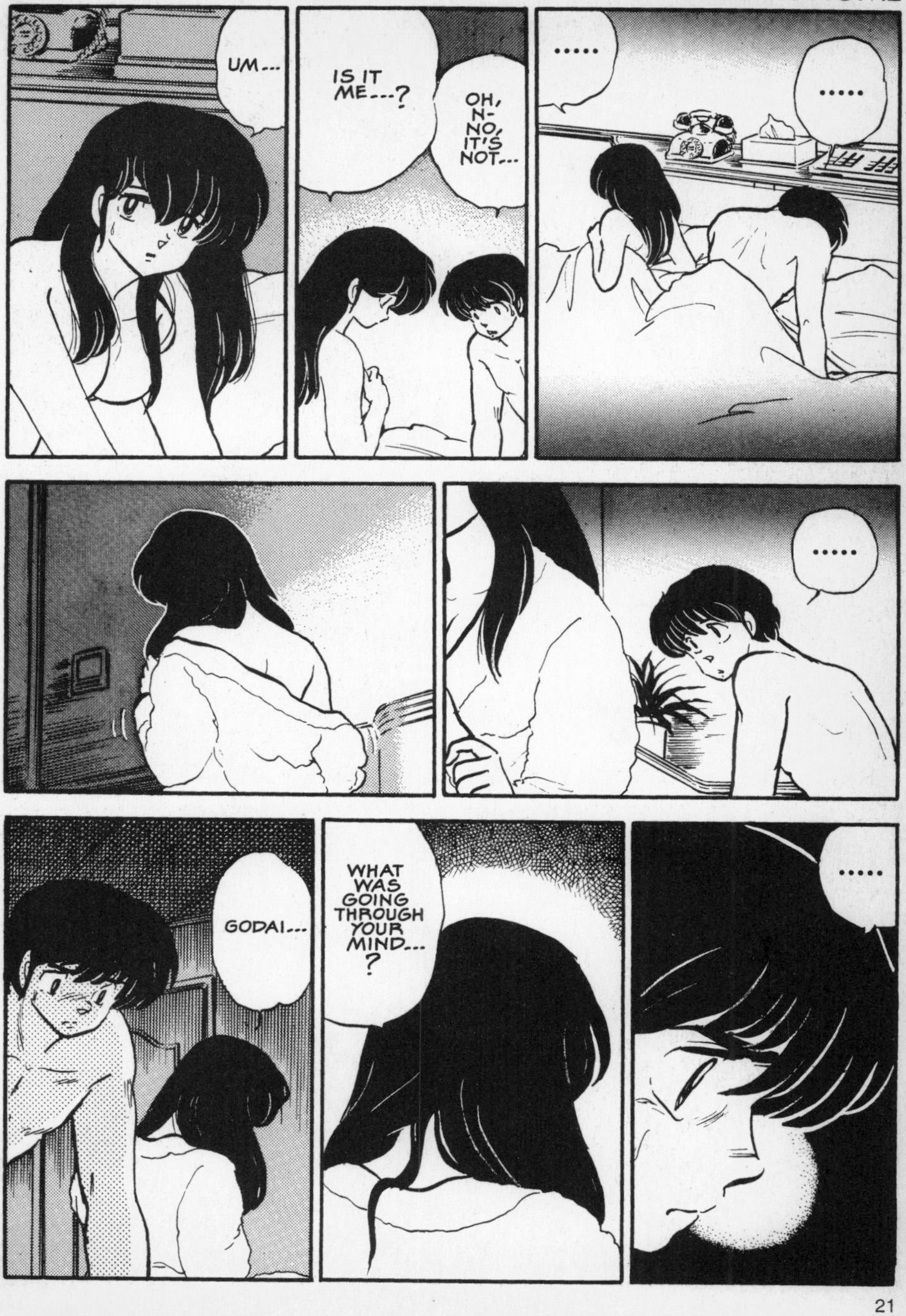
UM...
IS IT ME...?
OH, N-NO, IT'S NOT...
.....
.....
.....
GODAI...
WHAT WAS GOING THROUGH YOUR MIND...?
.....

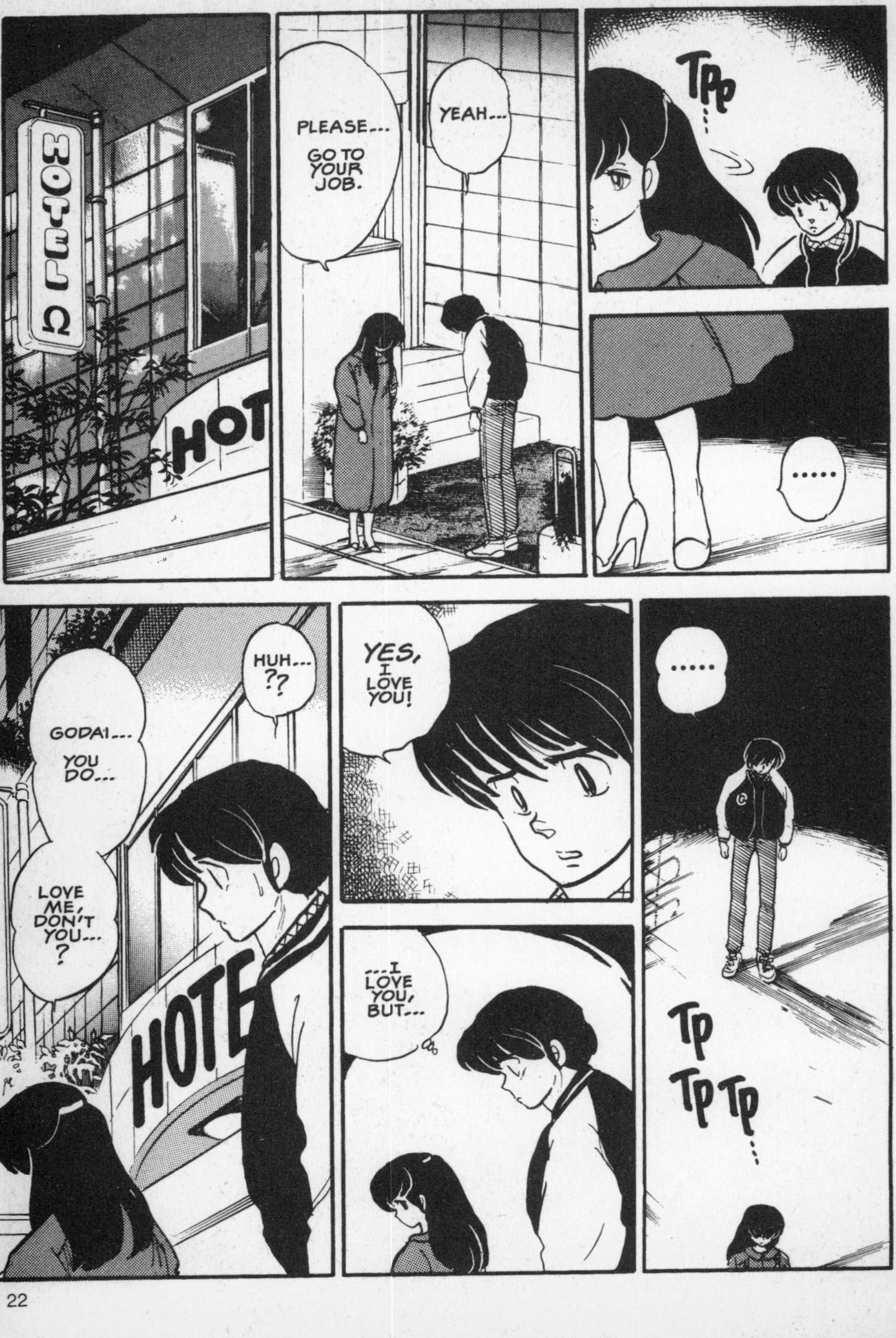
HOTEL Ω
HOT
PLEASE... GO TO YOUR JOB.
YEAH...
TPP...
......
GODAI... YOU DO...
LOVE ME, DON'T YOU...?
HUH...??
HOTEL Ω
HOTE
YES, I LOVE YOU!
...I LOVE YOU, BUT...
......
TP TP TP...

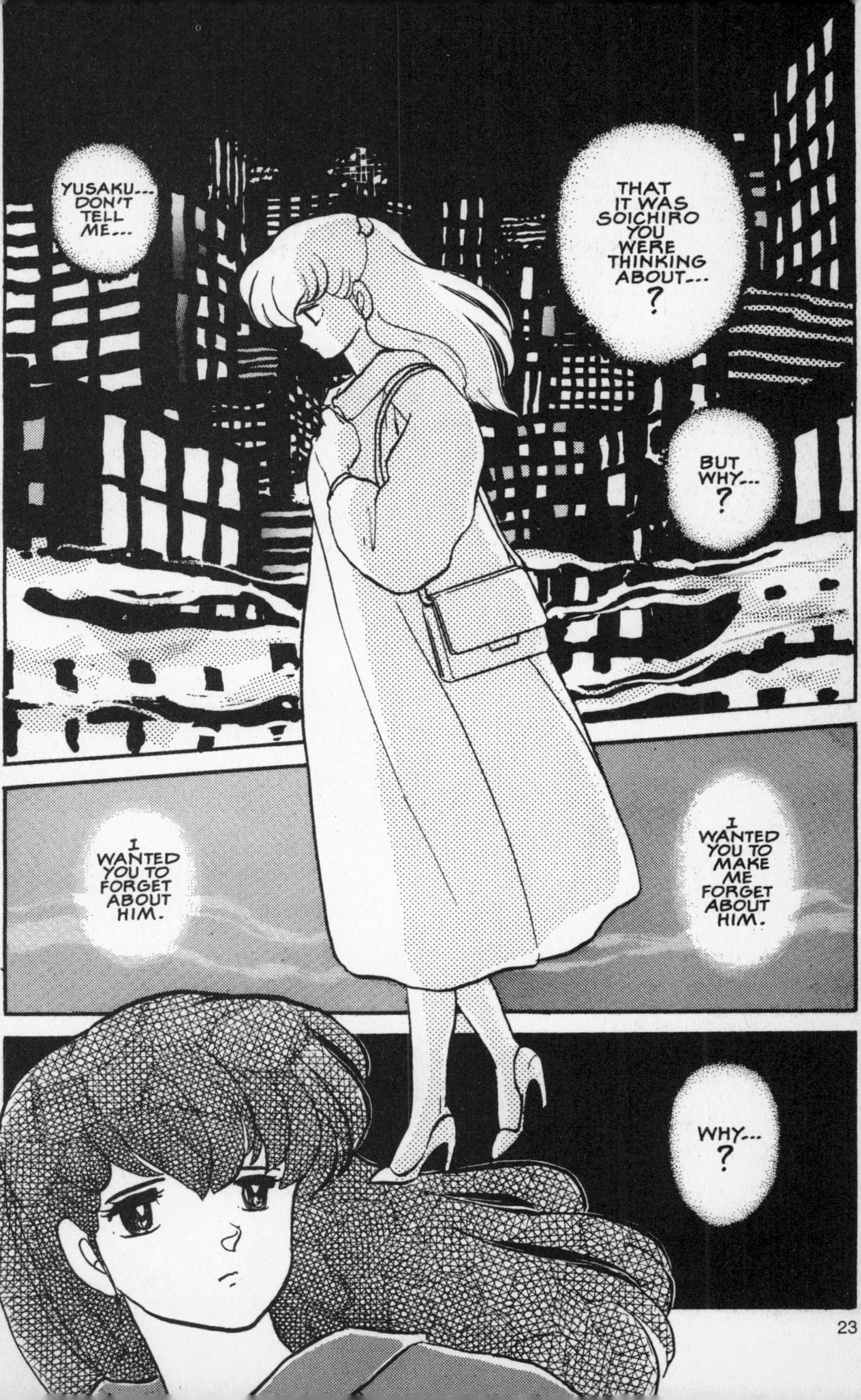
YUSAKU... DON'T TELL ME...
THAT IT WAS SOICHIRO YOU WERE THINKING ABOUT...?
BUT WHY...?
I WANTED YOU TO FORGET ABOUT HIM.
I WANTED YOU TO MAKE ME FORGET ABOUT HIM.
WHY...?

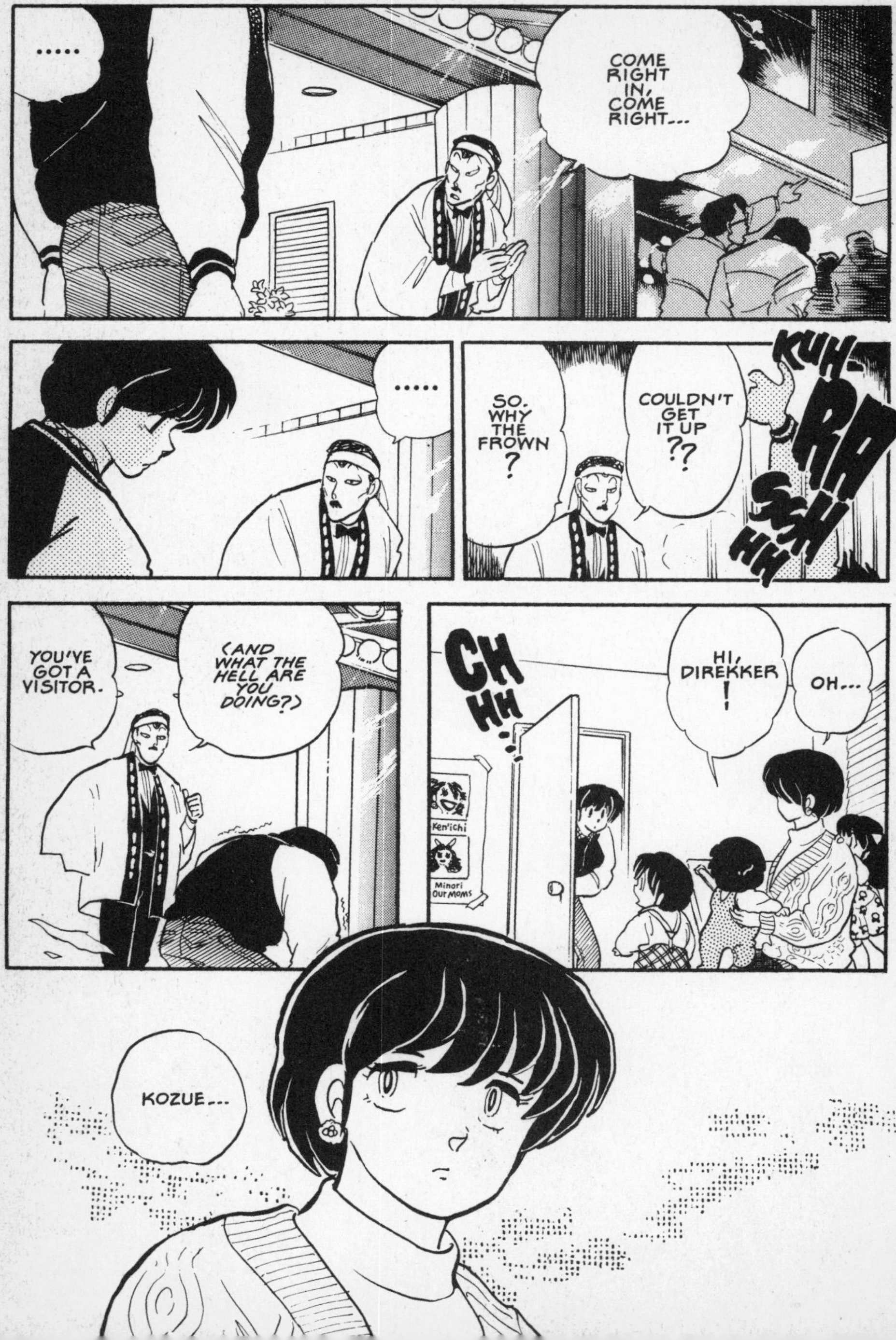
......
COME RIGHT IN, COME RIGHT...
......
SO. WHY THE FROWN ?
COULDN'T GET IT UP ??
KUH-RA
SSH HH
YOU'VE GOT A VISITOR.
(AND WHAT THE HELL ARE YOU DOING?)
CH HH
Ken'ichi
Minori
Our Moms
HI, DIREKKER !
OH...
KOZUE...

PART TWO
THE TRUTH

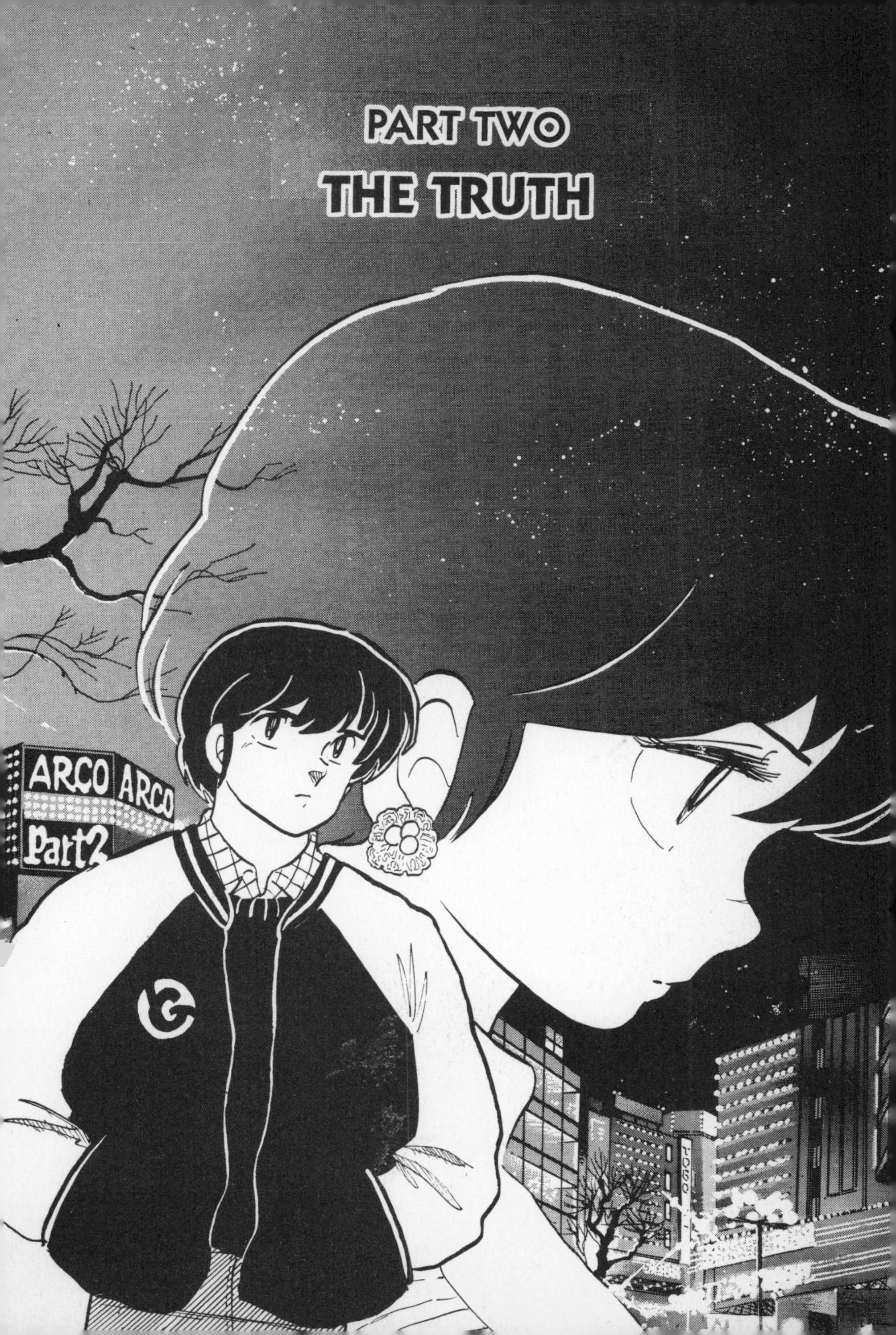
ARCO ARCO
Part2

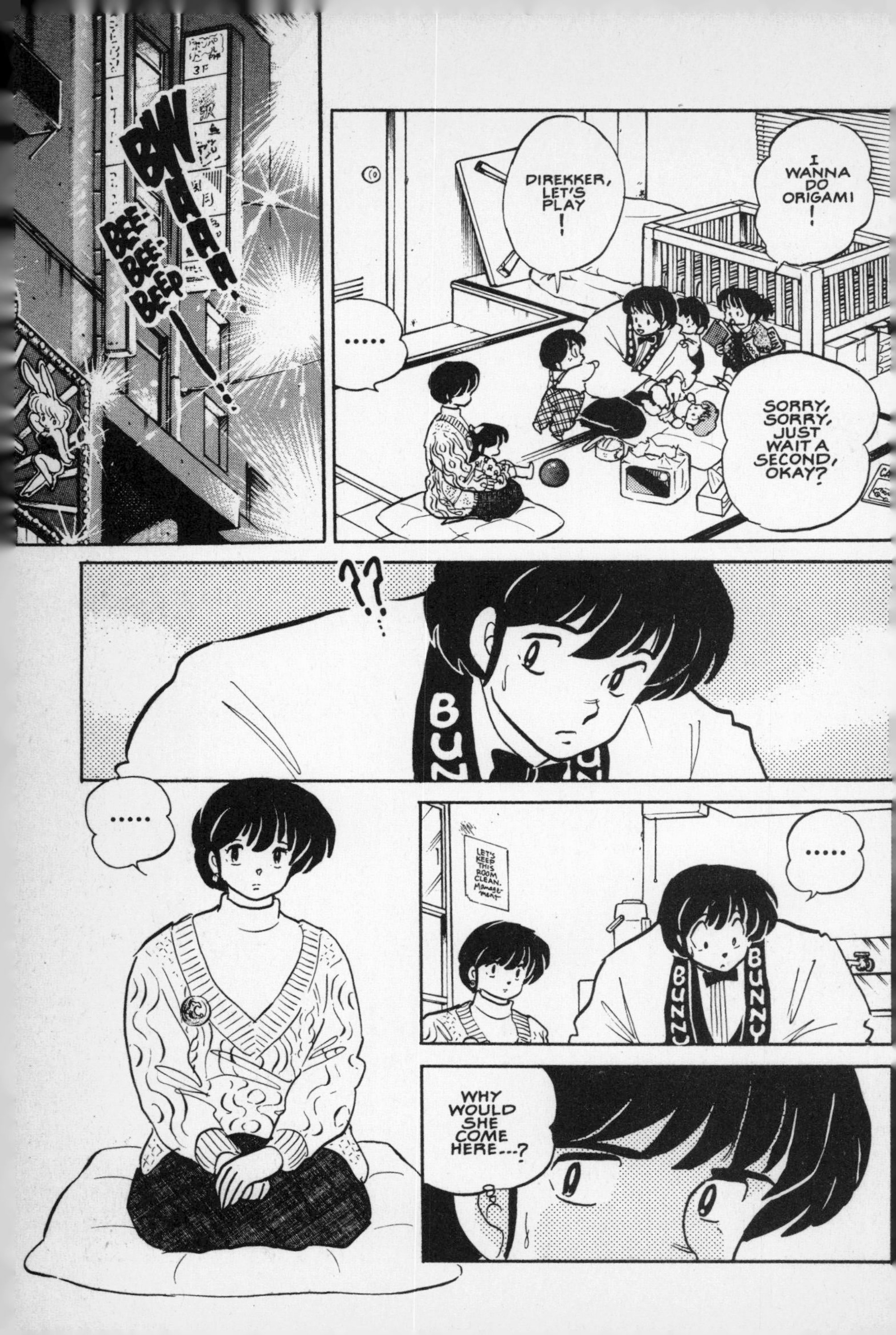
BWAAAH!
BEE-BEE-BEEP!!
DIREKKER, LET'S PLAY!
I WANNA DO ORIGAMI!
.....
SORRY, SORRY, JUST WAIT A SECOND, OKAY?
??
.....
LET'S KEEP THIS ROOM CLEAN. Management
.....
WHY WOULD SHE COME HERE...?

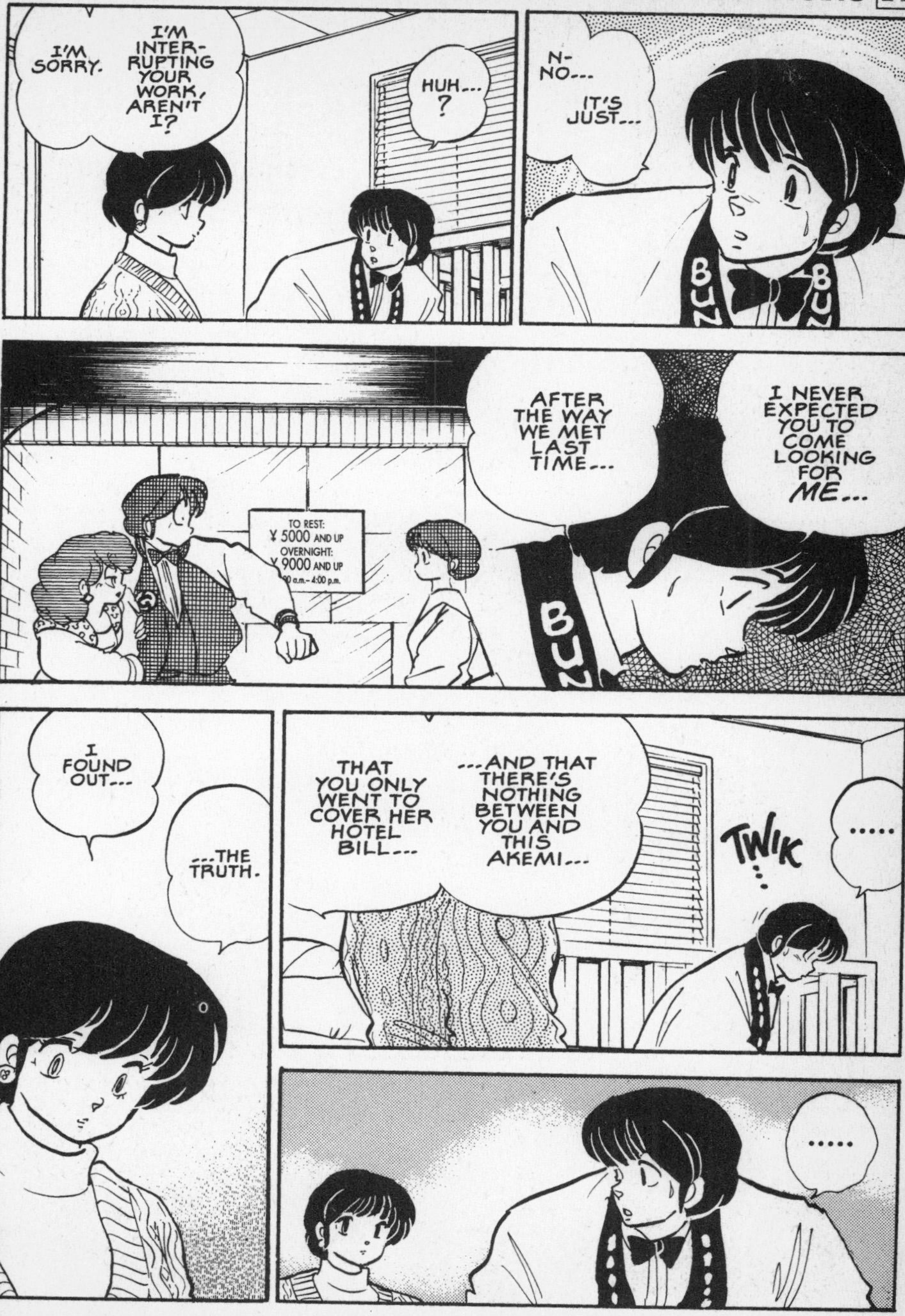
I'M SORRY.
I'M INTERRUPTING YOUR WORK, AREN'T I?
HUH... ?
N-NO... IT'S JUST...
TO REST: ¥ 5000 AND UP
OVERNIGHT: ¥ 9000 AND UP
AFTER THE WAY WE MET LAST TIME...
I NEVER EXPECTED YOU TO COME LOOKING FOR ME...
I FOUND OUT...
...THE TRUTH.
THAT YOU ONLY WENT TO COVER HER HOTEL BILL...
...AND THAT THERE'S NOTHING BETWEEN YOU AND THIS AKEMI...
TWIK
.....
.....

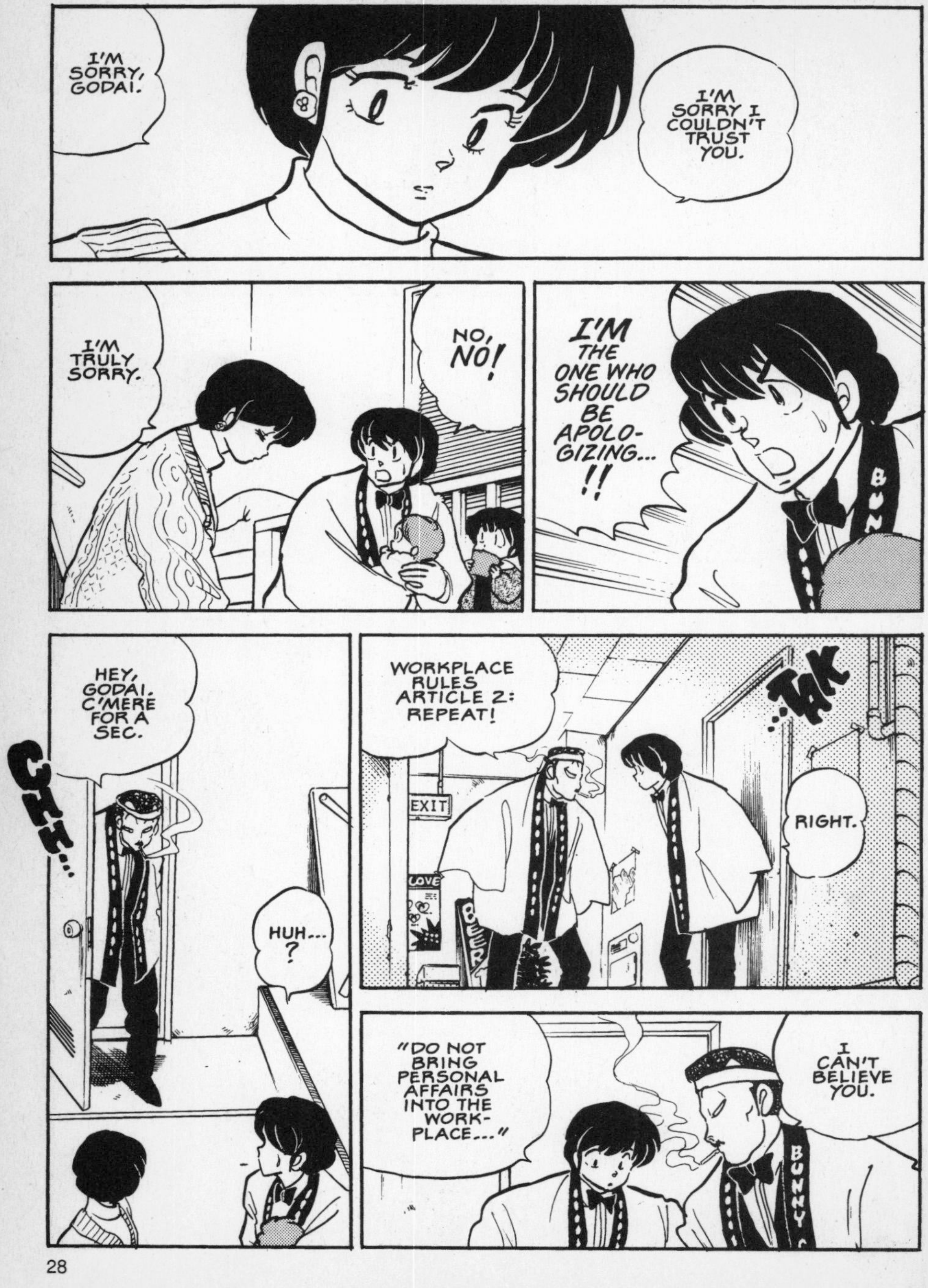
I'M SORRY, GODAI.
I'M SORRY I COULDN'T TRUST YOU.
I'M TRULY SORRY.
NO, NO!
I'M THE ONE WHO SHOULD BE APOLOGIZING...!!
BUN
CHHH...
HEY, GODAI. C'MERE FOR A SEC.
HUH...?
WORKPLACE RULES ARTICLE 2: REPEAT!
...TAK
EXIT
LOVE
BEER
RIGHT.
"DO NOT BRING PERSONAL AFFAIRS INTO THE WORK-PLACE..."
I CAN'T BELIEVE YOU.
BUNNY

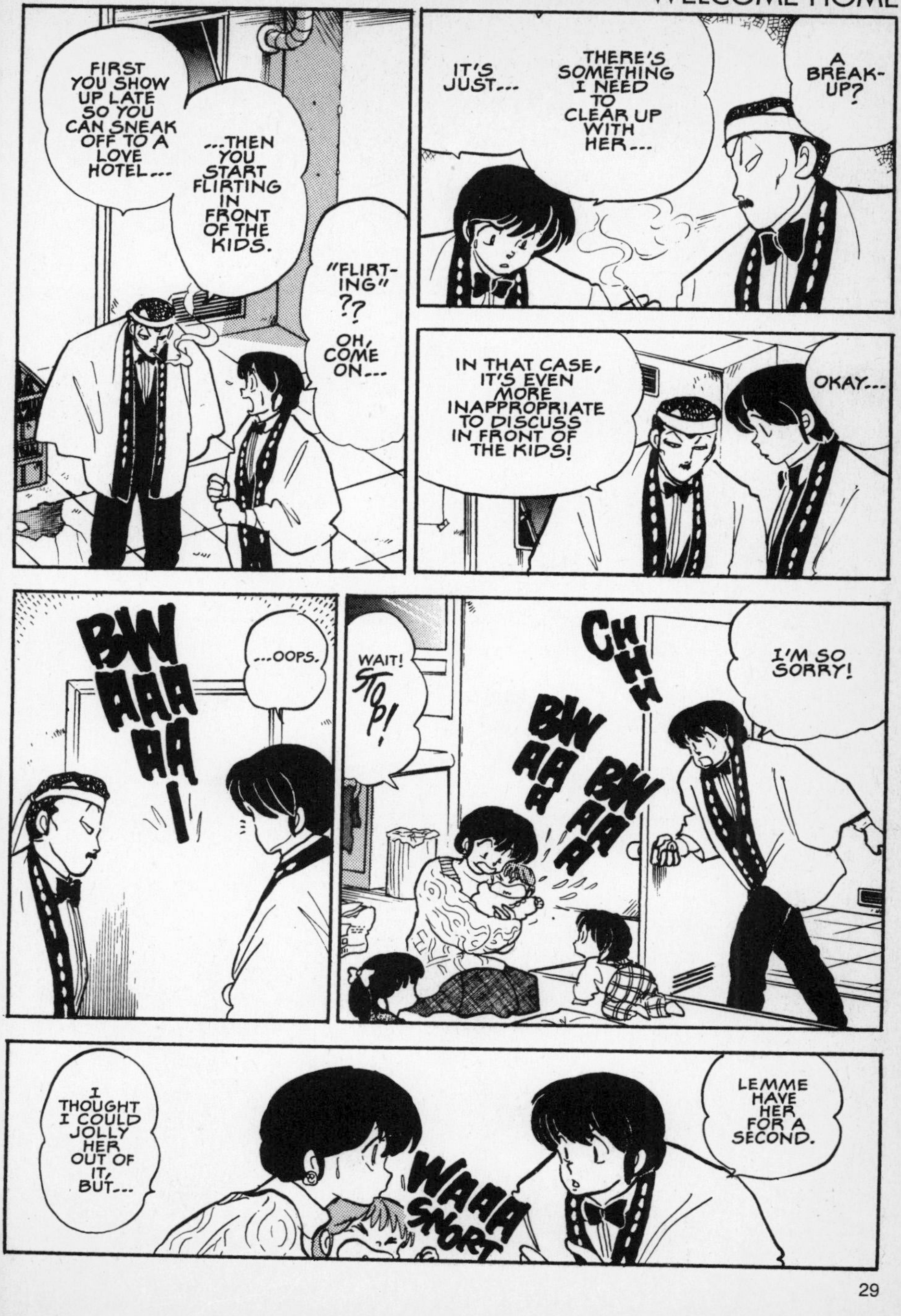
FIRST YOU SHOW UP LATE SO YOU CAN SNEAK OFF TO A LOVE HOTEL...
...THEN YOU START FLIRTING IN FRONT OF THE KIDS.
"FLIRTING" ??
OH, COME ON...
IT'S JUST...
THERE'S SOMETHING I NEED TO CLEAR UP WITH HER...
A BREAK-UP?
IN THAT CASE, IT'S EVEN MORE INAPPROPRIATE TO DISCUSS IN FRONT OF THE KIDS!
OKAY...
...OOPS.
WAIT!
STOP!
I'M SO SORRY!
I THOUGHT I COULD JOLLY HER OUT OF IT, BUT...
WAAAA
SNORT
LEMME HAVE HER FOR A SECOND.

SHH
SHH
SHH
SHH...

CH CH CH CH

.....

WOW... THAT WAS AMAZING, GODAI!

HUH?

THROB!

OH, NO, IT'S NOTHING.

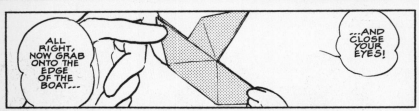

ALL RIGHT, NOW GRAB ONTO THE EDGE OF THE BOAT...

...AND CLOSE YOUR EYES!

UH-OH!

THAT'S FUNNY...

WHY ARE YOU HOLDING ONTO THE SAIL NOW?!

WEEEEE- HAHAHA

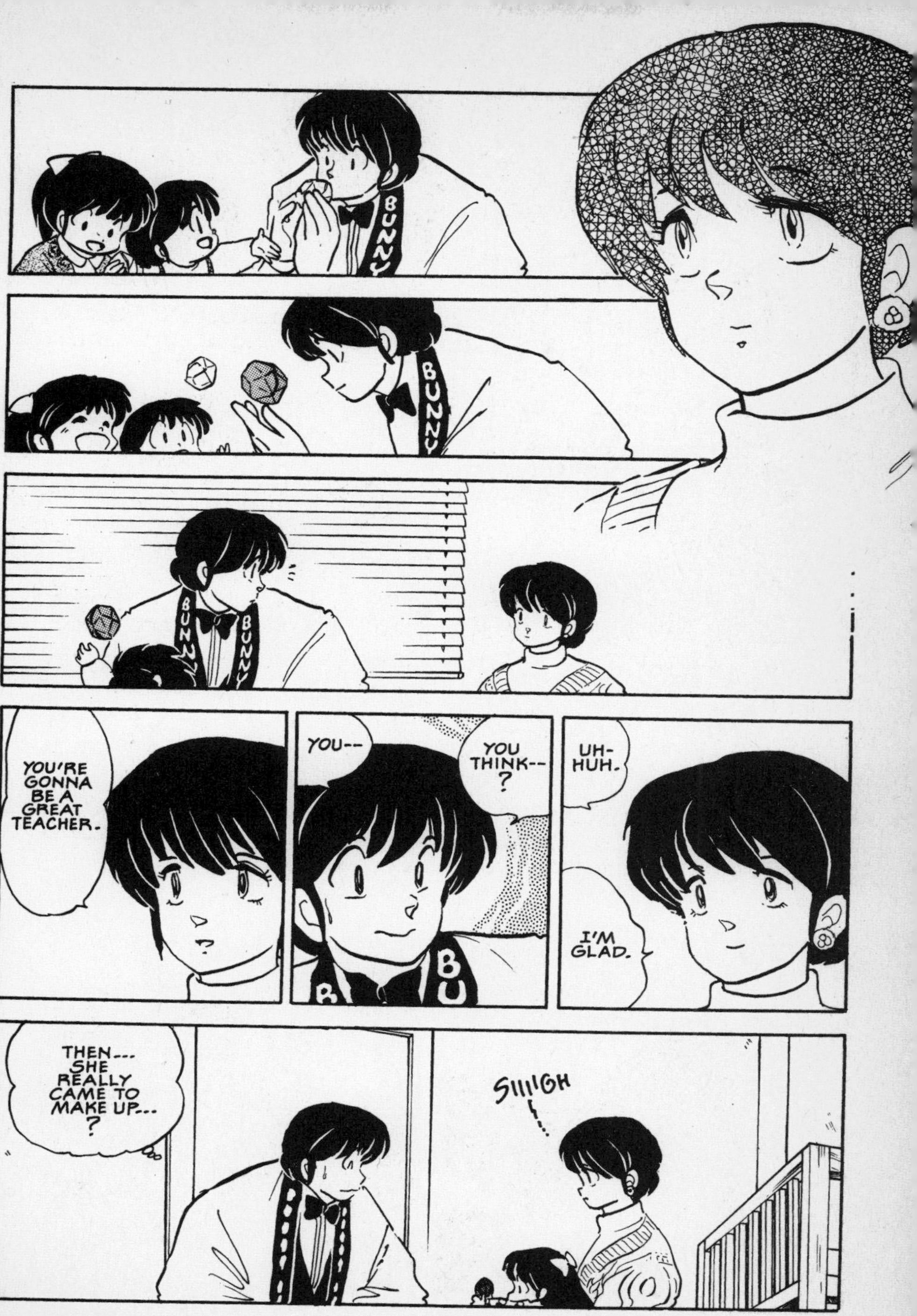
BUNNY
BUNNY
BUNNY
BUNNY
YOU'RE GONNA BE A GREAT TEACHER.
YOU--
YOU THINK--?
UH-HUH.
I'M GLAD.
THEN... SHE REALLY CAME TO MAKE UP...?
SIIIGH

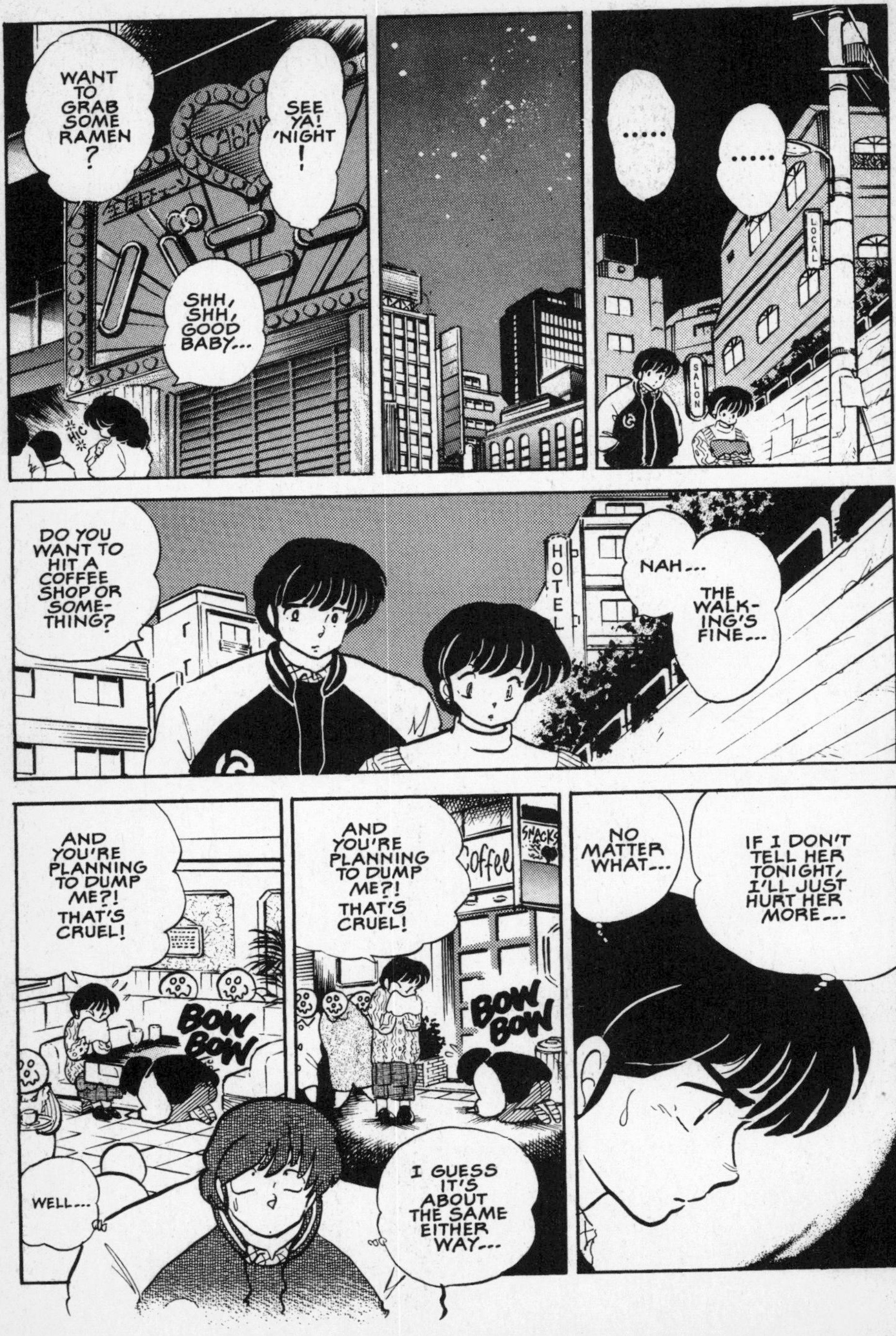
WANT TO GRAB SOME RAMEN?
SEE YA! 'NIGHT!
SHH, SHH, GOOD BABY...
HIC
......
......
LOCAL
SALON
DO YOU WANT TO HIT A COFFEE SHOP OR SOME-THING?
HOTEL
NAH... THE WALK-ING'S FINE...
AND YOU'RE PLANNING TO DUMP ME?! THAT'S CRUEL!
BOW BOW
WELL...
AND YOU'RE PLANNING TO DUMP ME?! THAT'S CRUEL!
Coffee
SNACKS
BOW BOW
I GUESS IT'S ABOUT THE SAME EITHER WAY...
NO MATTER WHAT...
IF I DON'T TELL HER TONIGHT, I'LL JUST HURT HER MORE...

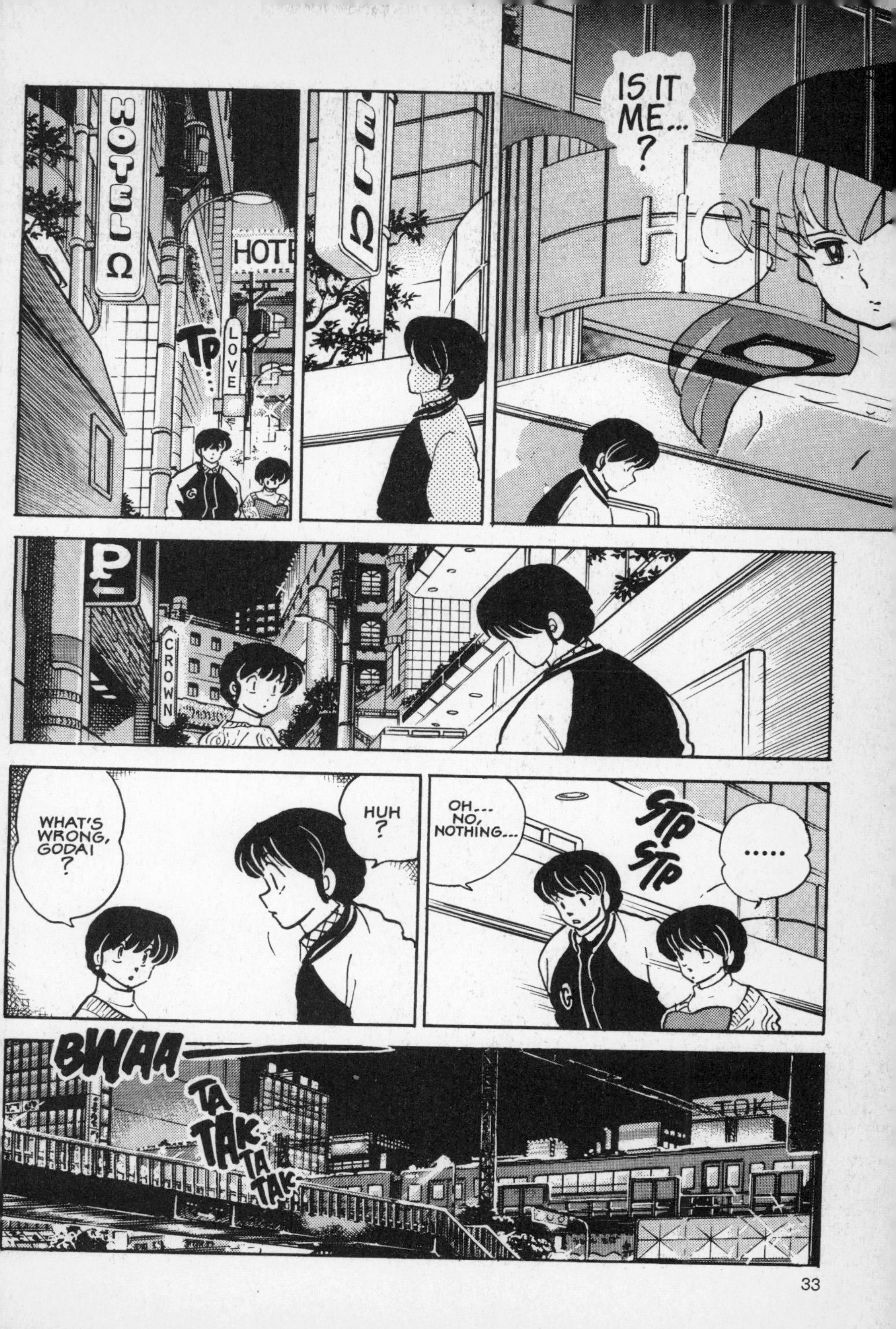

HOTEL Ω
HOTE
LOVE
TP...
EL Ω
IS IT ME... ?
HOT
P
CROWN
WHAT'S WRONG, GODAI ?
HUH ?
OH... NO, NOTHING...
STP STP
.....
BWAA
TA TAK TA TAK
TOK

AREN'T YOU COLD?

BWAAAAEEEEE!

NOPE, I'M FINE.

.....

KOZUE... UM... YOU SEE...

OH!

LOOK!

THE MOON'S SO PRETTY!

.....

Y-YEAH... REAL PRETTY.

LISTEN, KOZUE... SEE...

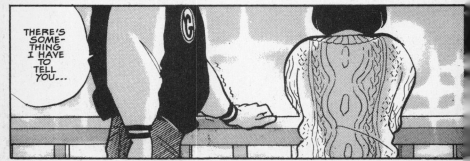

THERE'S SOMETHING I HAVE TO TELL YOU...

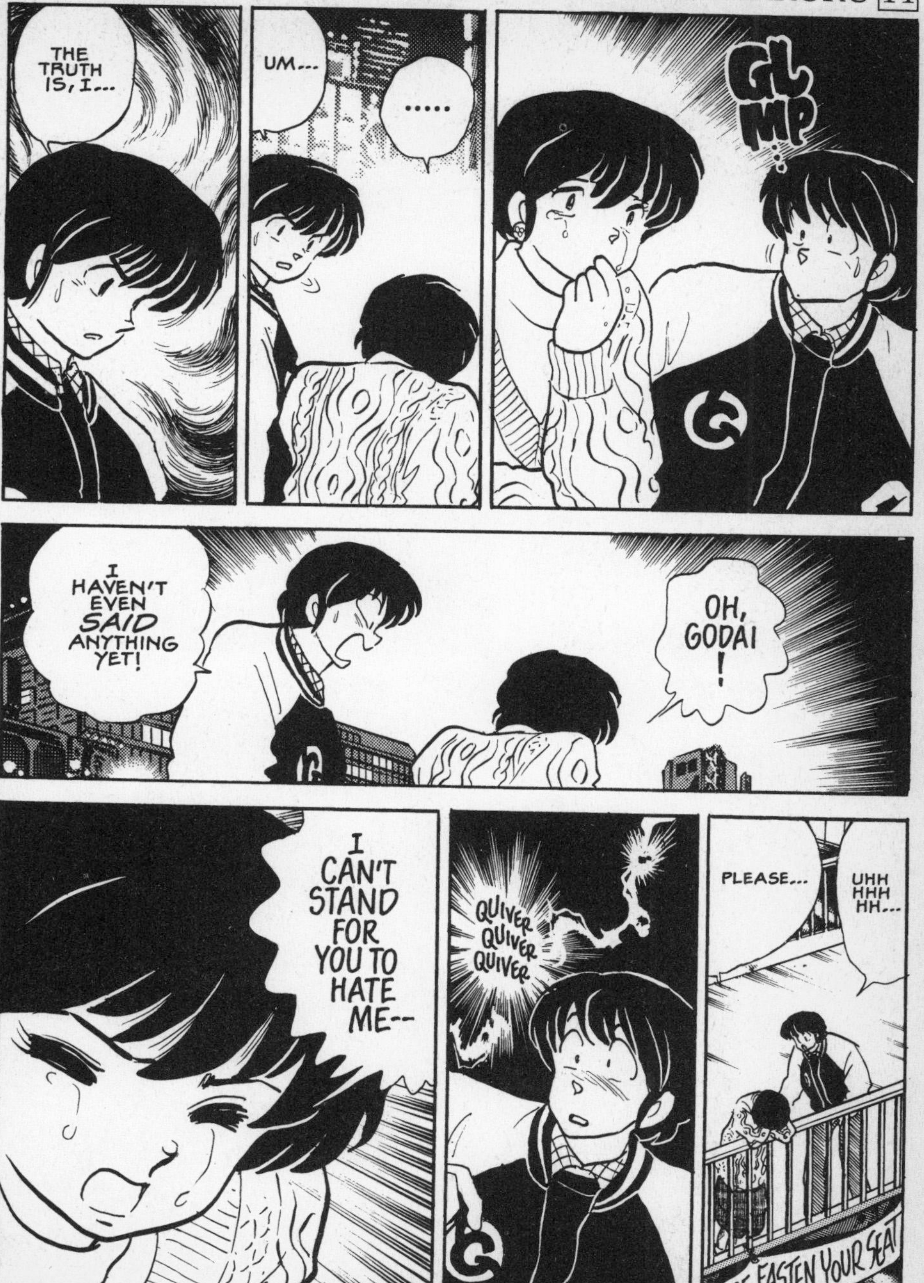
THE TRUTH IS, I...
UM...
......
GLMP
I HAVEN'T EVEN SAID ANYTHING YET!
OH, GODAI!
I CAN'T STAND FOR YOU TO HATE ME--
QUIVER QUIVER QUIVER
PLEASE...
UHH HHH HH...
EASE FASTEN YOUR SEAT

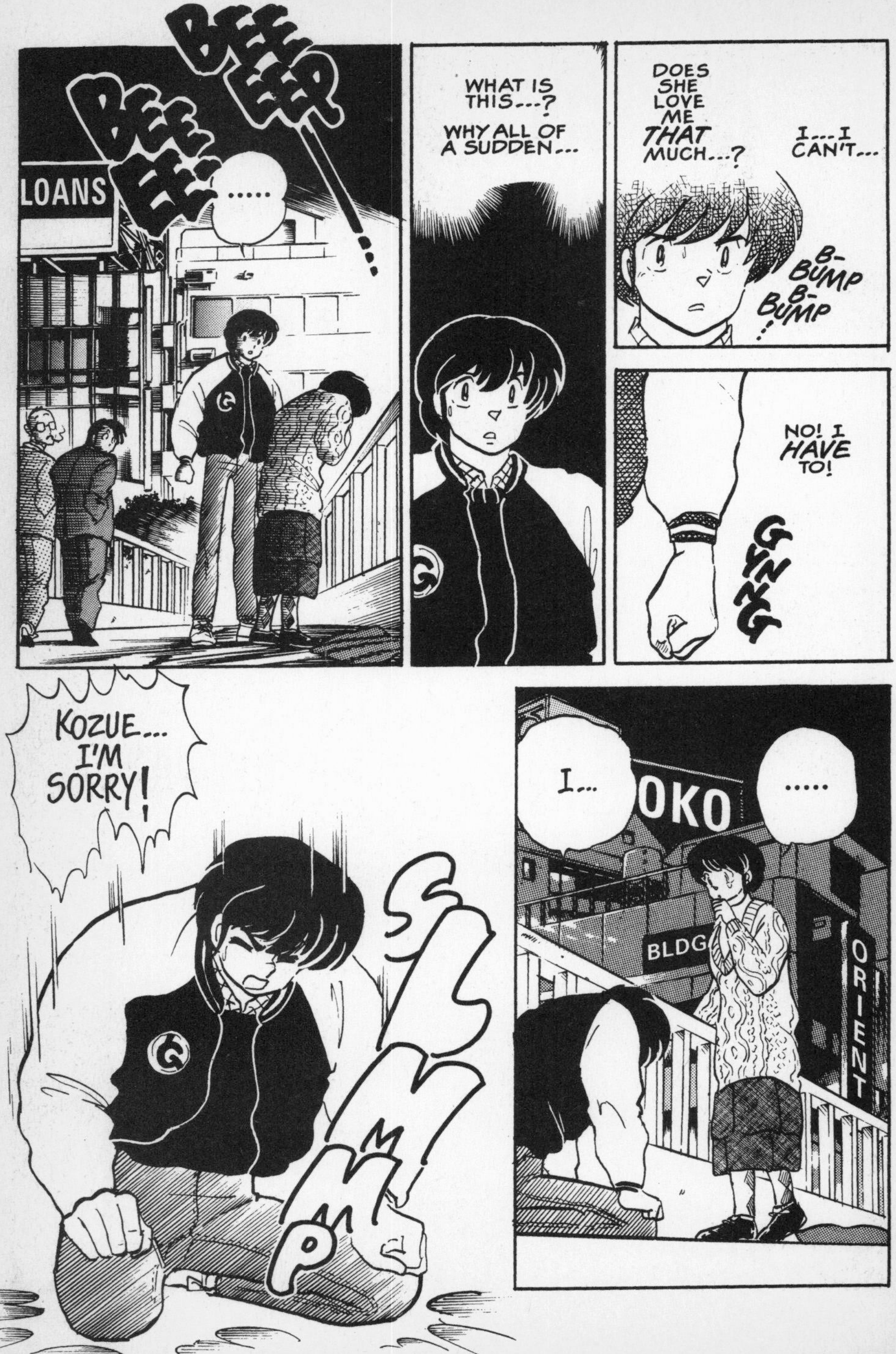
BEE EEP
BEE EE
LOANS
.....
WHAT IS THIS...?
WHY ALL OF A SUDDEN...
DOES SHE LOVE ME THAT MUCH...?
I... I CAN'T...
B-BUMP B-BUMP
NO! I HAVE TO!
GYNG
KOZUE... I'M SORRY!
SLUMMMP
I...
.....
OKO
BLDG
ORIENT

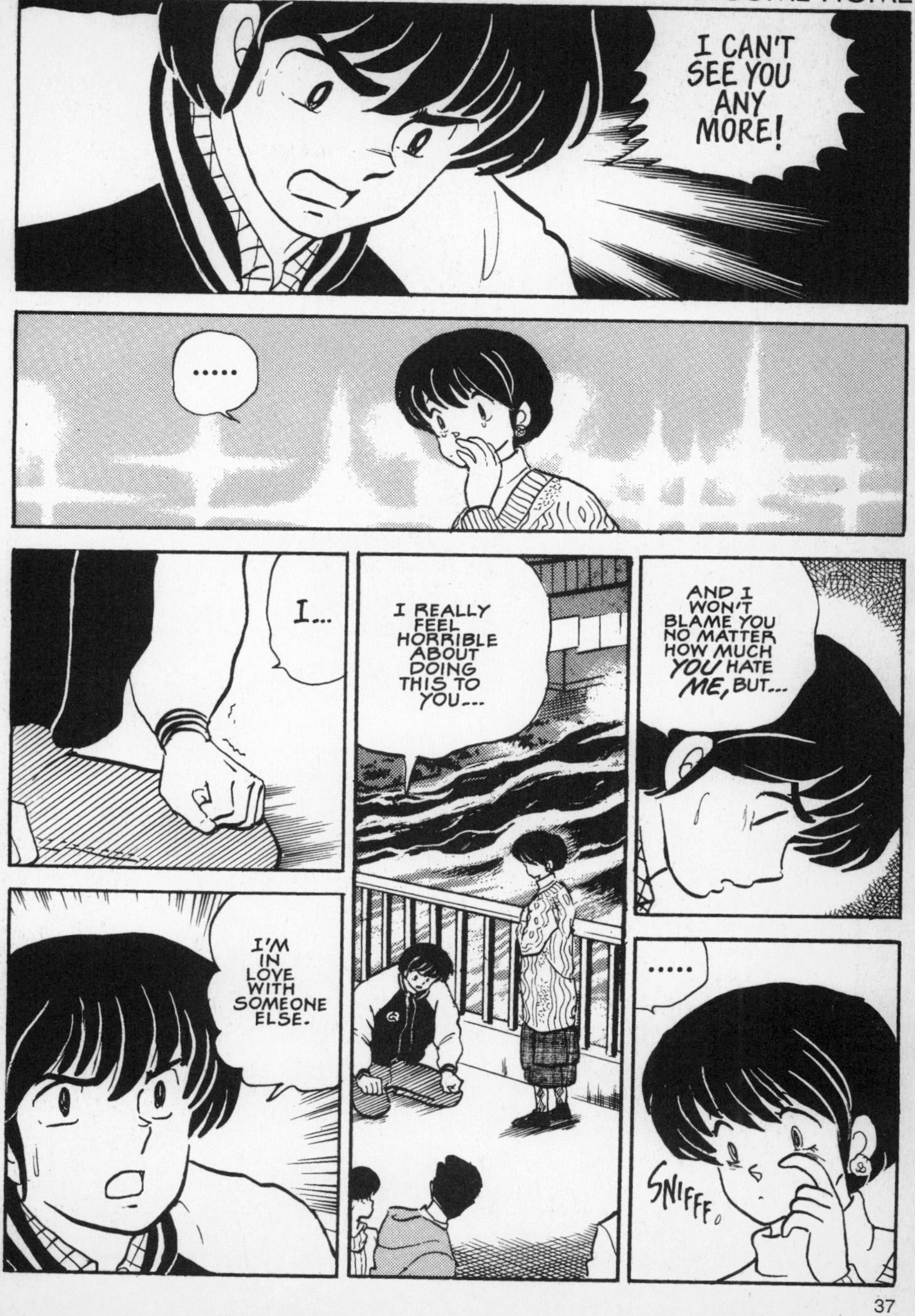
I CAN'T SEE YOU ANY MORE!
.....
I...
I REALLY FEEL HORRIBLE ABOUT DOING THIS TO YOU...
AND I WON'T BLAME YOU NO MATTER HOW MUCH YOU HATE ME, BUT...
I'M IN LOVE WITH SOMEONE ELSE.
.....
SNIFFFF

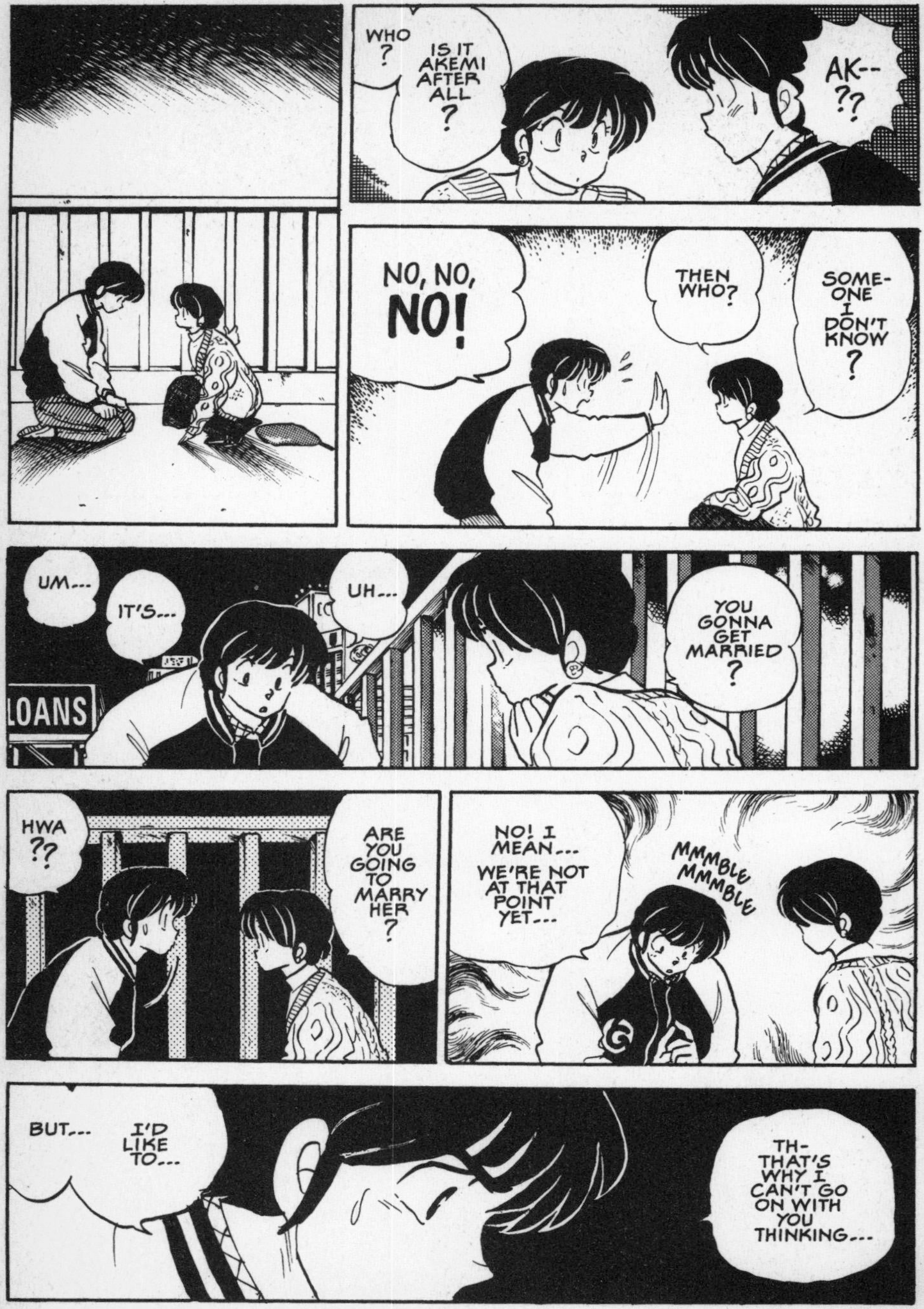
WHO ?
IS IT AKEMI AFTER ALL ?
AK-- ??
NO, NO, NO!
THEN WHO?
SOME-ONE I DON'T KNOW ?
UM...
IT'S...
UH...
LOANS
YOU GONNA GET MARRIED ?
HWA ??
ARE YOU GOING TO MARRY HER ?
NO! I MEAN... WE'RE NOT AT THAT POINT YET...
MMMBLE MMMBLE
BUT...
I'D LIKE TO...
TH-THAT'S WHY I CAN'T GO ON WITH YOU THINKING...

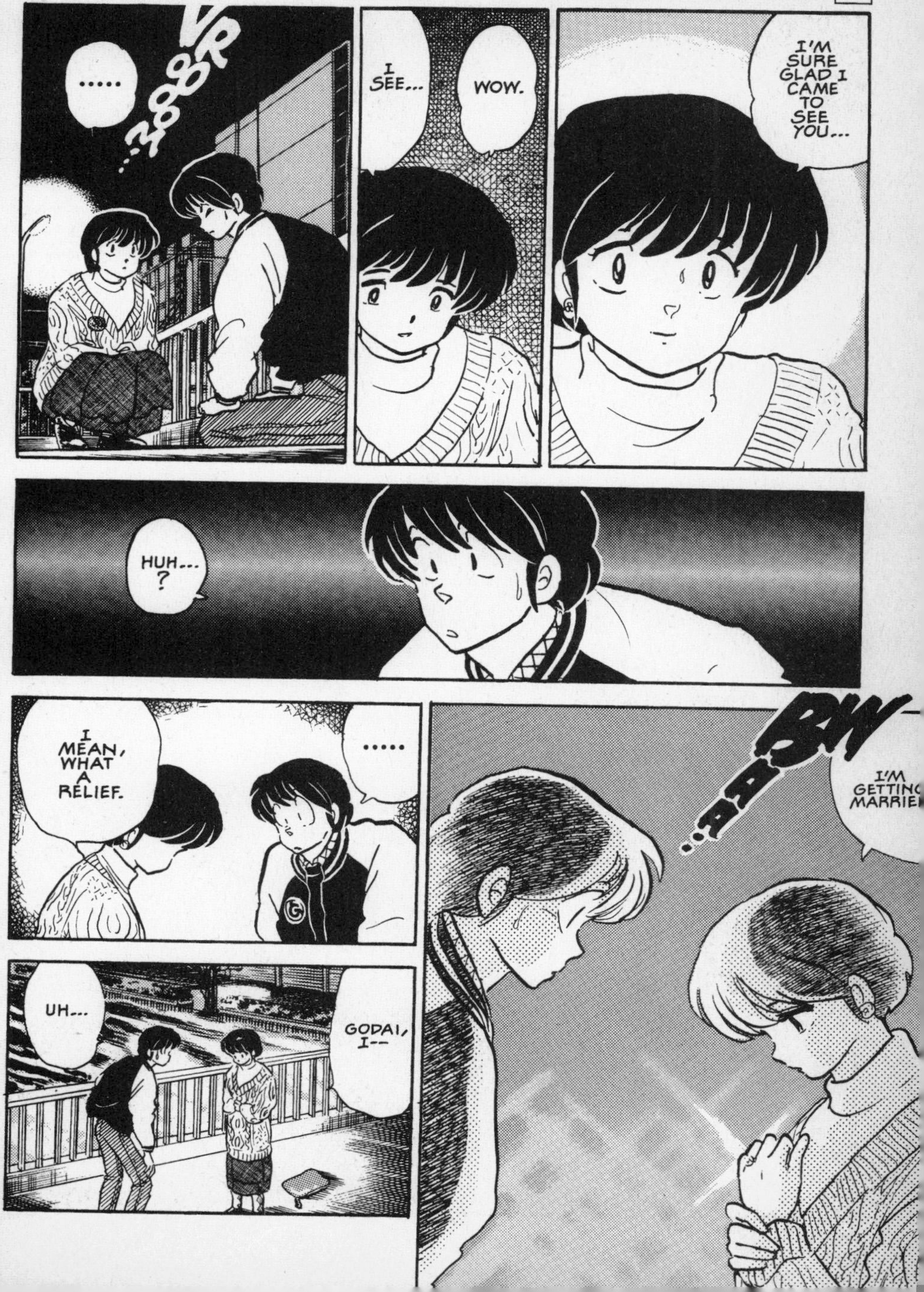
.....
I SEE...
WOW.
I'M SURE GLAD I CAME TO SEE YOU...
HUH... ?
I MEAN, WHAT A RELIEF.
.....
UH...
GODAI, I--
I'M GETTING MARRIE

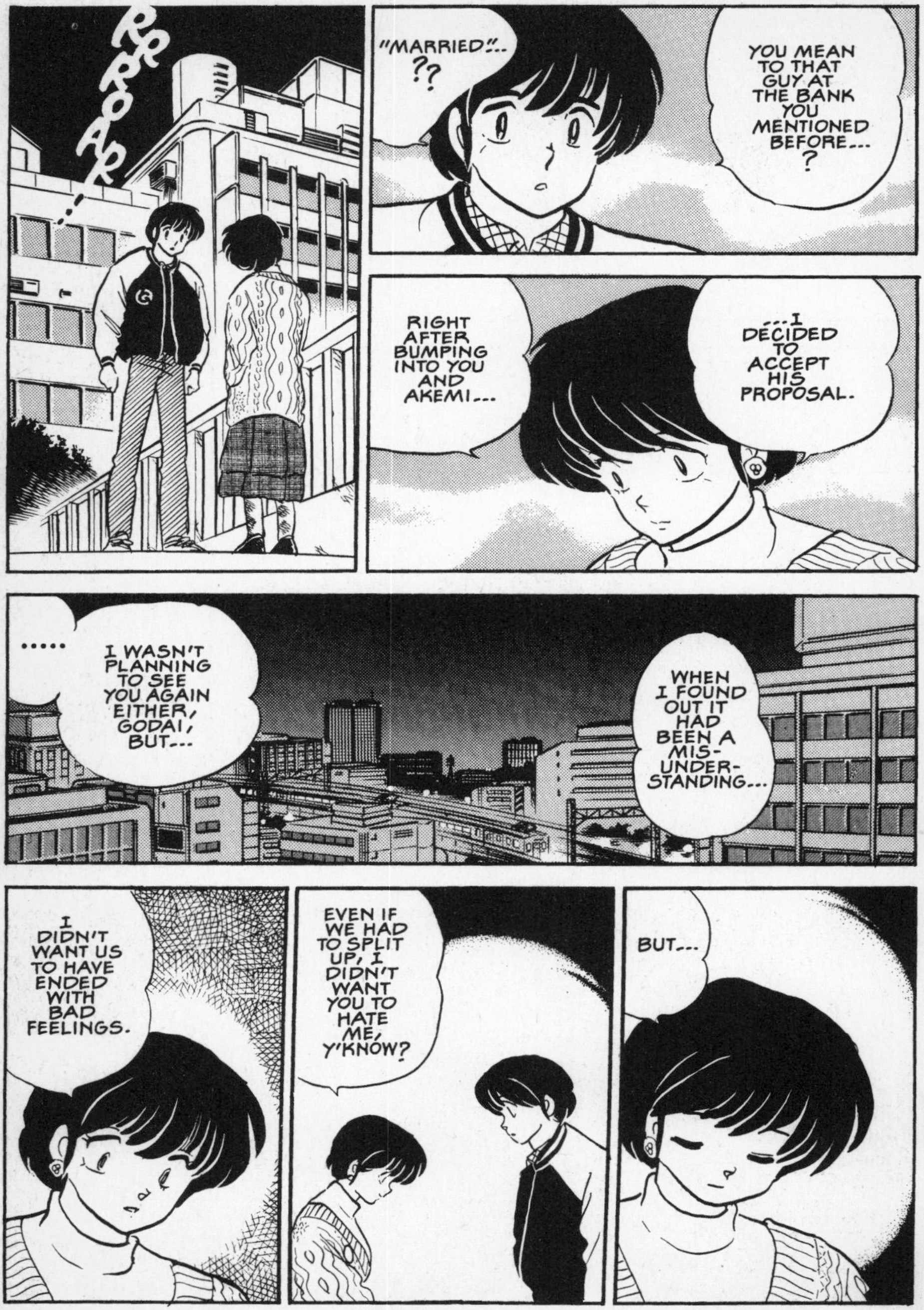
RRROAR!!
"MARRIED"!..
??
YOU MEAN TO THAT GUY AT THE BANK YOU MENTIONED BEFORE...?
RIGHT AFTER BUMPING INTO YOU AND AKEMI...
...I DECIDED TO ACCEPT HIS PROPOSAL.
.....
I WASN'T PLANNING TO SEE YOU AGAIN EITHER, GODAI, BUT...
WHEN I FOUND OUT IT HAD BEEN A MIS-UNDER-STANDING...
I DIDN'T WANT US TO HAVE ENDED WITH BAD FEELINGS.
EVEN IF WE HAD TO SPLIT UP, I DIDN'T WANT YOU TO HATE ME, Y'KNOW?
BUT...

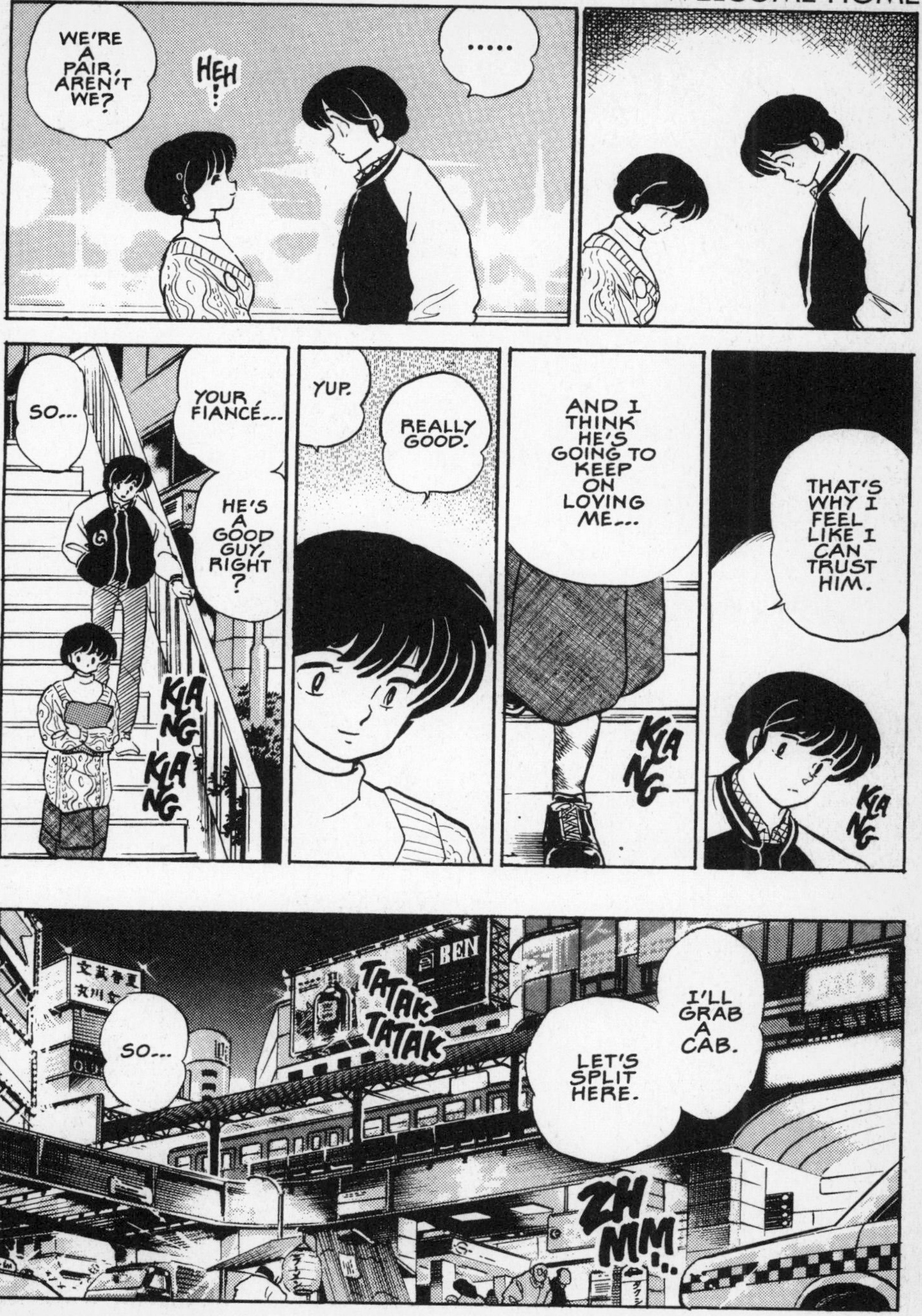
WE'RE A PAIR, AREN'T WE?
HEH
.....
SO...
YOUR FIANCÉ...
HE'S A GOOD GUY, RIGHT?
KLANG KLANG
YUP.
REALLY GOOD.
AND I THINK HE'S GOING TO KEEP ON LOVING ME...
KLANG
THAT'S WHY I FEEL LIKE I CAN TRUST HIM.
KLANG
SO...
TATAK TATAK
I'LL GRAB A CAB.
LET'S SPLIT HERE.
ZHMM...

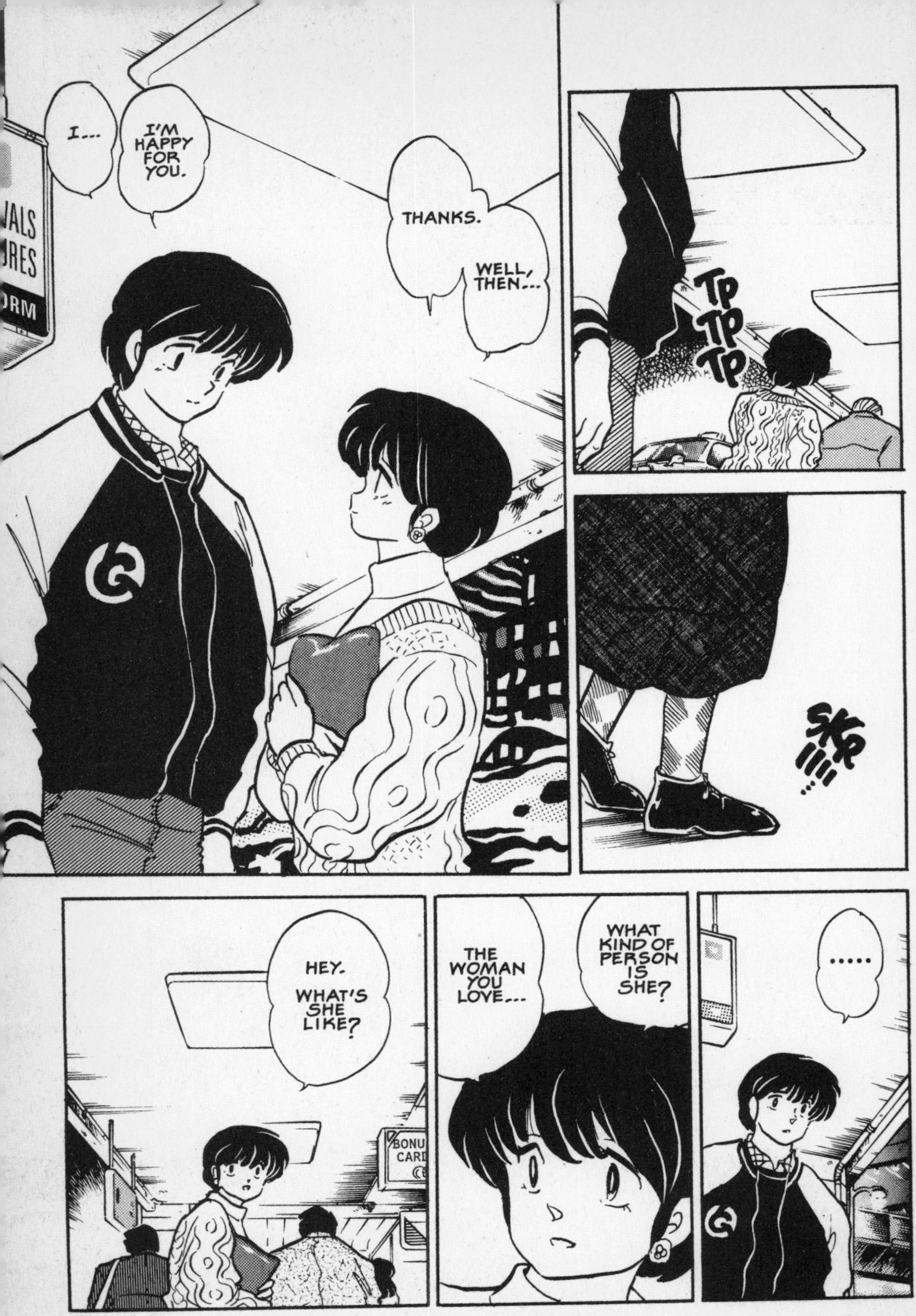
I...
I'M HAPPY FOR YOU.
THANKS.
WELL, THEN...
TP TP TP
SKR!!!!...
HEY.
WHAT'S SHE LIKE?
BONU CARD
THE WOMAN YOU LOVE...
WHAT KIND OF PERSON IS SHE?
.....

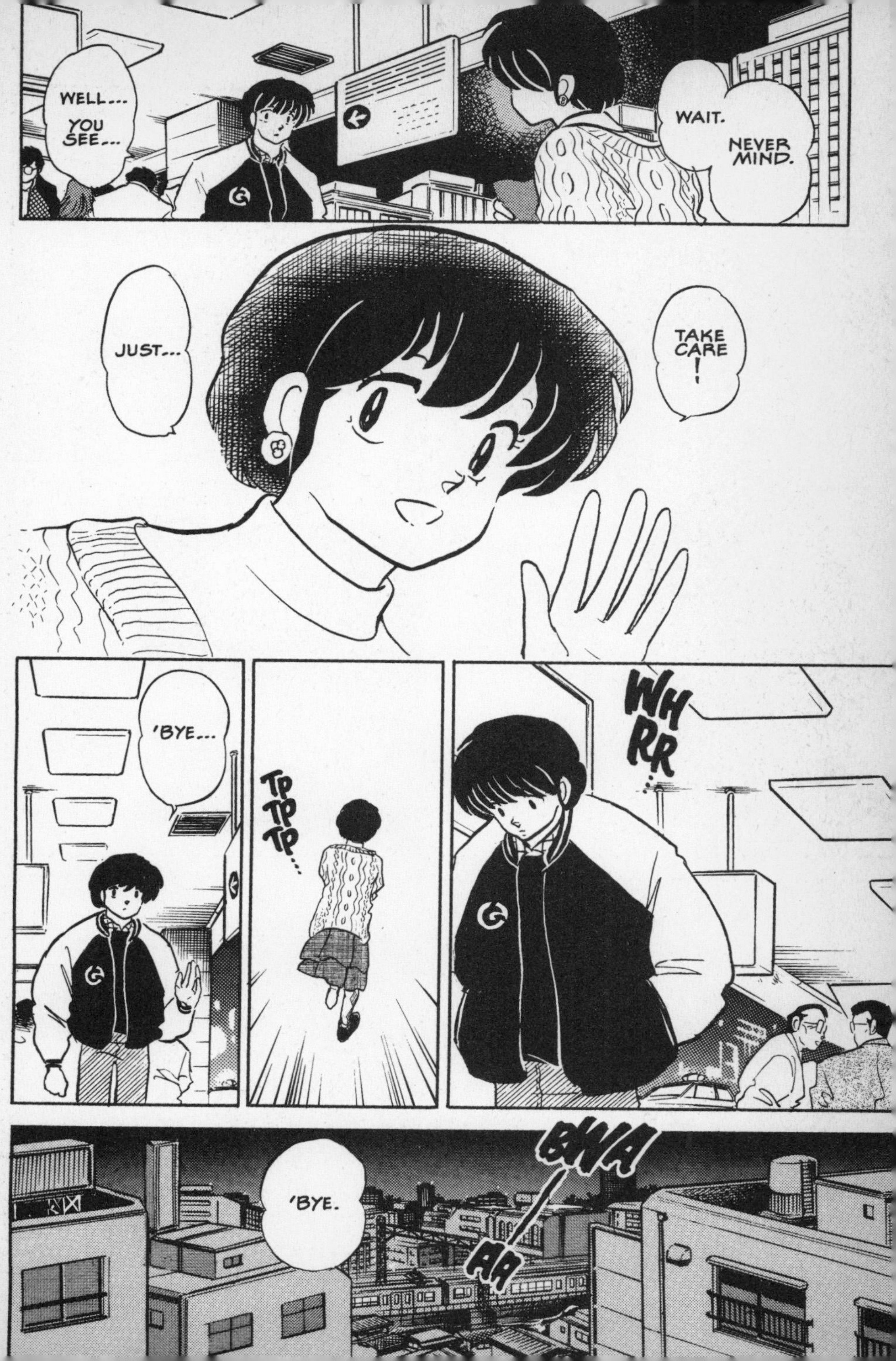
WELL... YOU SEE...
WAIT.
NEVER MIND.
JUST...
TAKE CARE!
'BYE...
TP TP TP...
WHRR...
'BYE.
BWA-AA

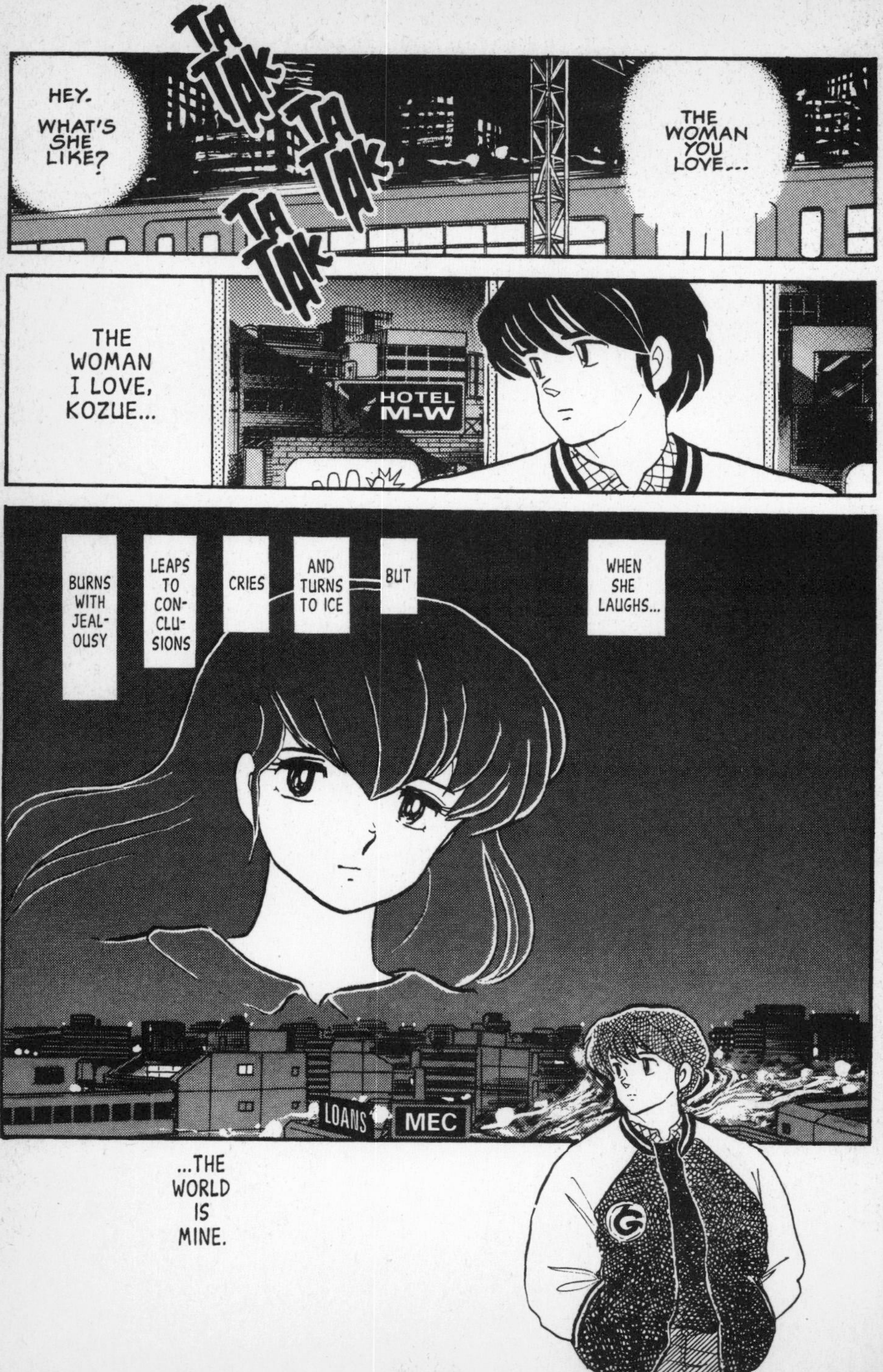
HEY. WHAT'S SHE LIKE?
TA TAK TA TAK TA TAK
THE WOMAN YOU LOVE...
THE WOMAN I LOVE, KOZUE...
HOTEL M-W
BURNS WITH JEAL-OUSY
LEAPS TO CON-CLU-SIONS
CRIES
AND TURNS TO ICE
BUT
WHEN SHE LAUGHS...
LOANS
MEC
...THE WORLD IS MINE.

PART THREE
SACRED VOWS

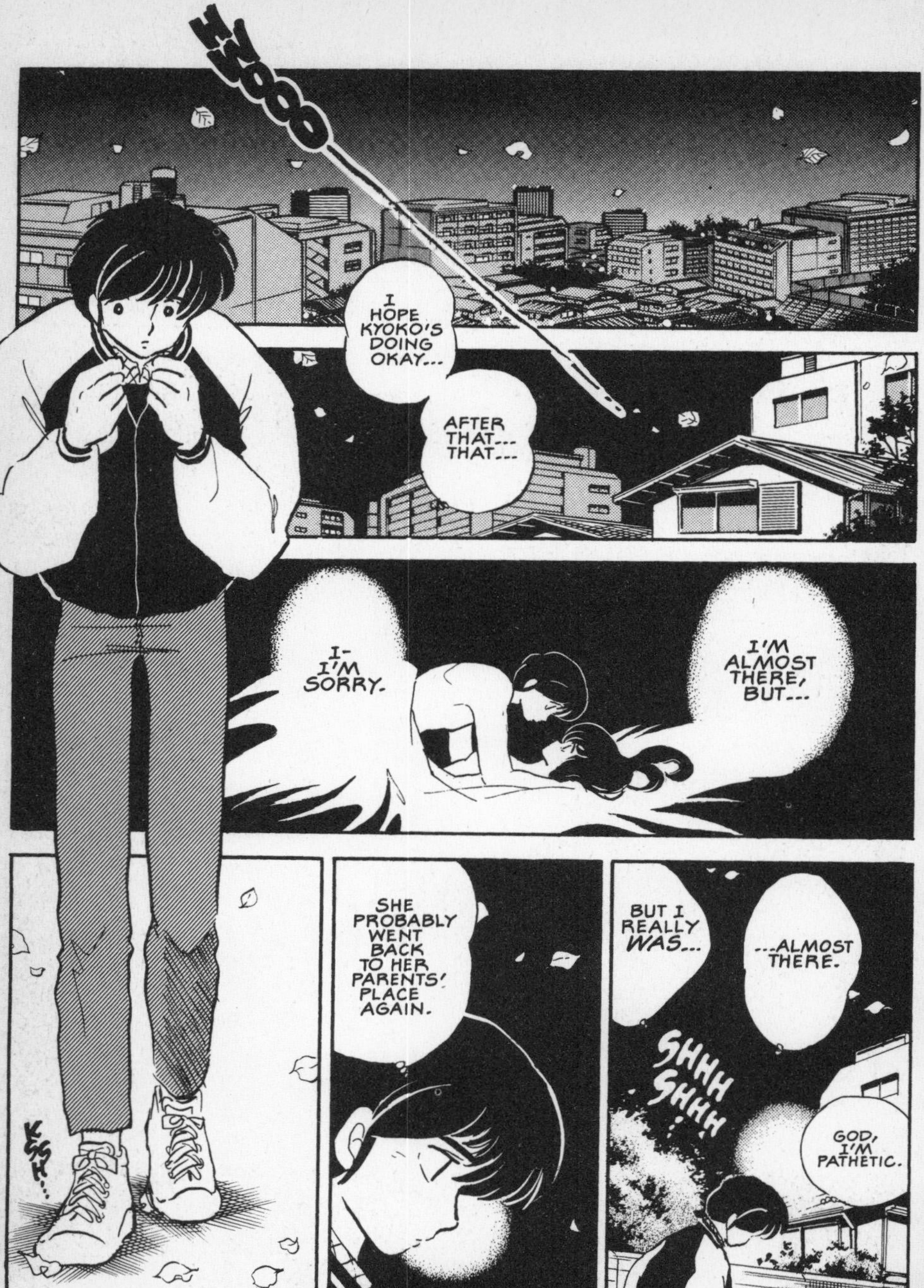
HYUOOO
I HOPE KYOKO'S DOING OKAY...
AFTER THAT... THAT...
I- I'M SORRY.
I'M ALMOST THERE, BUT...
KSSH...
SHE PROBABLY WENT BACK TO HER PARENTS' PLACE AGAIN.
BUT I REALLY WAS...
...ALMOST THERE.
SHHH SHHH
GOD, I'M PATHETIC.

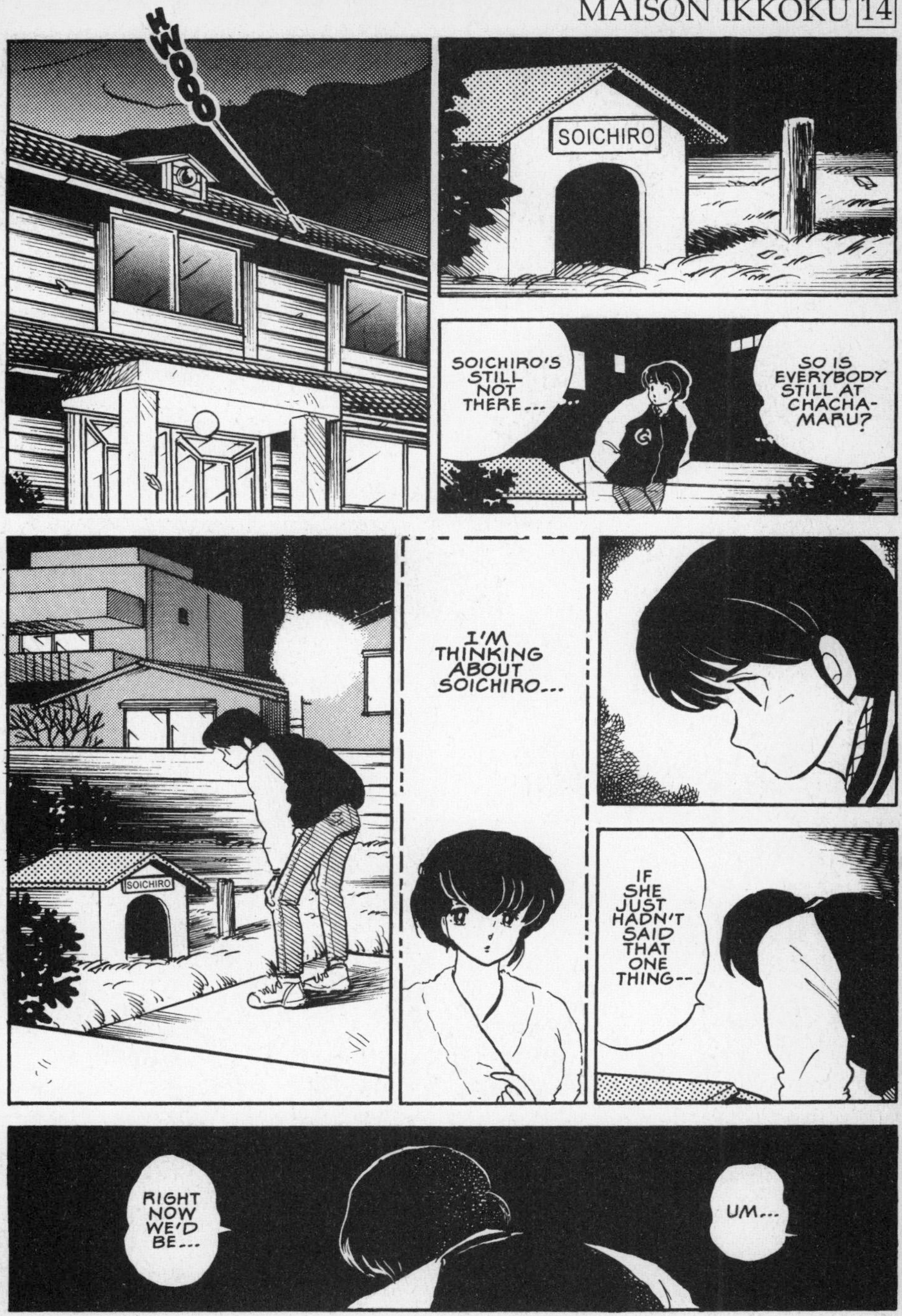
HWOOO
SOICHIRO
SOICHIRO'S STILL NOT THERE...
SO IS EVERYBODY STILL AT CHACHA-MARU?
SOICHIRO
I'M THINKING ABOUT SOICHIRO...
IF SHE JUST HADN'T SAID THAT ONE THING--
RIGHT NOW WE'D BE...
UM...

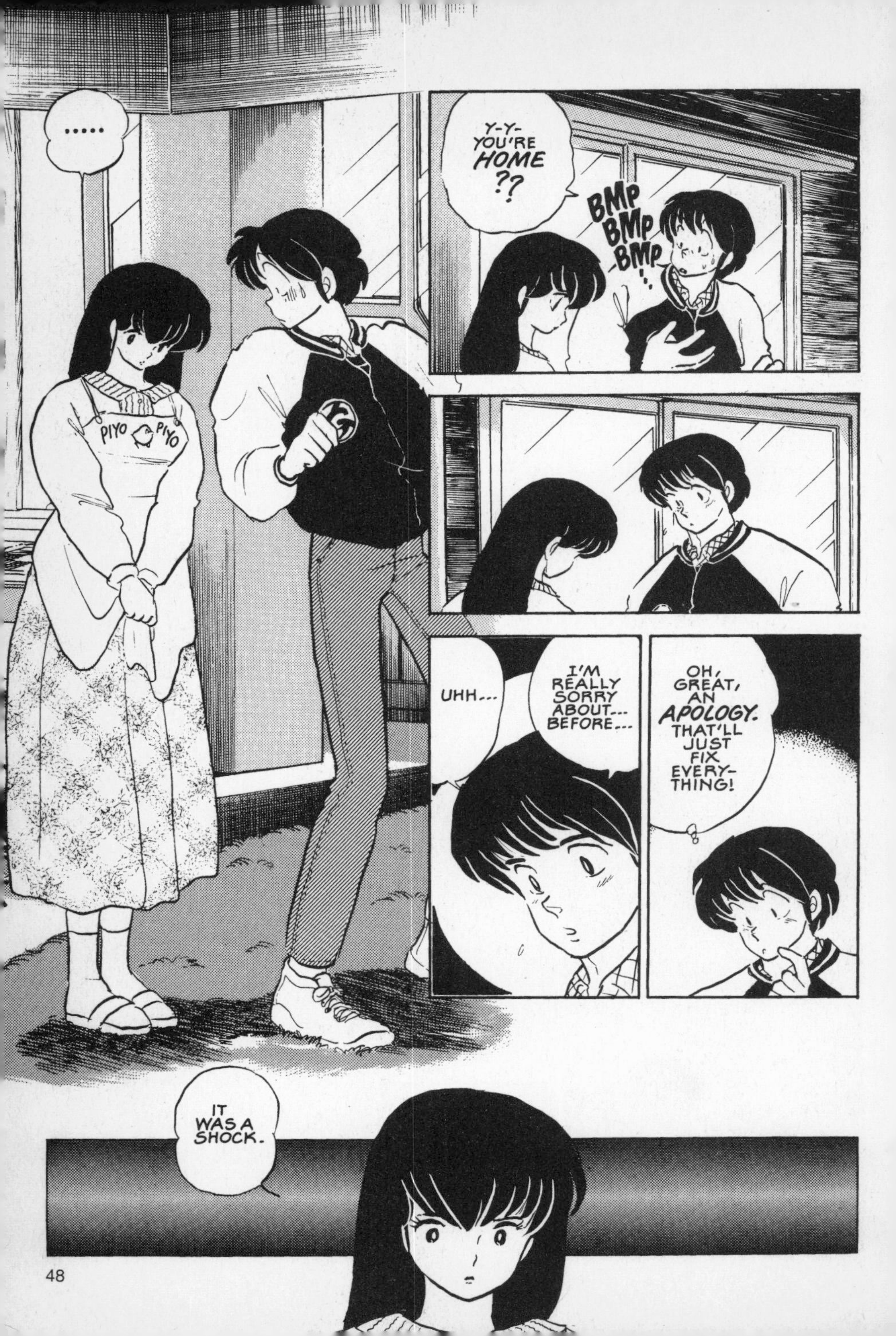

......
Y-Y-YOU'RE HOME ??
BMP BMP BMP
UHH...
I'M REALLY SORRY ABOUT... BEFORE...
OH, GREAT, AN APOLOGY. THAT'LL JUST FIX EVERYTHING!
IT WAS A SHOCK.

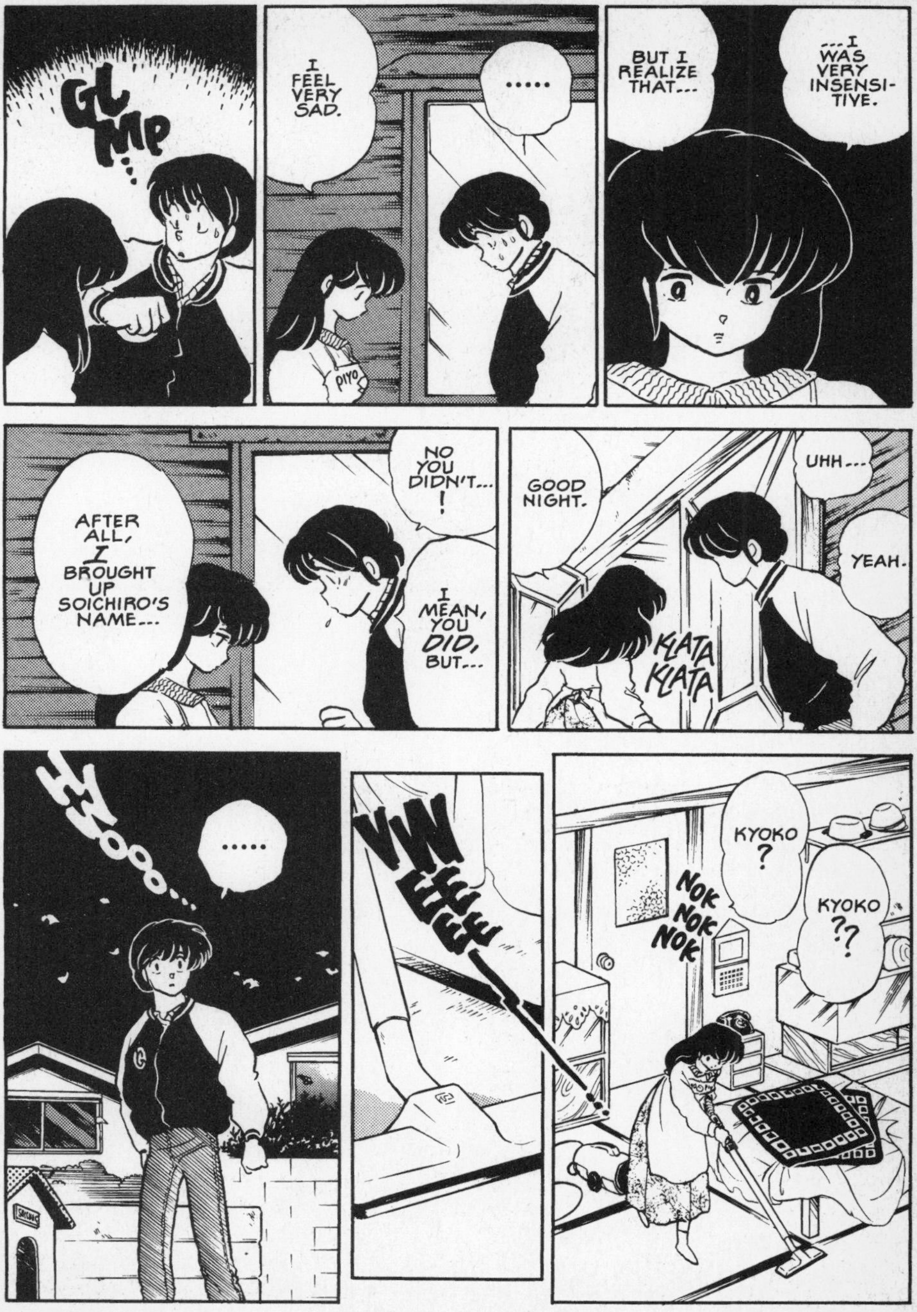
GLMP
I FEEL VERY SAD.
.....
BUT I REALIZE THAT...
...I WAS VERY INSENSI-TIVE.
AFTER ALL, I BROUGHT UP SOICHIRO'S NAME...
NO YOU DIDN'T... !
I MEAN, YOU DID, BUT...
GOOD NIGHT.
UHH...
YEAH.
KLATA KLATA
HYOOO...
.....
VWEEEE
KYOKO ?
NOK NOK NOK
KYOKO ??

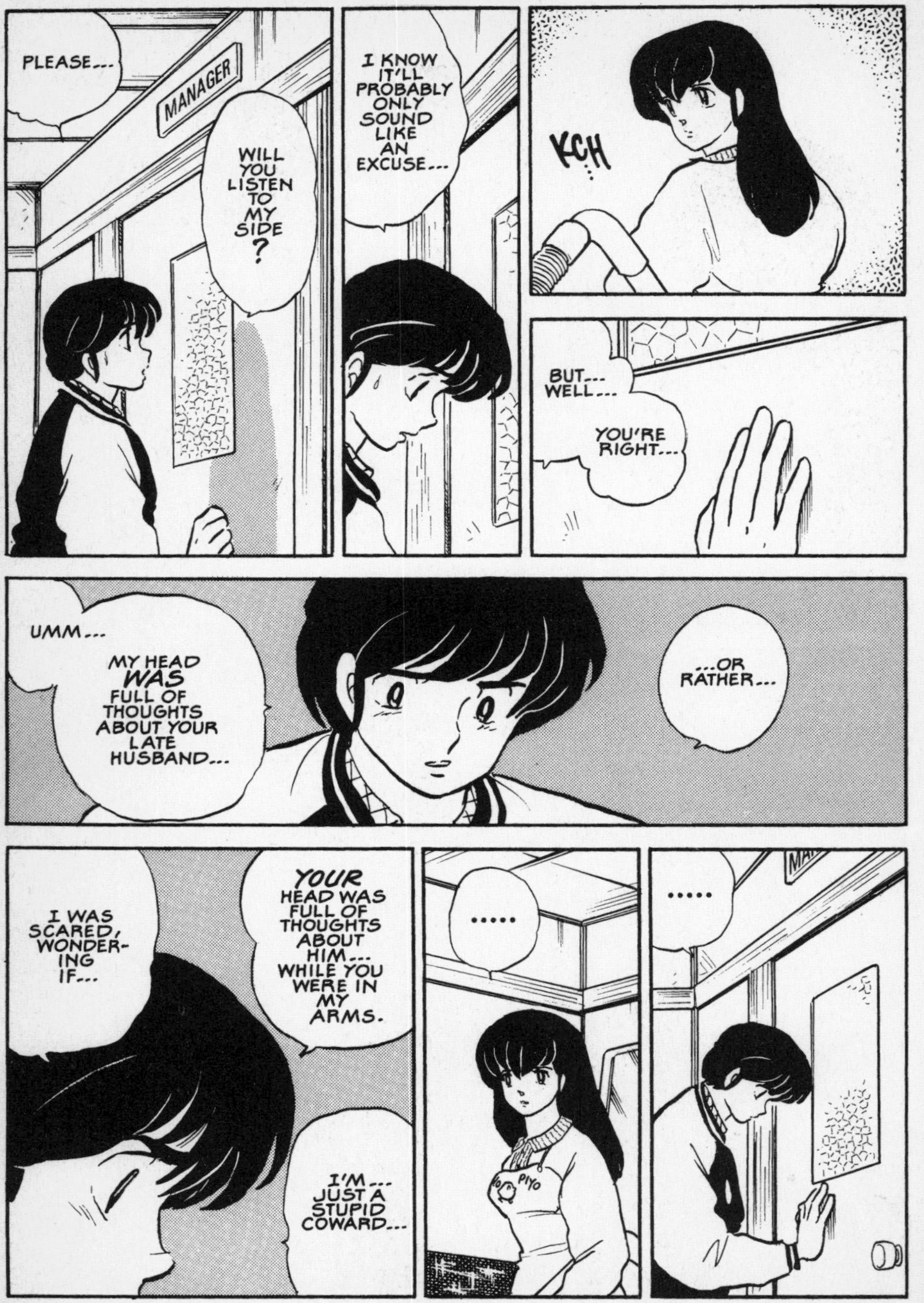
PLEASE...
MANAGER
WILL YOU LISTEN TO MY SIDE?
I KNOW IT'LL PROBABLY ONLY SOUND LIKE AN EXCUSE...
KCH
BUT... WELL...
YOU'RE RIGHT...
UMM...
MY HEAD WAS FULL OF THOUGHTS ABOUT YOUR LATE HUSBAND...
...OR RATHER...
I WAS SCARED, WONDER-ING IF...
YOUR HEAD WAS FULL OF THOUGHTS ABOUT HIM... WHILE YOU WERE IN MY ARMS.
I'M... JUST A STUPID COWARD...
.....
PIYO
.....

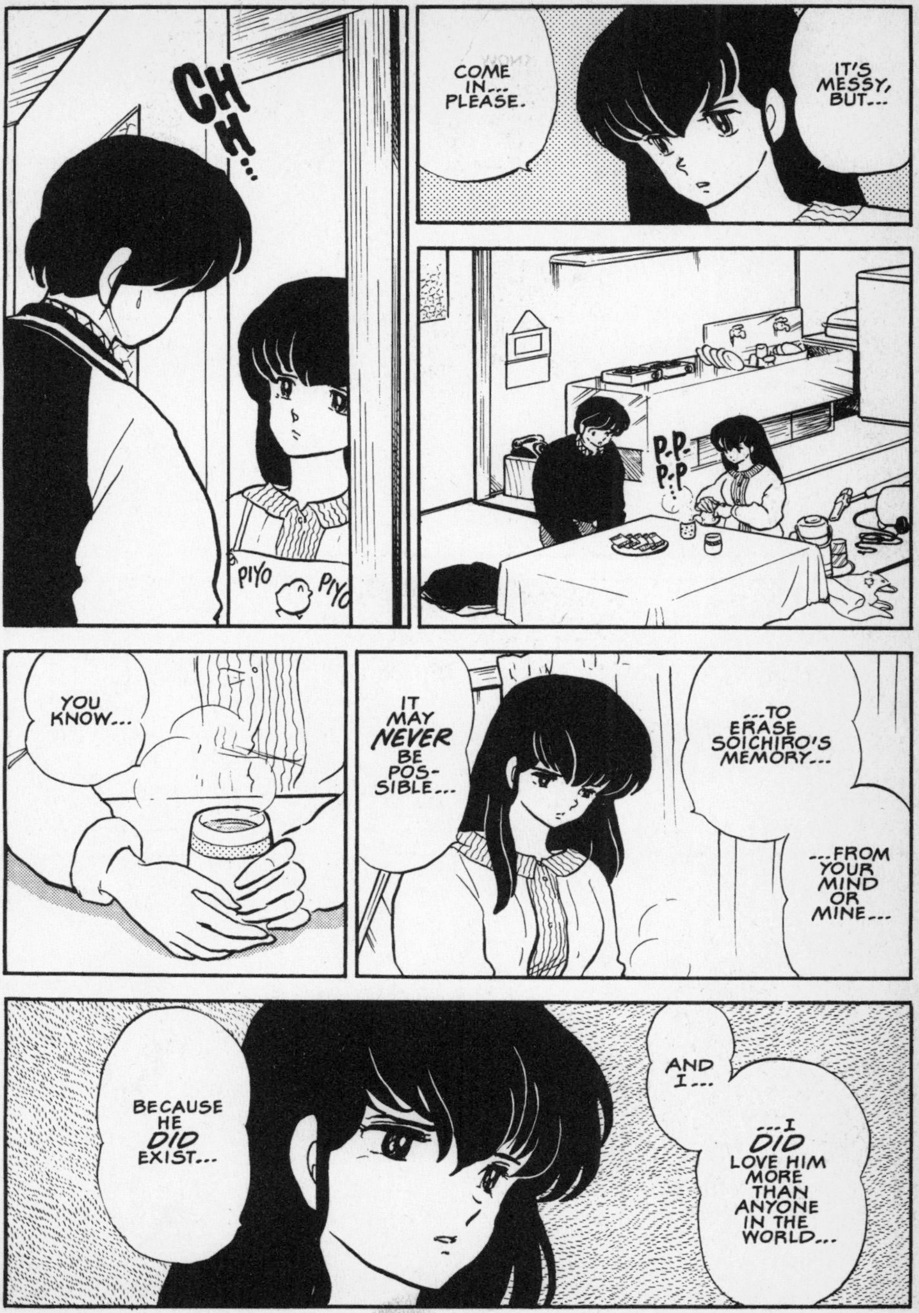
CHH...
PIYO PIYO
COME IN... PLEASE.
IT'S MESSY, BUT...
P-P-P-P
YOU KNOW...
IT MAY NEVER BE POSSIBLE...
...TO ERASE SOICHIRO'S MEMORY...
...FROM YOUR MIND OR MINE...
BECAUSE HE DID EXIST...
AND I...
...I DID LOVE HIM MORE THAN ANYONE IN THE WORLD...

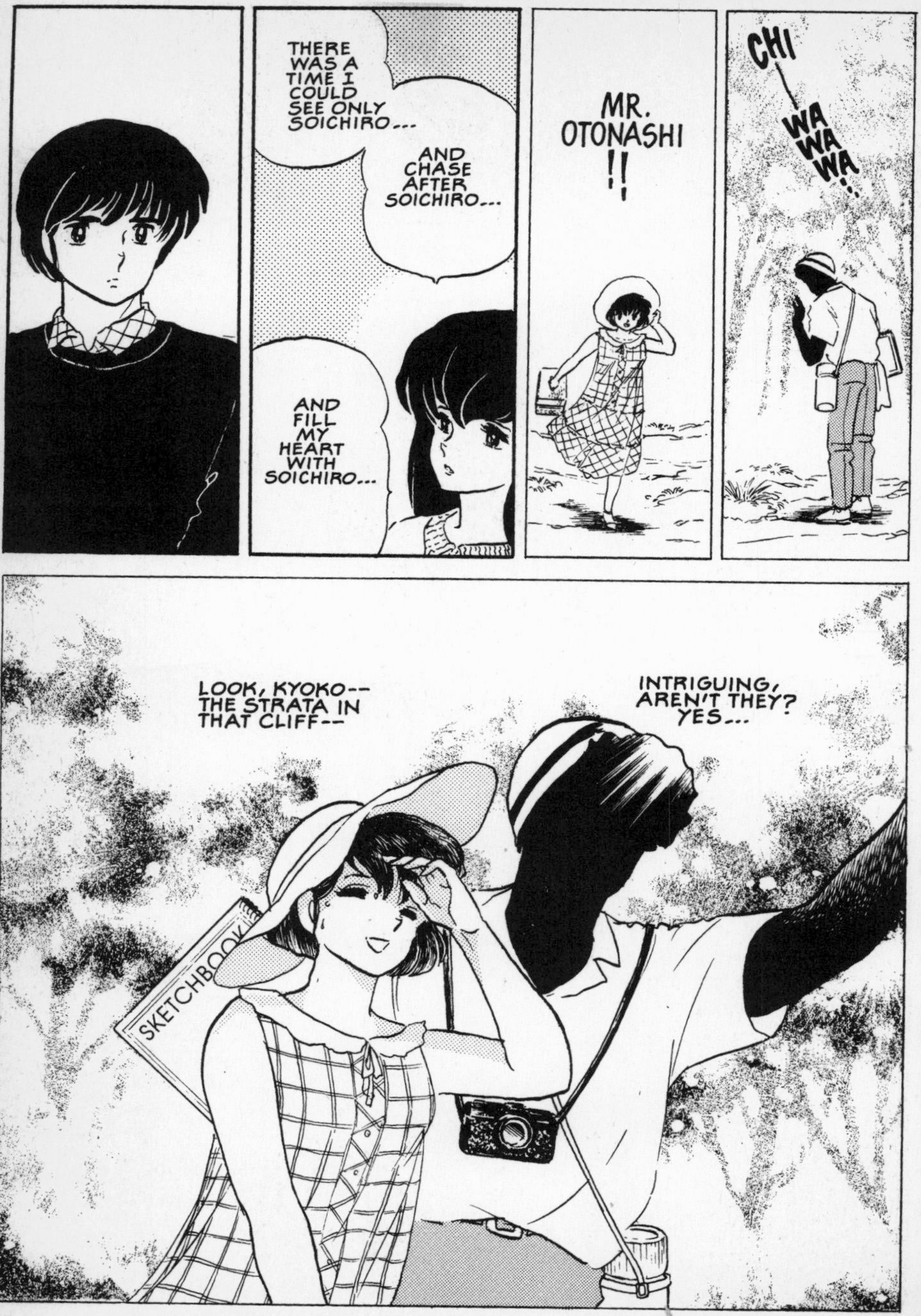
THERE WAS A TIME I COULD SEE ONLY SOICHIRO...
AND CHASE AFTER SOICHIRO...
AND FILL MY HEART WITH SOICHIRO...
MR. OTONASHI !!
CHI-WA WA WA WA...
LOOK, KYOKO-- THE STRATA IN THAT CLIFF--
INTRIGUING, AREN'T THEY? YES...
SKETCHBOOK

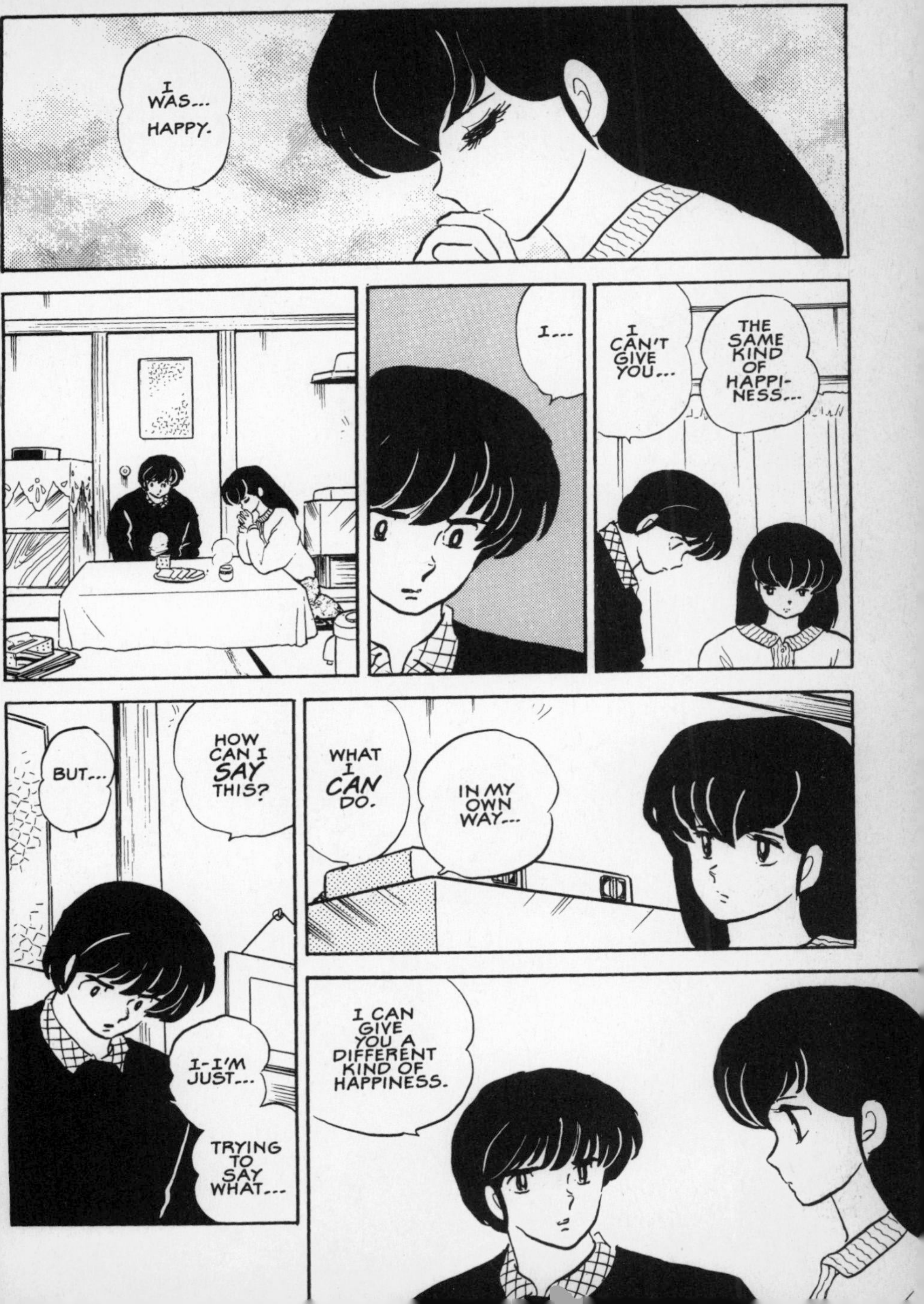
I WAS... HAPPY.
I...
I CAN'T GIVE YOU...
THE SAME KIND OF HAPPI-NESS...
BUT...
HOW CAN I SAY THIS?
I-I'M JUST...
TRYING TO SAY WHAT...
WHAT I CAN DO.
IN MY OWN WAY...
I CAN GIVE YOU A DIFFERENT KIND OF HAPPINESS.

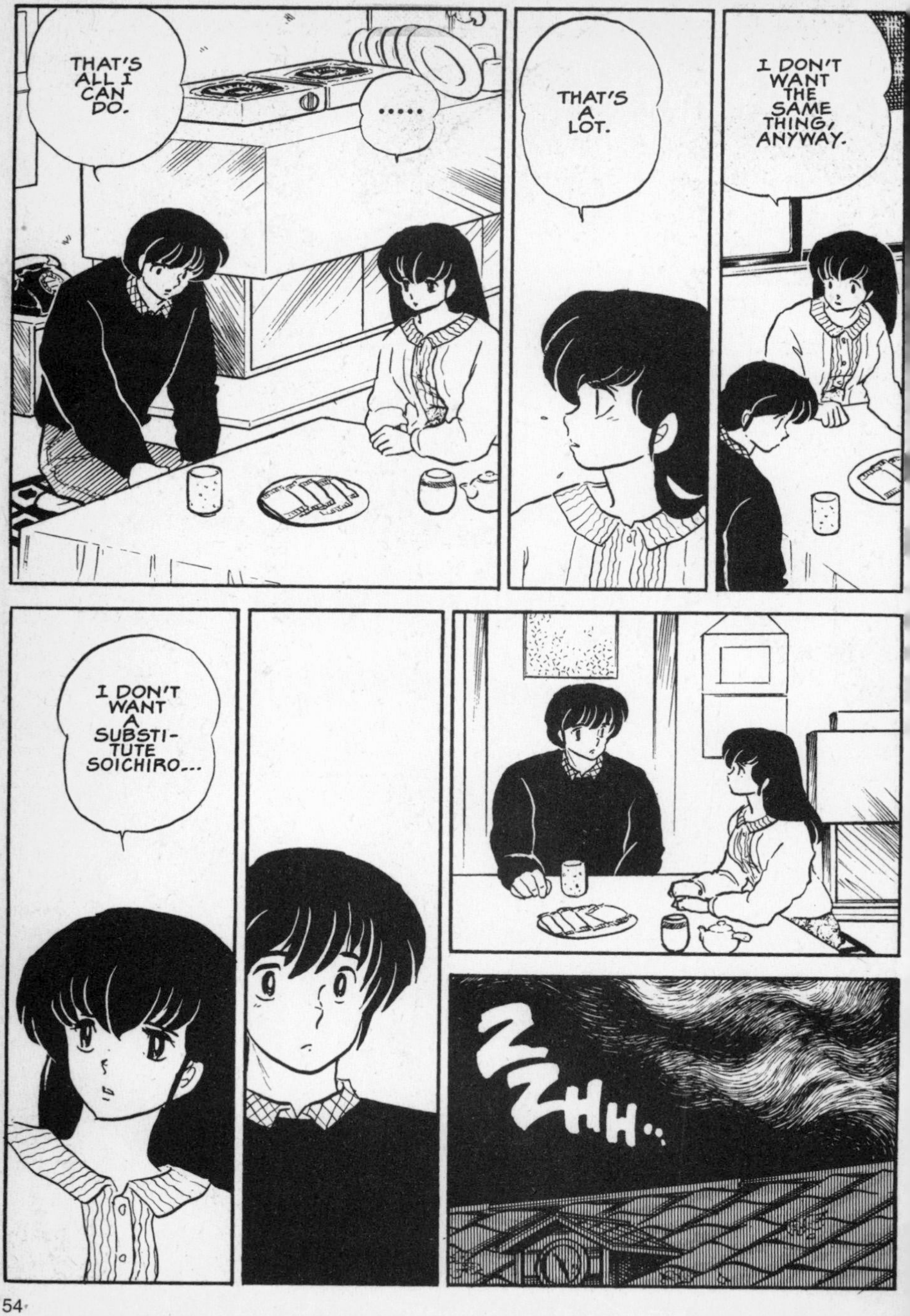
THAT'S ALL I CAN DO.
......
THAT'S A LOT.
I DON'T WANT THE SAME THING, ANYWAY.
I DON'T WANT A SUBSTI- TUTE SOICHIRO...
ZZHHH..

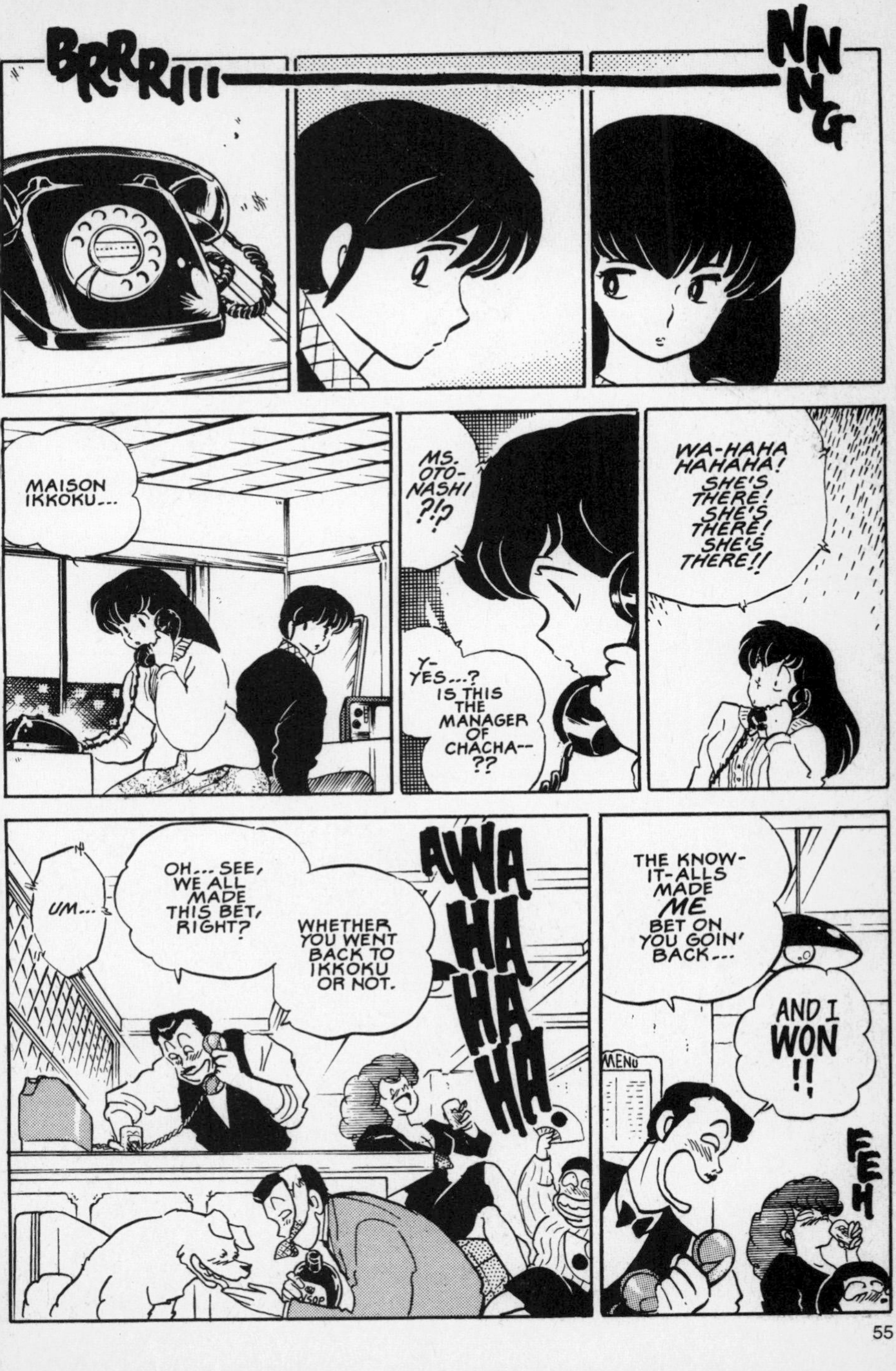
BRRRIII——NNNG
MAISON IKKOKU...
MS. OTO-NASHI ?!?
Y-YES...? IS THIS THE MANAGER OF CHACHA--??
WA-HAHA HAHAHA! SHE'S THERE! SHE'S THERE! SHE'S THERE!!
UM...
OH... SEE, WE ALL MADE THIS BET, RIGHT?
WHETHER YOU WENT BACK TO IKKOKU OR NOT.
AWAHAHAHAHA!
MENU
VSOP
THE KNOW-IT-ALLS MADE ME BET ON YOU GOIN' BACK...
AND I WON!!
FEH

WAHAHAHA

AWRIGHT! TONIGHT THE DRINKS ARE ON THE HOUSE!!

OH, YEAH--?!?

BWA-HA-HA

ZHOOM

WHAT... IN THE WORLD...?

THEY ALL STILL AT IT?

CH NG

EXPLOITING AKEMI'S BOSS, IT SEEMS.

YEAH?

THEY'RE SO SHAMELESS.

MAYBE I SHOULD GO BACK AND PICK UP SOICHIRO...

I MEAN, MY DOG, YOU KNOW...

HUH?

56

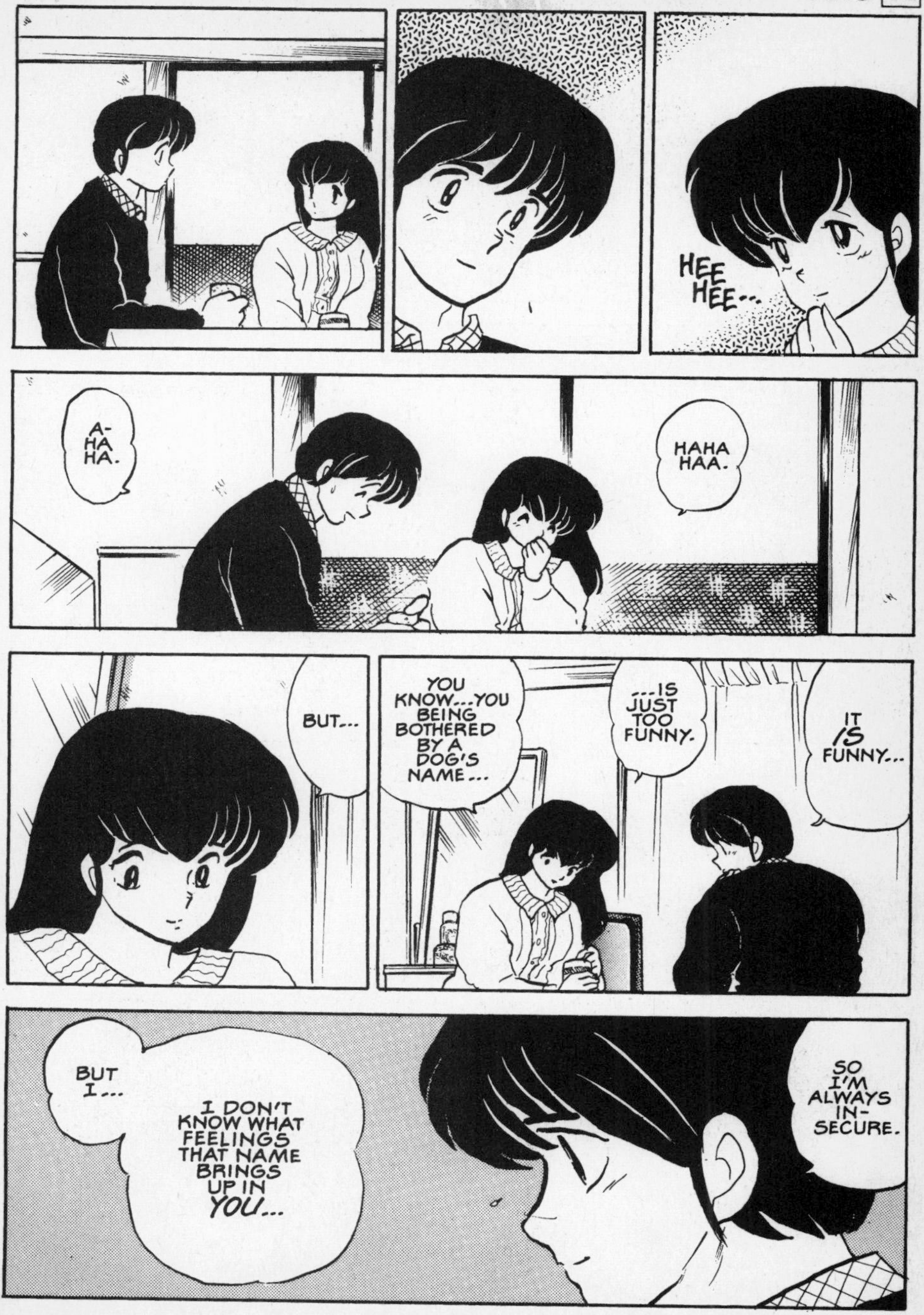
HEE HEE...
A-HA HA.
HAHA HAA.
BUT...
YOU KNOW...YOU BEING BOTHERED BY A DOG'S NAME...
...IS JUST TOO FUNNY.
IT IS FUNNY...
BUT I...
I DON'T KNOW WHAT FEELINGS THAT NAME BRINGS UP IN YOU...
SO I'M ALWAYS IN-SECURE.

AT THIS RATE... I'LL ALWAYS BE INSECURE.

.....

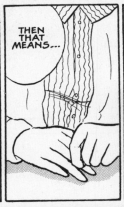

THEN THAT MEANS...

...WE'LL NEVER BE TOGETHER.

BEFORE WE ENTERED THAT HOTEL, YOU ACCUSED ME OF NOT *TRUSTING* YOU.

BUT *YOU*...

YOU DON'T TRUST *ME,* EITHER!!

TH-THAT'S...

THAT'S NOT FAIR, GODAI.

WHAT AM I SUPPOSED TO DO ?

ZZ HH

PLIP PLUP

PLIP PLIP PLIP PLIP

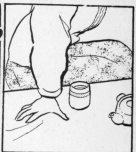

PLIP PLIP PLIP

DO I HAVE TO BEG...

"PLEASE MAKE LOVE TO ME..."

BEFORE YOU CAN FEEL SECURE ?

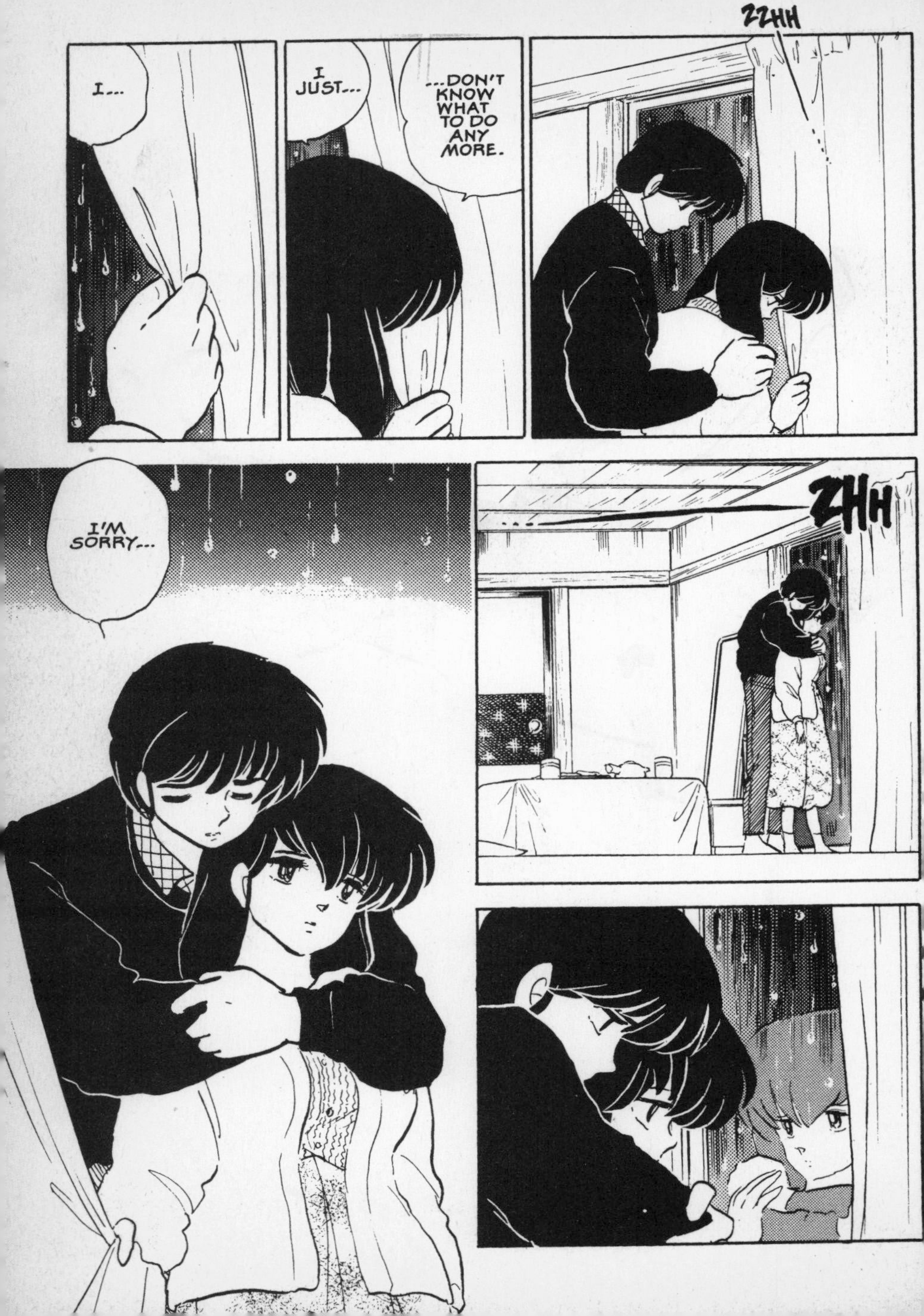

I...
I JUST...
...DON'T KNOW WHAT TO DO ANY MORE.
ZZHH
I'M SORRY...
ZHH

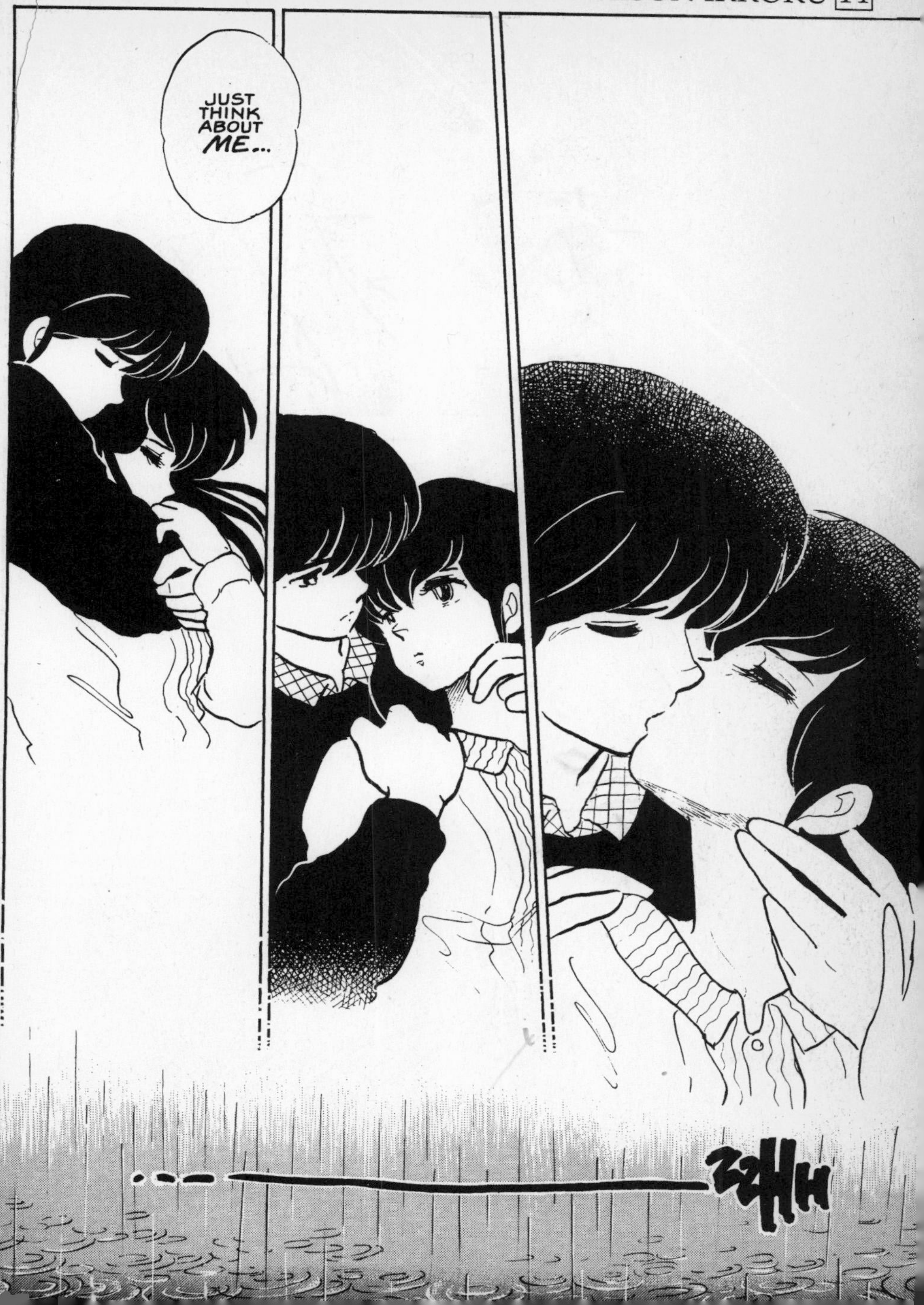
JUST THINK ABOUT ME...
ZZAHH

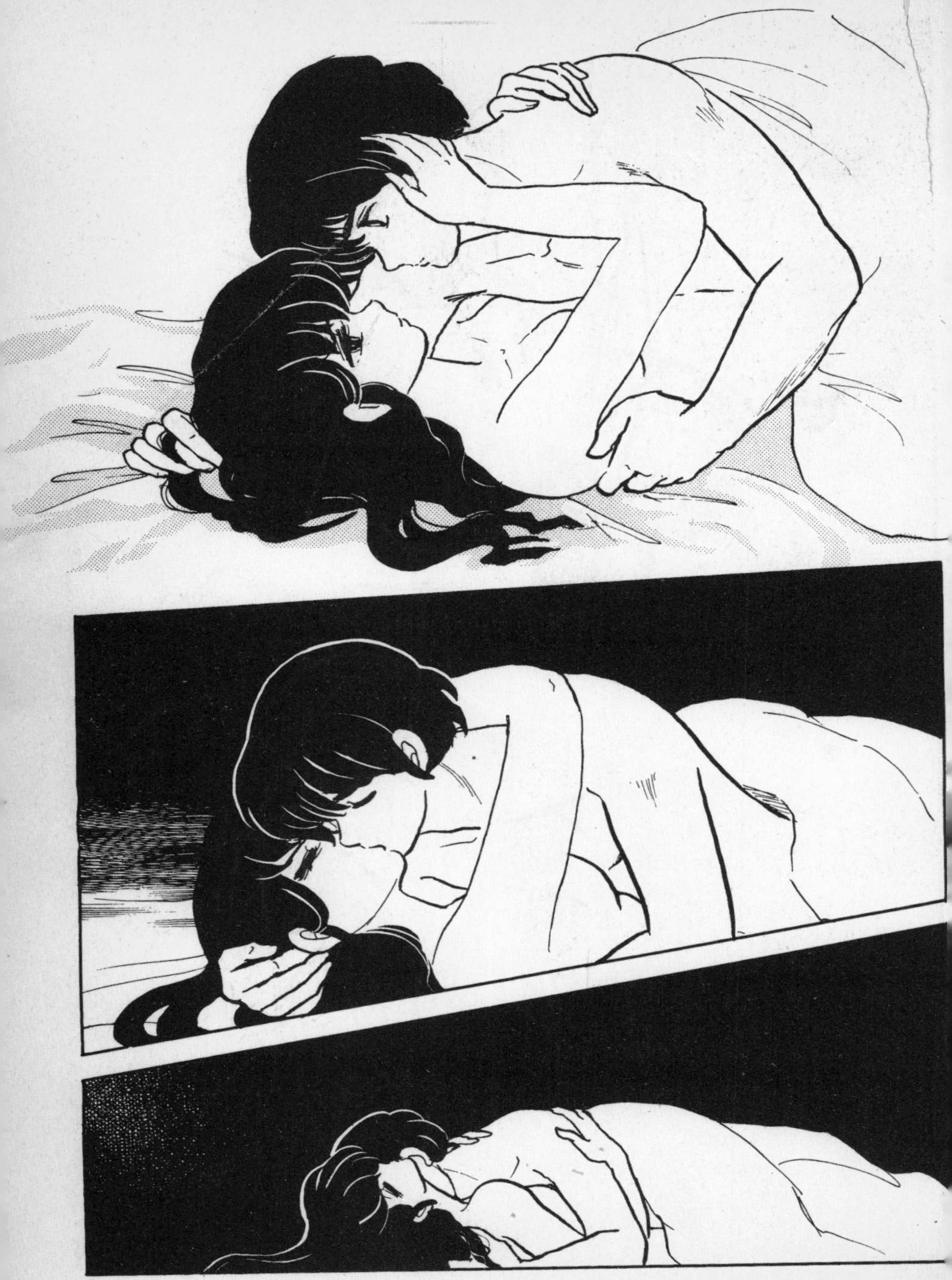

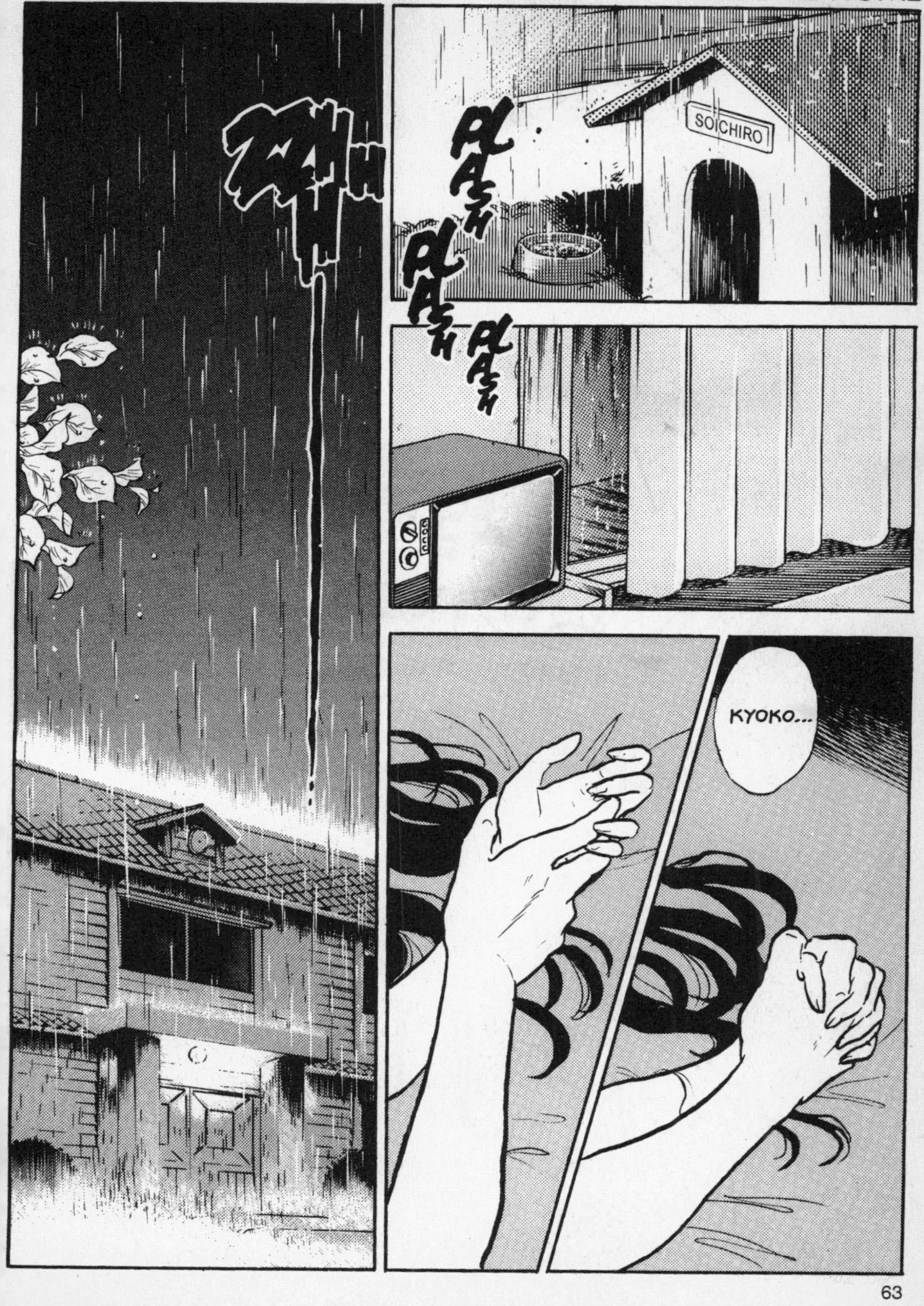
ZZAHH
PLASH
PLASH
PLASH
SOICHIRO
KYOKO...

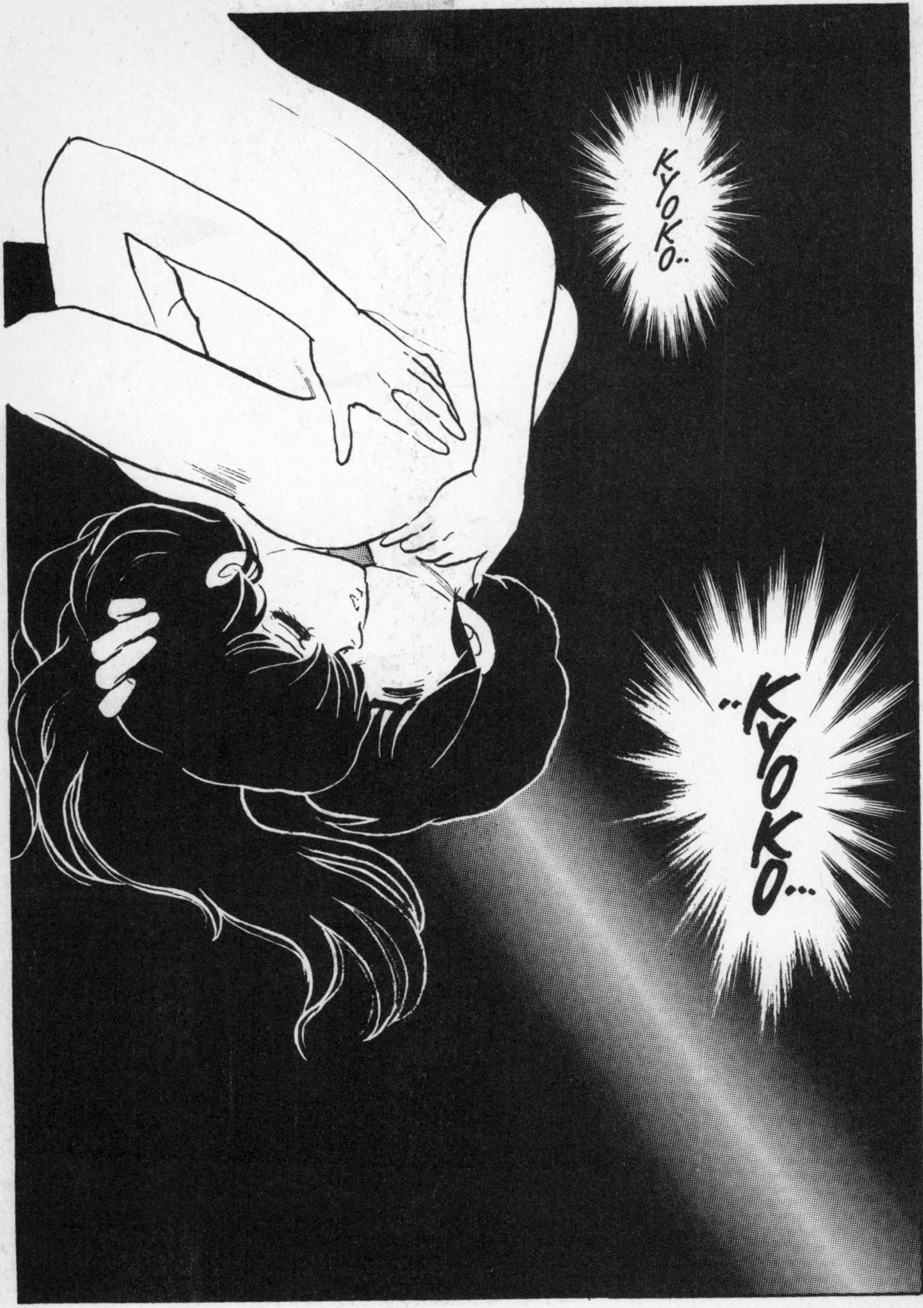
KYOKO..
..KYOKO...

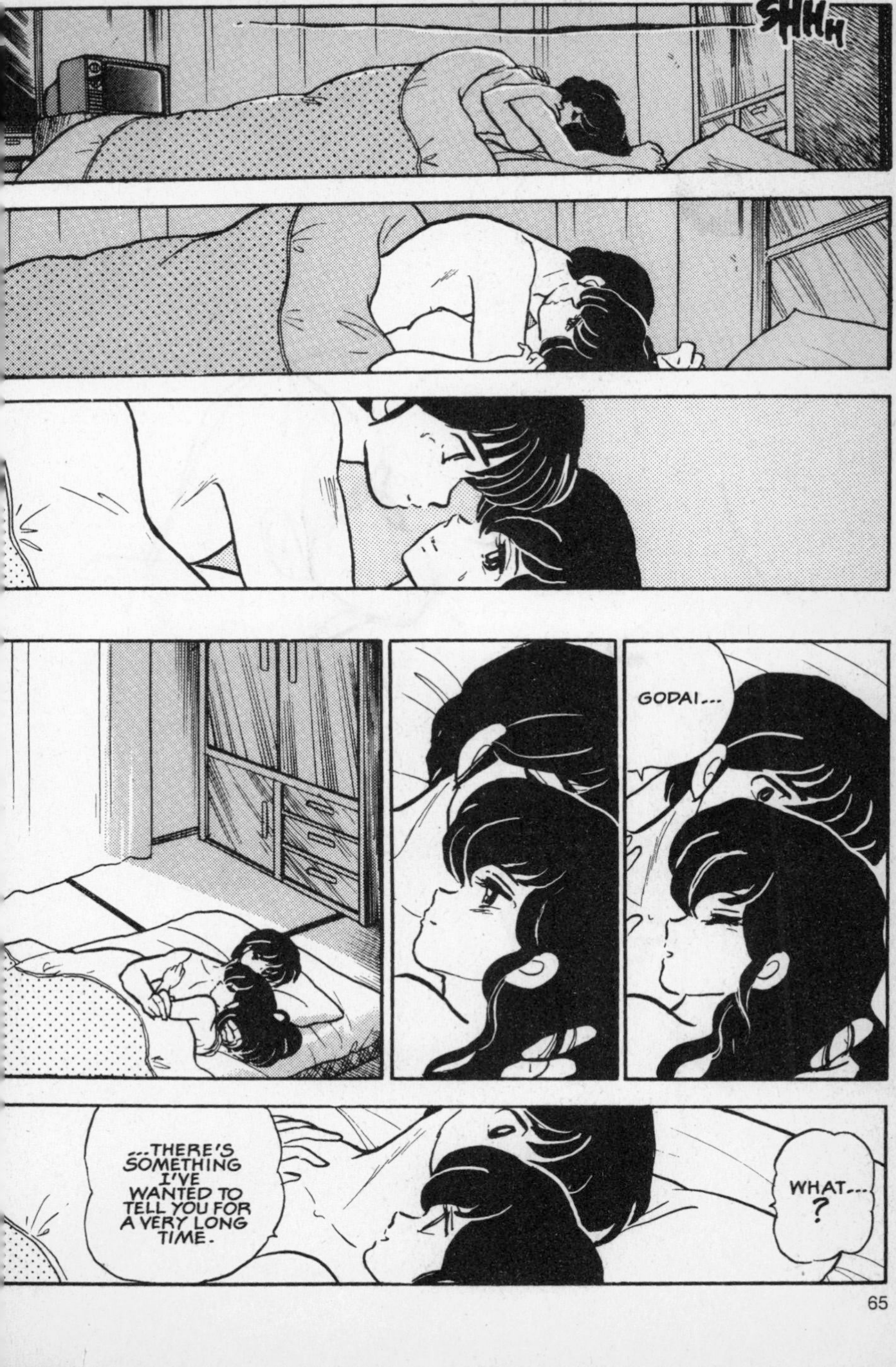
SHHH
GODAI...
...THERE'S SOMETHING I'VE WANTED TO TELL YOU FOR A VERY LONG TIME.
WHAT...?

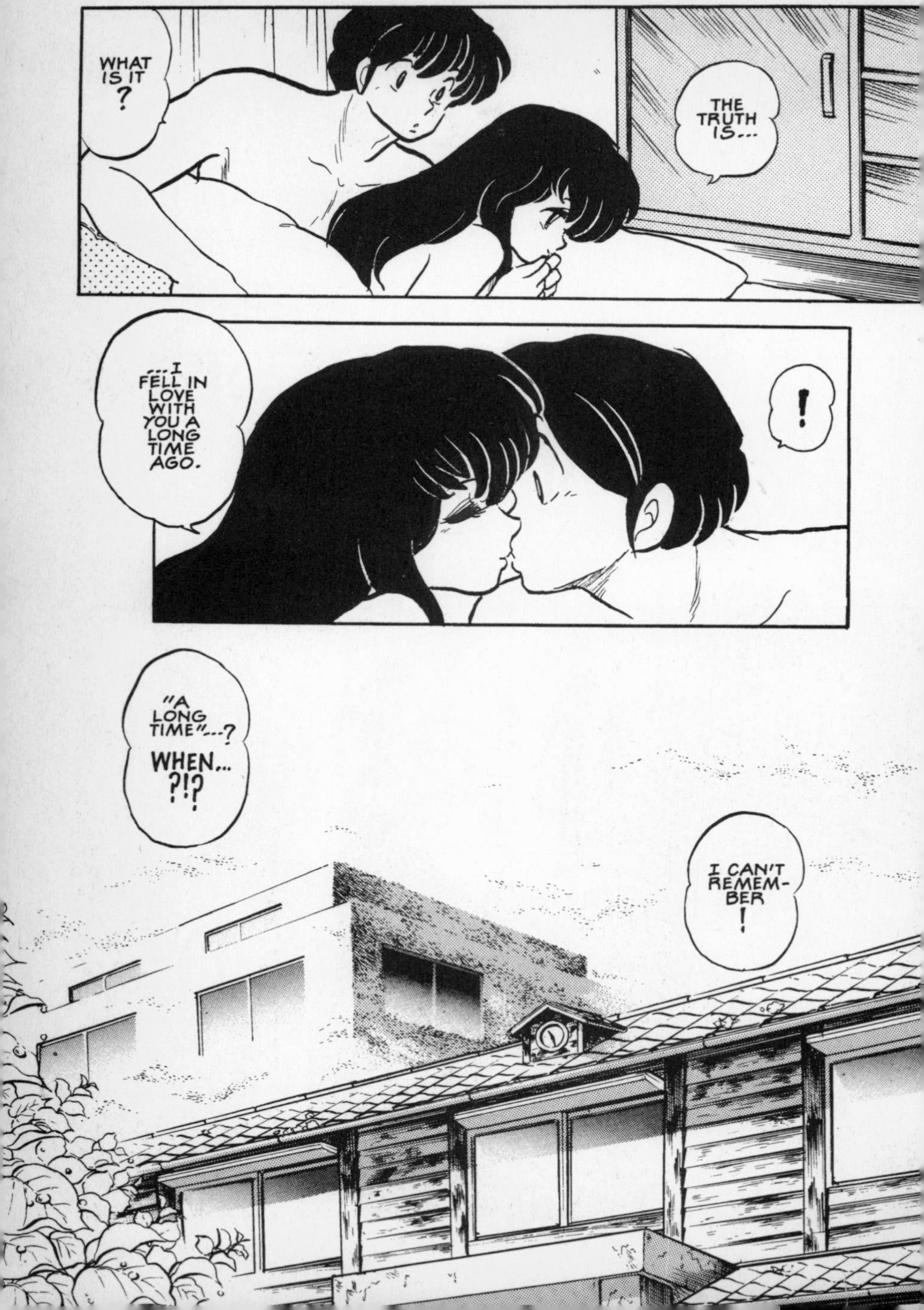
WHAT IS IT ?
THE TRUTH IS...
...I FELL IN LOVE WITH YOU A LONG TIME AGO.
!
"A LONG TIME"...?
WHEN... ?!?
I CAN'T REMEMBER !

PART FOUR
LOVE CALL

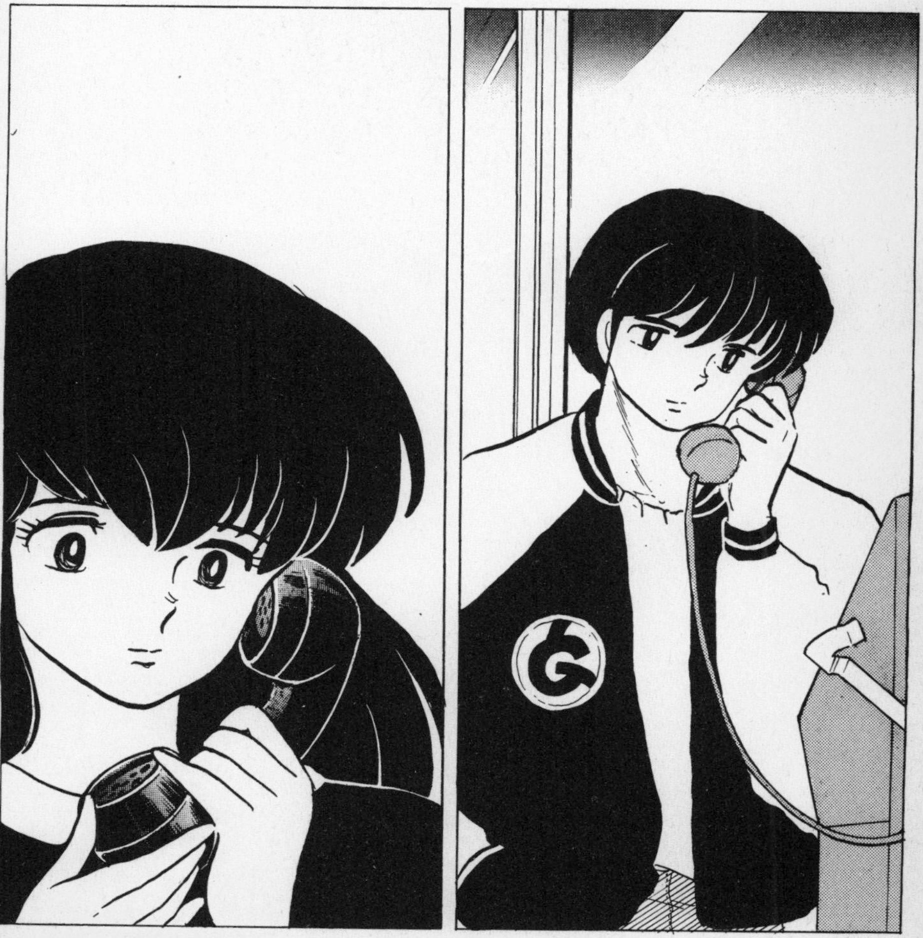

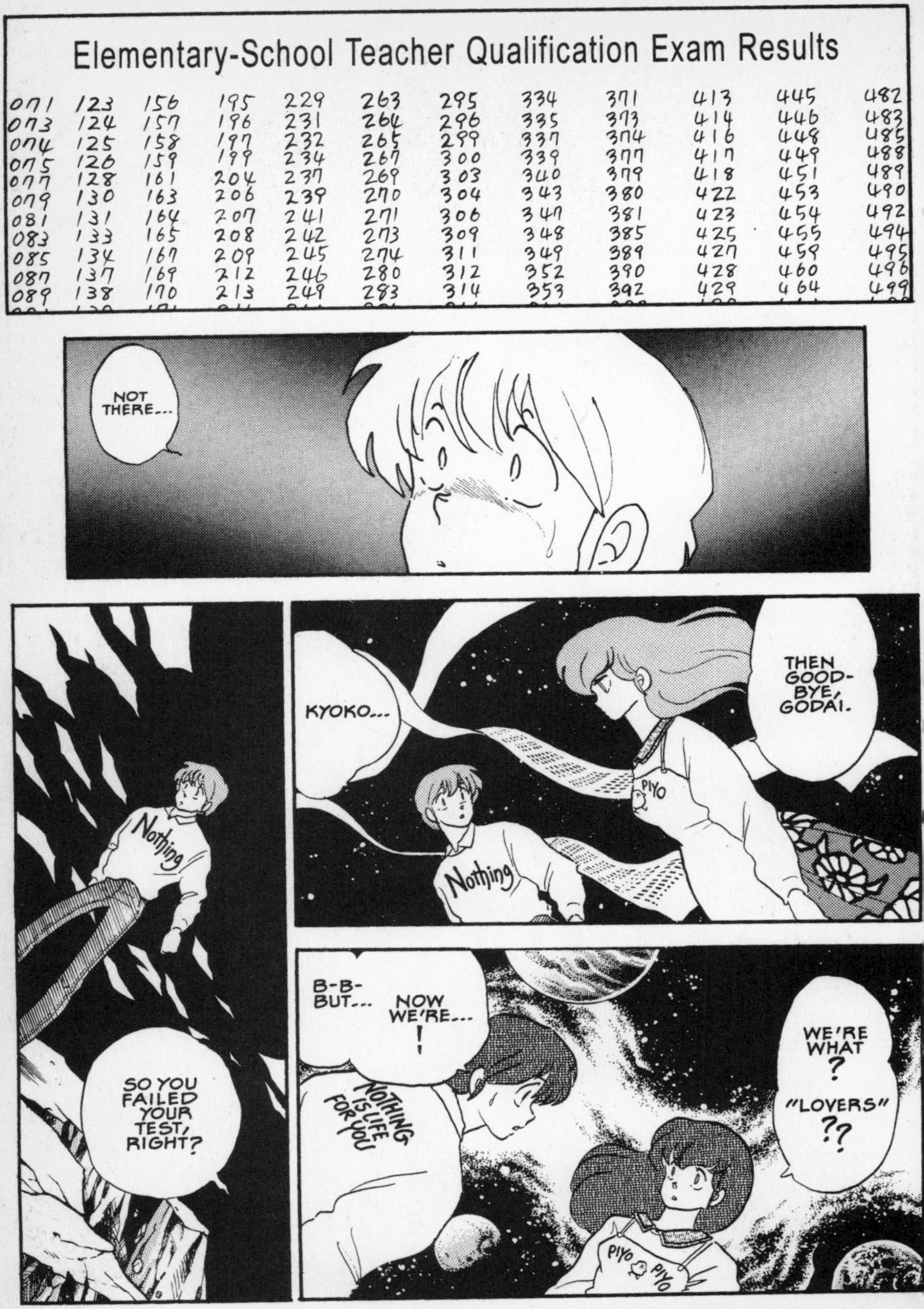
Elementary-School Teacher Qualification Exam Results
071 123 156 195 229 263 295 334 371 413 445 482
073 124 157 196 231 264 296 335 373 414 446 483
074 125 158 197 232 265 299 337 374 416 448 485
075 126 159 199 234 267 300 339 377 417 449 488
077 128 161 204 237 269 303 340 379 418 451 489
079 130 163 206 239 270 304 343 380 422 453 490
081 131 164 207 241 271 306 347 381 423 454 492
083 133 165 208 242 273 309 348 385 425 455 494
085 134 167 209 245 274 311 349 389 427 459 495
087 137 169 212 246 280 312 352 390 428 460 496
089 138 170 213 249 283 314 353 392 429 464 499
NOT THERE...
Nothing
SO YOU FAILED YOUR TEST, RIGHT?
KYOKO...
THEN GOOD-BYE, GODAI.
Nothing
PIYO
B-B-BUT...
NOW WE'RE...!
NOTHING IS LIFE FOR YOU
WE'RE WHAT? "LOVERS"??
PIYO PIYO

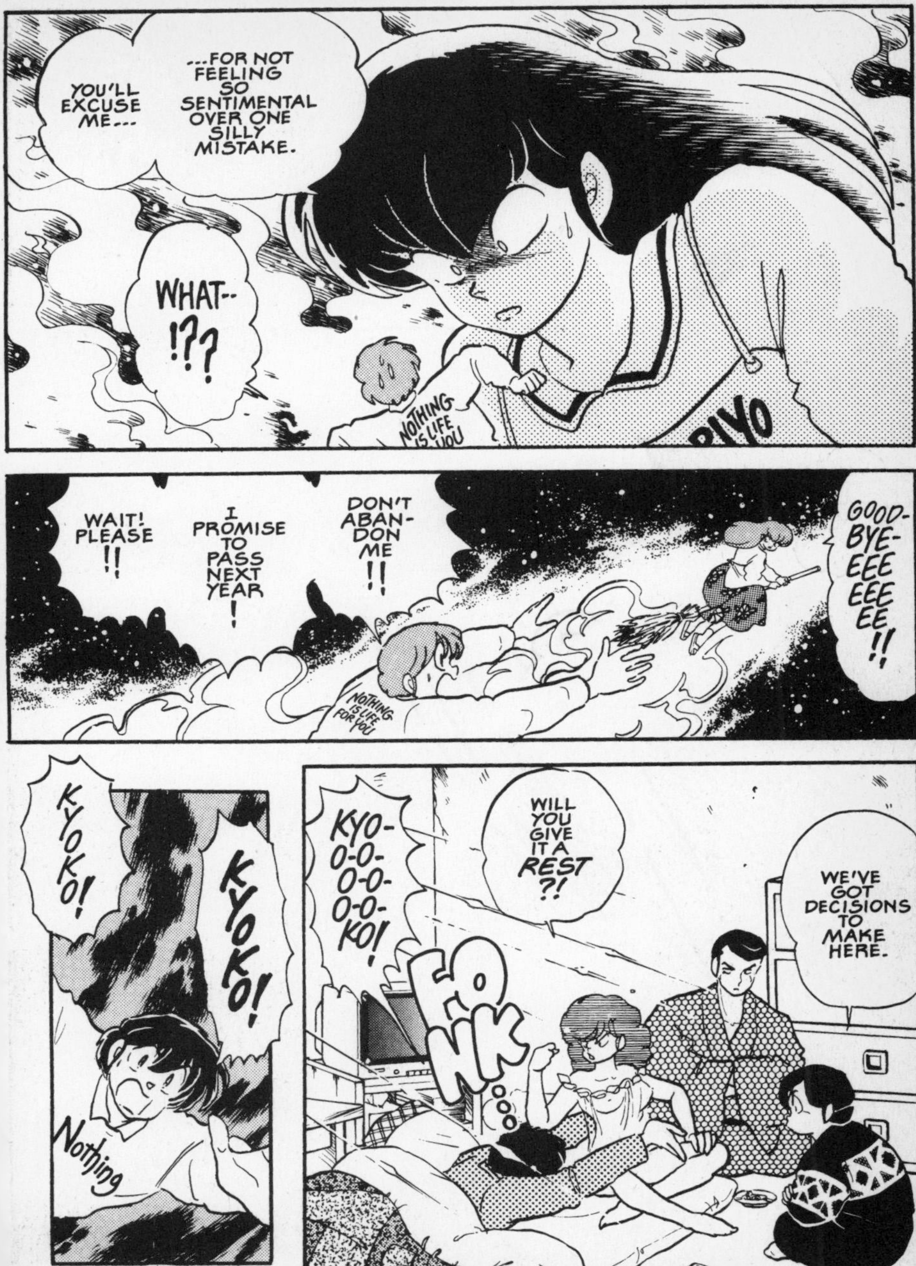
YOU'LL EXCUSE ME---
---FOR NOT FEELING SO SENTIMENTAL OVER ONE SILLY MISTAKE.
WHAT--!??
NOTHING IS LIFE YOU
PIYO
WAIT! PLEASE!!
I PROMISE TO PASS NEXT YEAR!
DON'T ABANDON ME!!
GOOD-BYE-EEEEEEEEE!!
NOTHING IS LIFE FOR YOU
KYOKO!
KYOKO!
Nothing
KYO-O-O-O-O-O-O-KO!
WILL YOU GIVE IT A REST?!
WE'VE GOT DECISIONS TO MAKE HERE.
FONK

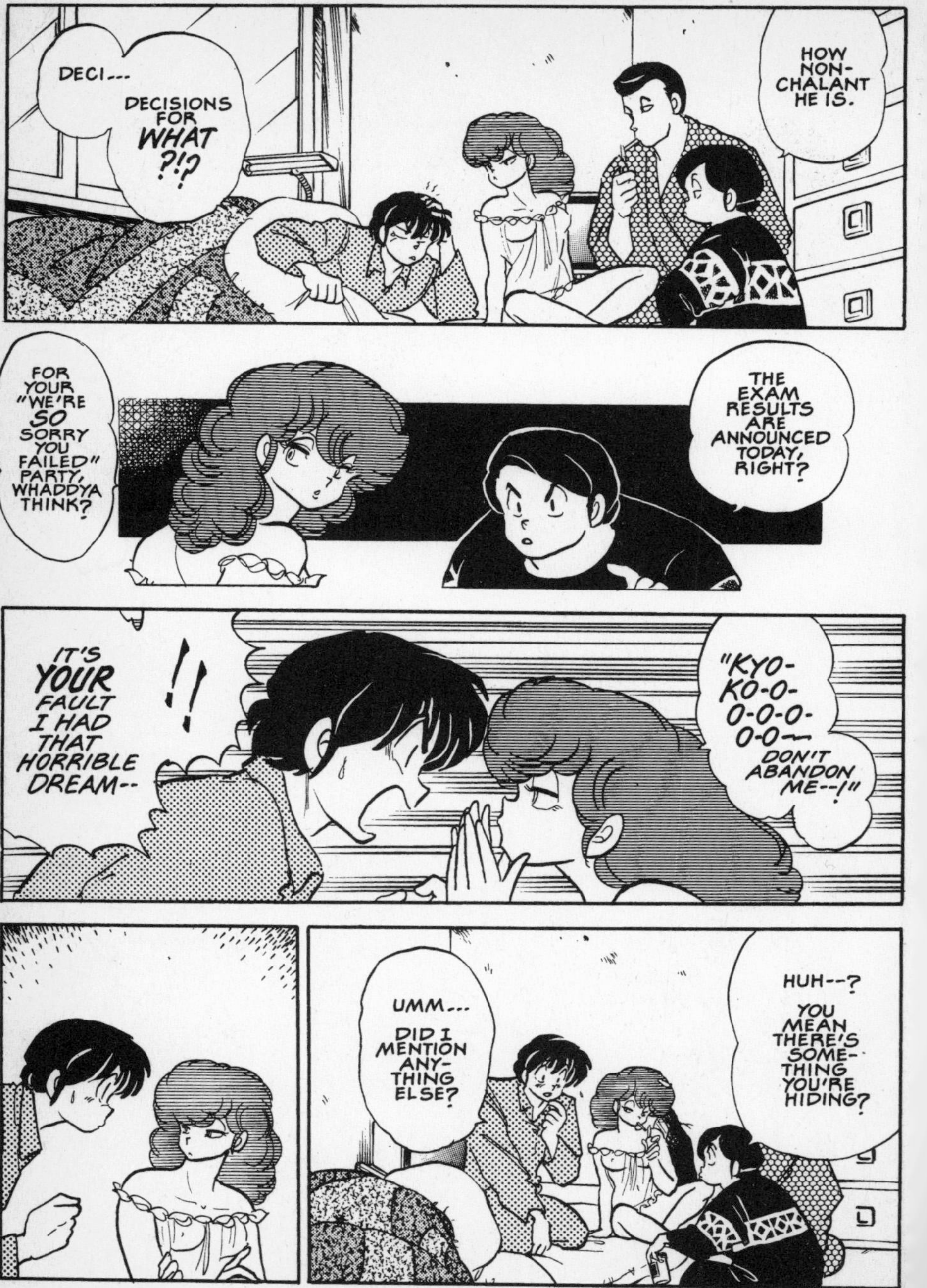
DECI...
DECISIONS FOR WHAT ?!?
HOW NON-CHALANT HE IS.
FOR YOUR "WE'RE SO SORRY YOU FAILED" PARTY, WHADDYA THINK?
THE EXAM RESULTS ARE ANNOUNCED TODAY, RIGHT?
IT'S YOUR FAULT I HAD THAT HORRIBLE DREAM--
!!
"KYO-KO-O-O-O-O-O-O-O-- DON'T ABANDON ME--!"
UMM... DID I MENTION ANY-THING ELSE?
HUH--? YOU MEAN THERE'S SOME-THING YOU'RE HIDING?

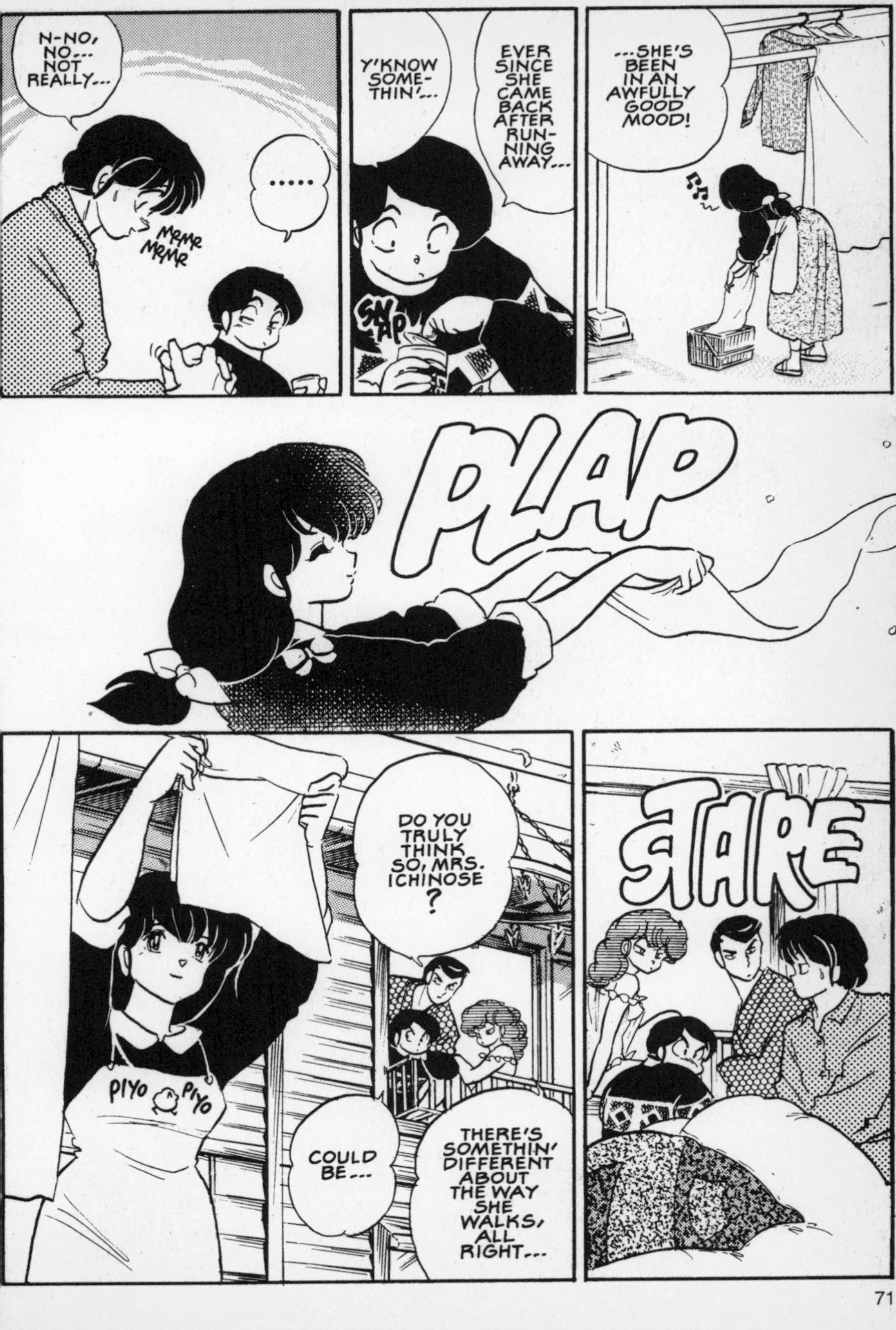
N-NO, NO... NOT REALLY...
......
MRMR MRMR
Y'KNOW SOME-THIN'...
EVER SINCE SHE CAME BACK AFTER RUN-NING AWAY...
SNAP
...SHE'S BEEN IN AN AWFULLY GOOD MOOD!
PLAP
DO YOU TRULY THINK SO, MRS. ICHINOSE?
PIYO PIYO
COULD BE...
THERE'S SOMETHIN' DIFFERENT ABOUT THE WAY SHE WALKS, ALL RIGHT...
STARE

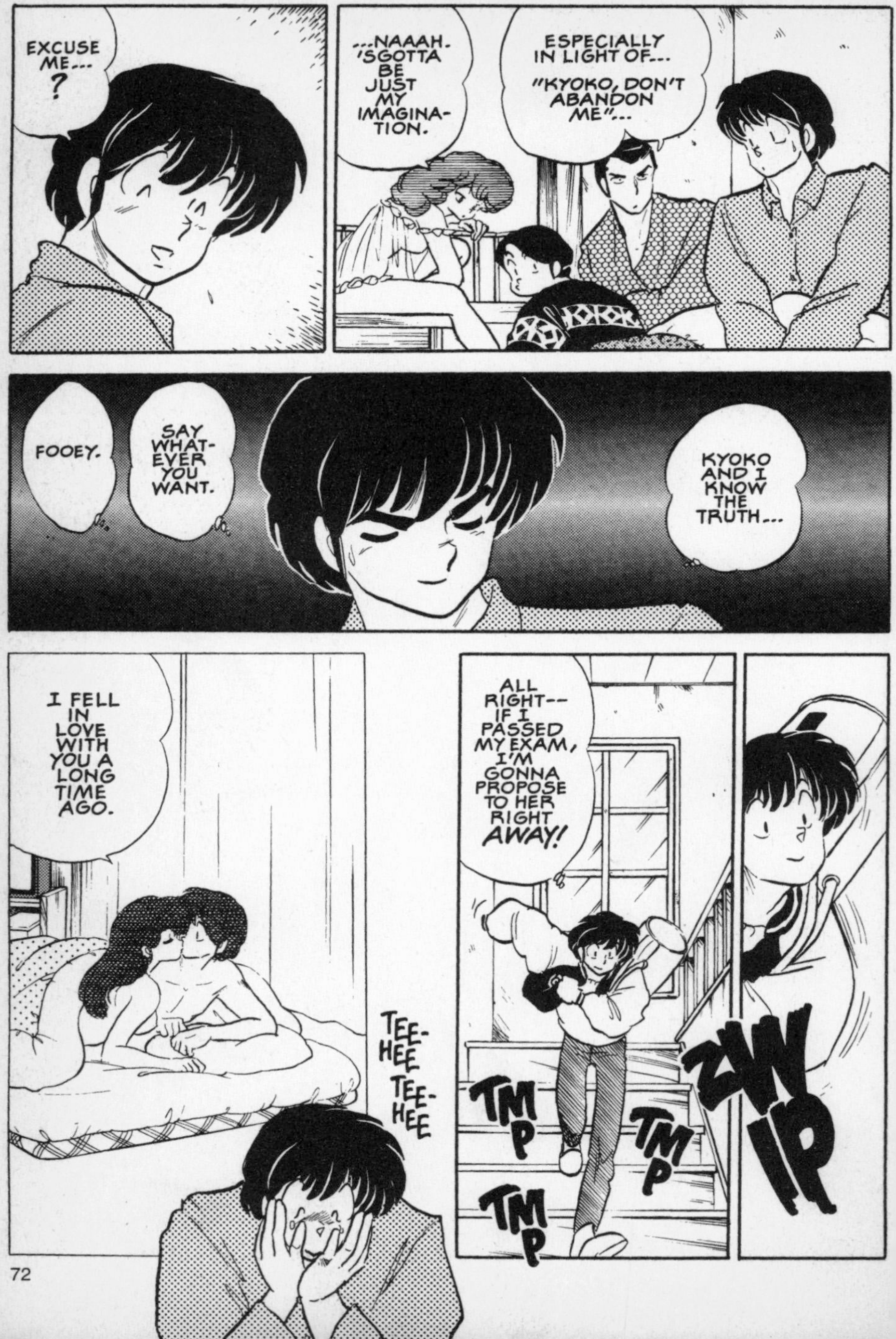
EXCUSE ME...?
...NAAAH. 'SGOTTA BE JUST MY IMAGINATION.
ESPECIALLY IN LIGHT OF...
"KYOKO, DON'T ABANDON ME"...
FOOEY.
SAY WHATEVER YOU WANT.
KYOKO AND I KNOW THE TRUTH...
I FELL IN LOVE WITH YOU A LONG TIME AGO.
TEE-HEE TEE-HEE
ALL RIGHT--IF I PASSED MY EXAM, I'M GONNA PROPOSE TO HER RIGHT AWAY!
TMP
TMP
TMP
ZWIP

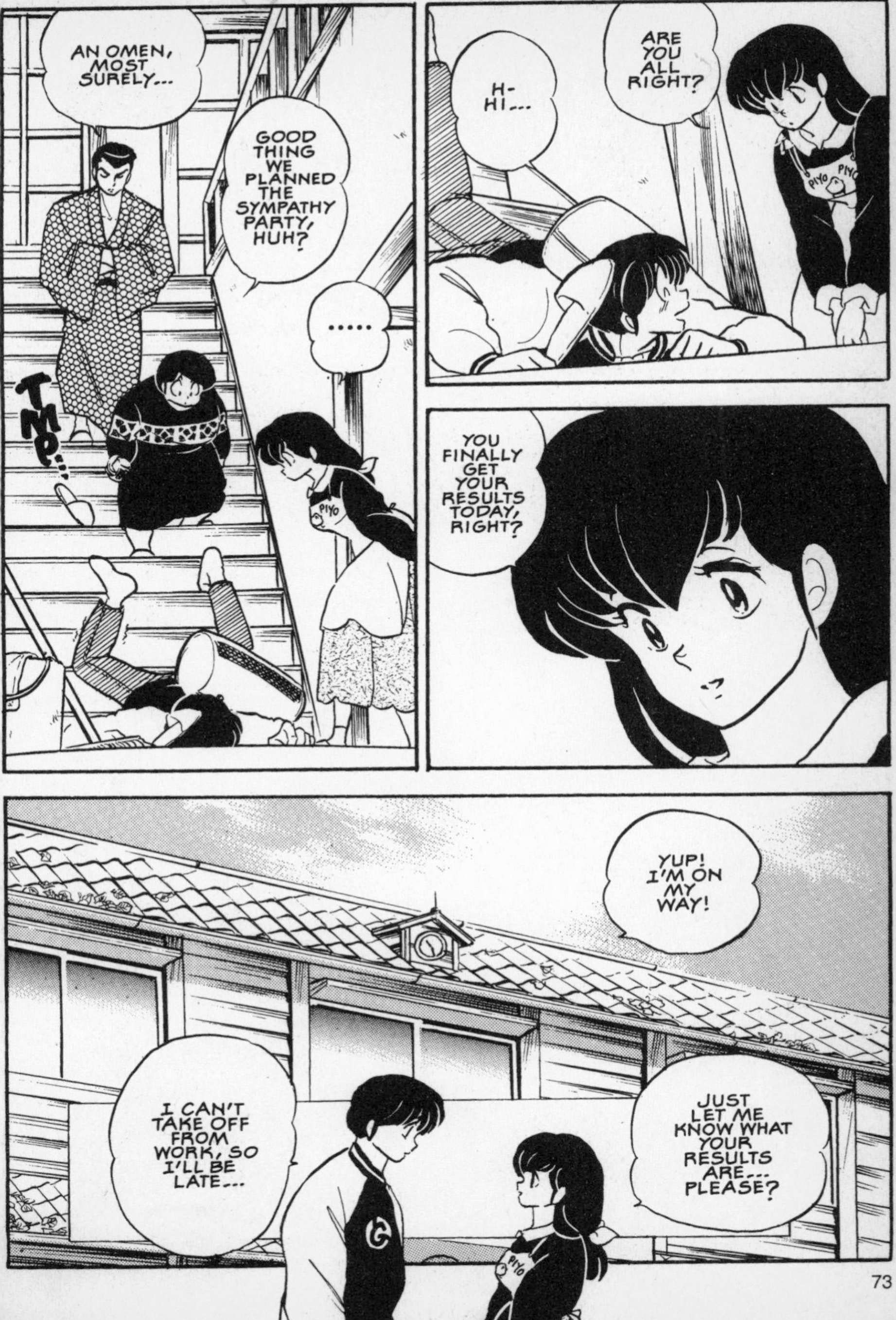
AN OMEN, MOST SURELY...
GOOD THING WE PLANNED THE SYMPATHY PARTY, HUH?
.....
TMP...
ARE YOU ALL RIGHT?
H-HI...
YOU FINALLY GET YOUR RESULTS TODAY, RIGHT?
YUP! I'M ON MY WAY!
I CAN'T TAKE OFF FROM WORK, SO I'LL BE LATE...
JUST LET ME KNOW WHAT YOUR RESULTS ARE... PLEASE?

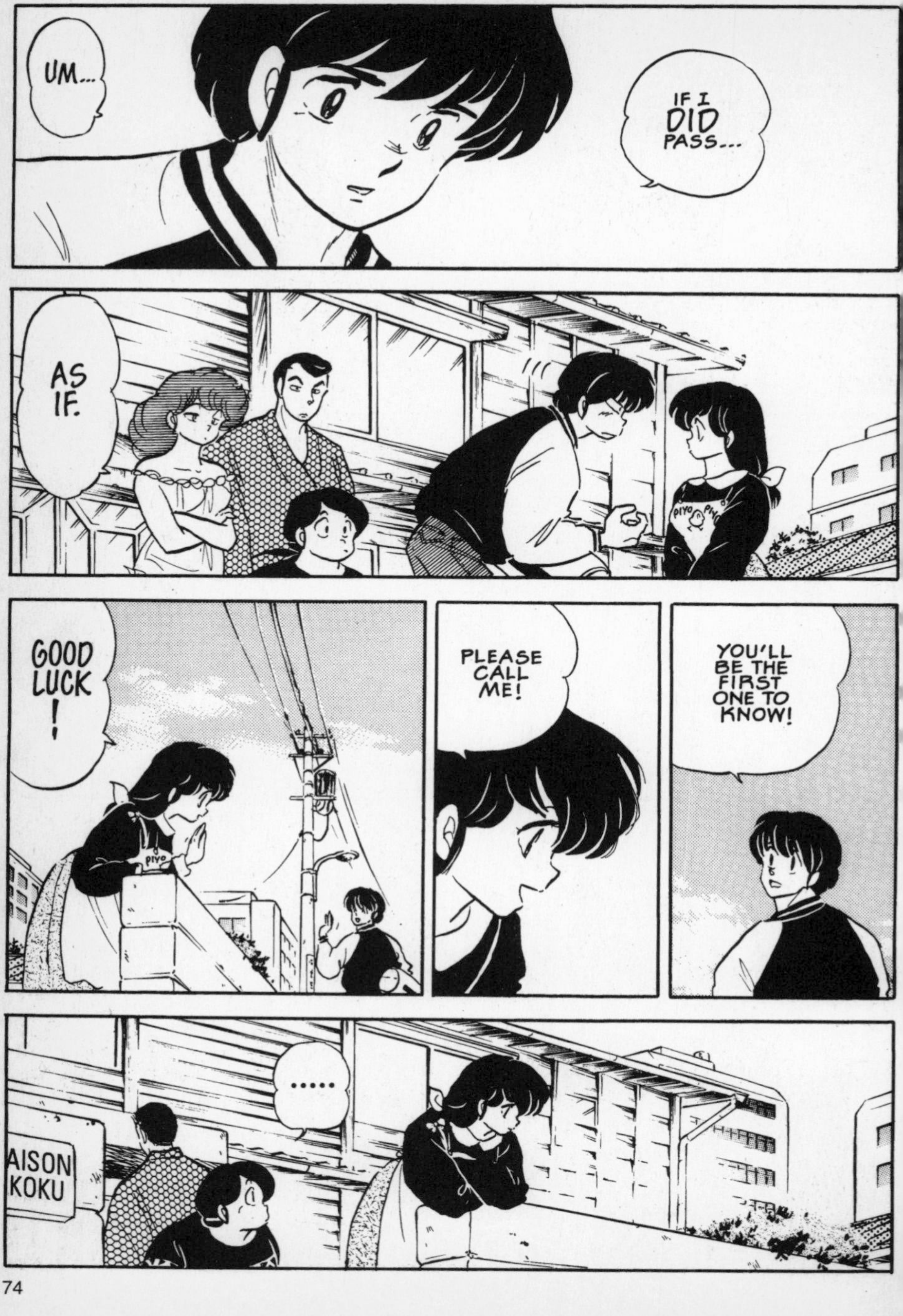
UM...
IF I DID PASS...
AS IF.
GOOD LUCK !
PLEASE CALL ME!
YOU'LL BE THE FIRST ONE TO KNOW!
AISON KOKU
.....

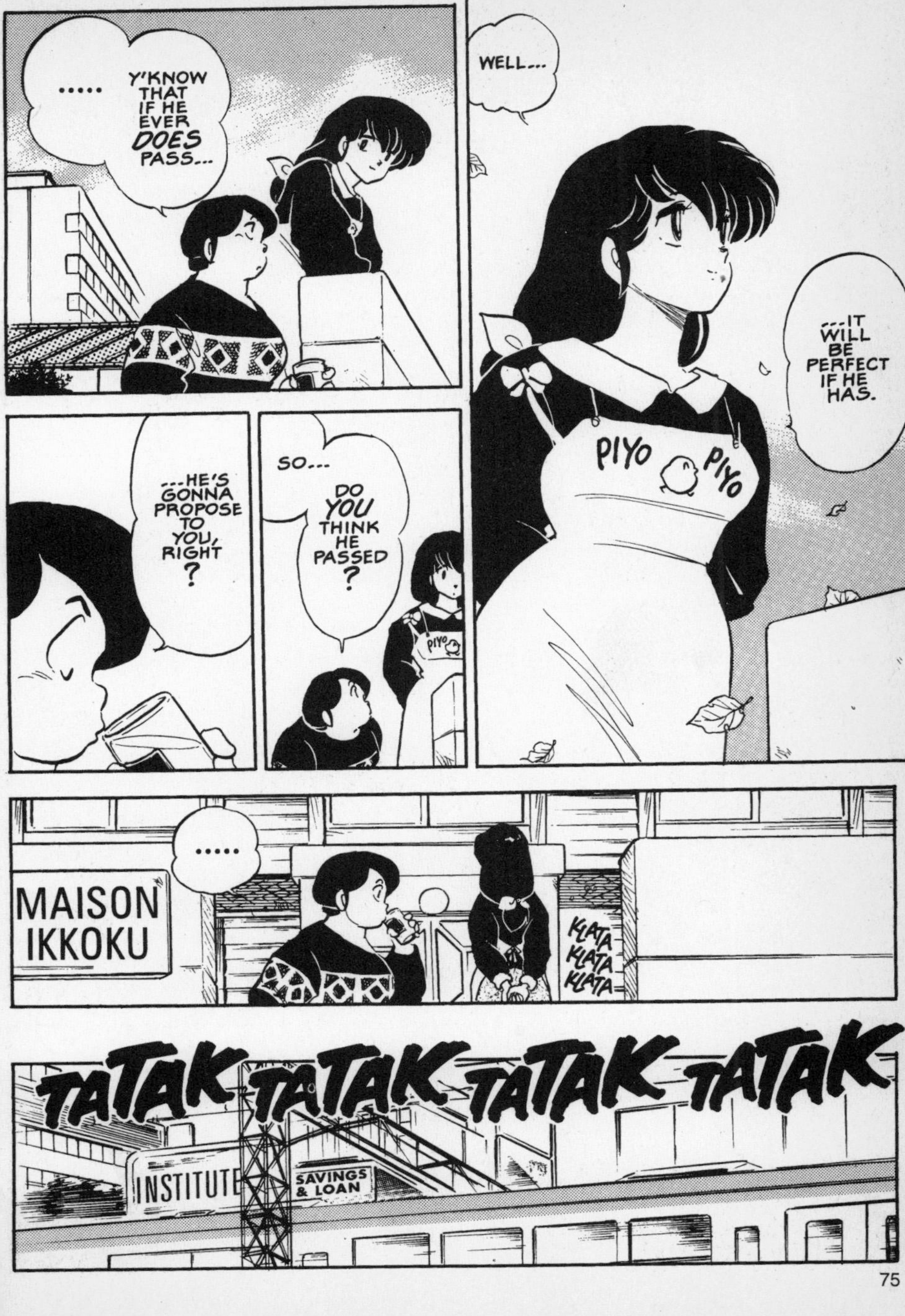
.....
Y'KNOW THAT IF HE EVER DOES PASS...
...HE'S GONNA PROPOSE TO YOU, RIGHT?
SO...
DO YOU THINK HE PASSED?
PIYO
WELL...
PIYO PIYO
...IT WILL BE PERFECT IF HE HAS.
.....
MAISON IKKOKU
KLATA KLATA KLATA
TATAK TATAK TATAK TATAK
INSTITUTE
SAVINGS & LOAN

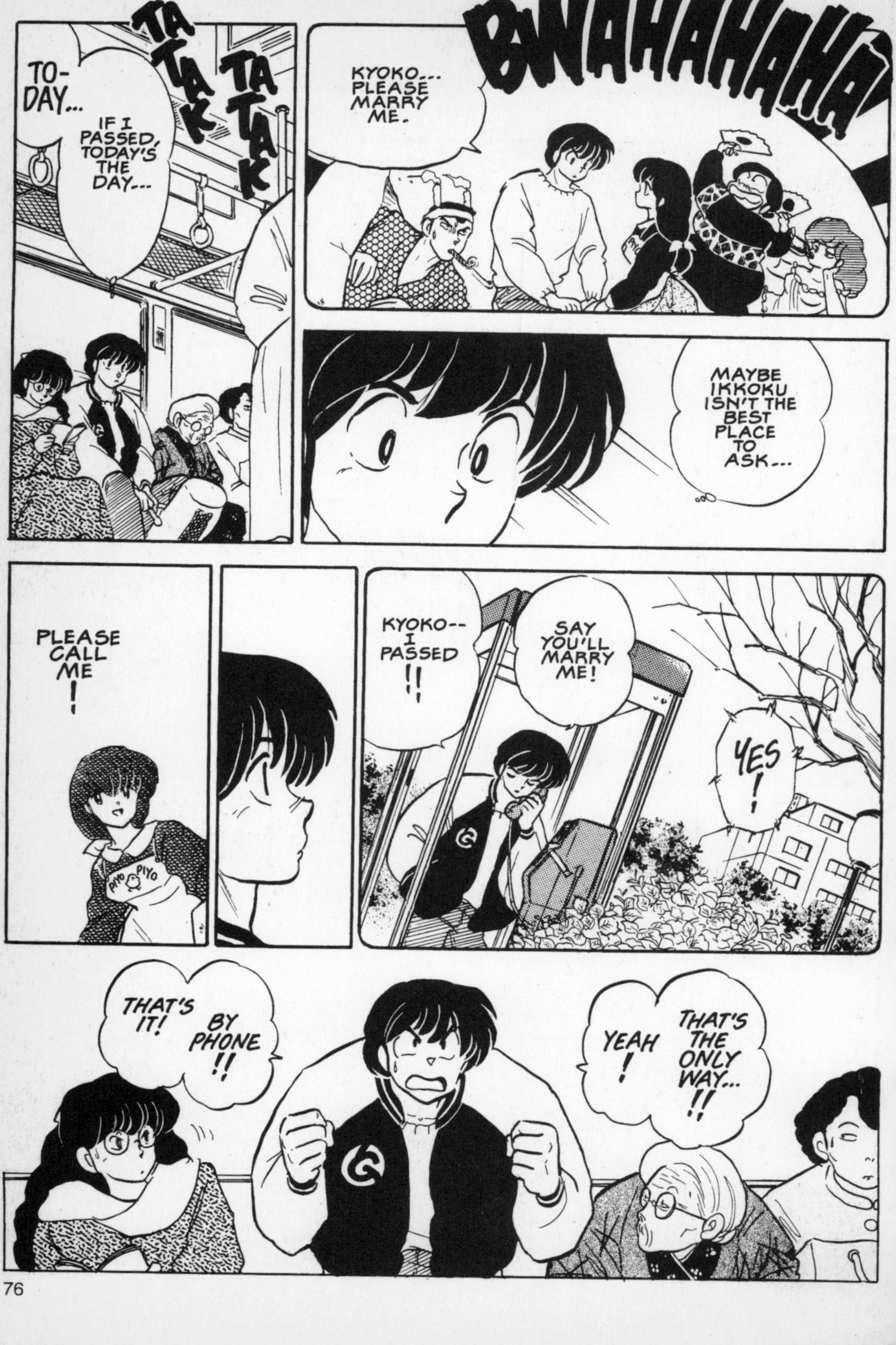
TO-DAY...
TA TAK TA TAK
IF I PASSED, TODAY'S THE DAY...
KYOKO... PLEASE MARRY ME.
BWAHAHAHAHA!
MAYBE IKKOKU ISN'T THE BEST PLACE TO ASK...
PLEASE CALL ME!
KYOKO-- I PASSED!!
SAY YOU'LL MARRY ME!
YES!
PIYO PIYO
THAT'S IT! BY PHONE!!
YEAH! THAT'S THE ONLY WAY...!!

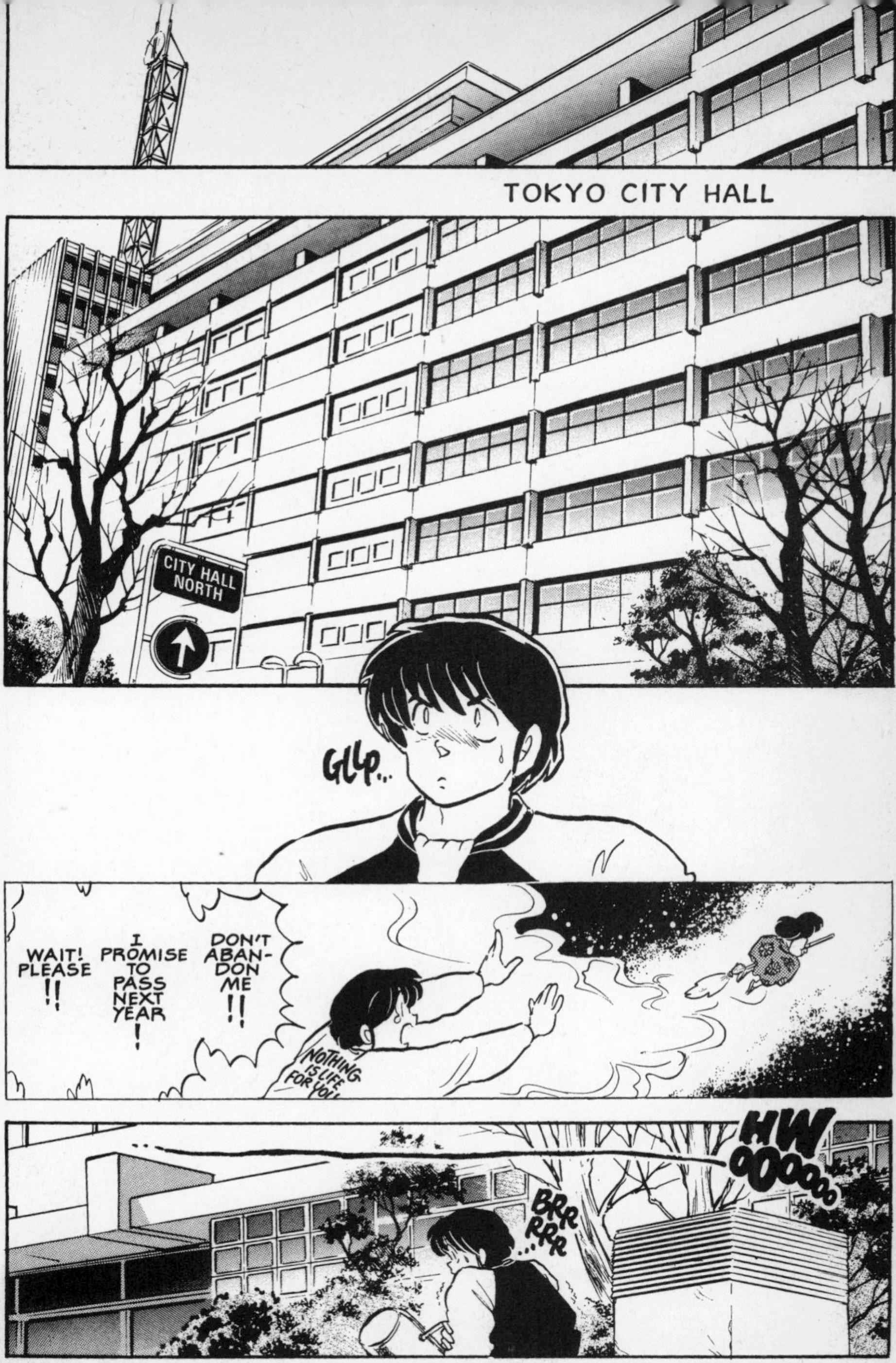
TOKYO CITY HALL
CITY HALL NORTH
GULP...
WAIT! PLEASE!!
I PROMISE TO PASS NEXT YEAR!
DON'T ABANDON ME!!
HWOOOOOO
BRRRRR...

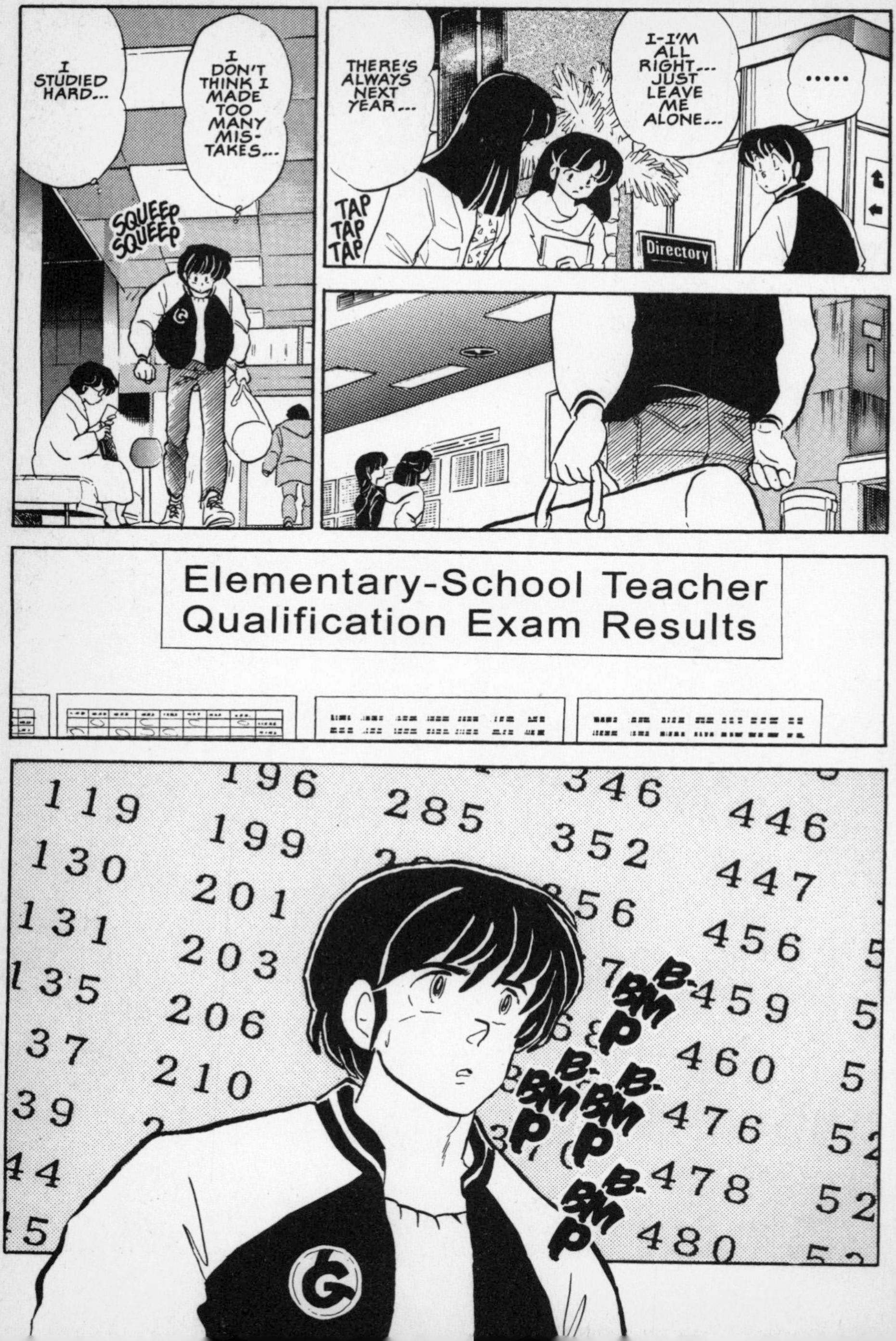
I STUDIED HARD...
I DON'T THINK I MADE TOO MANY MIS-TAKES...
SQUEEP SQUEEP
THERE'S ALWAYS NEXT YEAR...
TAP TAP TAP
I-I'M ALL RIGHT... JUST LEAVE ME ALONE...
......
Directory
Elementary-School Teacher Qualification Exam Results
B-BMP
B-BMP
B-BMP
B-BMP

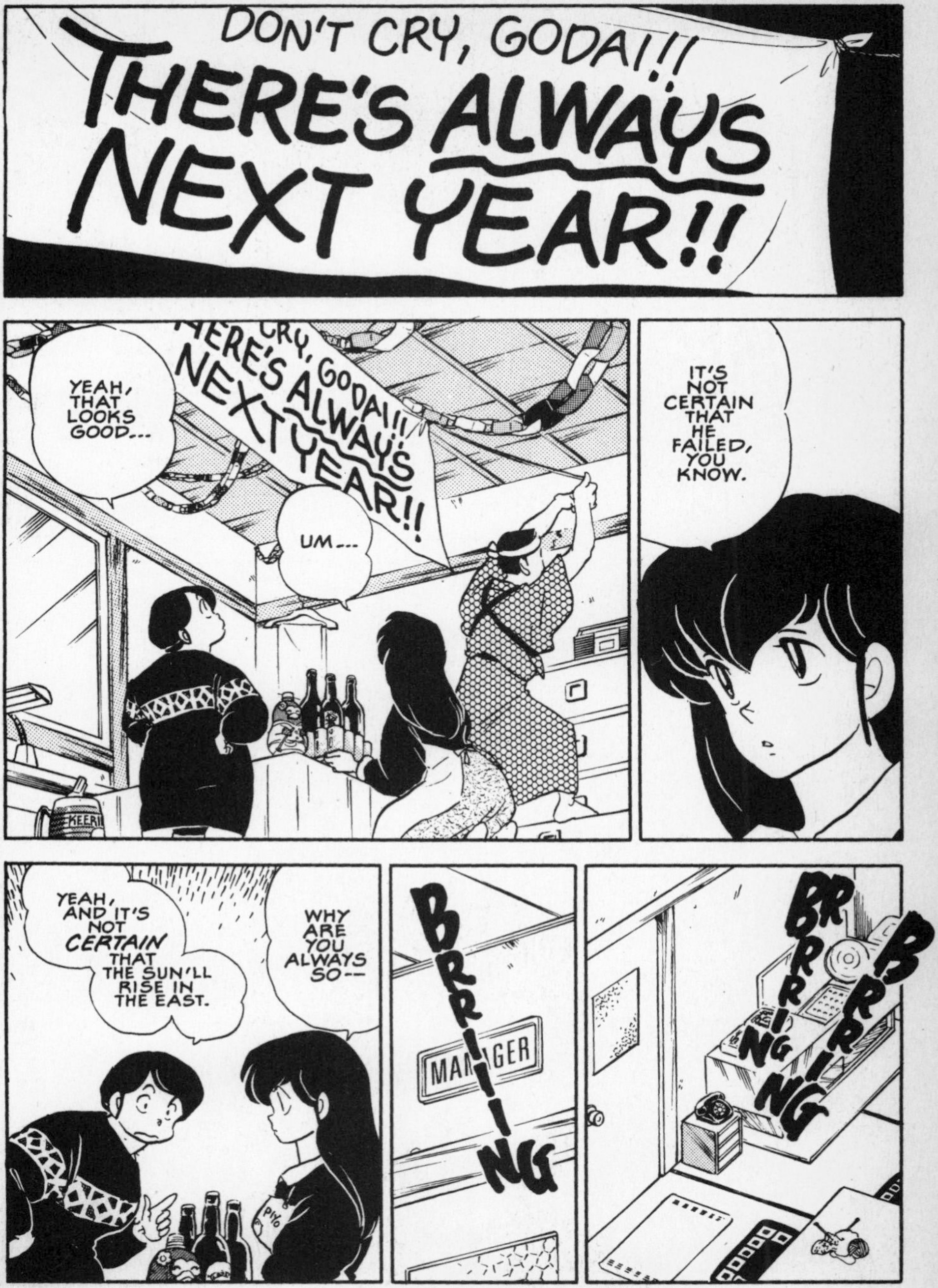
DON'T CRY, GODAI!!
THERE'S ALWAYS NEXT YEAR!!
YEAH, THAT LOOKS GOOD...
UM...
IT'S NOT CERTAIN THAT HE FAILED, YOU KNOW.
YEAH, AND IT'S NOT CERTAIN THAT THE SUN'LL RISE IN THE EAST.
WHY ARE YOU ALWAYS SO--
BRRRIIIING
MANAGER
BRRRING
BRRRING

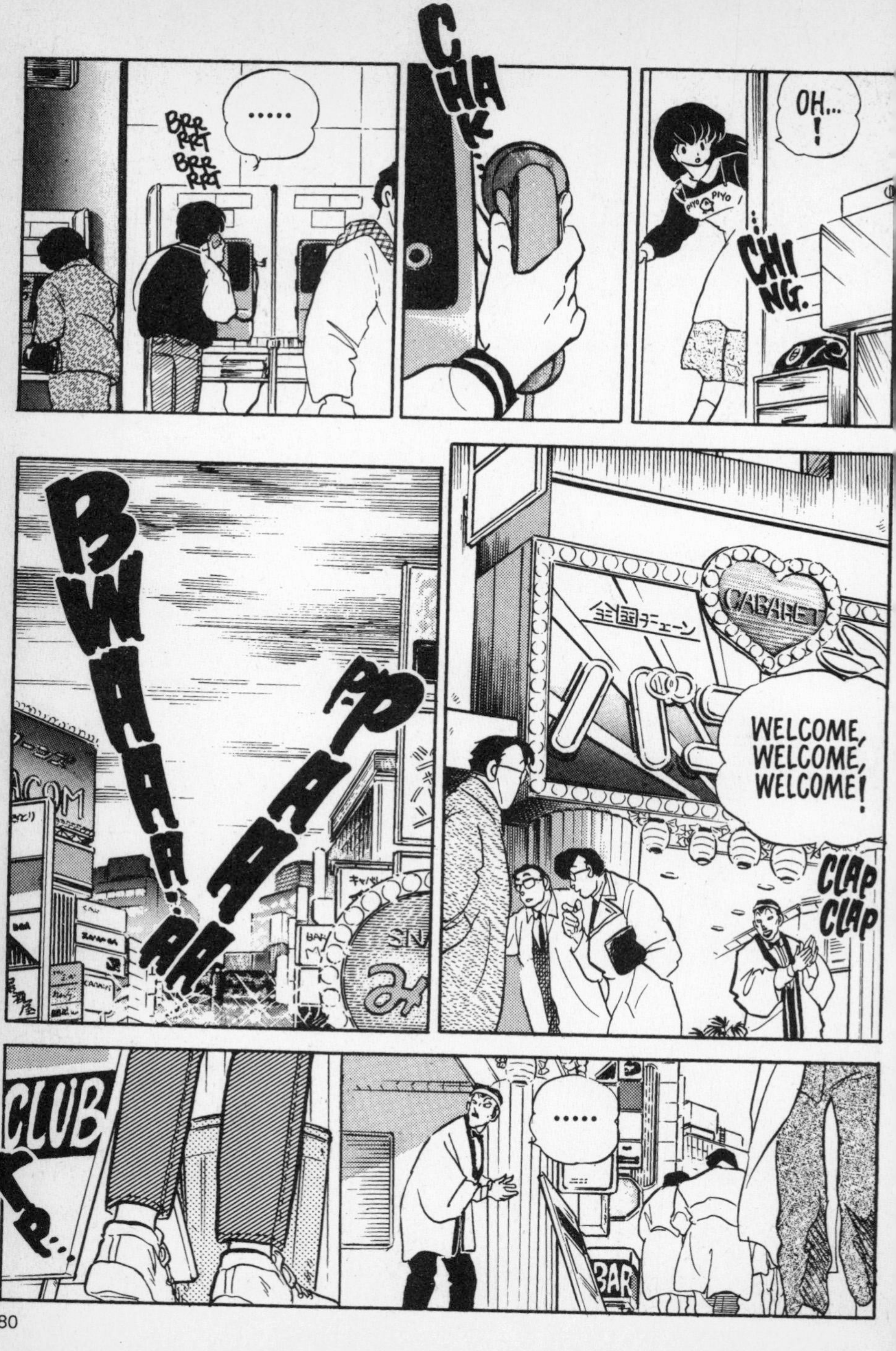
BRR RRT BRR RRT
......
CHAK...
OH... !
CHING.
BWAAAA..AA
PPAAAA
全国チェーン
CABARET
WELCOME, WELCOME, WELCOME!
CLAP CLAP
CLUB
TP..
......
BAR

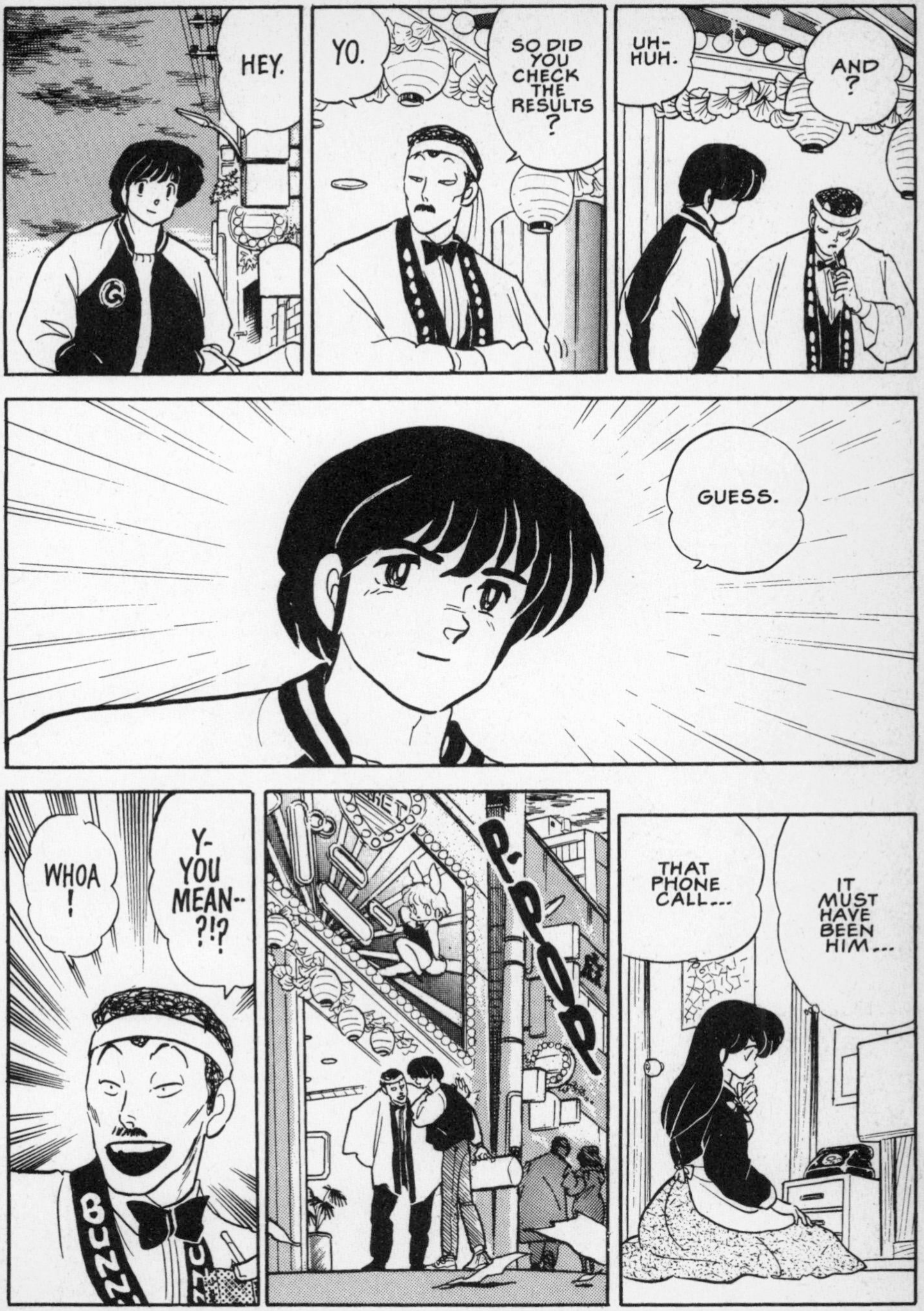
HEY.
YO.
SO DID YOU CHECK THE RESULTS ?
UH-HUH.
AND ?
GUESS.
WHOA !
Y-YOU MEAN-- ?!?
P'POOP
THAT PHONE CALL...
IT MUST HAVE BEEN HIM...

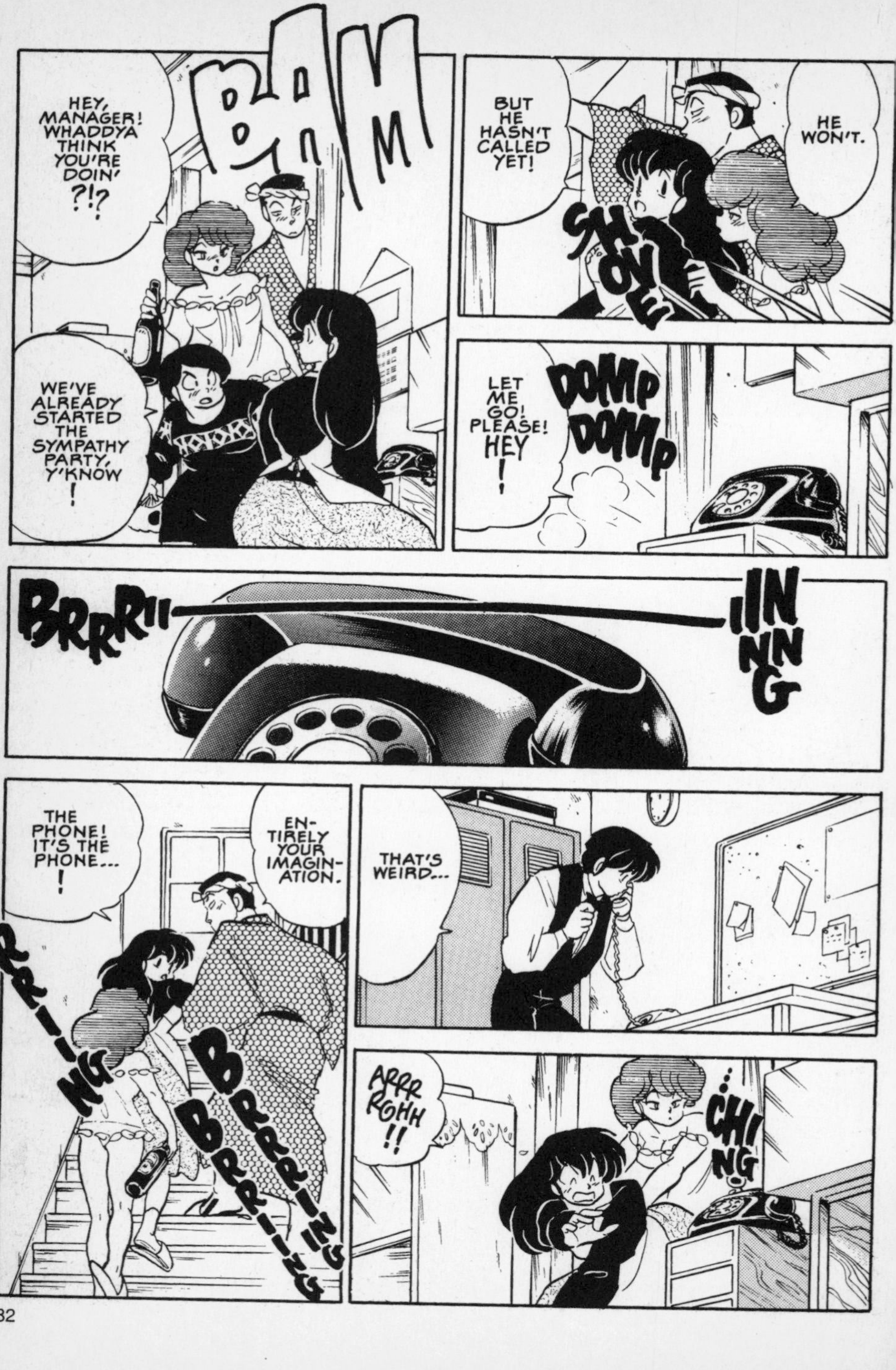
BAM
BOOM
HEY, MANAGER! WHADDYA THINK YOU'RE DOIN' ?!?
WE'VE ALREADY STARTED THE SYMPATHY PARTY, Y'KNOW!
BUT HE HASN'T CALLED YET!
SHOVE
HE WON'T.
LET ME GO! PLEASE! HEY!
DOMP DOMP
BRRRII—IINNNNG
THE PHONE! IT'S THE PHONE...!
ENTIRELY YOUR IMAGINATION.
BRRIIING
BBRRRRING
BRRRING
THAT'S WEIRD...
ARRRRGHH!!
...CHING

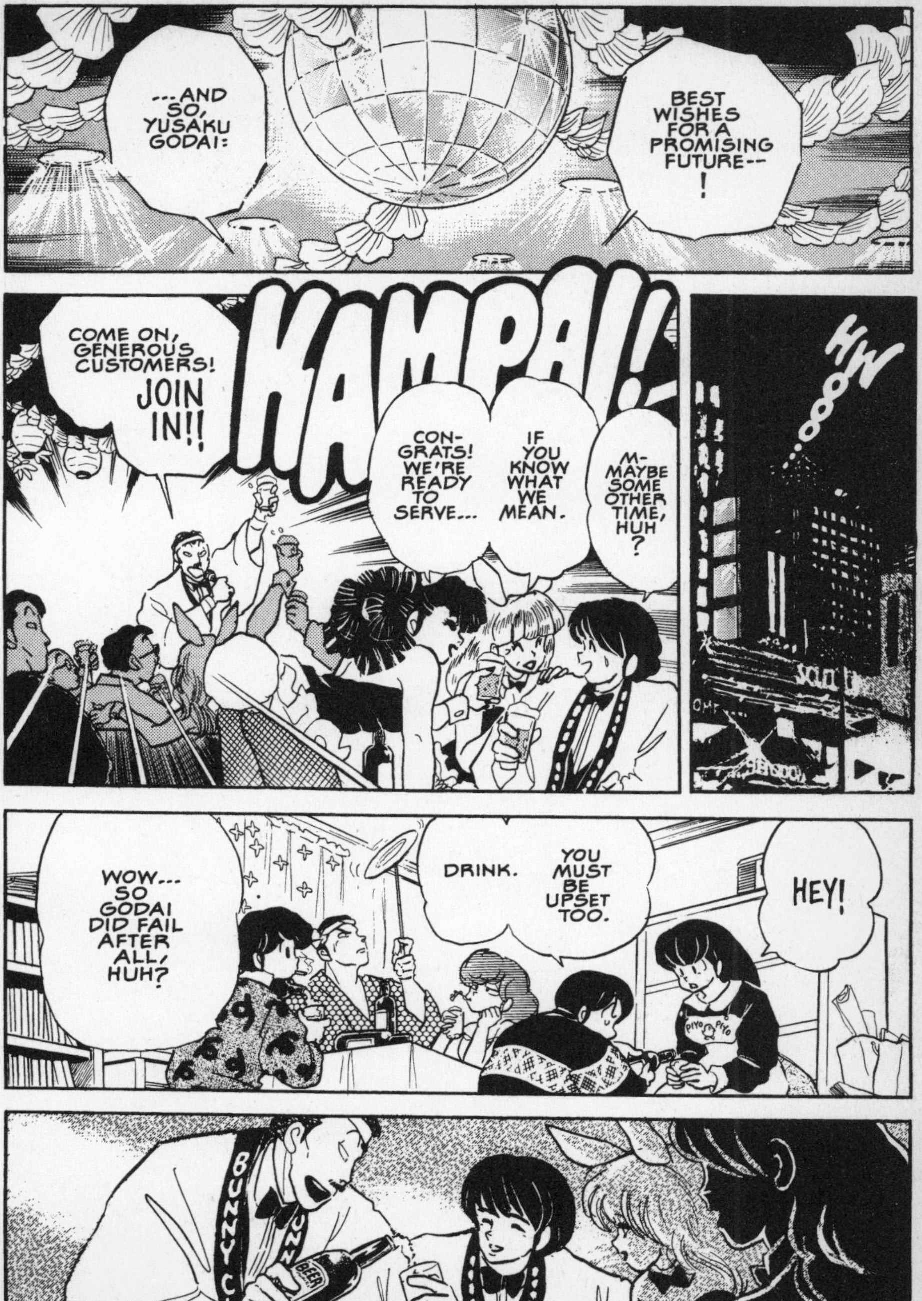
---AND SO, YUSAKU GODAI:
BEST WISHES FOR A PROMISING FUTURE--!
COME ON, GENEROUS CUSTOMERS! JOIN IN!!
KAMPAI!
CON-GRATS! WE'RE READY TO SERVE...
IF YOU KNOW WHAT WE MEAN.
M-MAYBE SOME OTHER TIME, HUH?
WOW... SO GODAI DID FAIL AFTER ALL, HUH?
DRINK.
YOU MUST BE UPSET TOO.
HEY!

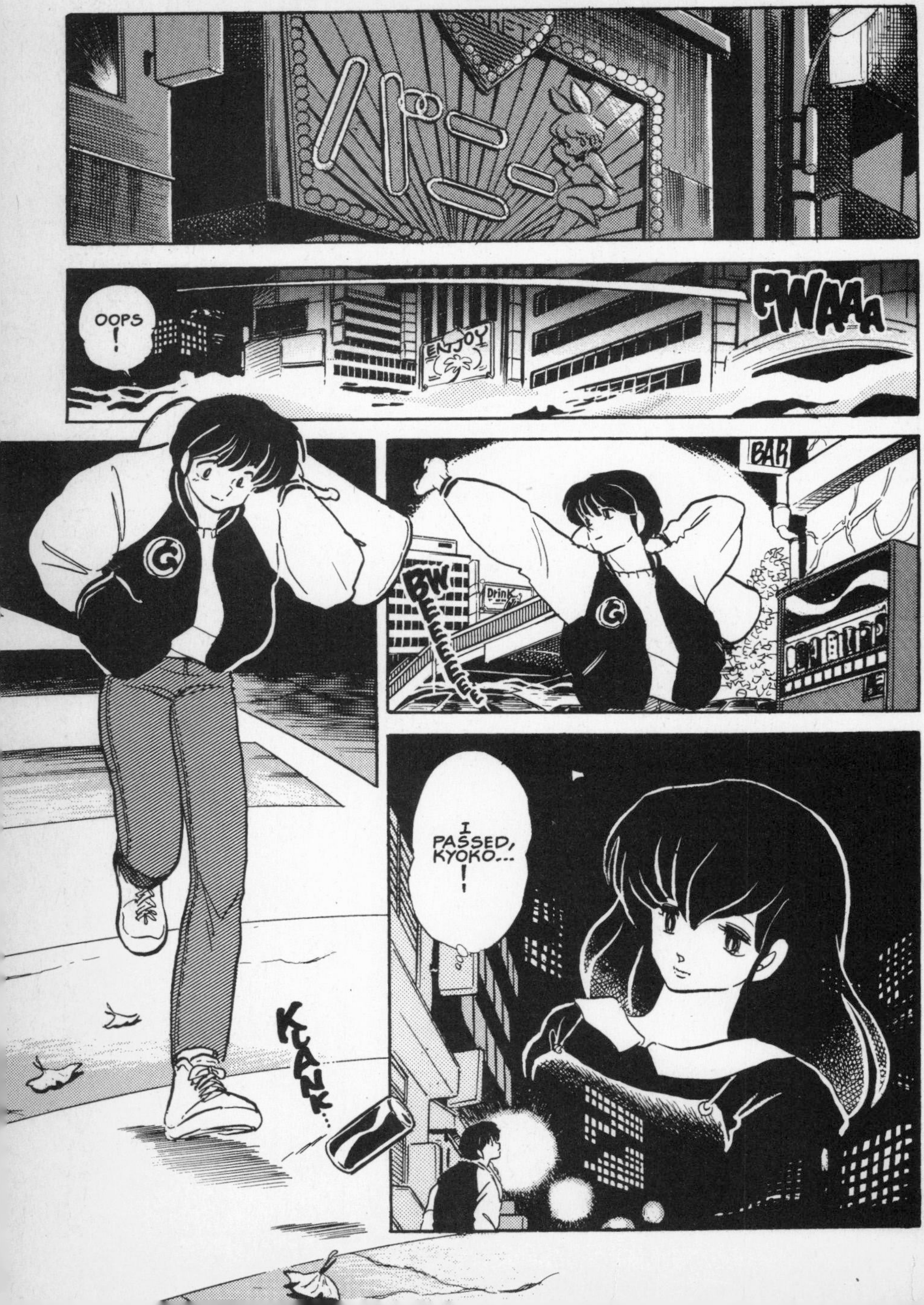
OOPS
!
PWAAAA
ENJOY
KLANK...
BAR
Drink
BWEEEEEEEE
I PASSED, KYOKO...
!

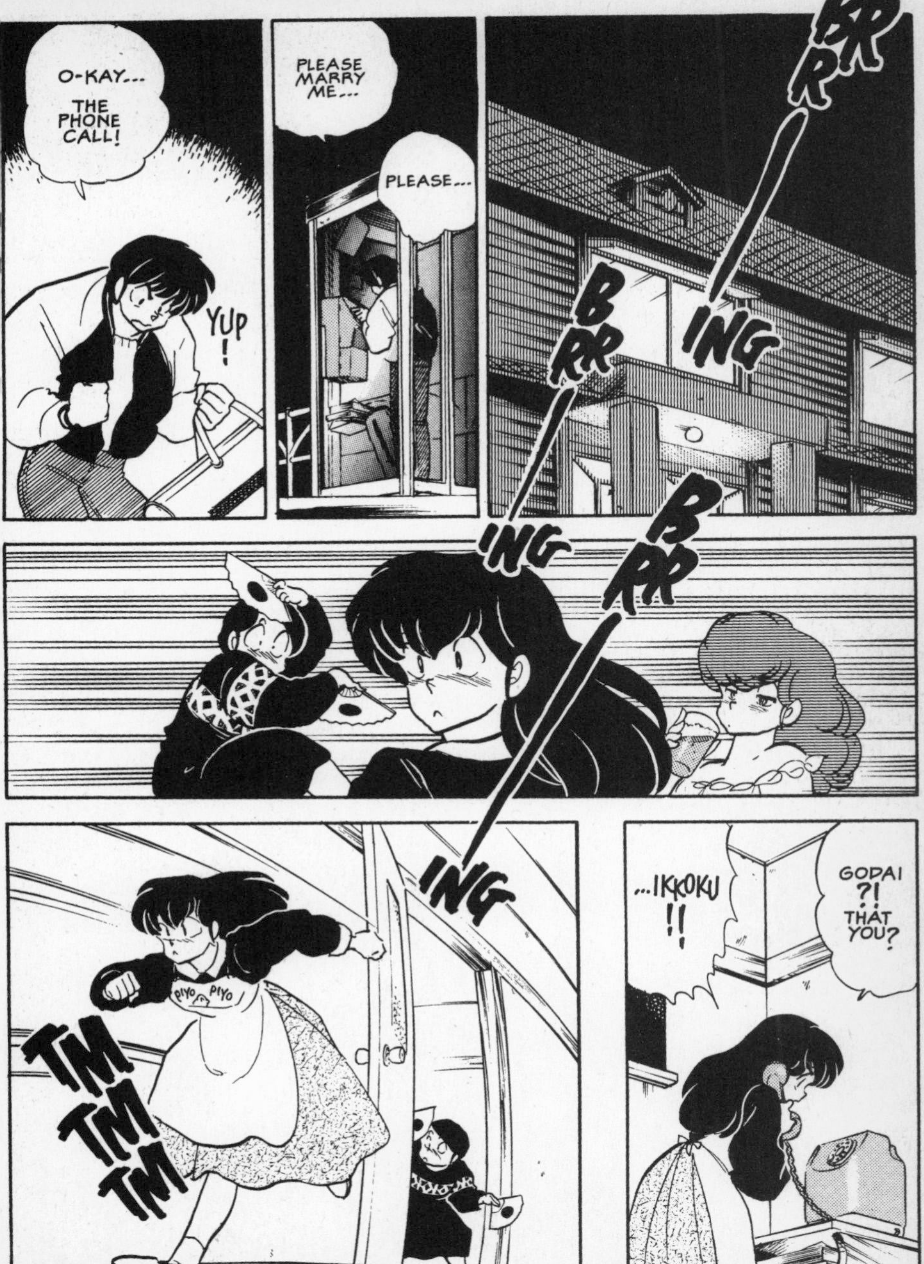
O-KAY... THE PHONE CALL!
YUP!
PLEASE MARRY ME...
PLEASE...
BRRR
ING
BRRR
ING
BRRR
ING
TM TM TM
PIYO PIYO
...IKKOKU!!
GODAI?! THAT YOU?

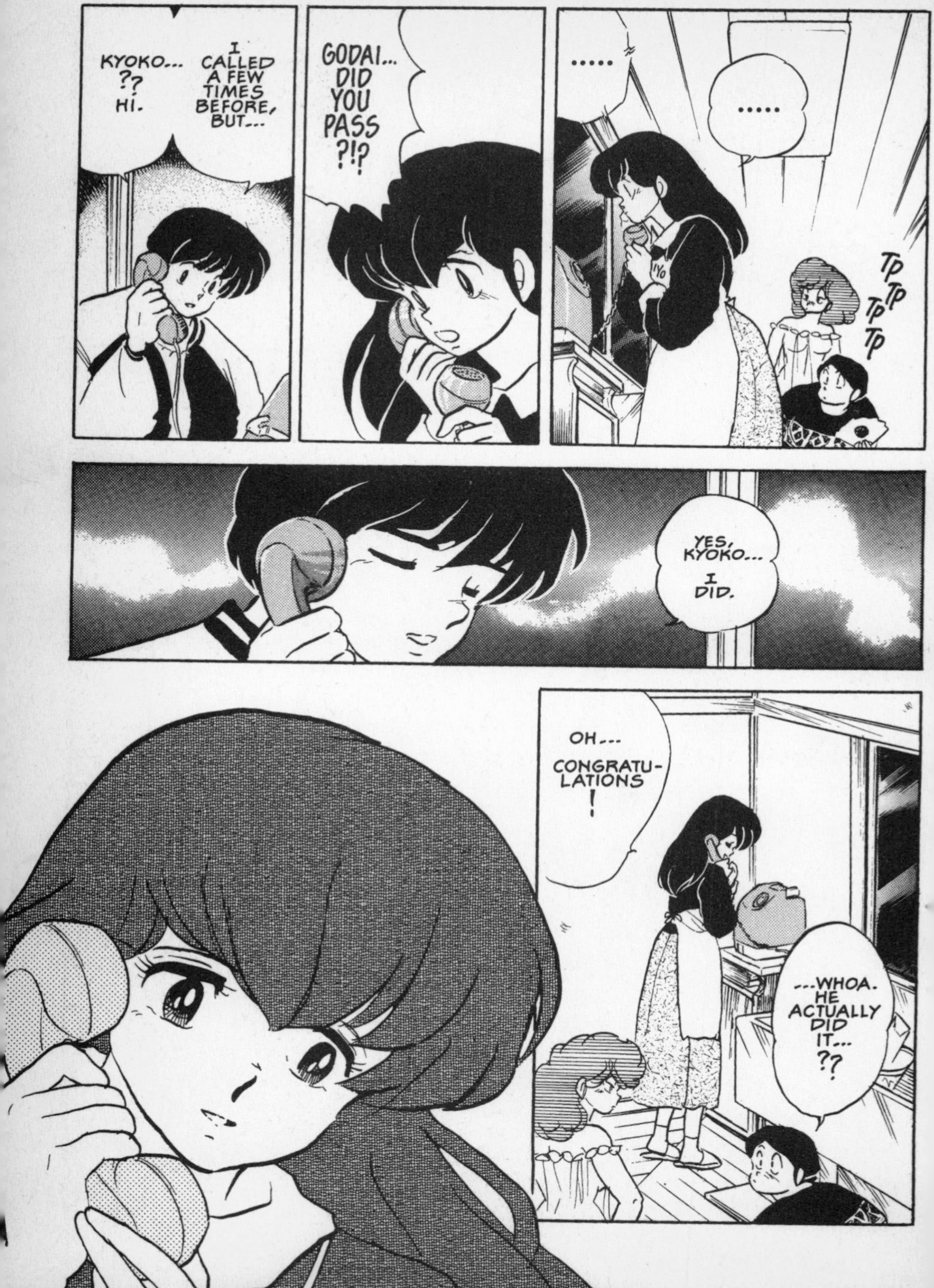
KYOKO... ?? HI.
I CALLED A FEW TIMES BEFORE, BUT...
GODAI... DID YOU PASS ?!?
.....
.....
IYO
TP TP TP TP
YES, KYOKO... I DID.
OH... CONGRATULATIONS !
...WHOA. HE ACTUALLY DID IT... ??

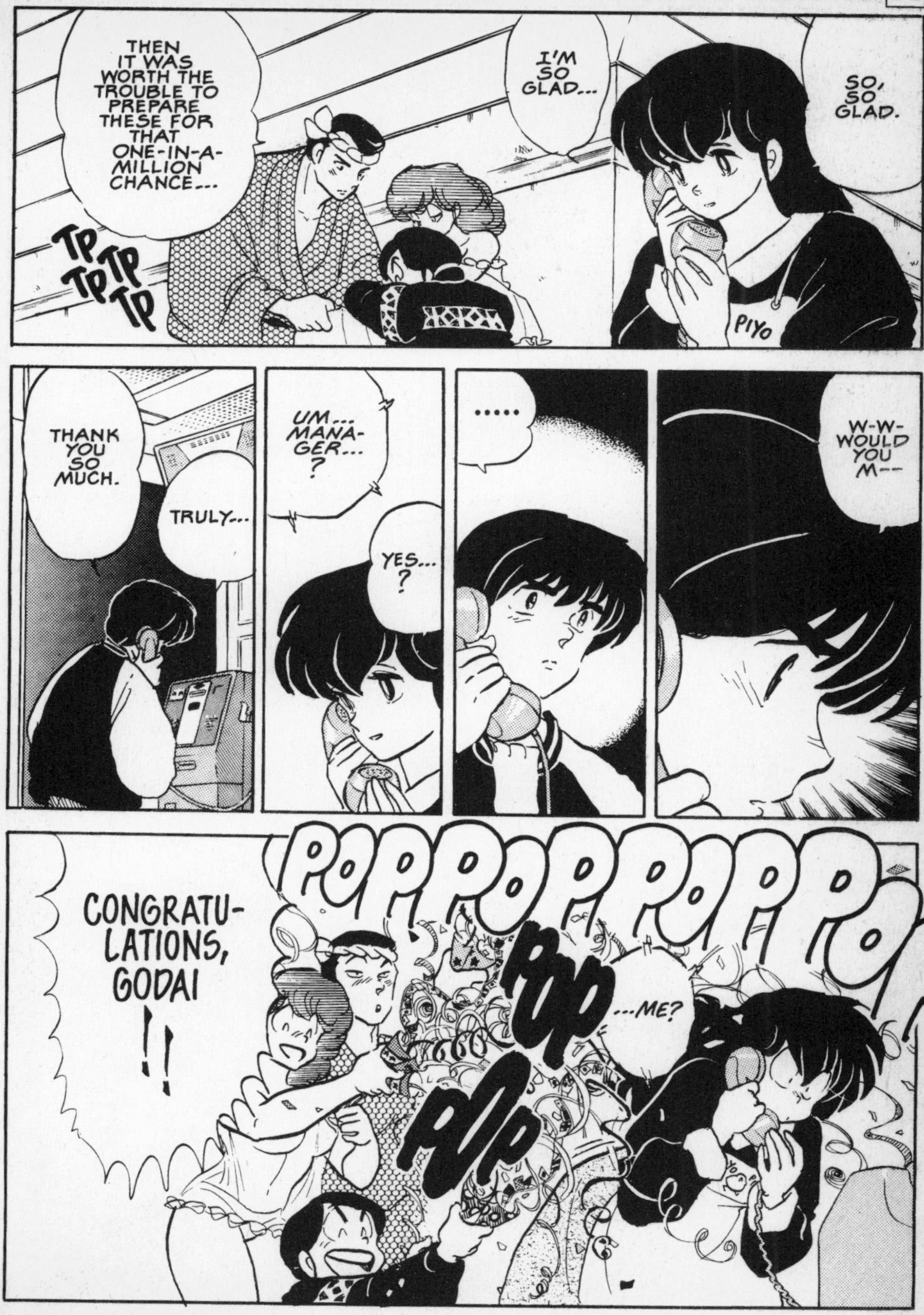
THEN IT WAS WORTH THE TROUBLE TO PREPARE THESE FOR THAT ONE-IN-A-MILLION CHANCE...
TP TP TP TP TP
I'M SO GLAD...
SO, SO GLAD.
PIYO
THANK YOU SO MUCH.
TRULY...
UM... MANAGER...?
YES...?
.....
W-W-WOULD YOU M--
CONGRATULATIONS, GODAI !!
POP POP POP POP POP POP POP
POP
POP
...ME?

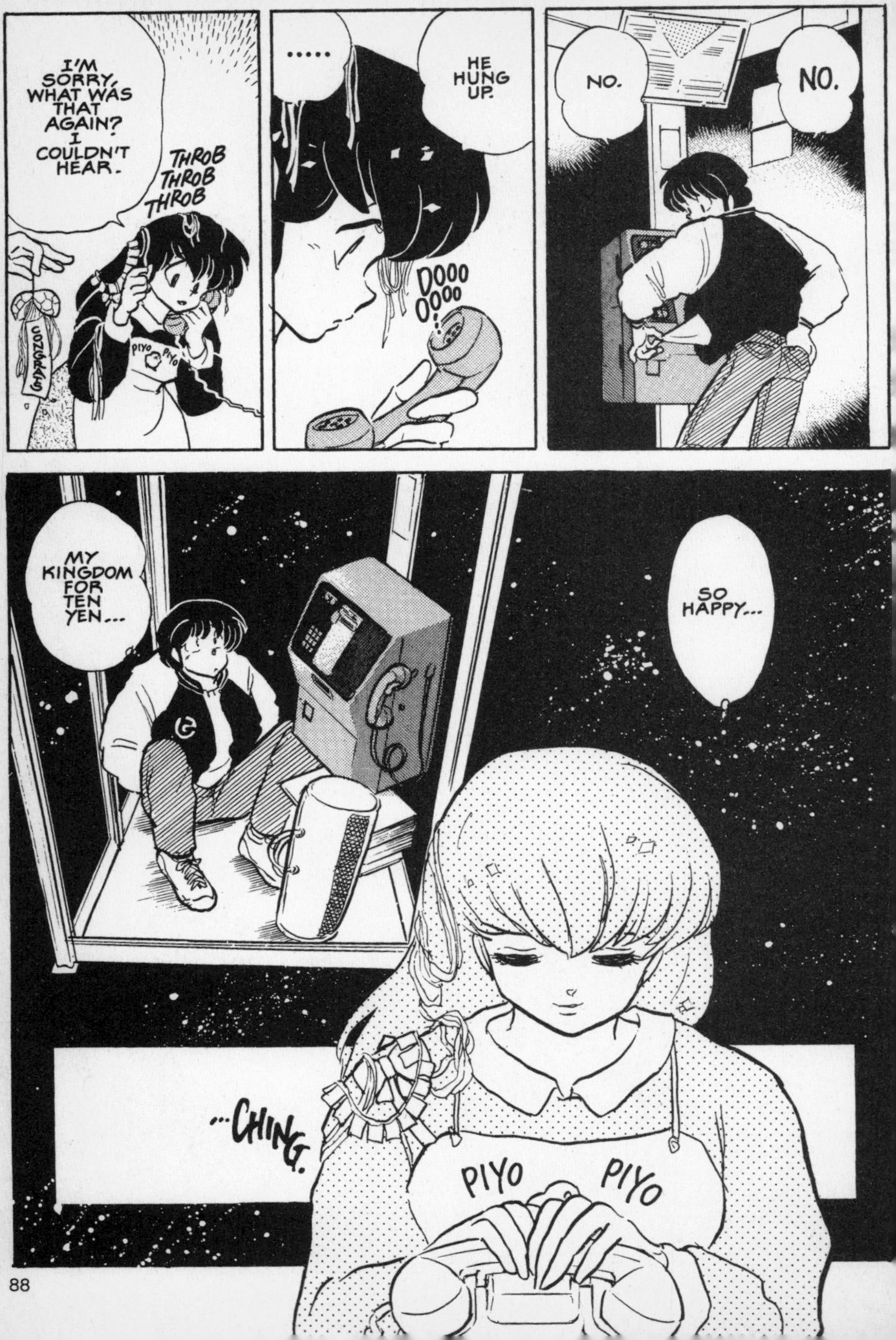

I'M SORRY, WHAT WAS THAT AGAIN? I COULDN'T HEAR.
THROB THROB THROB
CONGRATS
PIYO PIYO
.....
HE HUNG UP.
DOOOOOOO
NO.
NO.
MY KINGDOM FOR TEN YEN...
SO HAPPY...
...CHING.
PIYO PIYO

PART FIVE
WAIT FOR ME TONIGHT

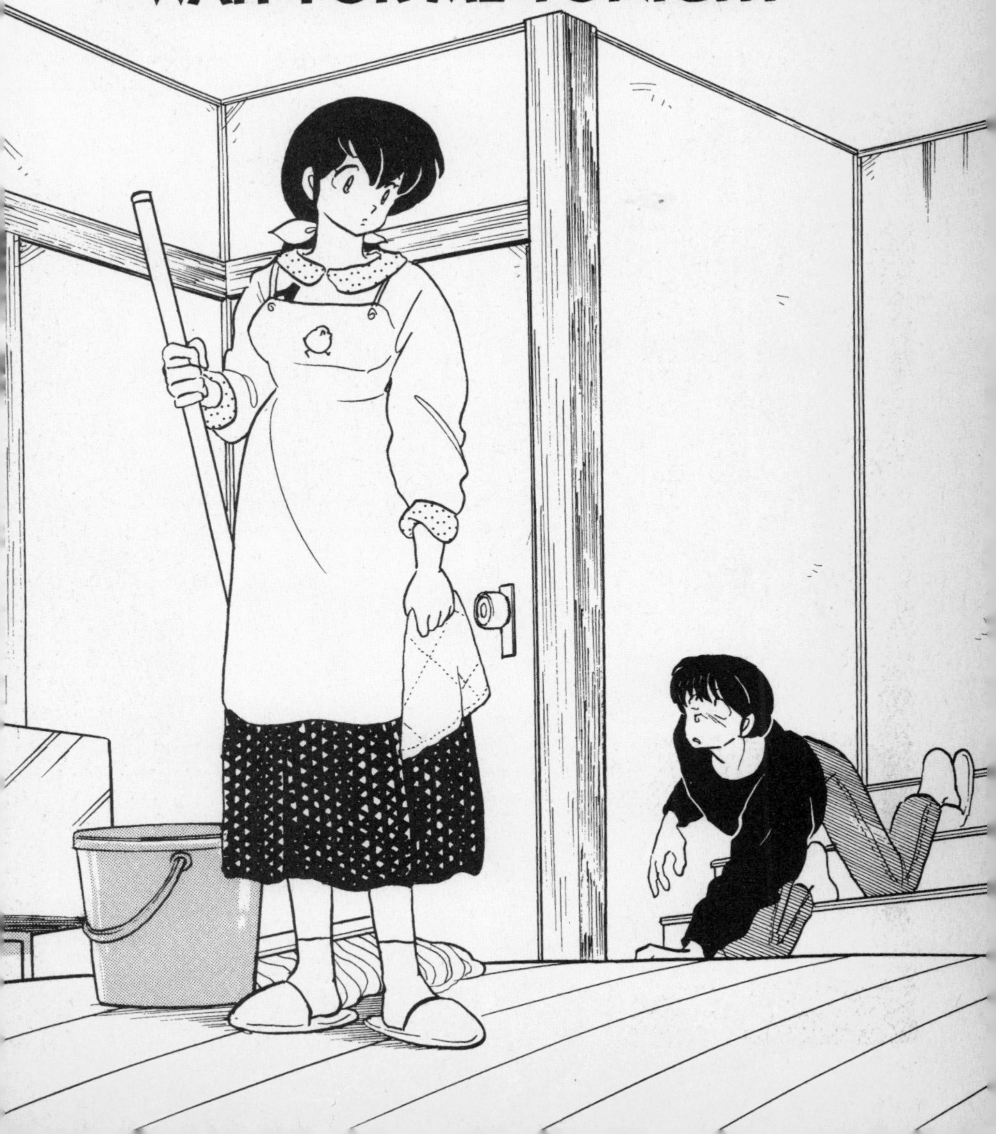

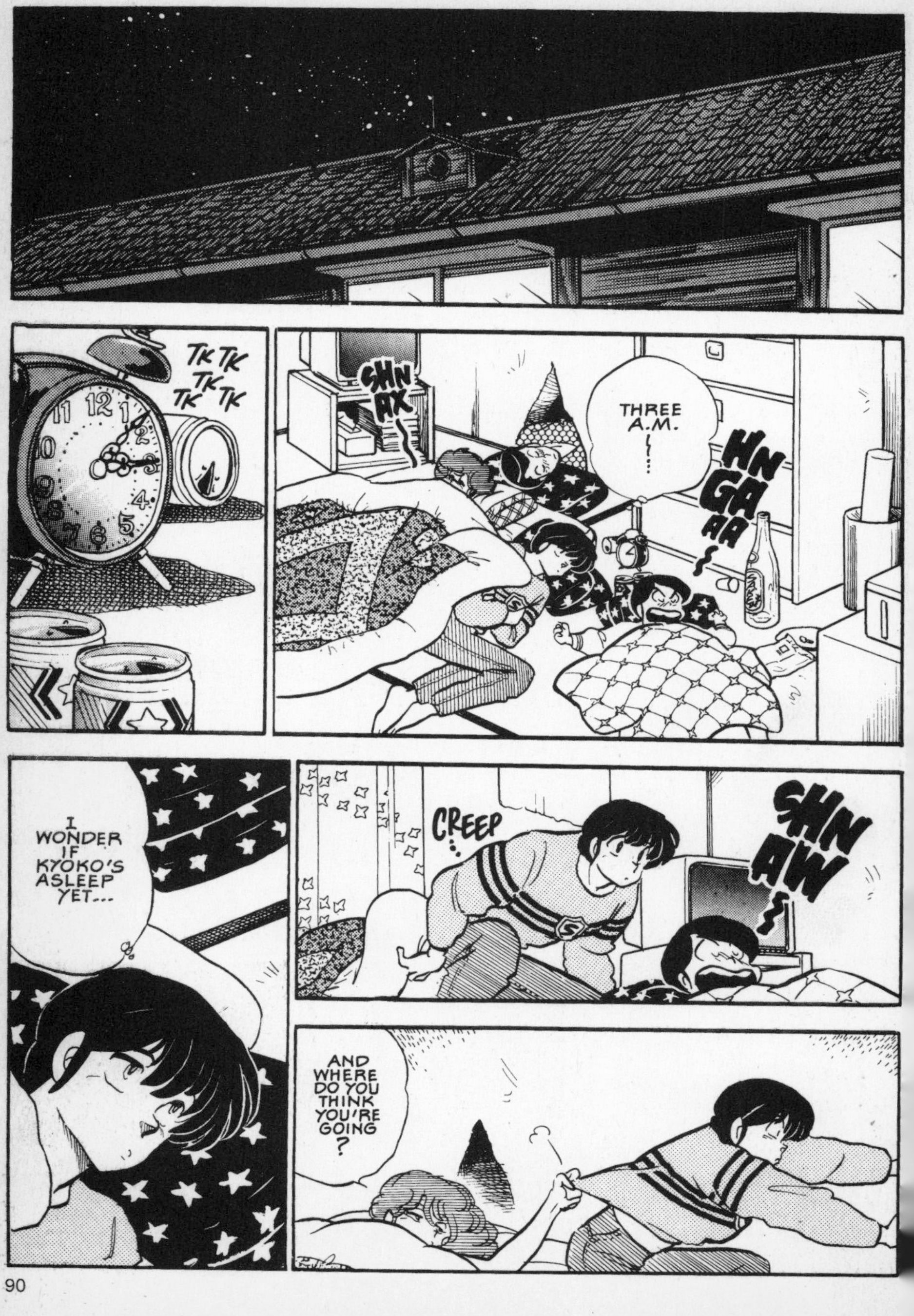
TK TK TK TK TK
SHN AX
THREE A.M. ...
HN GA AA
I WONDER IF KYOKO'S ASLEEP YET...
CREEP
SHN AW
AND WHERE DO YOU THINK YOU'RE GOING?

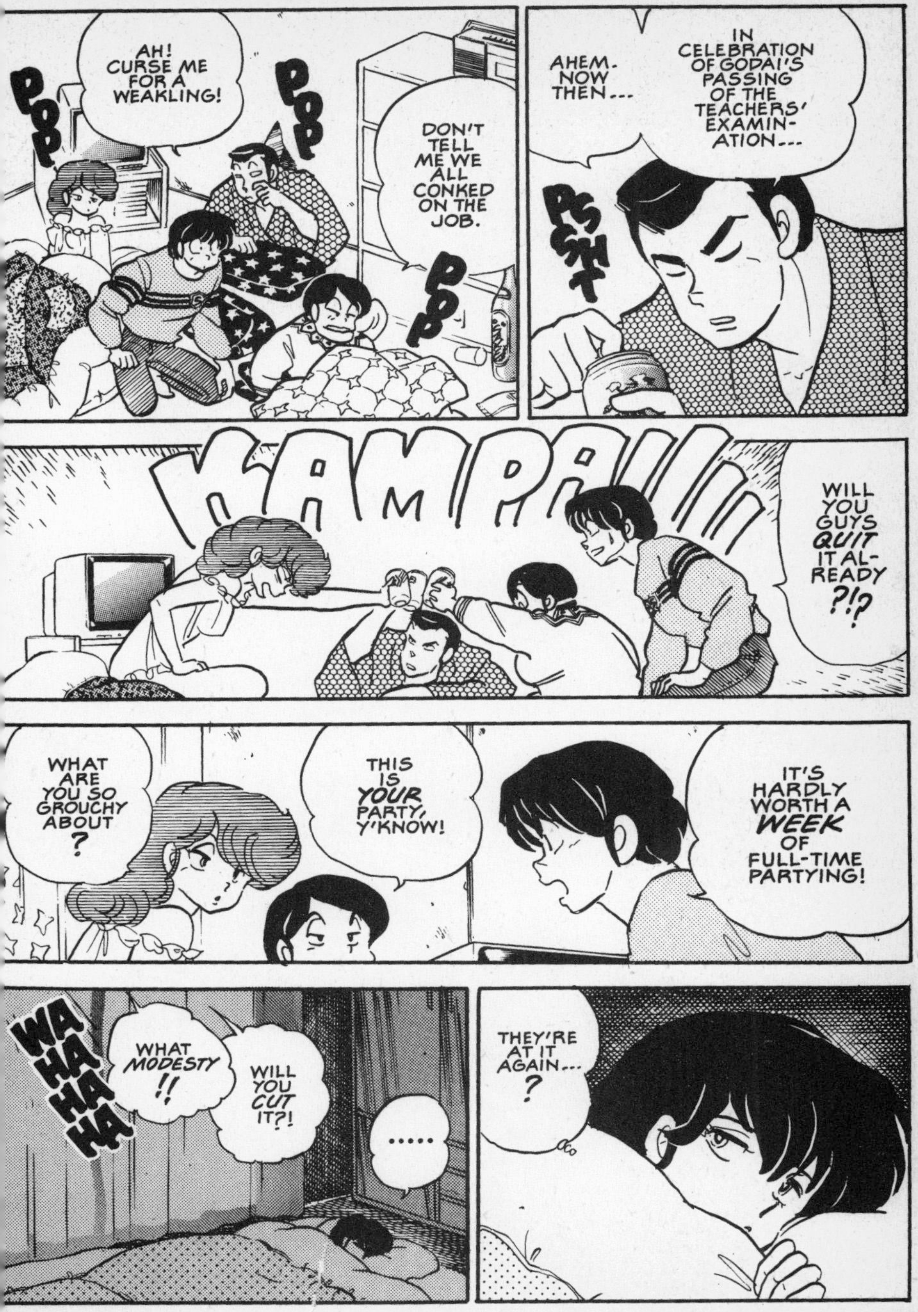
AH! CURSE ME FOR A WEAKLING!
POP
POP
DON'T TELL ME WE ALL CONKED ON THE JOB.
POP
AHEM. NOW THEN...
IN CELEBRATION OF GODAI'S PASSING OF THE TEACHERS' EXAMINATION...
PSSHT
KAMPAI!!
WILL YOU GUYS QUIT IT ALREADY ?!?
WHAT ARE YOU SO GROUCHY ABOUT ?
THIS IS YOUR PARTY, Y'KNOW!
IT'S HARDLY WORTH A WEEK OF FULL-TIME PARTYING!
WAHAHAHA
WHAT MODESTY !!
WILL YOU CUT IT?!
......
THEY'RE AT IT AGAIN... ?

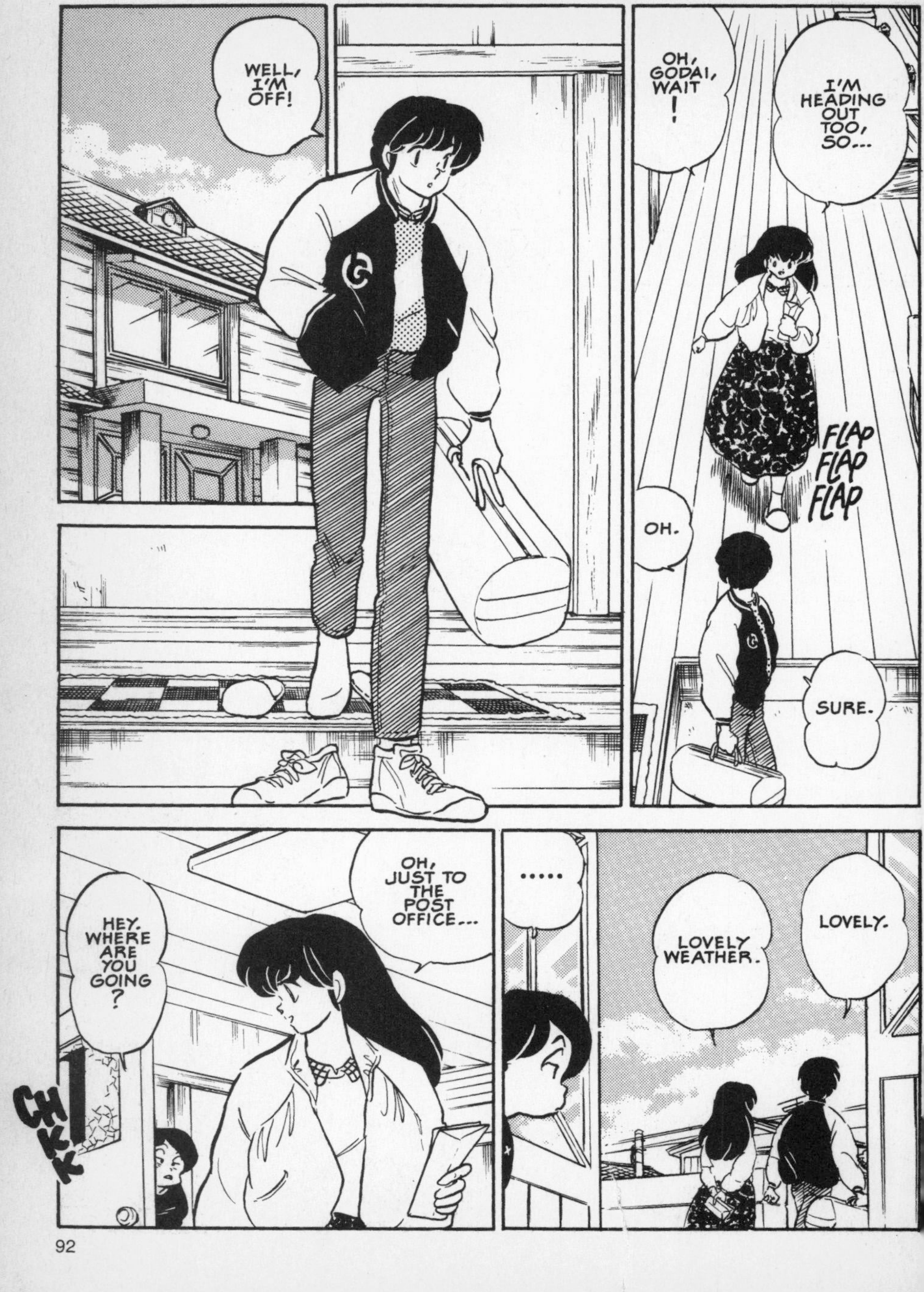
WELL, I'M OFF!
OH, GODAI, WAIT!
I'M HEADING OUT TOO, SO...
FLAP FLAP FLAP
OH.
SURE.
CHKK
HEY. WHERE ARE YOU GOING?
OH, JUST TO THE POST OFFICE...
.....
LOVELY WEATHER.
LOVELY.

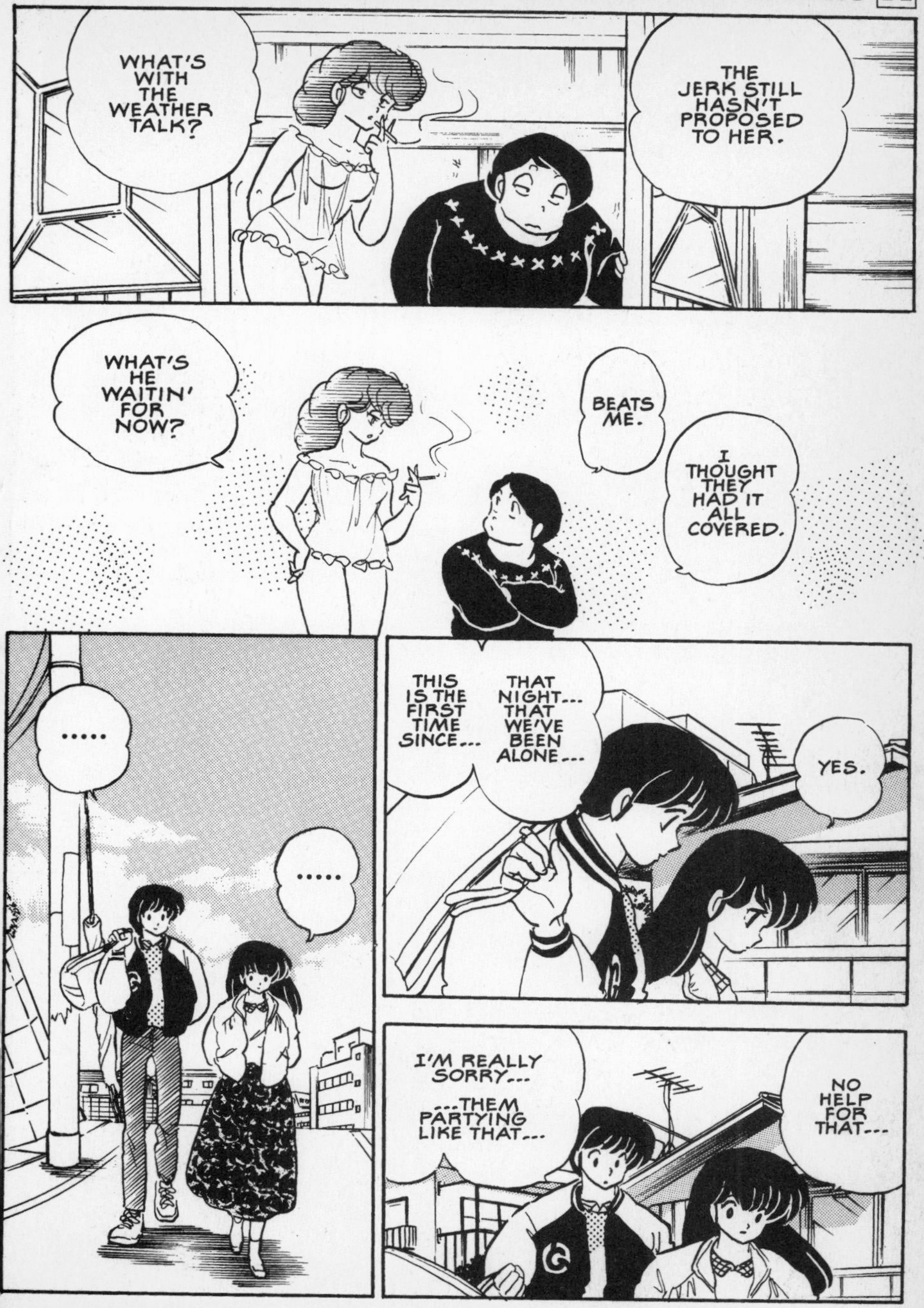
WHAT'S WITH THE WEATHER TALK?
THE JERK STILL HASN'T PROPOSED TO HER.
WHAT'S HE WAITIN' FOR NOW?
BEATS ME.
I THOUGHT THEY HAD IT ALL COVERED.
.....
.....
THIS IS THE FIRST TIME SINCE... THAT NIGHT... THAT WE'VE BEEN ALONE...
YES.
I'M REALLY SORRY... ...THEM PARTYING LIKE THAT...
NO HELP FOR THAT...

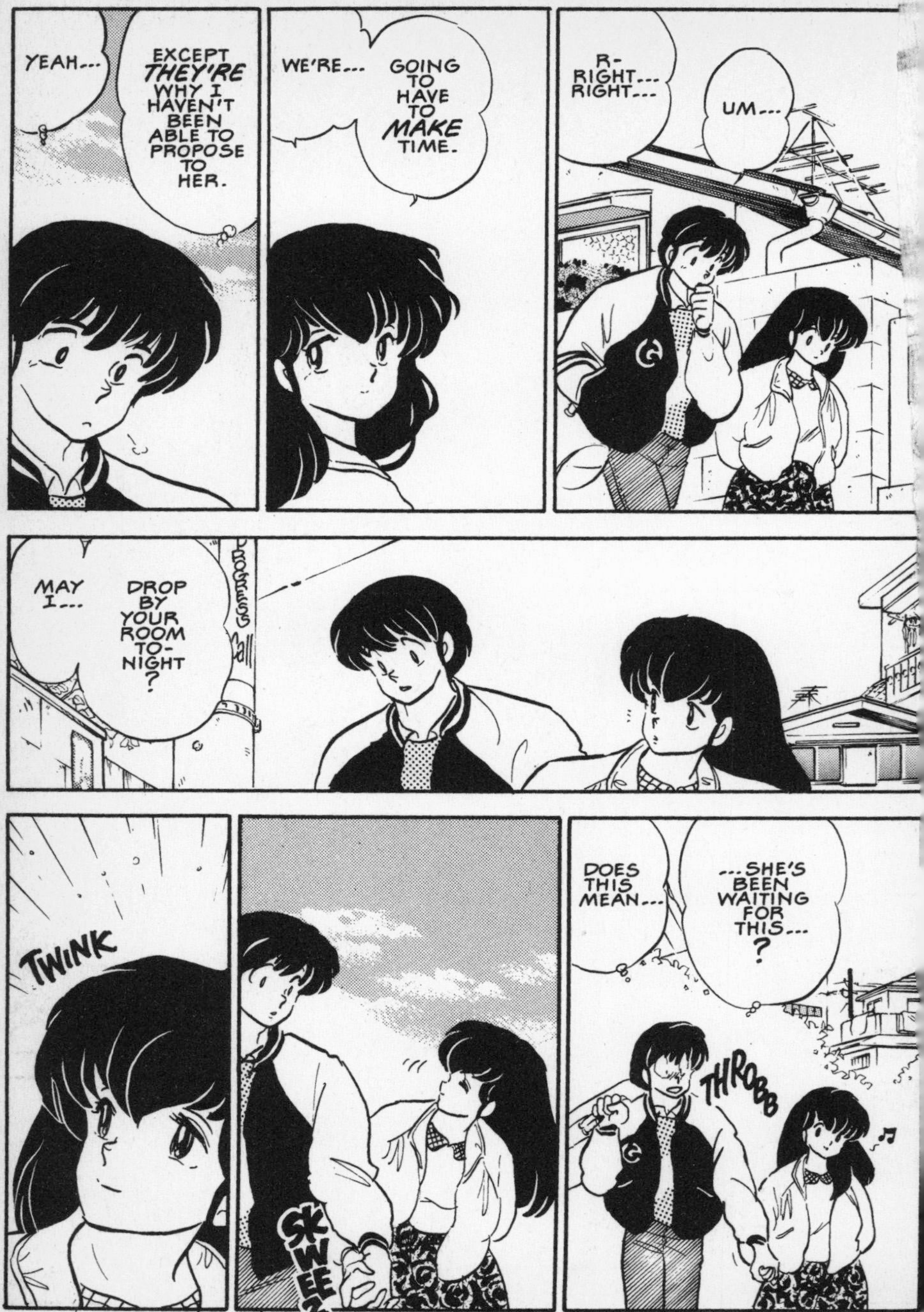
YEAH...
EXCEPT THEY'RE WHY I HAVEN'T BEEN ABLE TO PROPOSE TO HER.
WE'RE...
GOING TO HAVE TO MAKE TIME.
R- RIGHT... RIGHT...
UM...
MAY I...
DROP BY YOUR ROOM TO-NIGHT ?
PROGRESS
Call
TWINK
SKWEEZ
DOES THIS MEAN...
...SHE'S BEEN WAITING FOR THIS... ?
THROBB

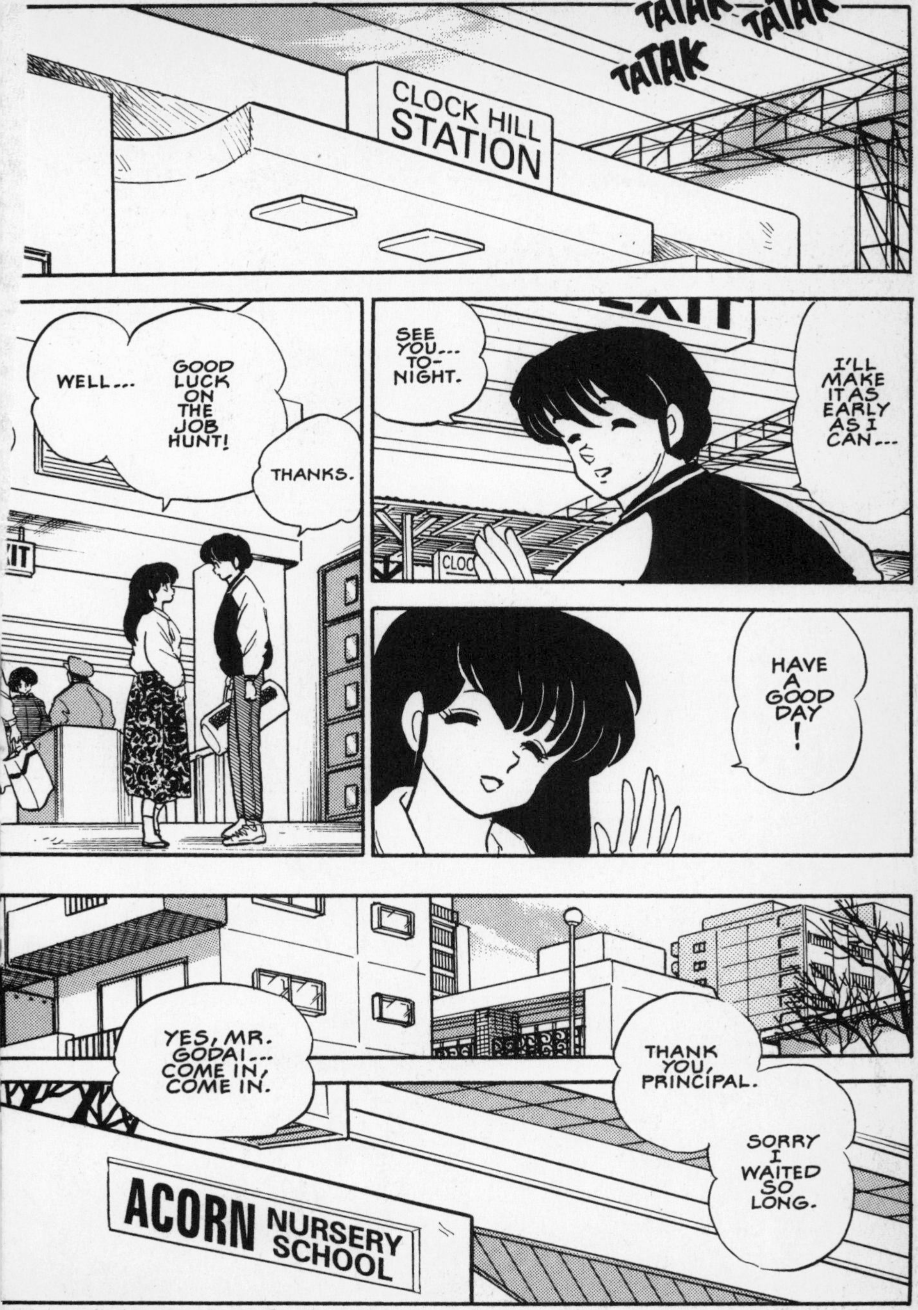

TATAK TATAK TATAK
CLOCK HILL STATION
WELL...
GOOD LUCK ON THE JOB HUNT!
THANKS.
EXIT
SEE YOU... TO-NIGHT.
EXIT
I'LL MAKE IT AS EARLY AS I CAN...
HAVE A GOOD DAY!
YES, MR. GODAI... COME IN, COME IN.
THANK YOU, PRINCIPAL.
SORRY I WAITED SO LONG.
ACORN NURSERY SCHOOL

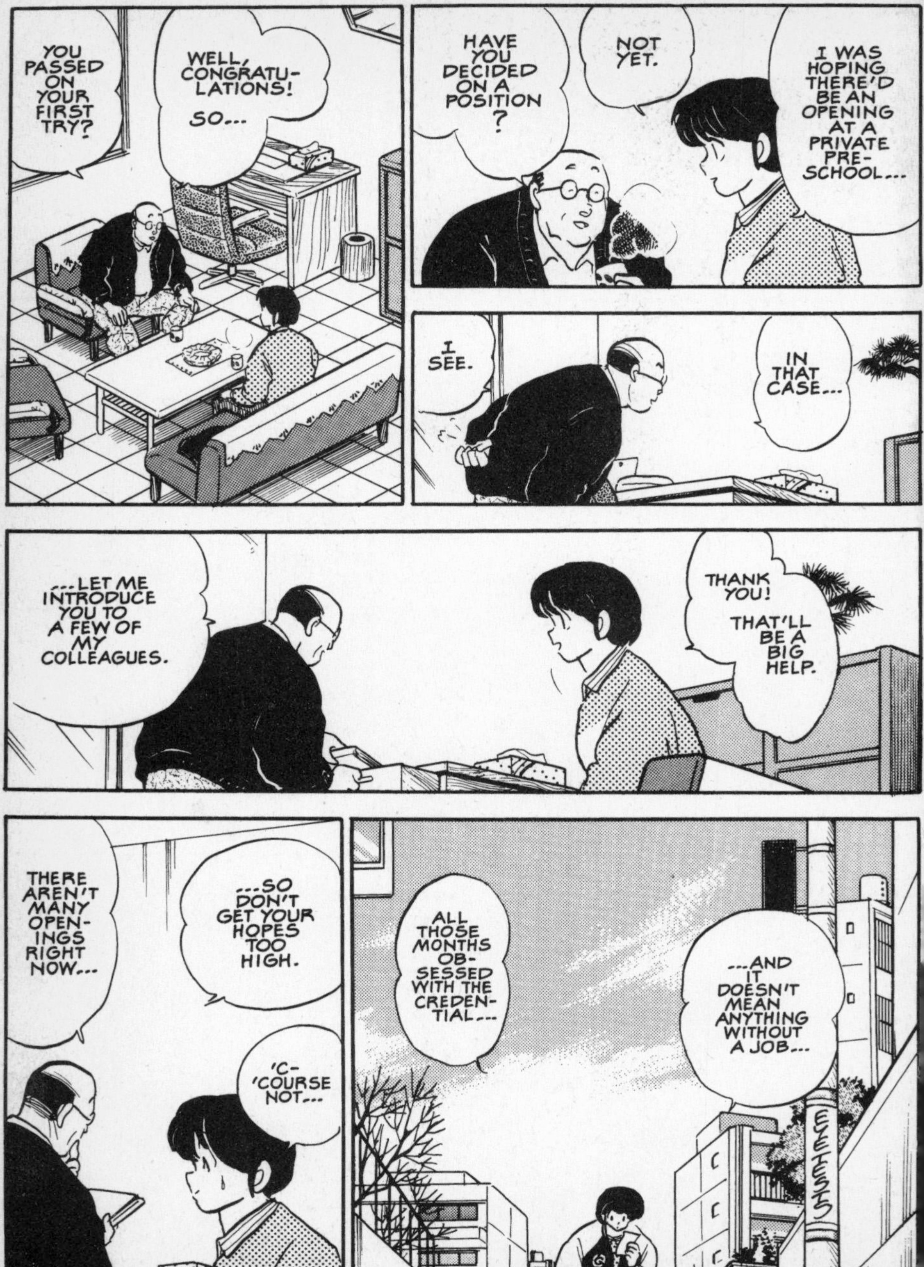
YOU PASSED ON YOUR FIRST TRY?
WELL, CONGRATU-LATIONS!
SO...
HAVE YOU DECIDED ON A POSITION ?
NOT YET.
I WAS HOPING THERE'D BE AN OPENING AT A PRIVATE PRE-SCHOOL...
I SEE.
IN THAT CASE...
...LET ME INTRODUCE YOU TO A FEW OF MY COLLEAGUES.
THANK YOU!
THAT'LL BE A BIG HELP.
THERE AREN'T MANY OPEN-INGS RIGHT NOW...
...SO DON'T GET YOUR HOPES TOO HIGH.
'C-'COURSE NOT...
ALL THOSE MONTHS OB-SESSED WITH THE CREDEN-TIAL...
...AND IT DOESN'T MEAN ANYTHING WITHOUT A JOB...
EYE TESTS

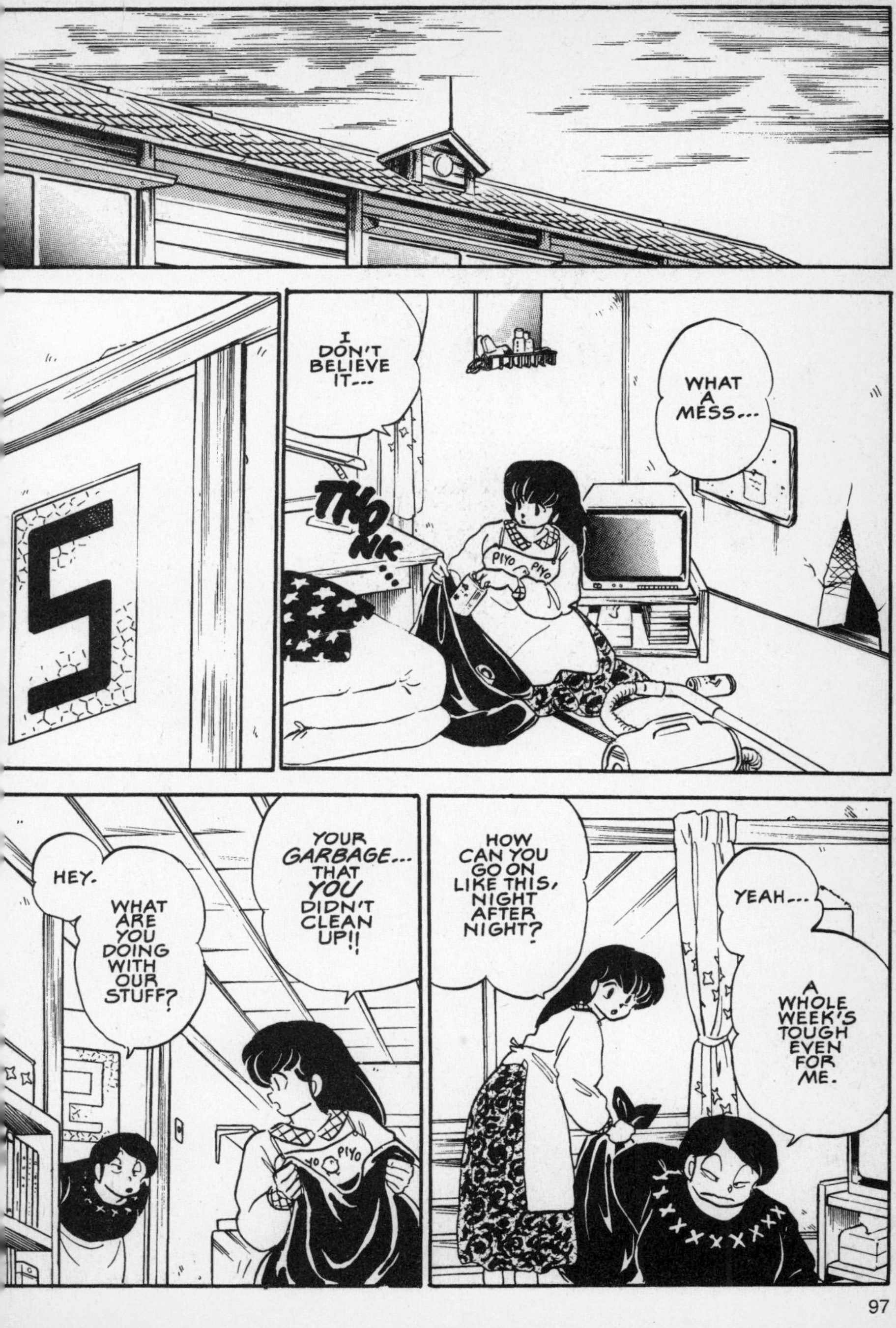
I DON'T BELIEVE IT...
THONK...
PIYO PIYO
WHAT A MESS...
HEY.
WHAT ARE YOU DOING WITH OUR STUFF?
YOUR GARBAGE... THAT YOU DIDN'T CLEAN UP!!
HOW CAN YOU GO ON LIKE THIS, NIGHT AFTER NIGHT?
YEAH...
A WHOLE WEEK'S TOUGH EVEN FOR ME.

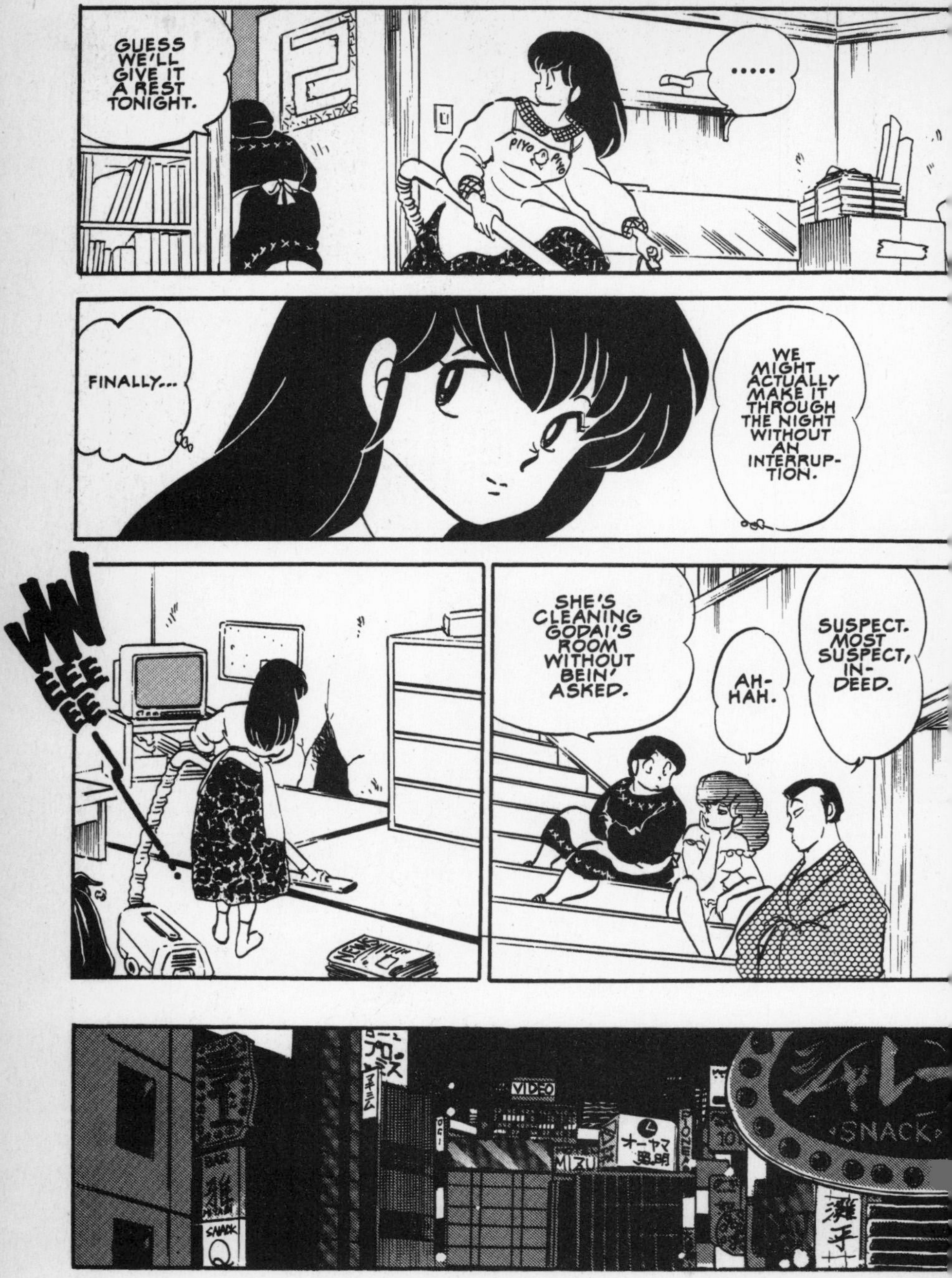
GUESS WE'LL GIVE IT A REST TONIGHT.
.....
PIYO PIYO
FINALLY...
WE MIGHT ACTUALLY MAKE IT THROUGH THE NIGHT WITHOUT AN INTERRUP-TION.
WWEEEEE
SHE'S CLEANING GODAI'S ROOM WITHOUT BEIN' ASKED.
AH-HAH.
SUSPECT. MOST SUSPECT, INDEED.
VIDEO
SNACK
オーヤマ
照明
MISU
BAR
SNACK
Q

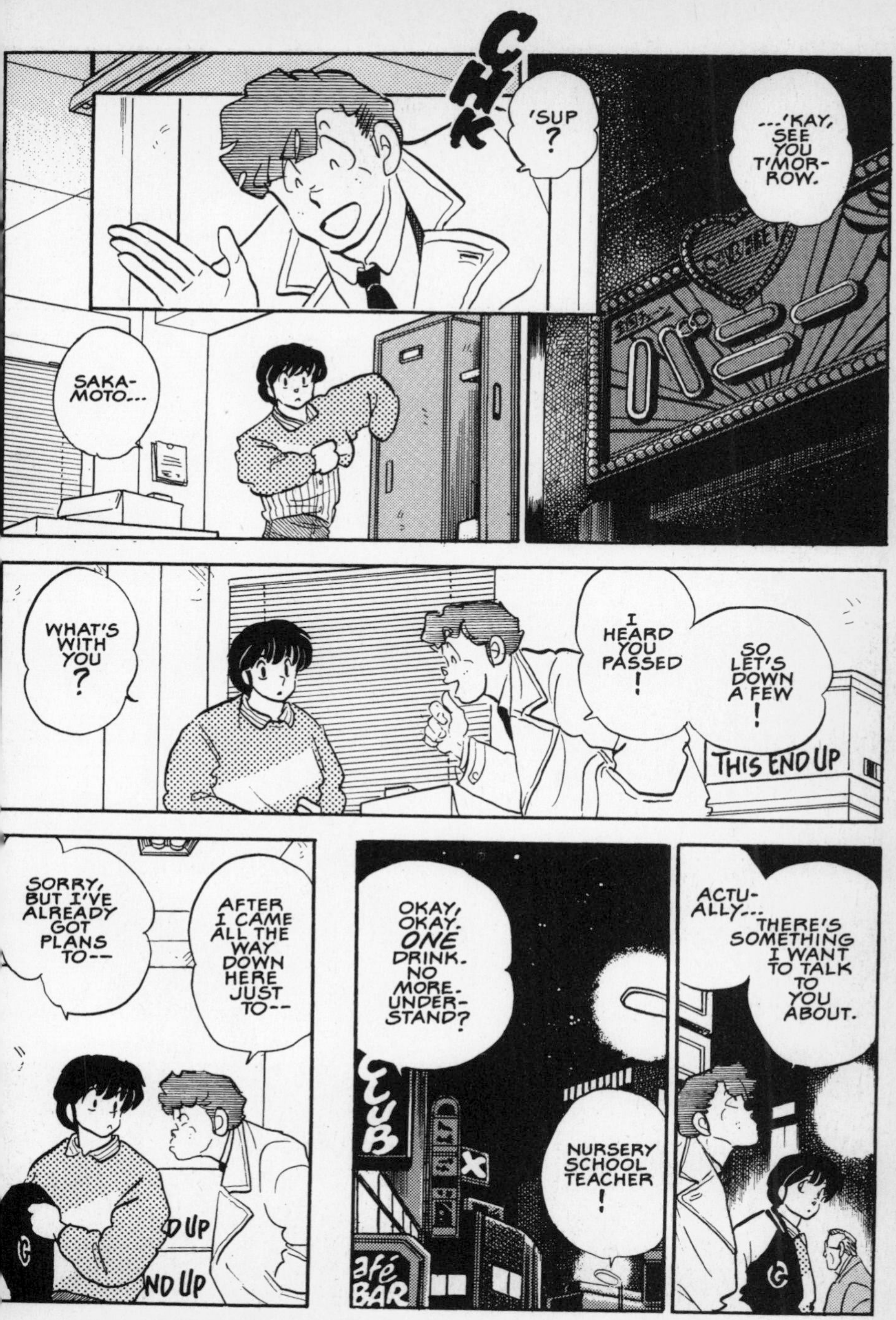
CHK
'SUP?
SAKAMOTO...
...'KAY, SEE YOU T'MORROW.
WHAT'S WITH YOU?
I HEARD YOU PASSED!
SO LET'S DOWN A FEW!
THIS END UP
SORRY, BUT I'VE ALREADY GOT PLANS TO--
AFTER I CAME ALL THE WAY DOWN HERE JUST TO--
OKAY, OKAY. *ONE* DRINK. NO MORE. UNDERSTAND?
NURSERY SCHOOL TEACHER!
ACTUALLY... THERE'S SOMETHING I WANT TO TALK TO YOU ABOUT.

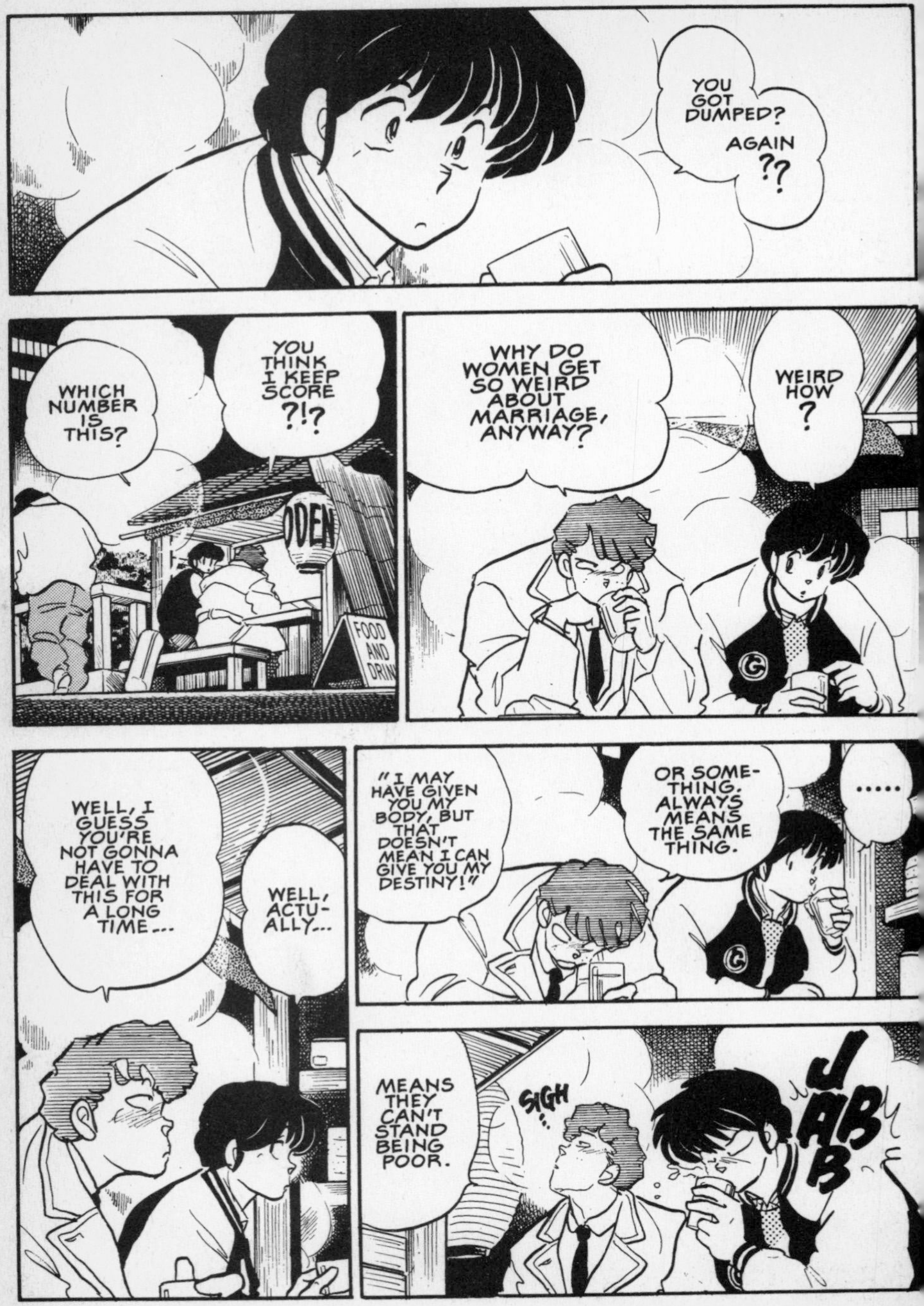

YOU GOT DUMPED? AGAIN ??
WHICH NUMBER IS THIS?
YOU THINK I KEEP SCORE ?!?
ODEN
FOOD AND DRIN
WHY DO WOMEN GET SO WEIRD ABOUT MARRIAGE, ANYWAY?
WEIRD HOW ?
"I MAY HAVE GIVEN YOU MY BODY, BUT THAT DOESN'T MEAN I CAN GIVE YOU MY DESTINY!"
OR SOME-THING. ALWAYS MEANS THE SAME THING.
.....
WELL, I GUESS YOU'RE NOT GONNA HAVE TO DEAL WITH THIS FOR A LONG TIME...
WELL, ACTU-ALLY...
MEANS THEY CAN'T STAND BEING POOR.
SIGH
JAB

WE POOR MEN...

WOMEN PLAY WITH US LIKE TOYS...

BUT WILL *WE* EVER KNOW THE JOYS OF MARRIAGE? EH?!

KUH-LATTA

WHAT'S *WE* GOT TO DO WITH IT?!?

DAMN AKIKO... DAMN ITSUKO... DAMN UKIKO...

SOBB SOBB SOBB

DAMN ELLIE... DAMN ORIE...

SOBB SOBB SOBB SOBB SOBB

YOU GONNA DO THE WHOLE CATA- LOGUE...?

ME, I'M A ONE- KYOKO MAN...

AND SHE'S WAITING FOR ME TO PROPOSE TO HER...

I THINK.

I WORK! I HAVE A DECENT JOB!

BUT DO YOU EVER *GO* TO IT?

LET'S GO DRINK- ING!

LET'S LICK EACH OTHER'S WOUNDS !

OHHH, NO.

I TOLD YOU...

DONK

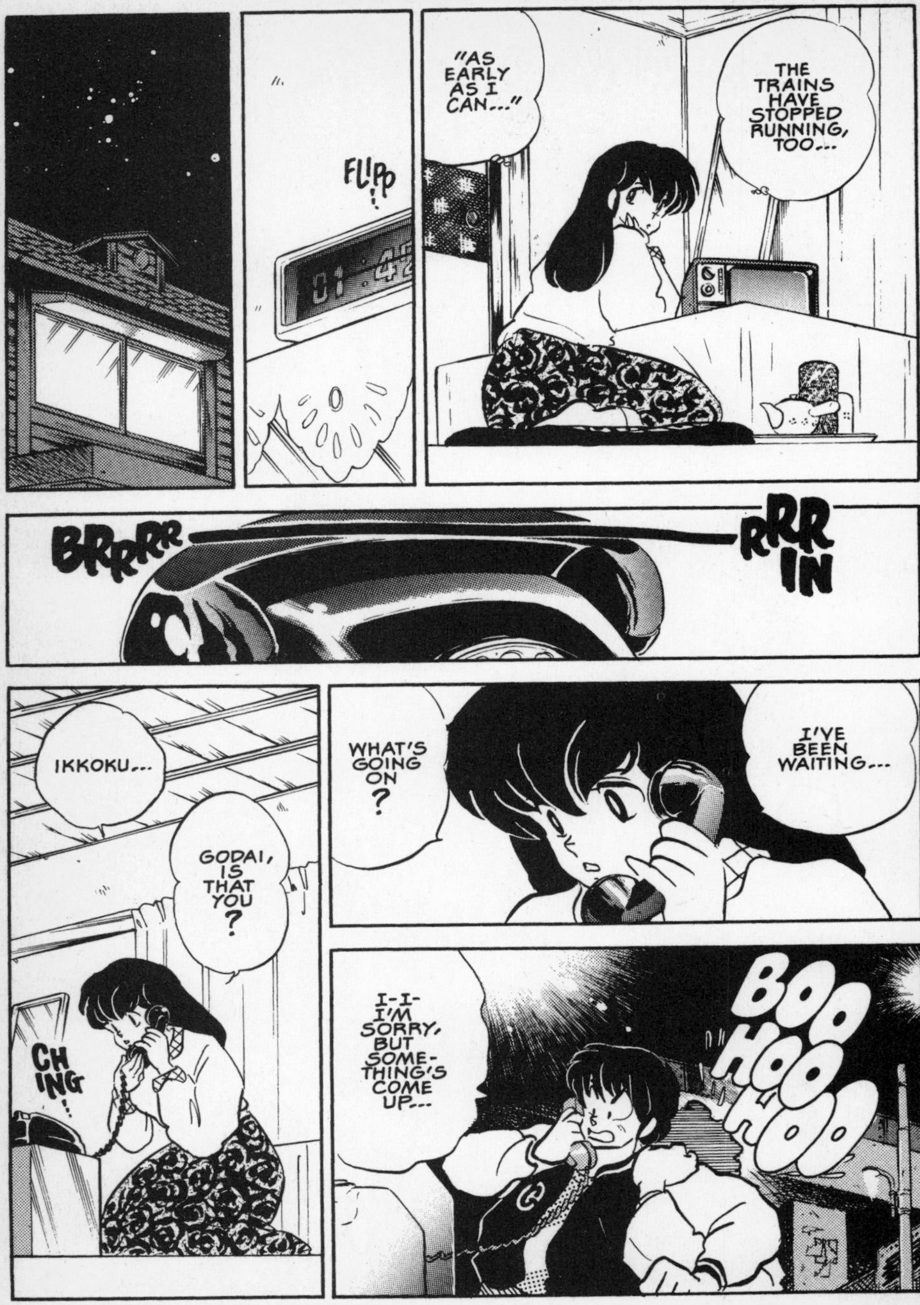
FLIPP
"AS EARLY AS I CAN..."
THE TRAINS HAVE STOPPED RUNNING, TOO...
BRRRRR——RRRIN
IKKOKU...
GODAI, IS THAT YOU?
CHING!!
WHAT'S GOING ON?
I'VE BEEN WAITING...
I-I-I'M SORRY, BUT SOME-THING'S COME UP...
BOO HOO HOO HOO

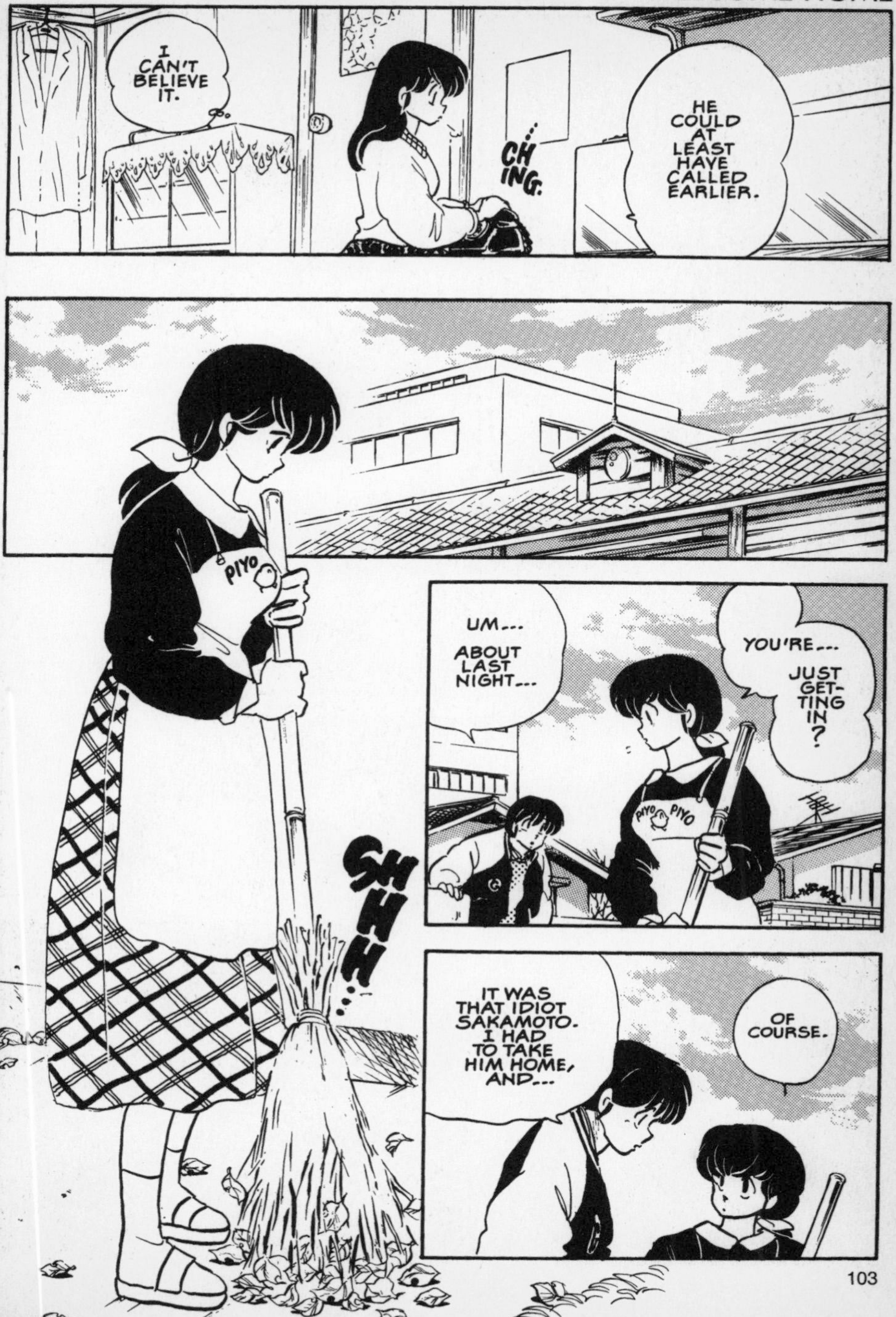
I CAN'T BELIEVE IT.
...CHING.
HE COULD AT LEAST HAVE CALLED EARLIER.
SHHHH...
UM... ABOUT LAST NIGHT...
YOU'RE... JUST GETTING IN?
IT WAS THAT IDIOT SAKAMOTO. I HAD TO TAKE HIM HOME, AND...
OF COURSE.

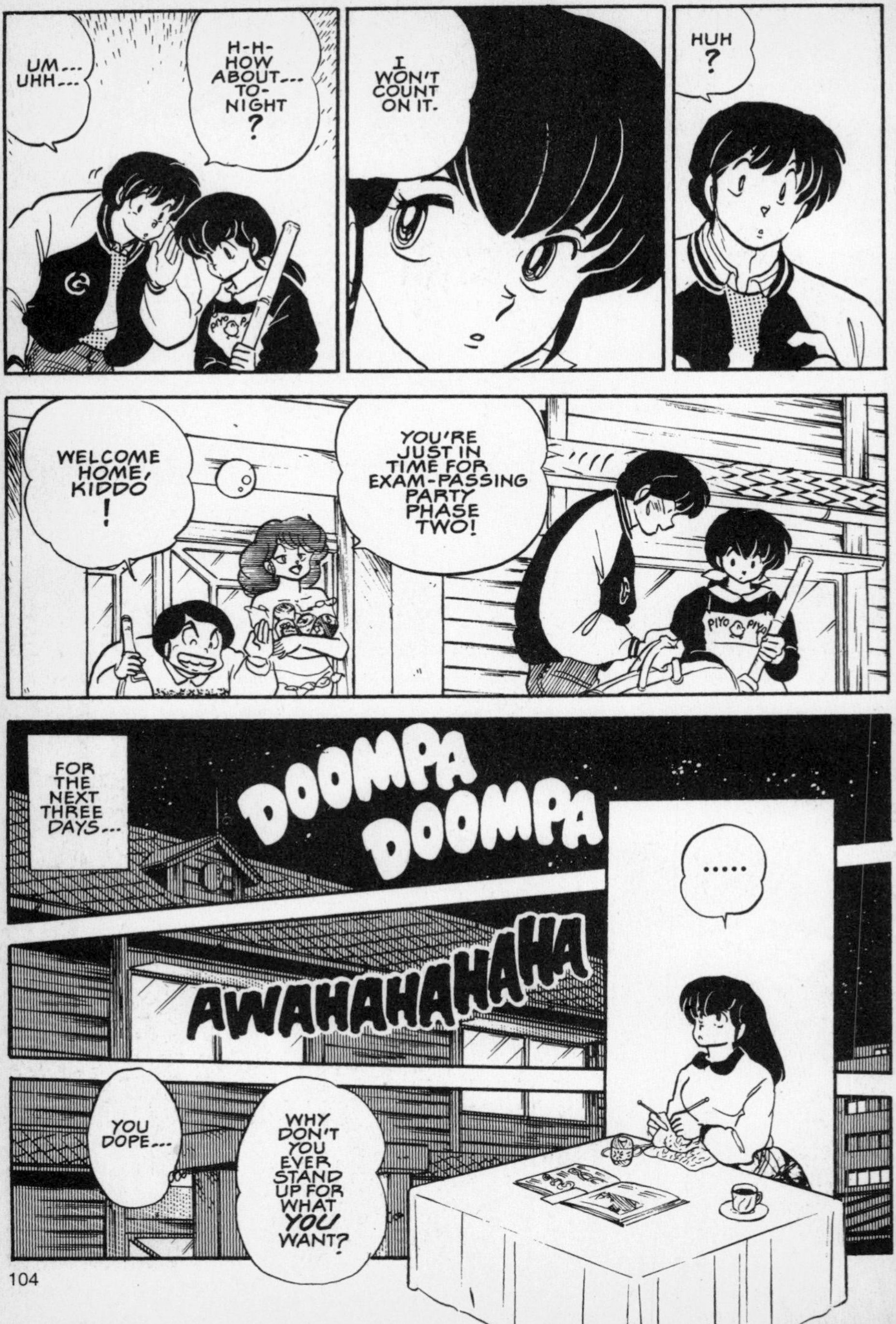
UM... UHH...
H-H-HOW ABOUT... TO-NIGHT?
I WON'T COUNT ON IT.
HUH?
WELCOME HOME, KIDDO!
YOU'RE JUST IN TIME FOR EXAM-PASSING PARTY PHASE TWO!
PIYO PIYO
FOR THE NEXT THREE DAYS...
DOOMPA DOOMPA
AWAHAHAHAHA
......
YOU DOPE...
WHY DON'T YOU EVER STAND UP FOR WHAT YOU WANT?

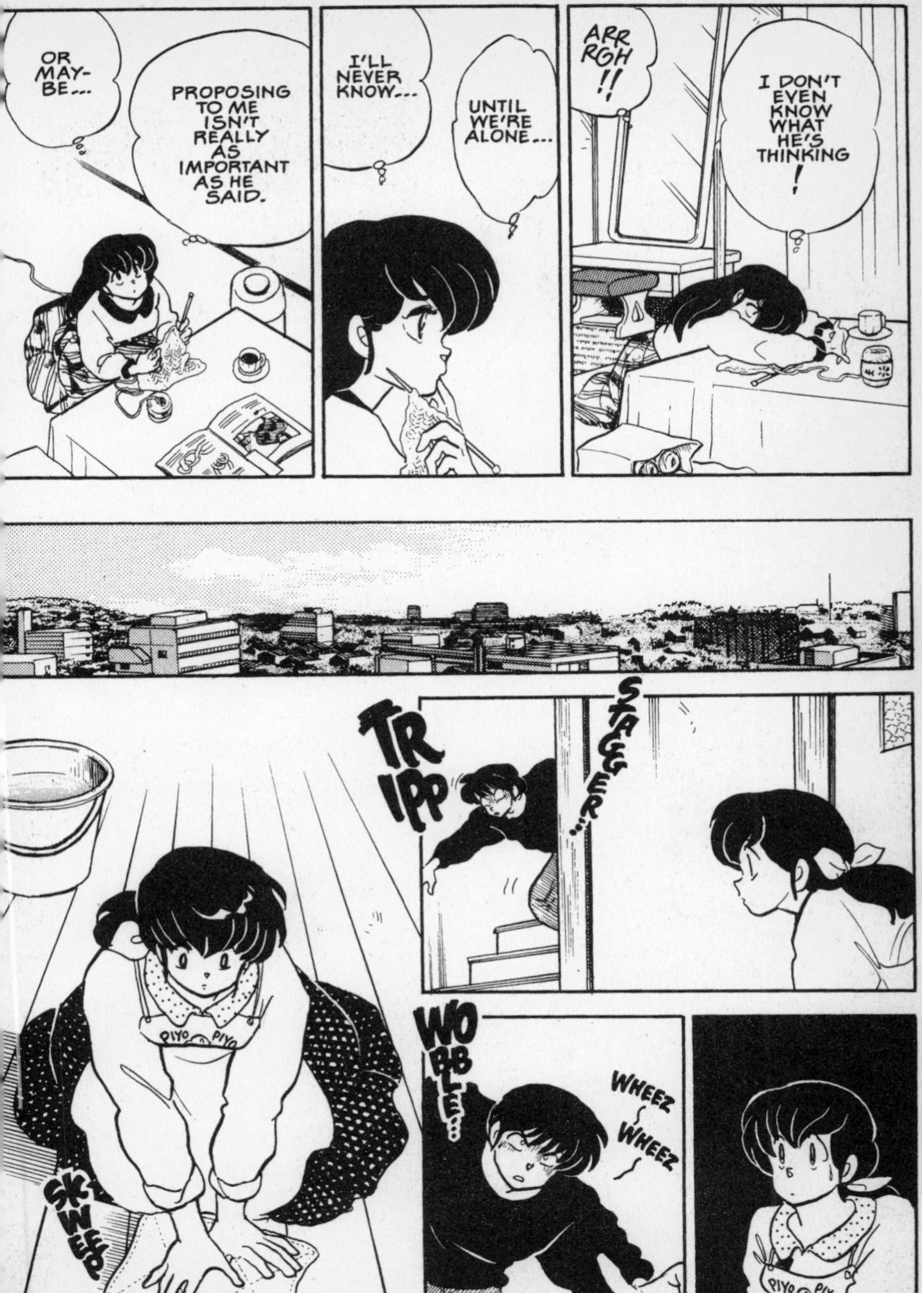
OR MAYBE...
PROPOSING TO ME ISN'T REALLY AS IMPORTANT AS HE SAID.
I'LL NEVER KNOW...
UNTIL WE'RE ALONE...
ARRRGH!!
I DON'T EVEN KNOW WHAT HE'S THINKING!
PIYO PIYO
SKWEEP
TRIPP
STAGGER..
WOBBLE...
WHEEZ WHEEZ
PIYO PIYO

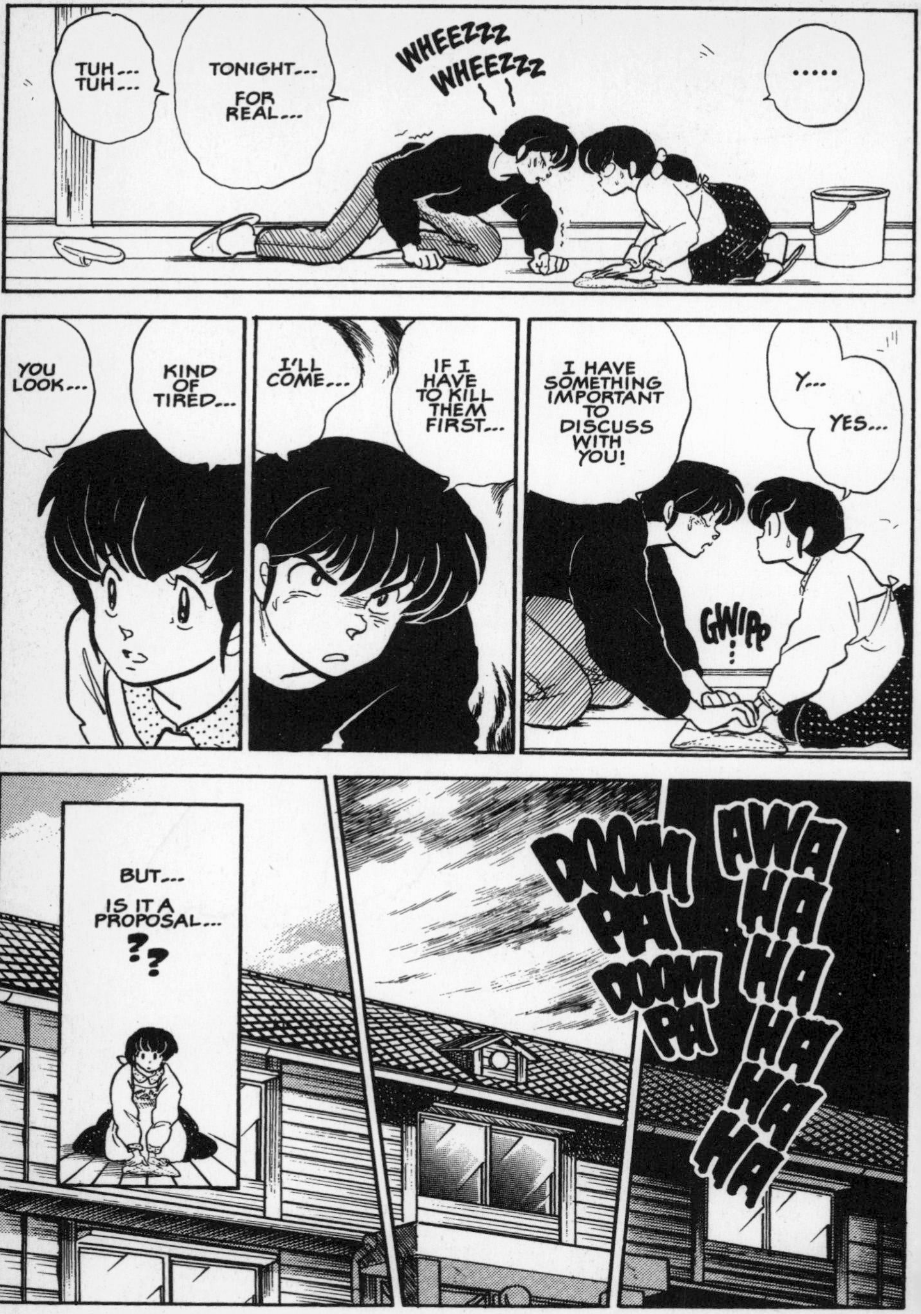
TUH... TUH...
TONIGHT... FOR REAL...
WHEEZZZ WHEEZZZ
.....
YOU LOOK...
KIND OF TIRED...
I'LL COME...
IF I HAVE TO KILL THEM FIRST...
I HAVE SOMETHING IMPORTANT TO DISCUSS WITH YOU!
Y... YES...
GWIPP
BUT... IS IT A PROPOSAL... ??
DOOM PA DOOM PA
AWA HA HA HA HA HA HA

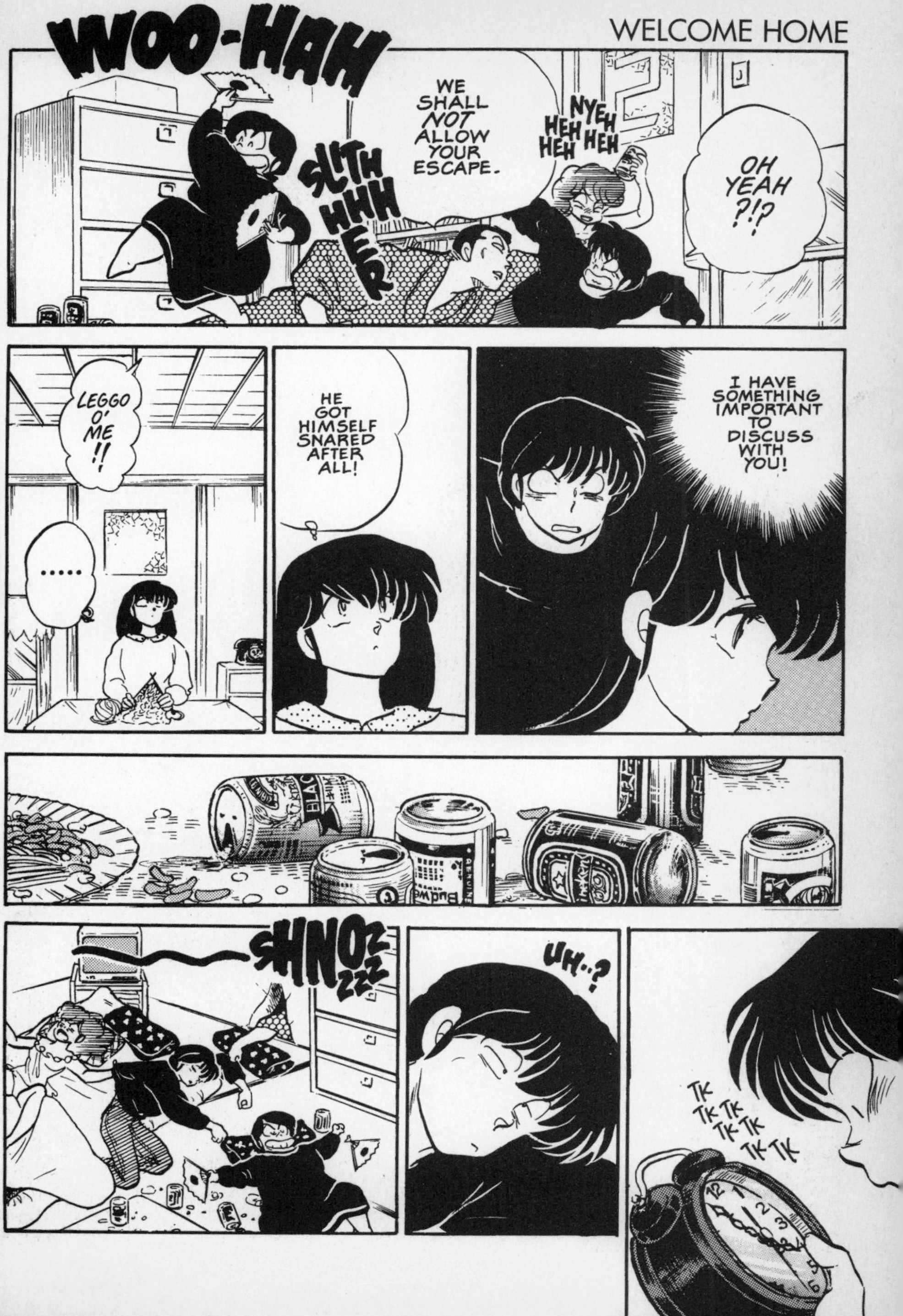
WOO-HAH
SLITHHHHER
WE SHALL NOT ALLOW YOUR ESCAPE.
NYEH HEH HEH HEH HEH
OH YEAH ?!?
LEGGO O' ME !!
.....
HE GOT HIMSELF SNARED AFTER ALL!
I HAVE SOMETHING IMPORTANT TO DISCUSS WITH YOU!
SHNOZZZZ
UH..?
TK TK TK TK TK TK TK TK

KYOKO
?

MANAGER

KYOKO
!!

NOK
NOK
NOK

SHE
MUST'VE
GONE
TO---

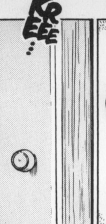

KR
EEE
...

GLA
RRR!!

YAA
AA!

LIAR!!

P-P-
PLEASE
FOR-
GIVE
ME
!

I
THOUGHT
YOU HAD
SOMETHING
"IMPOR-
TANT"
TO
DISCUSS
!

I---I---
I DO!
BUT---
BUT---
BUT---

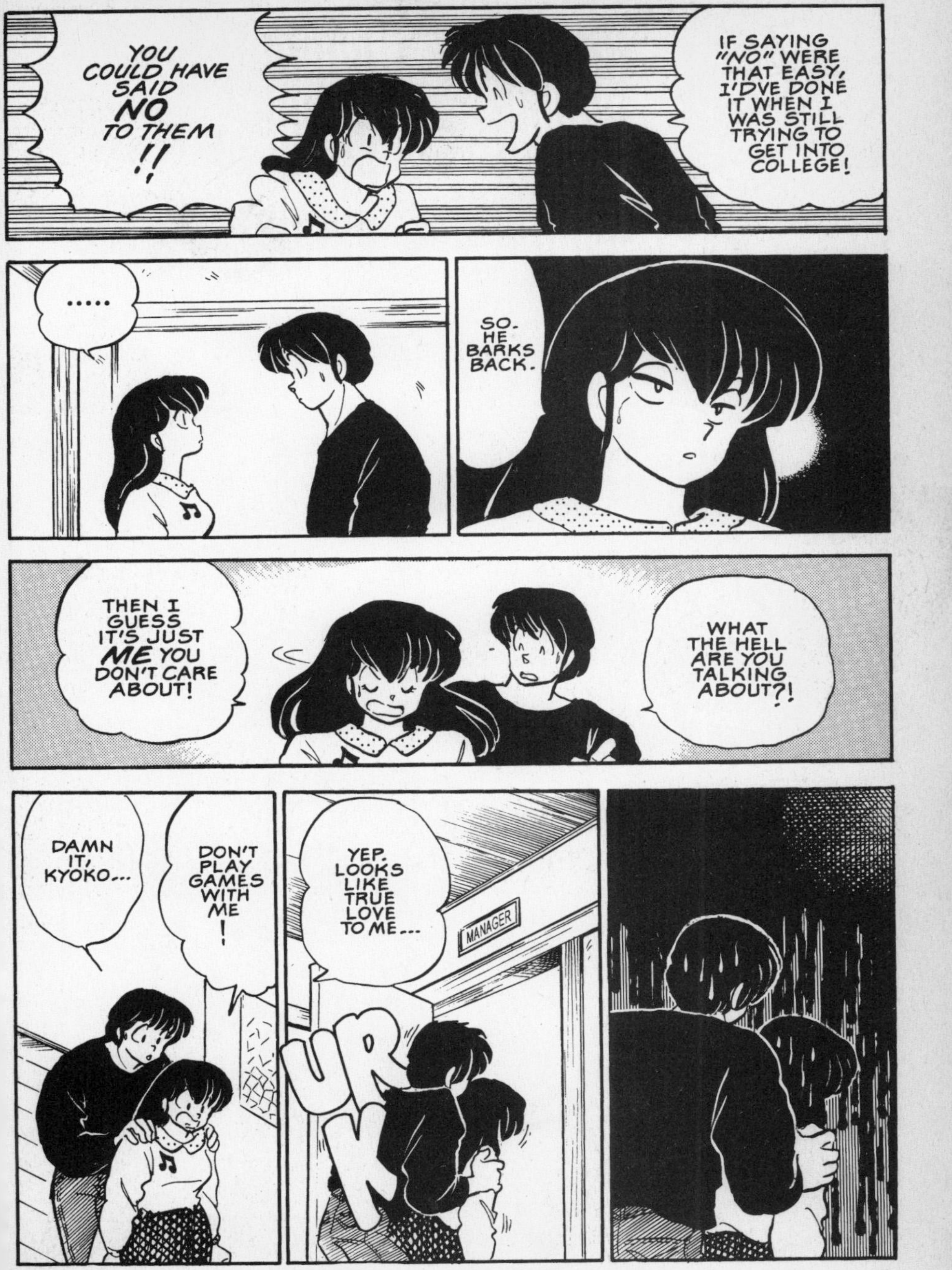
YOU COULD HAVE SAID NO TO THEM !!
IF SAYING "NO" WERE THAT EASY, I'DVE DONE IT WHEN I WAS STILL TRYING TO GET INTO COLLEGE!
.....
SO. HE BARKS BACK.
THEN I GUESS IT'S JUST ME YOU DON'T CARE ABOUT!
WHAT THE HELL ARE YOU TALKING ABOUT?!
DAMN IT, KYOKO...
DON'T PLAY GAMES WITH ME !
YEP. LOOKS LIKE TRUE LOVE TO ME...
MANAGER
URK

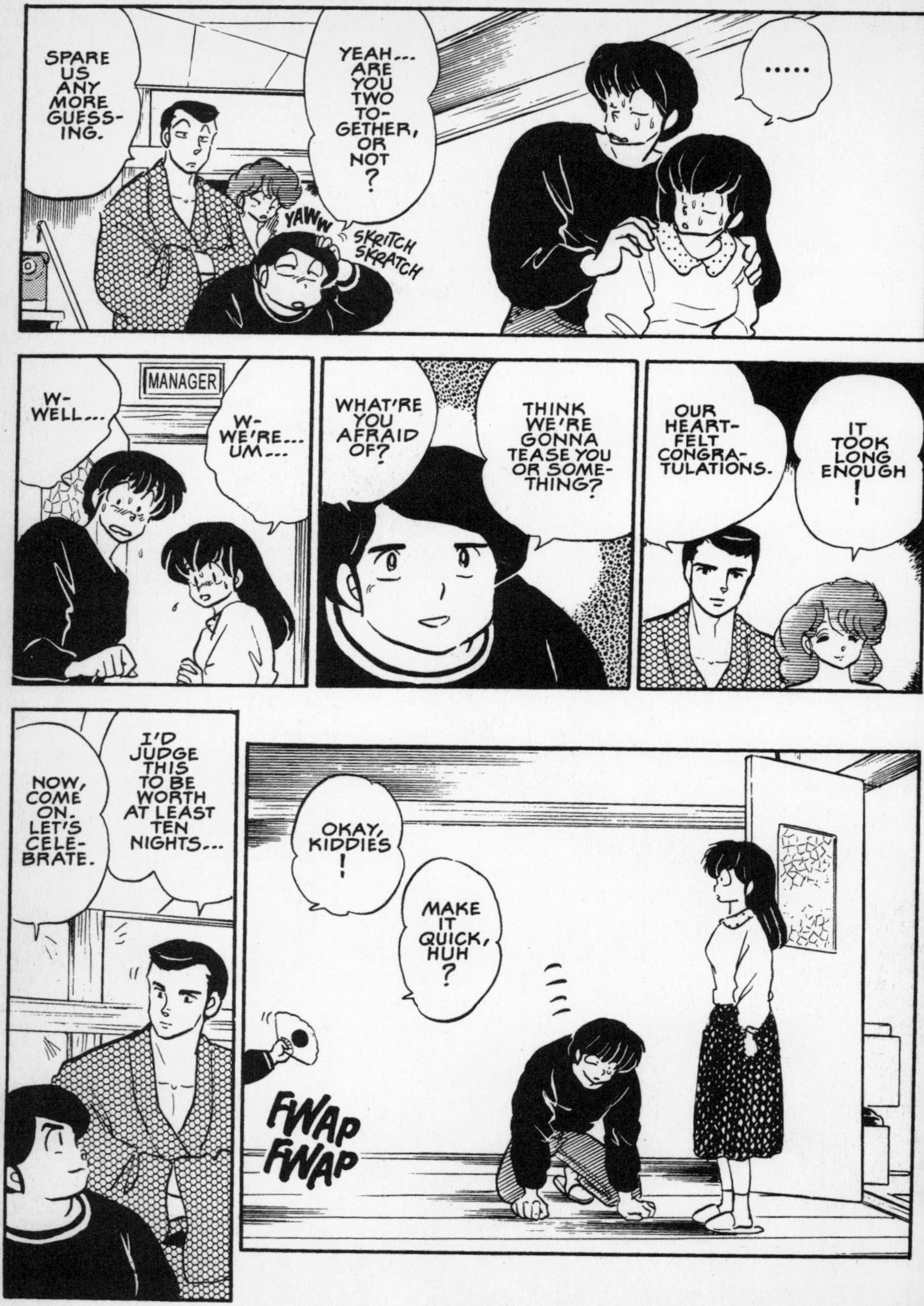
SPARE US ANY MORE GUESSING.
YEAH... ARE YOU TWO TOGETHER, OR NOT?
YAWW
SKRITCH SKRATCH
.....
MANAGER
W-WELL...
W-WE'RE... UM...
WHAT'RE YOU AFRAID OF?
THINK WE'RE GONNA TEASE YOU OR SOMETHING?
OUR HEARTFELT CONGRATULATIONS.
IT TOOK LONG ENOUGH!
NOW, COME ON. LET'S CELEBRATE.
I'D JUDGE THIS TO BE WORTH AT LEAST TEN NIGHTS...
OKAY, KIDDIES!
MAKE IT QUICK, HUH?
FWAP FWAP

PART SIX

SYMPATHY

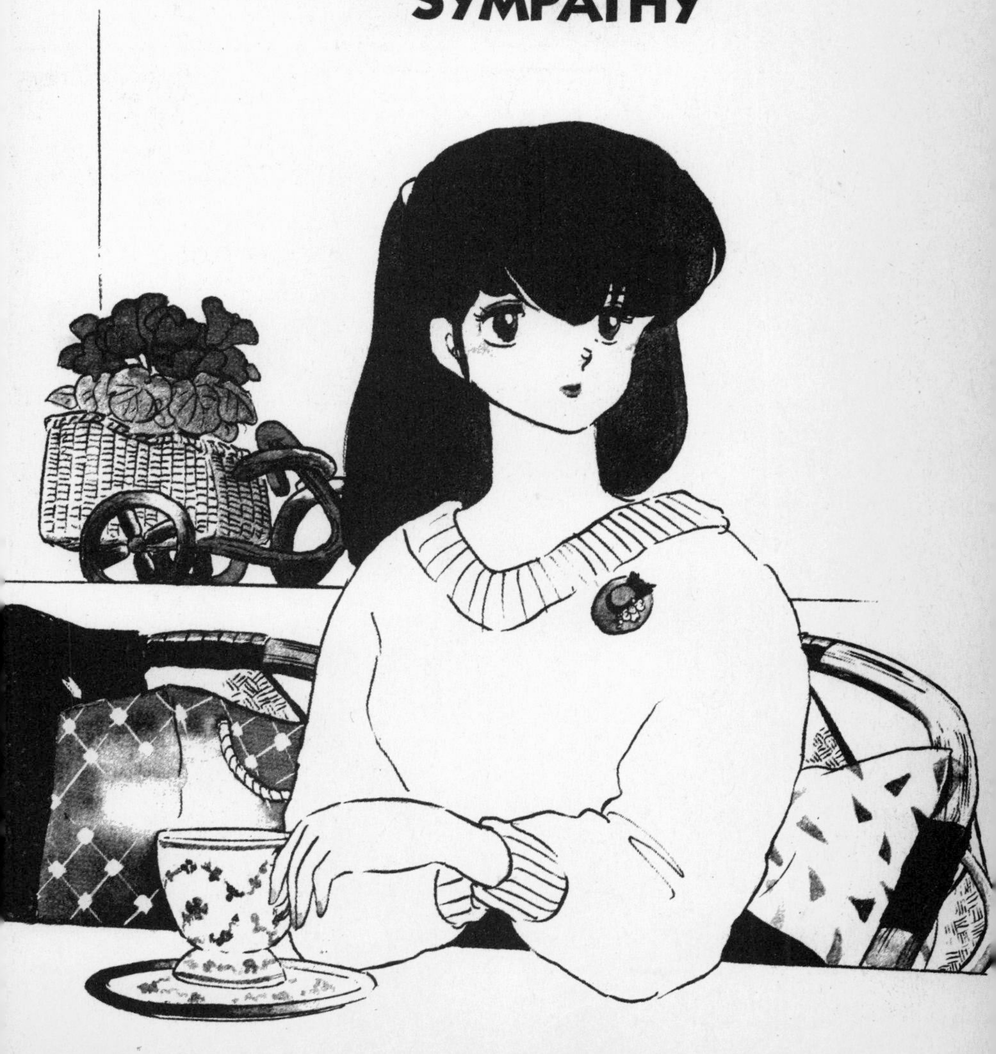

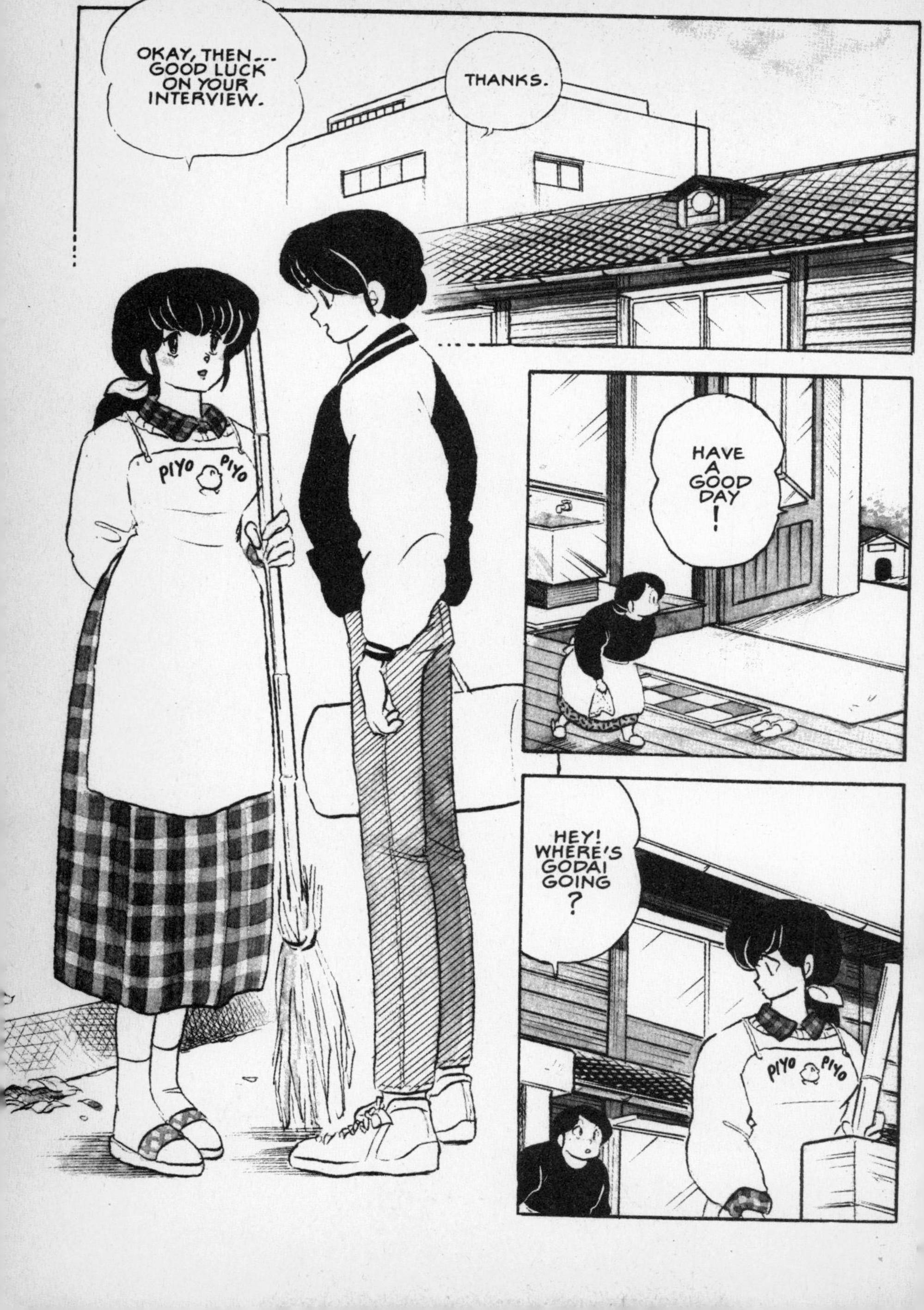
OKAY, THEN... GOOD LUCK ON YOUR INTERVIEW.
THANKS.
PIYO PIYO
HAVE A GOOD DAY!
HEY! WHERE'S GODAI GOING?
PIYO PIYO

PRE-SCHOOL INTERVIEWS, HE SAID.

WITH REFERRALS FROM THE PRINCIPAL OF THE SCHOOL WHERE HE USED TO WORK.

ACORN NURSERY SCHOOL

PRINCIPAL? IT'S KUROKI.

NOK NOK NOK NOK

WELL, COME IN, COME IN.

WHAT IS IT, KUROKI?

I THOUGHT I SHOULD LET YOU KNOW...

I'M...

PLANNING TO GET MARRIED.

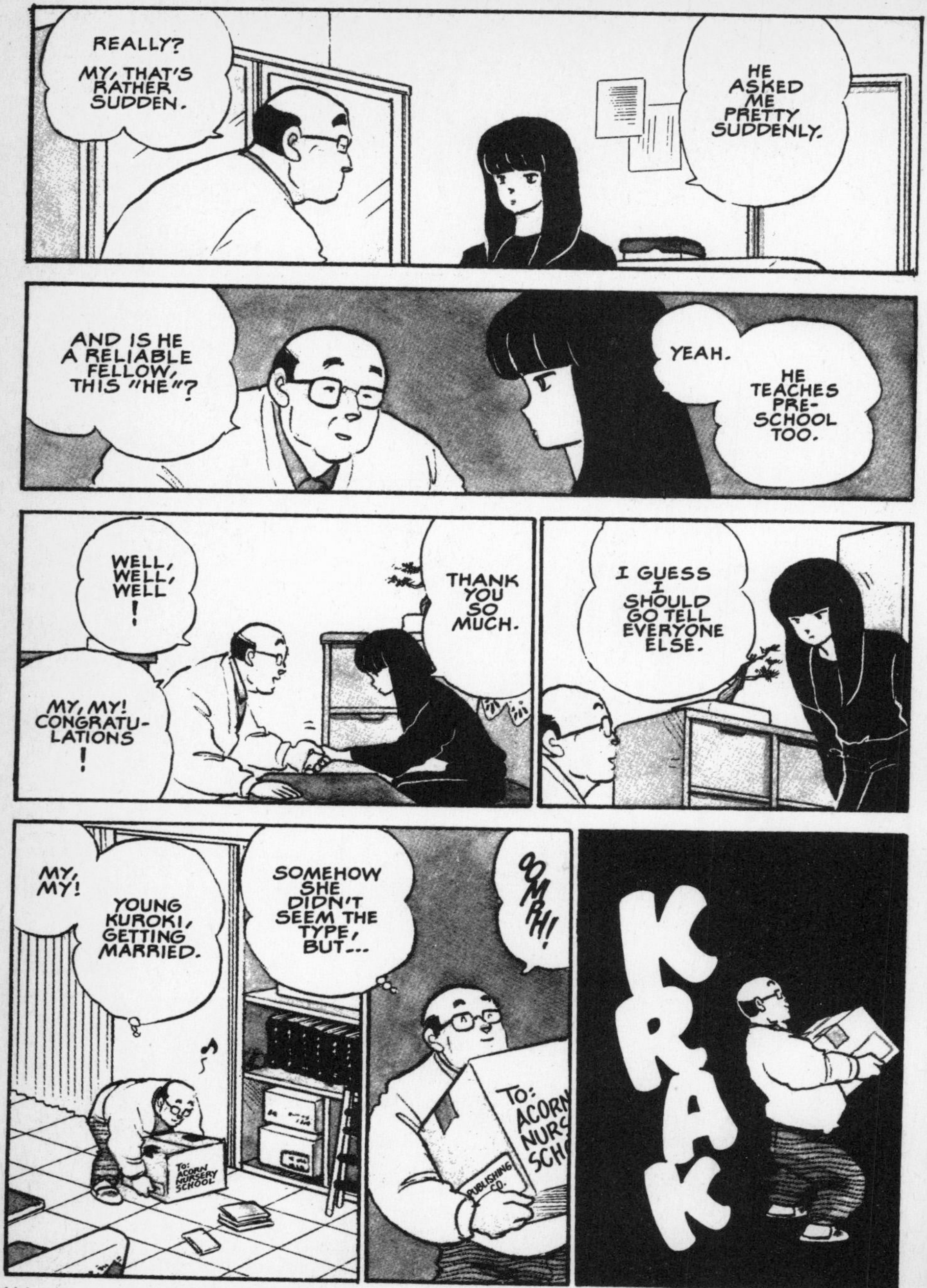
REALLY? MY, THAT'S RATHER SUDDEN.
HE ASKED ME PRETTY SUDDENLY.
AND IS HE A RELIABLE FELLOW, THIS "HE"?
YEAH.
HE TEACHES PRE-SCHOOL TOO.
WELL, WELL, WELL!
MY, MY! CONGRATULATIONS!
THANK YOU SO MUCH.
I GUESS I SHOULD GO TELL EVERYONE ELSE.
MY, MY!
YOUNG KUROKI, GETTING MARRIED.
TO: ACORN NURSERY SCHOOL
SOMEHOW SHE DIDN'T SEEM THE TYPE, BUT...
OOMPH!!
TO: ACORN NURS SCH
PUBLISHING CO.
KRAK

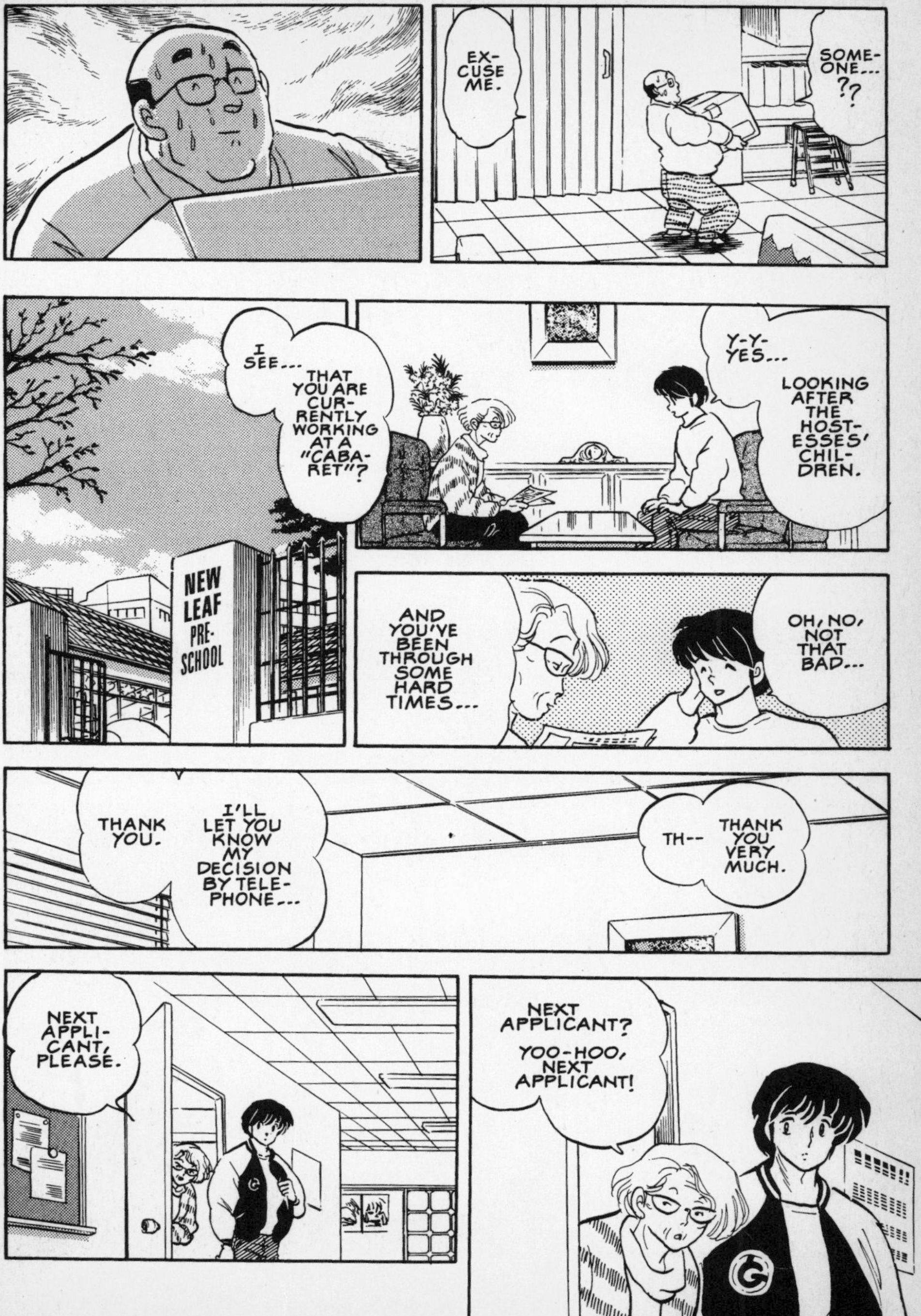
EX-CUSE ME.
SOME-ONE... ??
NEW LEAF PRE-SCHOOL
I SEE... THAT YOU ARE CUR-RENTLY WORKING AT A "CABA-RET"?
Y-Y-YES... LOOKING AFTER THE HOST-ESSES' CHIL-DREN.
AND YOU'VE BEEN THROUGH SOME HARD TIMES...
OH, NO, NOT THAT BAD...
THANK YOU. I'LL LET YOU KNOW MY DECISION BY TELE-PHONE...
TH-- THANK YOU VERY MUCH.
NEXT APPLI-CANT, PLEASE.
NEXT APPLICANT? YOO-HOO, NEXT APPLICANT!

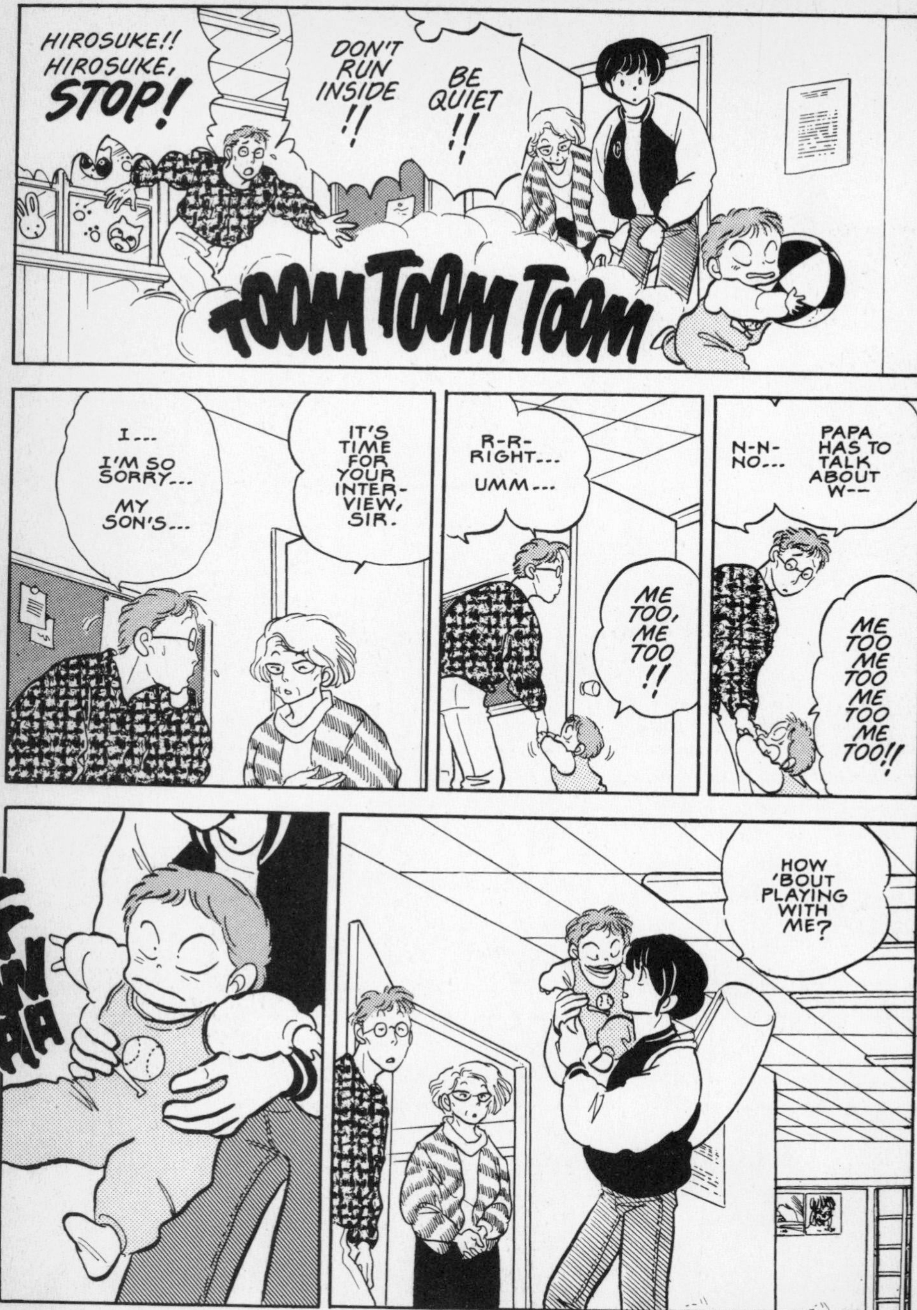
HIROSUKE!! HIROSUKE, STOP!
DON'T RUN INSIDE !!
BE QUIET !!
TOOM TOOM TOOM
I... I'M SO SORRY... MY SON'S...
IT'S TIME FOR YOUR INTER-VIEW, SIR.
R-R-RIGHT... UMM...
ME TOO, ME TOO !!
N-N-NO...
PAPA HAS TO TALK ABOUT W--
ME TOO ME TOO ME TOO ME TOO!!
FWAA
HOW 'BOUT PLAYING WITH ME?

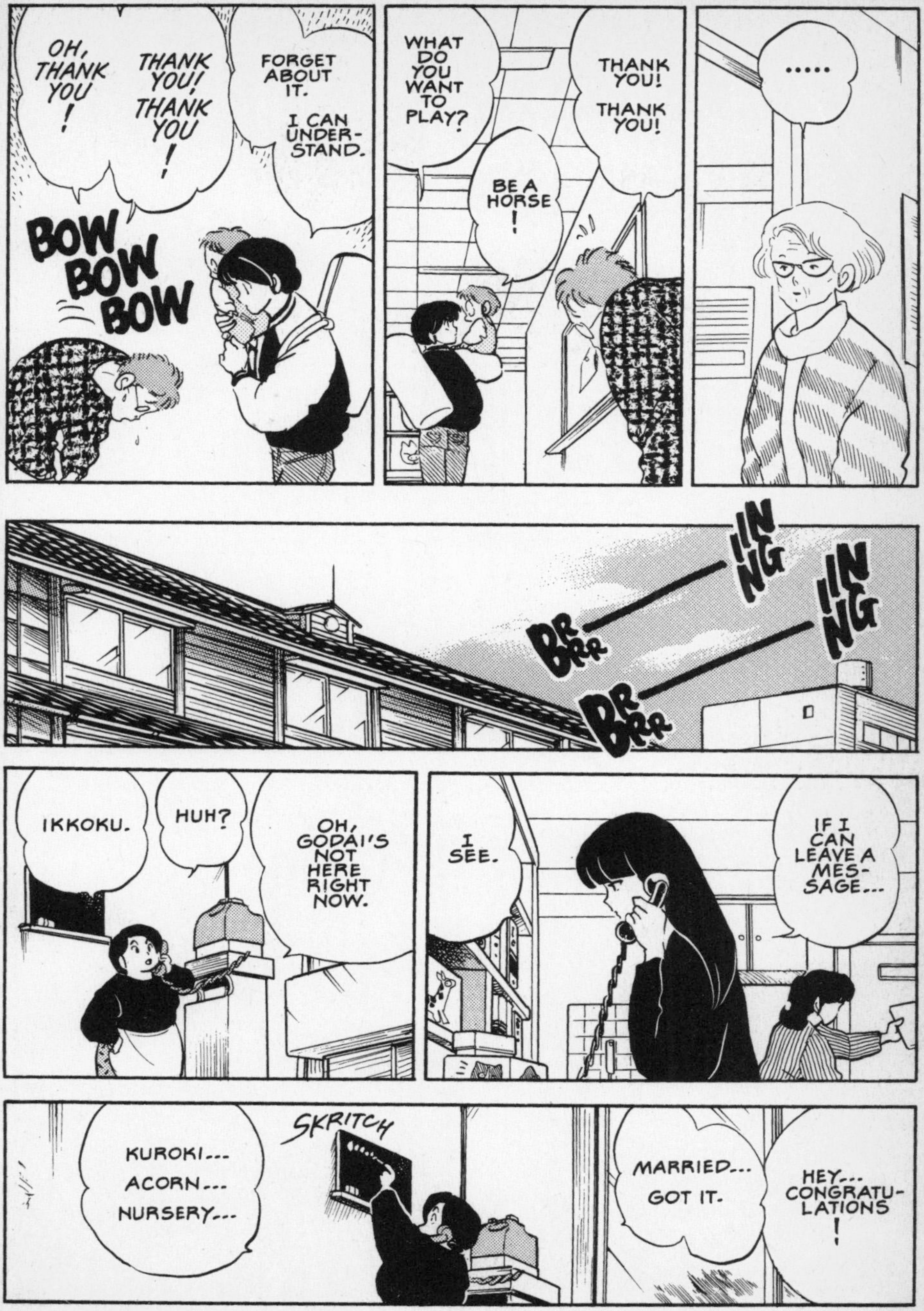
OH, THANK YOU!
THANK YOU! THANK YOU!
FORGET ABOUT IT.
I CAN UNDERSTAND.
BOW BOW BOW
WHAT DO YOU WANT TO PLAY?
BE A HORSE!
THANK YOU!
THANK YOU!
.....
BRRR IING
BRRR IING
IKKOKU.
HUH?
OH, GODAI'S NOT HERE RIGHT NOW.
I SEE.
IF I CAN LEAVE A MESSAGE...
KUROKI... ACORN... NURSERY...
SKRITCH
MARRIED... GOT IT.
HEY... CONGRATULATIONS!

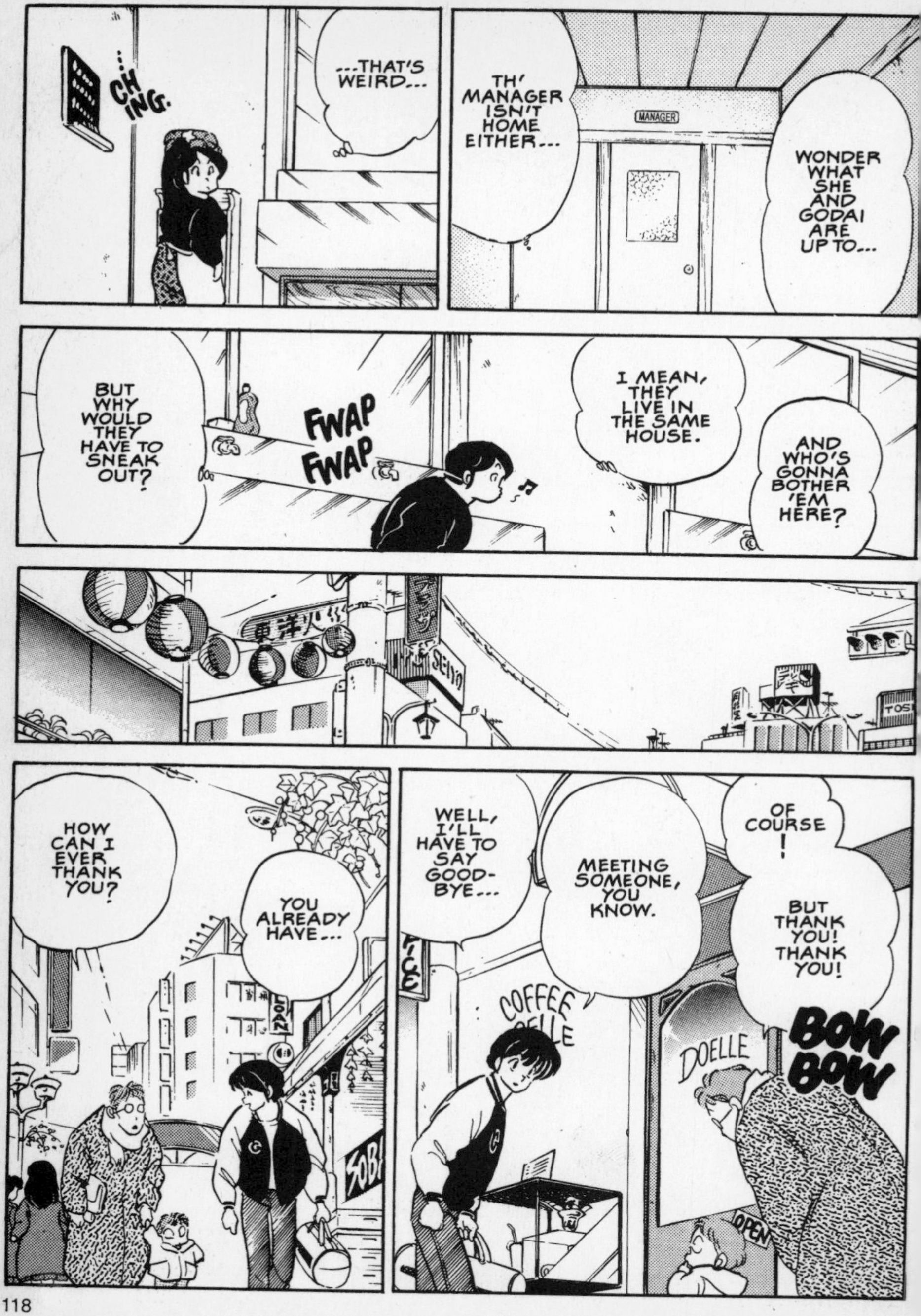
CHING.
...THAT'S WEIRD...
TH' MANAGER ISN'T HOME EITHER...
MANAGER
WONDER WHAT SHE AND GODAI ARE UP TO...
BUT WHY WOULD THEY HAVE TO SNEAK OUT?
FWAP FWAP
I MEAN, THEY LIVE IN THE SAME HOUSE.
AND WHO'S GONNA BOTHER 'EM HERE?
HOW CAN I EVER THANK YOU?
YOU ALREADY HAVE...
LOAN
SOBA
WELL, I'LL HAVE TO SAY GOOD-BYE...
MEETING SOMEONE, YOU KNOW.
OF COURSE!
BUT THANK YOU! THANK YOU!
COFFEE
DOELLE
BOW BOW
OPEN

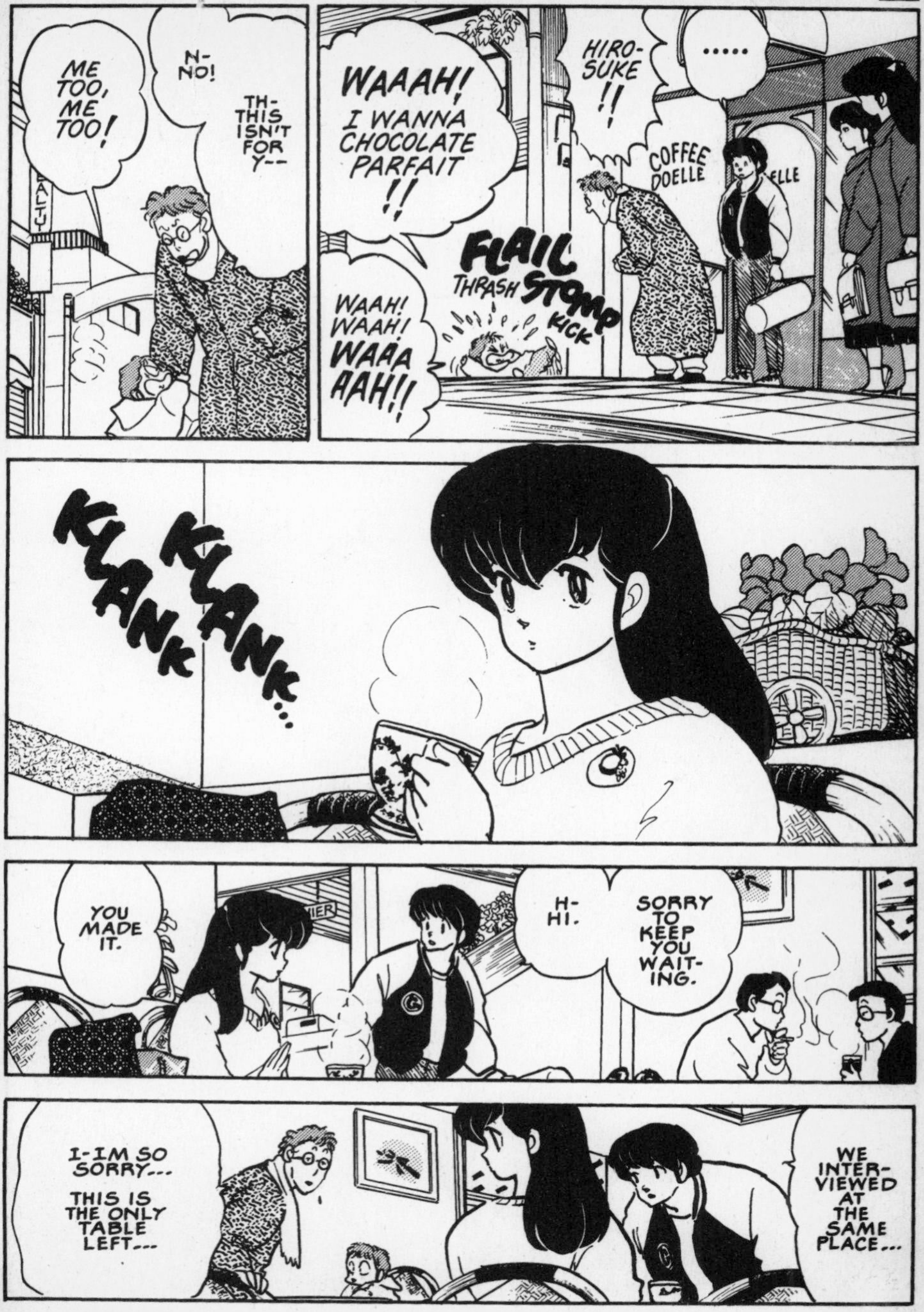
ME TOO, ME TOO!
N-NO!
TH-THIS ISN'T FOR Y--
WAAAH! I WANNA CHOCOLATE PARFAIT !!
WAAH! WAAH! WAAAAAH!!
FLAIL
THRASH
STOMP
KICK
HIRO-SUKE !!
.....
COFFEE DOELLE
ELLE
KLANK KLANK...
YOU MADE IT.
H-HI.
SORRY TO KEEP YOU WAITING.
I-IM SO SORRY...
THIS IS THE ONLY TABLE LEFT...
WE INTERVIEWED AT THE SAME PLACE...

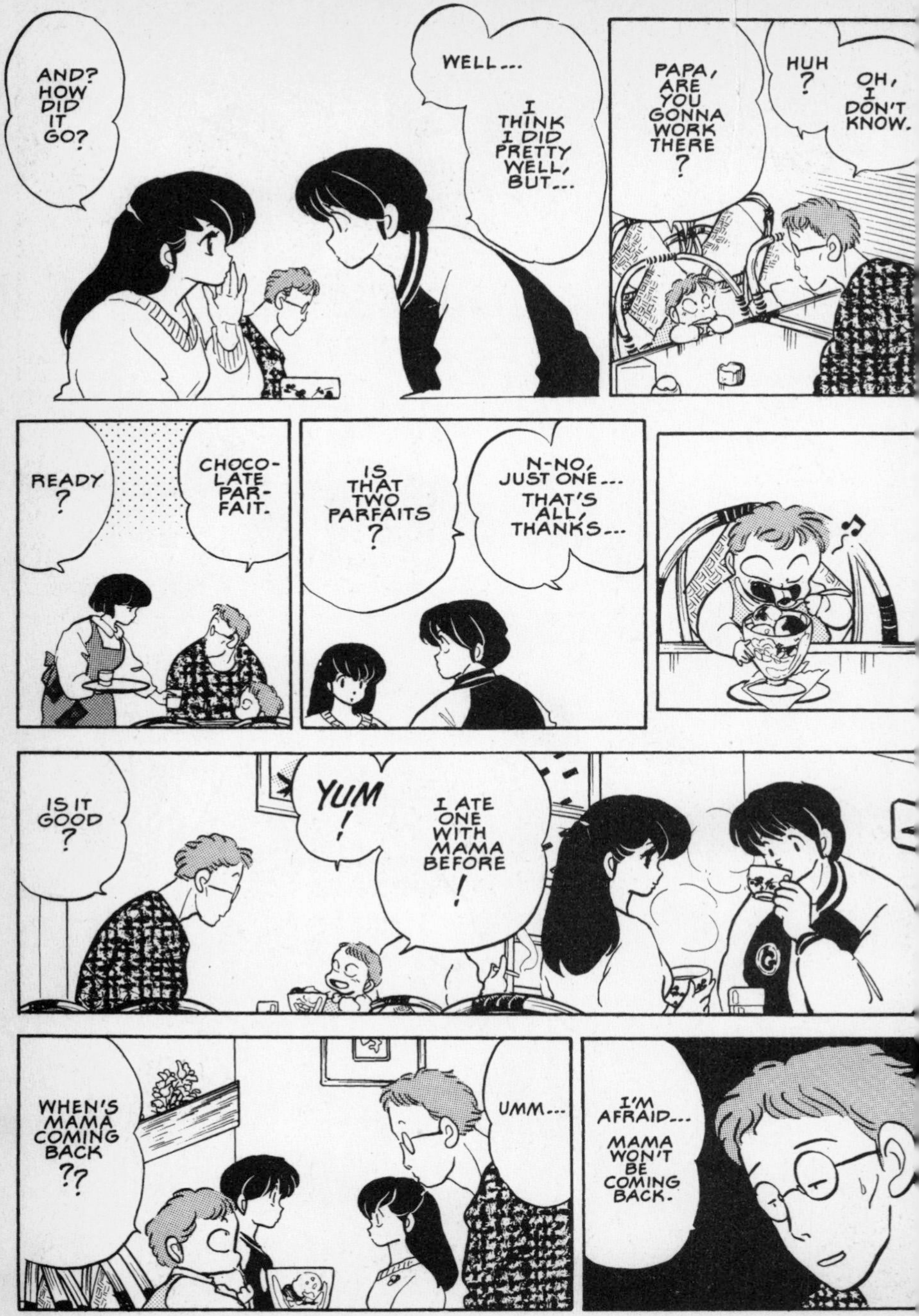
AND? HOW DID IT GO?
WELL...
I THINK I DID PRETTY WELL, BUT...
PAPA, ARE YOU GONNA WORK THERE?
HUH?
OH, I DON'T KNOW.
READY?
CHOCOLATE PARFAIT.
IS THAT TWO PARFAITS?
N-NO, JUST ONE... THAT'S ALL, THANKS...
IS IT GOOD?
YUM!
I ATE ONE WITH MAMA BEFORE!
WHEN'S MAMA COMING BACK??
UMM...
I'M AFRAID... MAMA WON'T BE COMING BACK.

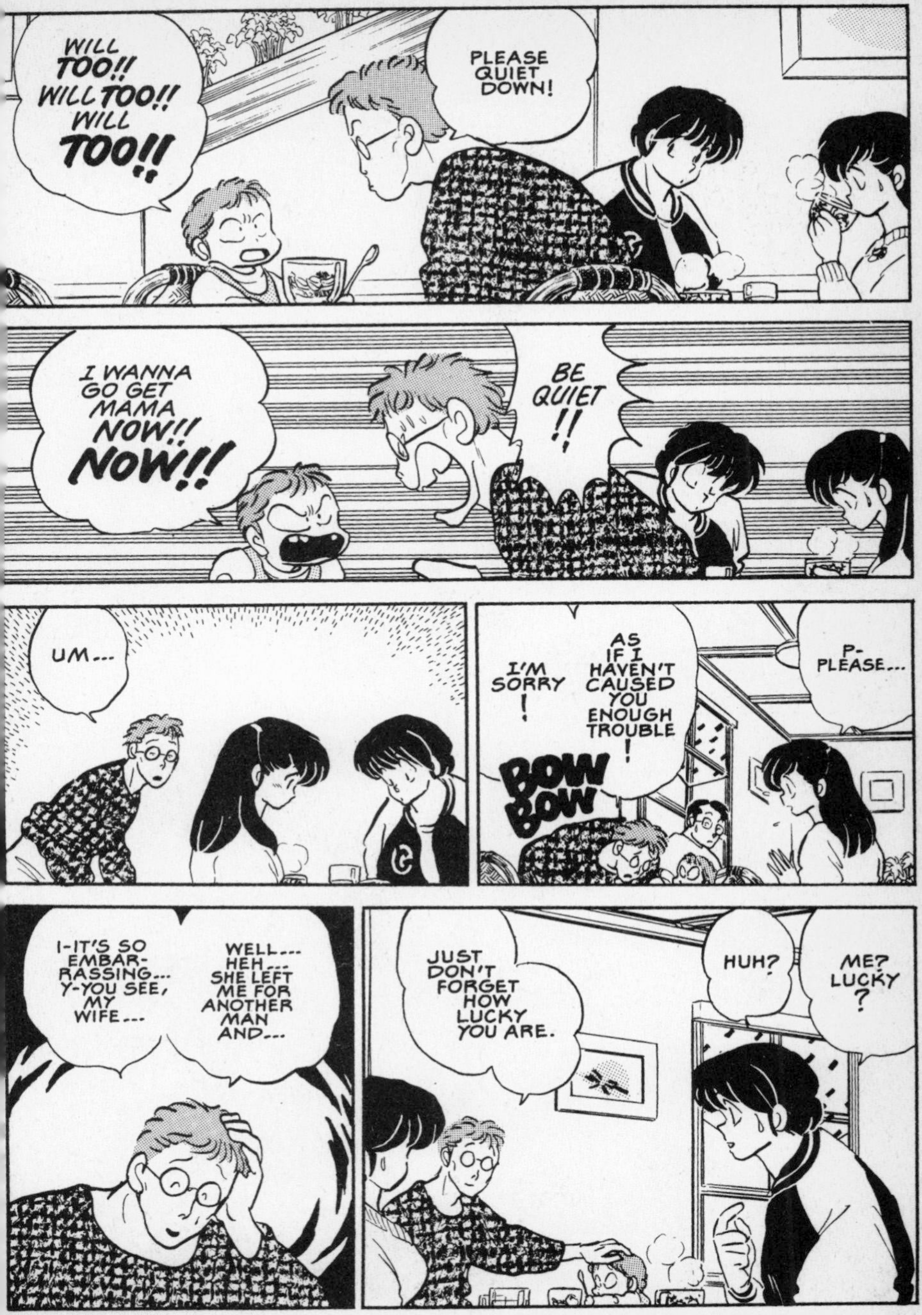
WILL TOO!! WILL TOO!! WILL TOO!!
PLEASE QUIET DOWN!
I WANNA GO GET MAMA NOW!! NOW!!
BE QUIET !!
UM...
I'M SORRY !
AS IF I HAVEN'T CAUSED YOU ENOUGH TROUBLE !
BOW BOW
P-PLEASE...
I-IT'S SO EMBARRASSING... Y-YOU SEE, MY WIFE...
WELL... HEH... SHE LEFT ME FOR ANOTHER MAN AND...
JUST DON'T FORGET HOW LUCKY YOU ARE.
HUH?
ME? LUCKY ?

YOUR WHOLE LIFE'S AHEAD OF YOU...

AND SUCH A LOVELY COMPANION TO SHARE IT...

COM... PANION... Y-Y-YEAH...

MAYBE SHE WILL BE, IF I CAN EVER...

AND TODAY...

I THINK YOU GOT YOURSELF A JOB.

GULP

HUH ??

THE PRINCIPAL WAS...

SPEAKING VERY HIGHLY OF YOU...

I FEEL KIND OF SORRY FOR HIM...

ME TOO.

RAISING A KID BY HIMSELF... THAT KID...

IT MUST BE HARD.

ICE CREAM

24 HRS.

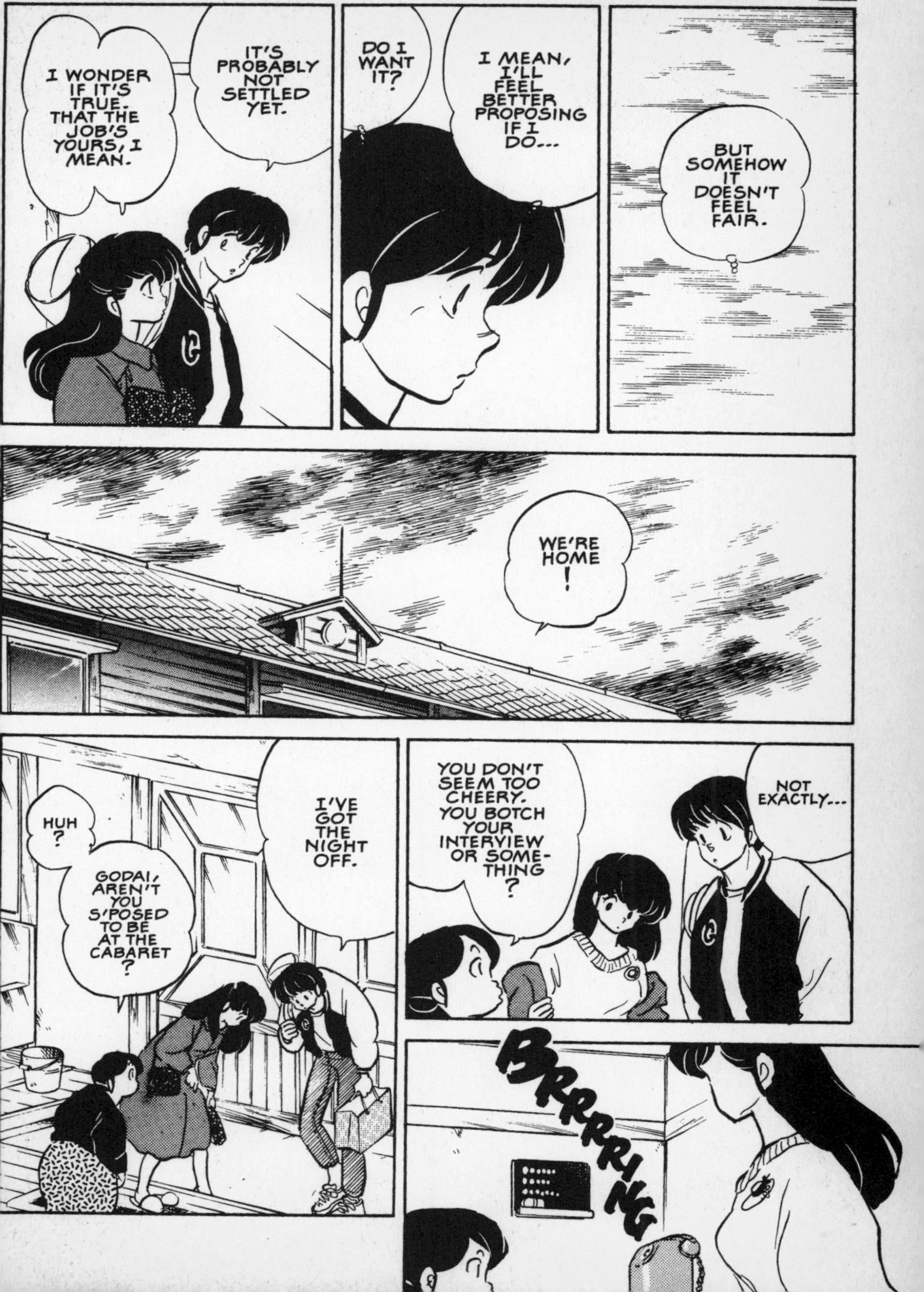
I WONDER IF IT'S TRUE. THAT THE JOB'S YOURS, I MEAN.
IT'S PROBABLY NOT SETTLED YET.
DO I WANT IT?
I MEAN, I'LL FEEL BETTER PROPOSING IF I DO...
BUT SOMEHOW IT DOESN'T FEEL FAIR.
WE'RE HOME!
HUH?
GODAI, AREN'T YOU S'POSED TO BE AT THE CABARET?
I'VE GOT THE NIGHT OFF.
YOU DON'T SEEM TOO CHEERY. YOU BOTCH YOUR INTERVIEW OR SOMETHING?
NOT EXACTLY...
BRRRRING

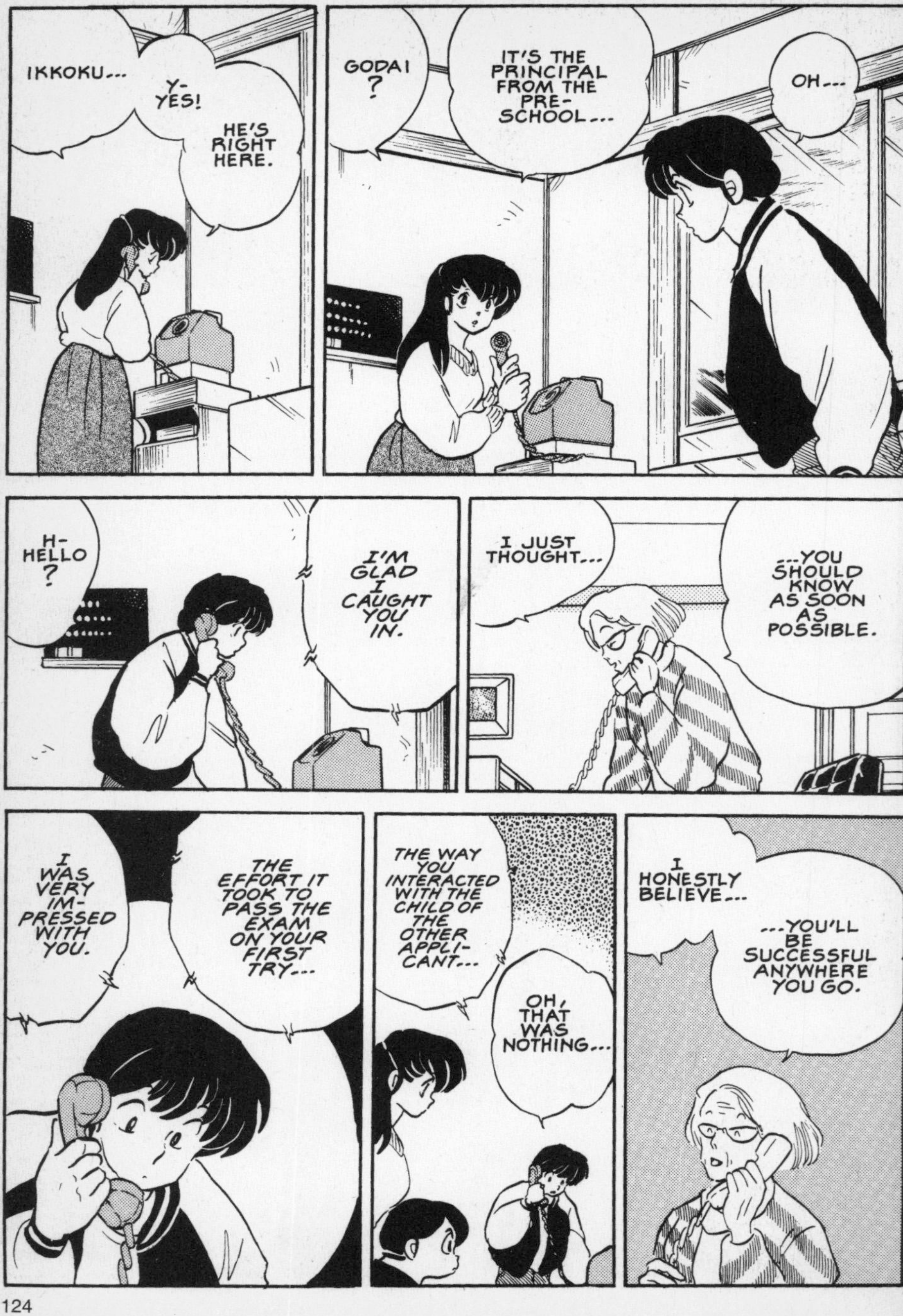
IKKOKU...
Y-YES!
HE'S RIGHT HERE.
GODAI?
IT'S THE PRINCIPAL FROM THE PRE-SCHOOL...
OH...
H-HELLO?
I'M GLAD I CAUGHT YOU IN.
I JUST THOUGHT...
...YOU SHOULD KNOW AS SOON AS POSSIBLE.
I WAS VERY IM-PRESSED WITH YOU.
THE EFFORT IT TOOK TO PASS THE EXAM ON YOUR FIRST TRY...
THE WAY YOU INTERACTED WITH THE CHILD OF THE OTHER APPLI-CANT...
OH, THAT WAS NOTHING...
I HONESTLY BELIEVE...
...YOU'LL BE SUCCESSFUL ANYWHERE YOU GO.

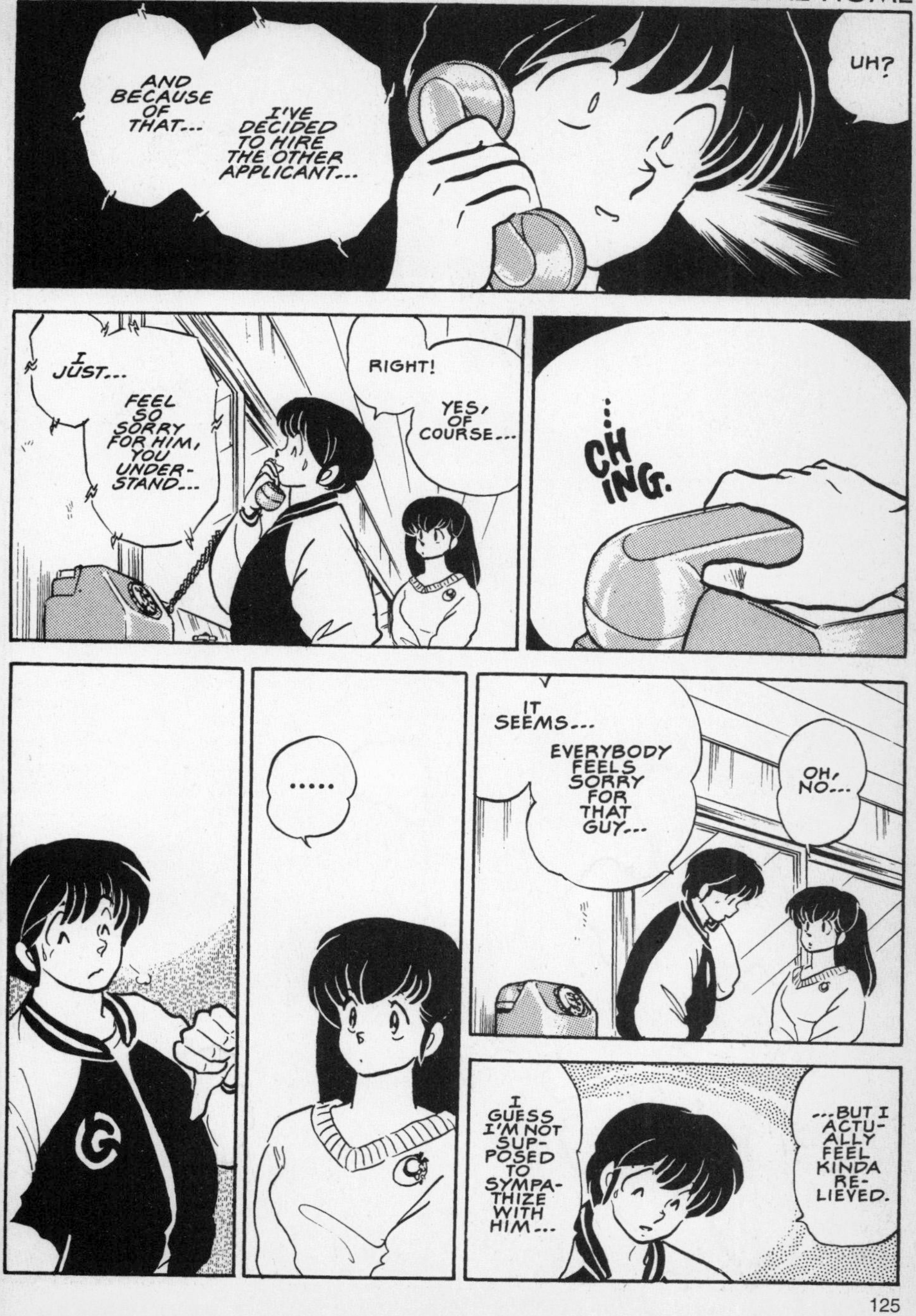
AND BECAUSE OF THAT...
I'VE DECIDED TO HIRE THE OTHER APPLICANT...
UH?
I JUST...
FEEL SO SORRY FOR HIM, YOU UNDERSTAND...
RIGHT!
YES, OF COURSE...
...CHING.
......
IT SEEMS...
EVERYBODY FEELS SORRY FOR THAT GUY...
OH, NO...
I GUESS I'M NOT SUPPOSED TO SYMPATHIZE WITH HIM...
...BUT I ACTUALLY FEEL KINDA RELIEVED.

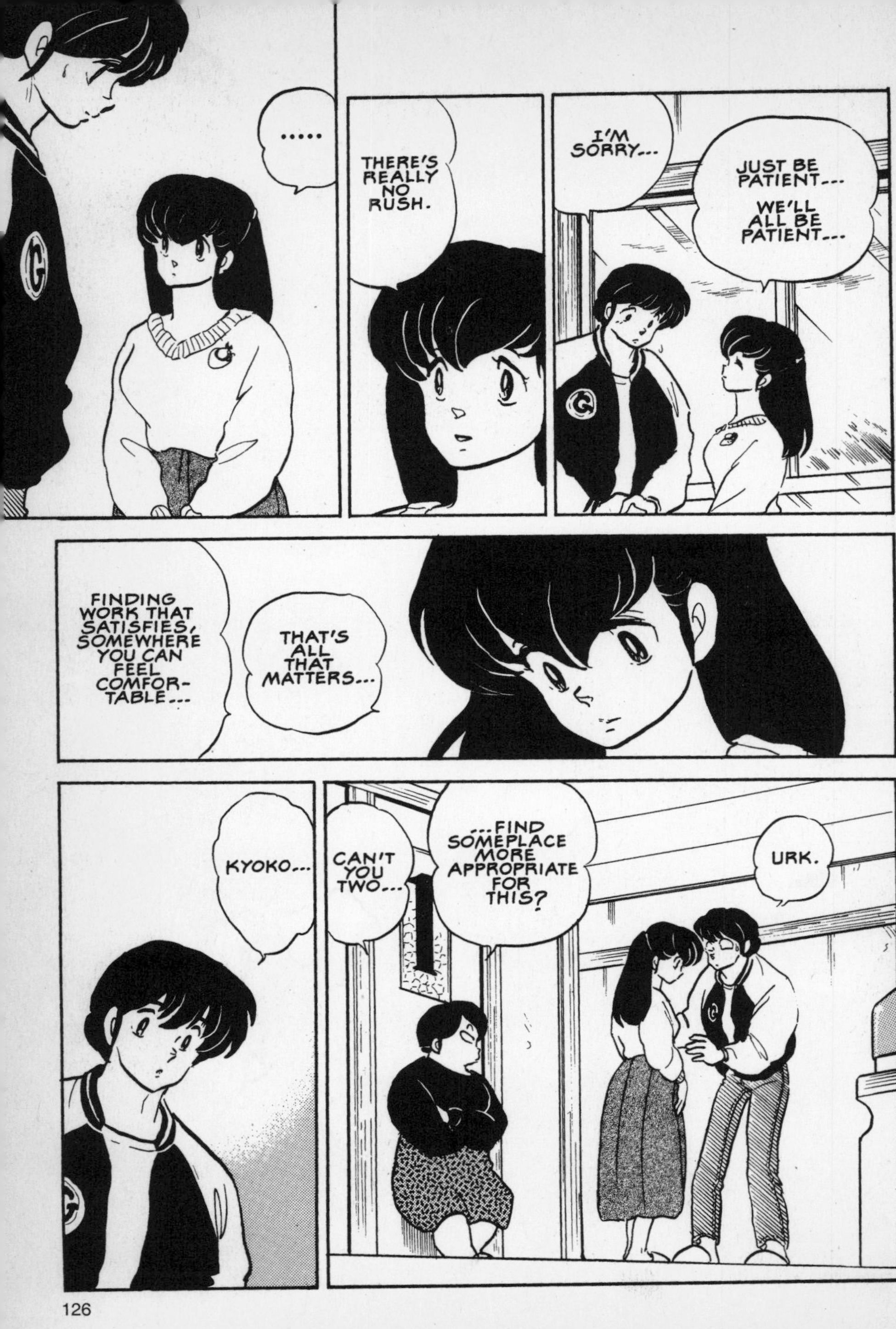
.....
THERE'S REALLY NO RUSH.
I'M SORRY...
JUST BE PATIENT...
WE'LL ALL BE PATIENT...
FINDING WORK THAT SATISFIES, SOMEWHERE YOU CAN FEEL COMFORTABLE...
THAT'S ALL THAT MATTERS...
KYOKO...
CAN'T YOU TWO...
...FIND SOMEPLACE MORE APPROPRIATE FOR THIS?
URK.

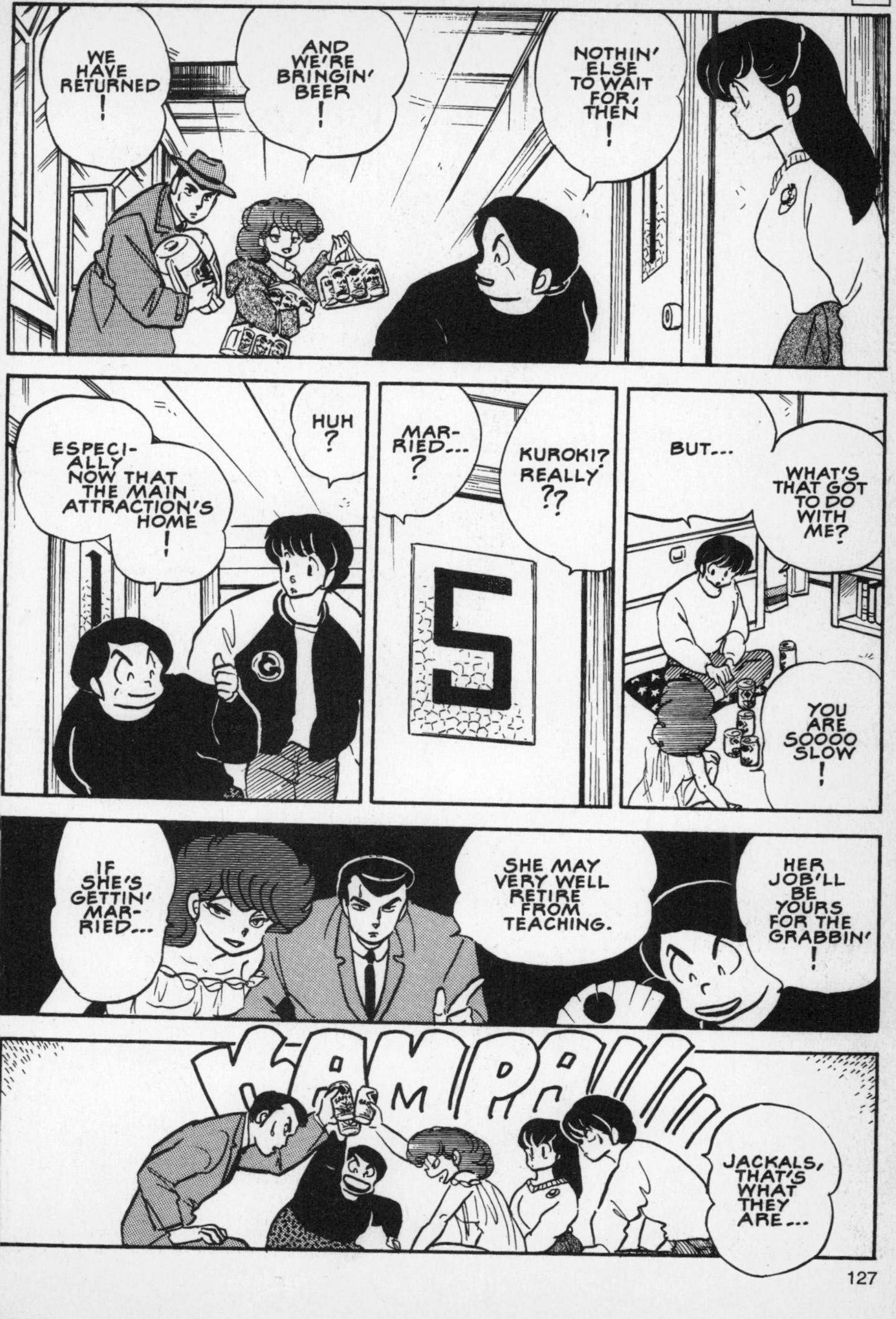
WE HAVE RETURNED !
AND WE'RE BRINGIN' BEER !
NOTHIN' ELSE TO WAIT FOR, THEN !
ESPECI-ALLY NOW THAT THE MAIN ATTRACTION'S HOME !
HUH ?
MAR-RIED... ?
KUROKI? REALLY ??
BUT...
WHAT'S THAT GOT TO DO WITH ME?
YOU ARE SOOOO SLOW !
IF SHE'S GETTIN' MAR-RIED...
SHE MAY VERY WELL RETIRE FROM TEACHING.
HER JOB'LL BE YOURS FOR THE GRABBIN' !
KAMPAI!!
JACKALS, THAT'S WHAT THEY ARE...

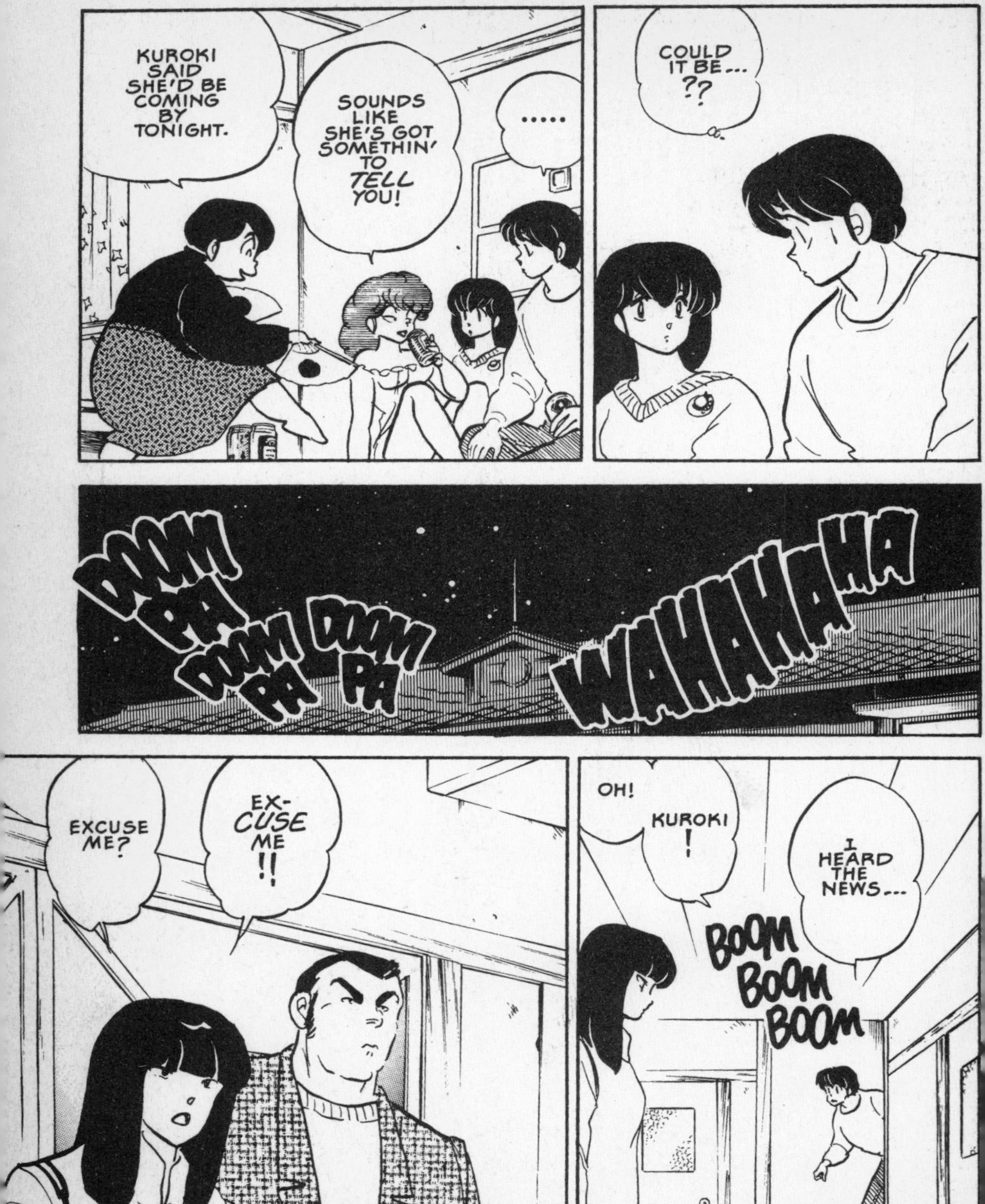
KUROKI SAID SHE'D BE COMING BY TONIGHT.
SOUNDS LIKE SHE'S GOT SOMETHIN' TO TELL YOU!
.....
COULD IT BE... ??
DOOM PA DOOM PA DOOM PA
WAHAHAHAHA
EXCUSE ME?
EX-CUSE ME !!
OH!
KUROKI !
I HEARD THE NEWS...
BOOM BOOM BOOM

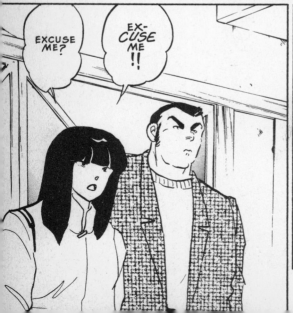

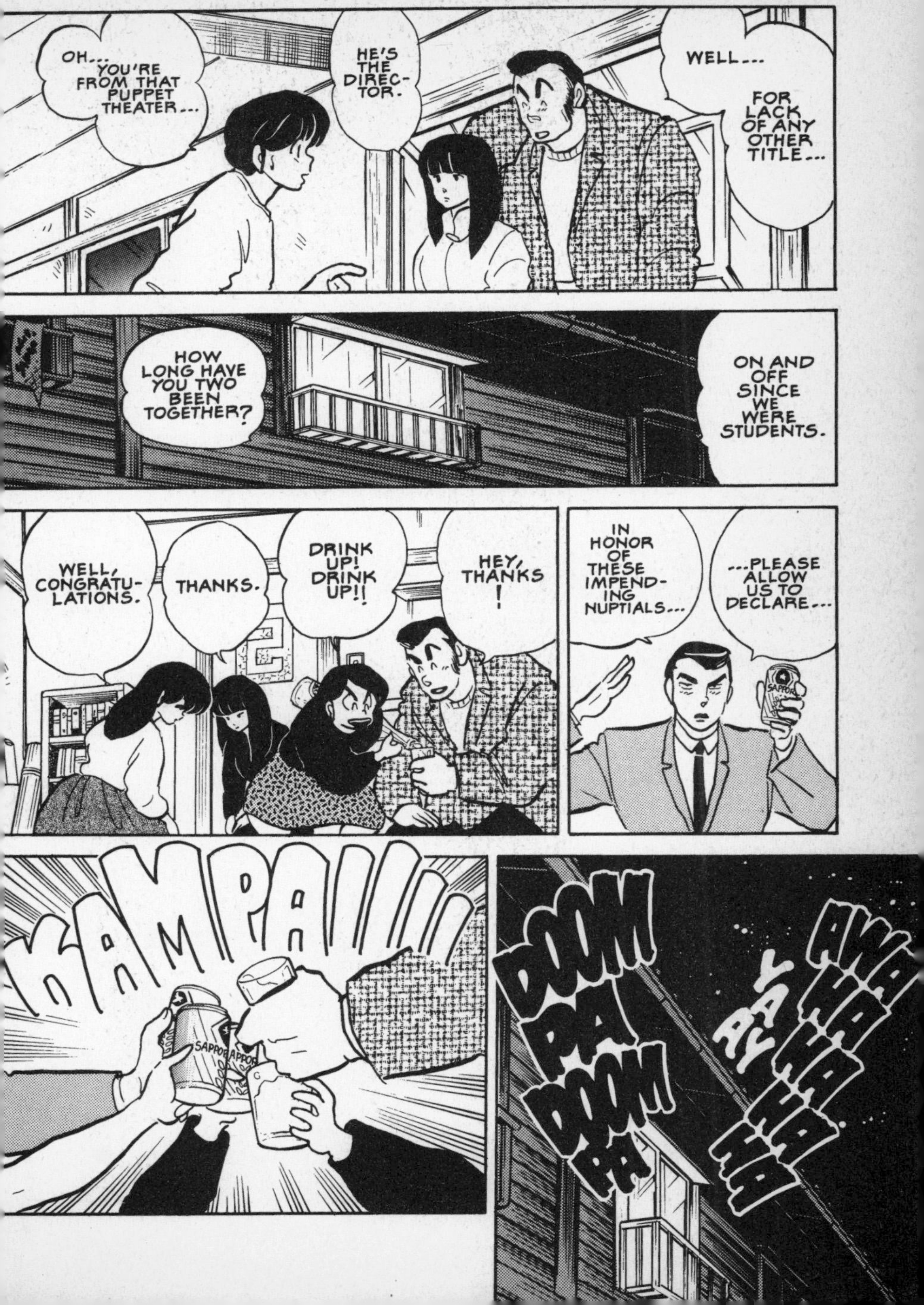
OH... YOU'RE FROM THAT PUPPET THEATER...
HE'S THE DIREC-TOR.
WELL...
FOR LACK OF ANY OTHER TITLE...
HOW LONG HAVE YOU TWO BEEN TOGETHER?
ON AND OFF SINCE WE WERE STUDENTS.
WELL, CONGRATU-LATIONS.
THANKS.
DRINK UP! DRINK UP!!
HEY, THANKS!
IN HONOR OF THESE IMPEND-ING NUPTIALS...
...PLEASE ALLOW US TO DECLARE...
KAMPAI!!!
DOOM PA DOOM PA
AWA HA HA HA HA

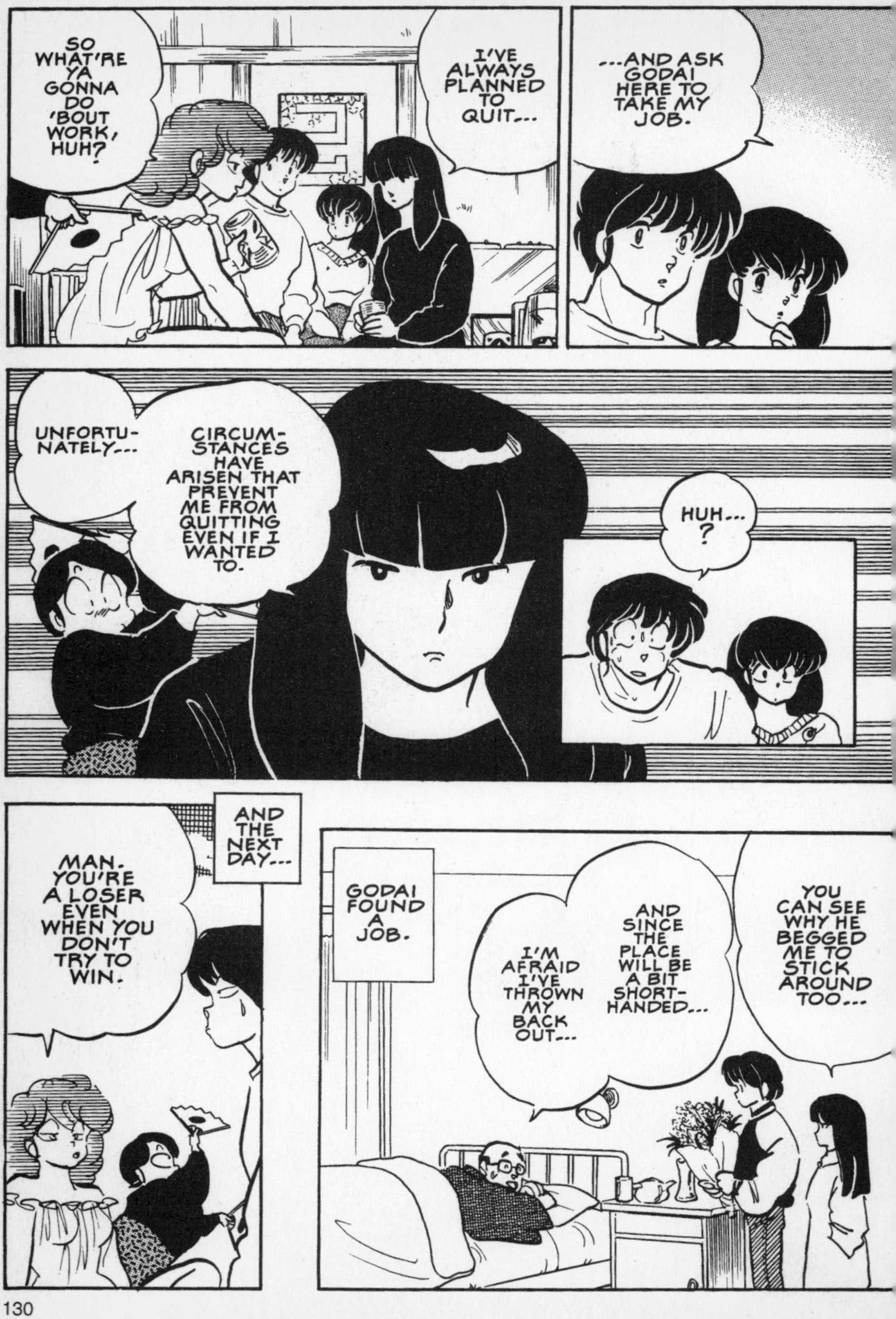
SO WHAT'RE YA GONNA DO 'BOUT WORK, HUH?
I'VE ALWAYS PLANNED TO QUIT...
...AND ASK GODAI HERE TO TAKE MY JOB.
UNFORTU-NATELY...
CIRCUM-STANCES HAVE ARISEN THAT PREVENT ME FROM QUITTING EVEN IF I WANTED TO.
HUH... ?
MAN. YOU'RE A LOSER EVEN WHEN YOU DON'T TRY TO WIN.
AND THE NEXT DAY...
GODAI FOUND A JOB.
I'M AFRAID I'VE THROWN MY BACK OUT...
AND SINCE THE PLACE WILL BE A BIT SHORT-HANDED...
YOU CAN SEE WHY HE BEGGED ME TO STICK AROUND TOO...

PART SEVEN
...IF IT EVER HAPPENS

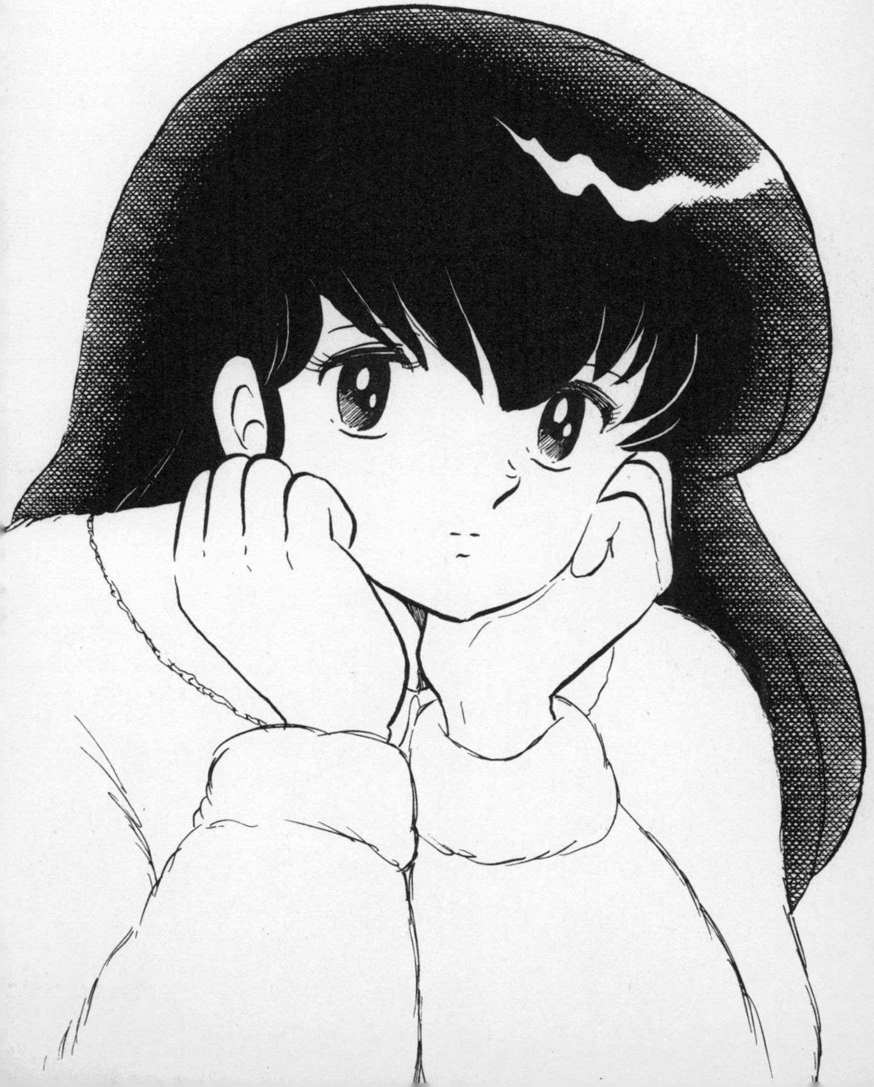

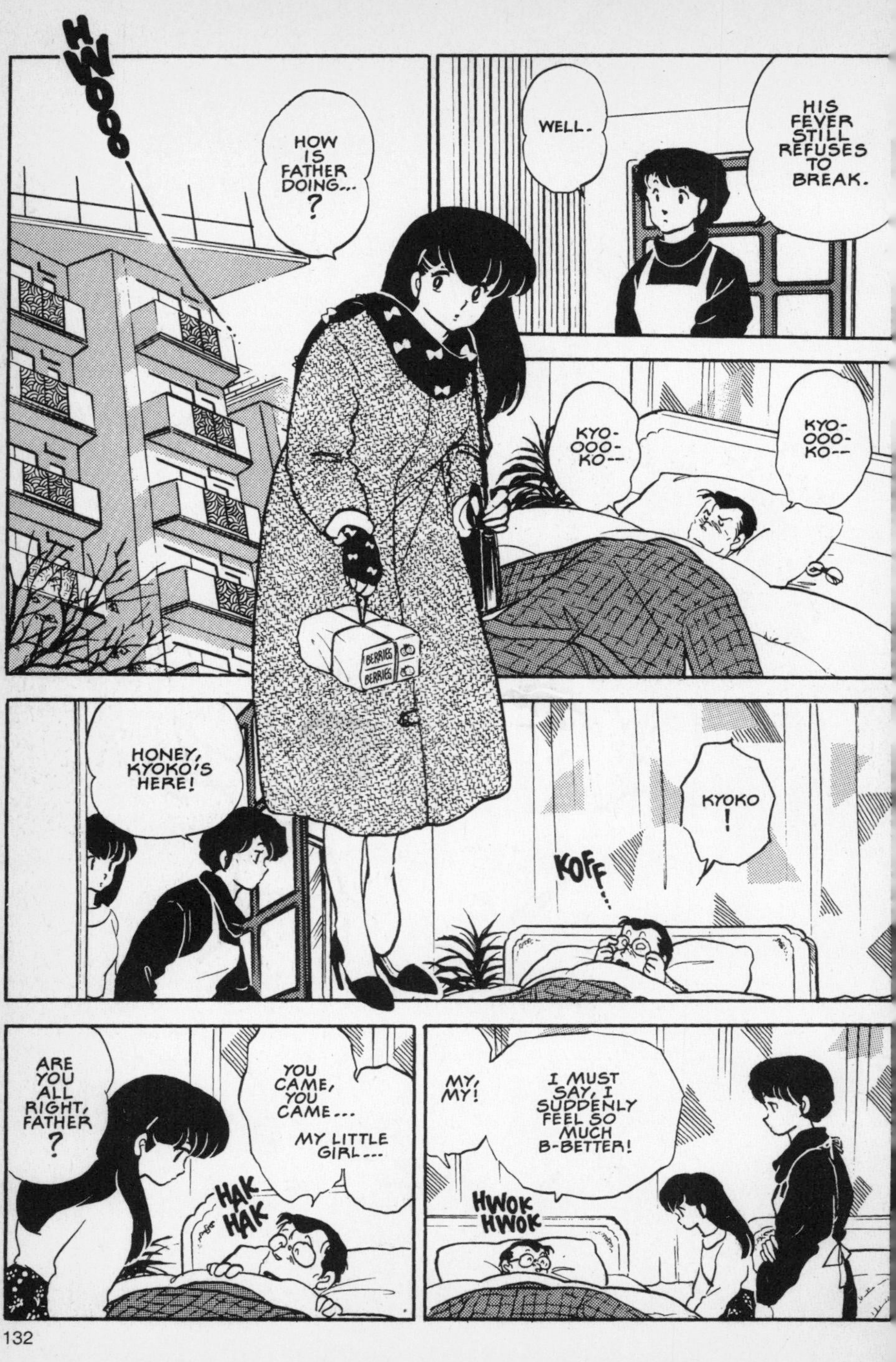
HWOOO
HOW IS FATHER DOING...?
BERRIES
BERRIES
WELL.
HIS FEVER STILL REFUSES TO BREAK.
KYO-OOO-KO--
KYO-OOO-KO--
HONEY, KYOKO'S HERE!
KYOKO!
KOFF
ARE YOU ALL RIGHT, FATHER?
YOU CAME, YOU CAME...
MY LITTLE GIRL...
HAK HAK
MY, MY!
I MUST SAY, I SUDDENLY FEEL SO MUCH B-BETTER!
HWOK HWOK

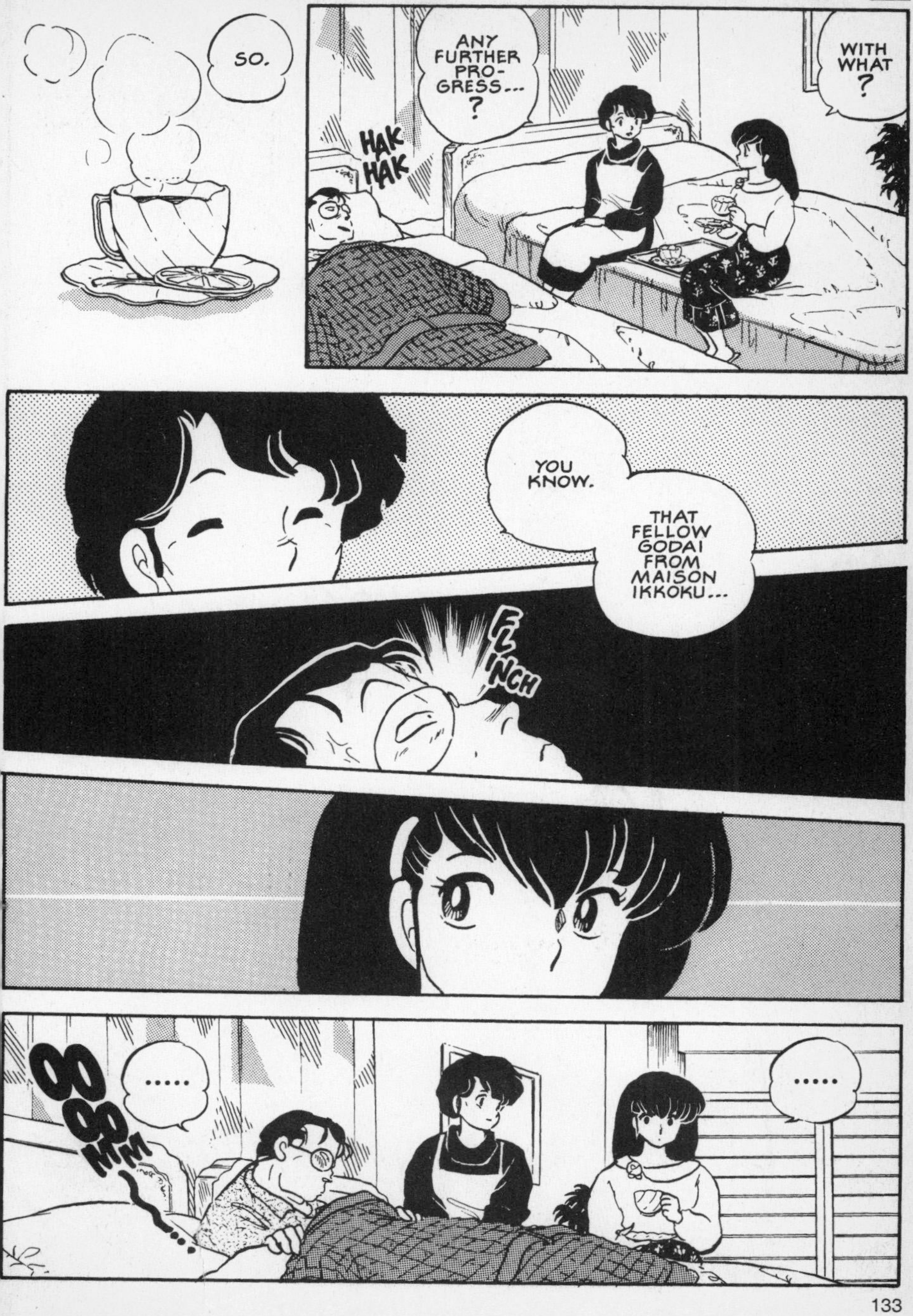
SO.
ANY FURTHER PRO-GRESS...?
HAK HAK
WITH WHAT?
YOU KNOW.
THAT FELLOW GODAI FROM MAISON IKKOKU...
FLINCH
OOOMM~...
.....
.....

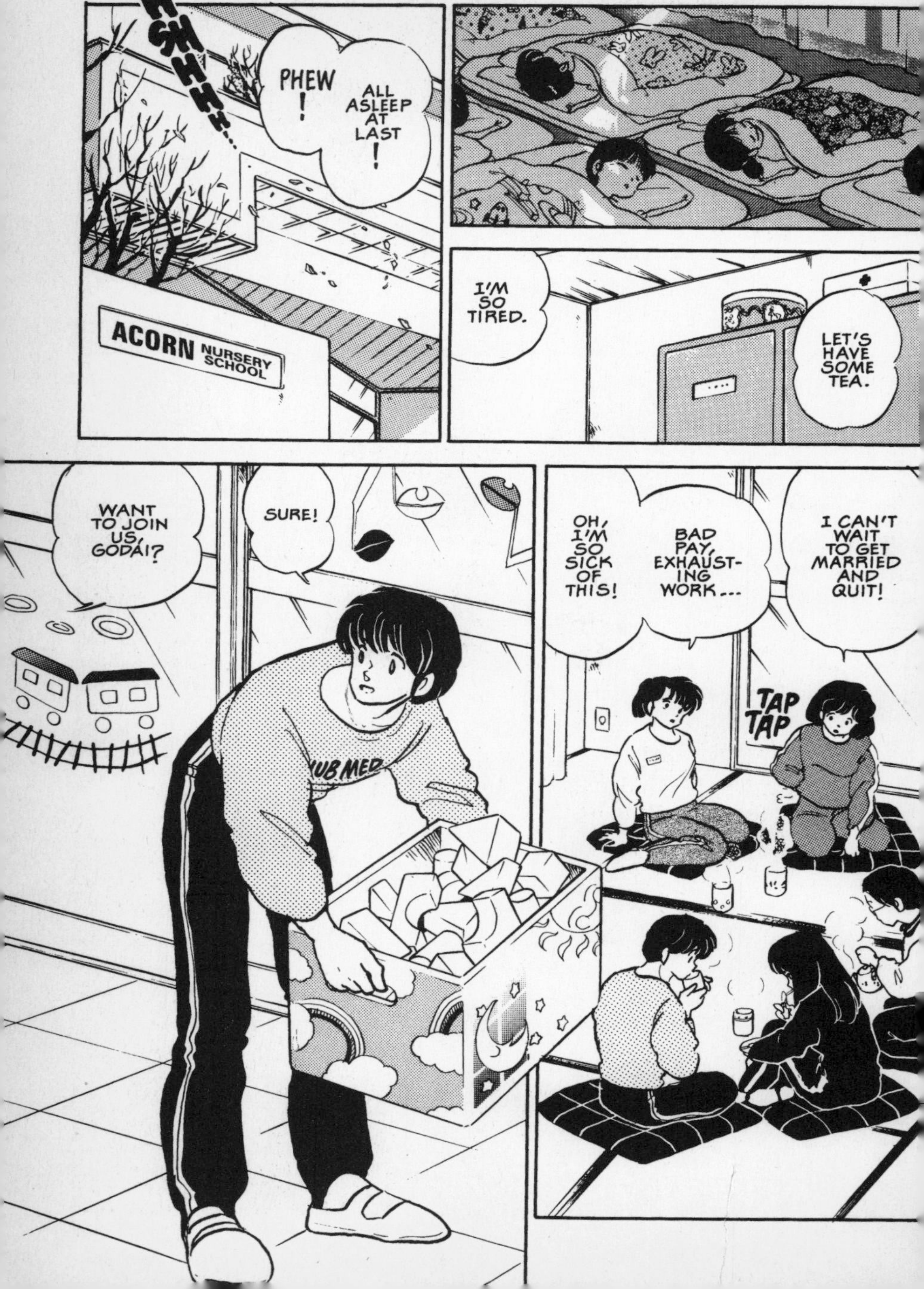
HSHHHH...
PHEW! ALL ASLEEP AT LAST!
ACORN NURSERY SCHOOL
I'M SO TIRED.
LET'S HAVE SOME TEA.
WANT TO JOIN US, GODAI?
SURE!
OH, I'M SO SICK OF THIS!
BAD PAY, EXHAUSTING WORK...
I CAN'T WAIT TO GET MARRIED AND QUIT!
TAP TAP

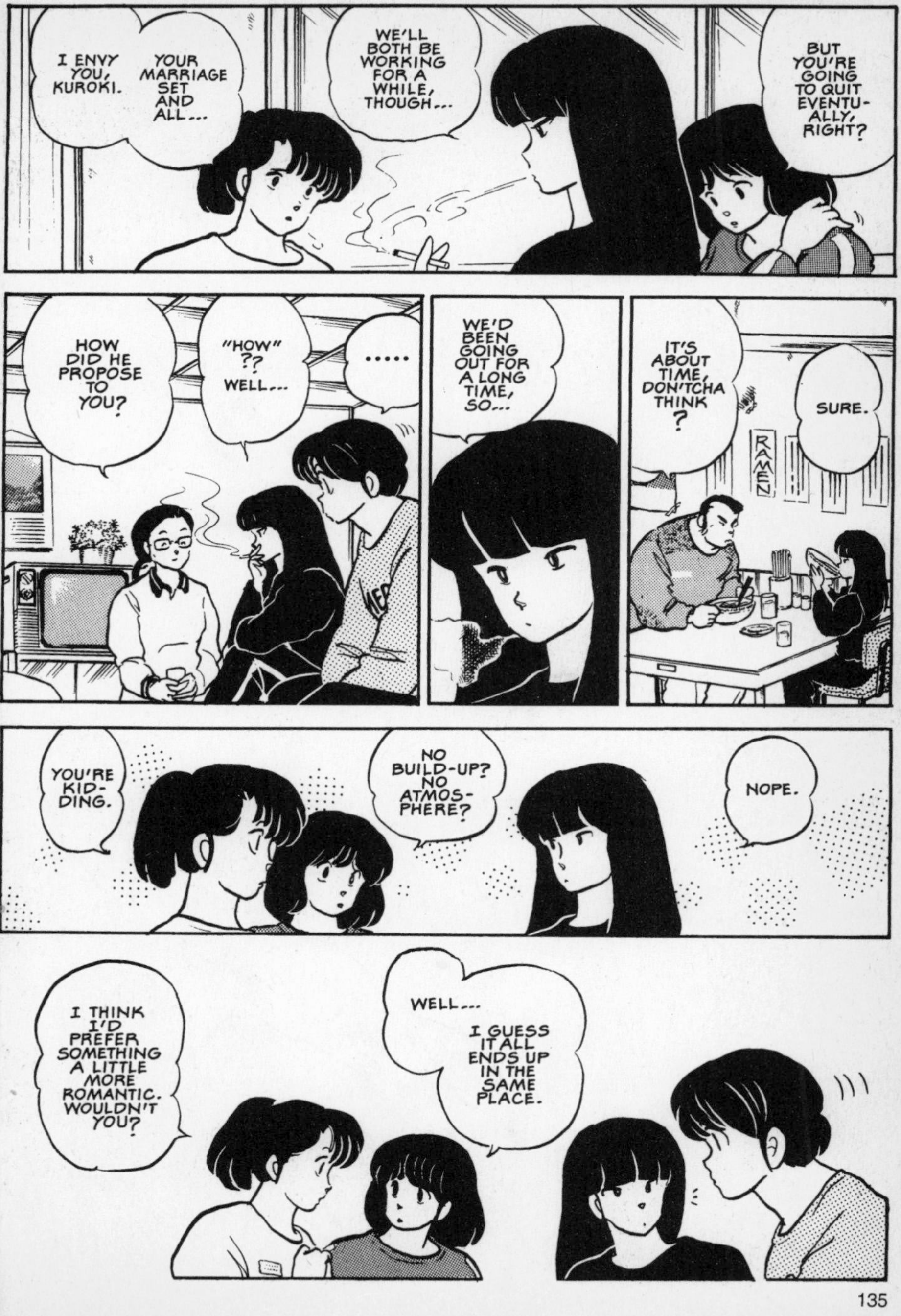

I ENVY YOU, KUROKI.
YOUR MARRIAGE SET AND ALL...
WE'LL BOTH BE WORKING FOR A WHILE, THOUGH...
BUT YOU'RE GOING TO QUIT EVENTU-ALLY, RIGHT?
HOW DID HE PROPOSE TO YOU?
"HOW"?? WELL...
.....
WE'D BEEN GOING OUT FOR A LONG TIME, SO...
IT'S ABOUT TIME, DON'TCHA THINK?
SURE.
RAMEN
YOU'RE KID-DING.
NO BUILD-UP? NO ATMOS-PHERE?
NOPE.
I THINK I'D PREFER SOMETHING A LITTLE MORE ROMANTIC. WOULDN'T YOU?
WELL...
I GUESS IT ALL ENDS UP IN THE SAME PLACE.

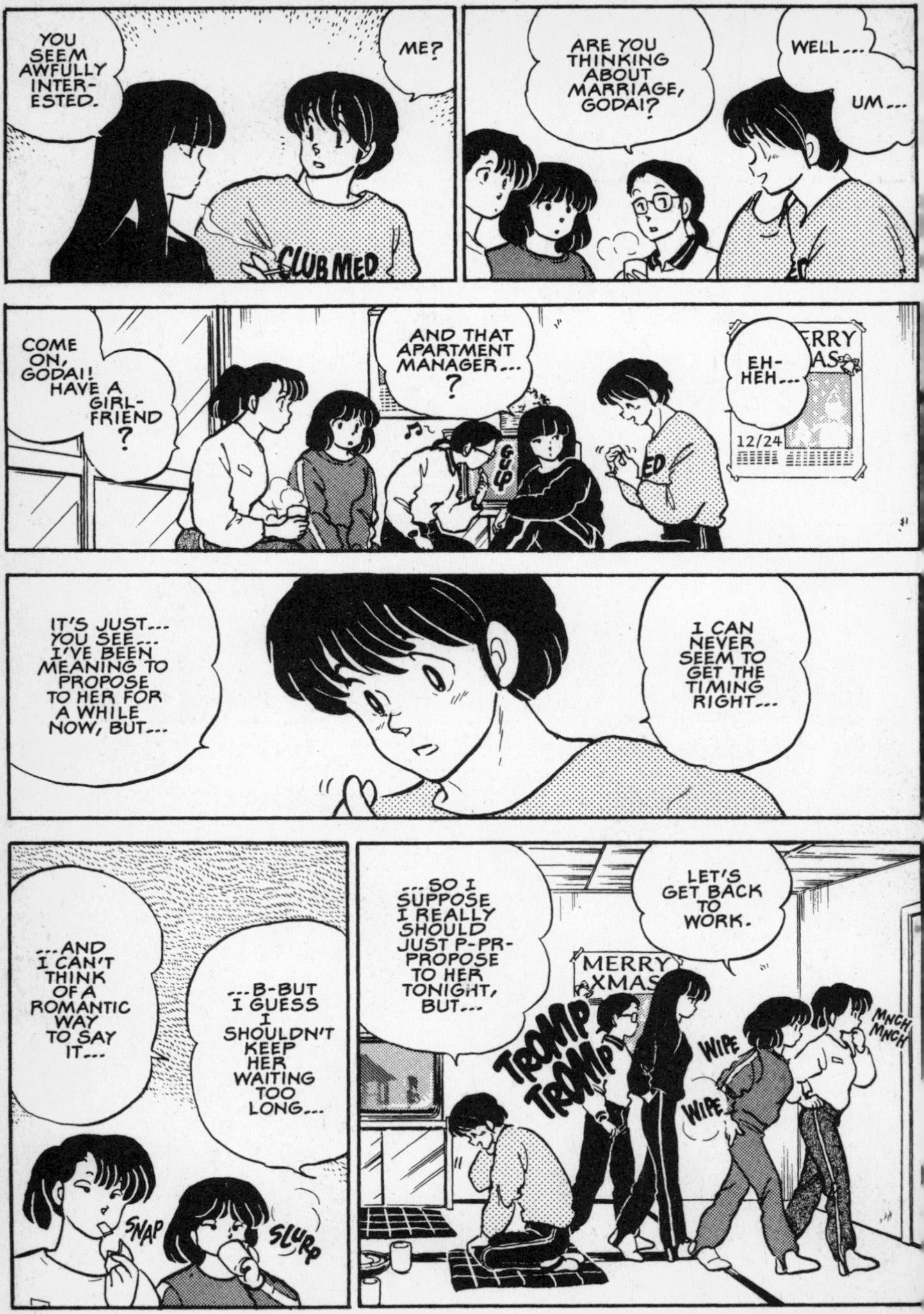
YOU SEEM AWFULLY INTER-ESTED.
ME?
CLUB MED
ARE YOU THINKING ABOUT MARRIAGE, GODAI?
WELL...
UM...
COME ON, GODAI! HAVE A GIRL-FRIEND ?
AND THAT APARTMENT MANAGER... ?
GULP
EH-HEH...
MERRY XMAS
12/24
IT'S JUST... YOU SEE... I'VE BEEN MEANING TO PROPOSE TO HER FOR A WHILE NOW, BUT...
I CAN NEVER SEEM TO GET THE TIMING RIGHT...
...AND I CAN'T THINK OF A ROMANTIC WAY TO SAY IT...
...B-BUT I GUESS I SHOULDN'T KEEP HER WAITING TOO LONG...
SNAP
SLURP
...SO I SUPPOSE I REALLY SHOULD JUST P-PR-PROPOSE TO HER TONIGHT, BUT...
LET'S GET BACK TO WORK.
MERRY XMAS
TROMP TROMP
WIPE
WIPE
MNCH MNCH

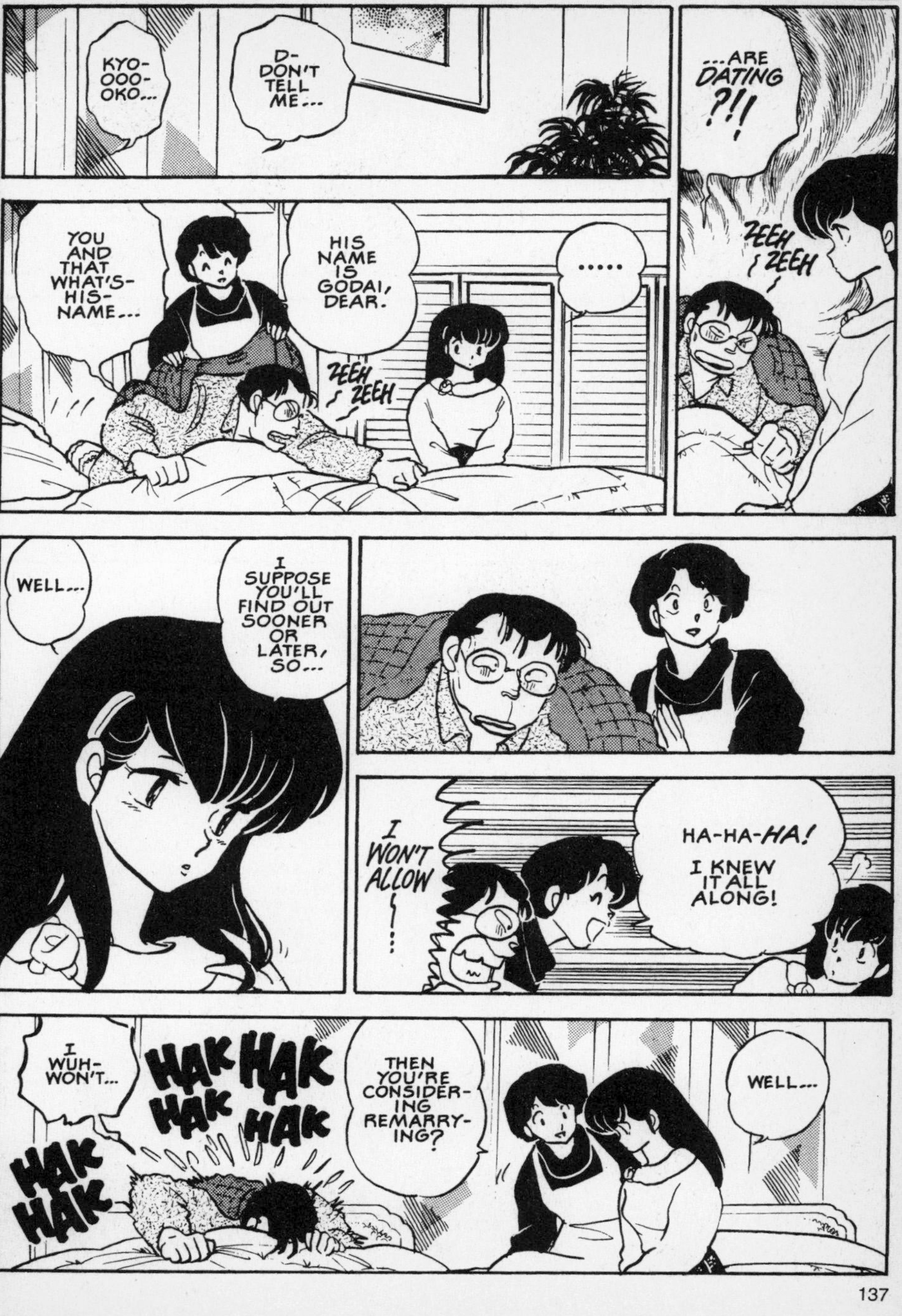
KYO-OOO-OKO...
D-DON'T TELL ME...
YOU AND THAT WHAT'S-HIS-NAME...
HIS NAME IS GODAI, DEAR.
.....
ZEEH ZEEH
...ARE DATING ?!!
ZEEH ZEEH
WELL...
I SUPPOSE YOU'LL FIND OUT SOONER OR LATER, SO...
I WON'T ALLOW...!
HA-HA-HA! I KNEW IT ALL ALONG!
I WUH-WON'T...
HAK HAK HAK HAK HAK HAK HAK HAK
THEN YOU'RE CONSIDERING REMARRYING?
WELL...

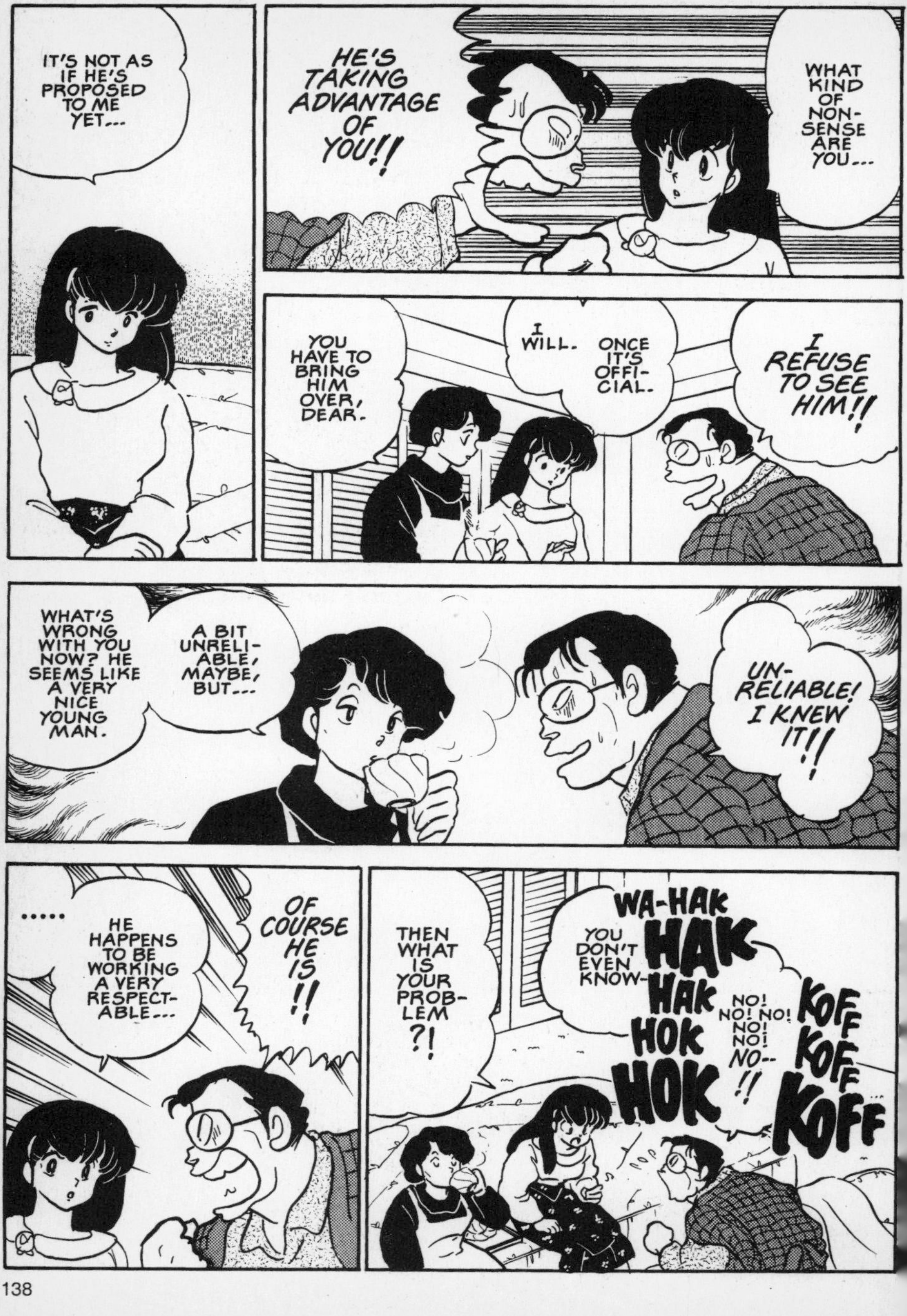

IT'S NOT AS IF HE'S PROPOSED TO ME YET...
HE'S TAKING ADVANTAGE OF YOU!!
WHAT KIND OF NON-SENSE ARE YOU...
YOU HAVE TO BRING HIM OVER, DEAR.
I WILL. ONCE IT'S OFFI-CIAL.
I REFUSE TO SEE HIM!!
WHAT'S WRONG WITH YOU NOW? HE SEEMS LIKE A VERY NICE YOUNG MAN.
A BIT UNRELI-ABLE, MAYBE, BUT...
UN-RELIABLE! I KNEW IT!!
.....
HE HAPPENS TO BE WORKING A VERY RESPECT-ABLE...
OF COURSE HE IS!!
THEN WHAT IS YOUR PROB-LEM?!
WA-HAK
YOU DON'T EVEN KNOW-
HAK HAK HOK HOK
NO! NO! NO! NO! NO! NO--!!
KOFF KOFF KOFF...

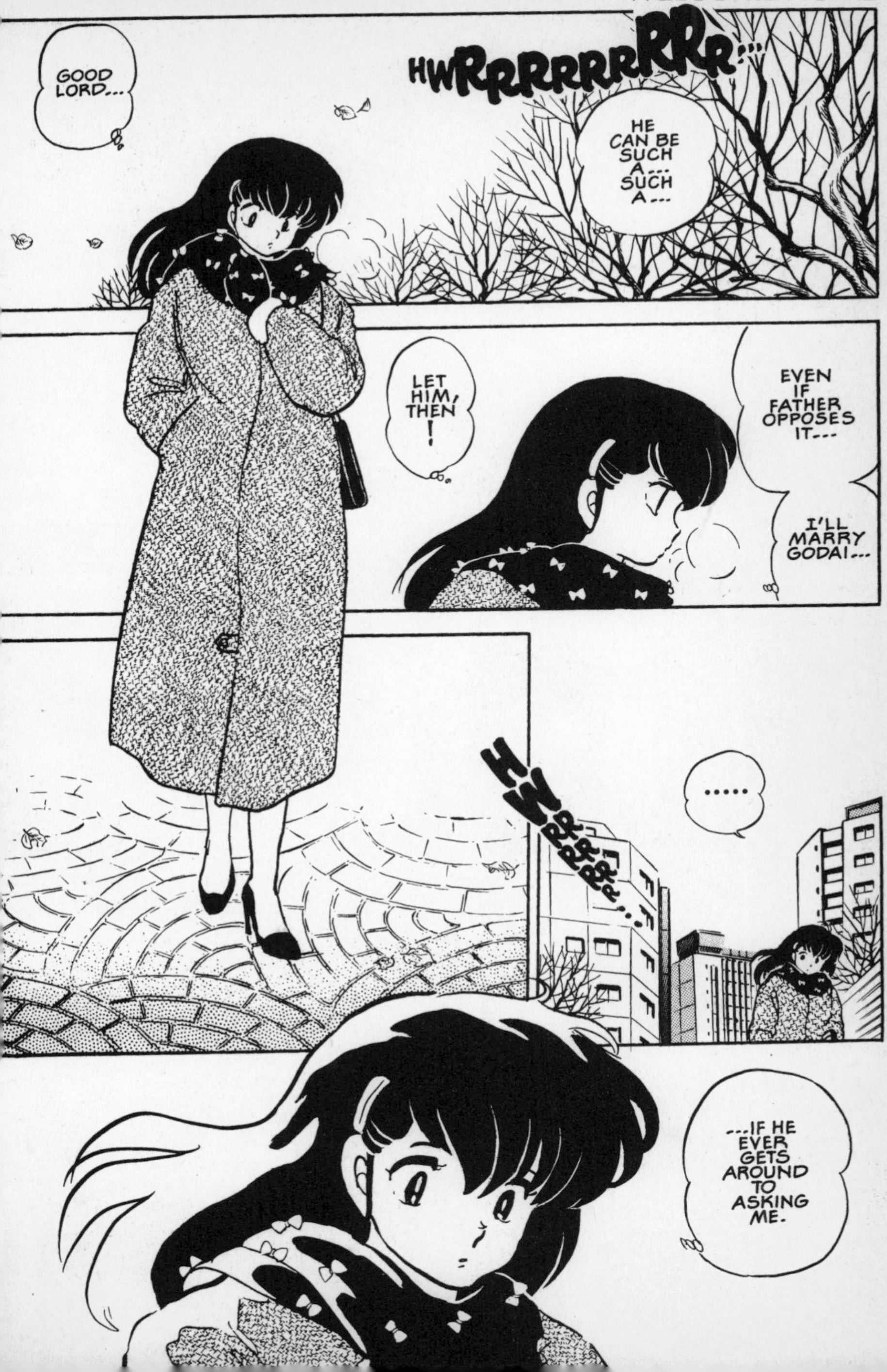
GOOD LORD...
HWRRRRRRRRR!!!
HE CAN BE SUCH A... SUCH A...
LET HIM, THEN!
EVEN IF FATHER OPPOSES IT...
I'LL MARRY GODAI...
HWRRRRRR!...
......
...IF HE EVER GETS AROUND TO ASKING ME.

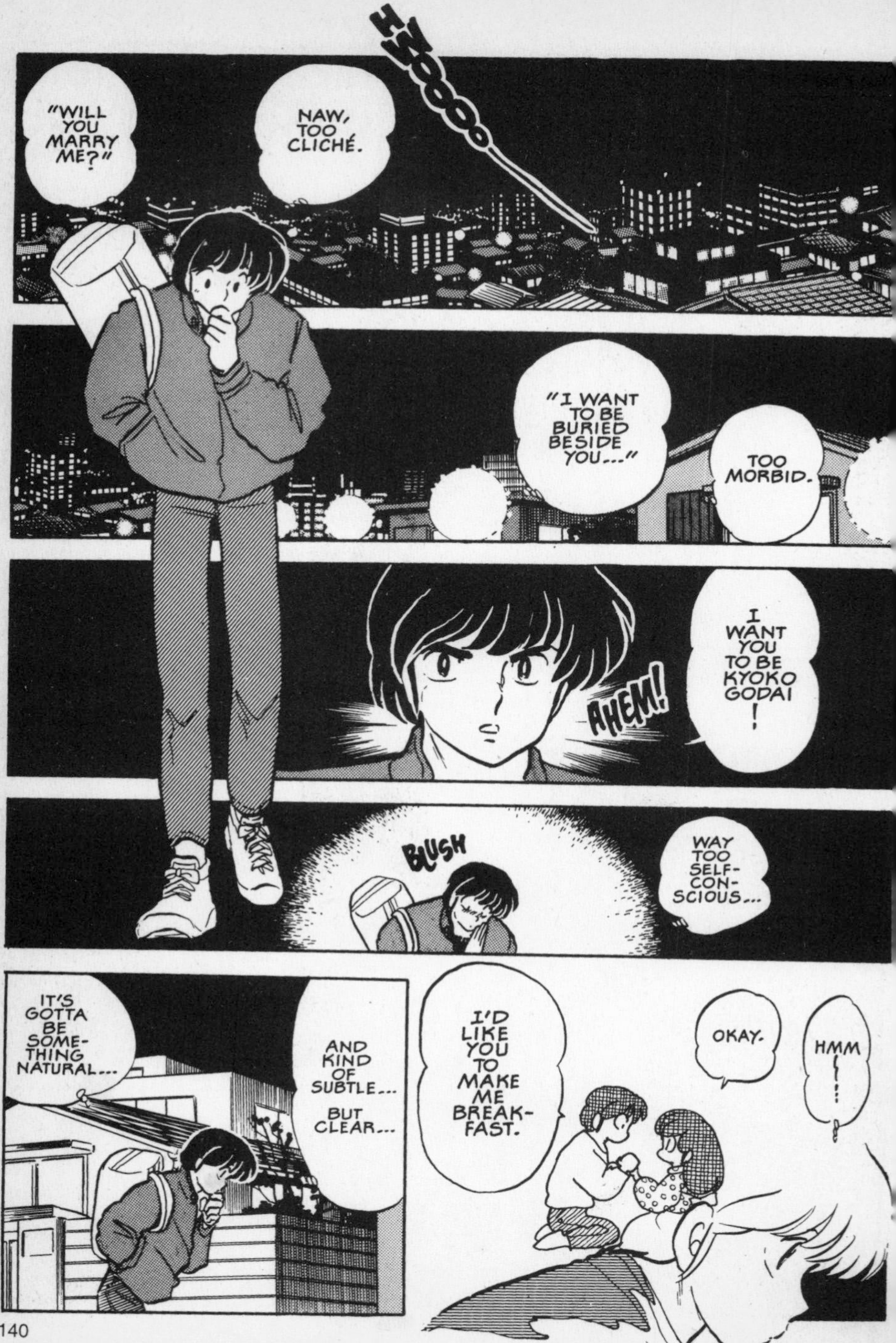
"WILL YOU MARRY ME?"
NAW, TOO CLICHÉ.
HWOOOOO
"I WANT TO BE BURIED BESIDE YOU..."
TOO MORBID.
AHEM!
I WANT YOU TO BE KYOKO GODAI!
BLUSH
WAY TOO SELF-CONSCIOUS...
IT'S GOTTA BE SOMETHING NATURAL...
AND KIND OF SUBTLE... BUT CLEAR...
I'D LIKE YOU TO MAKE ME BREAKFAST.
OKAY.
HMM!!

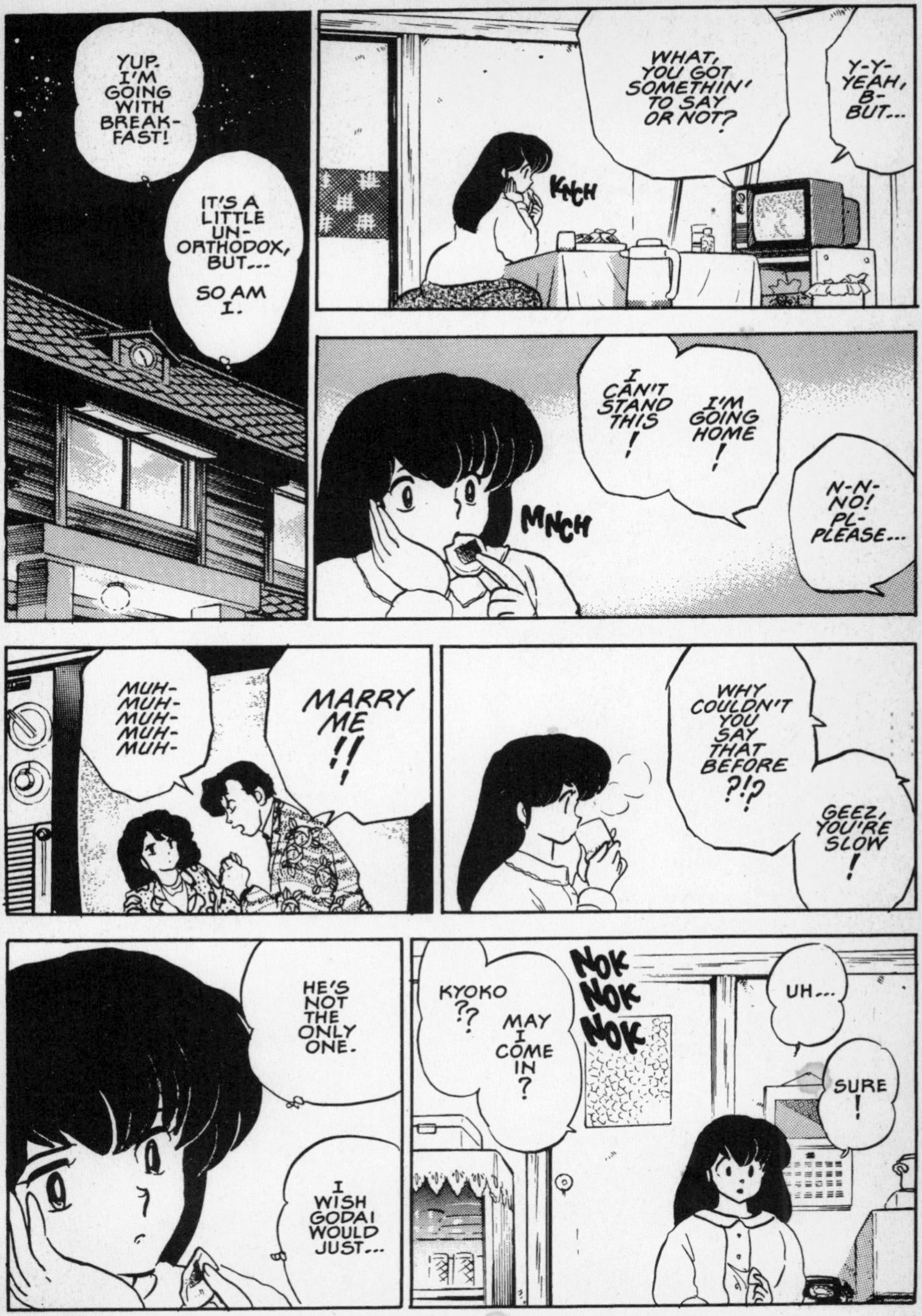
YUP. I'M GOING WITH BREAK-FAST!
IT'S A LITTLE UN-ORTHODOX, BUT... SO AM I.
KNCH
WHAT, YOU GOT SOMETHIN' TO SAY OR NOT?
Y-Y-YEAH, B-BUT...
MNCH
I CAN'T STAND THIS! I'M GOING HOME!
N-N-NO! PL-PLEASE...
MUH-MUH-MUH-MUH-MUH-
MARRY ME!!
WHY COULDN'T YOU SAY THAT BEFORE?!?
GEEZ, YOU'RE SLOW!
HE'S NOT THE ONLY ONE.
I WISH GODAI WOULD JUST...
NOK NOK NOK
KYOKO?? MAY I COME IN?
UH...
SURE!

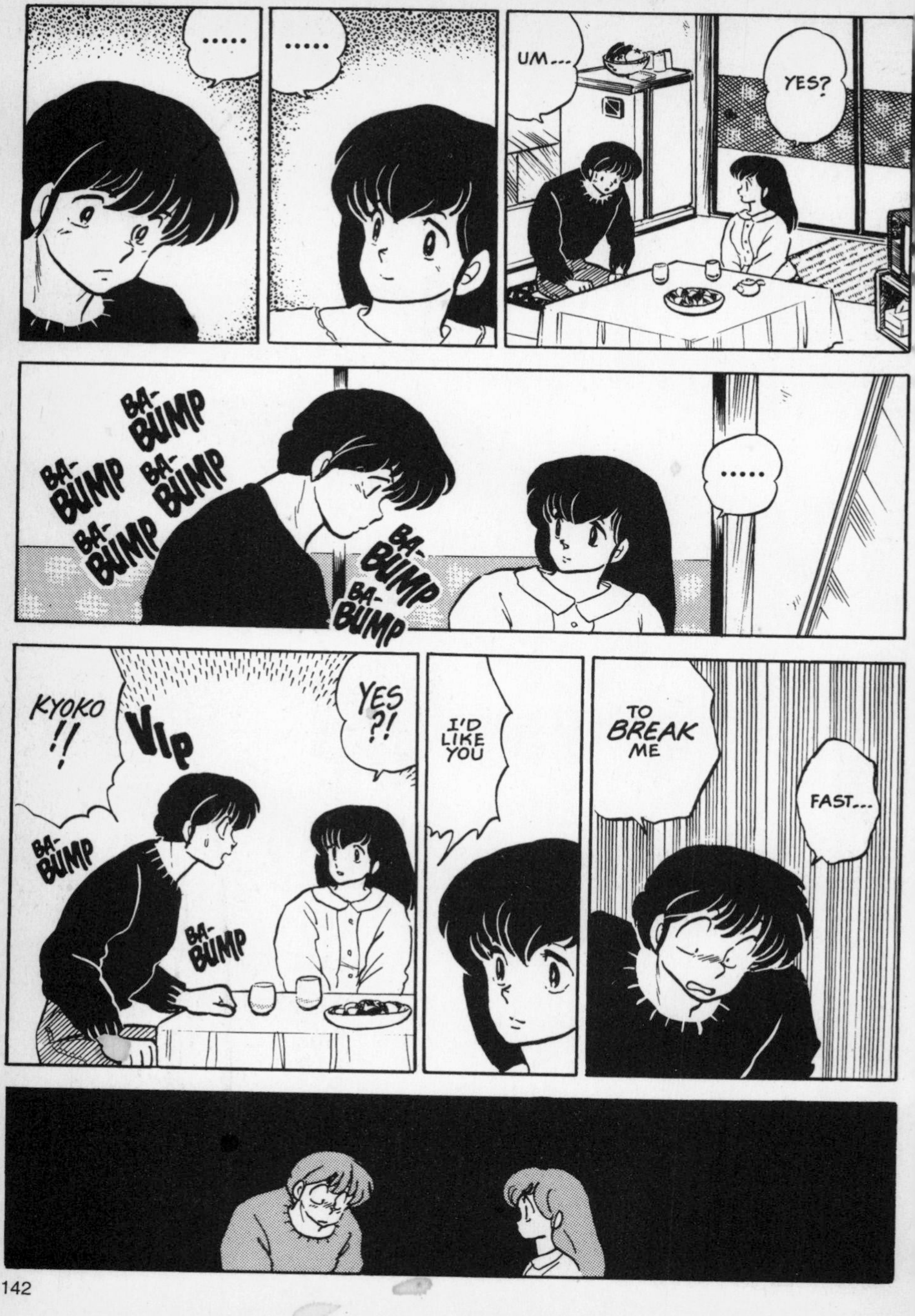

......
......
UM...
YES?
BA-BUMP
BA-BUMP
BA-BUMP
BA-BUMP
BA-BUMP
BA-BUMP
......
KYOKO !!
VIP
YES ?!
BA-BUMP
BA-BUMP
I'D LIKE YOU
TO BREAK ME
FAST...

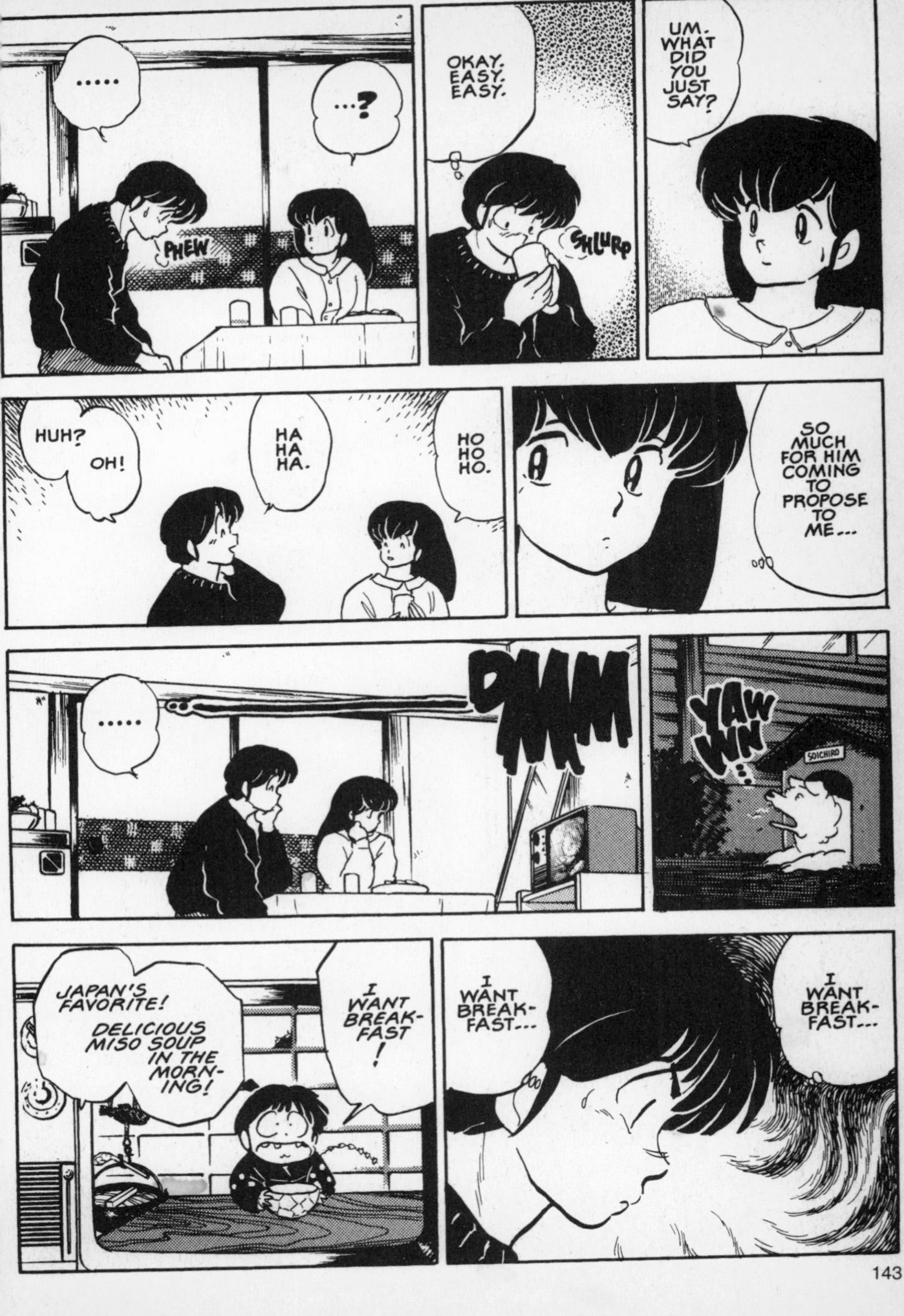
.....
...?
PHEW
OKAY. EASY. EASY.
SHLURP
UM. WHAT DID YOU JUST SAY?
HUH? OH!
HA HA HA.
HO HO HO.
SO MUCH FOR HIM COMING TO PROPOSE TO ME...
.....
DMM
YAWWN
SOICHIRO
JAPAN'S FAVORITE! DELICIOUS MISO SOUP IN THE MORNING!
I WANT BREAKFAST!
I WANT BREAK-FAST...
I WANT BREAK-FAST...

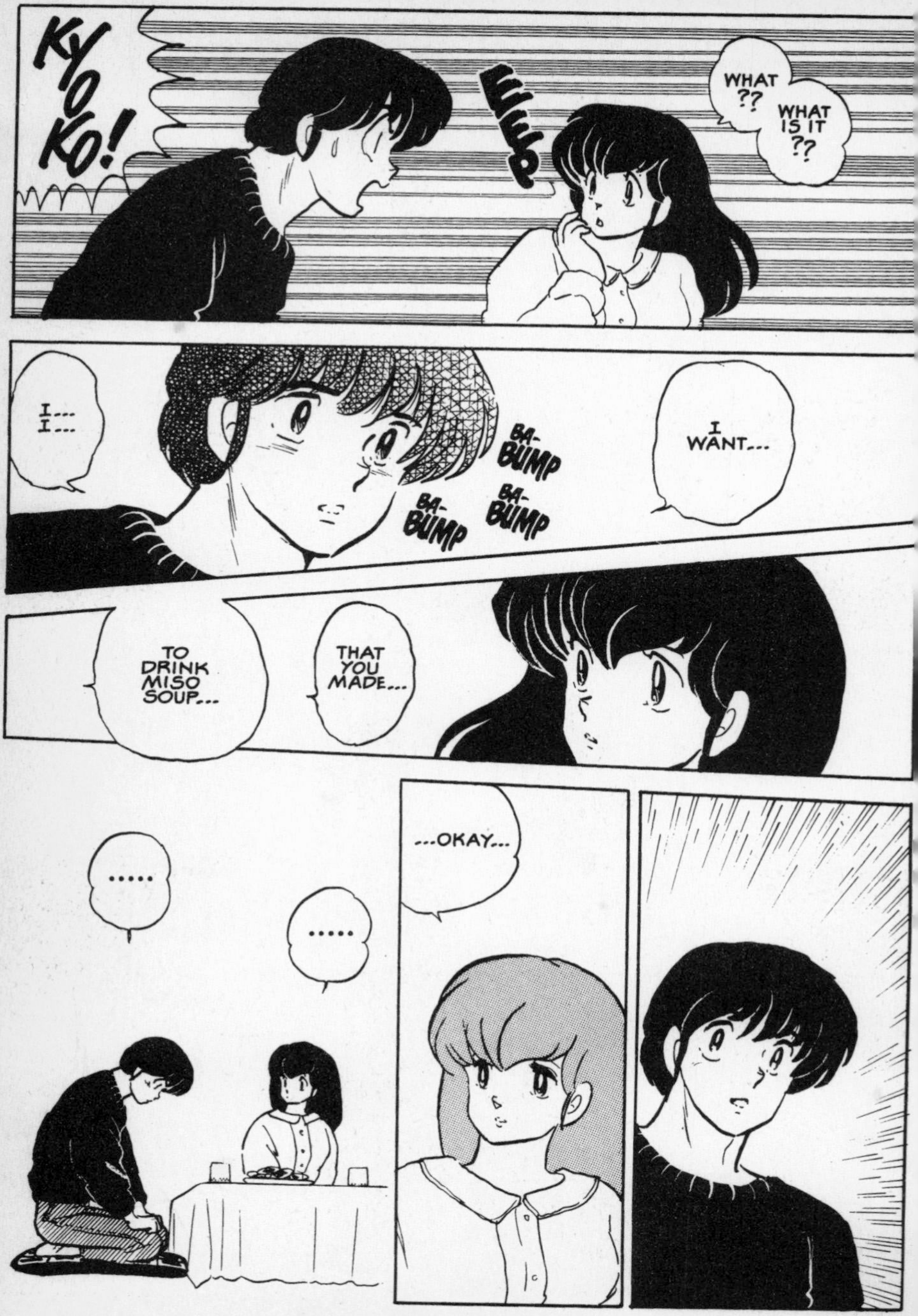
KYOKO!
EEEP
WHAT ??
WHAT IS IT ??
I... I...
BA-BUMP
BA-BUMP
BA-BUMP
I WANT...
TO DRINK MISO SOUP...
THAT YOU MADE...
......
......
...OKAY...

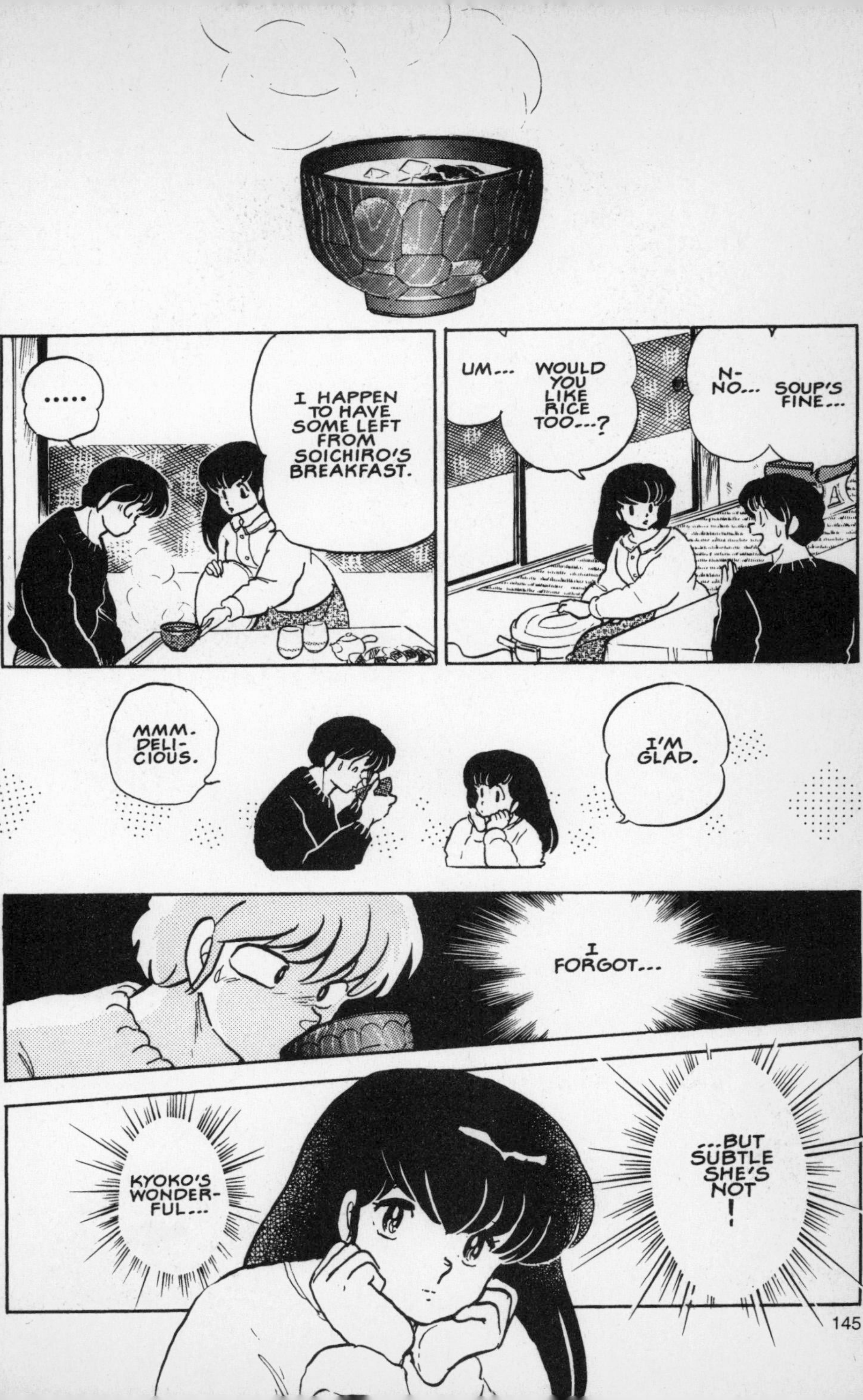
......
I HAPPEN TO HAVE SOME LEFT FROM SOICHIRO'S BREAKFAST.
UM... WOULD YOU LIKE RICE TOO...?
N- NO... SOUP'S FINE...
MMM- DELI- CIOUS.
I'M GLAD.
I FORGOT...
KYOKO'S WONDER- FUL...
...BUT SUBTLE SHE'S NOT !

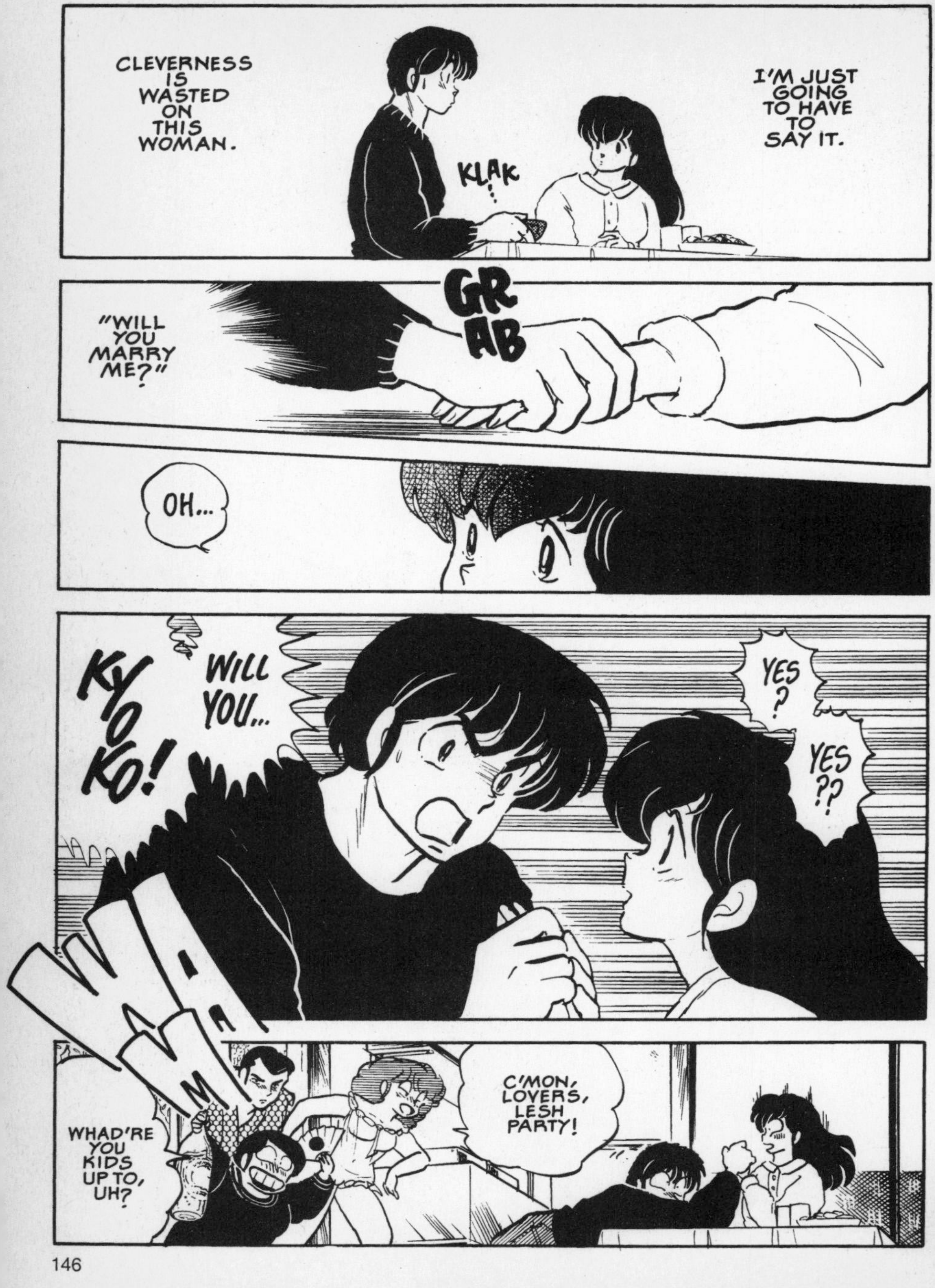
CLEVERNESS IS WASTED ON THIS WOMAN.
KLAK
I'M JUST GOING TO HAVE TO SAY IT.
"WILL YOU MARRY ME?"
GRAB
OH...
KYOKO!
WILL YOU...
YES?
YES??
WHA
WHAD'RE YOU KIDS UP TO, UH?
C'MON, LOVERS, LESH PARTY!

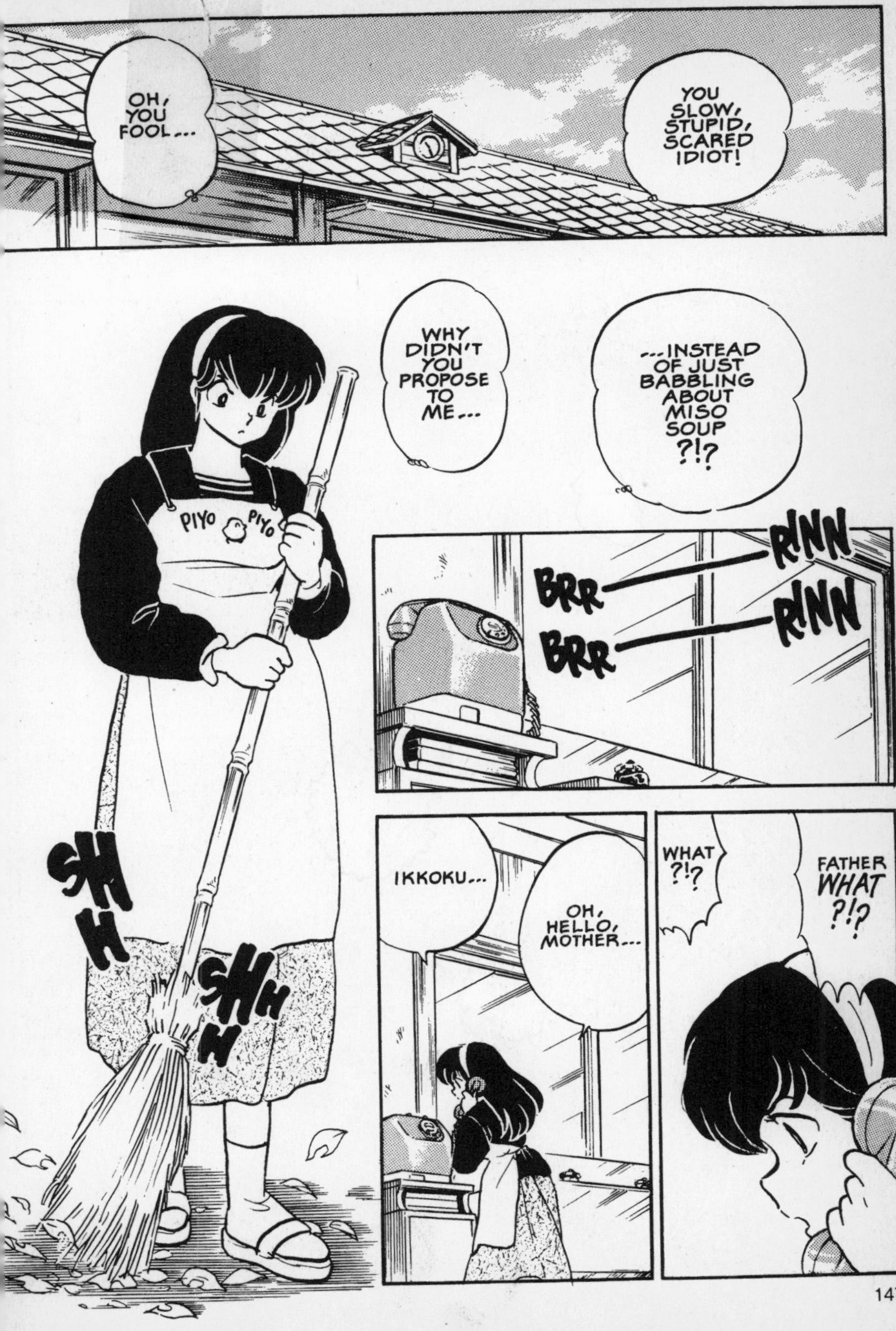
OH, YOU FOOL...
YOU SLOW, STUPID, SCARED IDIOT!
WHY DIDN'T YOU PROPOSE TO ME...
...INSTEAD OF JUST BABBLING ABOUT MISO SOUP ?!?
PIYO PIYO
SHH H
SHH H
BRR RINN
BRR RINN
IKKOKU...
OH, HELLO, MOTHER...
WHAT ?!?
FATHER WHAT ?!?

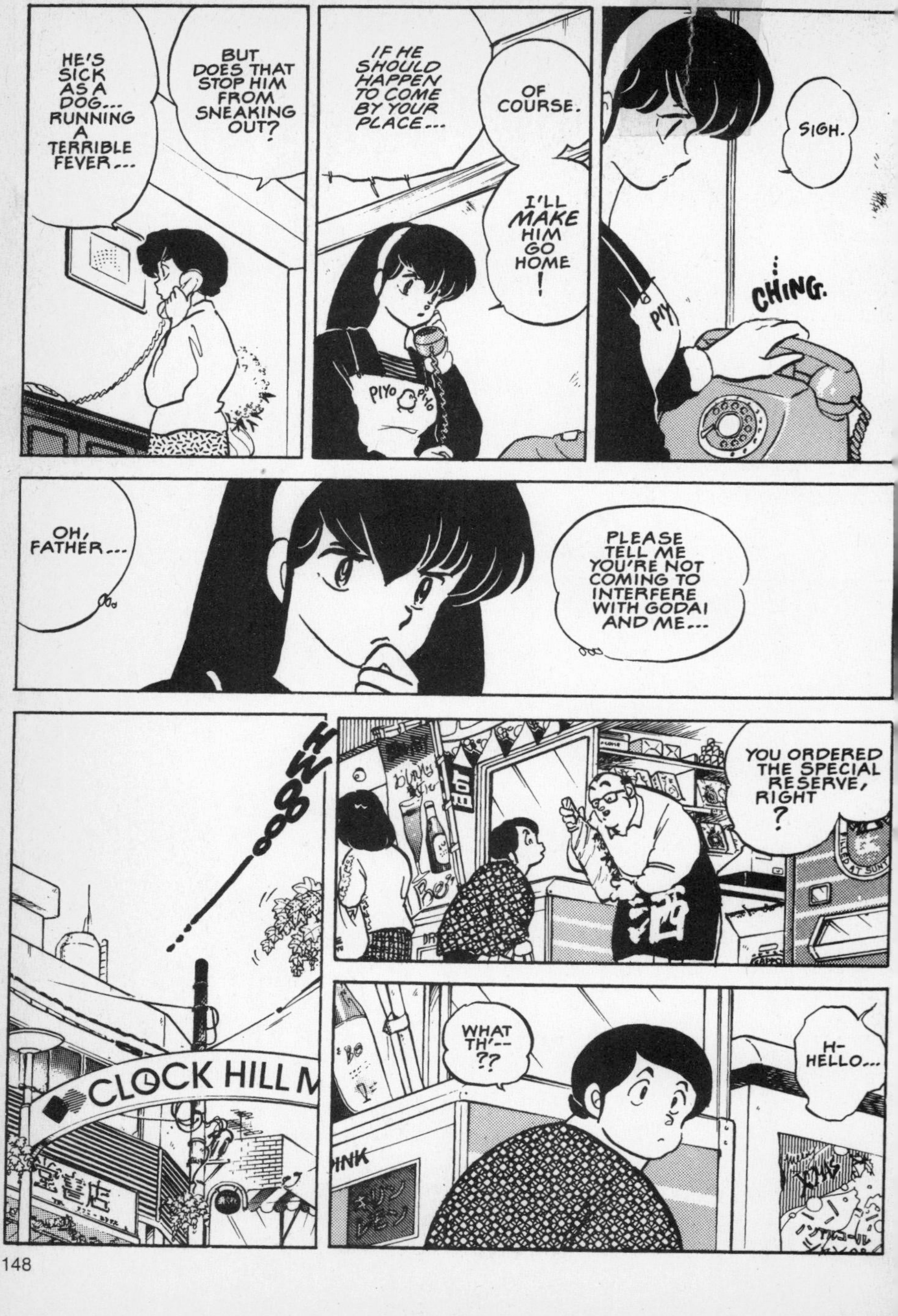
HE'S SICK AS A DOG... RUNNING A TERRIBLE FEVER...
BUT DOES THAT STOP HIM FROM SNEAKING OUT?
IF HE SHOULD HAPPEN TO COME BY YOUR PLACE...
OF COURSE.
I'LL MAKE HIM GO HOME!
SIGH.
CHING.
OH, FATHER...
PLEASE TELL ME YOU'RE NOT COMING TO INTERFERE WITH GODAI AND ME...
HWOOO---...
CLOCK HILL M
YOU ORDERED THE SPECIAL RESERVE, RIGHT?
WHAT TH'-- ??
H-HELLO...

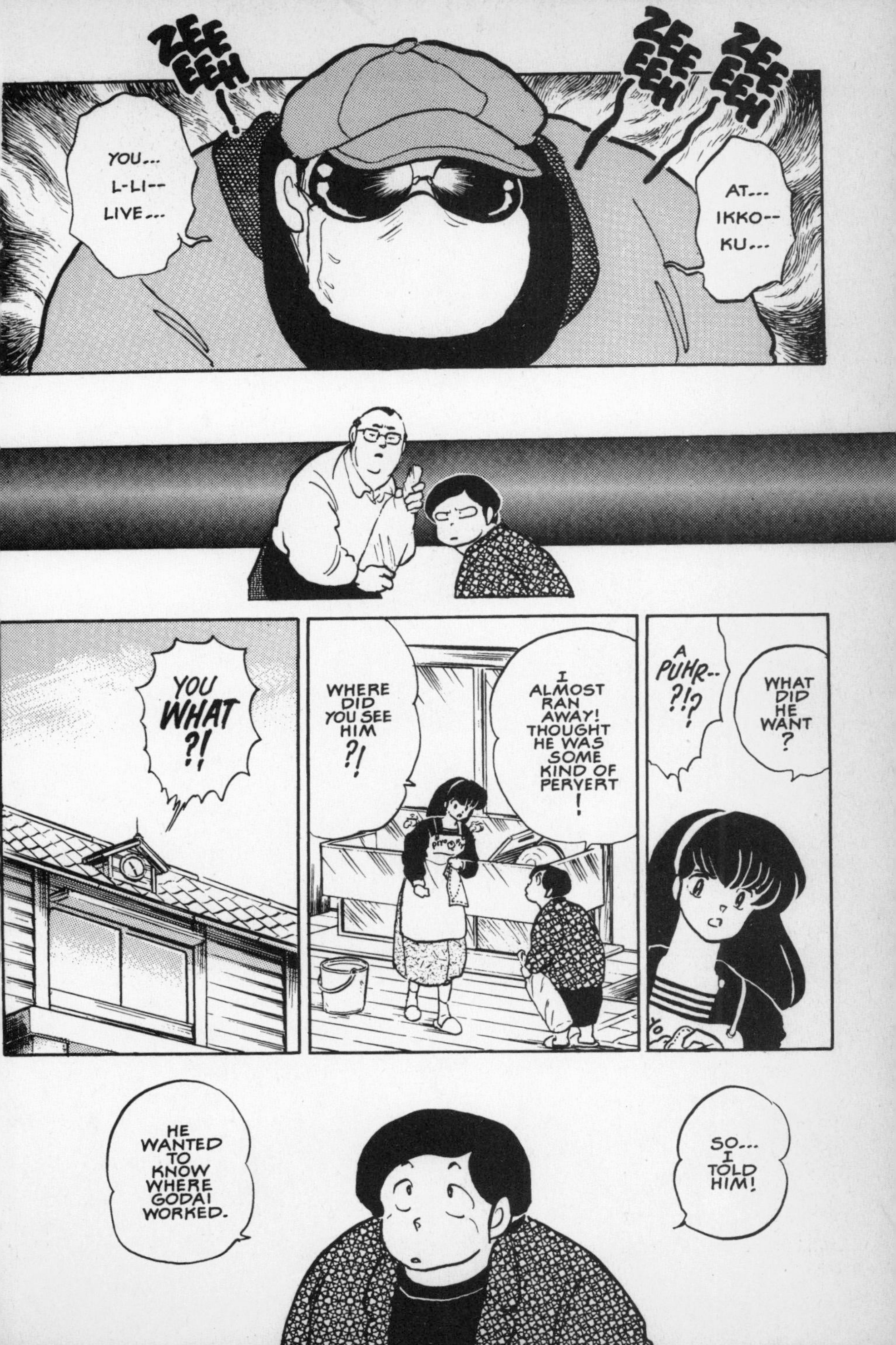
ZEE EEH!
YOU... L-LI-- LIVE...
ZEE EEH
ZEE EEH
AT... IKKO-- KU...
YOU WHAT ?!
WHERE DID YOU SEE HIM ?!
I ALMOST RAN AWAY! THOUGHT HE WAS SOME KIND OF PERVERT!
A PUHR-- ?!?
WHAT DID HE WANT?
HE WANTED TO KNOW WHERE GODAI WORKED.
SO... I TOLD HIM!

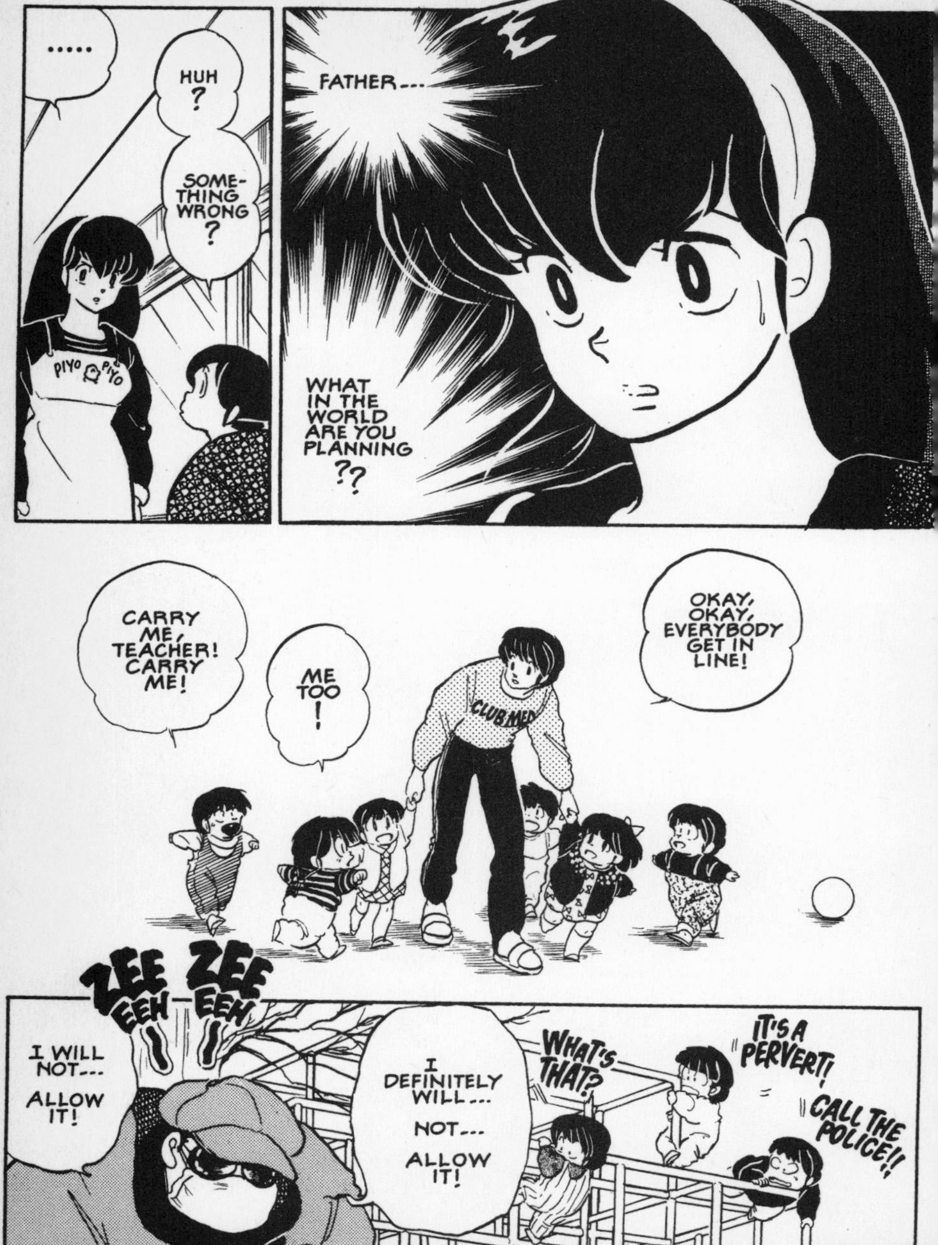

......
HUH?
SOMETHING WRONG?
FATHER...
WHAT IN THE WORLD ARE YOU PLANNING??
CARRY ME, TEACHER! CARRY ME!
ME TOO!
OKAY, OKAY, EVERYBODY GET IN LINE!
ZEE EEH!
ZEE EEH!
I WILL NOT... ALLOW IT!
I DEFINITELY WILL... NOT... ALLOW IT!
WHAT'S THAT?
IT'S A PERVERT!
CALL THE POLICE!!

PART EIGHT
PROMISES

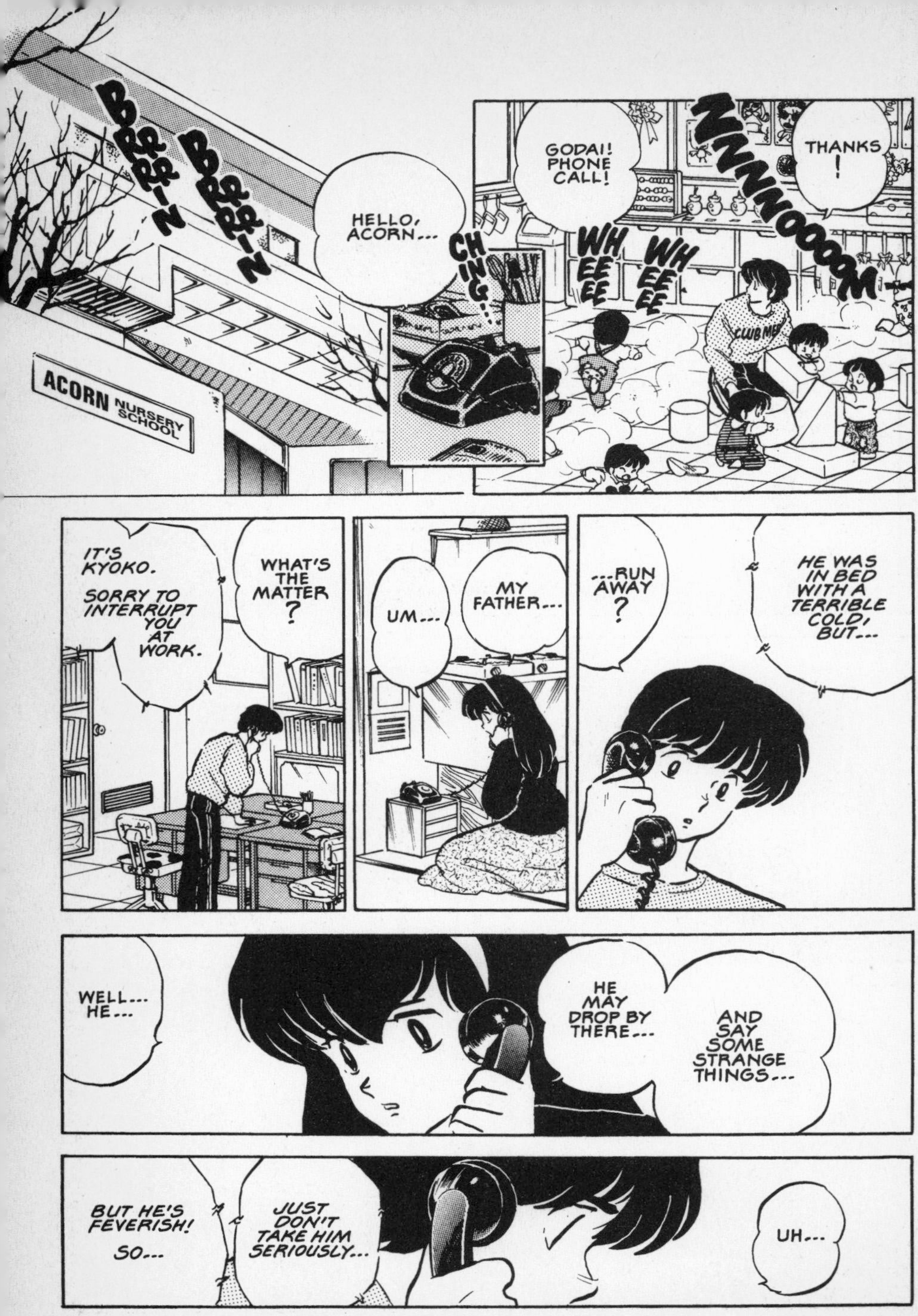
BRRR-RIN
BRRR-RIN
ACORN NURSERY SCHOOL
HELLO, ACORN...
CHING...
GODAI! PHONE CALL!
ZNNNOOOOM
THANKS!
WHEE
WHEE
CLUB MEN
IT'S KYOKO.
SORRY TO INTERRUPT YOU AT WORK.
WHAT'S THE MATTER?
UM...
MY FATHER...
...RUN AWAY?
HE WAS IN BED WITH A TERRIBLE COLD, BUT...
WELL... HE...
HE MAY DROP BY THERE...
AND SAY SOME STRANGE THINGS...
BUT HE'S FEVERISH! SO...
JUST DON'T TAKE HIM SERIOUSLY...
UH...

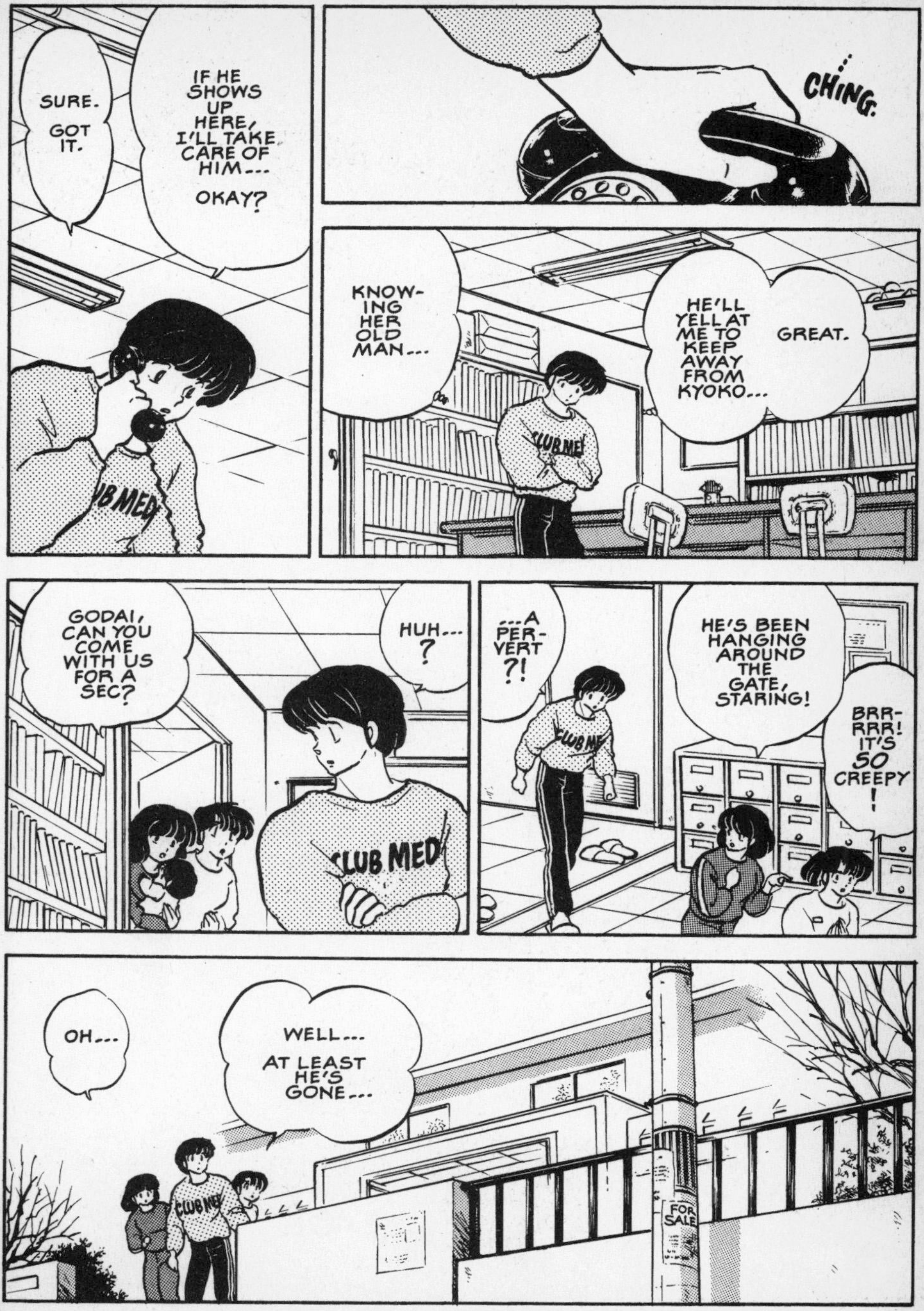
SURE. GOT IT.
IF HE SHOWS UP HERE, I'LL TAKE CARE OF HIM... OKAY?
CHING.
KNOWING HER OLD MAN...
HE'LL YELL AT ME TO KEEP AWAY FROM KYOKO...
GREAT.
GODAI, CAN YOU COME WITH US FOR A SEC?
HUH...?
...A PERVERT?!
HE'S BEEN HANGING AROUND THE GATE, STARING!
BRRRRR! IT'S SO CREEPY!
OH...
WELL... AT LEAST HE'S GONE...
FOR SALE

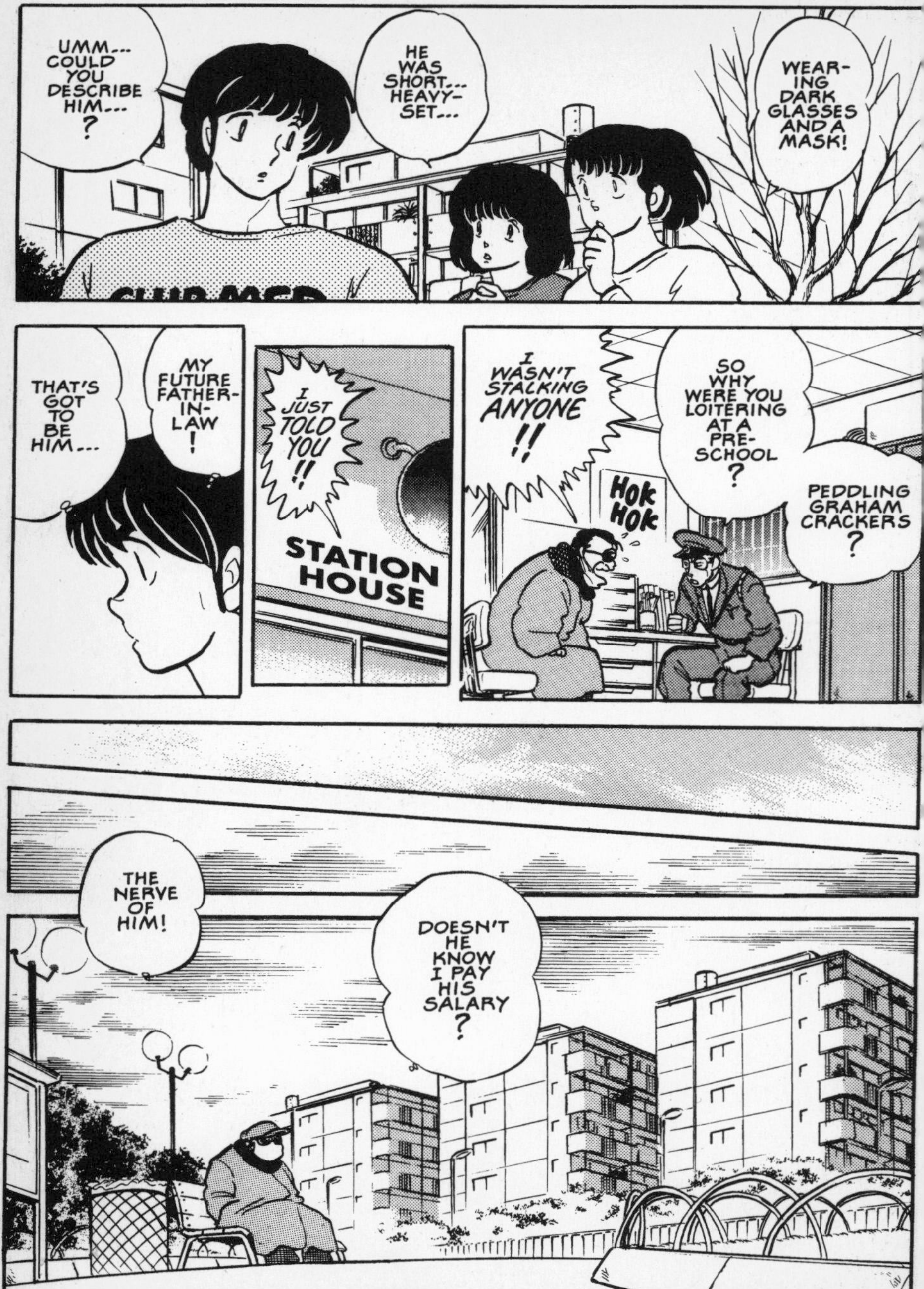
UMM... COULD YOU DESCRIBE HIM...?
HE WAS SHORT... HEAVY-SET...
WEAR-ING DARK GLASSES AND A MASK!
THAT'S GOT TO BE HIM...
MY FUTURE FATHER-IN-LAW!
I JUST TOLD YOU!!
STATION HOUSE
I WASN'T STALKING ANYONE!!
SO WHY WERE YOU LOITERING AT A PRE-SCHOOL?
HOK HOK
PEDDLING GRAHAM CRACKERS?
THE NERVE OF HIM!
DOESN'T HE KNOW I PAY HIS SALARY?

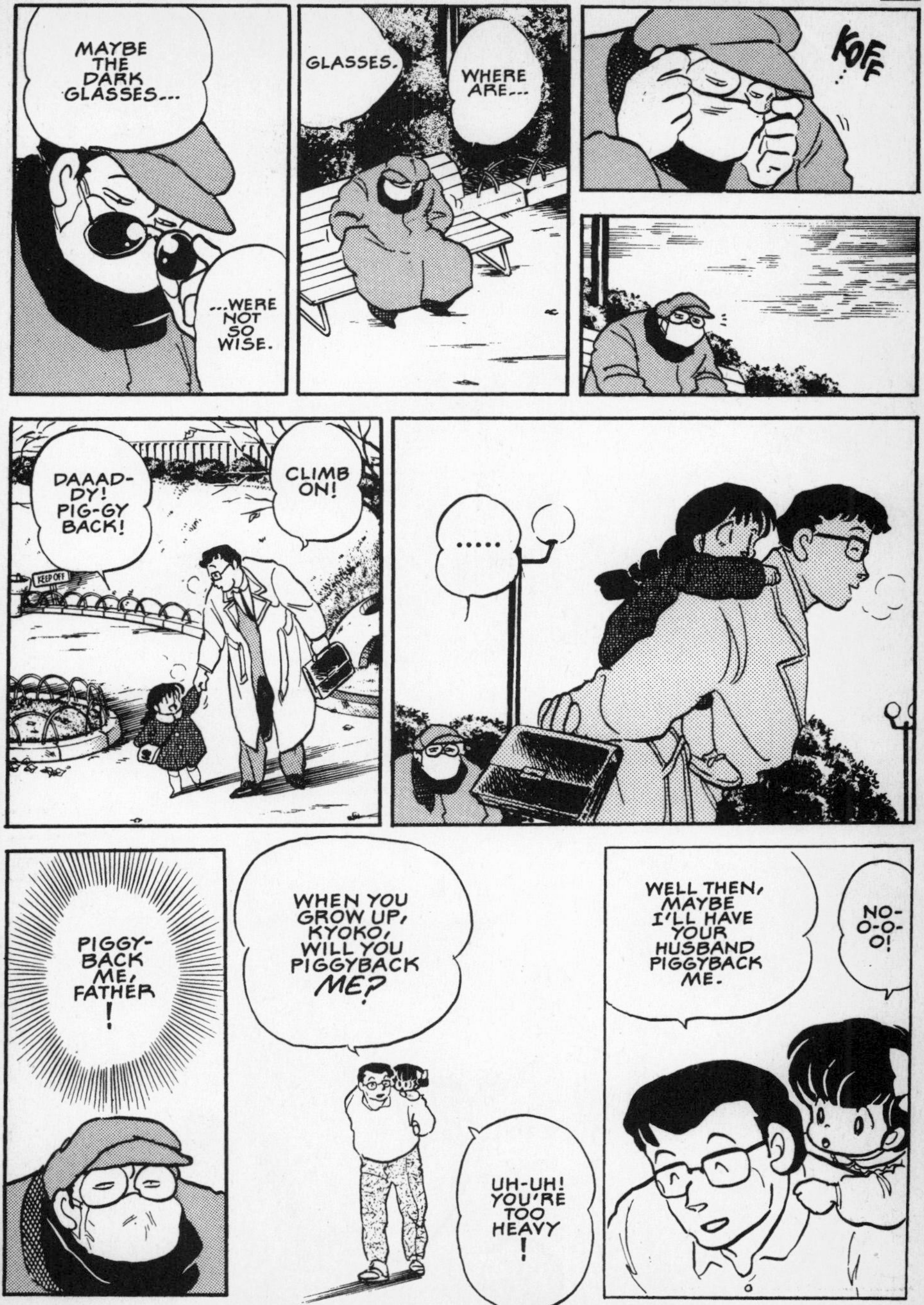
MAYBE THE DARK GLASSES...
...WERE NOT SO WISE.
WHERE ARE...
GLASSES.
KOFF
DAAAD-DY! PIG-GY BACK!
KEEP OFF
CLIMB ON!
.....
PIGGY-BACK ME, FATHER!
WHEN YOU GROW UP, KYOKO, WILL YOU PIGGYBACK ME?
UH-UH! YOU'RE TOO HEAVY!
WELL THEN, MAYBE I'LL HAVE YOUR HUSBAND PIGGYBACK ME.
NO-O-O-O!

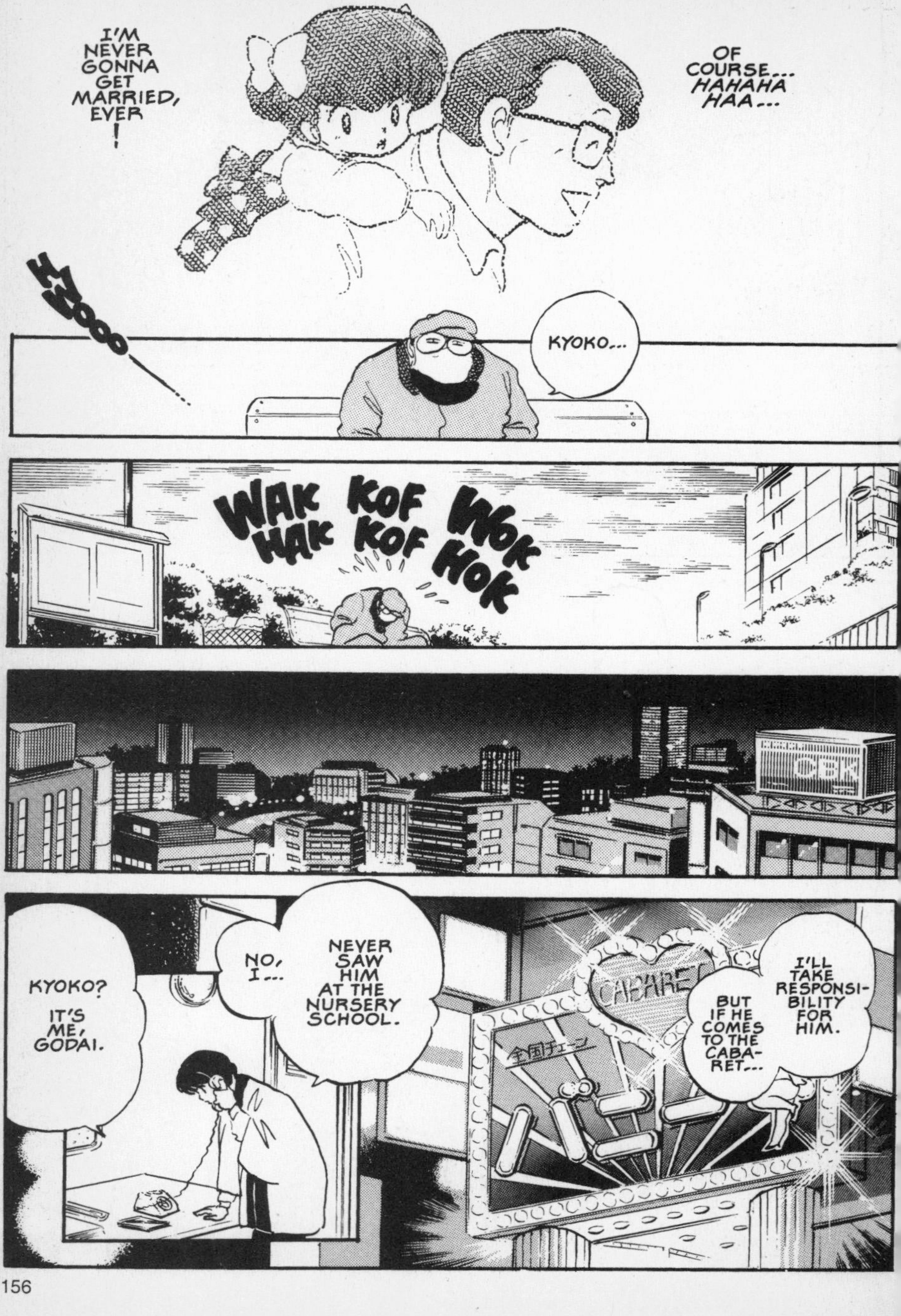

I'M NEVER GONNA GET MARRIED, EVER!
OF COURSE... HAHAHA HAA...
HYUOOO...
KYOKO...
WAK HAK
KOF KOF
WOK HOK
KYOKO? IT'S ME, GODAI.
NO, I...
NEVER SAW HIM AT THE NURSERY SCHOOL.
CABARET
全国チェーン
BUT IF HE COMES TO THE CABA-RET...
I'LL TAKE RESPONSI-BILITY FOR HIM.

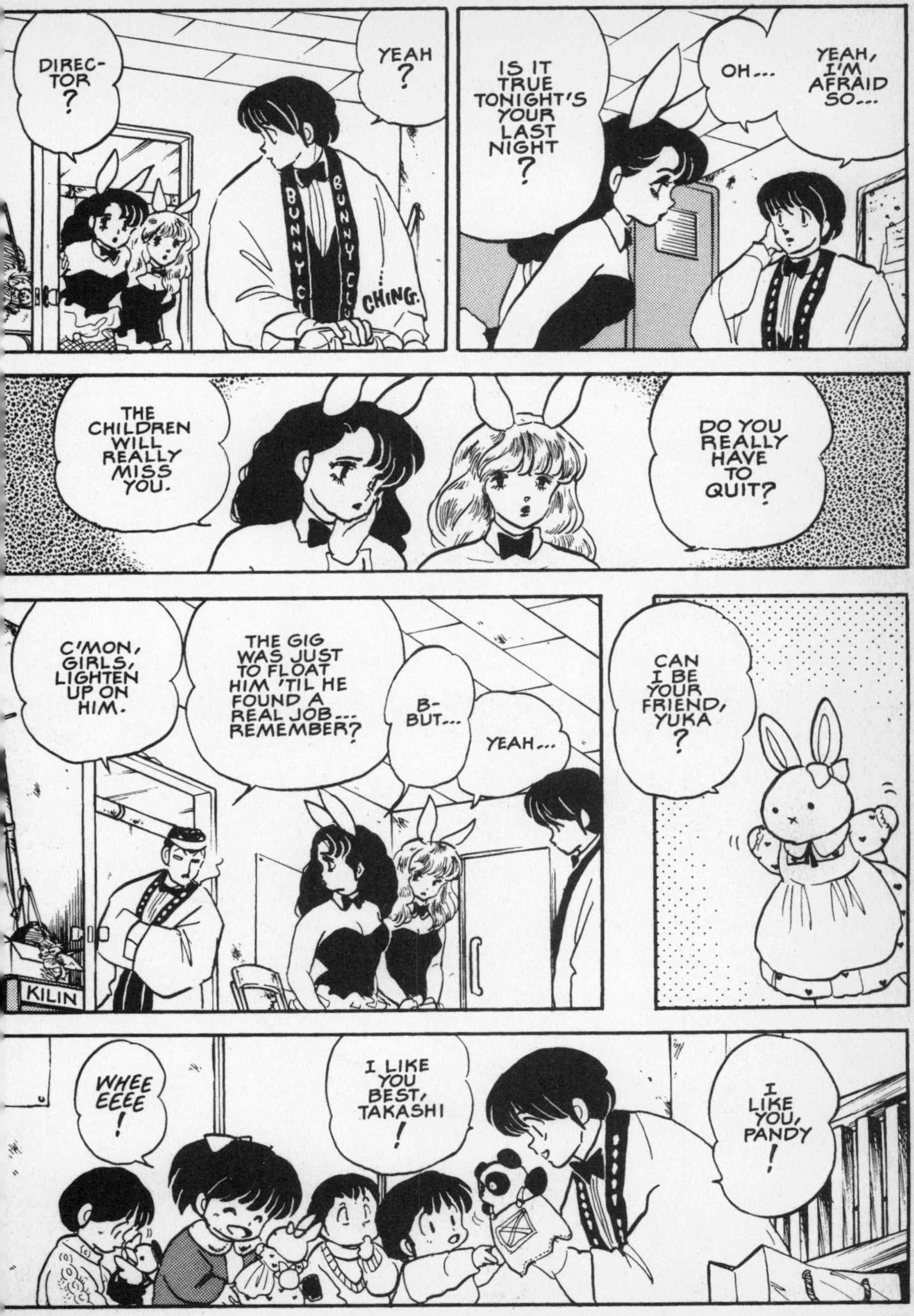
DIRECTOR-TOR?
YEAH?
CHING.
IS IT TRUE TONIGHT'S YOUR LAST NIGHT?
OH...
YEAH, I'M AFRAID SO...
THE CHILDREN WILL REALLY MISS YOU.
DO YOU REALLY HAVE TO QUIT?
C'MON, GIRLS, LIGHTEN UP ON HIM.
THE GIG WAS JUST TO FLOAT HIM 'TIL HE FOUND A REAL JOB... REMEMBER?
B-BUT...
YEAH...
KILIN
CAN I BE YOUR FRIEND, YUKA?
WHEE EEEE!
I LIKE YOU BEST, TAKASHI!
I LIKE YOU, PANDY!

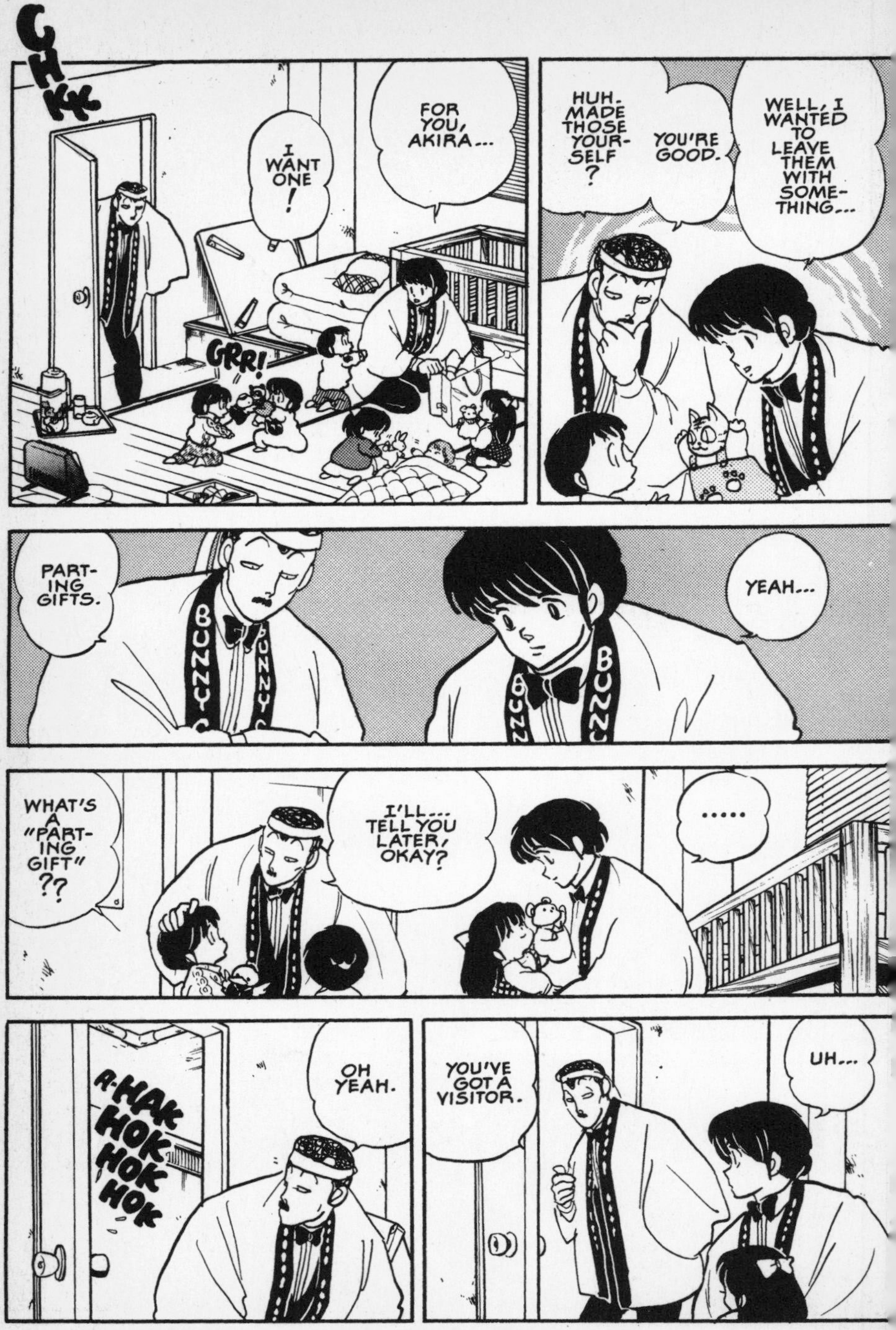

CHKK
I WANT ONE!
FOR YOU, AKIRA...
GRR!
HUH. MADE THOSE YOURSELF?
YOU'RE GOOD.
WELL, I WANTED TO LEAVE THEM WITH SOMETHING...
PARTING GIFTS.
YEAH...
WHAT'S A "PARTING GIFT"??
I'LL... TELL YOU LATER, OKAY?
.....
A-HAK HOK HOK HOK
OH YEAH.
YOU'VE GOT A VISITOR.
UH...

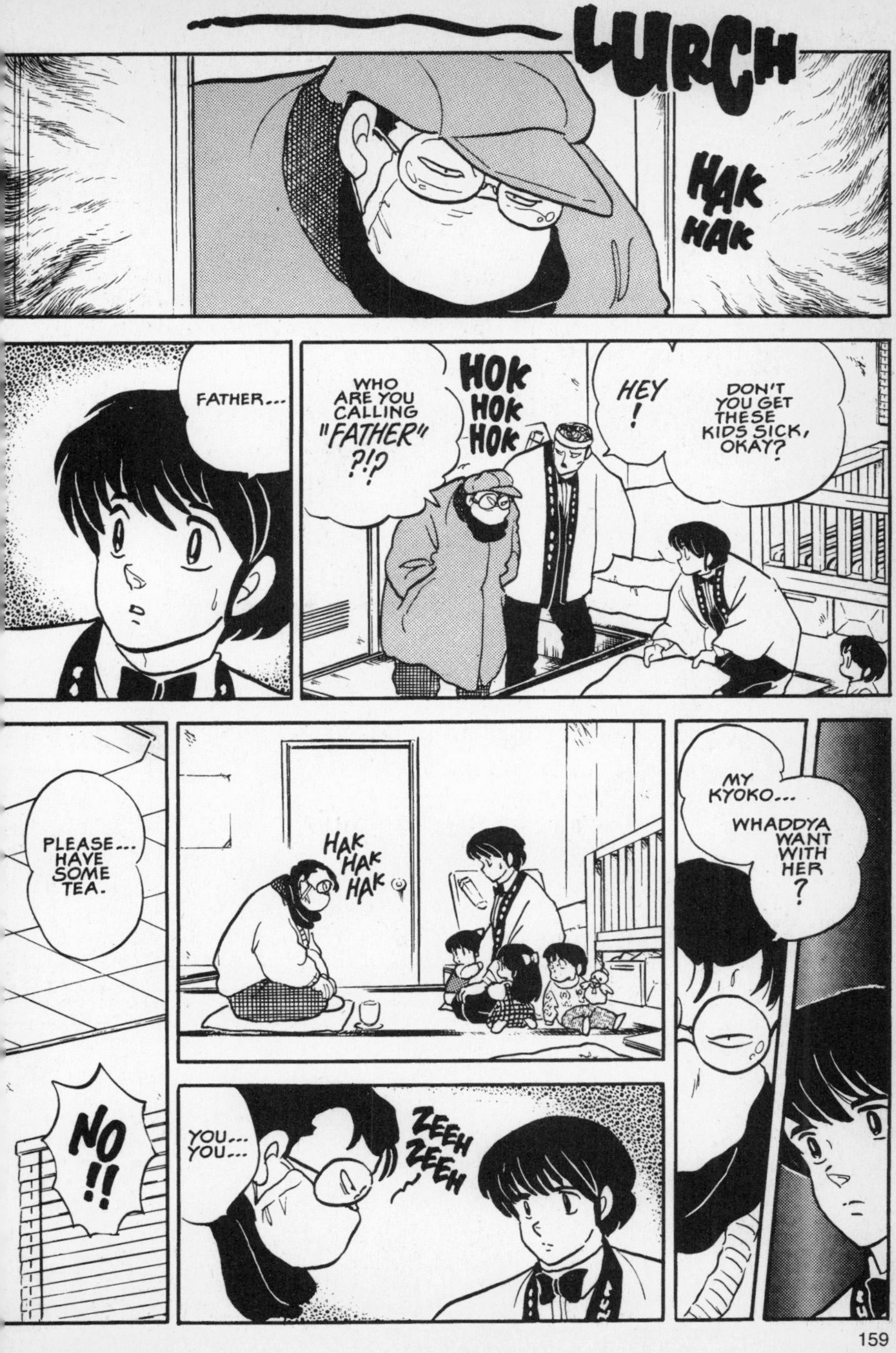
LURCH
HAK HAK
FATHER...
WHO ARE YOU CALLING "FATHER" ?!?
HOK HOK HOK
HEY!
DON'T YOU GET THESE KIDS SICK, OKAY?
PLEASE... HAVE SOME TEA.
HAK HAK HAK
NO!!
YOU... YOU...
ZEEH ZEEH
MY KYOKO...
WHADDYA WANT WITH HER?

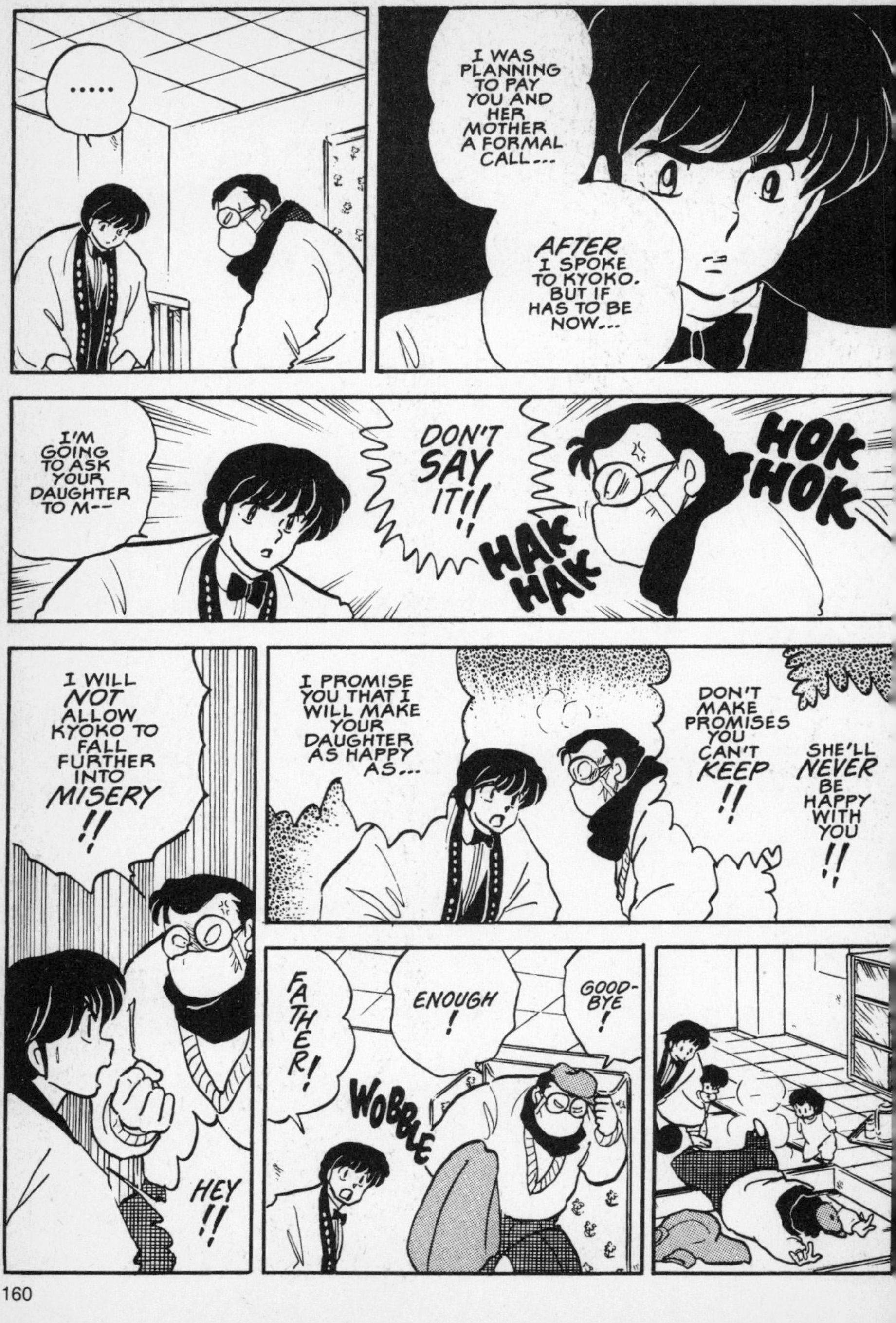

......
I WAS PLANNING TO PAY YOU AND HER MOTHER A FORMAL CALL...
AFTER I SPOKE TO KYOKO. BUT IF HAS TO BE NOW...
I'M GOING TO ASK YOUR DAUGHTER TO M--
DON'T SAY IT!!
HOK HOK
HAK HAK
I WILL NOT ALLOW KYOKO TO FALL FURTHER INTO MISERY!!
HEY!!
I PROMISE YOU THAT I WILL MAKE YOUR DAUGHTER AS HAPPY AS...
DON'T MAKE PROMISES YOU CAN'T KEEP!!
SHE'LL NEVER BE HAPPY WITH YOU!!
FATHER!
ENOUGH!
GOOD-BYE!
WOBBLE

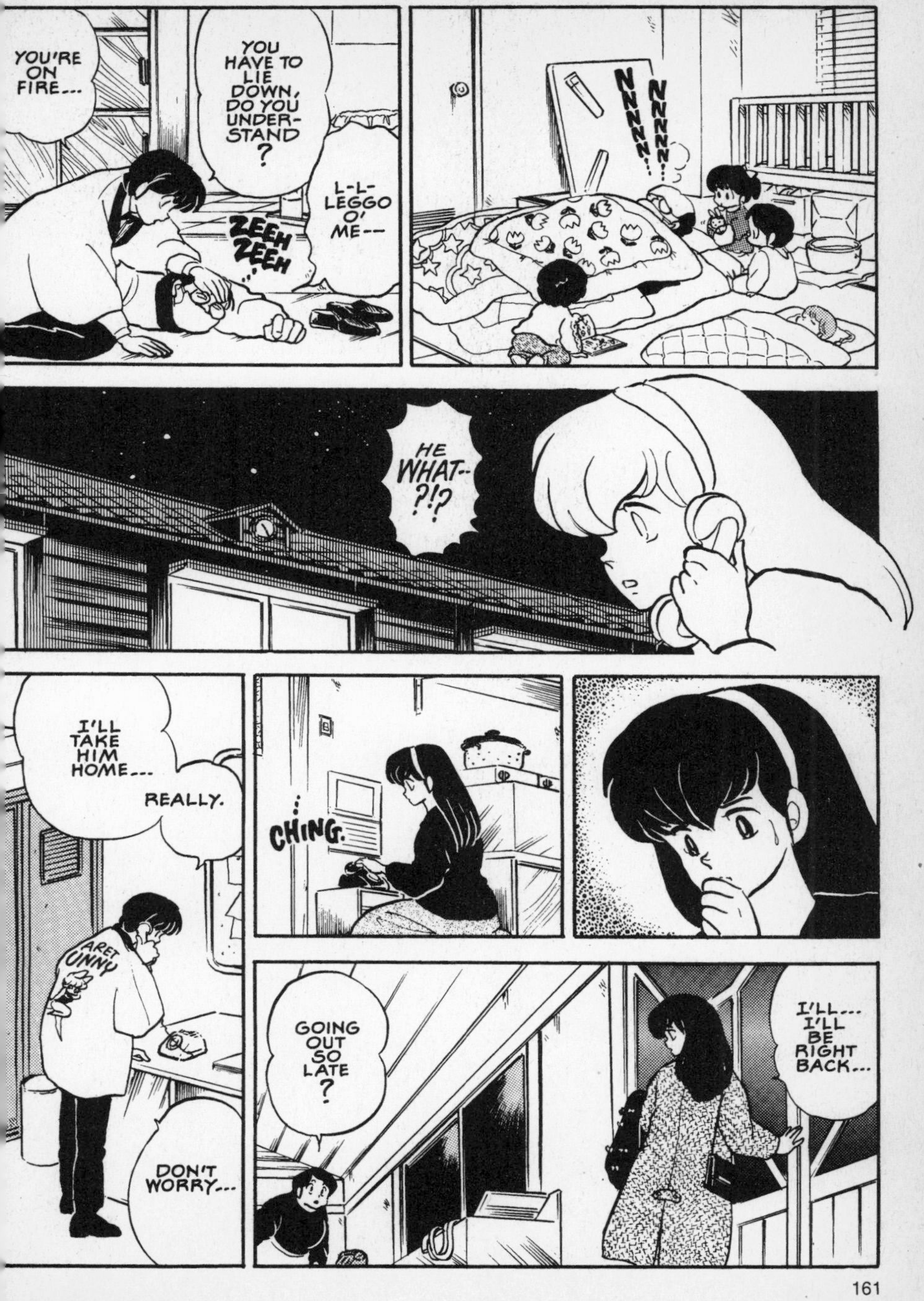
YOU'RE ON FIRE...
YOU HAVE TO LIE DOWN, DO YOU UNDERSTAND?
L-L-LEGGO O' ME--
ZEEH ZEEH
NNNNN!!
NNNNN!!
HE WHAT--?!?
I'LL TAKE HIM HOME...
REALLY.
DON'T WORRY...
CHING.
GOING OUT SO LATE?
I'LL... I'LL BE RIGHT BACK...

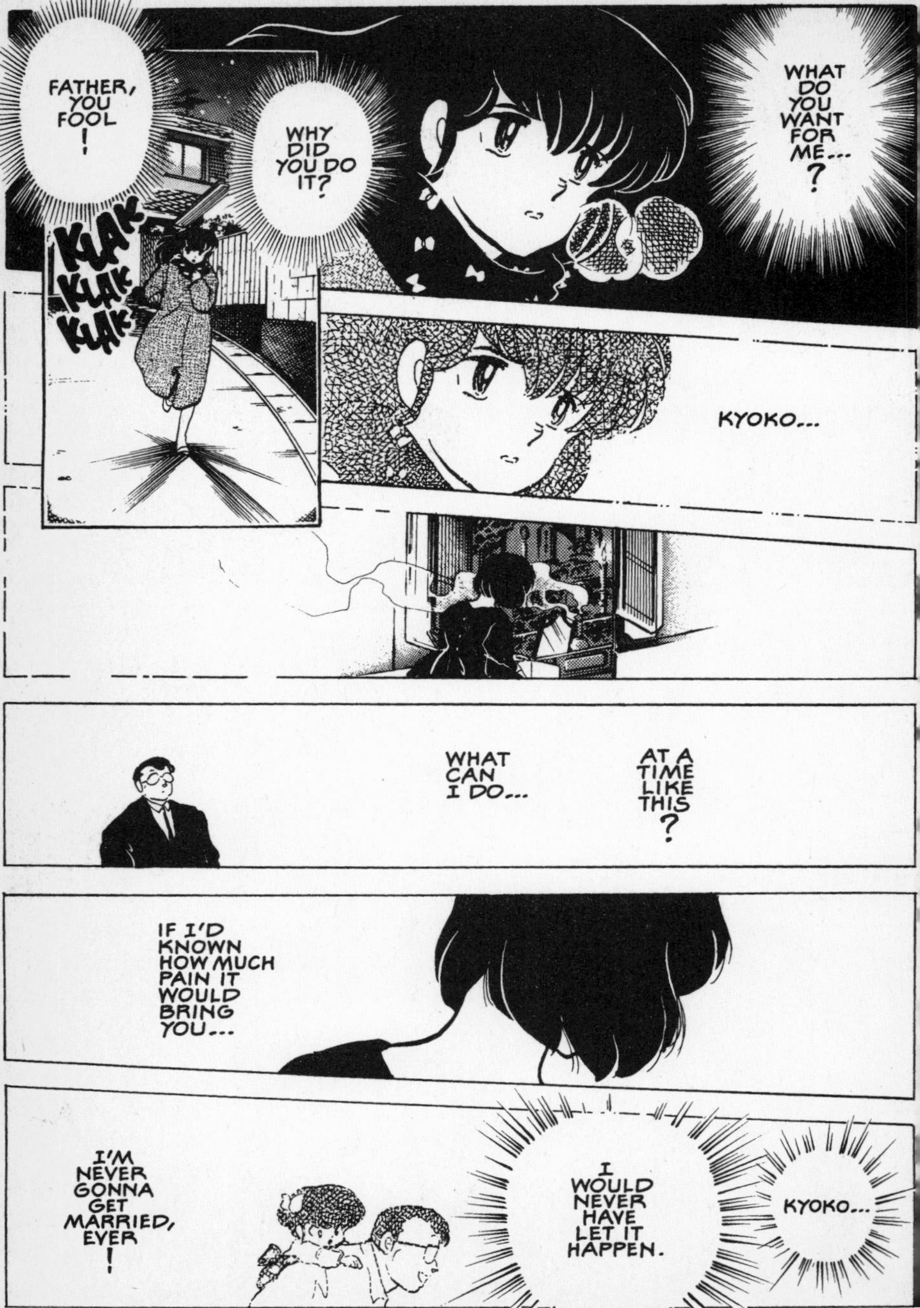
FATHER, YOU FOOL!
WHY DID YOU DO IT?
WHAT DO YOU WANT FOR ME...?
KLAK KLAK KLAK KLAK
KYOKO...
WHAT CAN I DO...
AT A TIME LIKE THIS?
IF I'D KNOWN HOW MUCH PAIN IT WOULD BRING YOU...
I'M NEVER GONNA GET MARRIED, EVER!
I WOULD NEVER HAVE LET IT HAPPEN.
KYOKO...

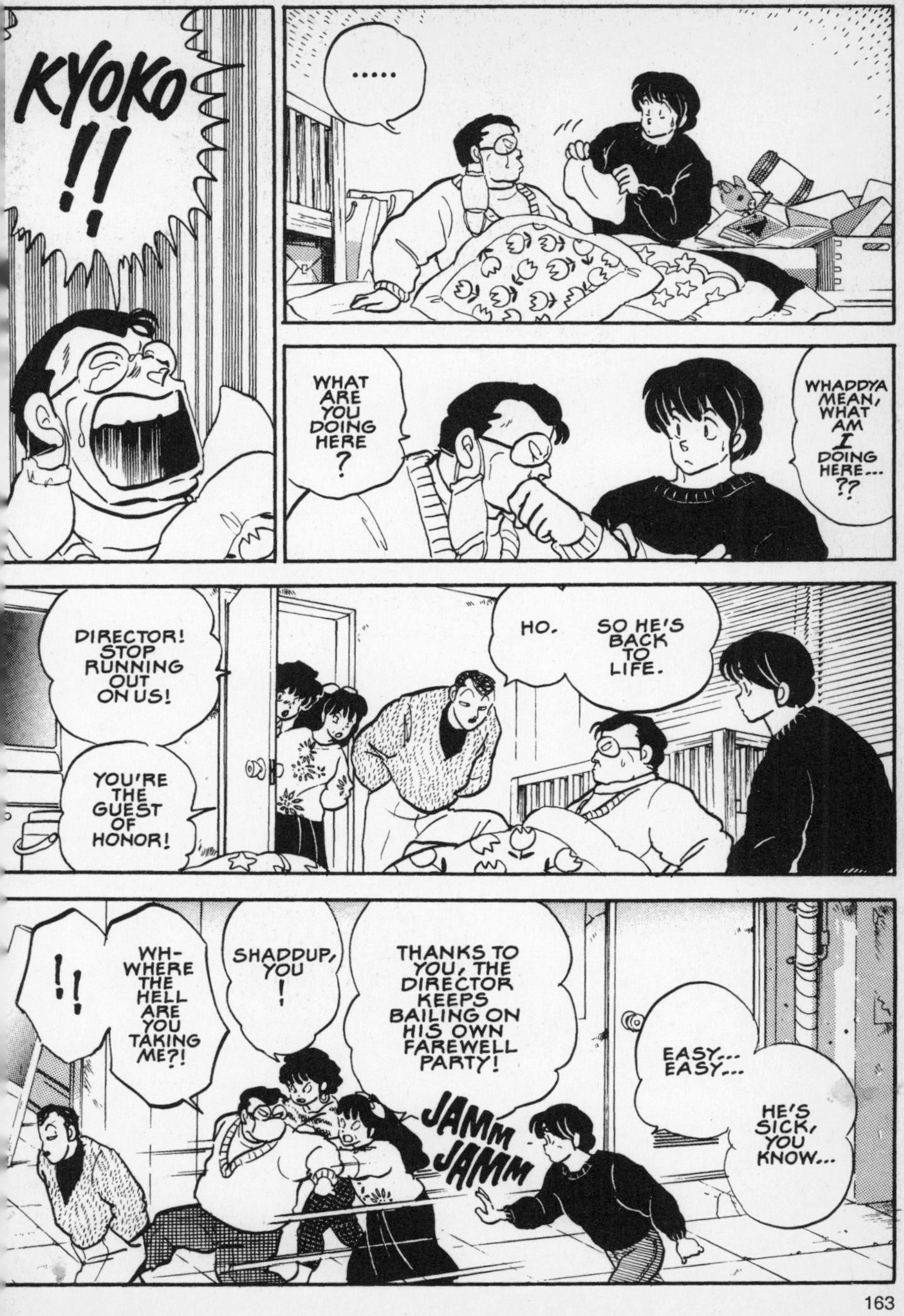
KYOKO !!
......
WHAT ARE YOU DOING HERE ?
WHADDYA MEAN, WHAT AM I DOING HERE... ??
DIRECTOR! STOP RUNNING OUT ON US!
YOU'RE THE GUEST OF HONOR!
HO. SO HE'S BACK TO LIFE.
!!
WH-WHERE THE HELL ARE YOU TAKING ME?!
SHADDUP, YOU !
THANKS TO YOU, THE DIRECTOR KEEPS BAILING ON HIS OWN FAREWELL PARTY!
JAMM JAMM
EASY... EASY...
HE'S SICK, YOU KNOW...

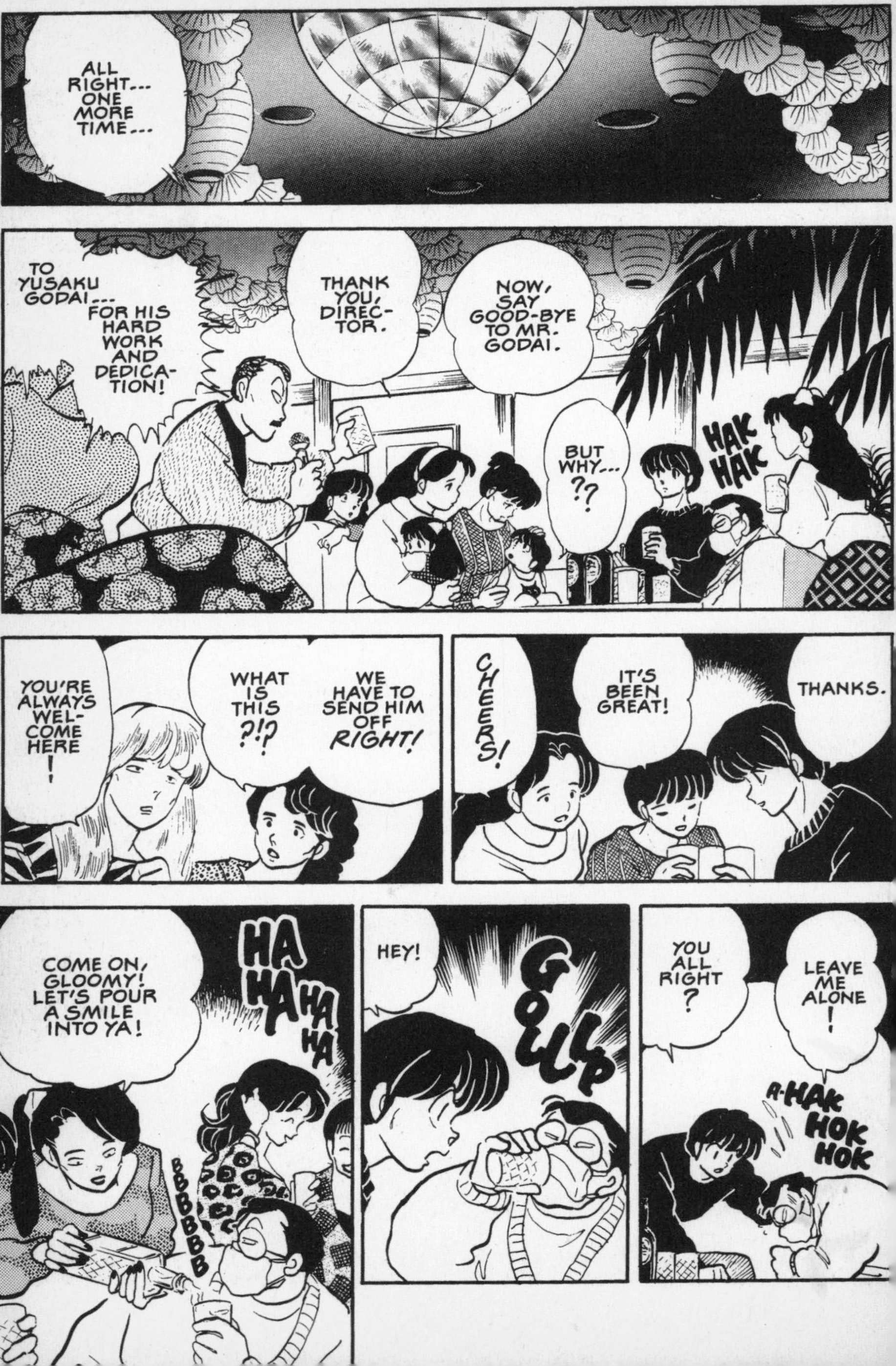
ALL RIGHT... ONE MORE TIME...
TO YUSAKU GODAI... FOR HIS HARD WORK AND DEDICATION!
THANK YOU, DIRECTOR.
NOW, SAY GOOD-BYE TO MR. GODAI.
BUT WHY...??
HAK HAK
YOU'RE ALWAYS WELCOME HERE!
WHAT IS THIS?!?
WE HAVE TO SEND HIM OFF RIGHT!
CHEERS!
IT'S BEEN GREAT!
THANKS.
COME ON, GLOOMY! LET'S POUR A SMILE INTO YA!
HA HA HA HA
BBBBBBB
HEY!
GULP
YOU ALL RIGHT?
LEAVE ME ALONE!
A-HAK HOK HOK

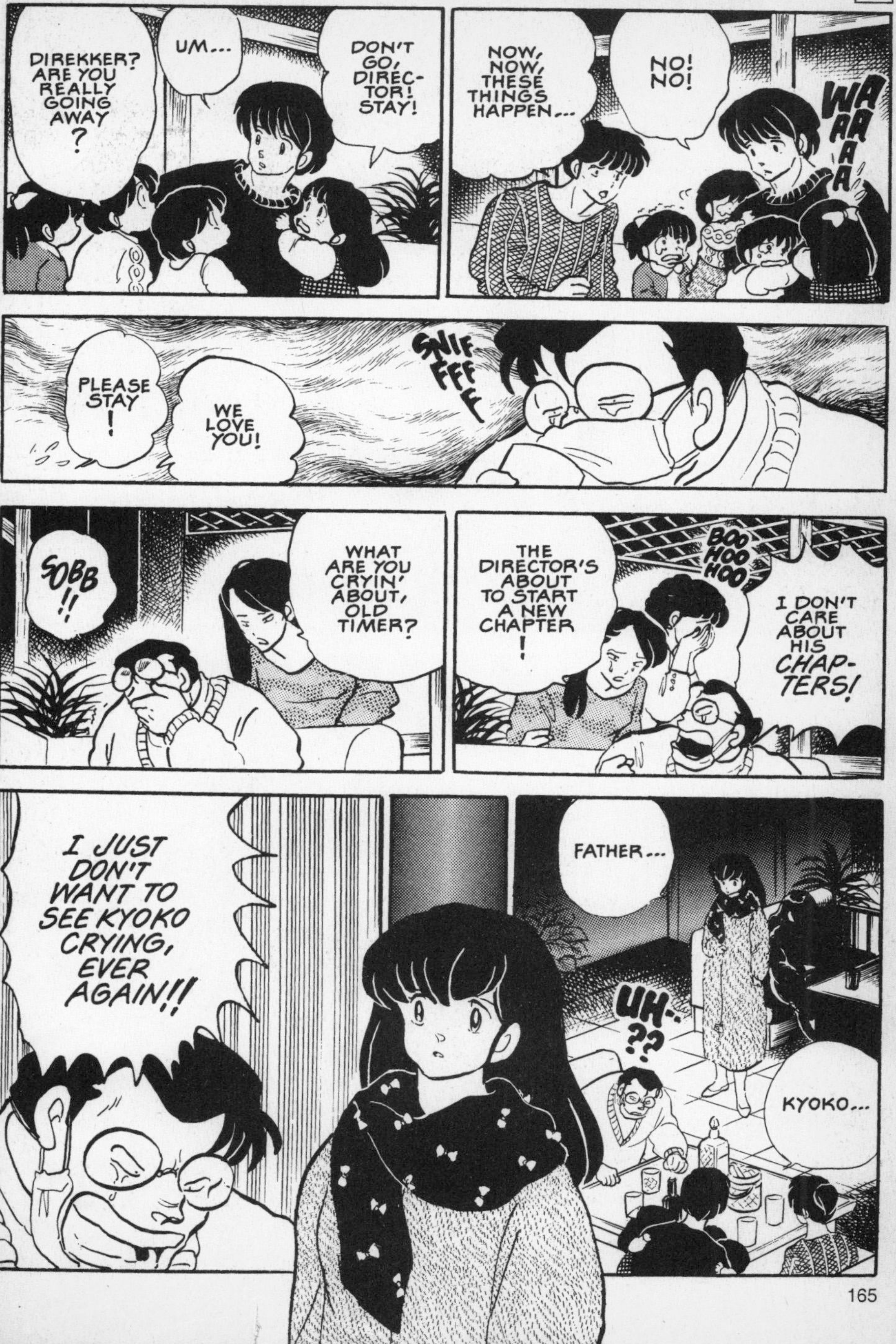
DIREKKER? ARE YOU REALLY GOING AWAY?
UM...
DON'T GO, DIRECTOR! STAY!
NOW, NOW, THESE THINGS HAPPEN...
NO! NO!
WAAAAA
PLEASE STAY!
WE LOVE YOU!
SNIFFFFF
SOBB!!
WHAT ARE YOU CRYIN' ABOUT, OLD TIMER?
THE DIRECTOR'S ABOUT TO START A NEW CHAPTER!
BOO HOO HOO
I DON'T CARE ABOUT HIS CHAPTERS!
I JUST DON'T WANT TO SEE KYOKO CRYING, EVER AGAIN!!
FATHER...
UH-??
KYOKO...

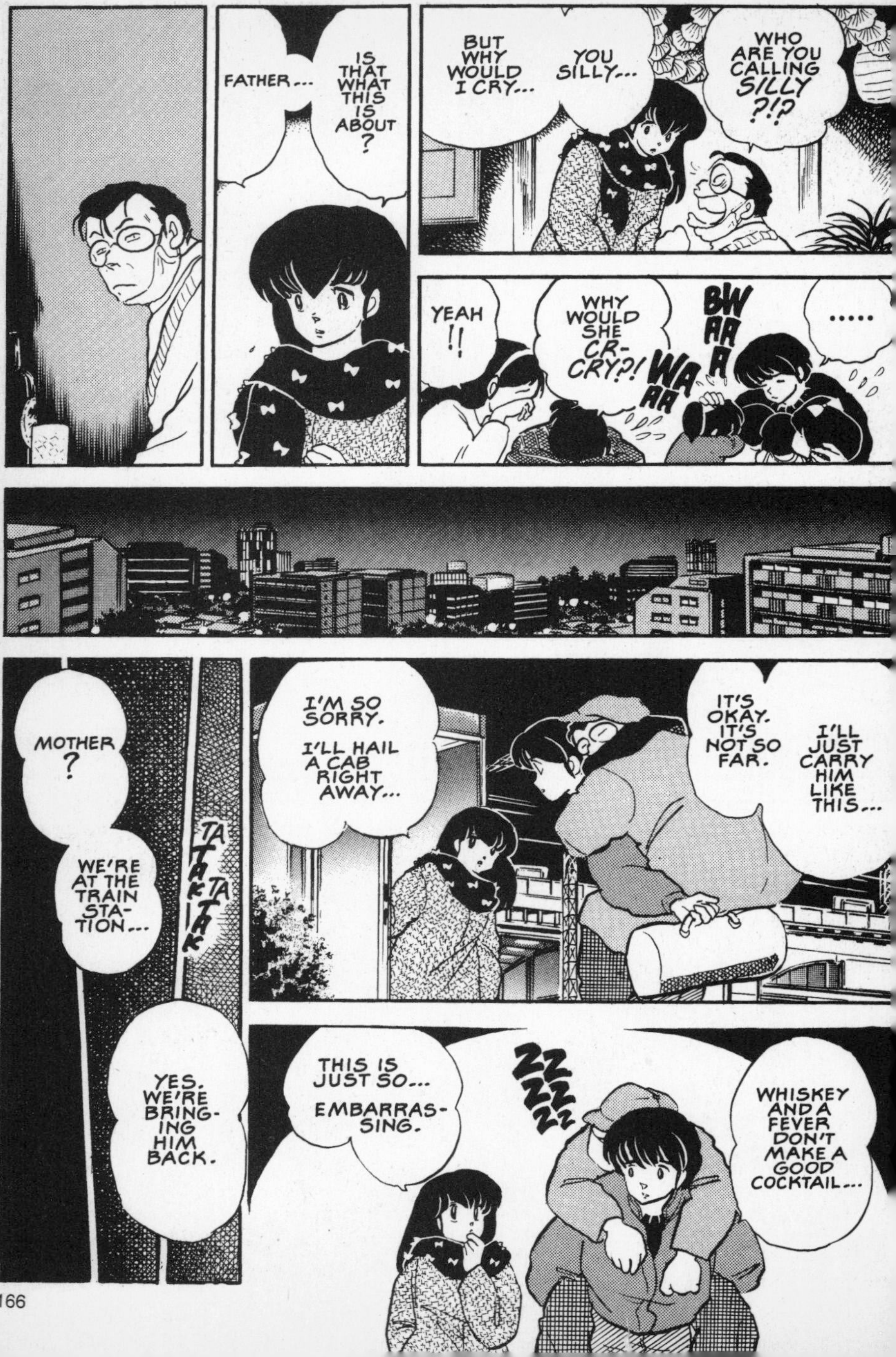
FATHER...
IS THAT WHAT THIS IS ABOUT ?
BUT WHY WOULD I CRY...
YOU SILLY...
WHO ARE YOU CALLING SILLY ?!?
YEAH !!
WHY WOULD SHE CR-CRY?!
BWAAA
WAAA
.....
MOTHER ?
WE'RE AT THE TRAIN STATION...
TA TAK TA TAK
I'M SO SORRY.
I'LL HAIL A CAB RIGHT AWAY...
IT'S OKAY. IT'S NOT SO FAR.
I'LL JUST CARRY HIM LIKE THIS...
YES. WE'RE BRINGING HIM BACK.
THIS IS JUST SO... EMBARRASSING.
ZZZZZ
WHISKEY AND A FEVER DON'T MAKE A GOOD COCKTAIL...

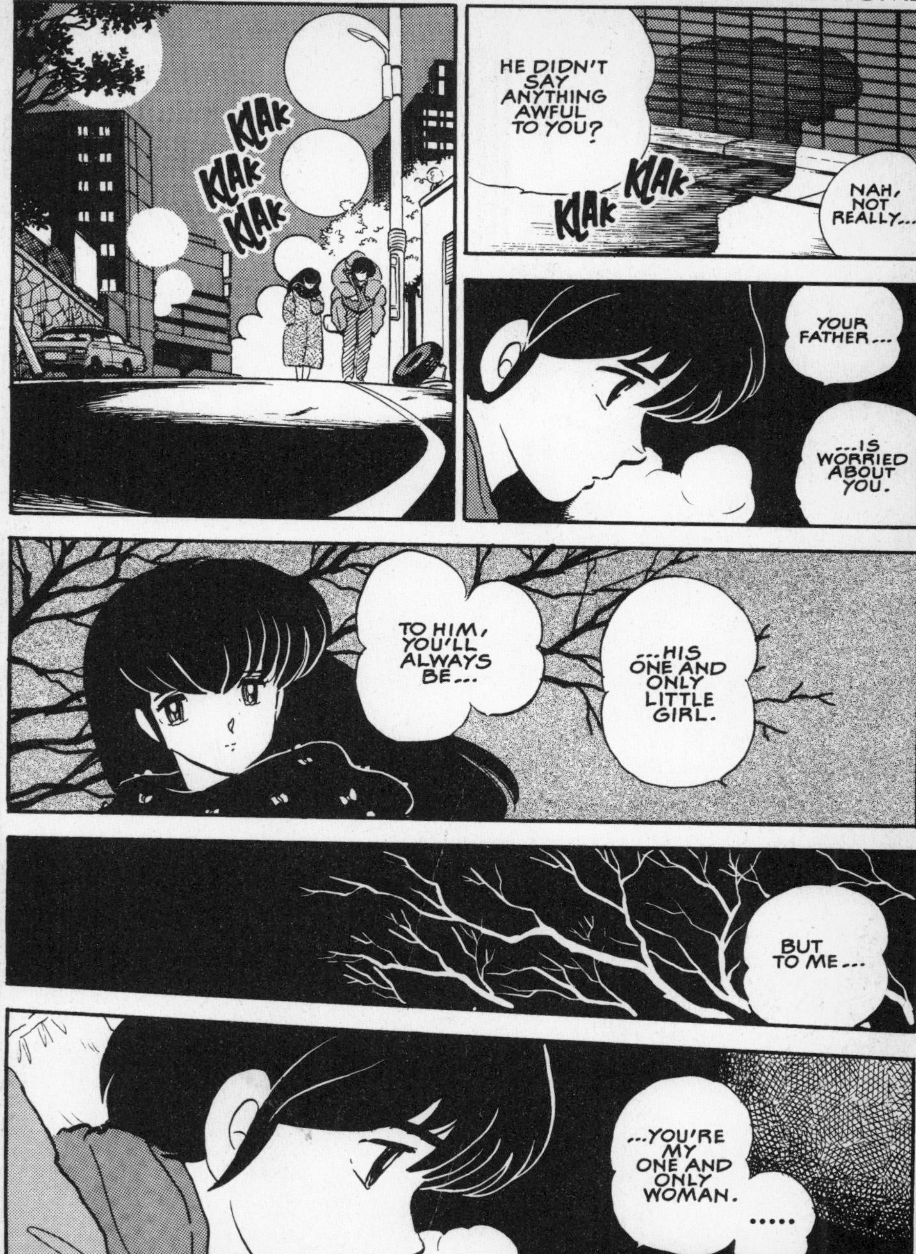
KLAK
KLAK
KLAK
HE DIDN'T SAY ANYTHING AWFUL TO YOU?
KLAK
KLAK
NAH, NOT REALLY...
YOUR FATHER...
...IS WORRIED ABOUT YOU.
TO HIM, YOU'LL ALWAYS BE...
...HIS ONE AND ONLY LITTLE GIRL.
BUT TO ME...
...YOU'RE MY ONE AND ONLY WOMAN.
.....

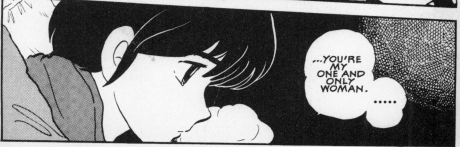

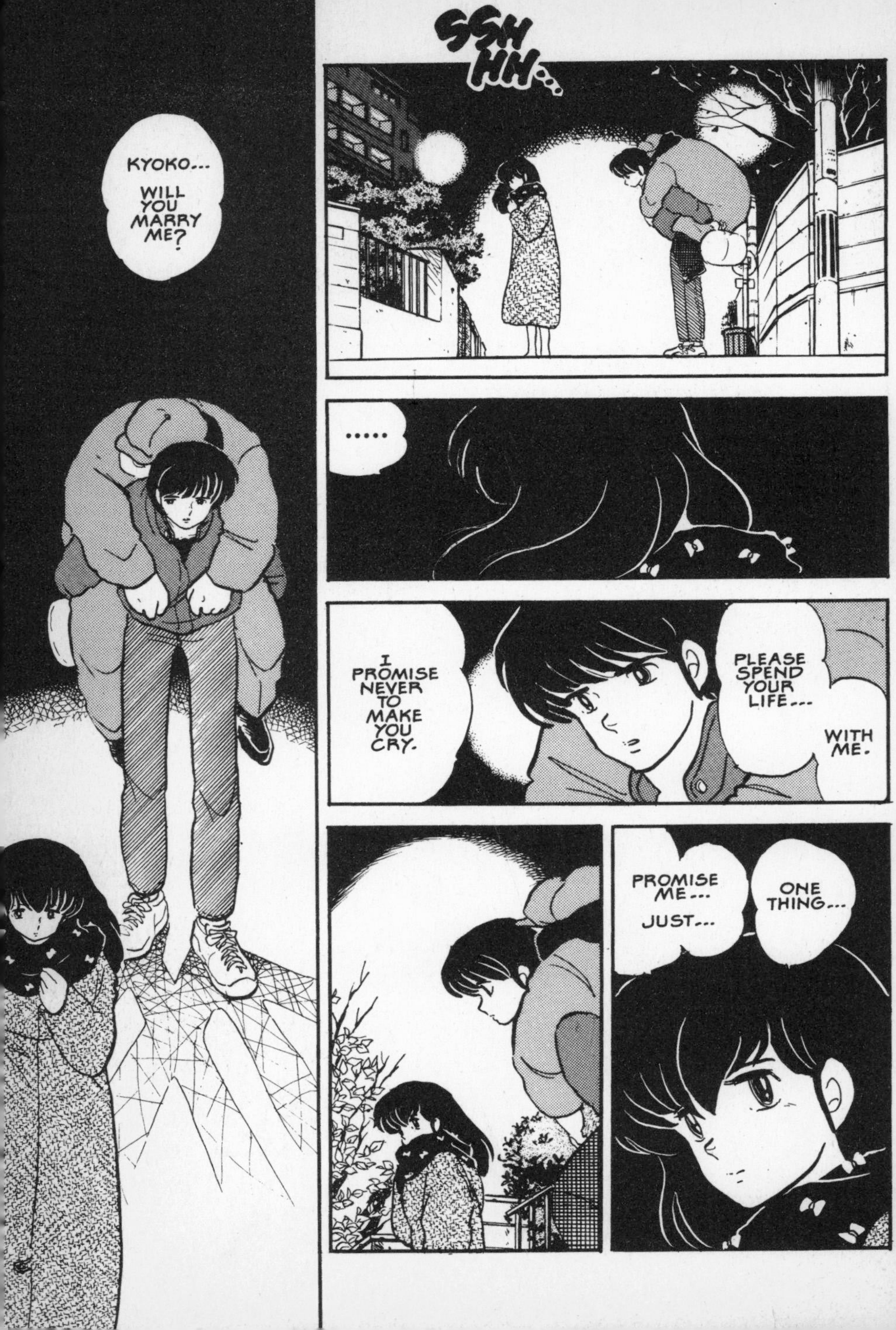
KYOKO...
WILL YOU MARRY ME?
SSHHH...
......
I PROMISE NEVER TO MAKE YOU CRY.
PLEASE SPEND YOUR LIFE...
WITH ME.
PROMISE ME...
JUST...
ONE THING...

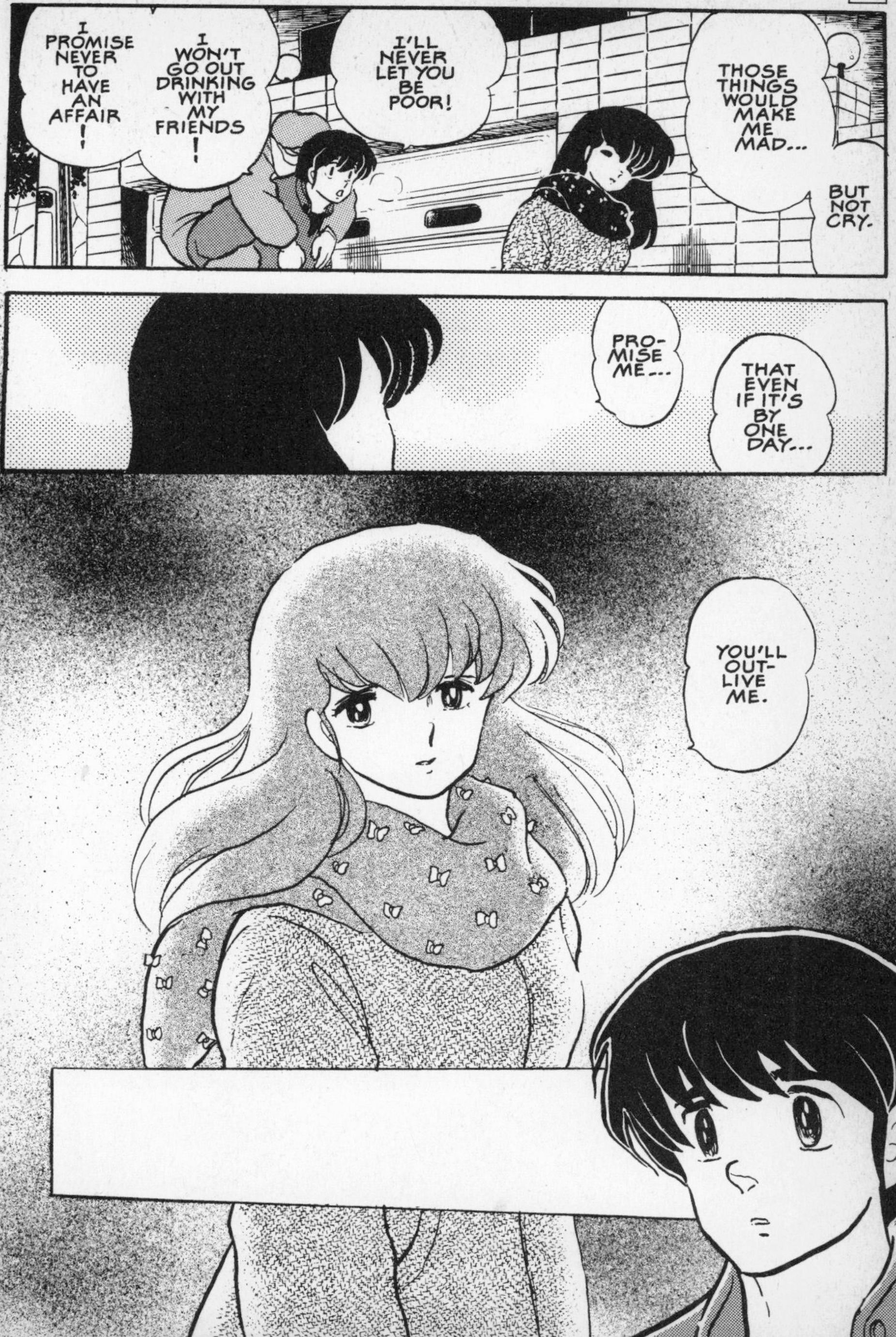
I PROMISE NEVER TO HAVE AN AFFAIR!
I WON'T GO OUT DRINKING WITH MY FRIENDS!
I'LL NEVER LET YOU BE POOR!
THOSE THINGS WOULD MAKE ME MAD...
BUT NOT CRY.
PROMISE ME...
THAT EVEN IF IT'S BY ONE DAY...
YOU'LL OUTLIVE ME.

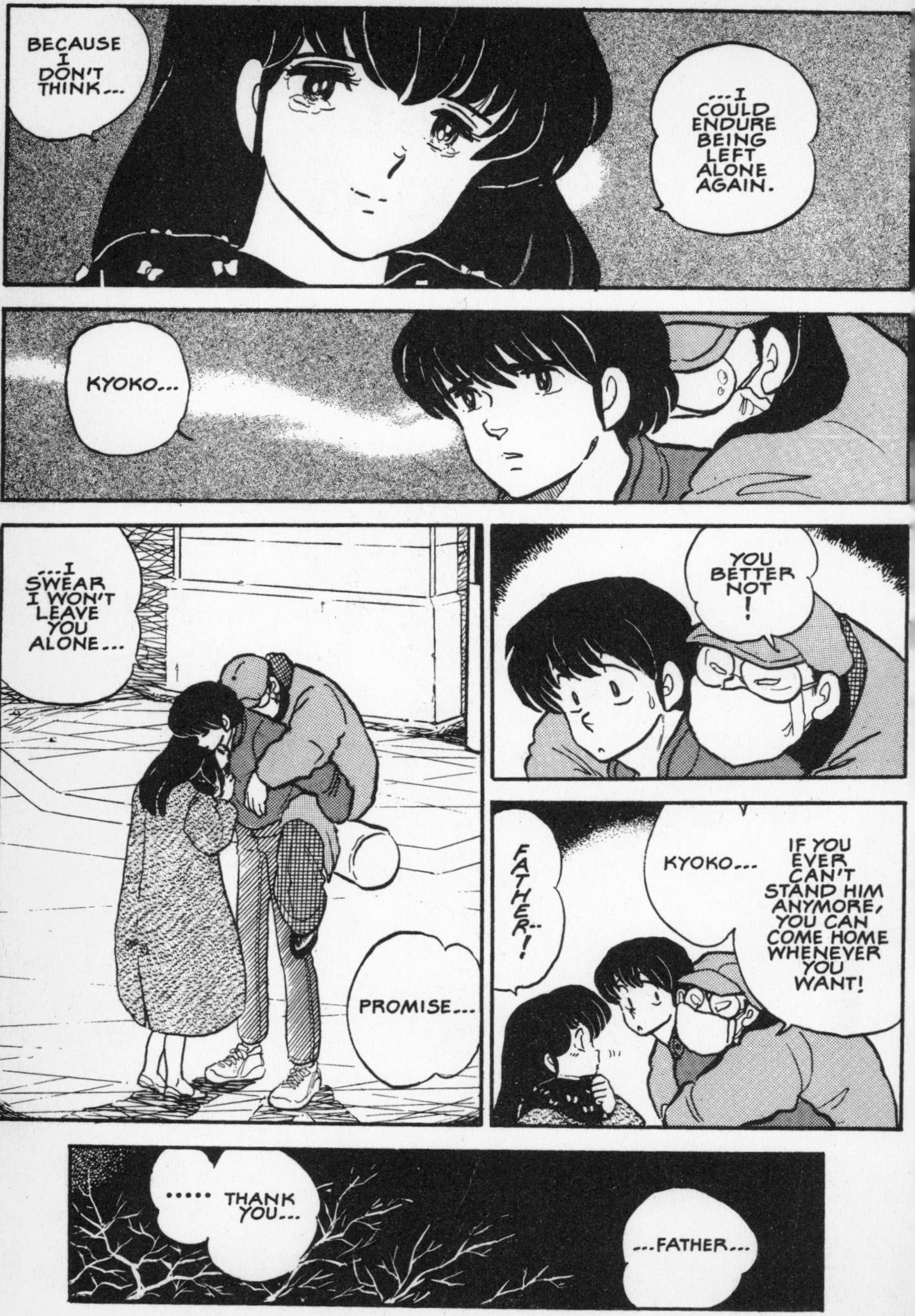
BECAUSE I DON'T THINK...
...I COULD ENDURE BEING LEFT ALONE AGAIN.
KYOKO...
...I SWEAR I WON'T LEAVE YOU ALONE...
PROMISE...
YOU BETTER NOT!
FATHER...!
KYOKO...
IF YOU EVER CAN'T STAND HIM ANYMORE, YOU CAN COME HOME WHENEVER YOU WANT!
..... THANK YOU...
...FATHER...

PART NINE
HEIRLOOMS

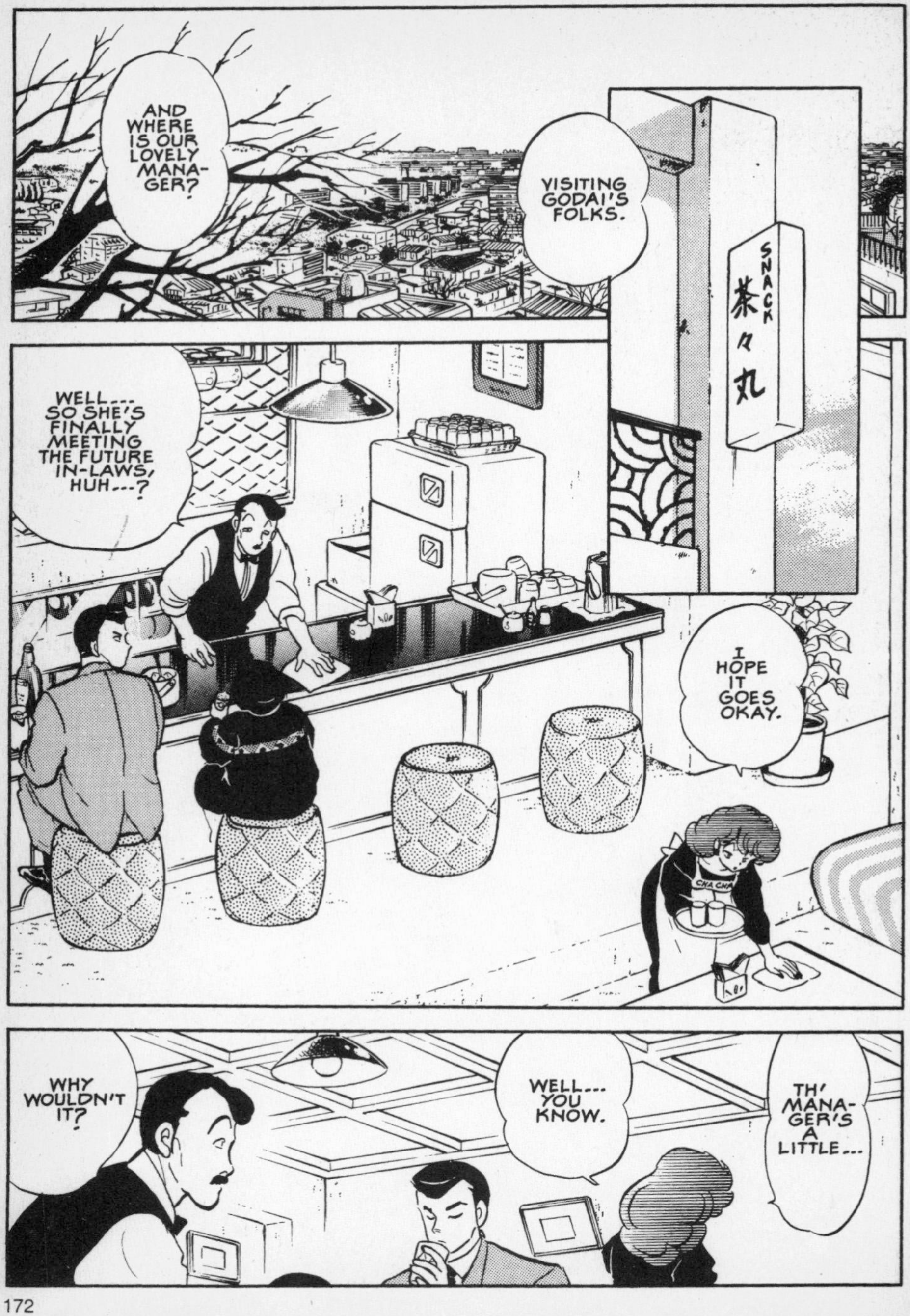
AND WHERE IS OUR LOVELY MANAGER?
VISITING GODAI'S FOLKS.
SNACK
茶々丸
WELL... SO SHE'S FINALLY MEETING THE FUTURE IN-LAWS, HUH...?
I HOPE IT GOES OKAY.
CHA CHA
WHY WOULDN'T IT?
WELL... YOU KNOW.
TH' MANAGER'S A LITTLE...

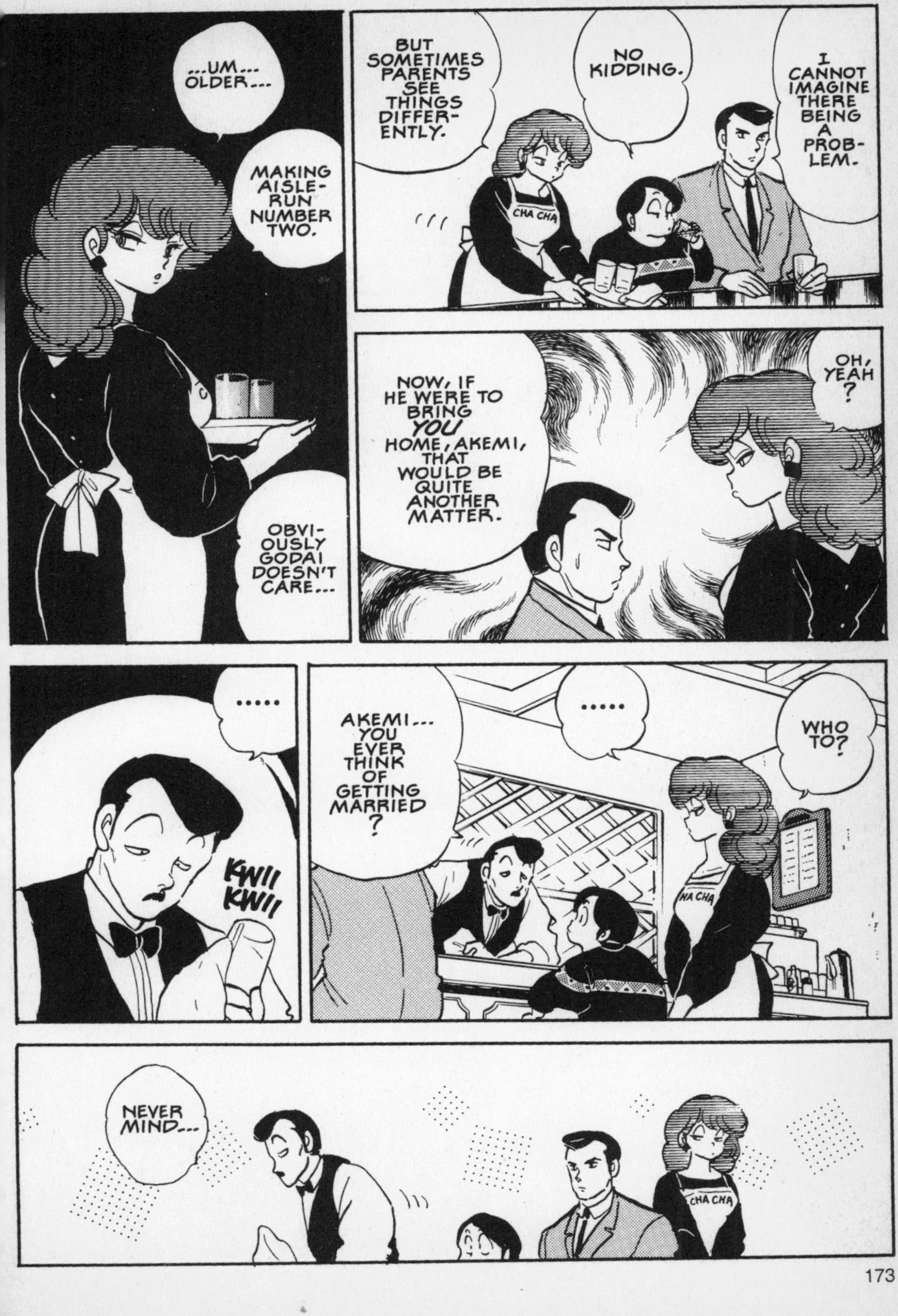
...UM... OLDER...
MAKING AISLE-RUN NUMBER TWO.
OBVIOUSLY GODAI DOESN'T CARE...
BUT SOMETIMES PARENTS SEE THINGS DIFFERENTLY.
NO KIDDING.
CHA CHA
I CANNOT IMAGINE THERE BEING A PROBLEM.
NOW, IF HE WERE TO BRING *YOU* HOME, AKEMI, THAT WOULD BE QUITE ANOTHER MATTER.
OH, YEAH?
.....
KWII KWII
AKEMI... YOU EVER THINK OF GETTING MARRIED?
.....
WHO TO?
NEVER MIND...
CHA CHA

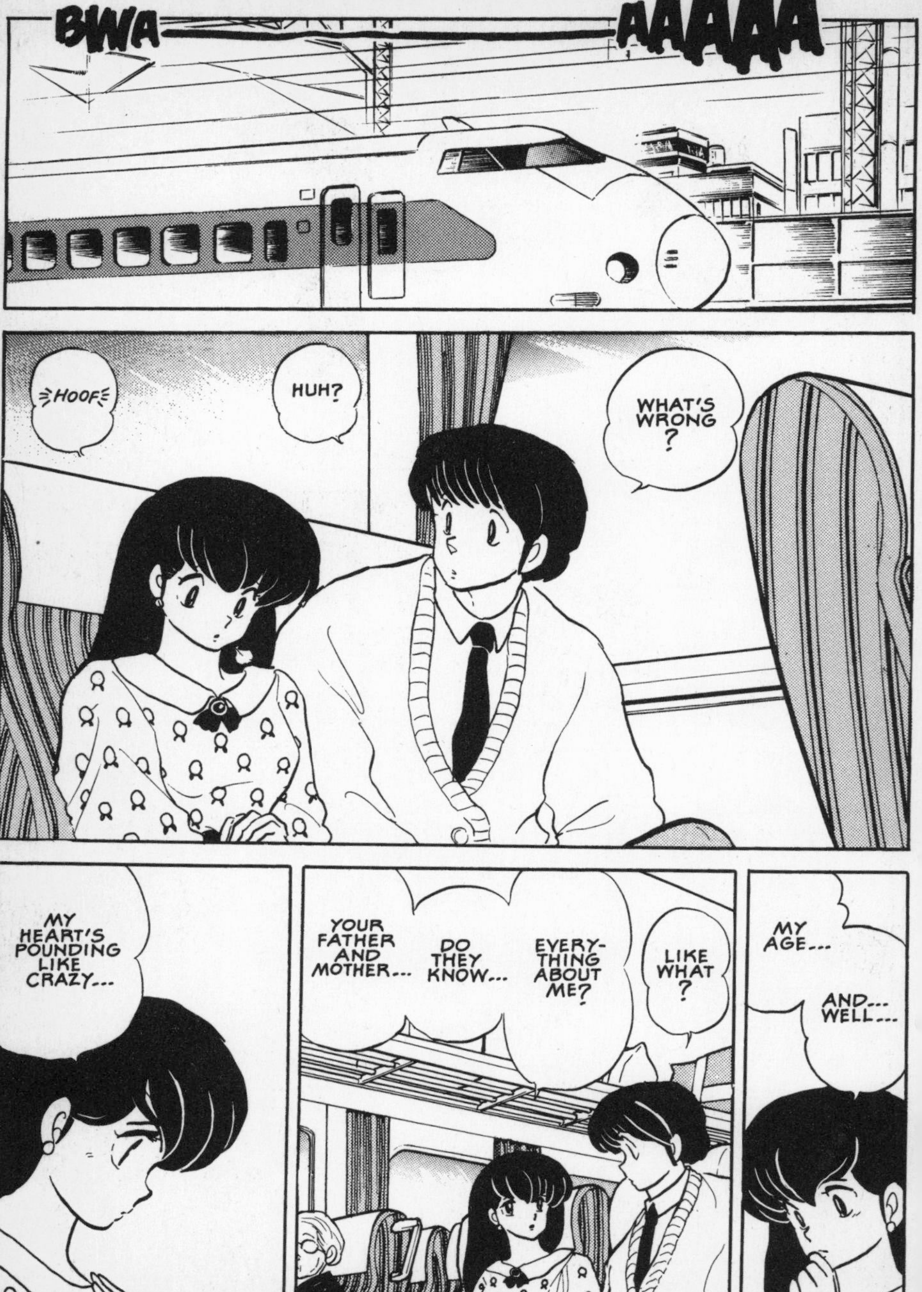
BWA—AAAAA
HOOF
HUH?
WHAT'S WRONG?
MY HEART'S POUNDING LIKE CRAZY...
YOUR FATHER AND MOTHER...
DO THEY KNOW...
EVERYTHING ABOUT ME?
LIKE WHAT?
MY AGE...
AND... WELL...

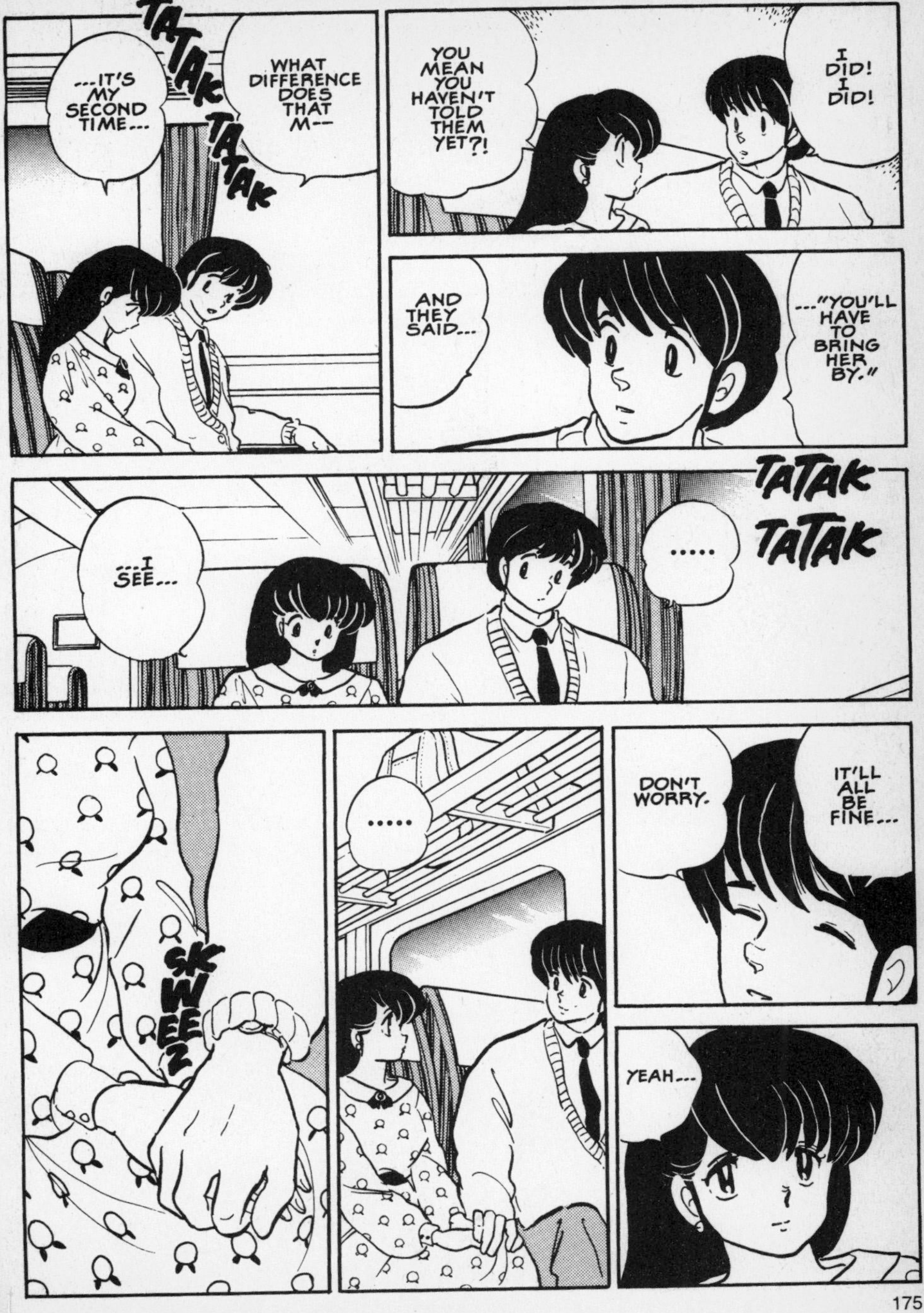
...IT'S MY SECOND TIME...
WHAT DIFFERENCE DOES THAT M--
TATAK TATAK TATAK
YOU MEAN YOU HAVEN'T TOLD THEM YET?!
I DID! I DID!
AND THEY SAID...
..."YOU'LL HAVE TO BRING HER BY."
...I SEE...
.....
TATAK TATAK
SKWEEZ
.....
DON'T WORRY.
IT'LL ALL BE FINE...
YEAH...

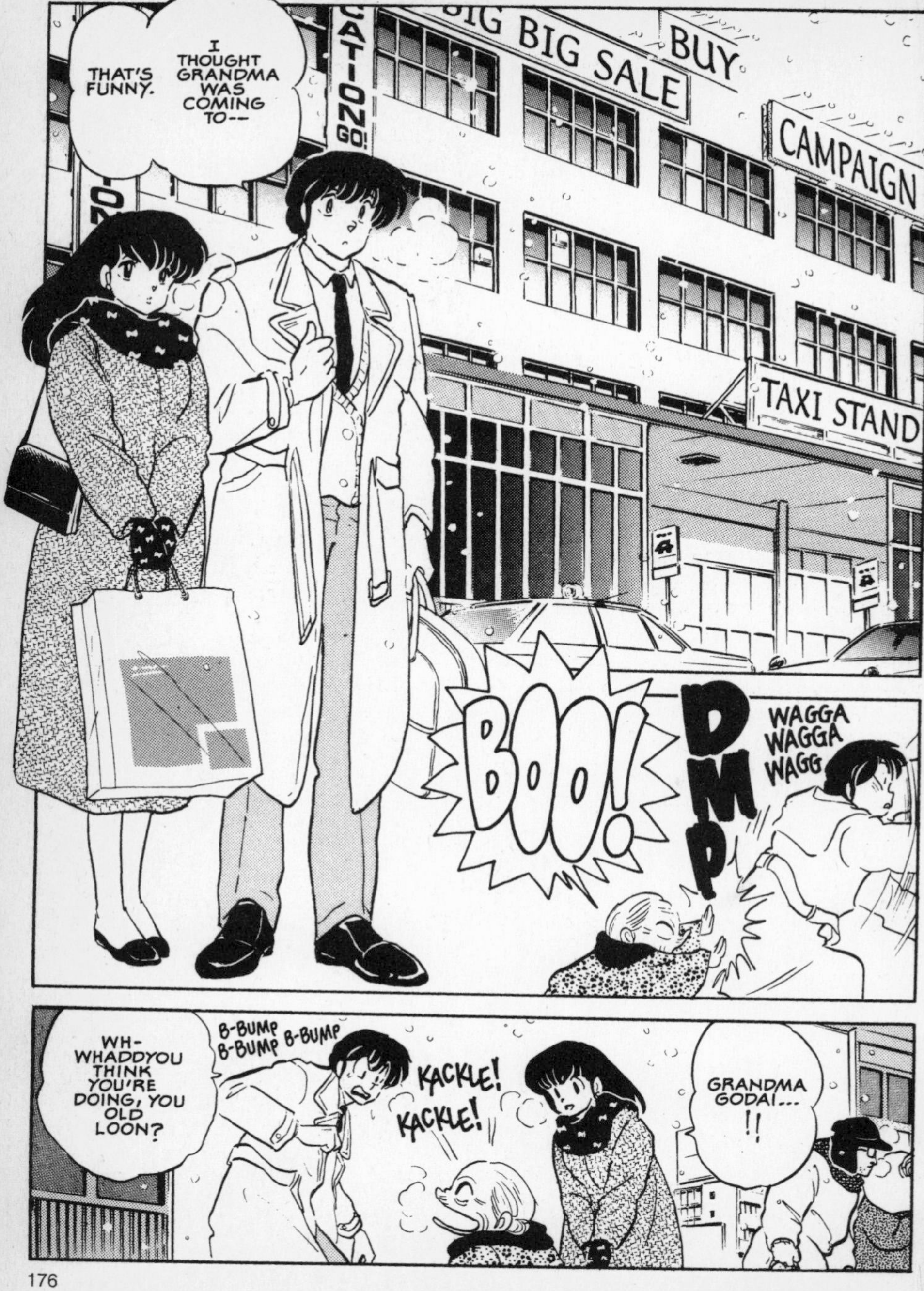
THAT'S FUNNY.
I THOUGHT GRANDMA WAS COMING TO--
CATION GO!
BIG BIG SALE
BUY
CAMPAIGN
TAXI STAND
BOO!
DMP
WAGGA WAGGA WAGG
WH-WHADDYOU THINK YOU'RE DOING, YOU OLD LOON?
B-BUMP B-BUMP B-BUMP
KACKLE! KACKLE!
GRANDMA GODAI...
!!

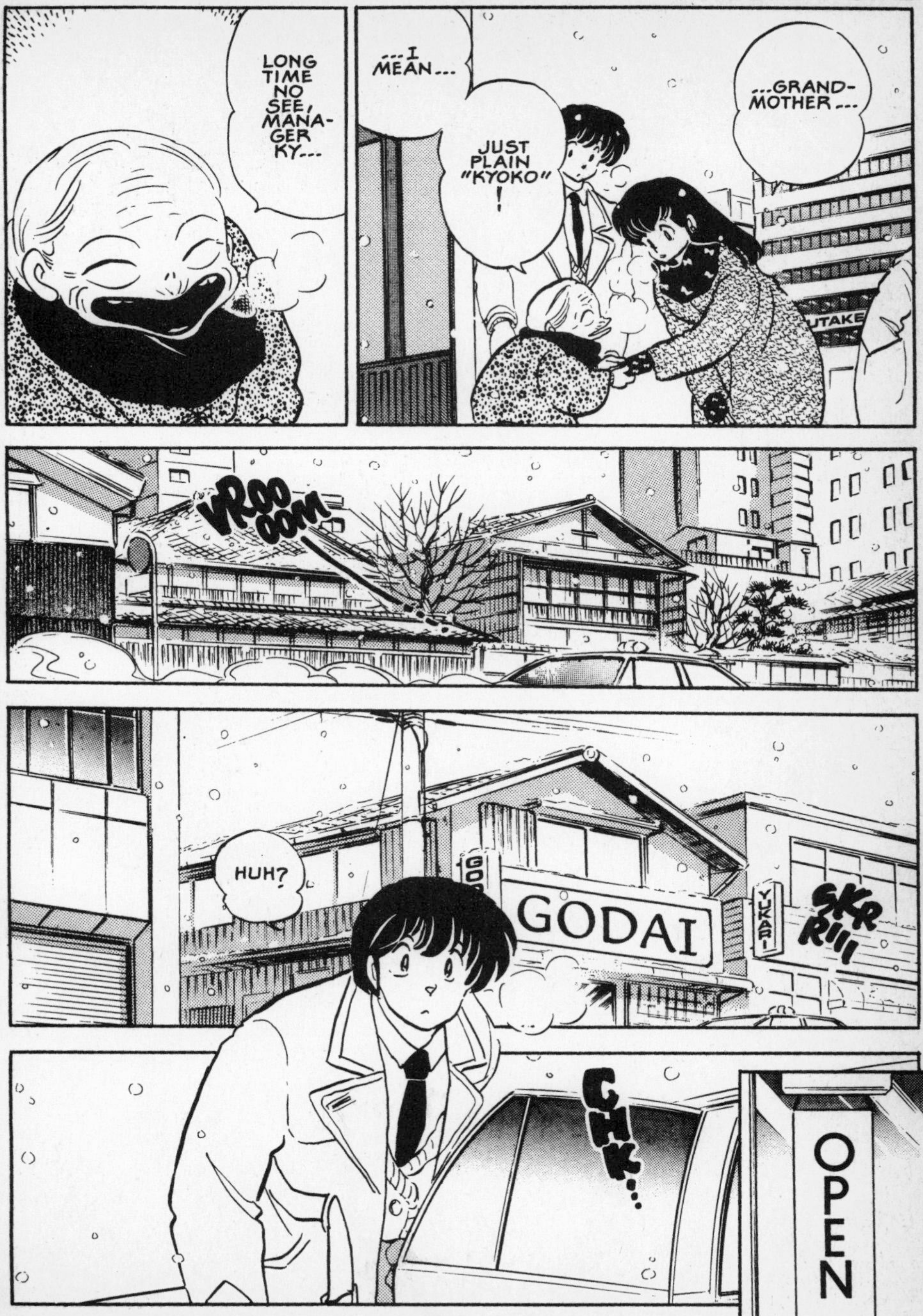
LONG TIME NO SEE, MANAGER KY...
...I MEAN...
JUST PLAIN "KYOKO"!
...GRANDMOTHER...
UTAKE
VROOOOM
HUH?
GODAI
YUKARI
SKRRIII
CHK...
OPEN

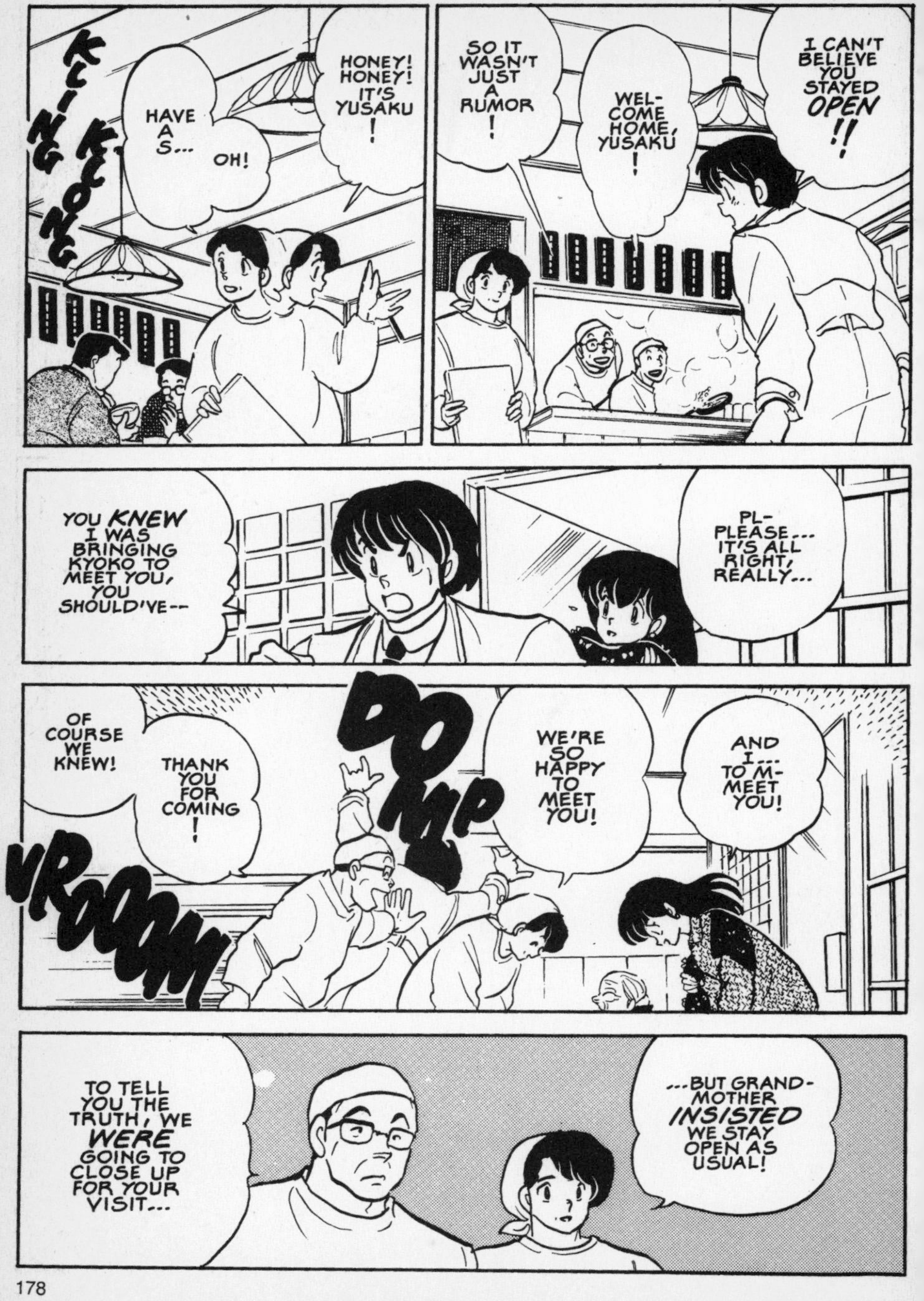
KLING KLONG
HAVE A S...
OH!
HONEY! HONEY! IT'S YUSAKU!
SO IT WASN'T JUST A RUMOR!
WEL-COME HOME, YUSAKU!
I CAN'T BELIEVE YOU STAYED OPEN!!
YOU KNEW I WAS BRINGING KYOKO TO MEET YOU, YOU SHOULD'VE--
PL-PLEASE... IT'S ALL RIGHT, REALLY...
VROOOM
OF COURSE WE KNEW!
THANK YOU FOR COMING!
DOMP
WE'RE SO HAPPY TO MEET YOU!
AND I... TO M-MEET YOU!
TO TELL YOU THE TRUTH, WE WERE GOING TO CLOSE UP FOR YOUR VISIT...
...BUT GRAND-MOTHER INSISTED WE STAY OPEN AS USUAL!

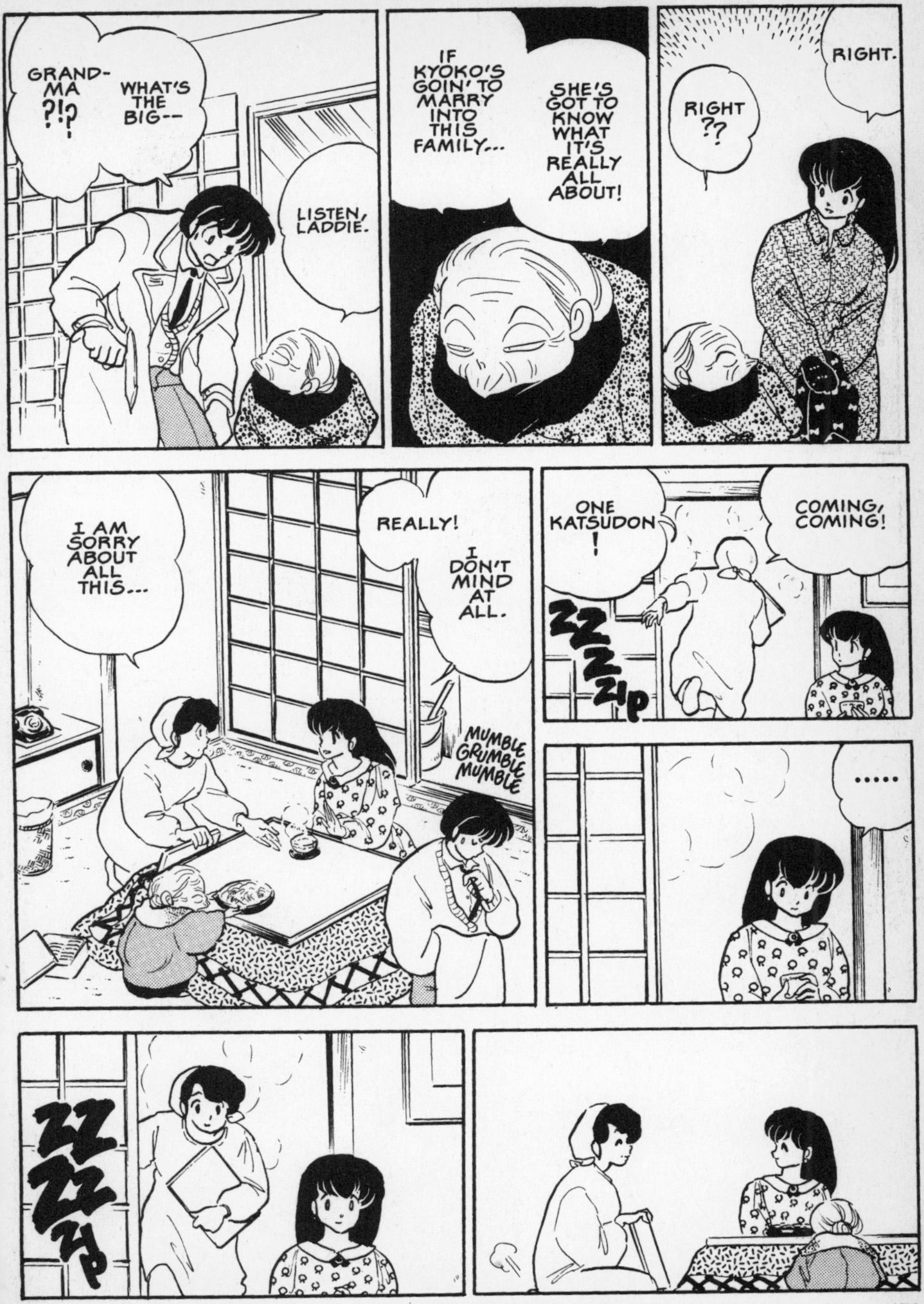
GRAND-MA ?!?
WHAT'S THE BIG--
LISTEN, LADDIE.
IF KYOKO'S GOIN' TO MARRY INTO THIS FAMILY...
SHE'S GOT TO KNOW WHAT IT'S REALLY ALL ABOUT!
RIGHT.
RIGHT ??
I AM SORRY ABOUT ALL THIS...
REALLY!
I DON'T MIND AT ALL.
MUMBLE GRUMBLE MUMBLE
ONE KATSUDON!
COMING, COMING!
ZZZZIP
.....
ZZZZZIP

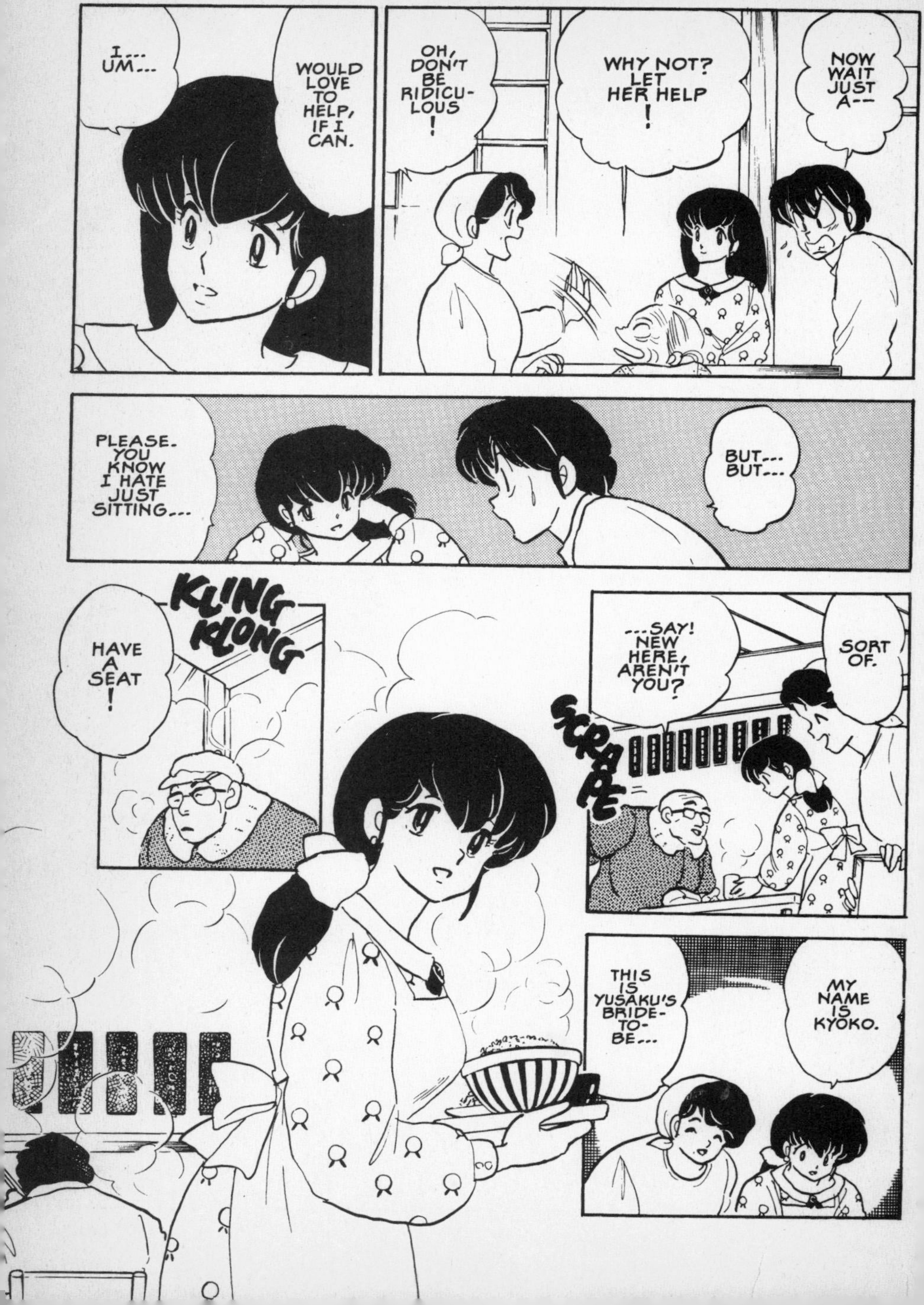

I... UM...
WOULD LOVE TO HELP, IF I CAN.
OH, DON'T BE RIDICU- LOUS !
WHY NOT? LET HER HELP !
NOW WAIT JUST A--
PLEASE. YOU KNOW I HATE JUST SITTING...
BUT... BUT...
KLING KLONG
HAVE A SEAT !
...SAY! NEW HERE, AREN'T YOU?
SORT OF.
SCRAPE
THIS IS YUSAKU'S BRIDE- TO- BE...
MY NAME IS KYOKO.

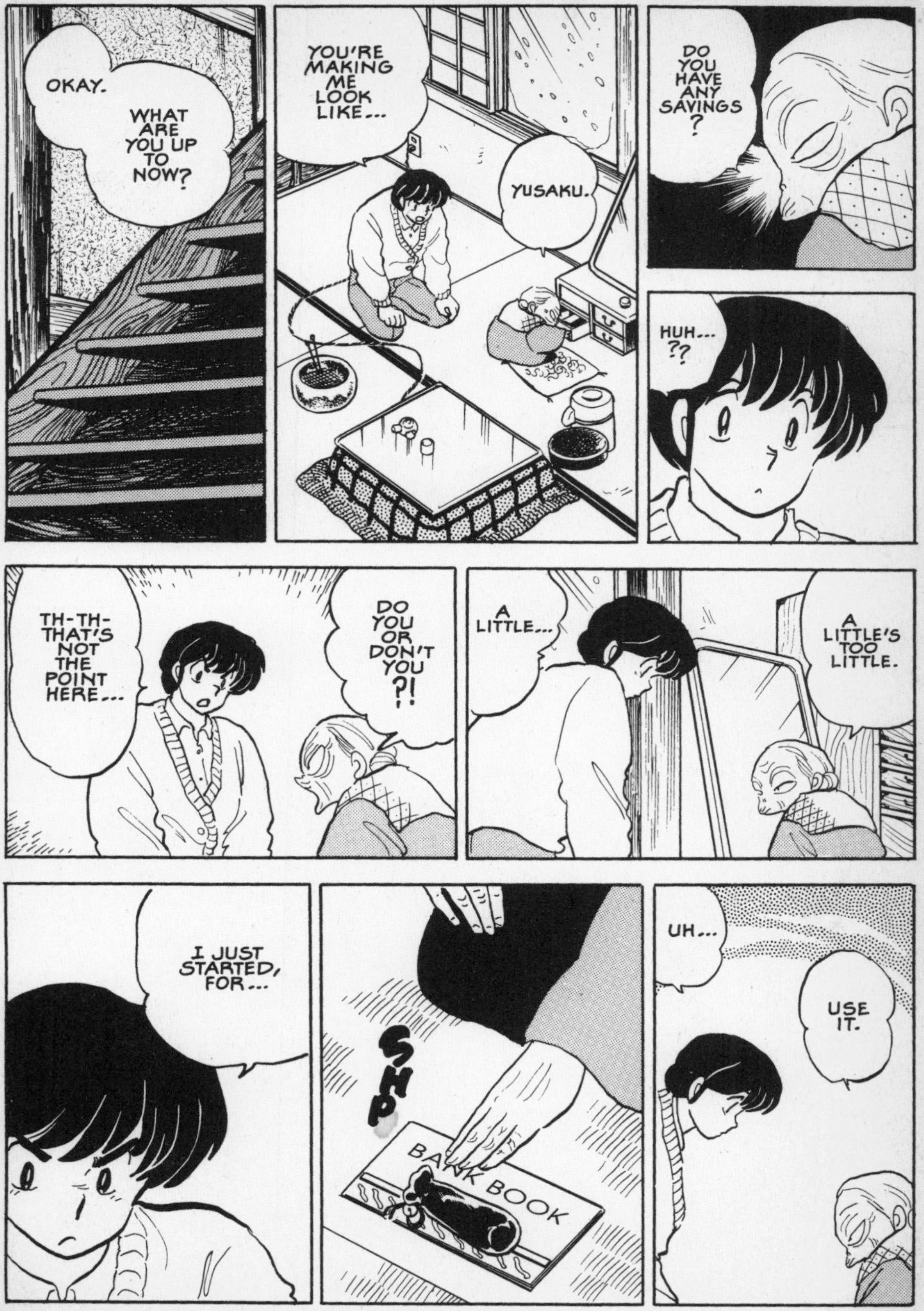
OKAY.
WHAT ARE YOU UP TO NOW?
YOU'RE MAKING ME LOOK LIKE...
YUSAKU.
DO YOU HAVE ANY SAVINGS?
HUH...??
TH-TH-THAT'S NOT THE POINT HERE...
DO YOU OR DON'T YOU?!
A LITTLE...
A LITTLE'S TOO LITTLE.
I JUST STARTED, FOR...
SHP
BANK BOOK
UH...
USE IT.

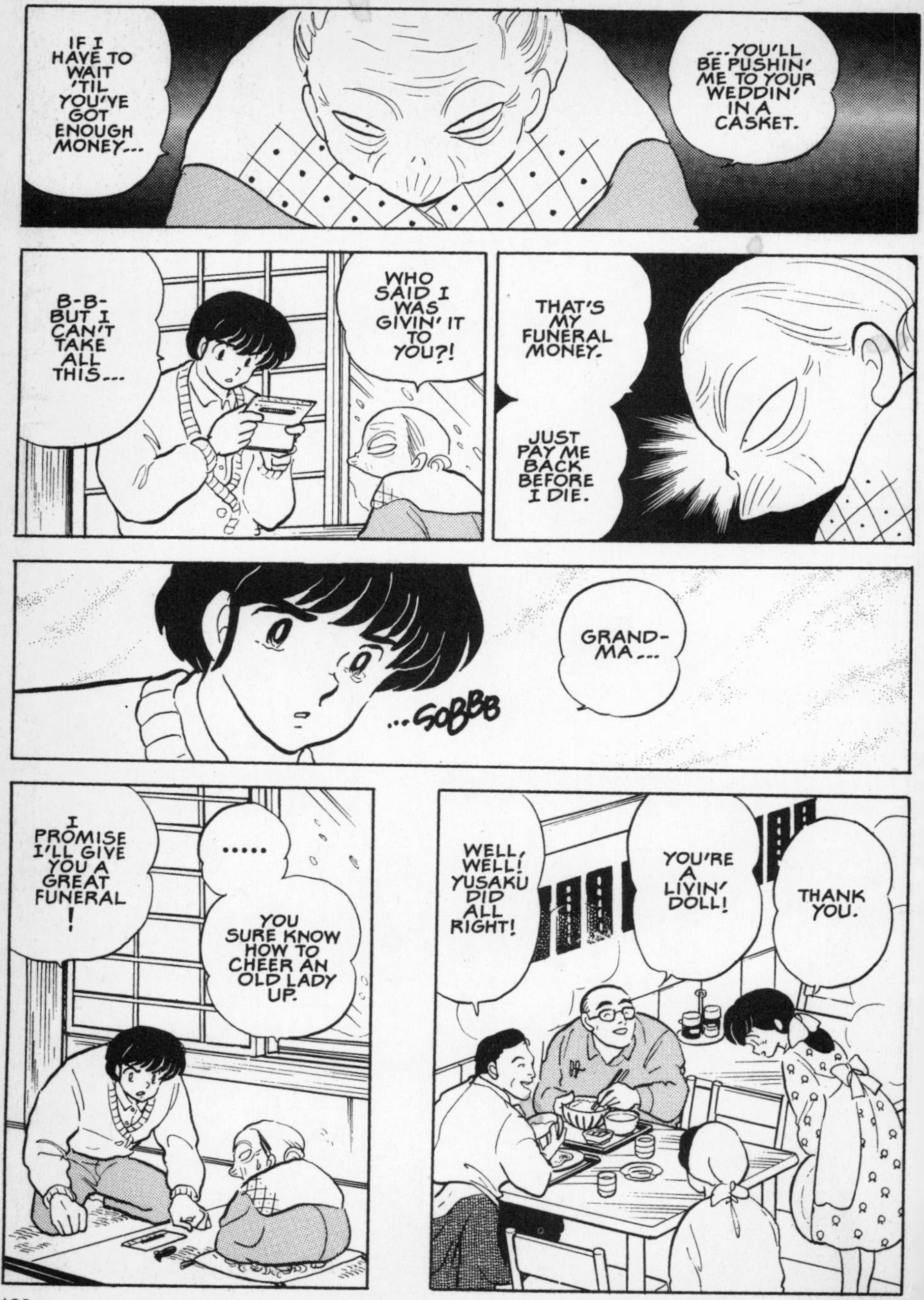
IF I HAVE TO WAIT 'TIL YOU'VE GOT ENOUGH MONEY...
...YOU'LL BE PUSHIN' ME TO YOUR WEDDIN' IN A CASKET.
B-B-BUT I CAN'T TAKE ALL THIS...
WHO SAID I WAS GIVIN' IT TO YOU?!
THAT'S MY FUNERAL MONEY.
JUST PAY ME BACK BEFORE I DIE.
GRAND-MA...
...SOBBB
I PROMISE I'LL GIVE YOU A GREAT FUNERAL!
.....
YOU SURE KNOW HOW TO CHEER AN OLD LADY UP.
WELL, WELL! YUSAKU DID ALL RIGHT!
YOU'RE A LIVIN' DOLL!
THANK YOU.

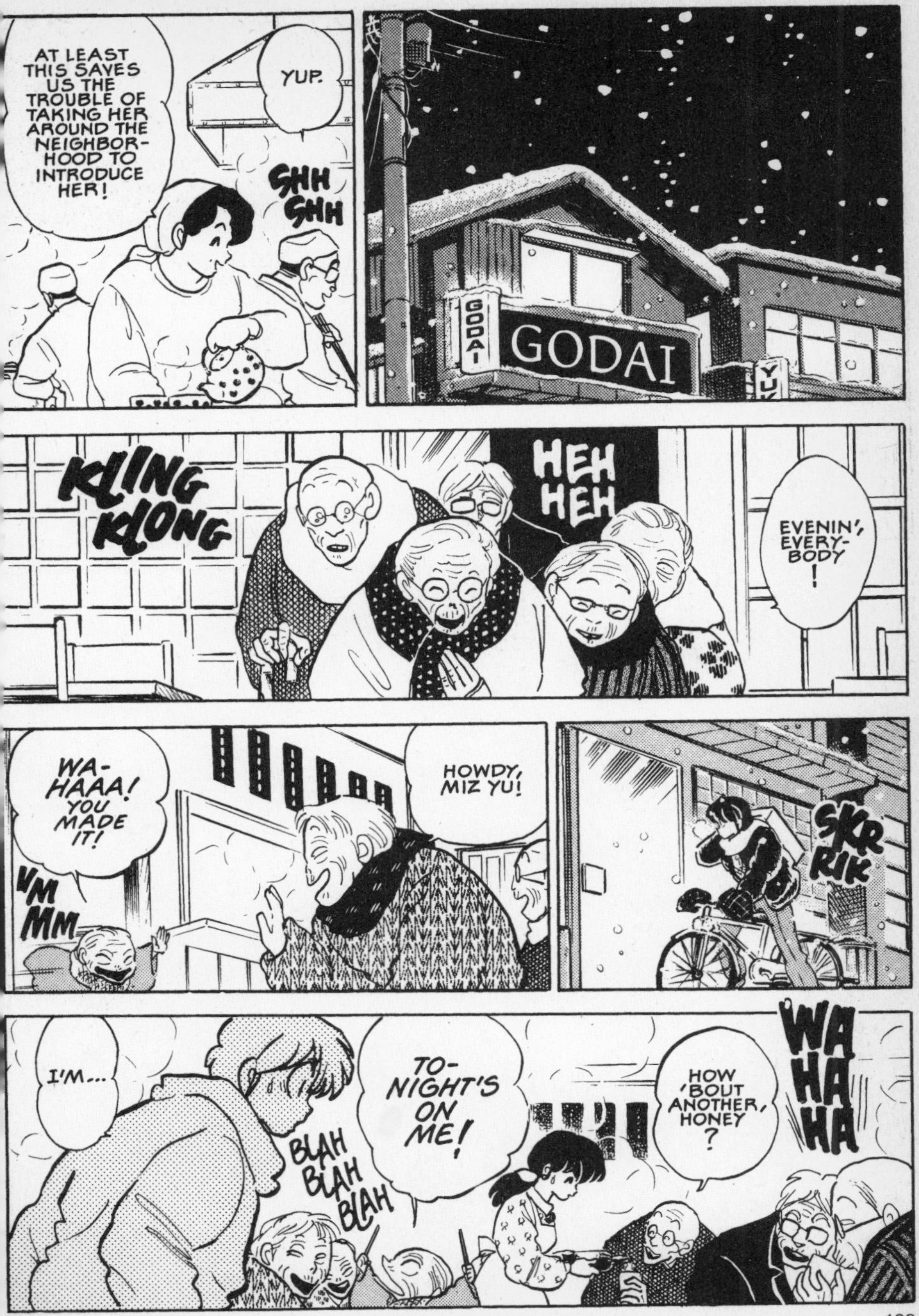
AT LEAST THIS SAVES US THE TROUBLE OF TAKING HER AROUND THE NEIGHBOR-HOOD TO INTRODUCE HER!
YUP.
SHH SHH
GODAI
GODAI
KLING KLONG
HEH HEH
EVENIN', EVERY-BODY!
WA-HAAA! YOU MADE IT!
MM MM
HOWDY, MIZ YU!
SKRRIK
I'M...
TO-NIGHT'S ON ME!
BLAH BLAH BLAH
HOW 'BOUT ANOTHER, HONEY?
WA HA HA HA

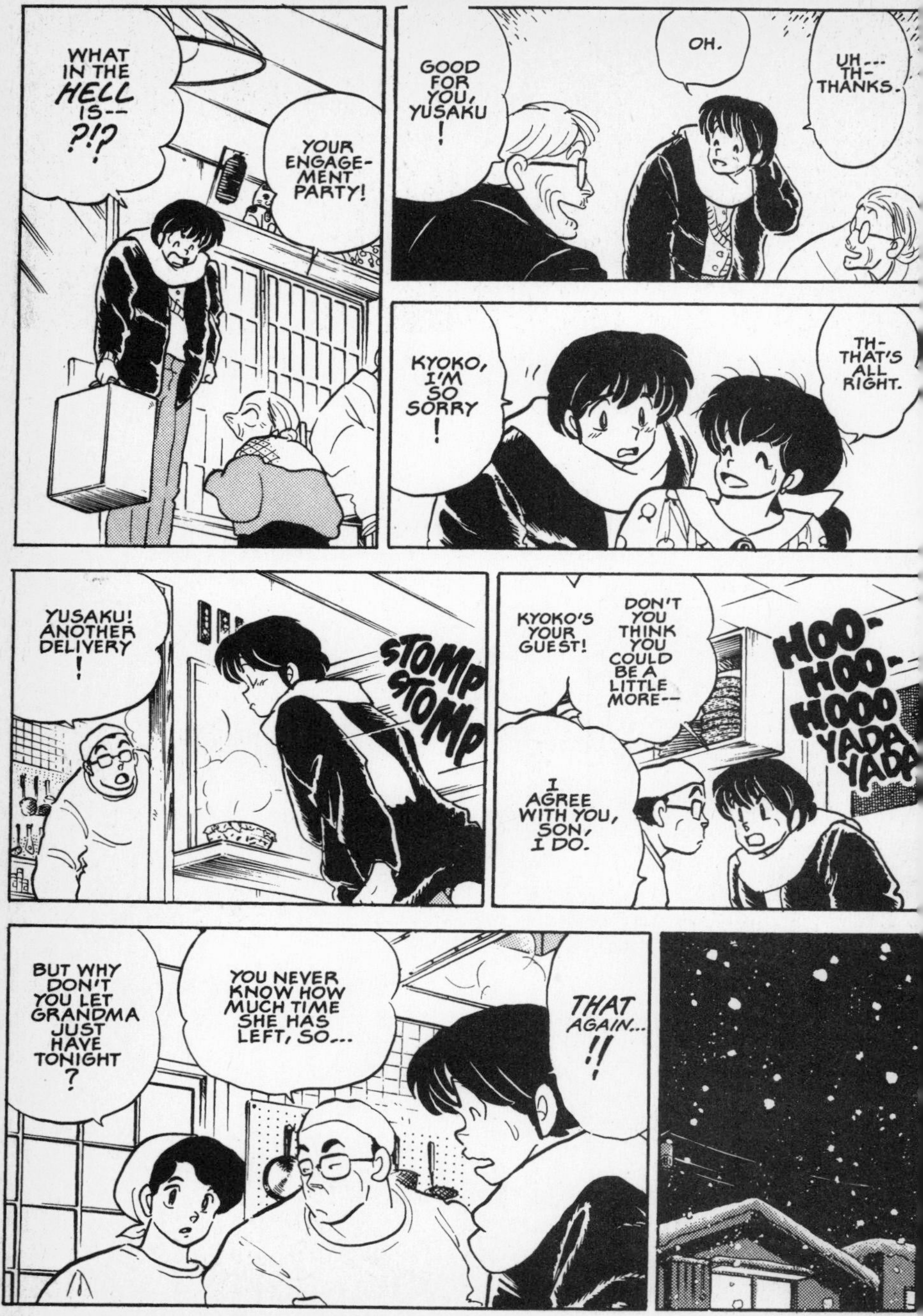
WHAT IN THE HELL IS-- ?!?
YOUR ENGAGEMENT PARTY!
GOOD FOR YOU, YUSAKU!
OH.
UH--- TH- THANKS.
KYOKO, I'M SO SORRY!
TH- THAT'S ALL RIGHT.
YUSAKU! ANOTHER DELIVERY!
STOMP STOMP
KYOKO'S YOUR GUEST!
DON'T YOU THINK YOU COULD BE A LITTLE MORE--
I AGREE WITH YOU, SON, I DO.
HOO-HOO-HOOO YADA YADA
BUT WHY DON'T YOU LET GRANDMA JUST HAVE TONIGHT?
YOU NEVER KNOW HOW MUCH TIME SHE HAS LEFT, SO...
THAT AGAIN...!!

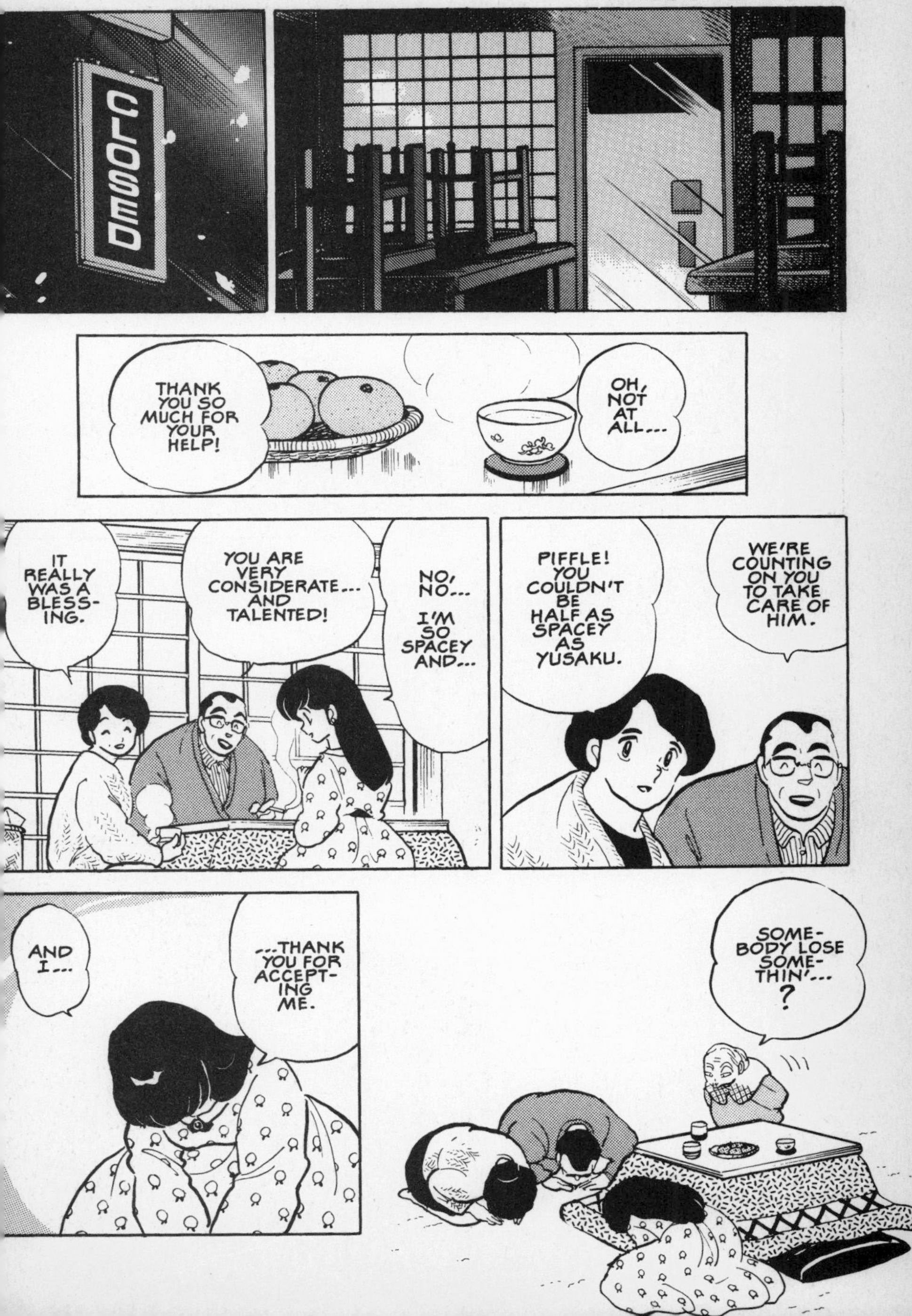
CLOSED
THANK YOU SO MUCH FOR YOUR HELP!
OH, NOT AT ALL...
IT REALLY WAS A BLESS-ING.
YOU ARE VERY CONSIDERATE... AND TALENTED!
NO, NO... I'M SO SPACEY AND...
PIFFLE! YOU COULDN'T BE HALF AS SPACEY AS YUSAKU.
WE'RE COUNTING ON YOU TO TAKE CARE OF HIM.
AND I...
...THANK YOU FOR ACCEPT-ING ME.
SOME-BODY LOSE SOME-THIN'... ?

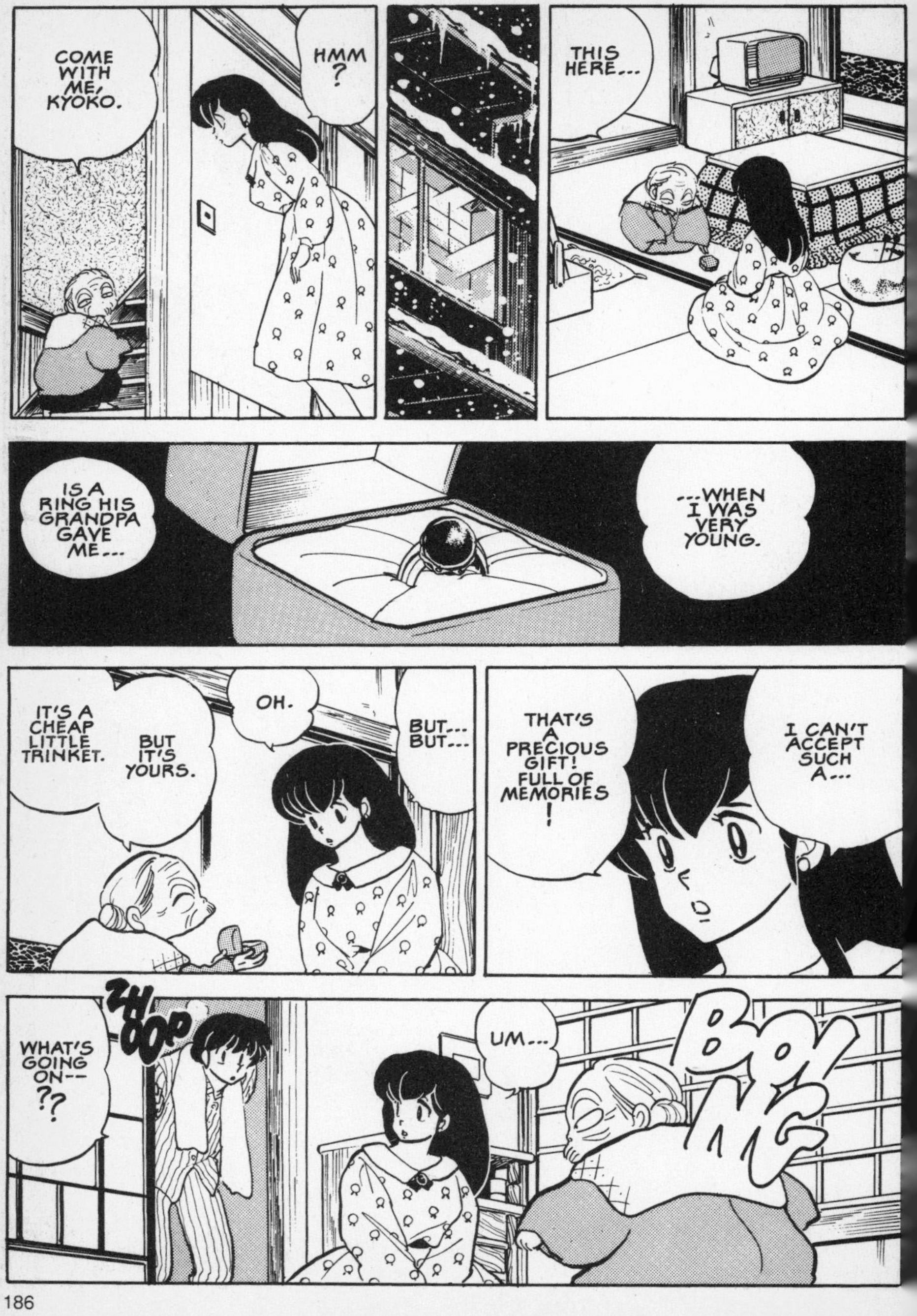
COME WITH ME, KYOKO.
HMM?
THIS HERE...
IS A RING HIS GRANDPA GAVE ME...
...WHEN I WAS VERY YOUNG.
IT'S A CHEAP LITTLE TRINKET.
BUT IT'S YOURS.
OH.
BUT... BUT...
THAT'S A PRECIOUS GIFT! FULL OF MEMORIES!
I CAN'T ACCEPT SUCH A...
WHAT'S GOING ON--??
ZHOOP
UM...
BOING

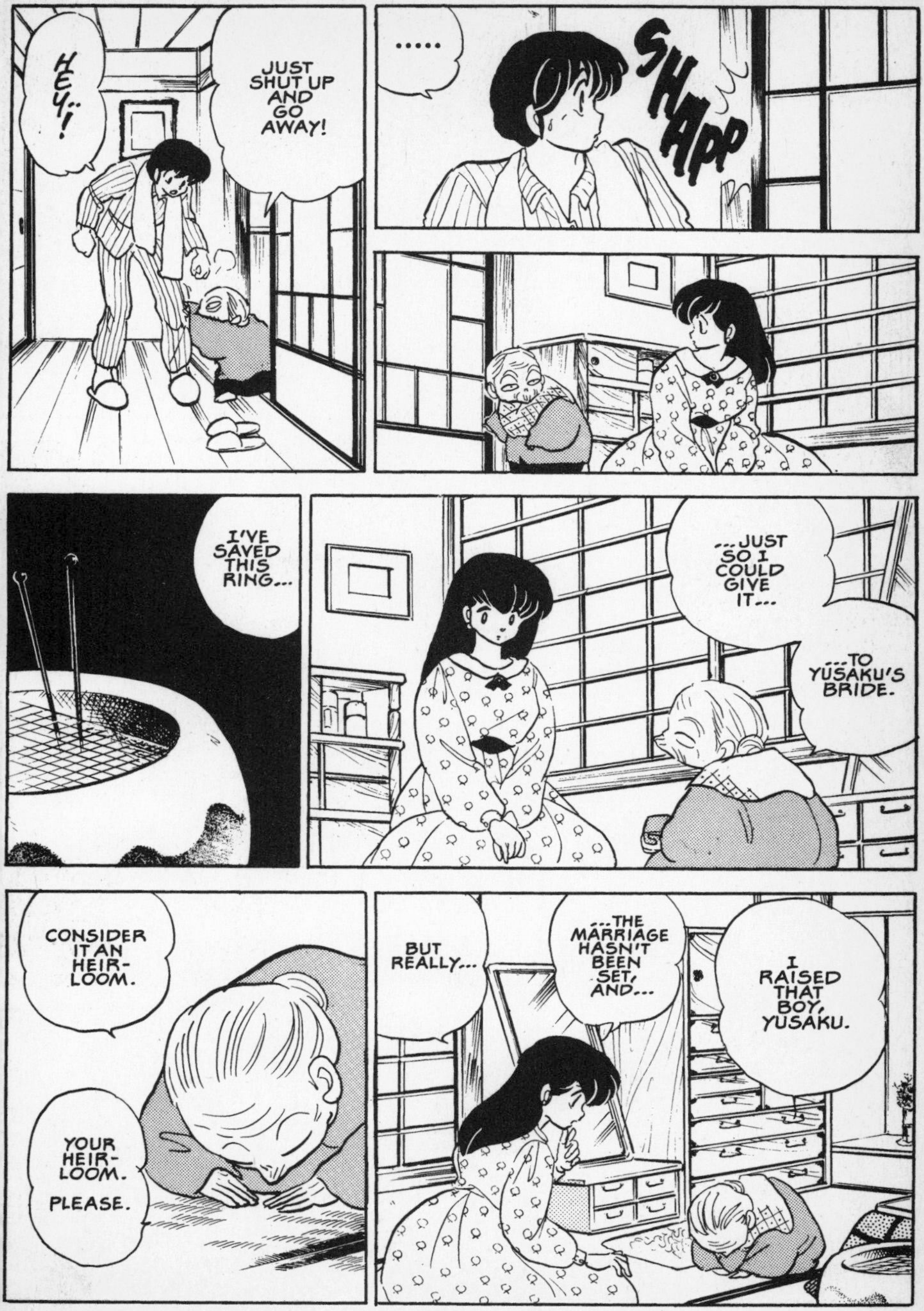
HEY..!
JUST SHUT UP AND GO AWAY!
.....
SHAPP
I'VE SAVED THIS RING...
...JUST SO I COULD GIVE IT...
...TO YUSAKU'S BRIDE.
CONSIDER IT AN HEIR-LOOM.
YOUR HEIR-LOOM.
PLEASE.
BUT REALLY...
...THE MARRIAGE HASN'T BEEN SET, AND...
I RAISED THAT BOY, YUSAKU.

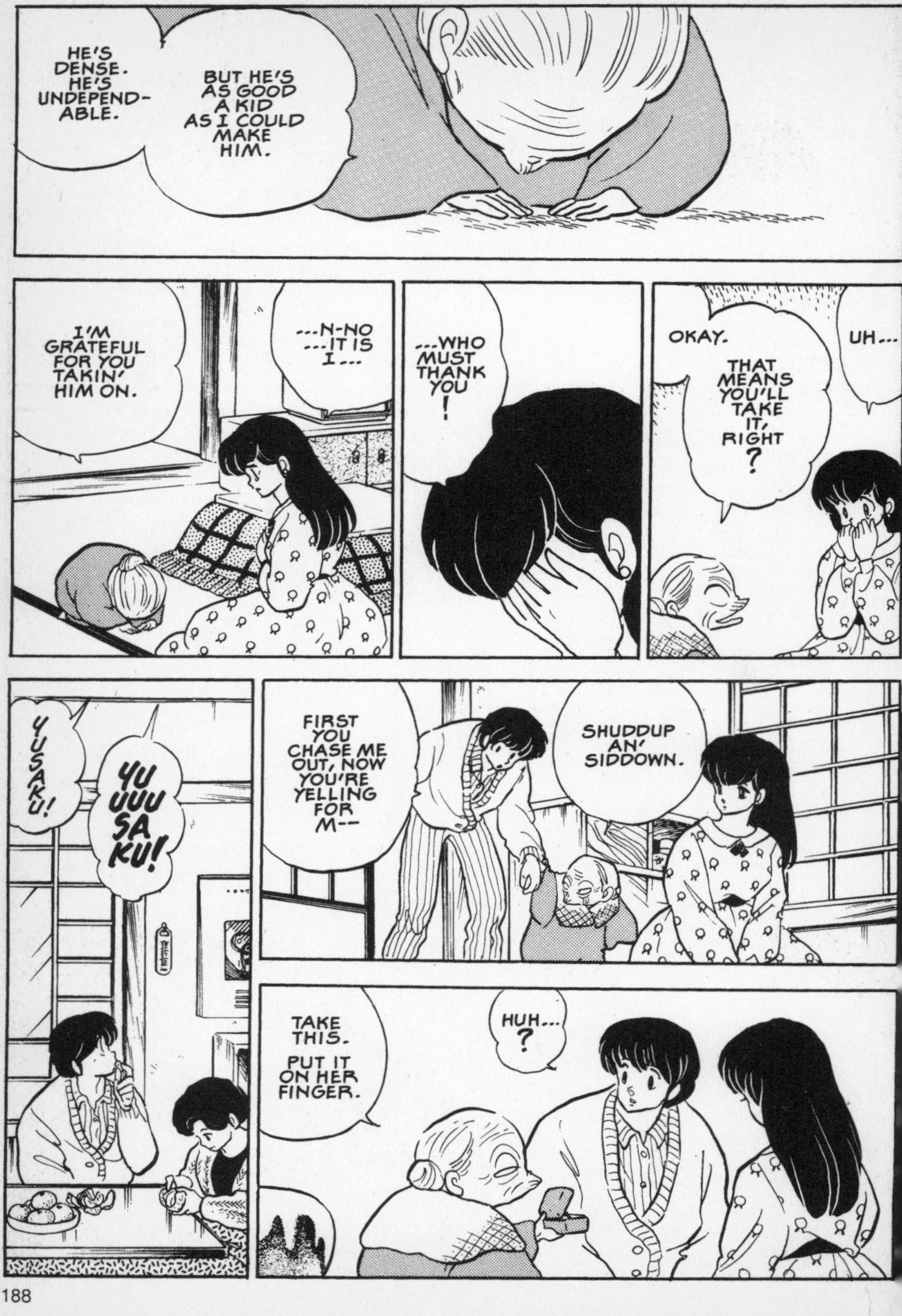
HE'S DENSE. HE'S UNDEPEND-ABLE.
BUT HE'S AS GOOD A KID AS I COULD MAKE HIM.
I'M GRATEFUL FOR YOU TAKIN' HIM ON.
---N-NO ---IT IS I---
---WHO MUST THANK YOU!
OKAY. THAT MEANS YOU'LL TAKE IT, RIGHT?
UH---
YUSAKU!
YU UUU SA KU!
FIRST YOU CHASE ME OUT, NOW YOU'RE YELLING FOR M--
SHUDDUP AN' SIDDOWN.
TAKE THIS. PUT IT ON HER FINGER.
HUH...?

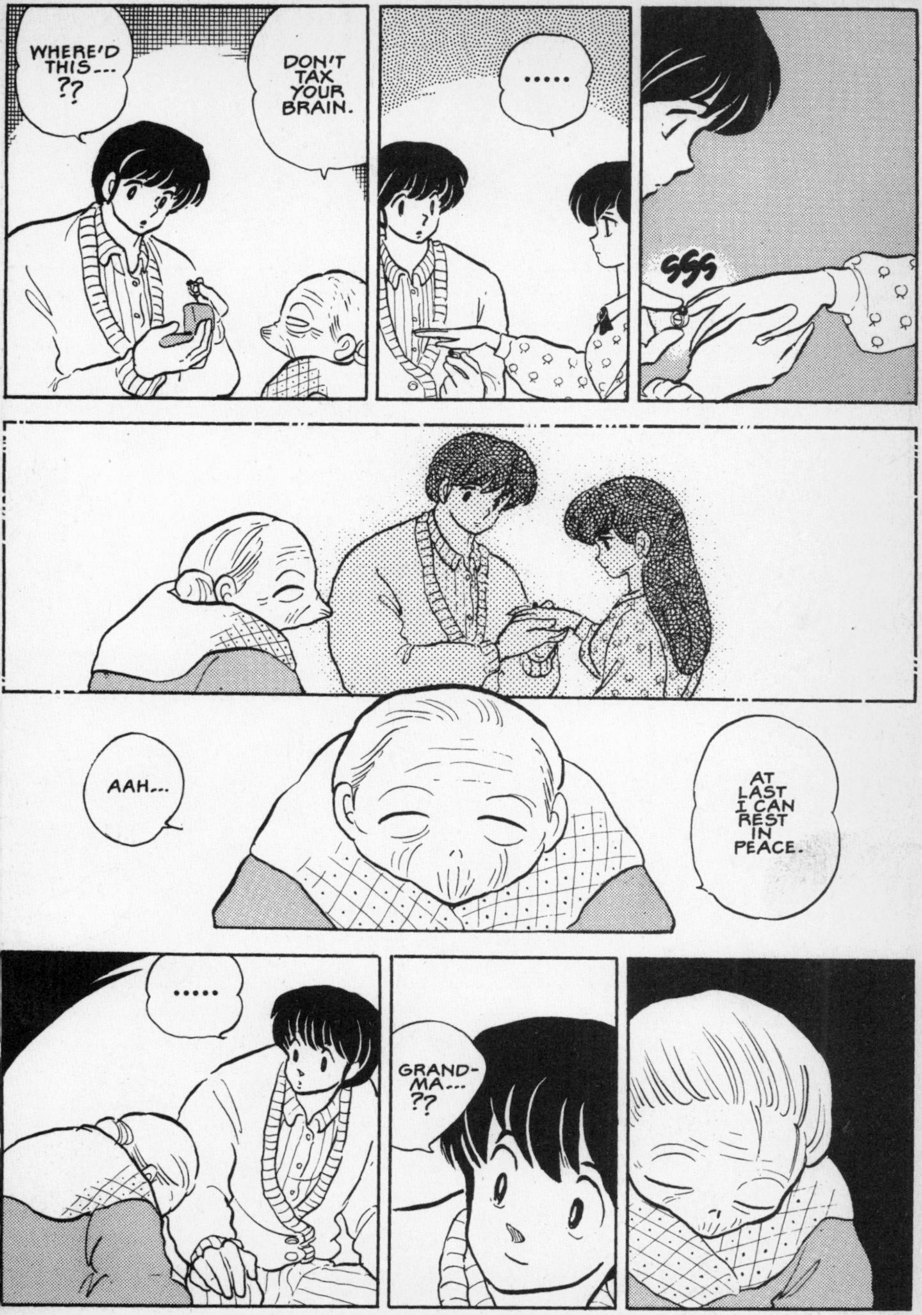
WHERE'D THIS... ??
DON'T TAX YOUR BRAIN.
.....
SSS
AAH...
AT LAST I CAN REST IN PEACE.
.....
GRAND-MA... ??

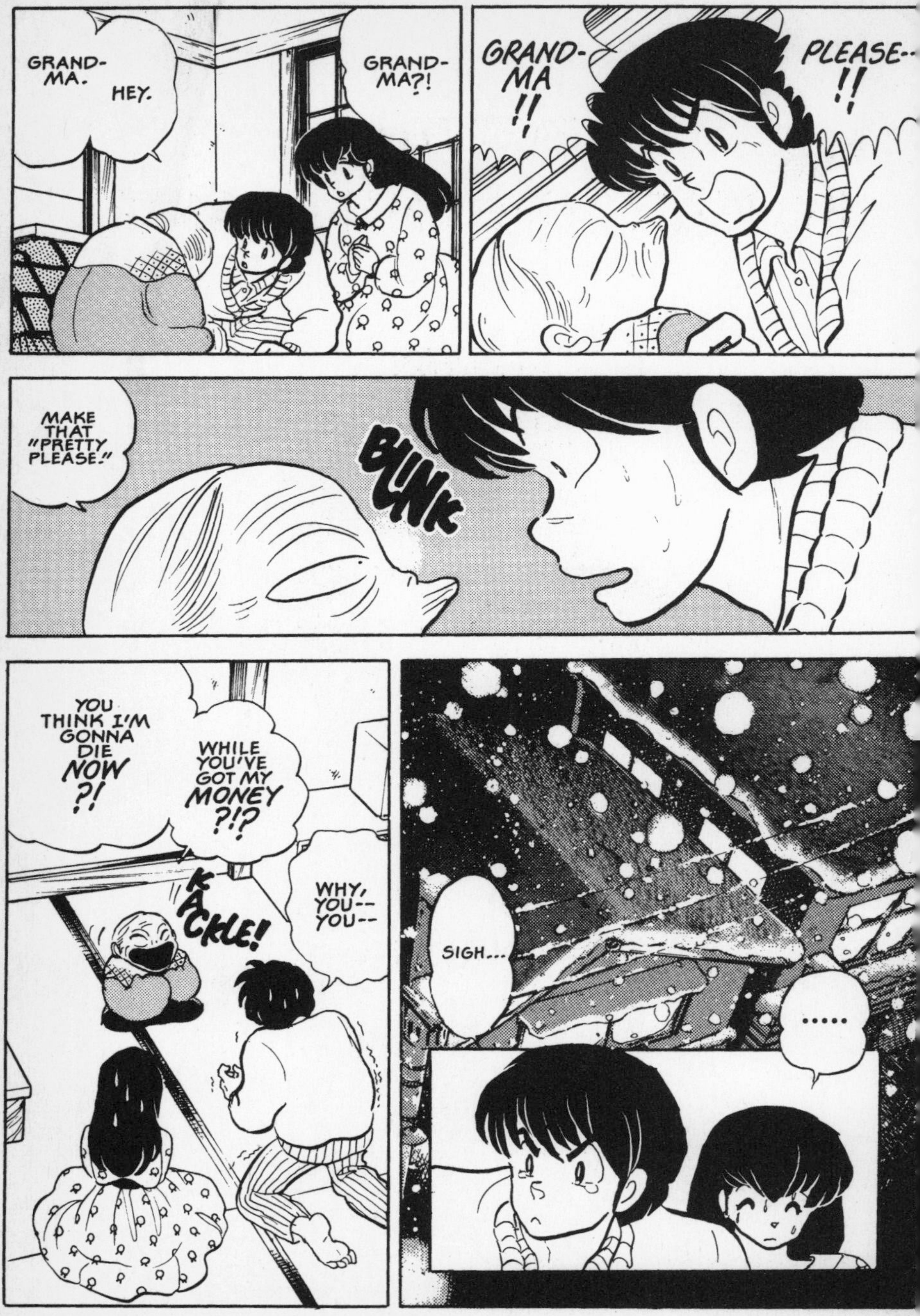
GRAND-MA. HEY.
GRAND-MA?!
GRAND-MA !!
PLEASE-- !!
MAKE THAT "PRETTY PLEASE."
BLINK
YOU THINK I'M GONNA DIE NOW ?!
WHILE YOU'VE GOT MY MONEY ?!?
KACKLE!
WHY, YOU-- YOU--
SIGH...
.....

PART TEN
BENEATH THE CHERRY TREE

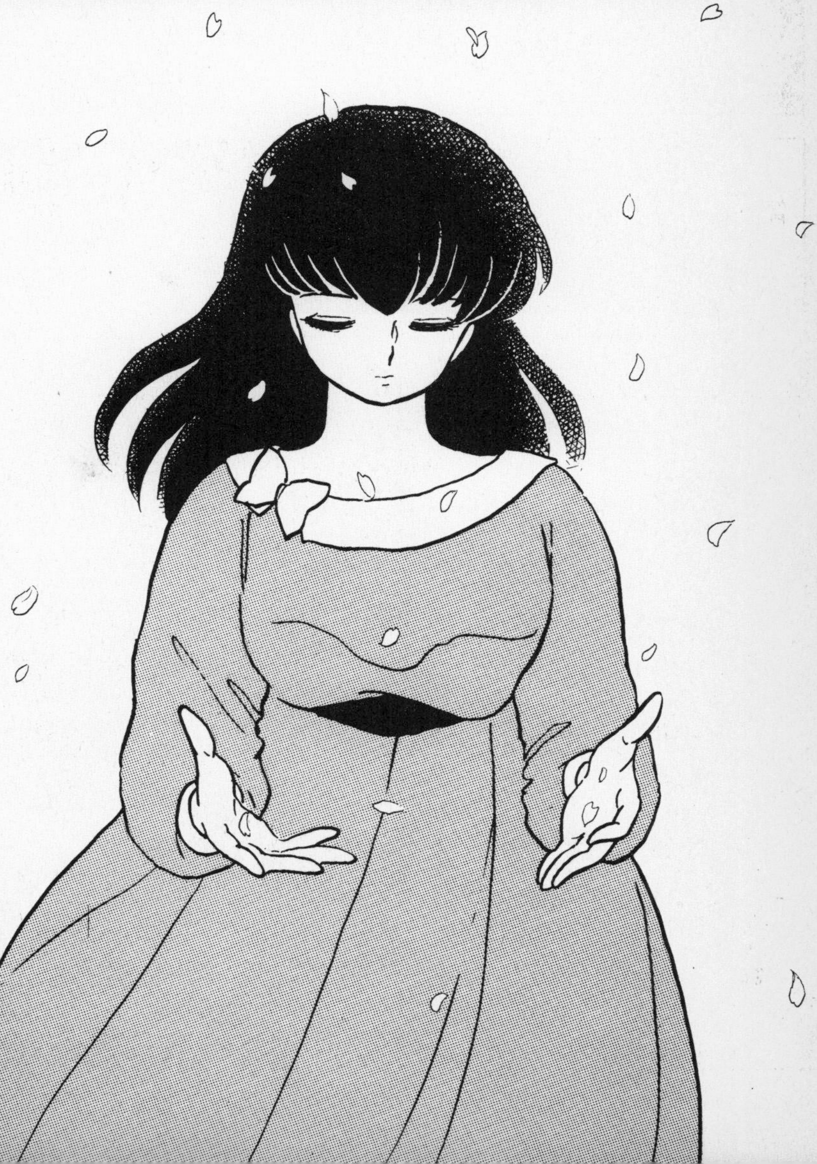

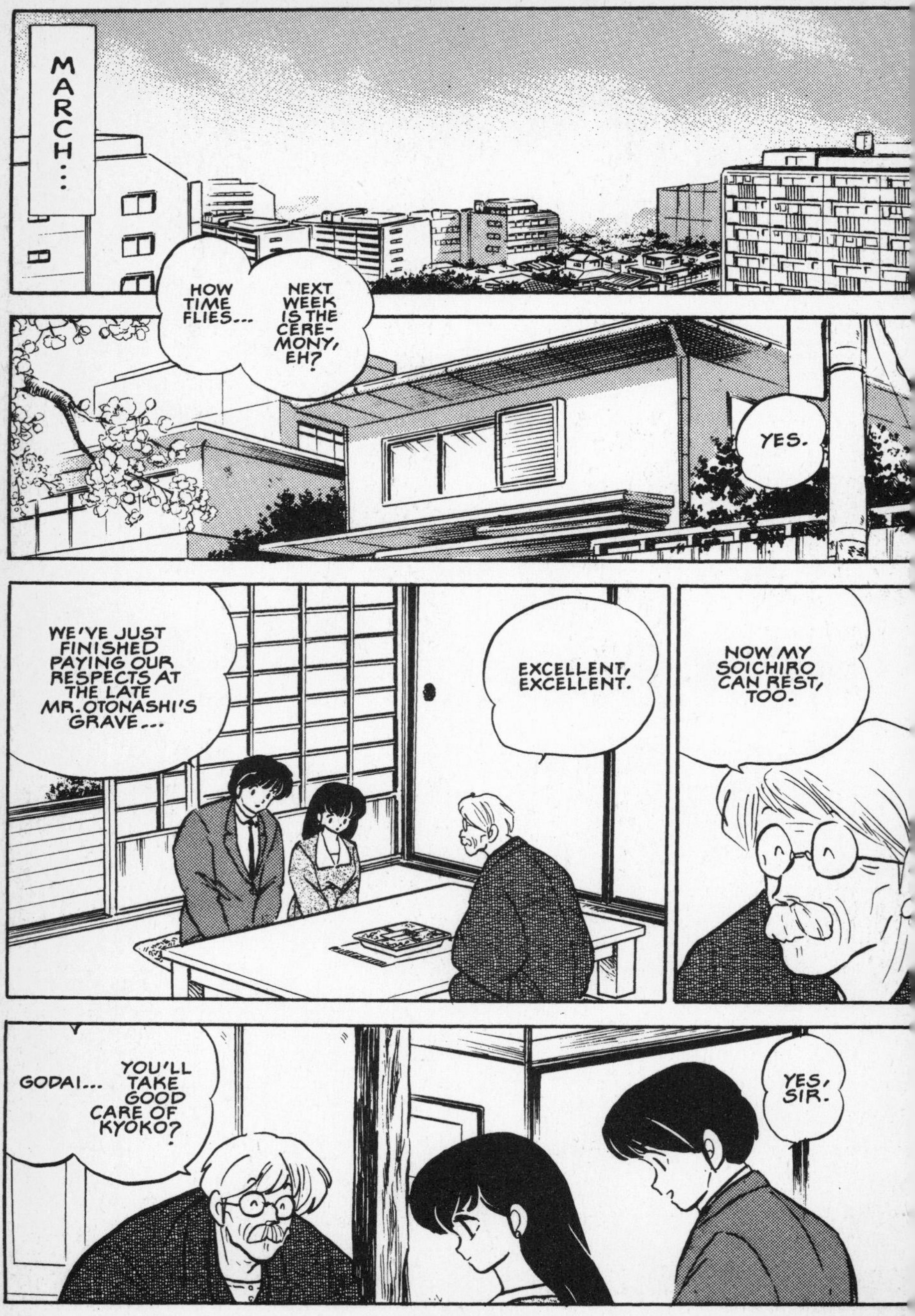
MARCH...
HOW TIME FLIES...
NEXT WEEK IS THE CERE-MONY, EH?
YES.
WE'VE JUST FINISHED PAYING OUR RESPECTS AT THE LATE MR. OTONASHI'S GRAVE...
EXCELLENT, EXCELLENT.
NOW MY SOICHIRO CAN REST, TOO.
GODAI...
YOU'LL TAKE GOOD CARE OF KYOKO?
YES, SIR.

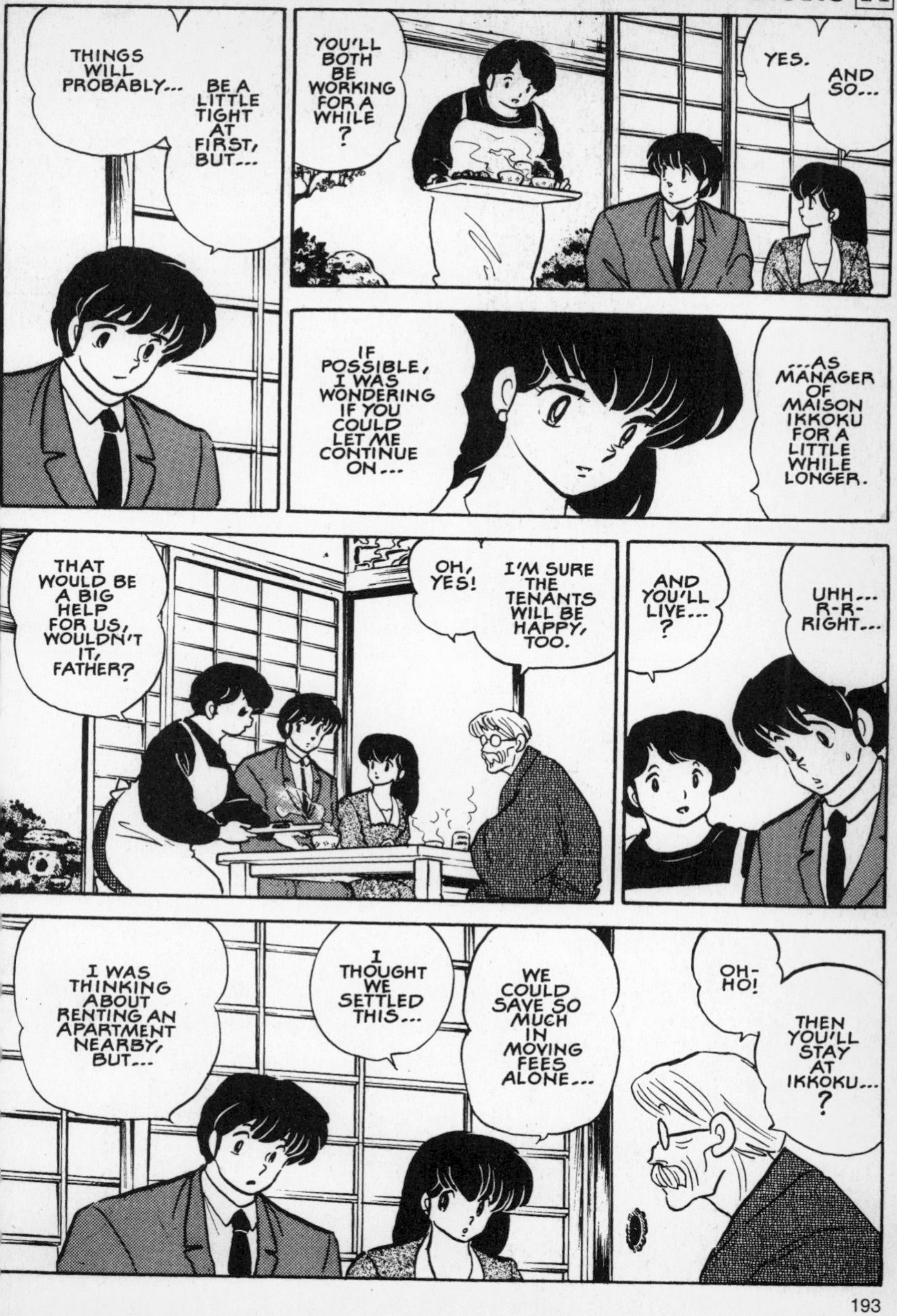
THINGS WILL PROBABLY... BE A LITTLE TIGHT AT FIRST, BUT...
YOU'LL BOTH BE WORKING FOR A WHILE ?
YES.
AND SO...
IF POSSIBLE, I WAS WONDERING IF YOU COULD LET ME CONTINUE ON...
...AS MANAGER OF MAISON IKKOKU FOR A LITTLE WHILE LONGER.
THAT WOULD BE A BIG HELP FOR US, WOULDN'T IT, FATHER?
OH, YES!
I'M SURE THE TENANTS WILL BE HAPPY, TOO.
AND YOU'LL LIVE... ?
UHH... R-R-RIGHT...
I WAS THINKING ABOUT RENTING AN APARTMENT NEARBY, BUT...
I THOUGHT WE SETTLED THIS...
WE COULD SAVE SO MUCH IN MOVING FEES ALONE...
OH-HO!
THEN YOU'LL STAY AT IKKOKU... ?

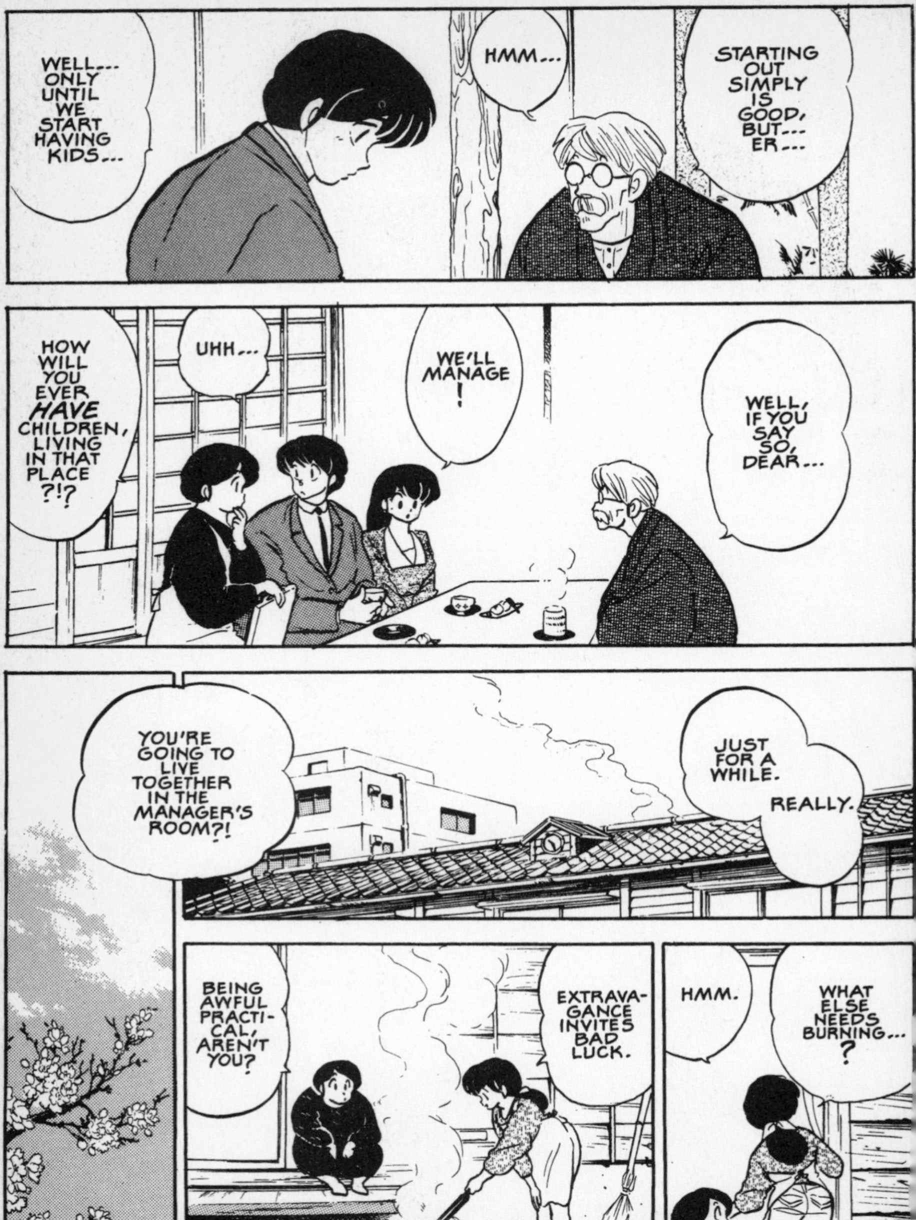
WELL... ONLY UNTIL WE START HAVING KIDS...
HMM...
STARTING OUT SIMPLY IS GOOD, BUT... ER...
HOW WILL YOU EVER *HAVE* CHILDREN, LIVING IN THAT PLACE ?!?
UHH...
WE'LL MANAGE!
WELL, IF YOU SAY SO, DEAR...
YOU'RE GOING TO LIVE TOGETHER IN THE MANAGER'S ROOM?!
JUST FOR A WHILE.
REALLY.
BEING AWFUL PRACTICAL, AREN'T YOU?
EXTRAVAGANCE INVITES BAD LUCK.
HMM.
WHAT ELSE NEEDS BURNING...?

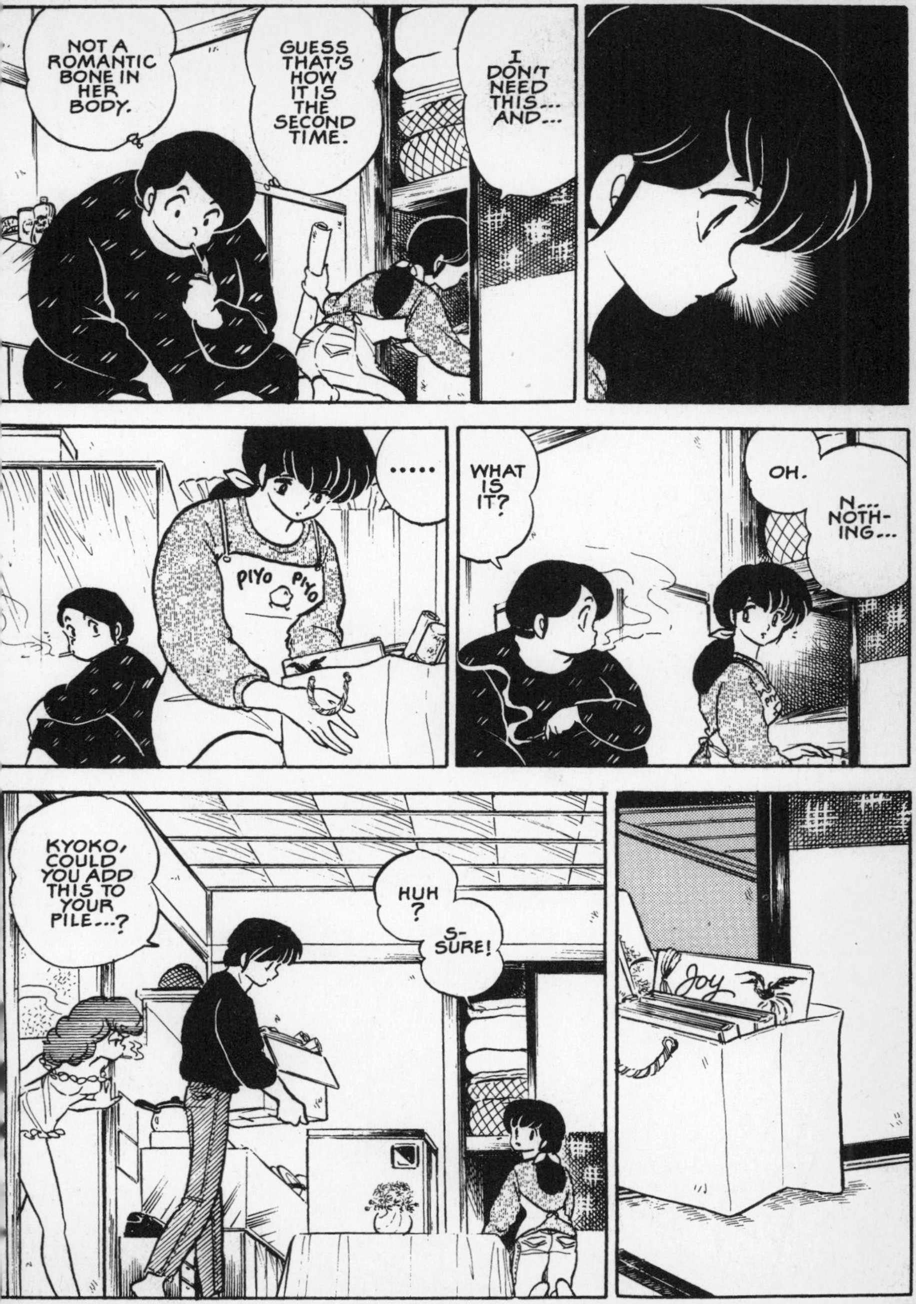
NOT A ROMANTIC BONE IN HER BODY.
GUESS THAT'S HOW IT IS THE SECOND TIME.
I DON'T NEED THIS... AND...
.....
WHAT IS IT?
OH.
N... NOTHING...
KYOKO, COULD YOU ADD THIS TO YOUR PILE...?
HUH?
S-SURE!
JOY

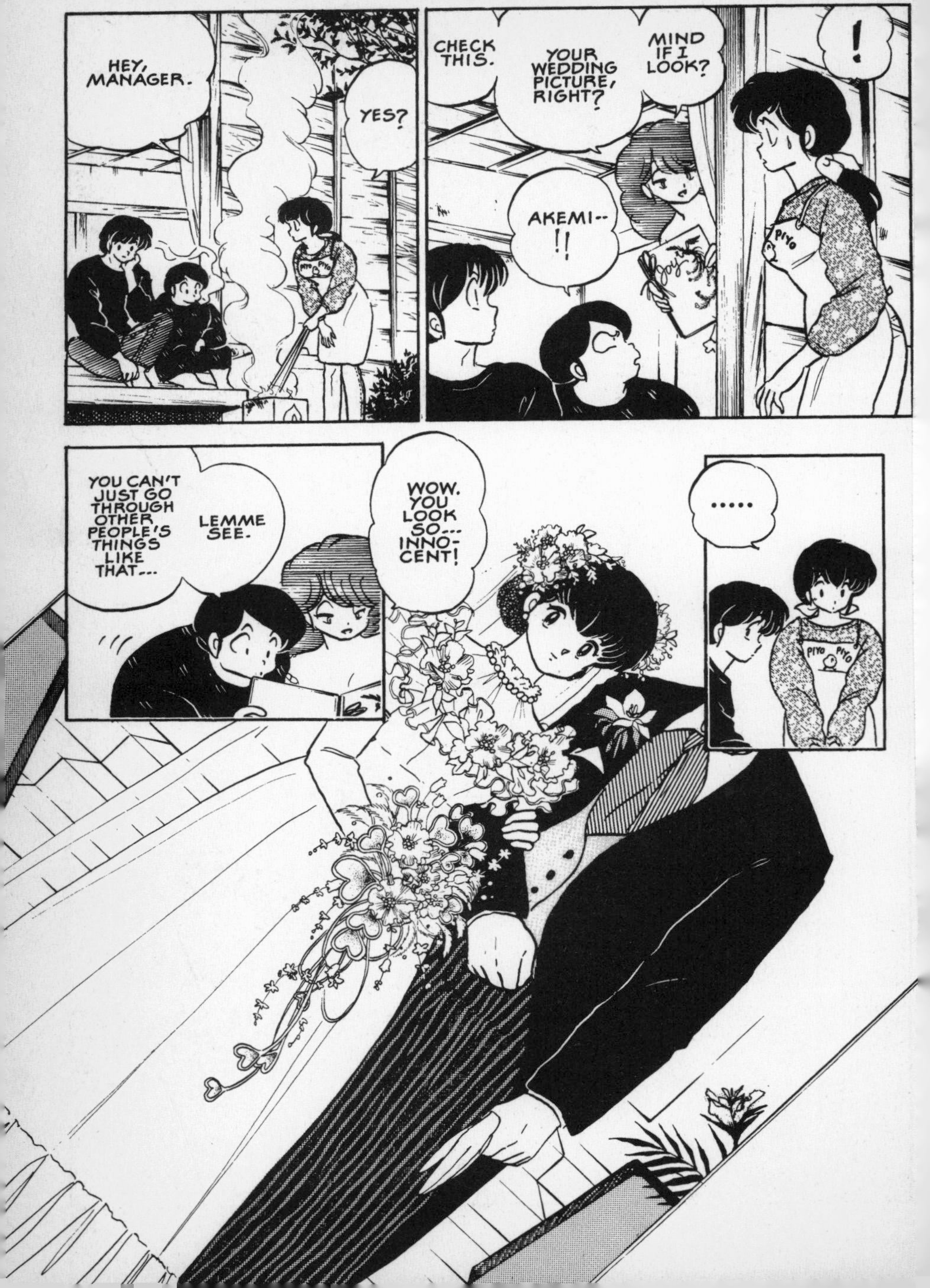
HEY, MANAGER.
YES?
CHECK THIS.
YOUR WEDDING PICTURE, RIGHT?
MIND IF I LOOK?
!
AKEMI-- !!
YOU CAN'T JUST GO THROUGH OTHER PEOPLE'S THINGS LIKE THAT...
LEMME SEE.
WOW. YOU LOOK SO... INNO-CENT!
.....
PIYO PIYO

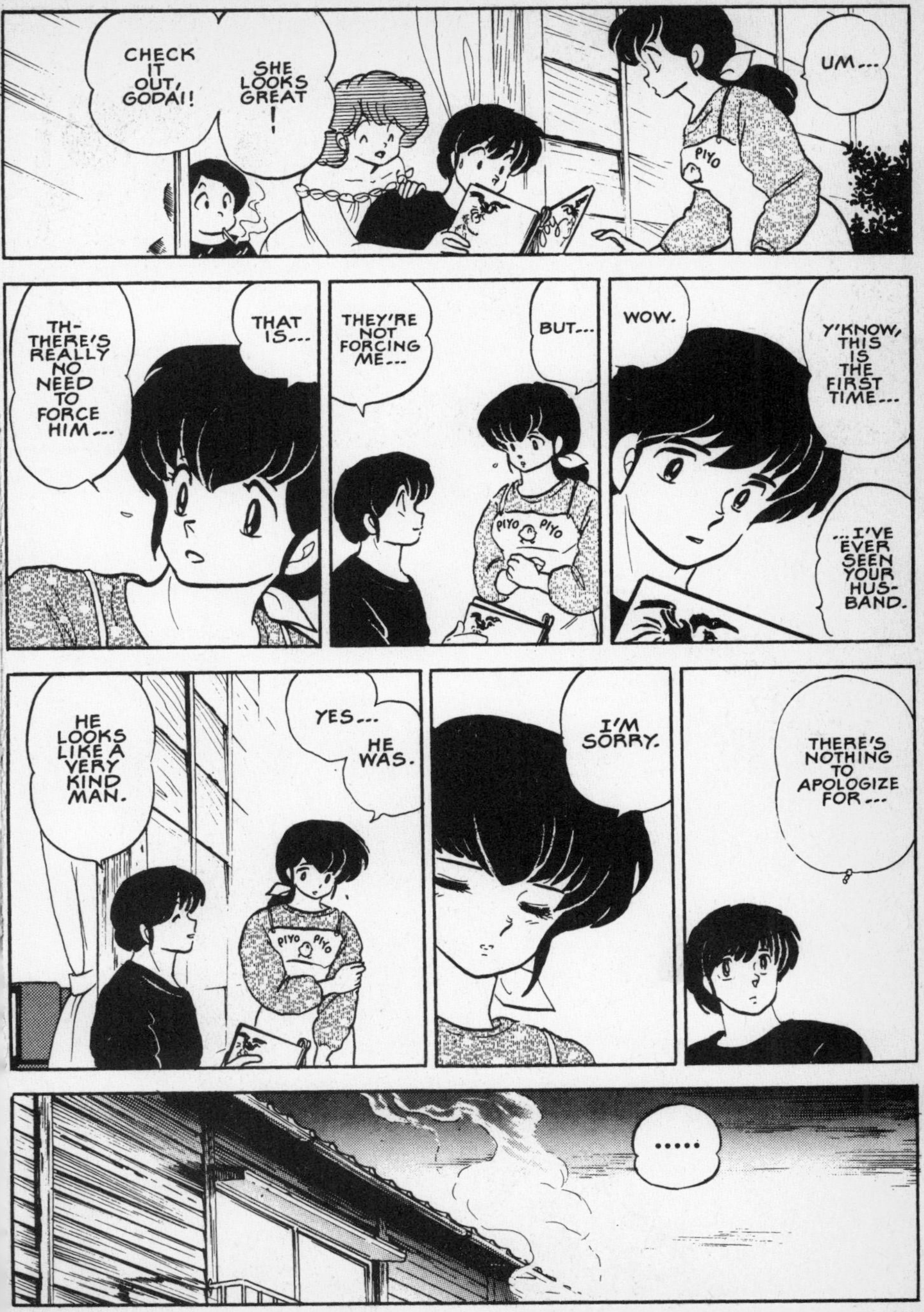
CHECK IT OUT, GODAI!
SHE LOOKS GREAT!
UM...
PIYO
TH-THERE'S REALLY NO NEED TO FORCE HIM...
THAT IS...
THEY'RE NOT FORCING ME...
BUT...
PIYO PIYO
WOW.
Y'KNOW, THIS IS THE FIRST TIME...
...I'VE EVER SEEN YOUR HUS-BAND.
HE LOOKS LIKE A VERY KIND MAN.
YES... HE WAS.
PIYO PIYO
I'M SORRY.
THERE'S NOTHING TO APOLOGIZE FOR...
......

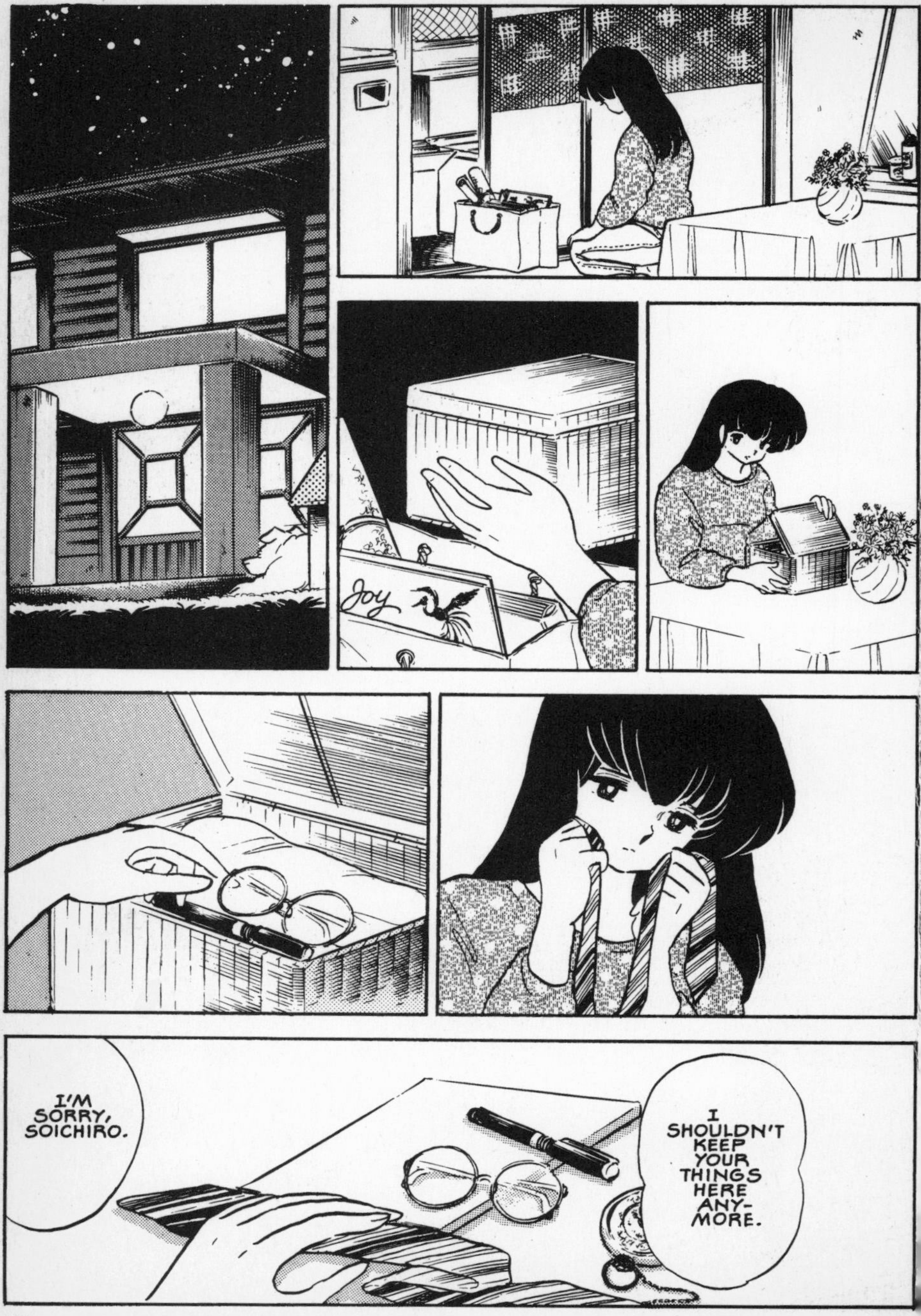
I'M SORRY, SOICHIRO.
I SHOULDN'T KEEP YOUR THINGS HERE ANY-MORE.

SHE DIDN'T HAVE TO FEEL SO SELF-CONSCIOUS...

...ABOUT HER WEDDING PHOTO.

I'M MARRYING HER FULLY AWARE OF THE SITUATION.

WHY WORRY?

UNLESS SHE REALLY HASN'T SETTLED HER OWN FEELINGS ABOUT IT...

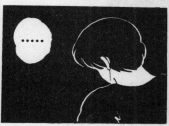

......

MANAGER

CHK...

TAP...

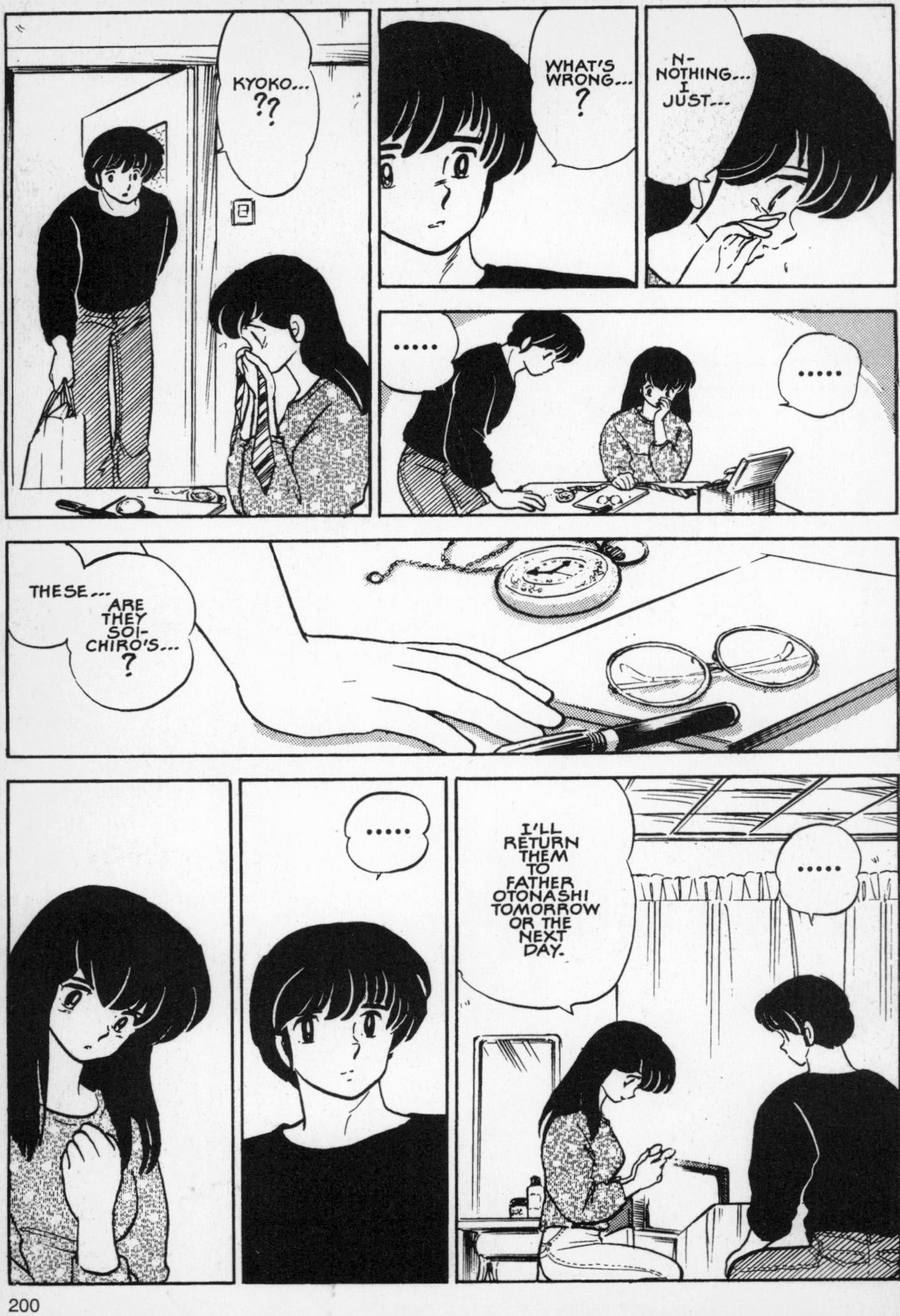
KYOKO... ??
WHAT'S WRONG... ?
N- NOTHING... I JUST...
.....
.....
THESE... ARE THEY SOI- CHIRO'S... ?
.....
I'LL RETURN THEM TO FATHER OTONASHI TOMORROW OR THE NEXT DAY.
.....

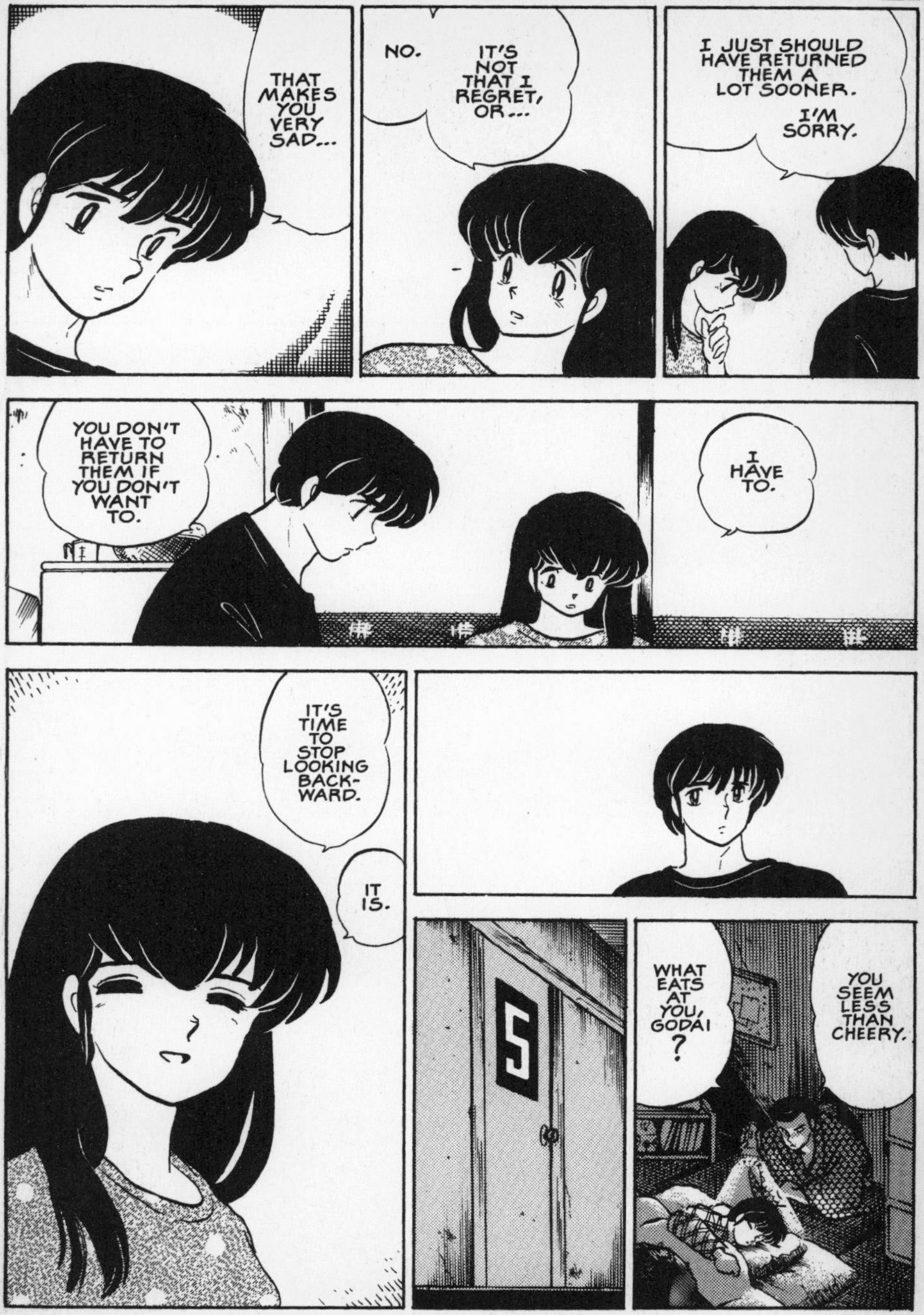
THAT MAKES YOU VERY SAD...
NO.
IT'S NOT THAT I REGRET, OR...
I JUST SHOULD HAVE RETURNED THEM A LOT SOONER.
I'M SORRY.
YOU DON'T HAVE TO RETURN THEM IF YOU DON'T WANT TO.
I HAVE TO.
IT'S TIME TO STOP LOOKING BACK-WARD.
IT IS.
5
WHAT EATS AT YOU, GODAI ?
YOU SEEM LESS THAN CHEERY.

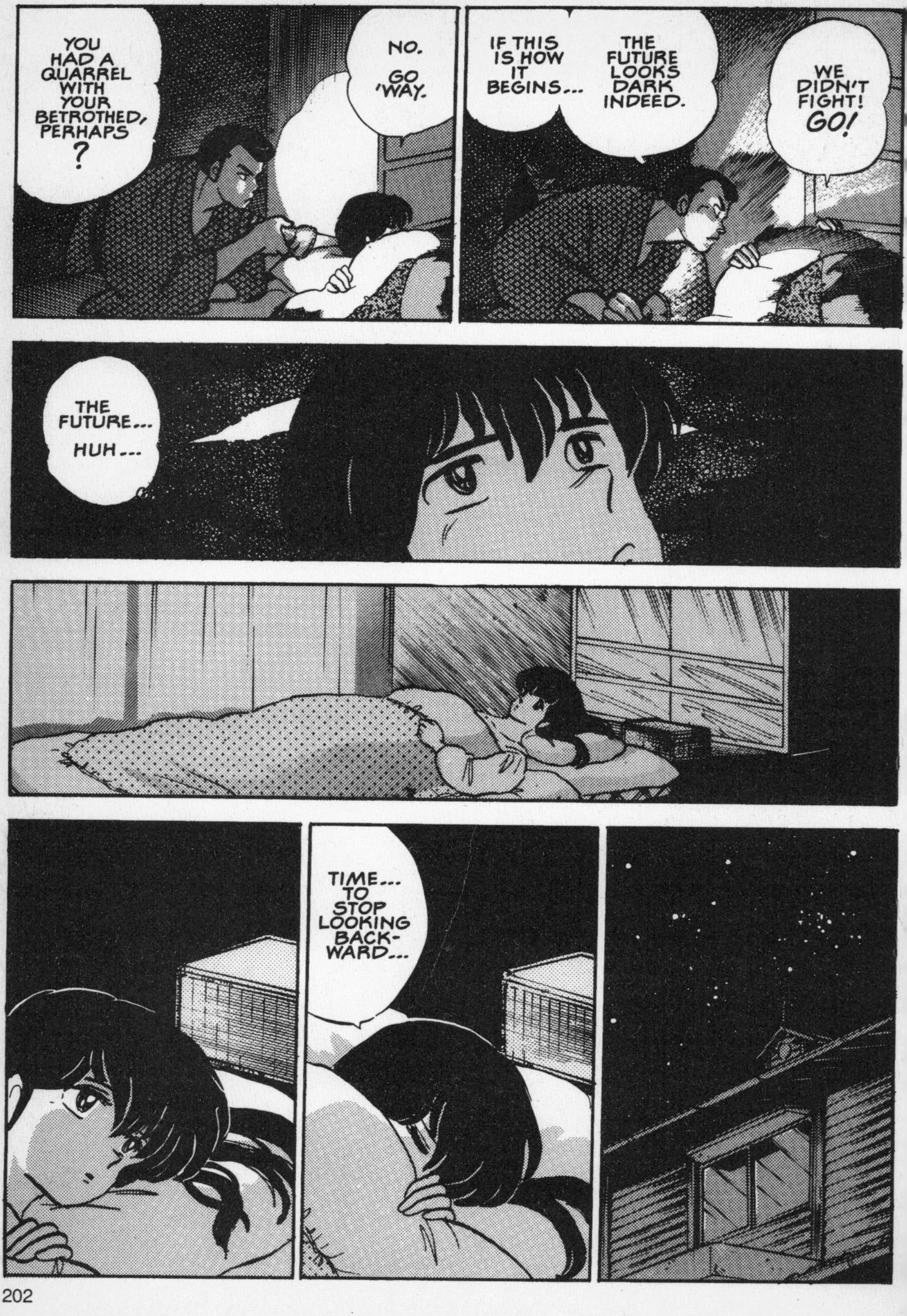
YOU HAD A QUARREL WITH YOUR BETROTHED, PERHAPS?
NO. GO 'WAY.
IF THIS IS HOW IT BEGINS...
THE FUTURE LOOKS DARK INDEED.
WE DIDN'T FIGHT! GO!
THE FUTURE... HUH...
TIME... TO STOP LOOKING BACKWARD...

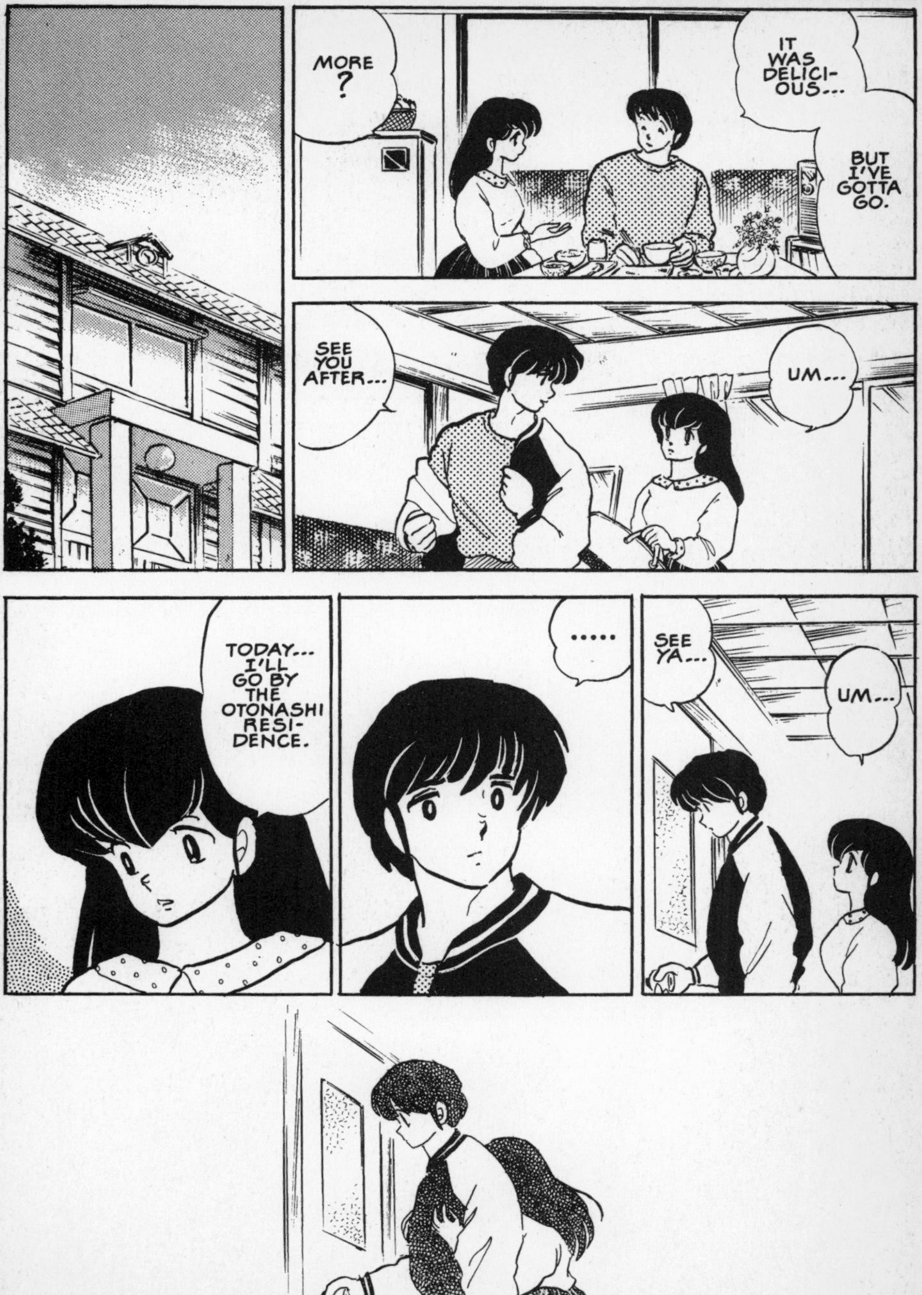
MORE?
IT WAS DELICI-OUS...
BUT I'VE GOTTA GO.
SEE YOU AFTER...
UM...
TODAY... I'LL GO BY THE OTONASHI RESI-DENCE.
.....
SEE YA...
UM...

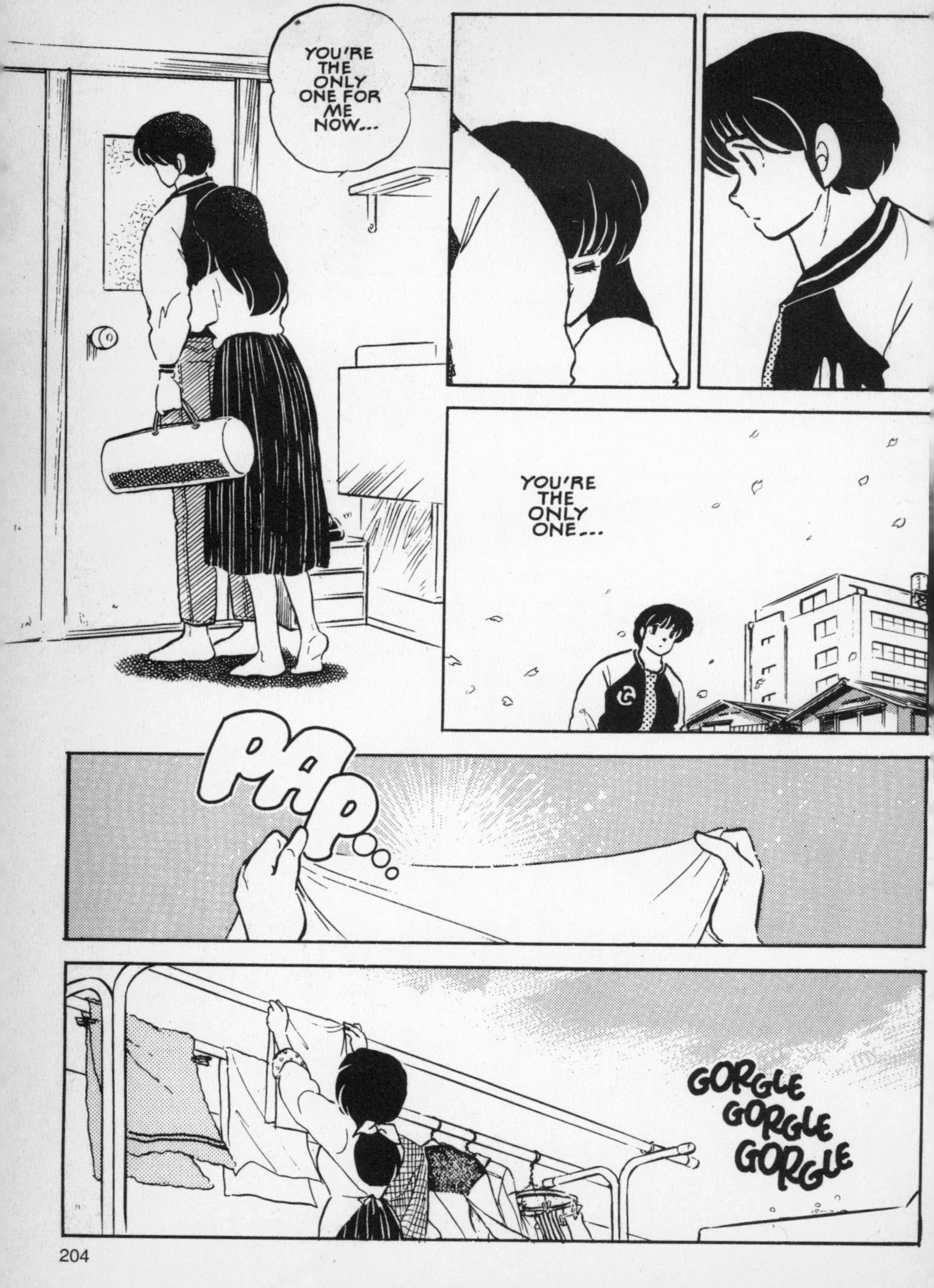
YOU'RE THE ONLY ONE FOR ME NOW...
YOU'RE THE ONLY ONE...
PAP...
GORGLE GORGLE GORGLE

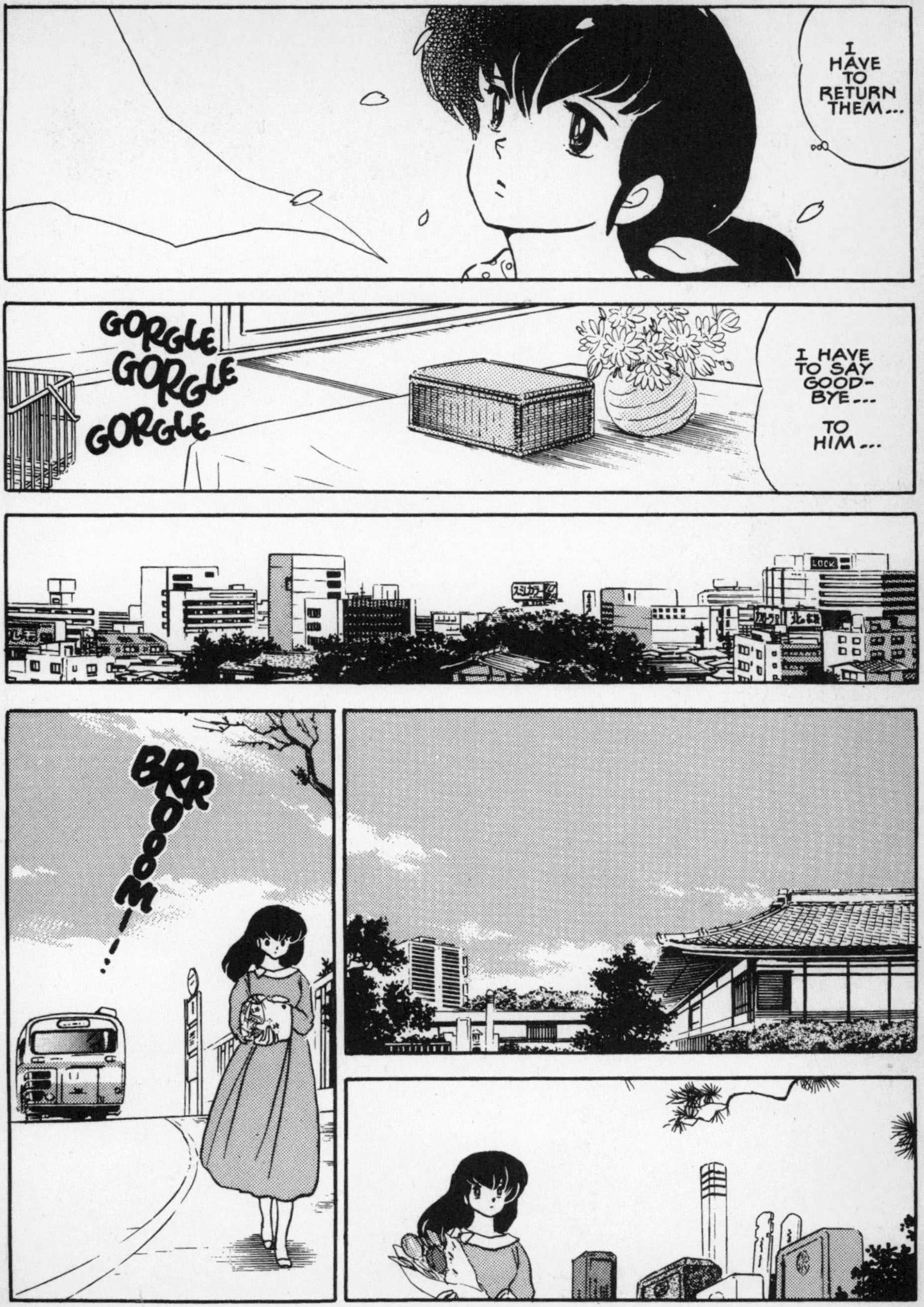
I HAVE TO RETURN THEM...
GORGLE GORGLE GORGLE
I HAVE TO SAY GOOD-BYE...
TO HIM...
BRRROOOOM!!...

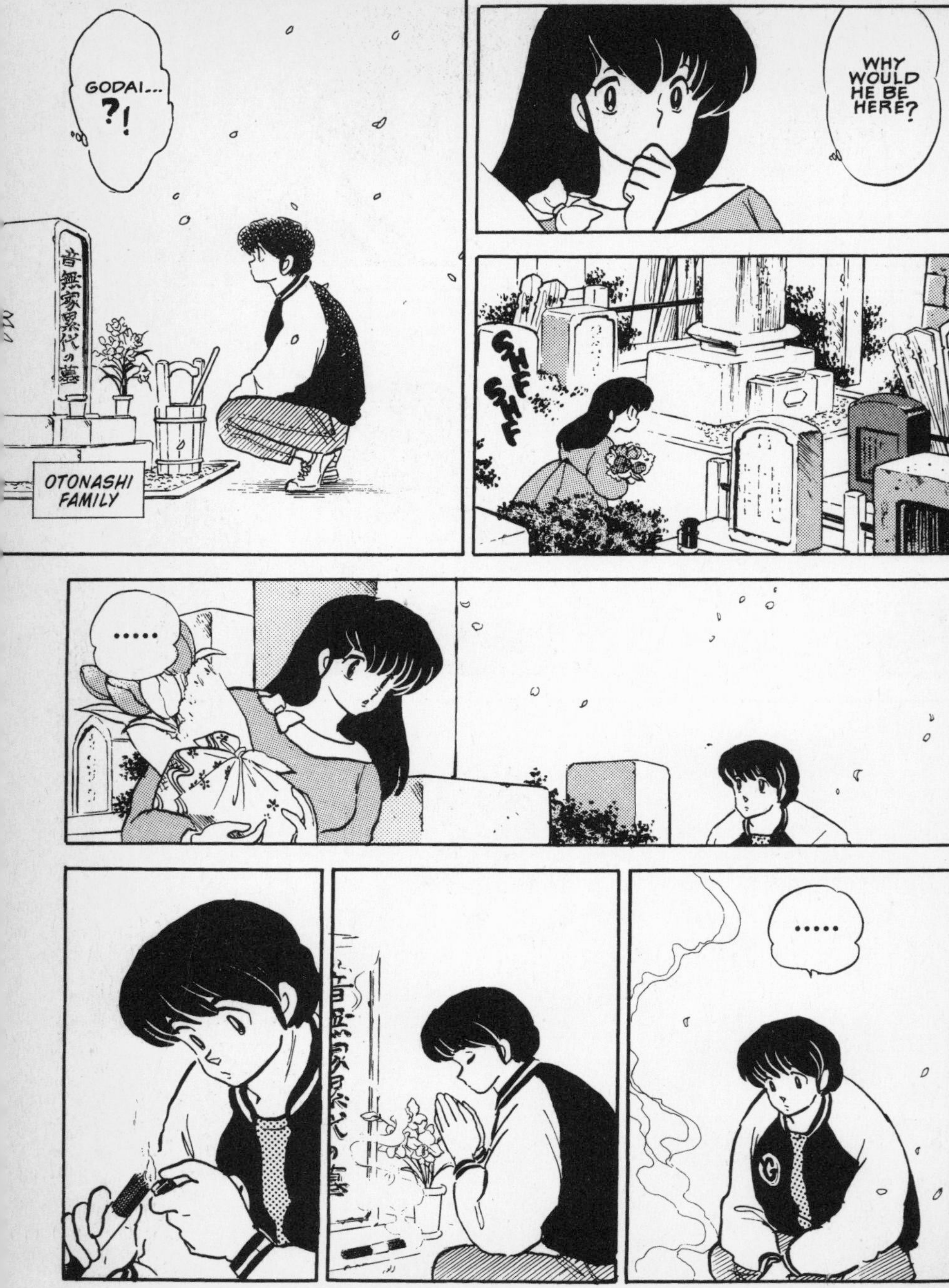
GODAI... ?!
音無家累代の墓
OTONASHI FAMILY
WHY WOULD HE BE HERE?
SHF SHF
.....
.....

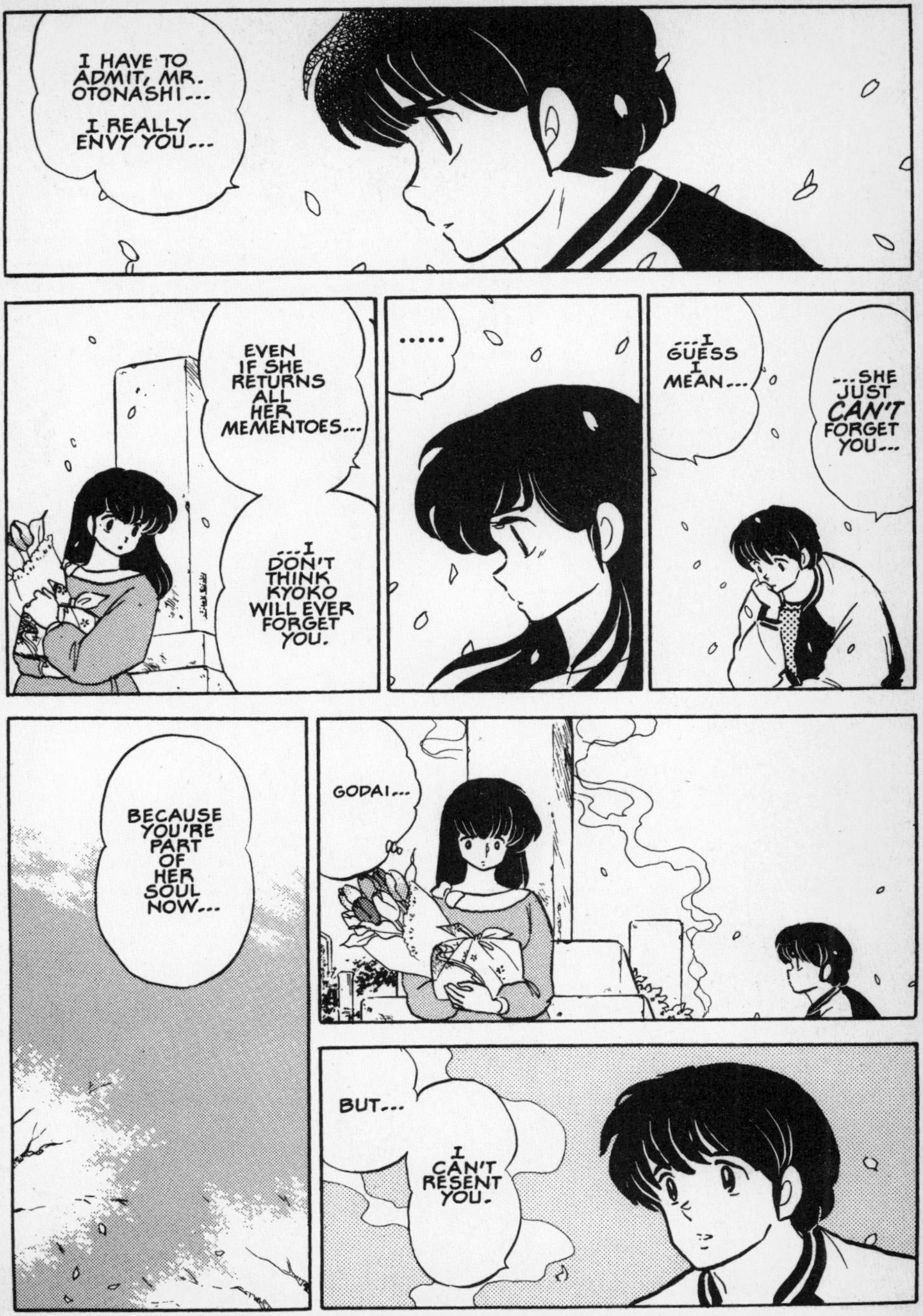
I HAVE TO ADMIT, MR. OTONASHI...
I REALLY ENVY YOU...
EVEN IF SHE RETURNS ALL HER MEMENTOES...
...I DON'T THINK KYOKO WILL EVER FORGET YOU.
.....
...I GUESS I MEAN...
...SHE JUST CAN'T FORGET YOU...
BECAUSE YOU'RE PART OF HER SOUL NOW...
GODAI...
BUT...
I CAN'T RESENT YOU.

YOU'VE BEEN A PART OF HER SINCE THE FIRST DAY I MET HER...

SO....

AND I STILL FELL IN LOVE WITH HER.

I'M TAKING YOU INTO MY LIFE TOO.

AS PART OF HER.

.....

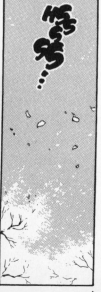

HSSSS...

SOICHIRO...

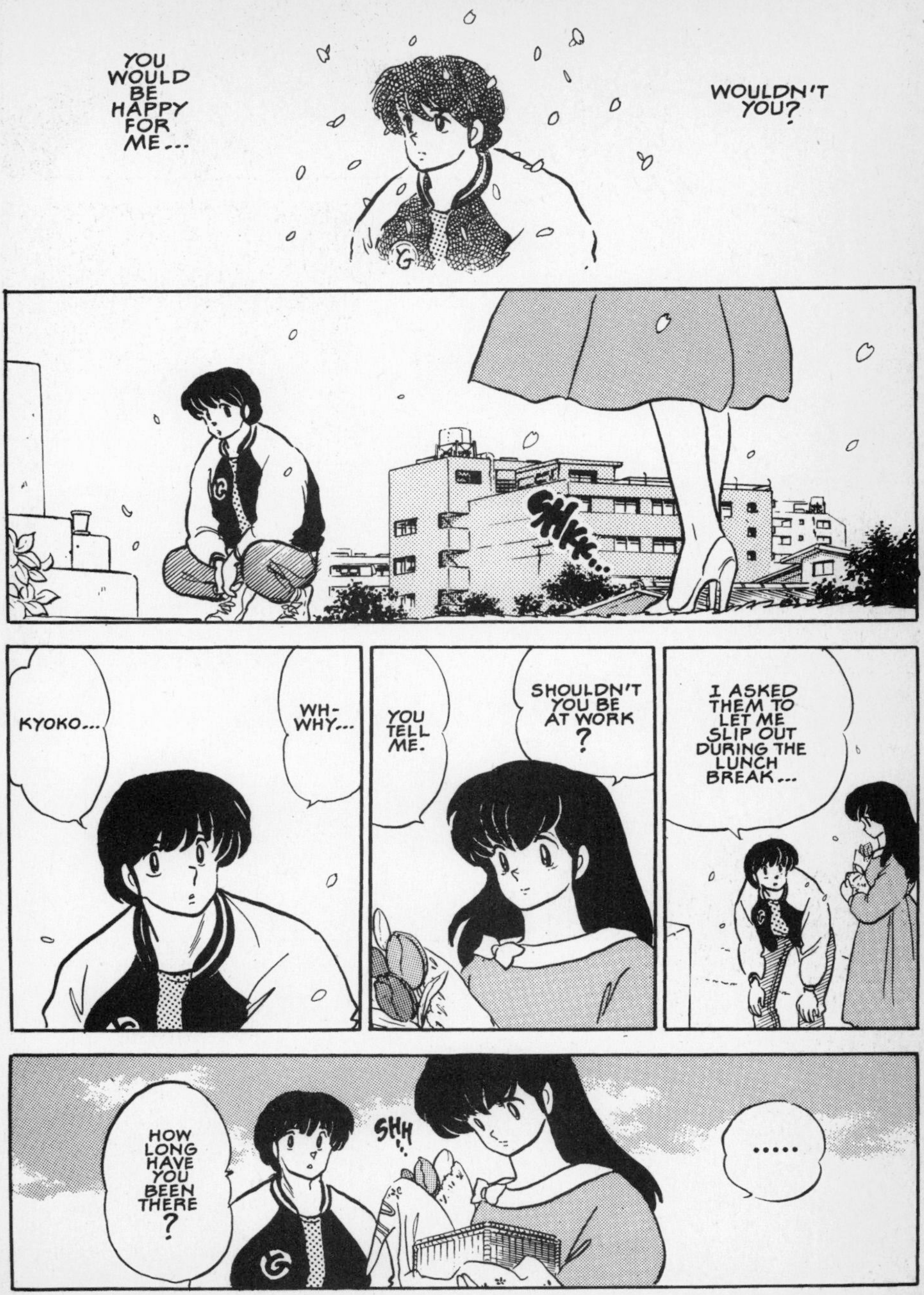

YOU WOULD BE HAPPY FOR ME...
WOULDN'T YOU?
SHKK...
KYOKO...
WH- WHY...
YOU TELL ME.
SHOULDN'T YOU BE AT WORK ?
I ASKED THEM TO LET ME SLIP OUT DURING THE LUNCH BREAK...
HOW LONG HAVE YOU BEEN THERE ?
SHH
.....

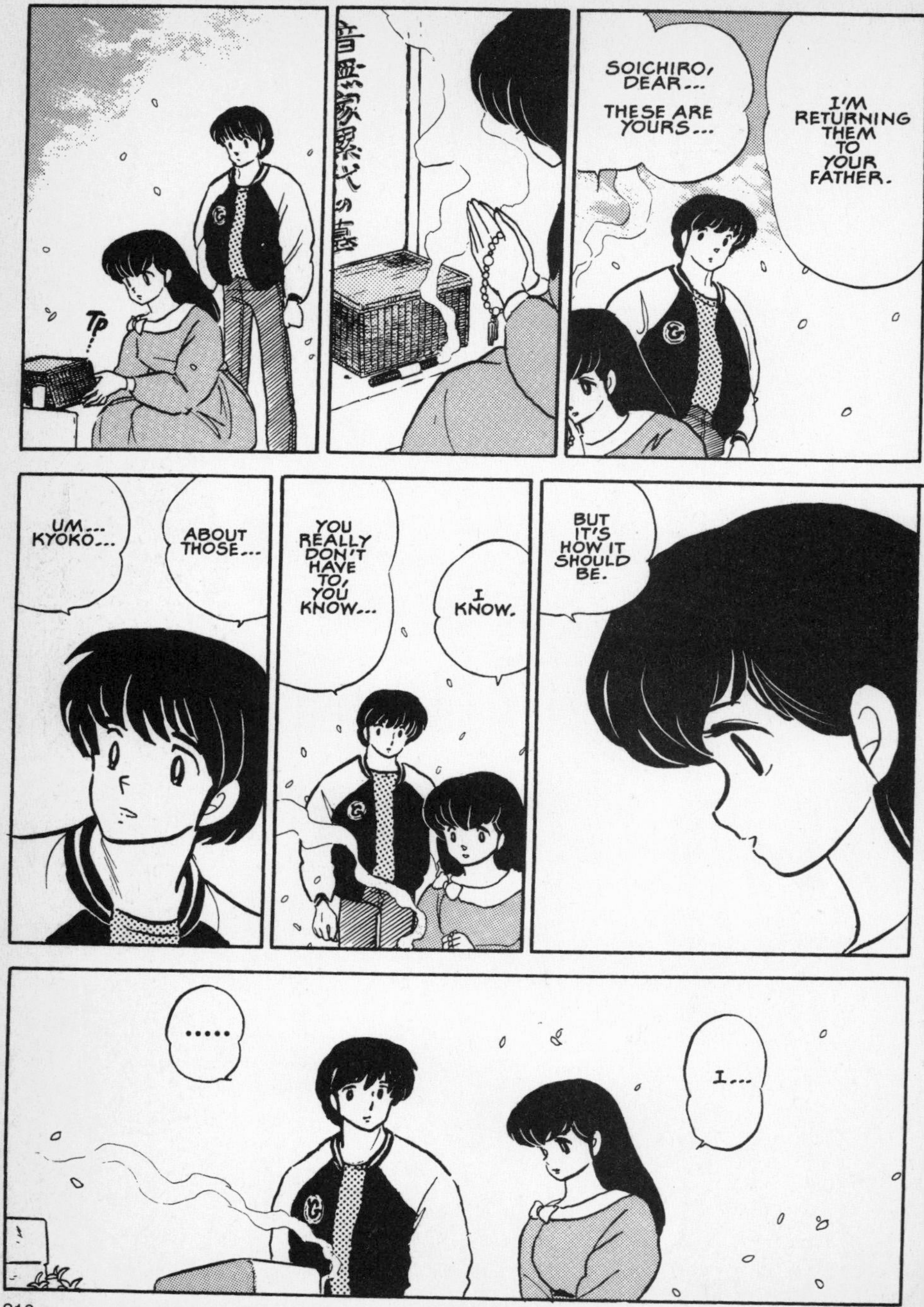
Tp
音無家累代の墓
SOICHIRO, DEAR...
THESE ARE YOURS...
I'M RETURNING THEM TO YOUR FATHER.
UM... KYOKO...
ABOUT THOSE...
YOU REALLY DON'T HAVE TO, YOU KNOW...
I KNOW.
BUT IT'S HOW IT SHOULD BE.
......
I...

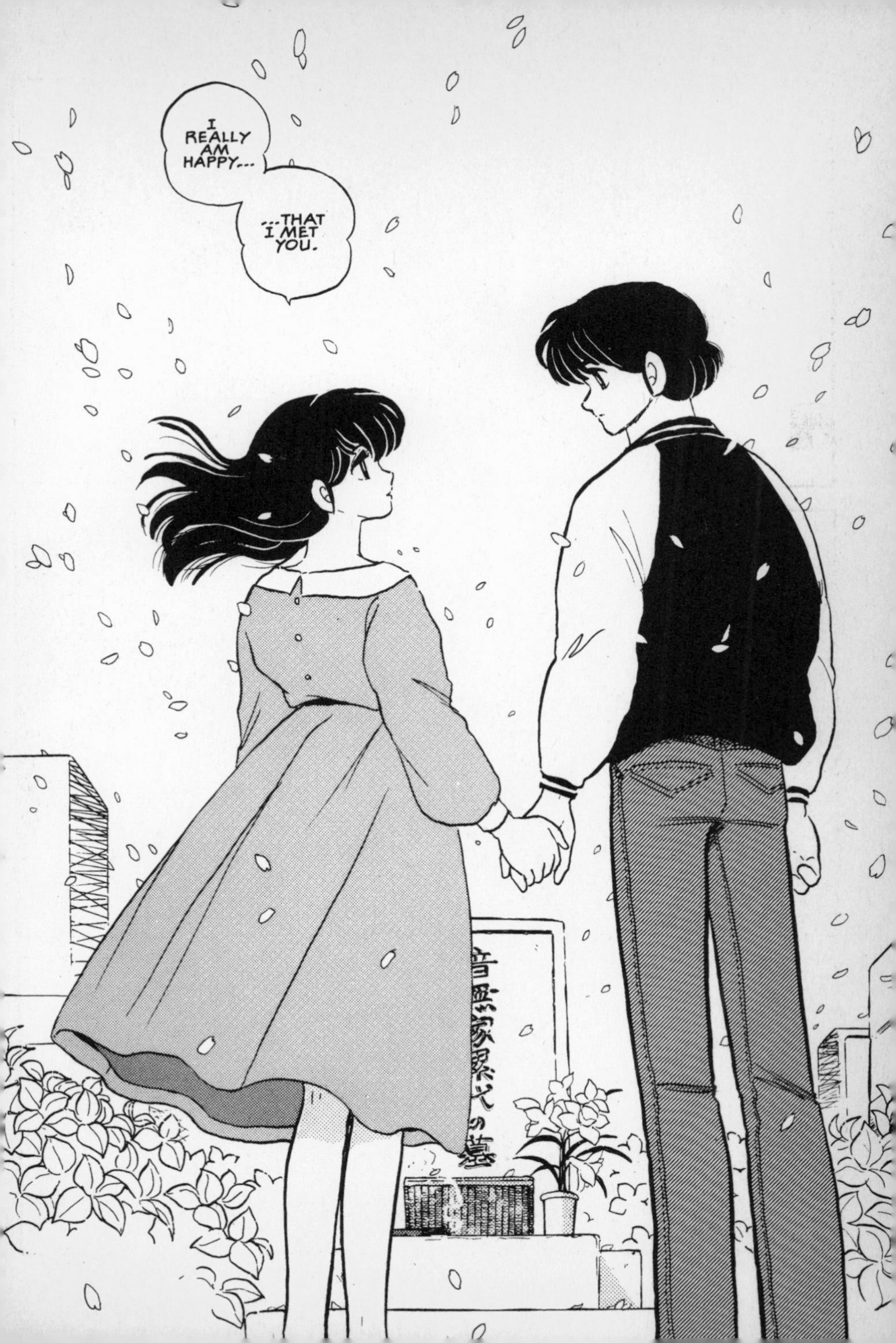
I REALLY AM HAPPY...
...THAT I MET YOU.

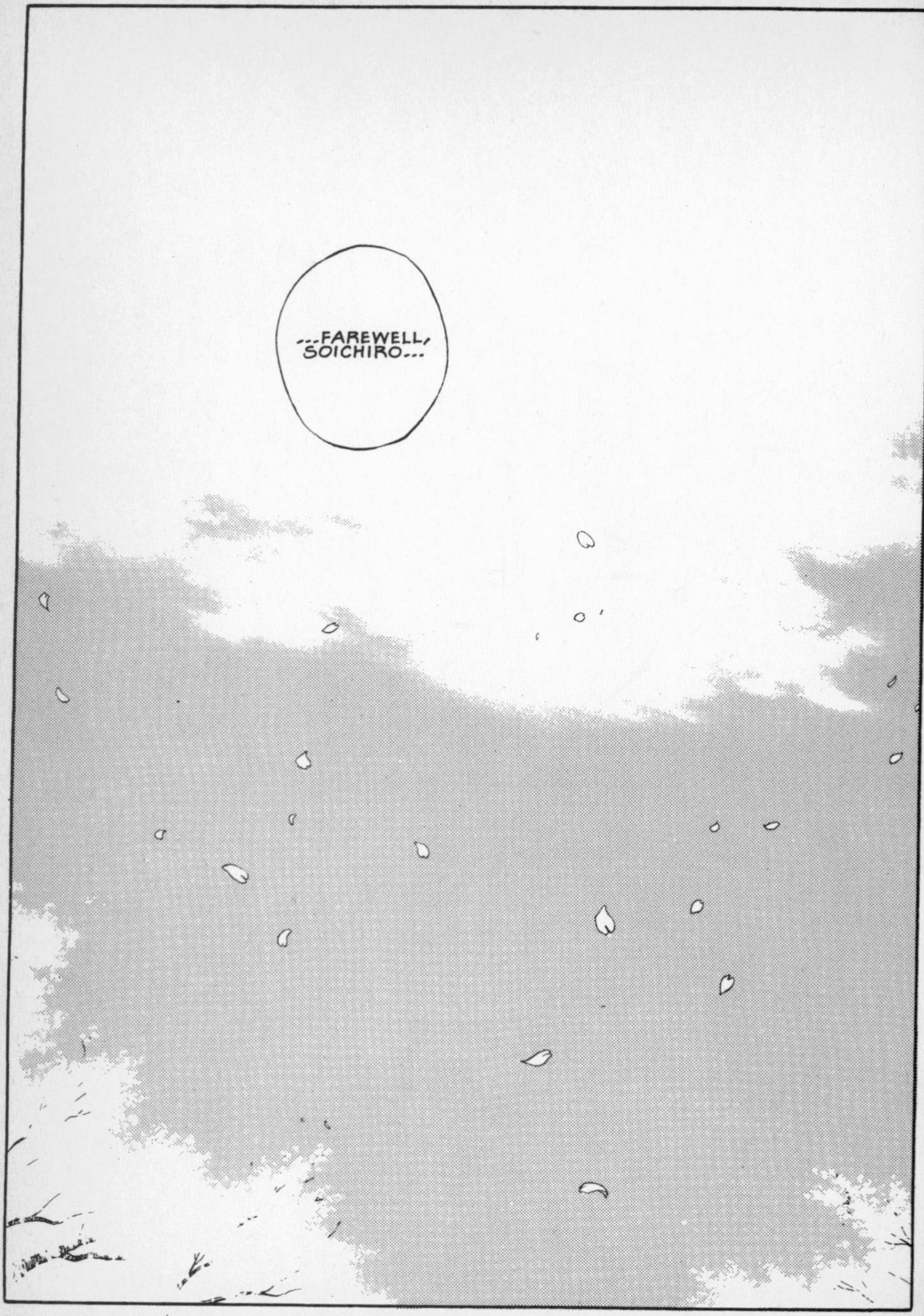
...FAREWELL, SOICHIRO...

PART ELEVEN

P.S. IKKOKU

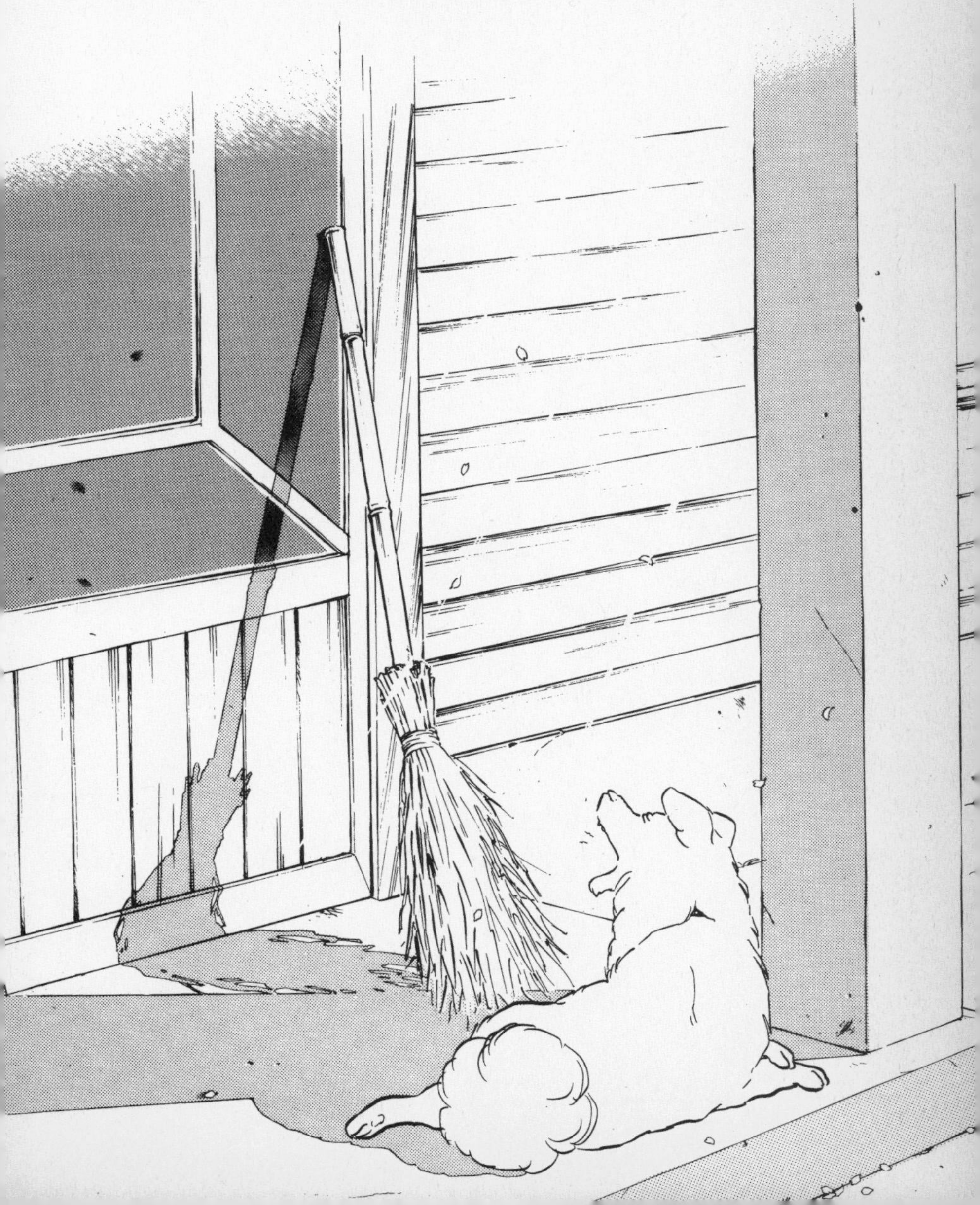

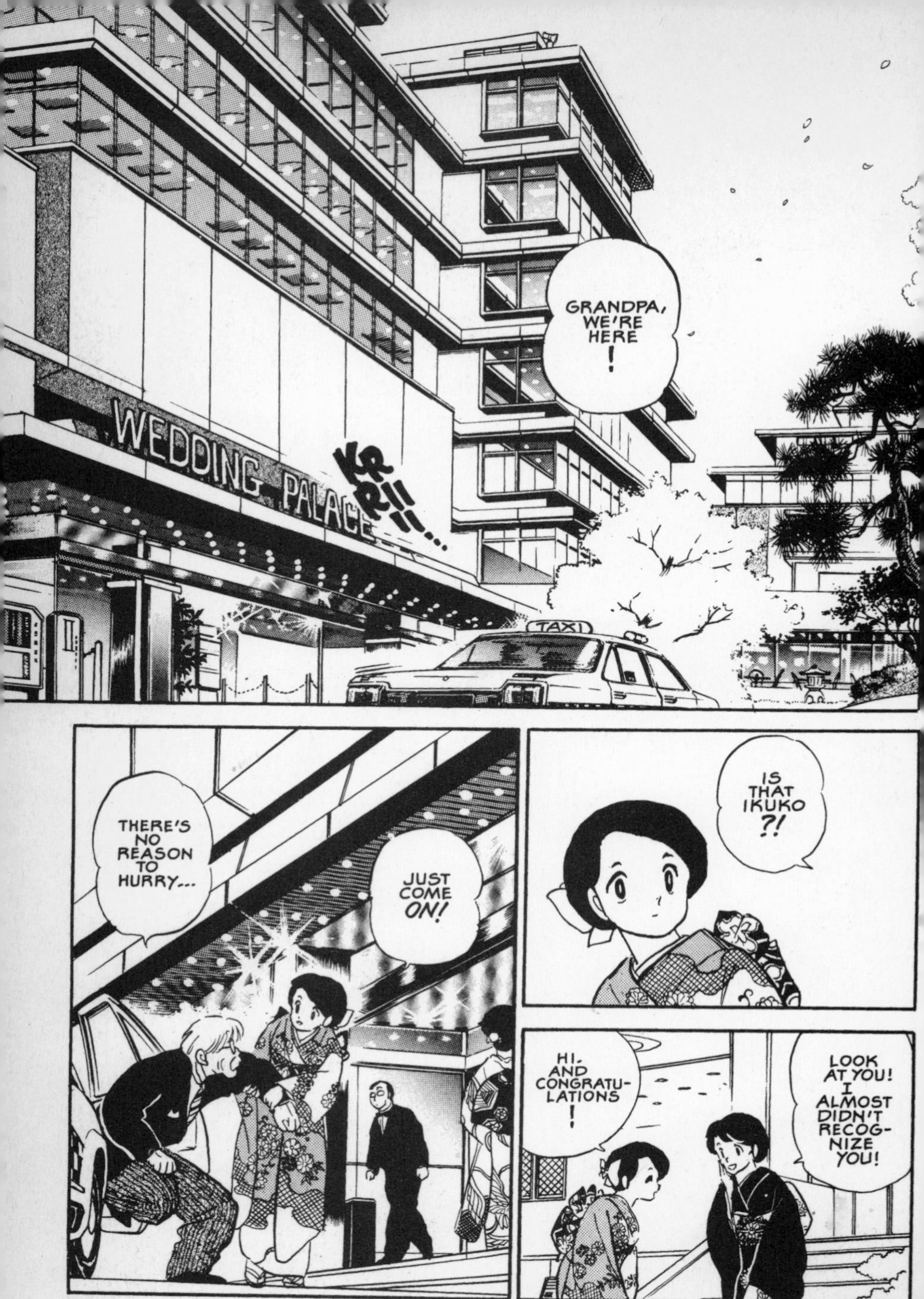
WEDDING PALACE
KRRII...
TAXI
GRANDPA, WE'RE HERE!
THERE'S NO REASON TO HURRY...
JUST COME ON!
IS THAT IKUKO ?!
HI. AND CONGRATULATIONS!
LOOK AT YOU! I ALMOST DIDN'T RECOGNIZE YOU!

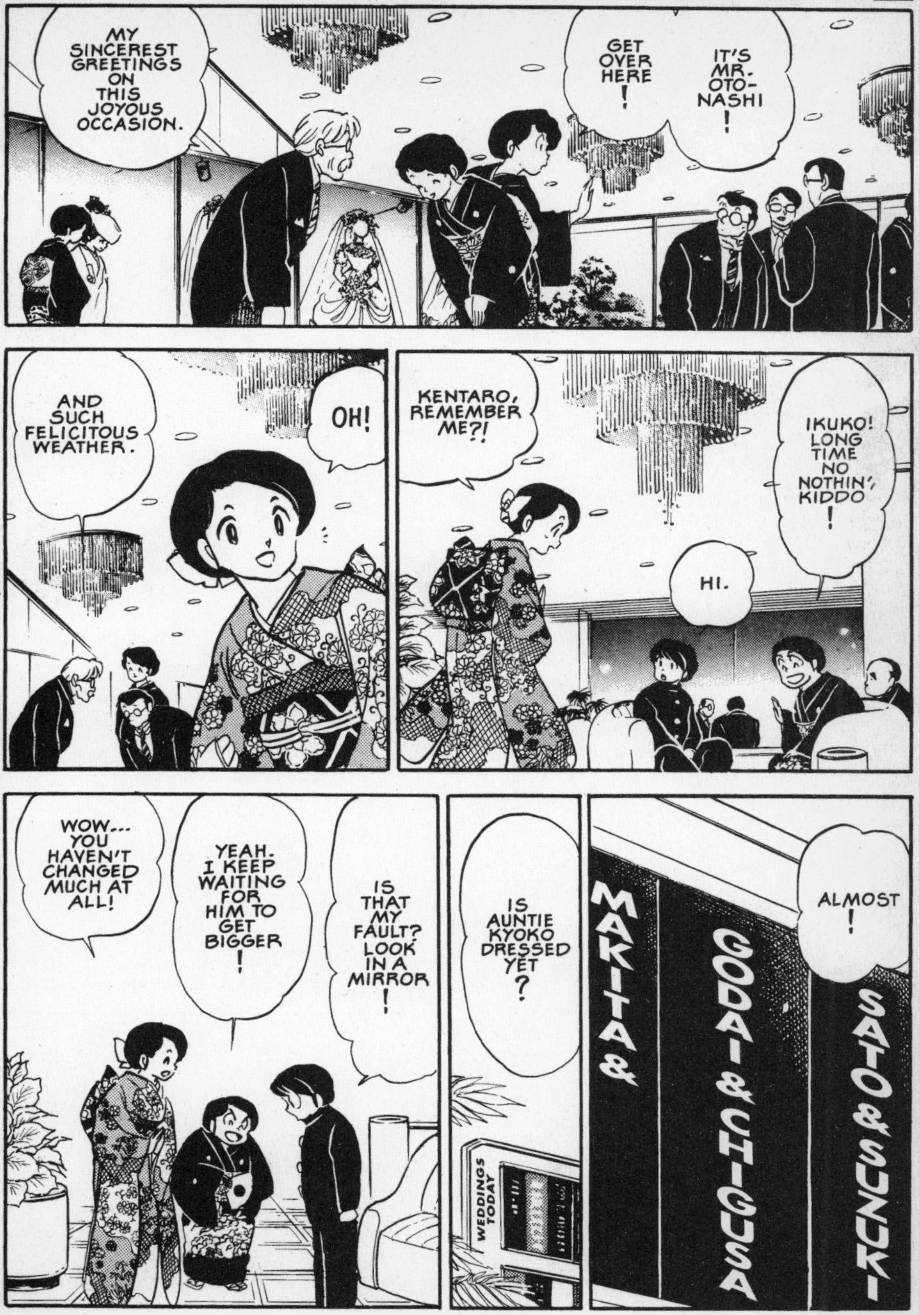
MY SINCEREST GREETINGS ON THIS JOYOUS OCCASION.
GET OVER HERE!
IT'S MR. OTONASHI!
AND SUCH FELICITOUS WEATHER.
OH!
KENTARO, REMEMBER ME?!
IKUKO! LONG TIME NO NOTHIN', KIDDO!
HI.
WOW... YOU HAVEN'T CHANGED MUCH AT ALL!
YEAH. I KEEP WAITING FOR HIM TO GET BIGGER!
IS THAT MY FAULT? LOOK IN A MIRROR!
IS AUNTIE KYOKO DRESSED YET?
WEDDINGS TODAY
MAKITA &
GODAI & CHIGUSA
SATO & SUZUKI
ALMOST!

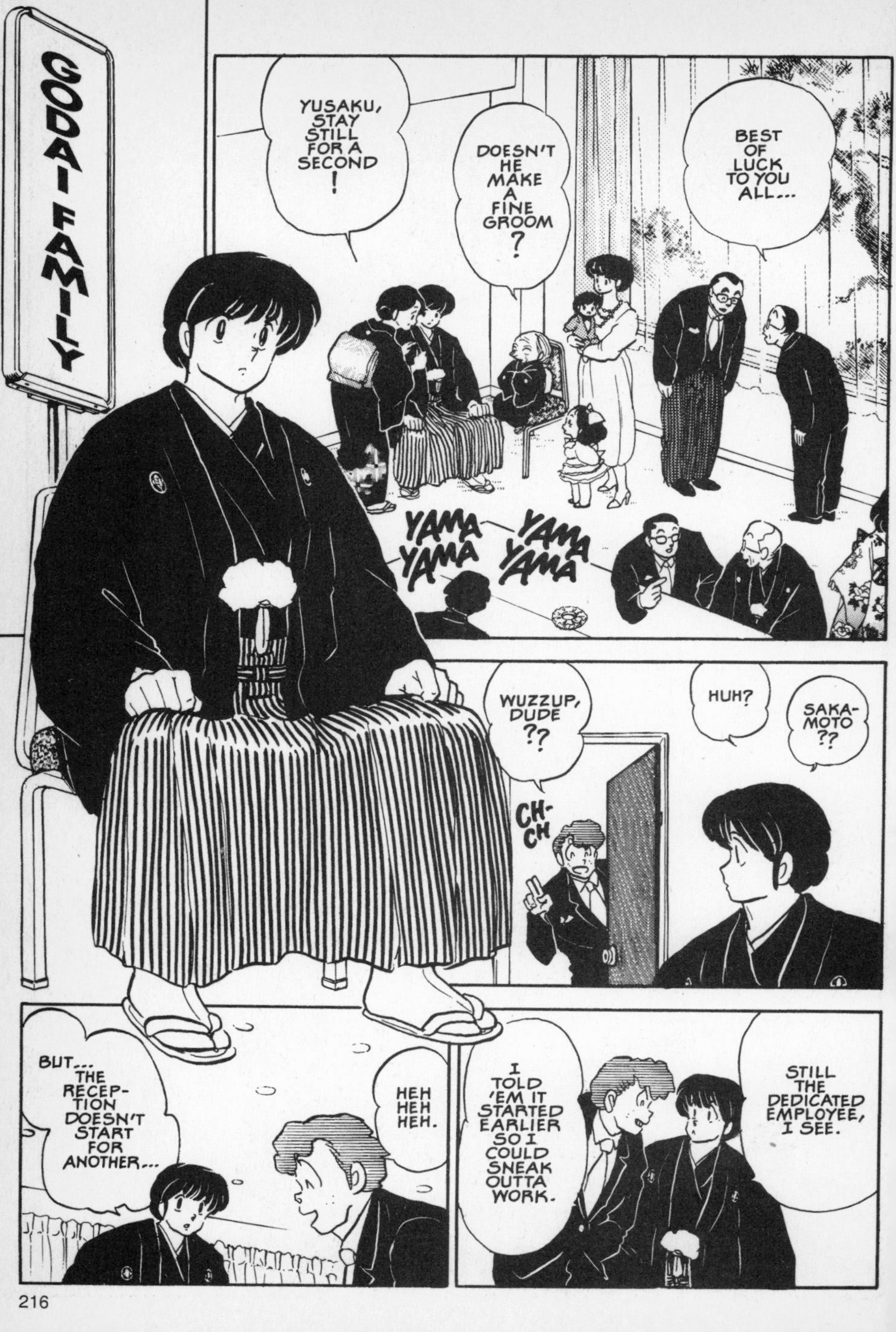

GODAI FAMILY
YUSAKU, STAY STILL FOR A SECOND!
DOESN'T HE MAKE A FINE GROOM?
BEST OF LUCK TO YOU ALL...
YAMA YAMA
YAMA YAMA
WUZZUP, DUDE??
CH-CH
HUH?
SAKAMOTO??
BUT... THE RECEPTION DOESN'T START FOR ANOTHER...
HEH HEH HEH.
I TOLD 'EM IT STARTED EARLIER SO I COULD SNEAK OUTTA WORK.
STILL THE DEDICATED EMPLOYEE, I SEE.

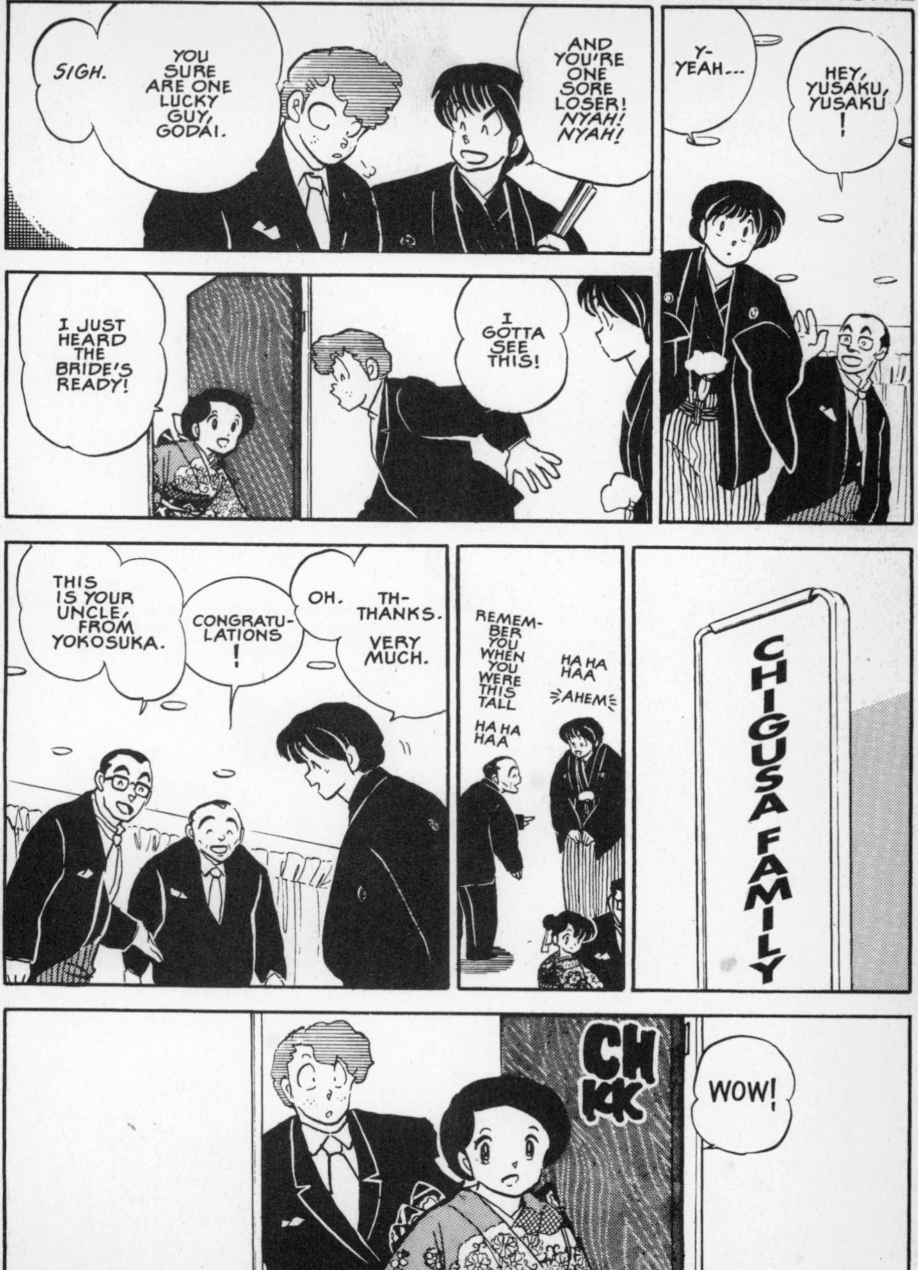
SIGH.
YOU SURE ARE ONE LUCKY GUY, GODAI.
AND YOU'RE ONE SORE LOSER! NYAH! NYAH!
Y-YEAH...
HEY, YUSAKU, YUSAKU!
I JUST HEARD THE BRIDE'S READY!
I GOTTA SEE THIS!
THIS IS YOUR UNCLE, FROM YOKOSUKA.
CONGRATULATIONS!
OH. TH-THANKS.
VERY MUCH.
REMEMBER YOU WHEN YOU WERE THIS TALL
HA HA HAA
AHEM
HA HA HAA
CHIGUSA FAMILY
CH KK
WOW!

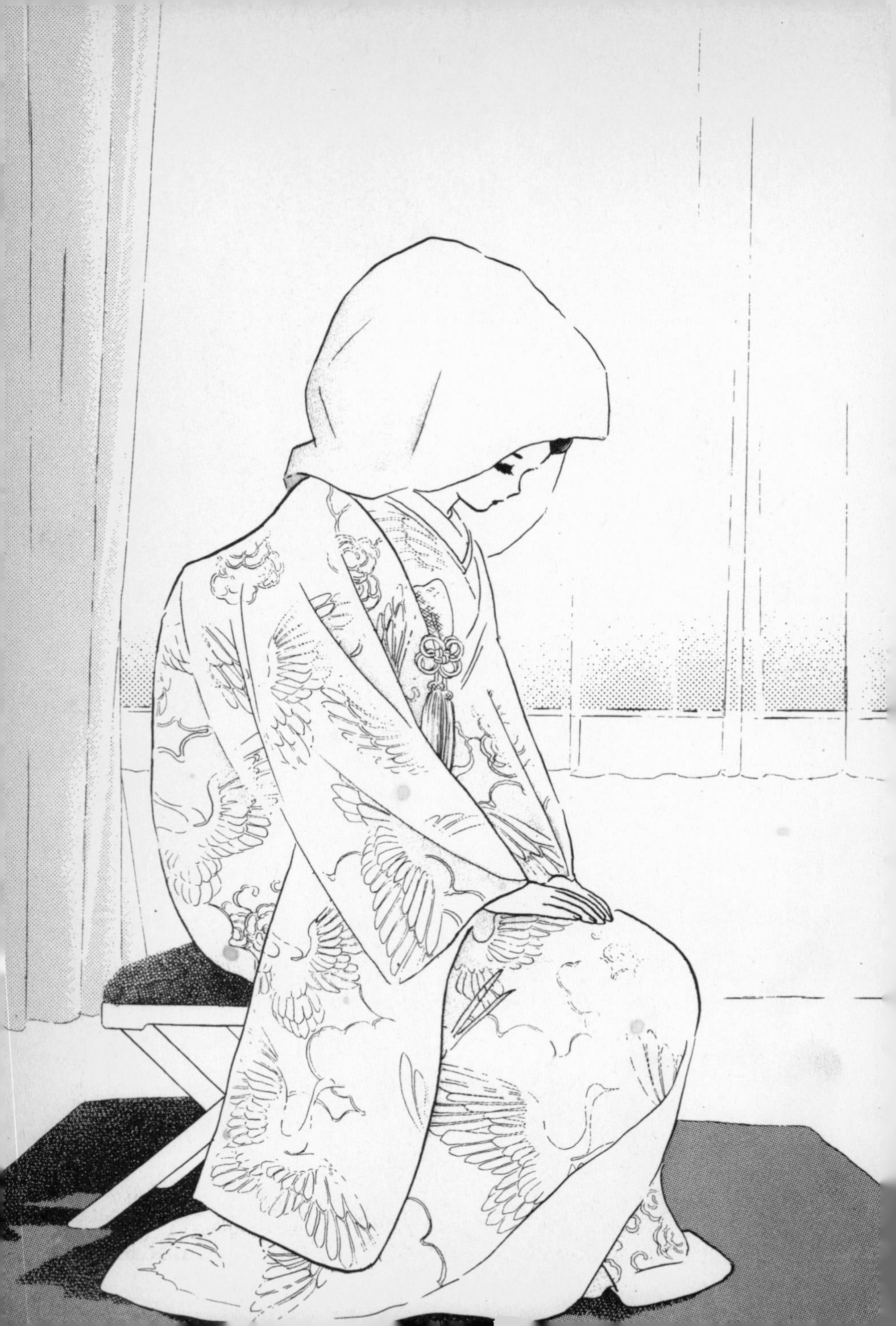

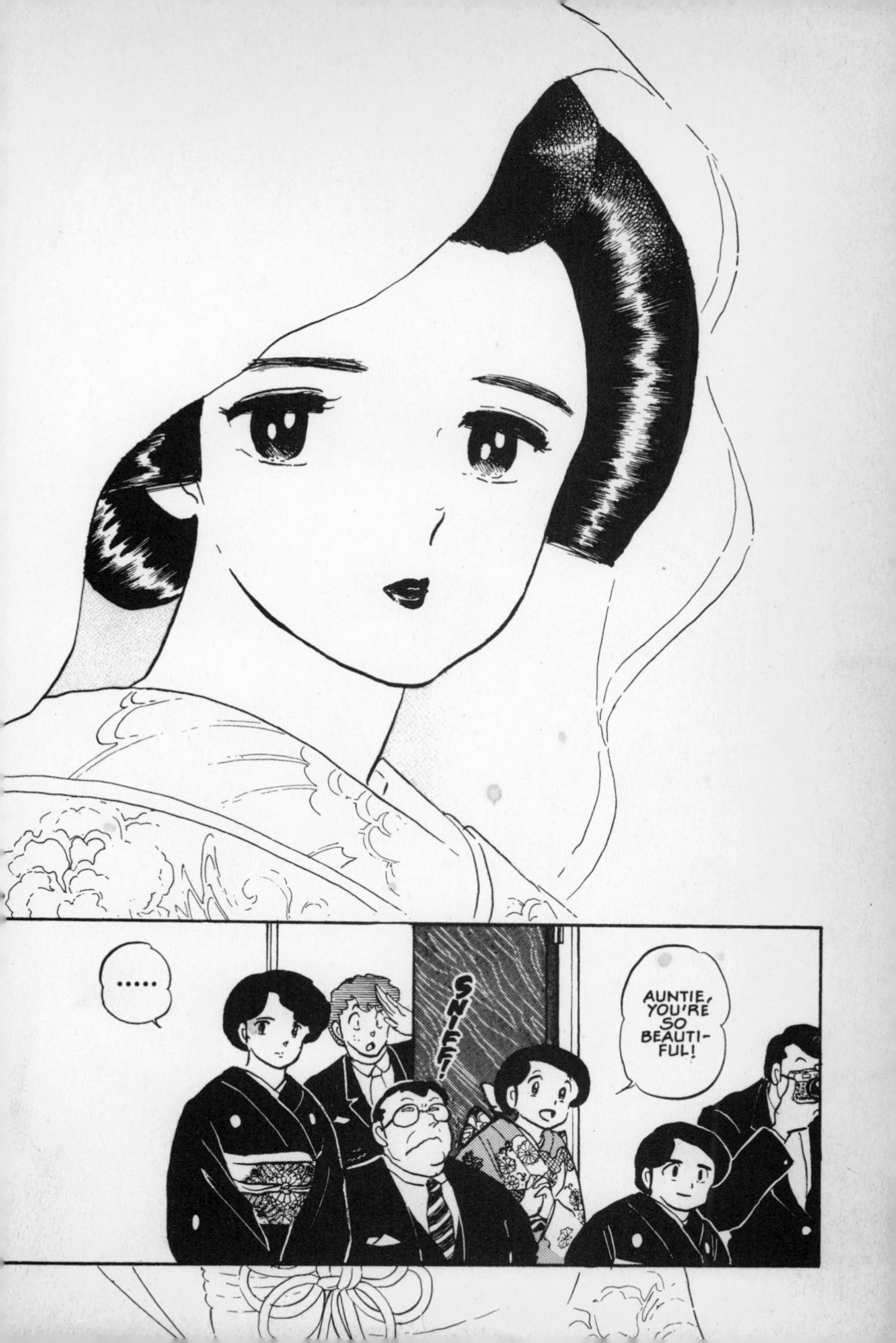
......
SNIFF!
AUNTIE, YOU'RE SO BEAUTIFUL!

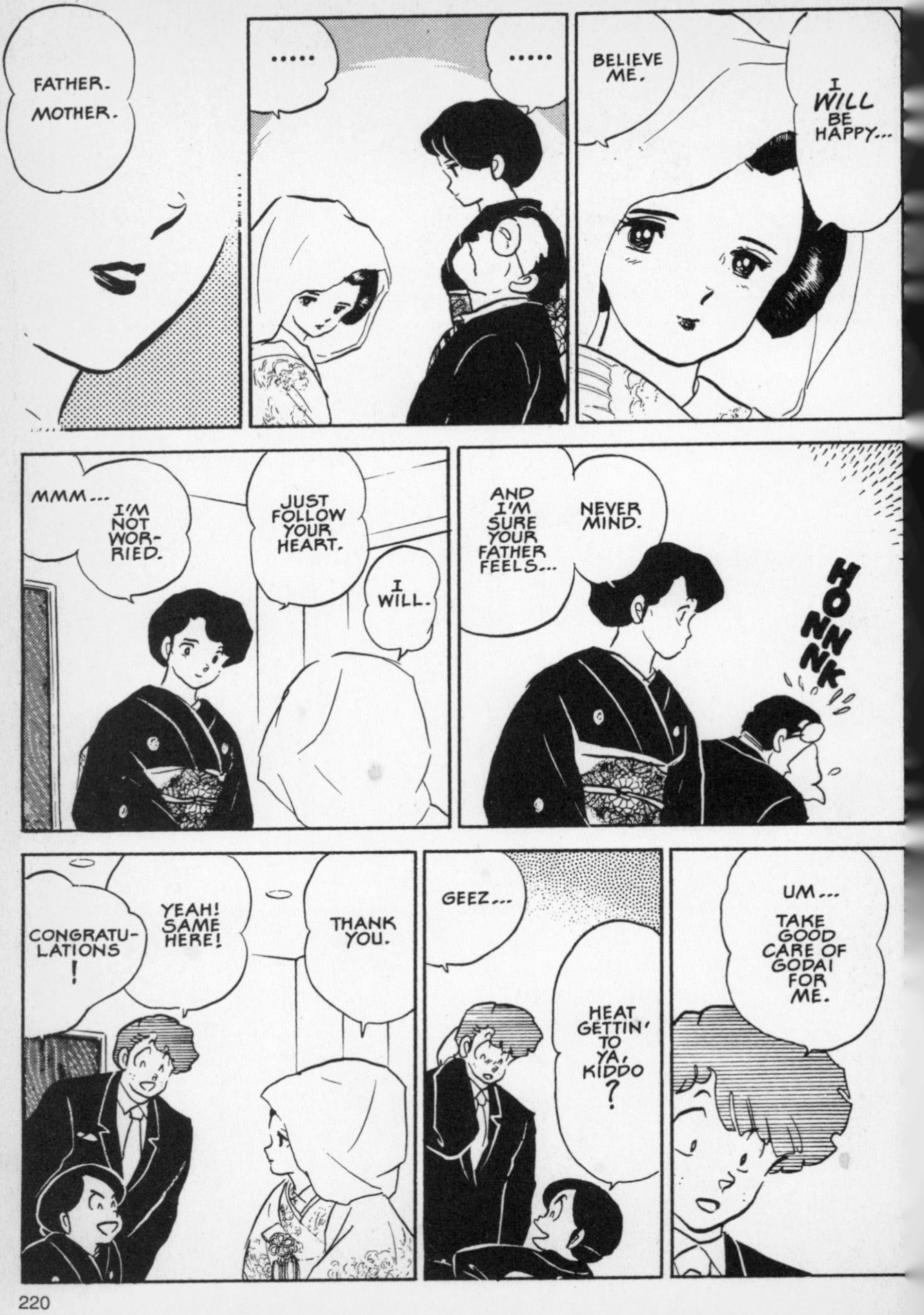
FATHER. MOTHER.
.....
.....
BELIEVE ME.
I WILL BE HAPPY...
MMM... I'M NOT WORRIED.
JUST FOLLOW YOUR HEART.
I WILL.
AND I'M SURE YOUR FATHER FEELS...
NEVER MIND.
HONNNK
CONGRATULATIONS!
YEAH! SAME HERE!
THANK YOU.
GEEZ...
HEAT GETTIN' TO YA, KIDDO?
UM...
TAKE GOOD CARE OF GODAI FOR ME.

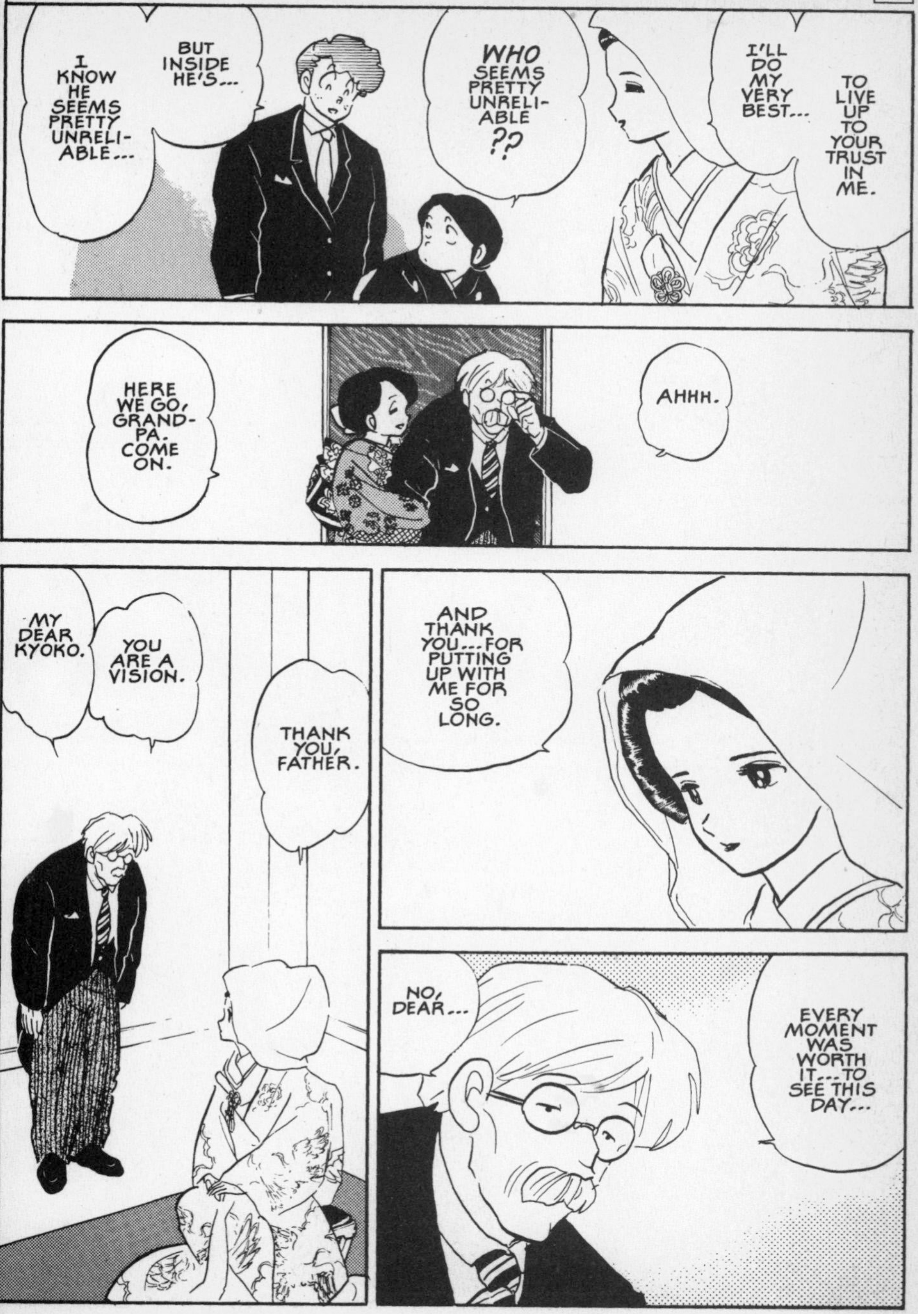
I KNOW HE SEEMS PRETTY UNRELI-ABLE...
BUT INSIDE HE'S...
WHO SEEMS PRETTY UNRELI-ABLE??
I'LL DO MY VERY BEST...
TO LIVE UP TO YOUR TRUST IN ME.
HERE WE GO, GRAND-PA. COME ON.
AHHH.
MY DEAR KYOKO.
YOU ARE A VISION.
THANK YOU, FATHER.
AND THANK YOU... FOR PUTTING UP WITH ME FOR SO LONG.
NO, DEAR...
EVERY MOMENT WAS WORTH IT... TO SEE THIS DAY...

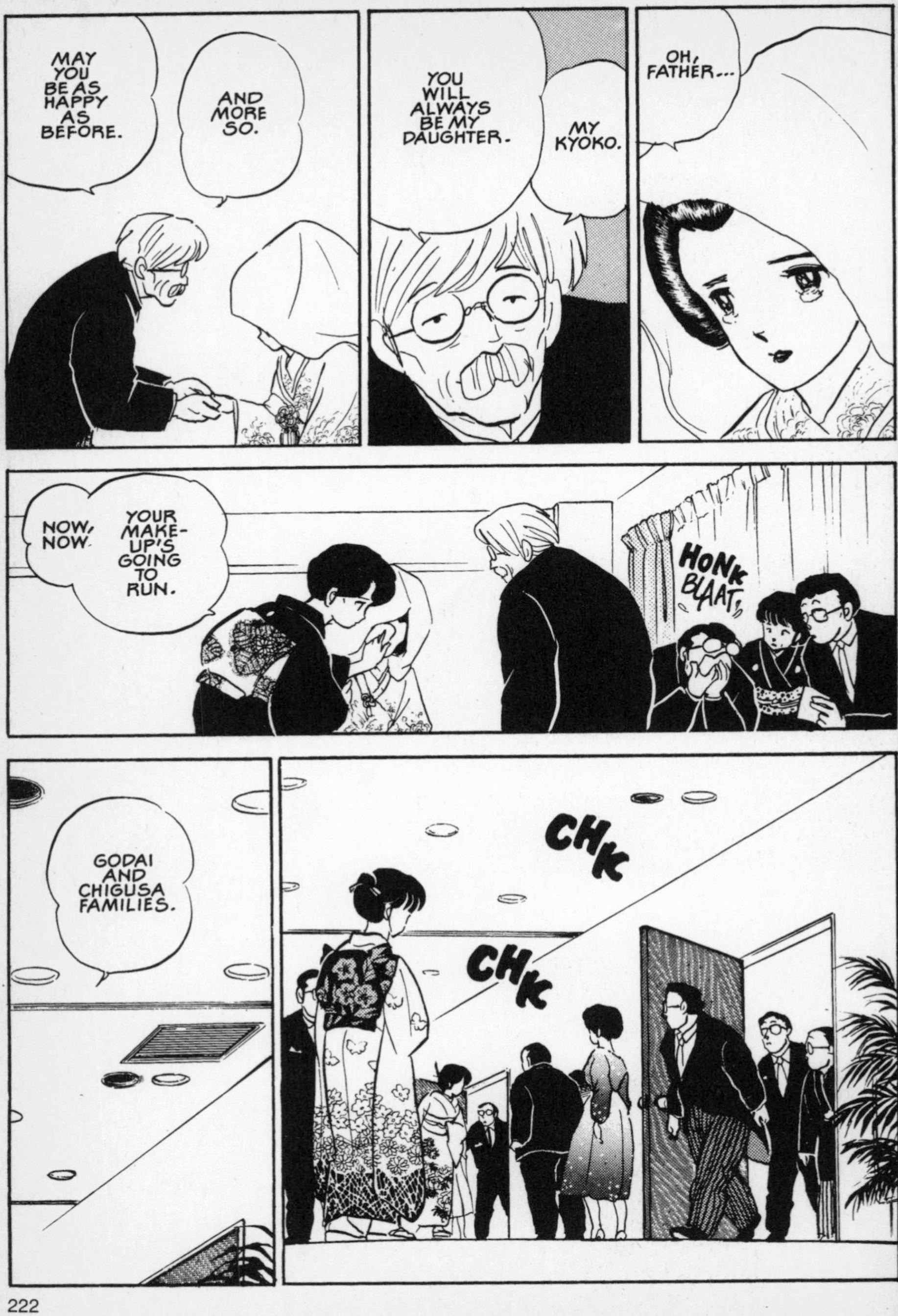
MAY YOU BE AS HAPPY AS BEFORE.
AND MORE SO.
YOU WILL ALWAYS BE MY DAUGHTER.
MY KYOKO.
OH, FATHER...
NOW, NOW.
YOUR MAKE-UP'S GOING TO RUN.
HONK
BLAAT
GODAI AND CHIGUSA FAMILIES.
CHK
CHK

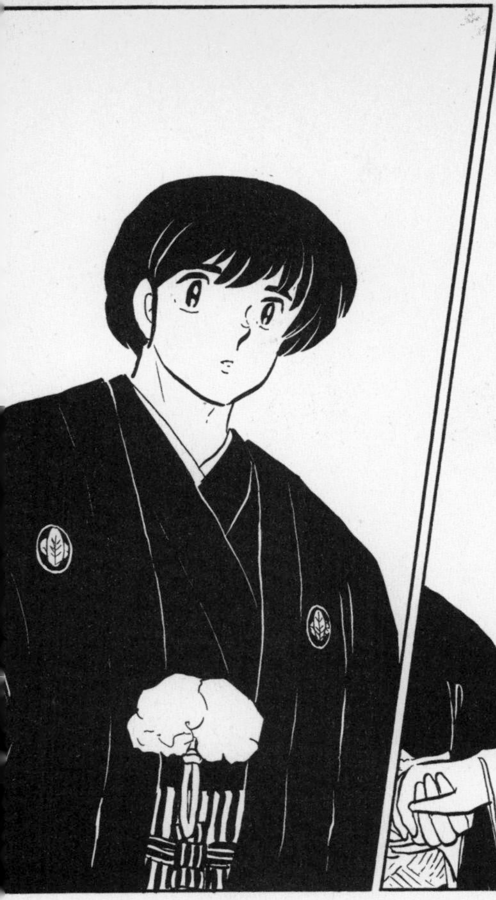

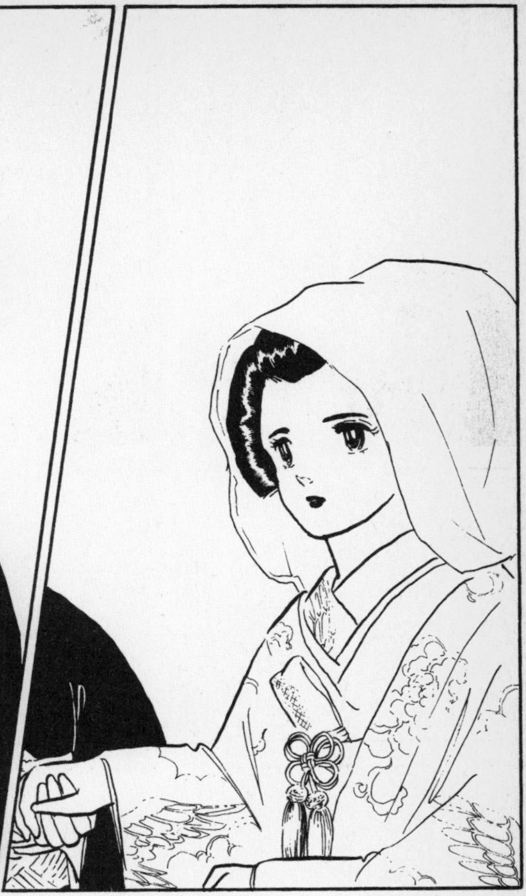

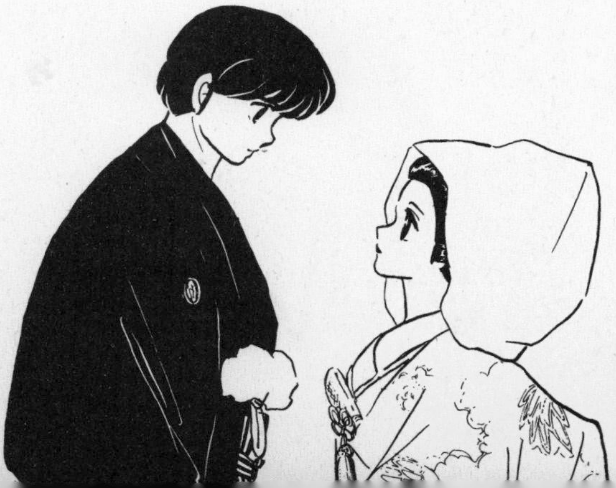

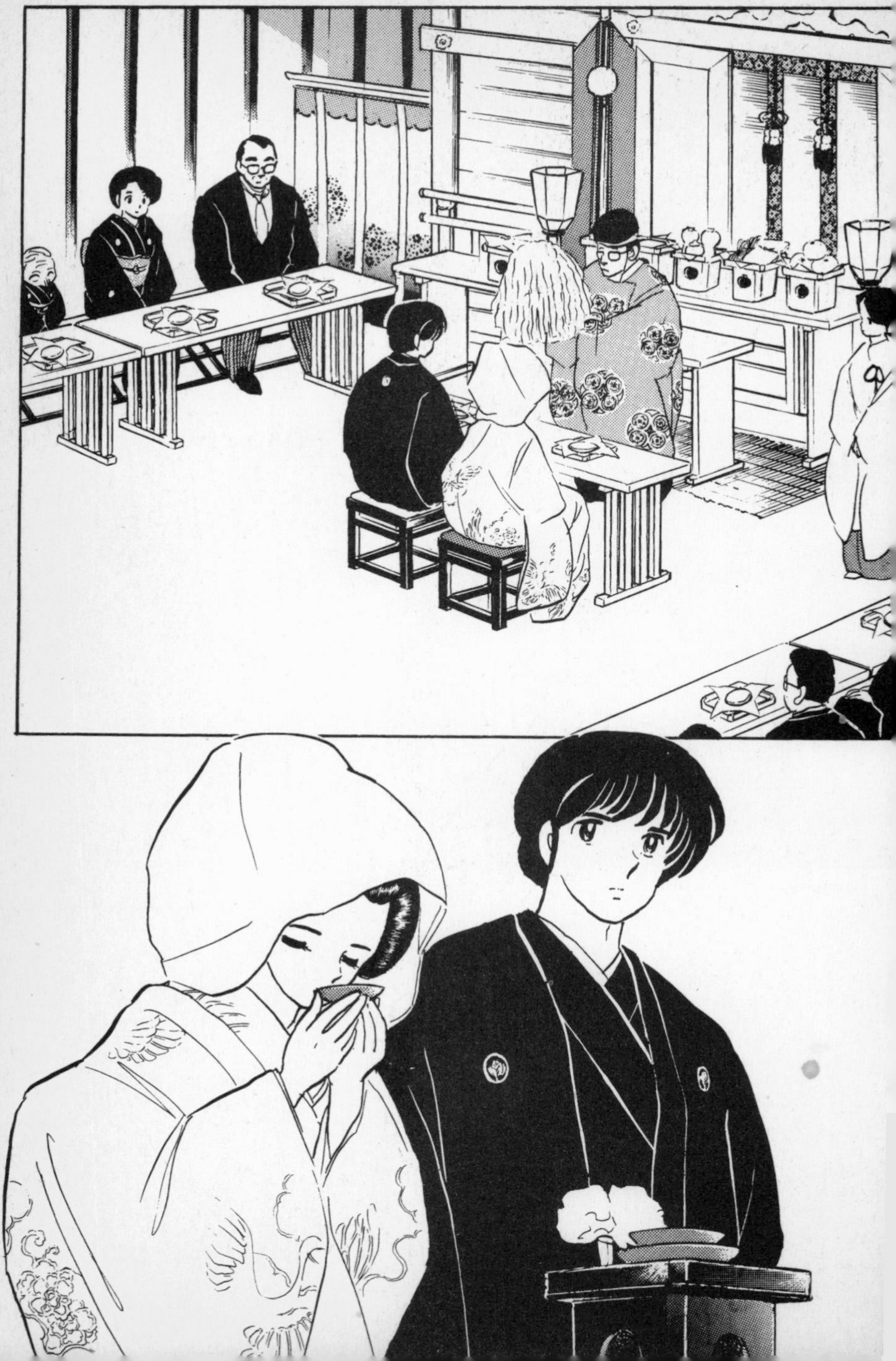

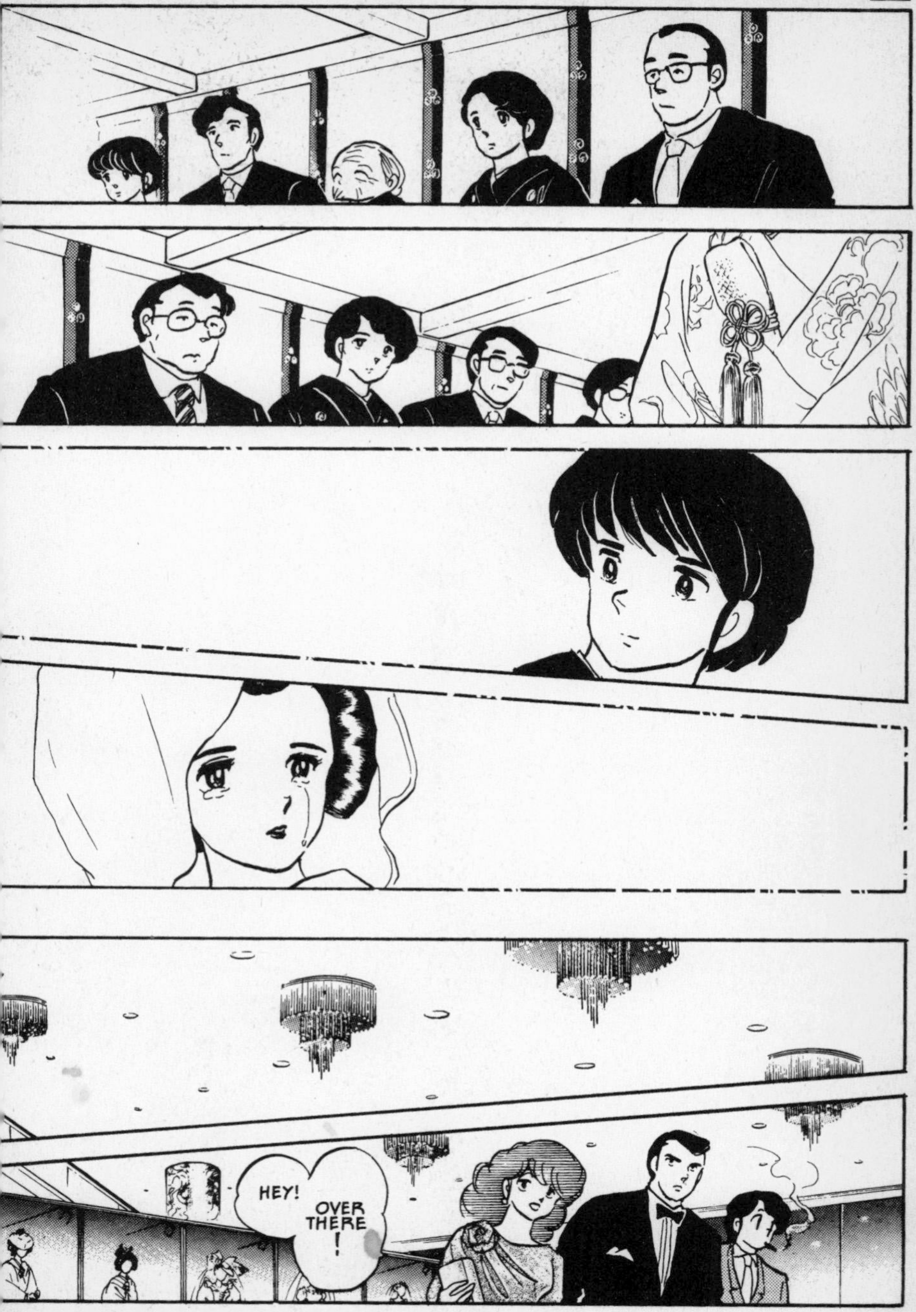
HEY! OVER THERE !

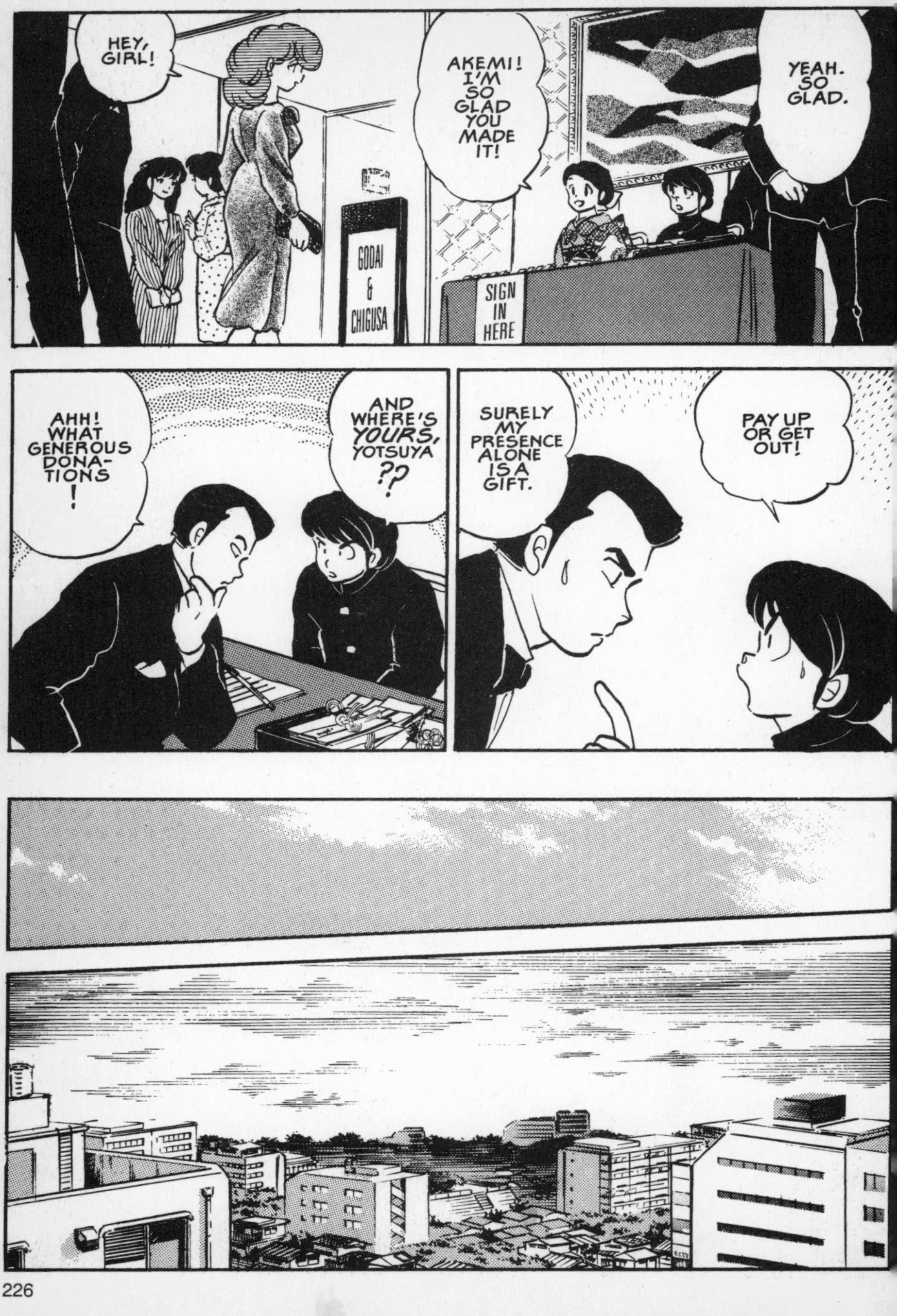
HEY, GIRL!
AKEMI! I'M SO GLAD YOU MADE IT!
YEAH. SO GLAD.
GODAI & CHIGUSA
SIGN IN HERE
AHH! WHAT GENEROUS DONATIONS!
AND WHERE'S YOURS, YOTSUYA??
SURELY MY PRESENCE ALONE IS A GIFT.
PAY UP OR GET OUT!

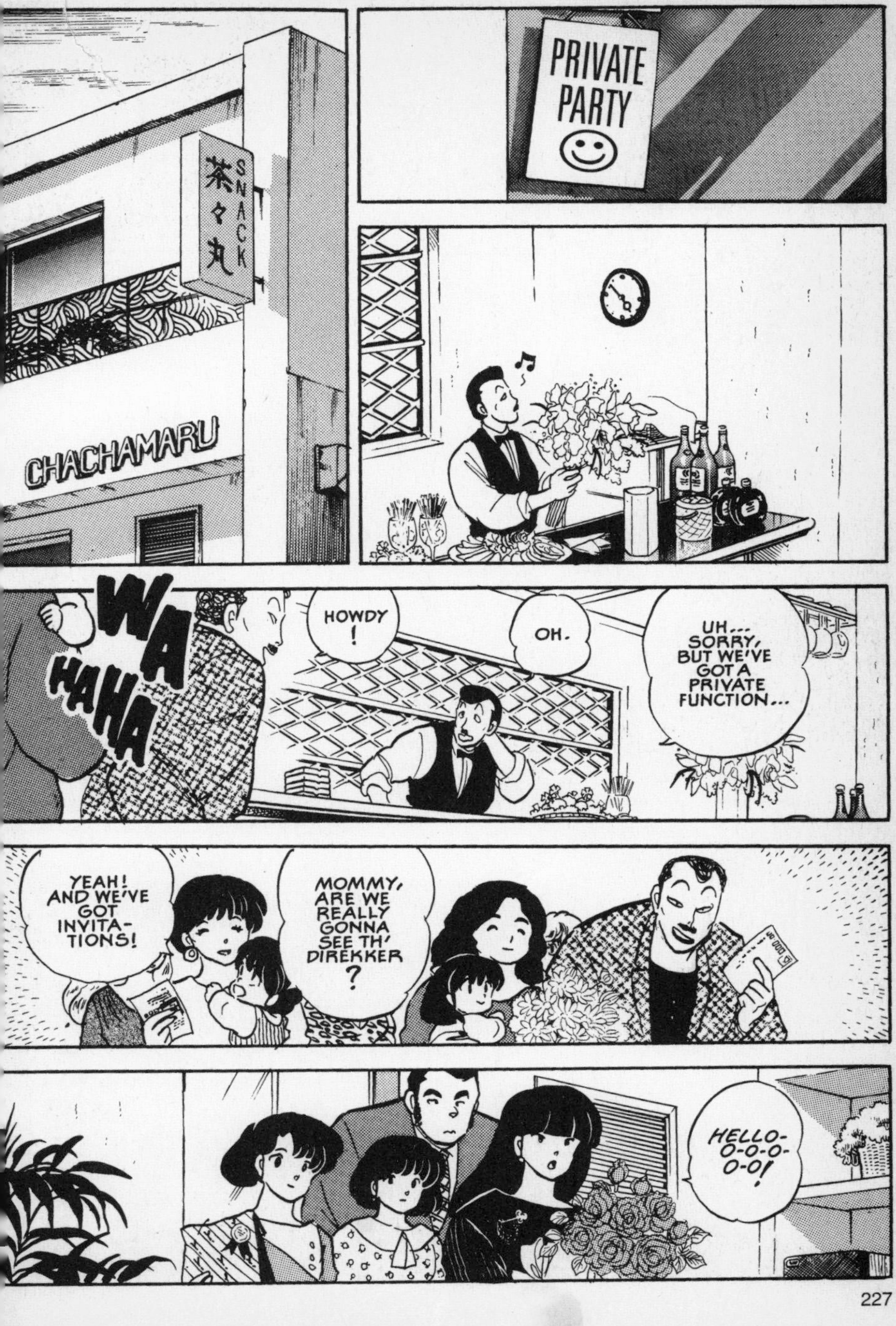
SNACK
茶々丸
CHACHAMARU
PRIVATE PARTY
WA HAHAHA
HOWDY!
OH.
UH... SORRY, BUT WE'VE GOT A PRIVATE FUNCTION...
YEAH! AND WE'VE GOT INVITA-TIONS!
MOMMY, ARE WE REALLY GONNA SEE TH' DIREKKER?
HELLO-O-O-O-O-O!

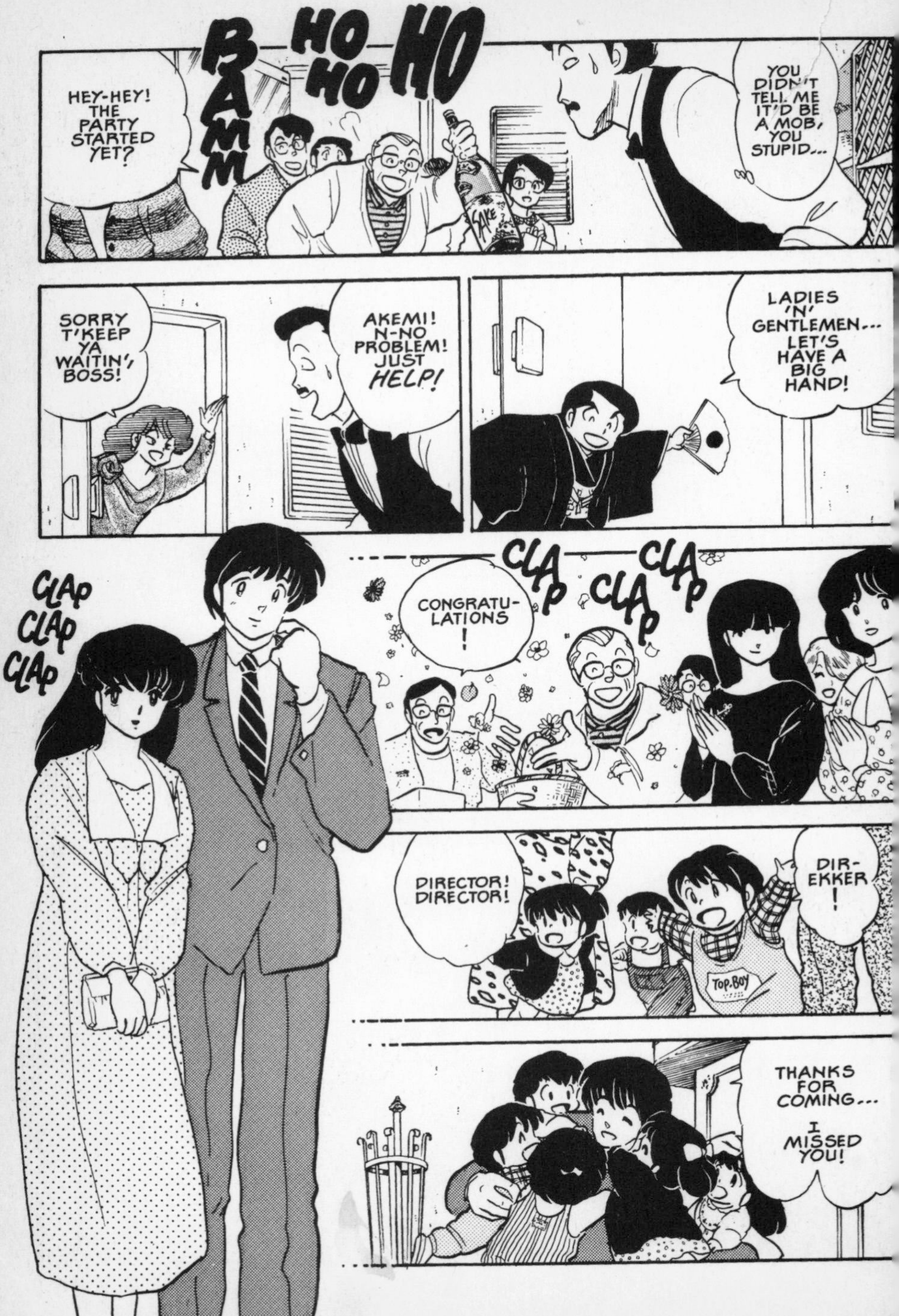
HEY-HEY! THE PARTY STARTED YET?
BAMM
HO HO HO HO
YOU DIDN'T TELL ME IT'D BE A MOB, YOU STUPID...
SORRY T'KEEP YA WAITIN', BOSS!
AKEMI! N-NO PROBLEM! JUST HELP!
LADIES 'N' GENTLEMEN... LET'S HAVE A BIG HAND!
CLAP CLAP CLAP
CLAP CLAP CLAP
CONGRATULATIONS!
DIRECTOR! DIRECTOR!
DIR-EKKER!
TOP.BOY
THANKS FOR COMING... I MISSED YOU!

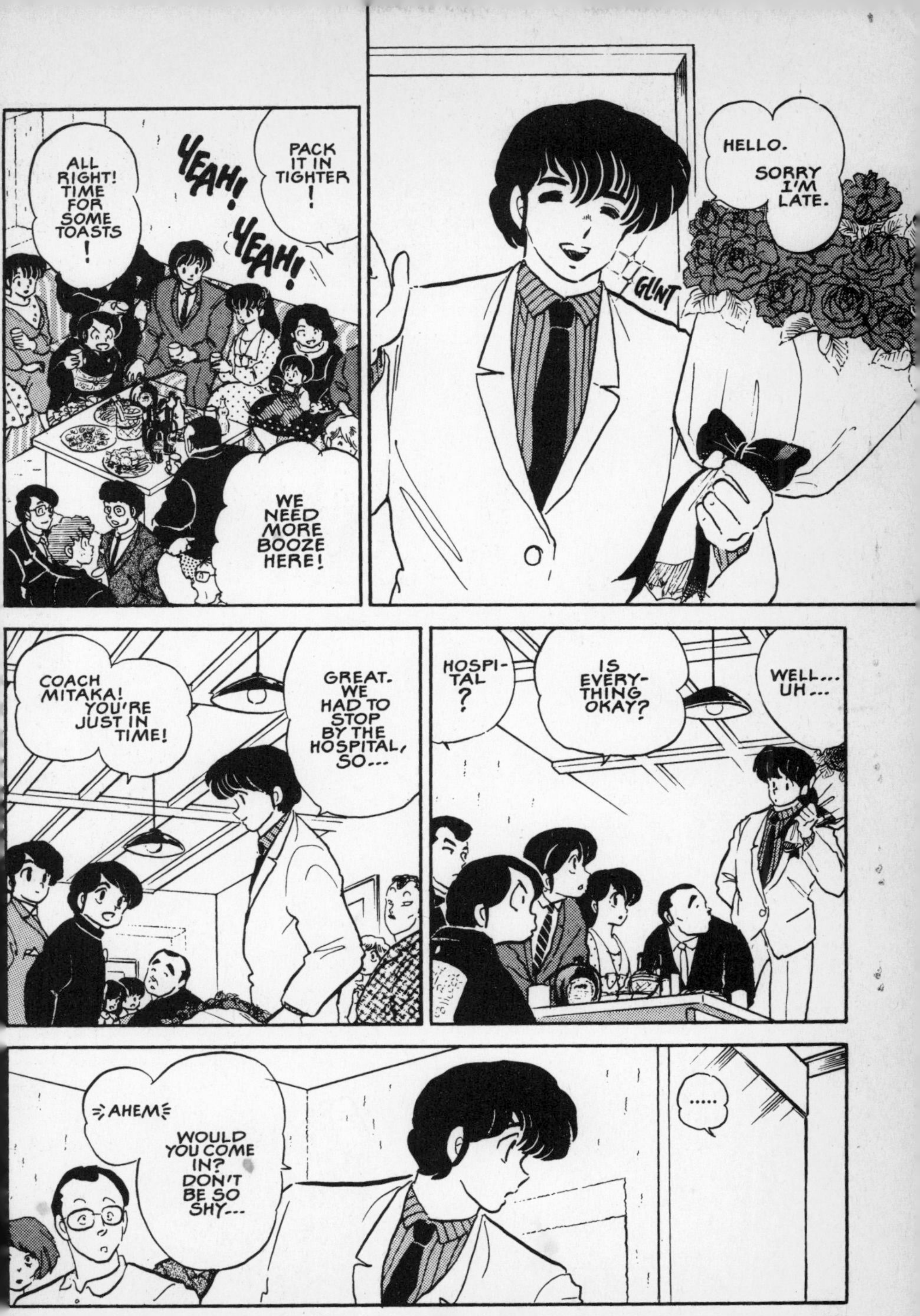
ALL RIGHT! TIME FOR SOME TOASTS!
YEAH! YEAH!
PACK IT IN TIGHTER!
WE NEED MORE BOOZE HERE!
HELLO.
SORRY I'M LATE.
GLINT
COACH MITAKA! YOU'RE JUST IN TIME!
GREAT. WE HAD TO STOP BY THE HOSPITAL, SO...
HOSPITAL?
IS EVERYTHING OKAY?
WELL... UH...
AHEM
WOULD YOU COME IN? DON'T BE SO SHY...
......

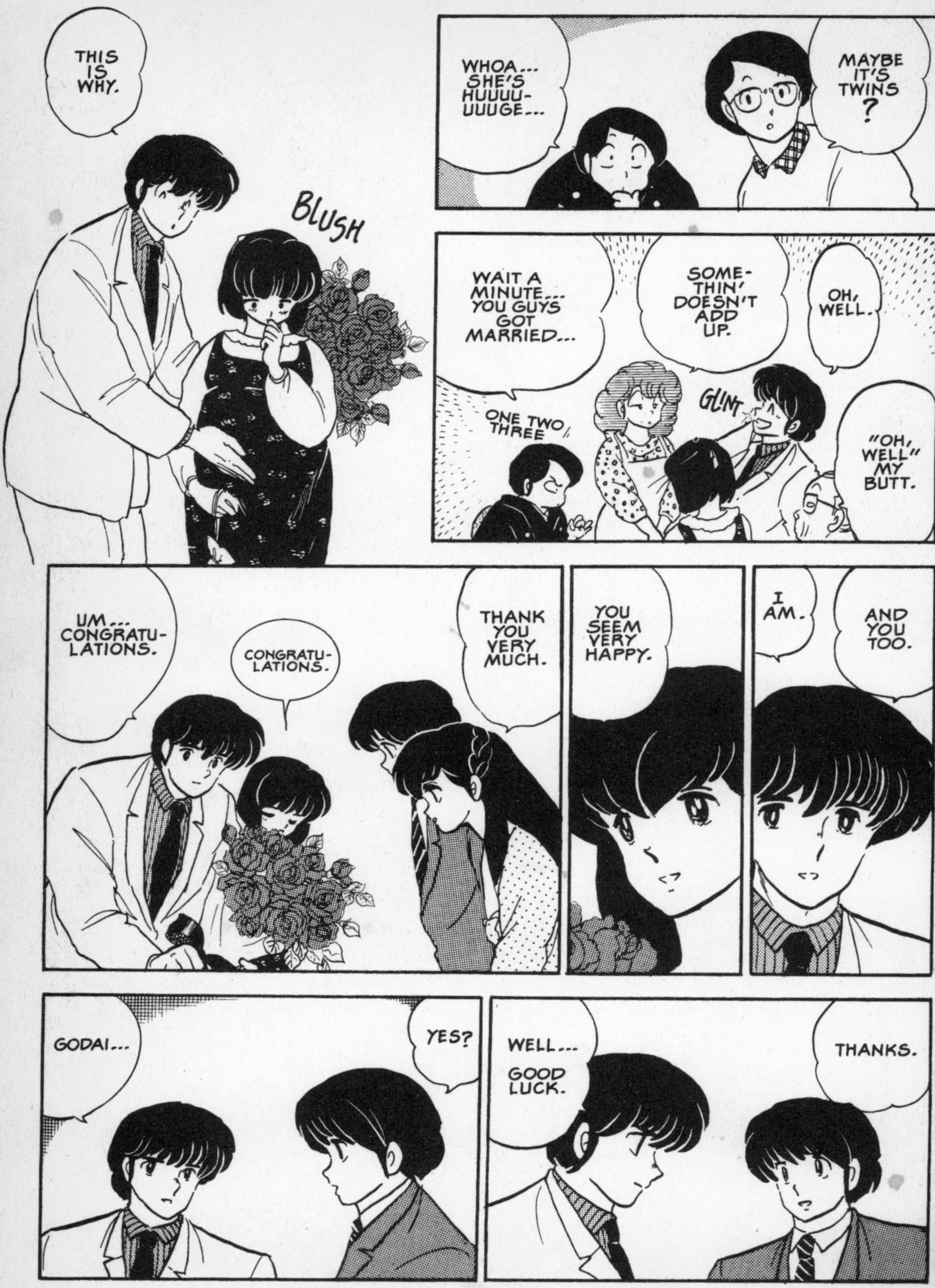
THIS IS WHY.
BLUSH
WHOA... SHE'S HUUUU-UUUGE...
MAYBE IT'S TWINS?
WAIT A MINUTE... YOU GUYS GOT MARRIED...
SOME-THIN' DOESN'T ADD UP.
OH, WELL.
ONE TWO THREE
GLINT
"OH, WELL" MY BUTT.
UM... CONGRATU-LATIONS.
CONGRATU-LATIONS.
THANK YOU VERY MUCH.
YOU SEEM VERY HAPPY.
I AM.
AND YOU TOO.
GODAI...
YES?
WELL...
GOOD LUCK.
THANKS.

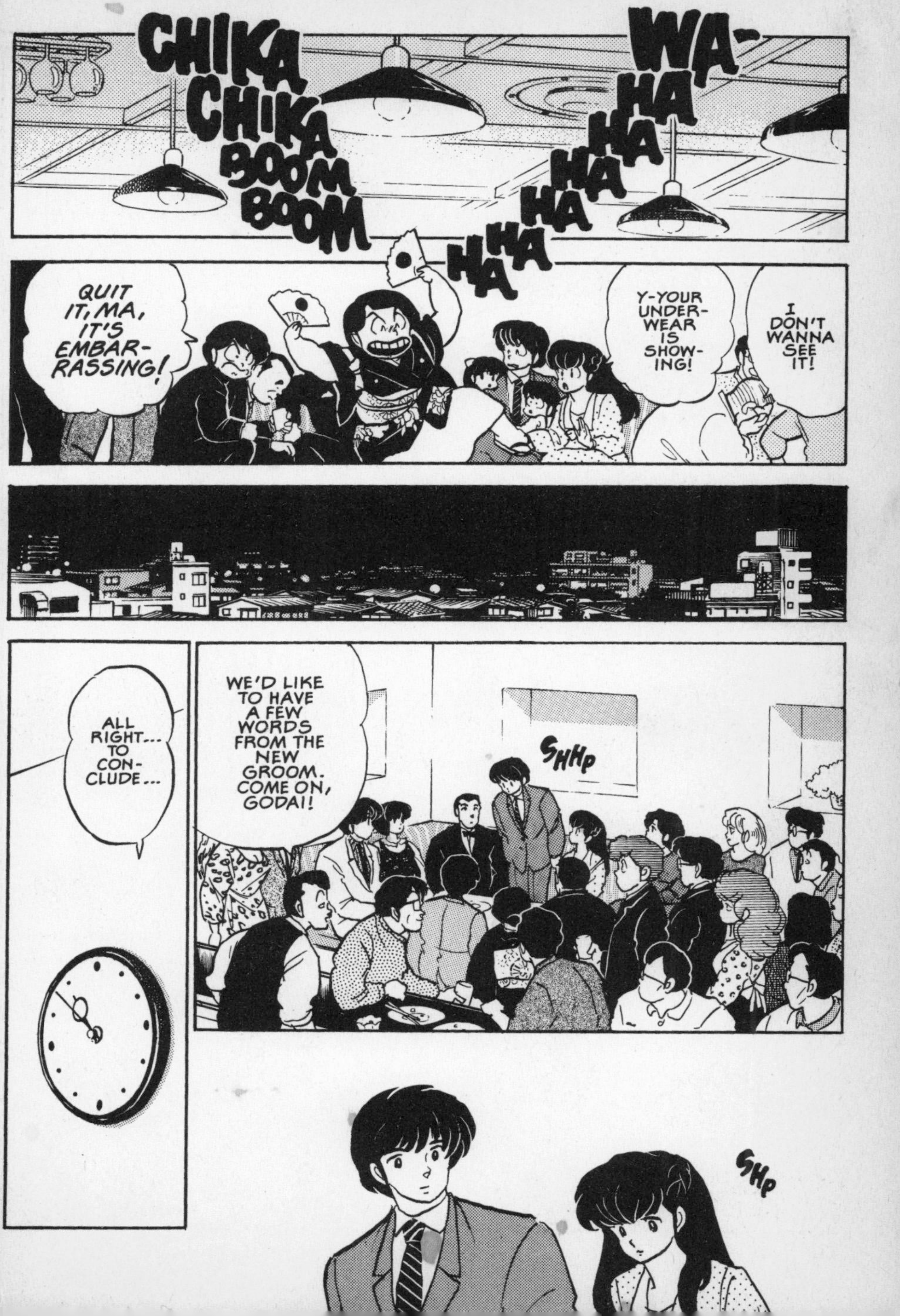
CHIKA CHIKA BOOM BOOM
WA-HA HA HA HA HA HA HA
QUIT IT, MA, IT'S EMBARRASSING!
Y-YOUR UNDERWEAR IS SHOWING!
I DON'T WANNA SEE IT!
ALL RIGHT... TO CONCLUDE...
WE'D LIKE TO HAVE A FEW WORDS FROM THE NEW GROOM. COME ON, GODAI!
SHHP
SHP

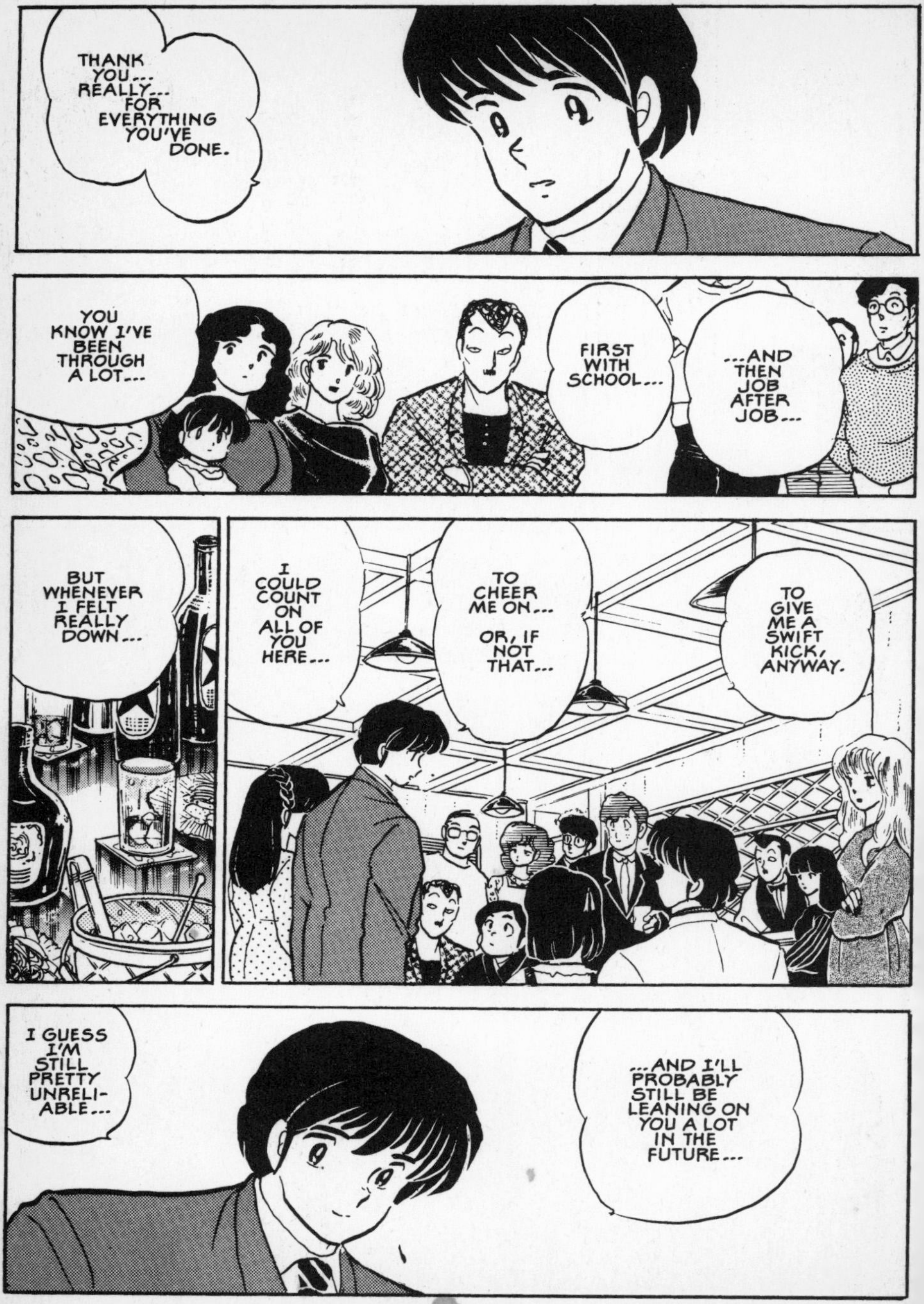
THANK YOU... REALLY... FOR EVERYTHING YOU'VE DONE.
YOU KNOW I'VE BEEN THROUGH A LOT...
FIRST WITH SCHOOL...
...AND THEN JOB AFTER JOB...
BUT WHENEVER I FELT REALLY DOWN...
I COULD COUNT ON ALL OF YOU HERE...
TO CHEER ME ON... OR, IF NOT THAT...
TO GIVE ME A SWIFT KICK, ANYWAY.
I GUESS I'M STILL PRETTY UNRELI-ABLE...
...AND I'LL PROBABLY STILL BE LEANING ON YOU A LOT IN THE FUTURE...

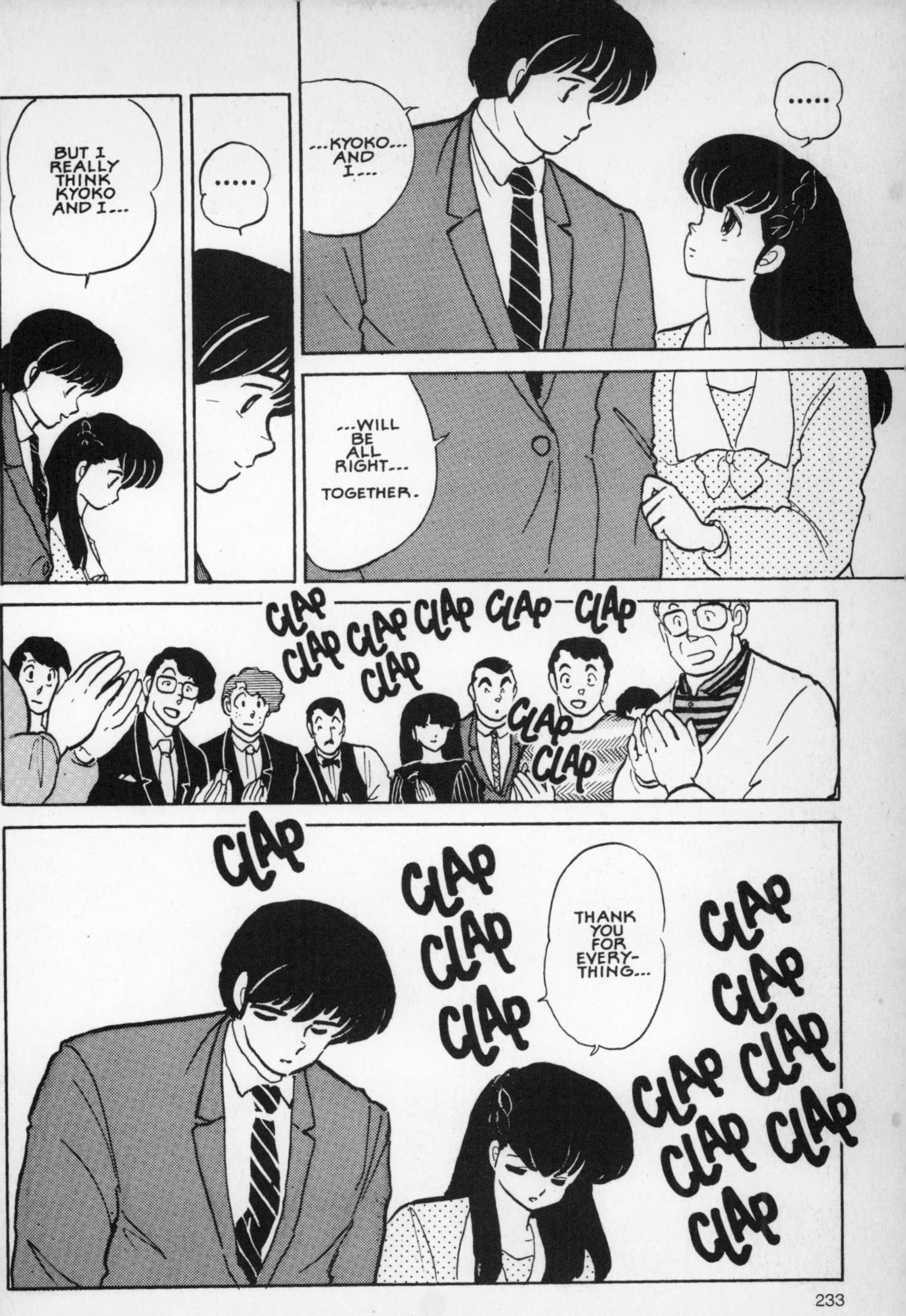

BUT I REALLY THINK KYOKO AND I...
......
...KYOKO... AND I...
......
...WILL BE ALL RIGHT... TOGETHER.
CLAP CLAP CLAP CLAP CLAP CLAP CLAP CLAP
CLAP CLAP
CLAP
CLAP CLAP CLAP
THANK YOU FOR EVERY-THING...
CLAP CLAP CLAP CLAP CLAP CLAP CLAP

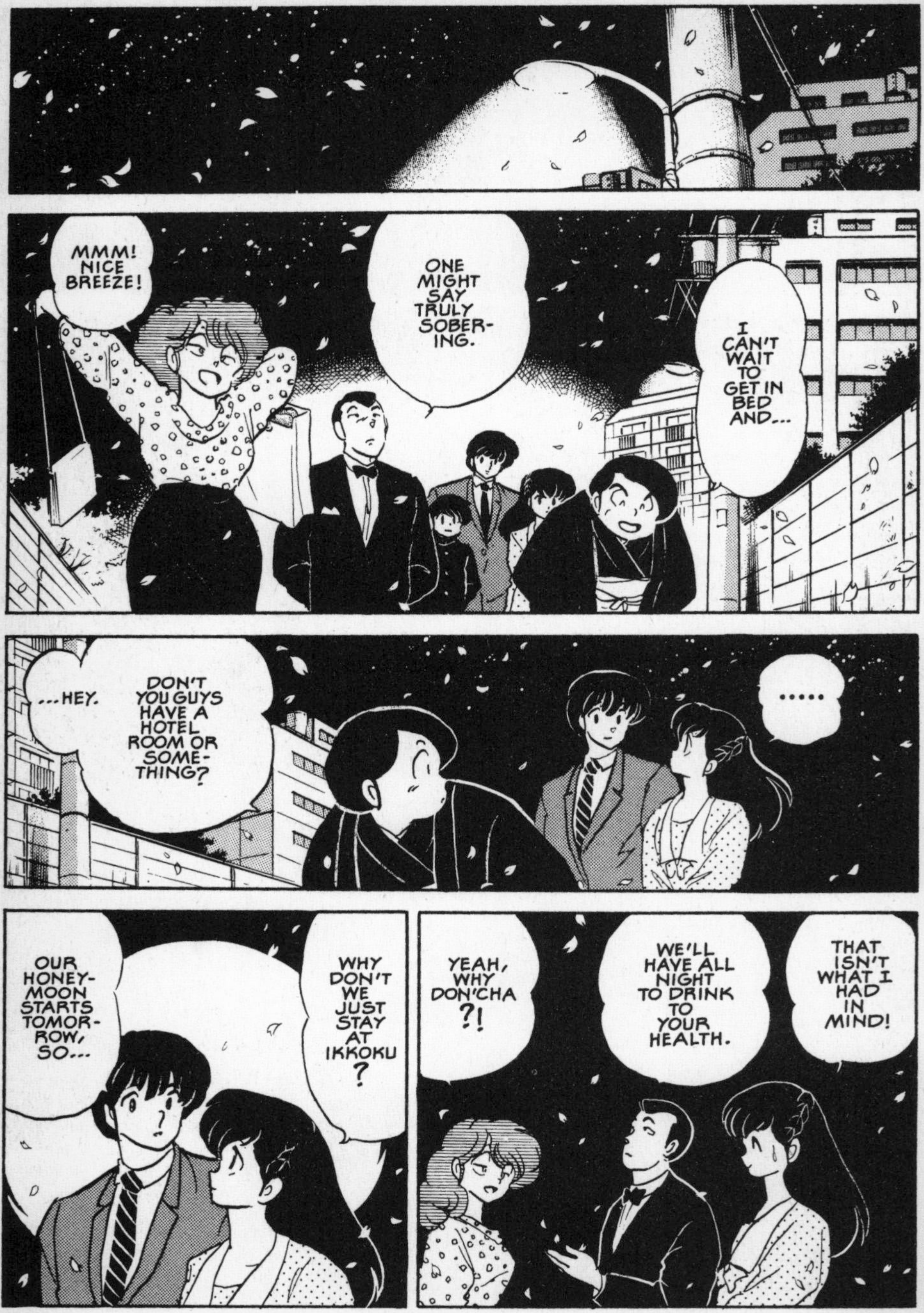
MMM! NICE BREEZE!
ONE MIGHT SAY TRULY SOBER-ING.
I CAN'T WAIT TO GET IN BED AND...
...HEY.
DON'T YOU GUYS HAVE A HOTEL ROOM OR SOME-THING?
.....
OUR HONEY-MOON STARTS TOMOR-ROW, SO...
WHY DON'T WE JUST STAY AT IKKOKU?
YEAH, WHY DON'CHA?!
WE'LL HAVE ALL NIGHT TO DRINK TO YOUR HEALTH.
THAT ISN'T WHAT I HAD IN MIND!

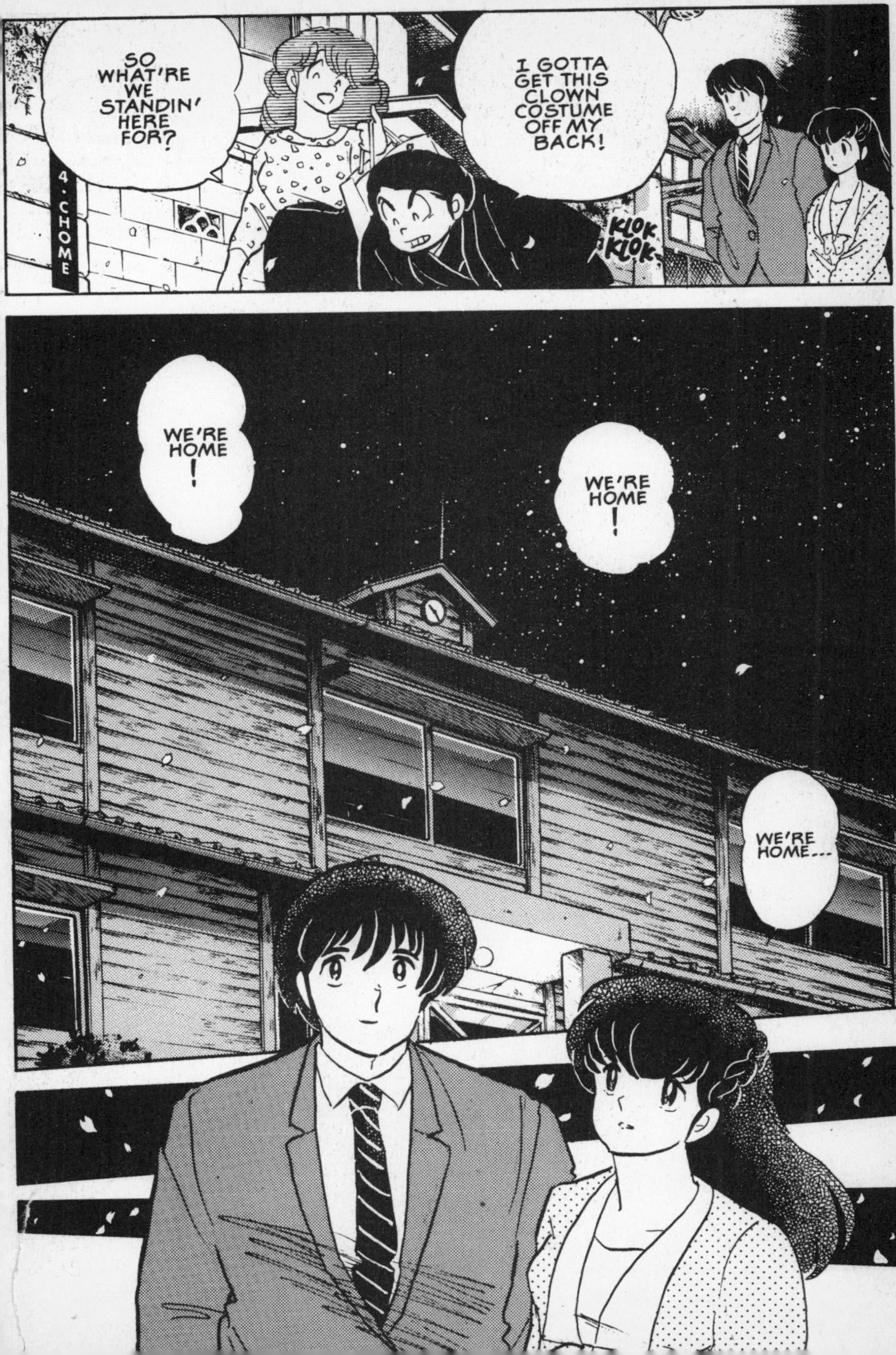
SO WHAT'RE WE STANDIN' HERE FOR?
4·CHOME
I GOTTA GET THIS CLOWN COSTUME OFF MY BACK!
KLOK KLOK
WE'RE HOME!
WE'RE HOME!
WE'RE HOME...

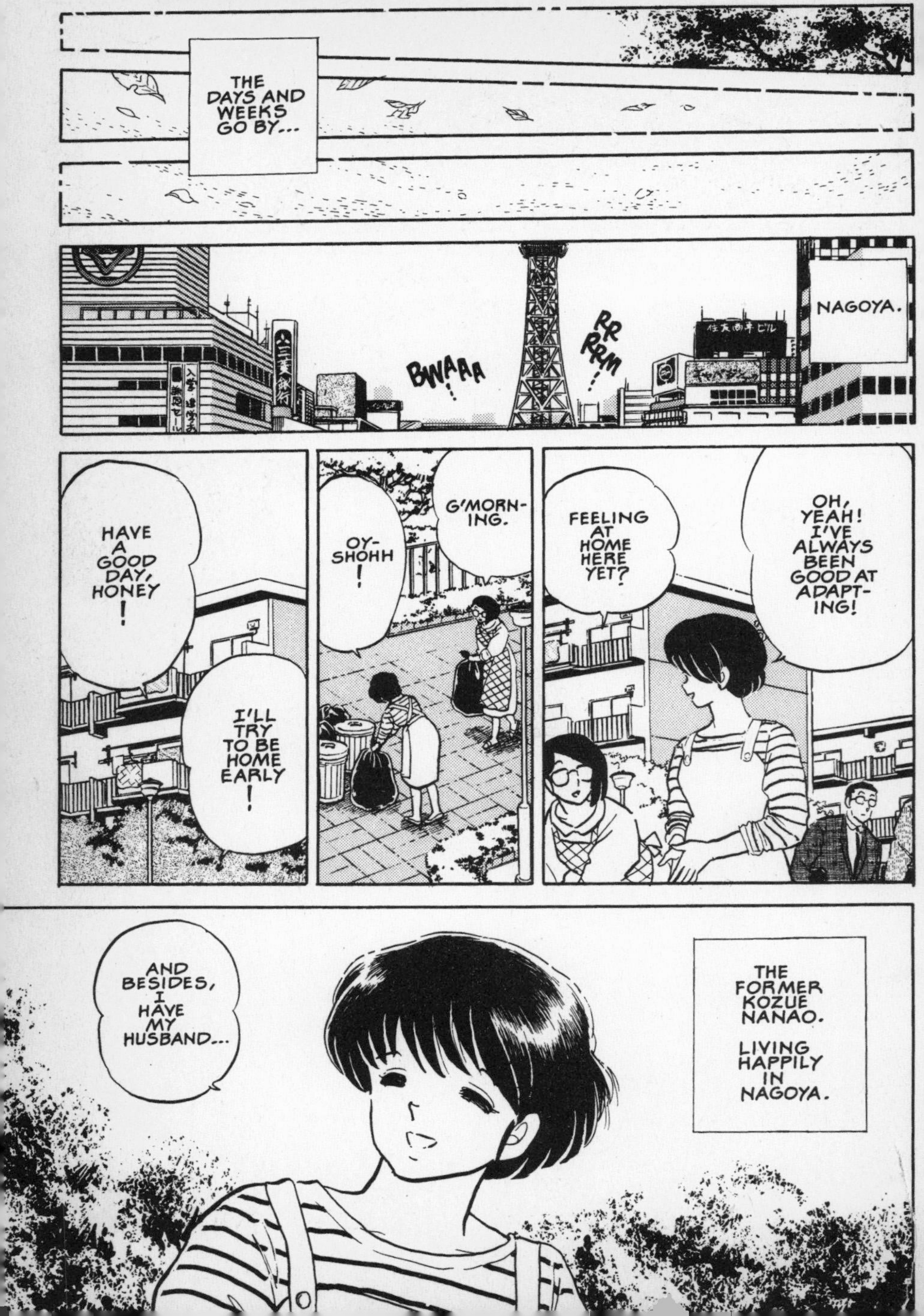
THE DAYS AND WEEKS GO BY...
BWAAAA!
RRRRM!
NAGOYA.
HAVE A GOOD DAY, HONEY!
I'LL TRY TO BE HOME EARLY!
OY-SHOHH!
G'MORN-ING.
FEELING AT HOME HERE YET?
OH, YEAH! I'VE ALWAYS BEEN GOOD AT ADAPT-ING!
AND BESIDES, I HAVE MY HUSBAND...
THE FORMER KOZUE NANAO.
LIVING HAPPILY IN NAGOYA.

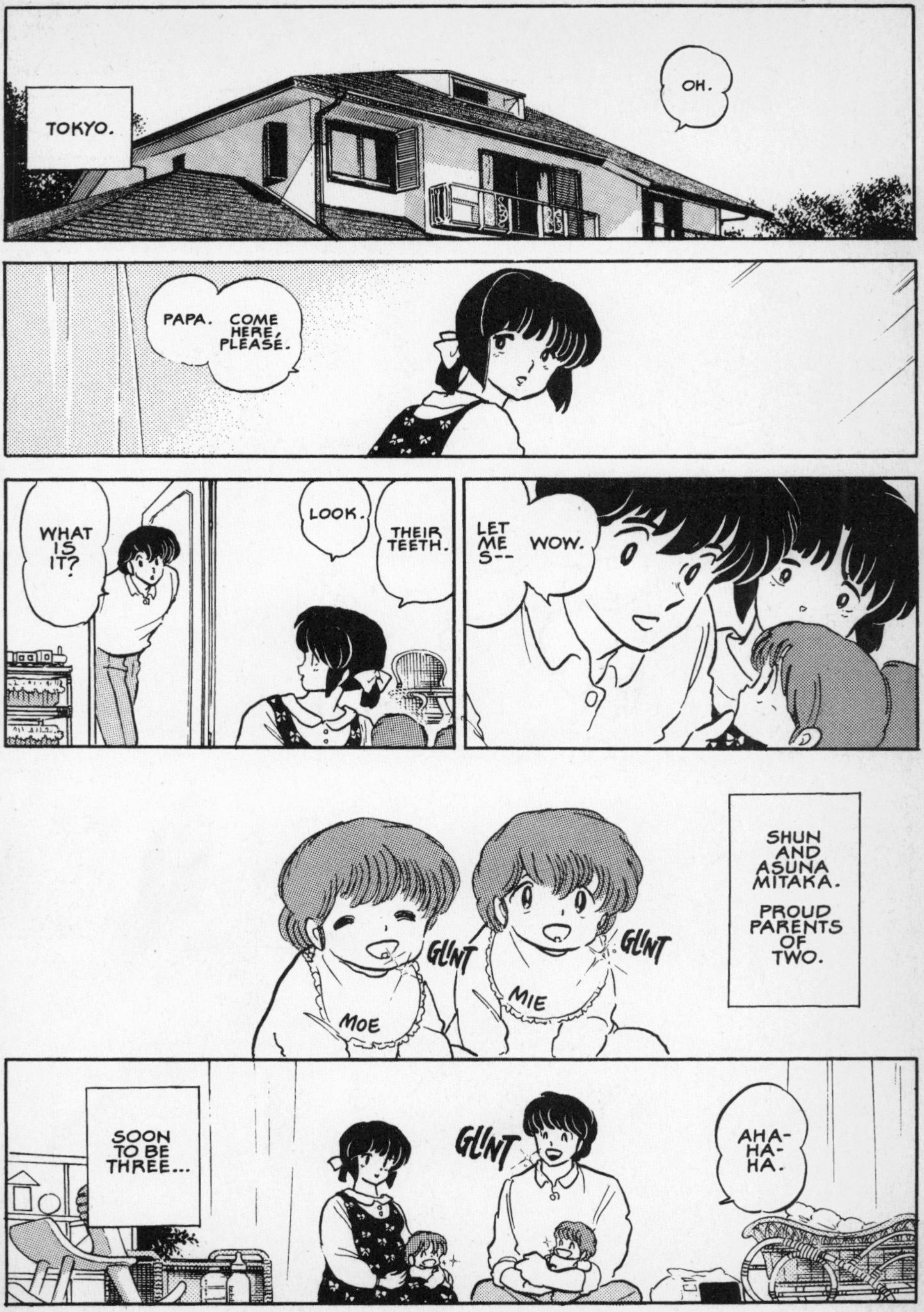
TOKYO.
OH.
PAPA. COME HERE, PLEASE.
WHAT IS IT?
LOOK.
THEIR TEETH.
LET ME S--
WOW.
GLINT
GLINT
MOE
MIE
SHUN AND ASUNA MITAKA. PROUD PARENTS OF TWO.
SOON TO BE THREE...
GLINT
AHA-HA-HA.

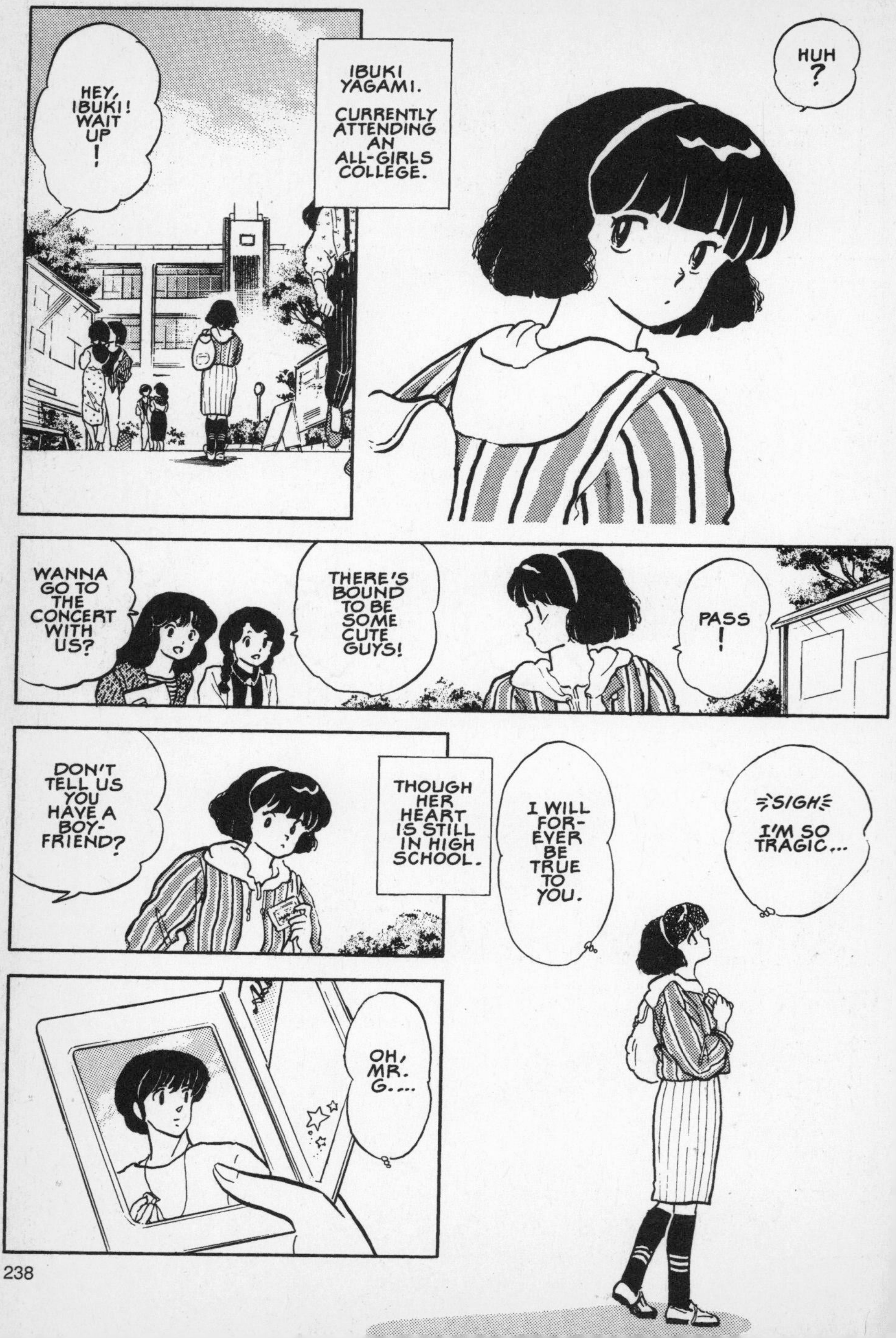

HEY, IBUKI! WAIT UP!
IBUKI YAGAMI. CURRENTLY ATTENDING AN ALL-GIRLS COLLEGE.
HUH?
WANNA GO TO THE CONCERT WITH US?
THERE'S BOUND TO BE SOME CUTE GUYS!
PASS!
DON'T TELL US YOU HAVE A BOY-FRIEND?
THOUGH HER HEART IS STILL IN HIGH SCHOOL.
OH, MR. G....
I WILL FOR-EVER BE TRUE TO YOU.
SIGH
I'M SO TRAGIC...

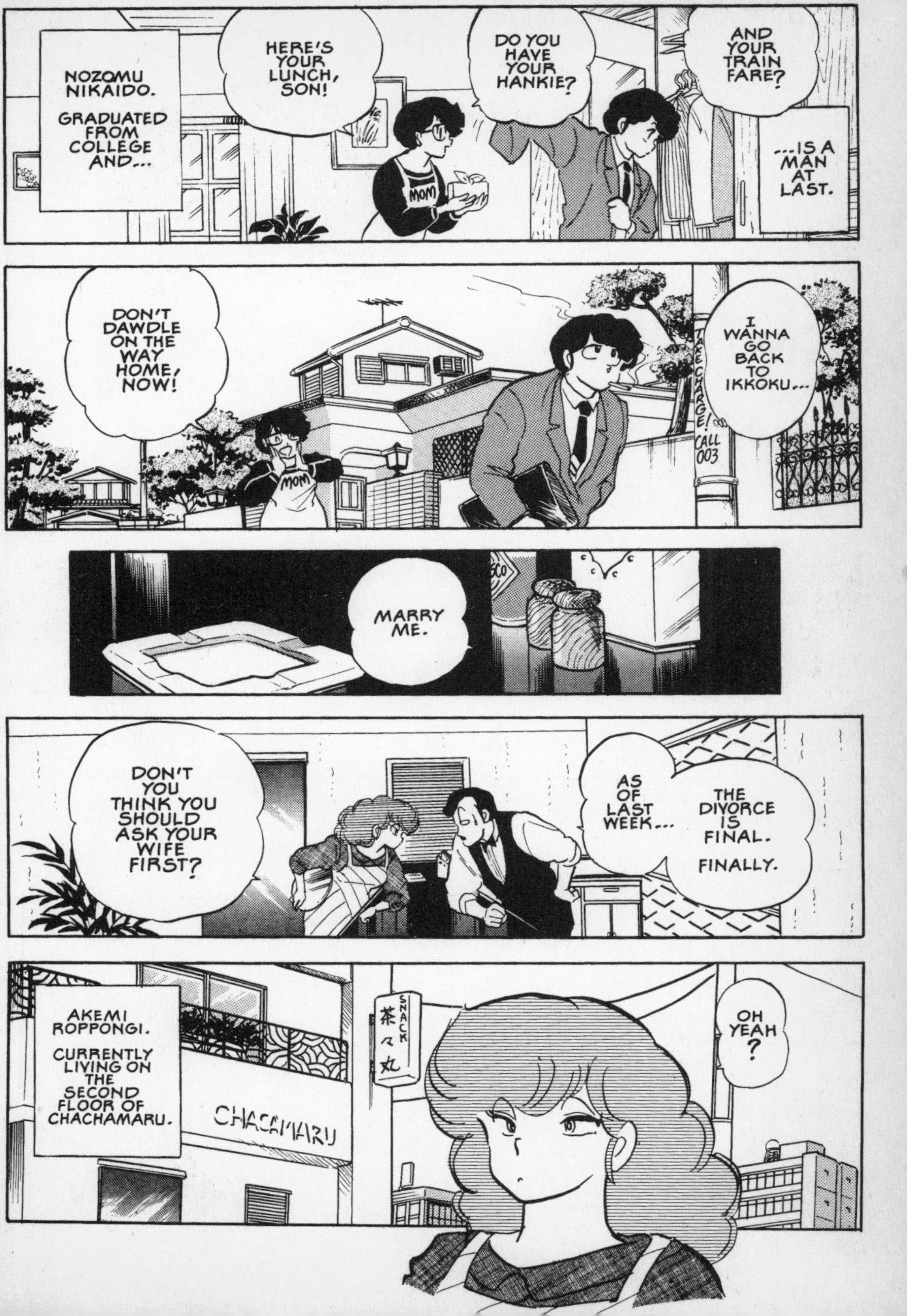
NOZOMU NIKAIDO.
GRADUATED FROM COLLEGE AND...
HERE'S YOUR LUNCH, SON!
DO YOU HAVE YOUR HANKIE?
AND YOUR TRAIN FARE?
...IS A MAN AT LAST.
DON'T DAWDLE ON THE WAY HOME, NOW!
TAKE CHARGE! CALL 003
I WANNA GO BACK TO IKKOKU...
MARRY ME.
DON'T YOU THINK YOU SHOULD ASK YOUR WIFE FIRST?
AS OF LAST WEEK...
THE DIVORCE IS FINAL.
FINALLY.
AKEMI ROPPONGI.
CURRENTLY LIVING ON THE SECOND FLOOR OF CHACHAMARU.
SNACK
茶々丸
CHACAMARU
OH YEAH?

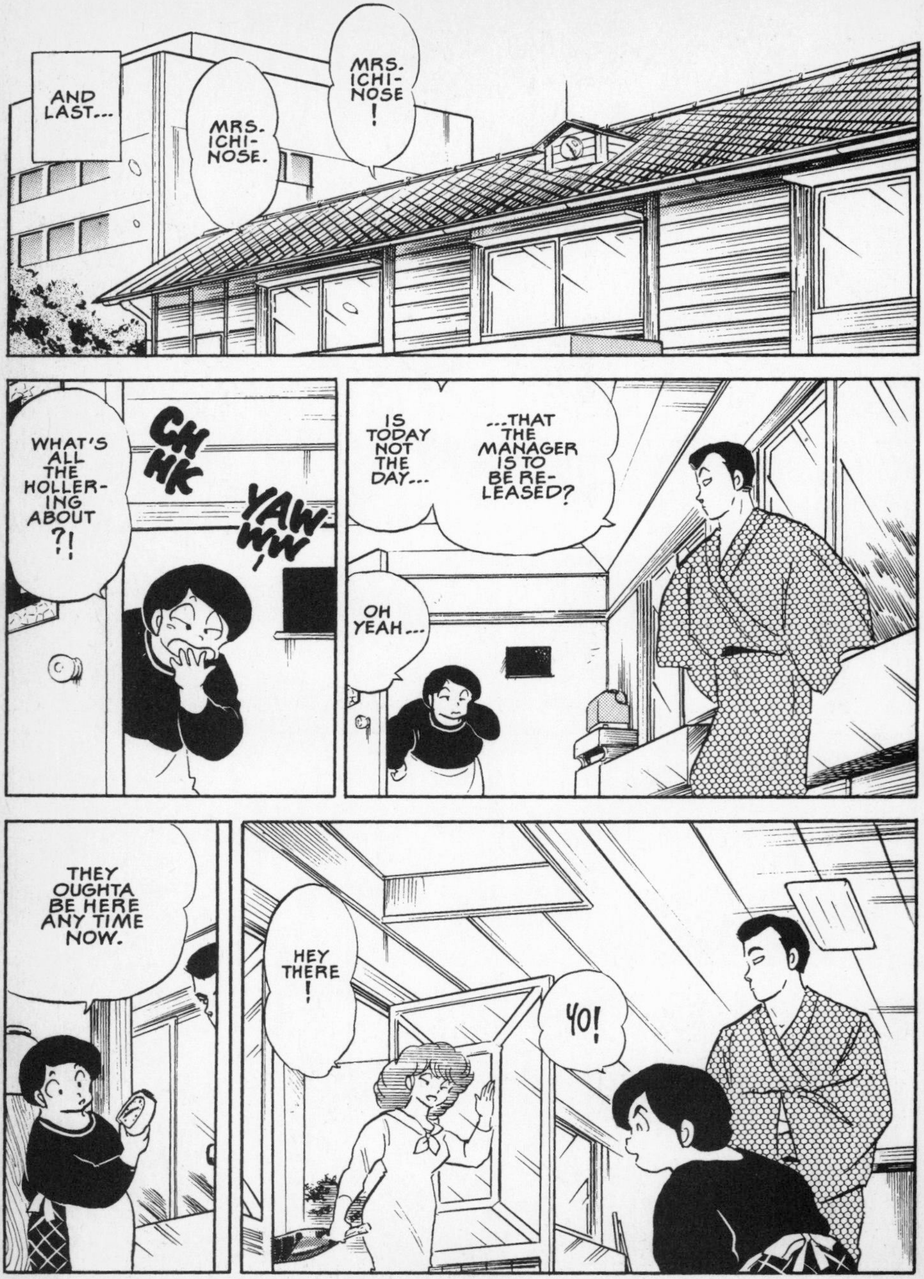
AND LAST...
MRS. ICHI-NOSE.
MRS. ICHI-NOSE!
WHAT'S ALL THE HOLLER-ING ABOUT ?!
CHHK
YAWWW
IS TODAY NOT THE DAY...
...THAT THE MANAGER IS TO BE RE-LEASED?
OH YEAH...
THEY OUGHTA BE HERE ANY TIME NOW.
HEY THERE!
YO!

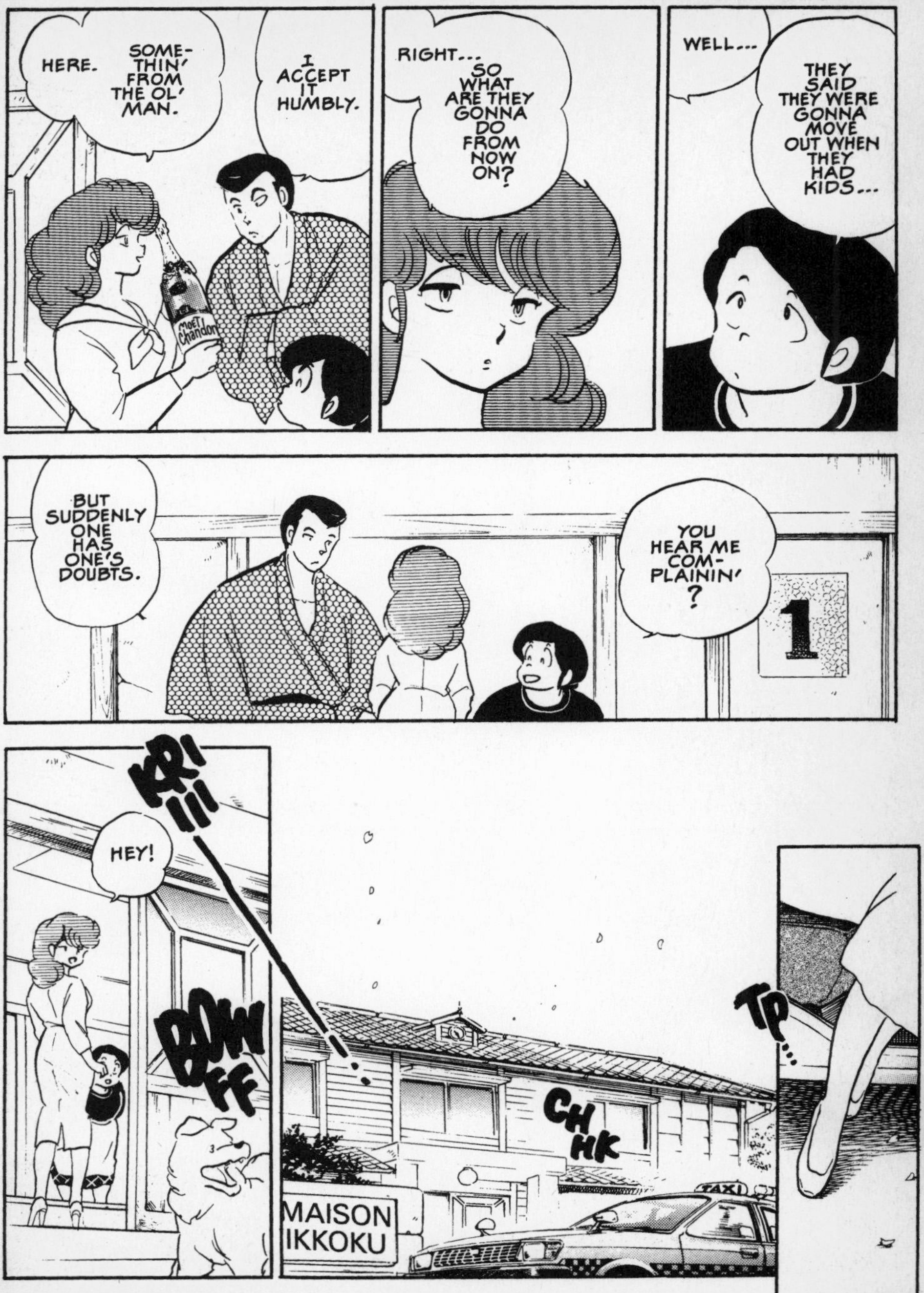
HERE.
SOME-THIN' FROM THE OL' MAN.
I ACCEPT IT HUMBLY.
Moet Chandon
RIGHT... SO WHAT ARE THEY GONNA DO FROM NOW ON?
WELL...
THEY SAID THEY WERE GONNA MOVE OUT WHEN THEY HAD KIDS...
BUT SUDDENLY ONE HAS ONE'S DOUBTS.
YOU HEAR ME COM-PLAININ'?
1
KRIIII
HEY!
BOWFF
CHHK
MAISON IKKOKU
TAXI
TP...

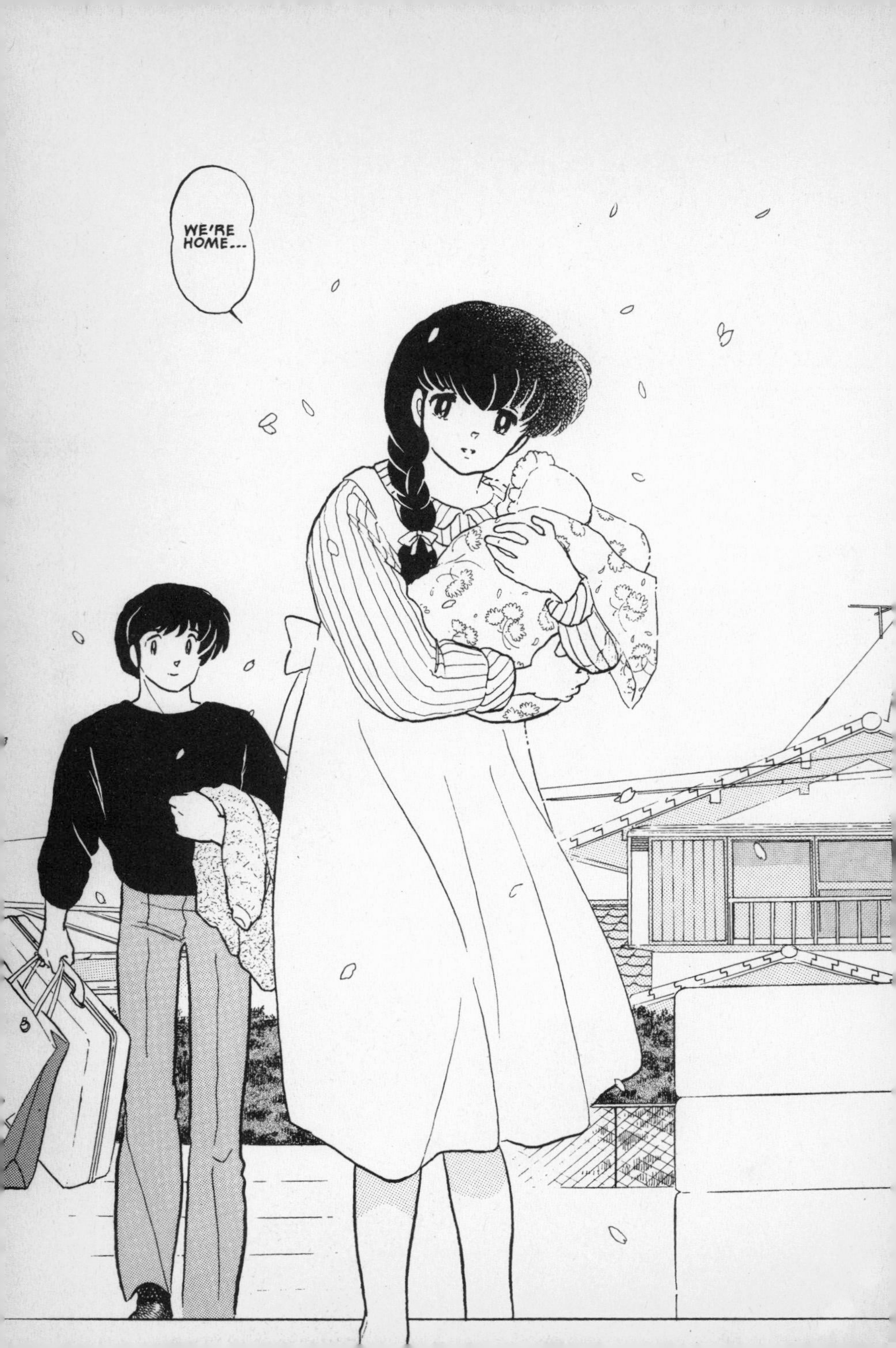
WE'RE HOME...

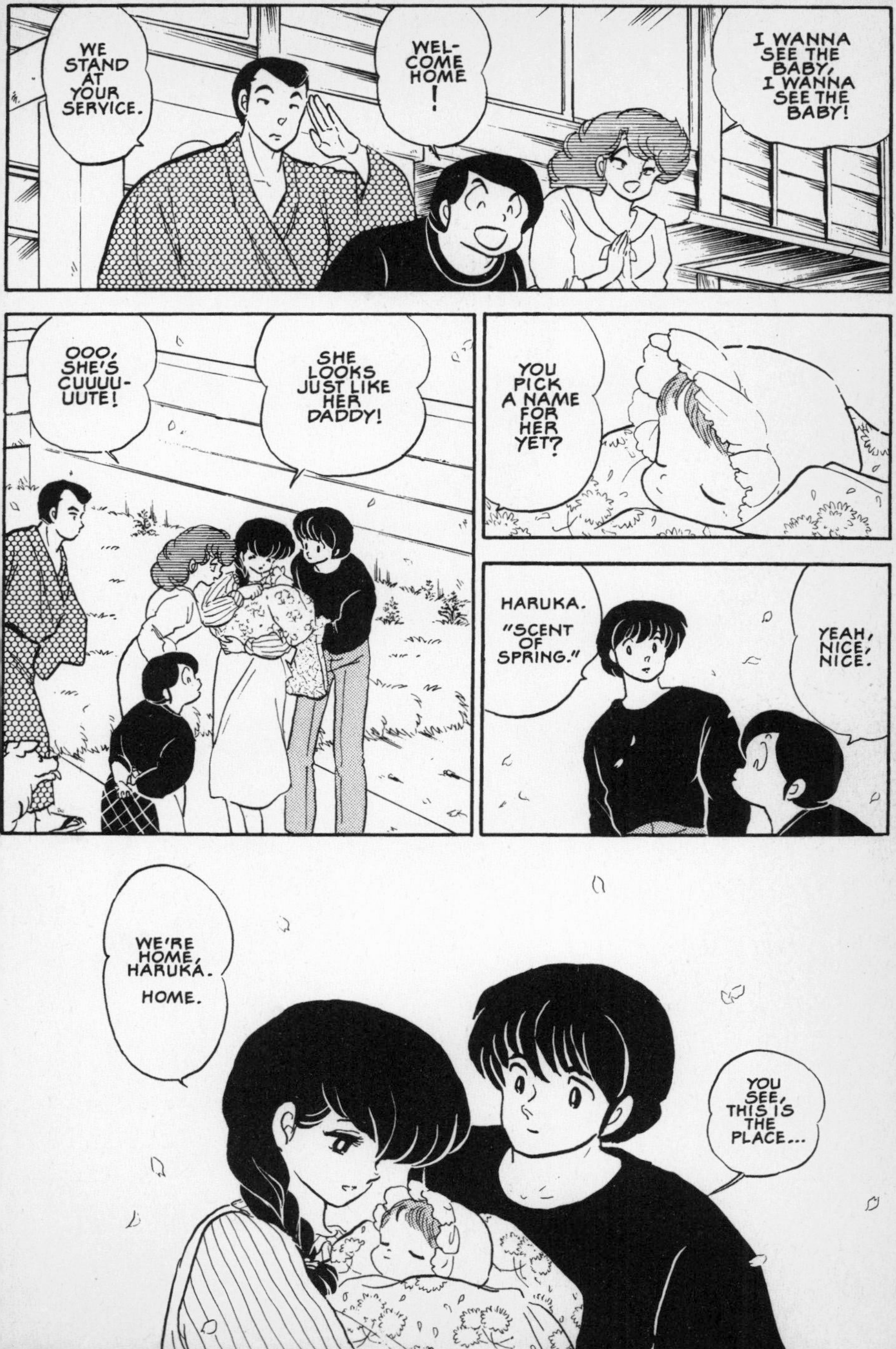
WE STAND AT YOUR SERVICE.
WEL-COME HOME!
I WANNA SEE THE BABY, I WANNA SEE THE BABY!
OOO, SHE'S CUUUU-UUTE!
SHE LOOKS JUST LIKE HER DADDY!
YOU PICK A NAME FOR HER YET?
HARUKA. "SCENT OF SPRING."
YEAH, NICE, NICE.
WE'RE HOME, HARUKA. HOME.
YOU SEE, THIS IS THE PLACE...

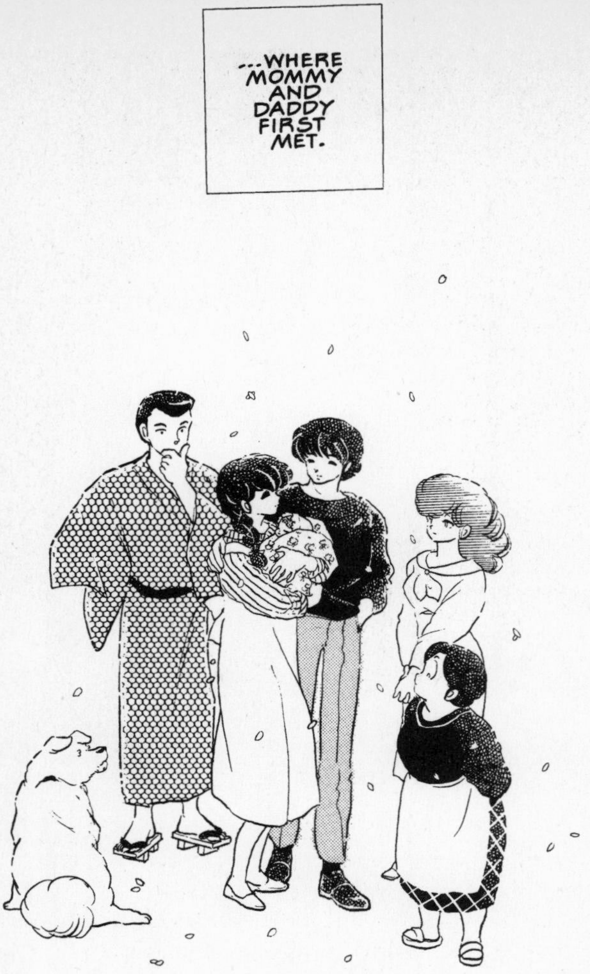
...WHERE MOMMY AND DADDY FIRST MET.

The End

Rumiko Takahashi

Rumiko Takahashi was born in 1957 in Niigata, Japan. She attended women's college in Tokyo, where she began studying comics with Kazuo Koike, author of *Crying Freeman*. In 1978, she won a prize in Shogakukan's annual "New Comic Artist Contest," and in that same year her boy-meets-alien comedy series *Lum*Urusei Yatsura* began appearing in the weekly manga magazine *Shônen Sunday*. This phenomenally successful series ran for nine years and sold over 22 million copies. Takahashi's later *Ranma 1/2* series enjoyed even greater popularity.

Takahashi is considered by many to be one of the world's most popular manga artists. With the publication of Volume 34 of her *Ranma 1/2* series in Japan, Takahashi's total sales passed one hundred million copies of her compiled works.

Takahashi's serial titles include *Lum*Urusei Yatsura*, *Ranma 1/2*, *One-Pound Gospel*, *Maison Ikkoku* and *Inu-Yasha*. Additionally, Takahashi has drawn many short stories which have been published in America under the title "Rumic Theater," and several installments of a saga known as her "Mermaid" series. Most of Takahashi's major stories have also been animated, and are widely available in translation worldwide. *Inu-Yasha* is her most recent serial story, first published in *Shônen Sunday* in 1996.

The Last Great Epic of the Human Race...
In a Dying Future, One Girl is the World's Last Hope...
From the creator of
"Kiki's Delivery Service" and "Princess Mononoke"
NAUSICAÄ
OF THE VALLEY OF WIND
story and art by Hayao Miyazaki
Nausicaä, a compassionate young princess who can commune with animals, battles to heal a world crippled by ecological disaster and war...
The complete story of Nausicaä is now available in 3 formats:
Perfect Collection Vol. 1~4 264~284 pages, $17.95 each
Nausicaä Box Set (4 Perfect Collections), $69.95
Original Collector's Editions Vol. 1 ($13.95), Vol. 4 ($13.95) Vol. 6 ($15.95), Vol. 7 (17.95)
"The best
AMR224-K
46 CA
Available at a comics store near you
Or order online at www.j-pop.com
Phone (800) 394-3042 • Fax (415) 546-7086
Ask for our free Viz Shop-By-Mail catalog!
©1994 NIBARIKI Co., Ltd. First published by Tokuma Shoten Publishing Co., Ltd. in Japan.